THREE KINGDOMS

Part One

MW00345421

THREE KINGDOMS

A Historical Novel

COMPLETE AND UNABRIDGED
Part One

———

Attributed to
Luo Guanzhong

Translated from the Chinese with
Afterword and Notes by
Moss Roberts

Foreword by John S. Service

———

UNIVERSITY OF CALIFORNIA PRESS / FOREIGN LANGUAGES PRESS
Berkeley Los Angeles London / Beijing

Calligraphy by Yang Xianyi.

Published by
University of California Press
Berkeley and Los Angeles, California
University of California Press, Ltd.
London, England
and by
Foreign Languages Press
Beijing, People's Republic of China
© 1991, 2004 by
The Regents of the University of California

Library of Congress Cataloging-in-Publication Data

Luo, Guanzhong, ca. 1330–ca. 1400.
    [San guo yan yi. English]
    Three kingdoms : a historical novel, complete and unabridged = [San guo yan yi] /
Attributed to Luo Guanzhong ; translated from the Chinese with afterword and notes
by Moss Roberts
      p. cm.
    Originally published: 1994.
    Parallel title in Chinese characters.
    ISBN 978-0-520-22478-0 (pbk. : pt. one : alk. paper) —
    ISBN 978-0-520-22503-9 (pbk. : pt. two : alk. paper)
      1. China—History—Three Kingdoms, 220–265—Fiction. I. Title: San guo yan yi.
II. Roberts, Moss, 1937– III. Title.

PL2690.S3E53 2004
895.1'346—dc22   2004043994

Printed in the United States of America

17   16   15   14   13   12   11   10   09   08
11   10   9   8   7   6   5   4   3

The paper used in this publication meets the minimum requirements of
ANSI/ NISO Z39.48-1992 (R 1997) (*Permanence of Paper*). ∞

Not for sale in the People's Republic of China.

CONTENTS

MAPS

ACKNOWLEDGMENTS

Moss Roberts

A number of people have made this project possible and helped bring it to completion—first of all my teachers, whose devotion to the subject matters of sinology has inspired me and guided my studies. Among the most influential were the late P. A. Boodberg, who instructed me in ancient Chinese and the connections between language and history, and W. T. de Bary, whose instruction in Chinese thought has stood me in good stead as a translator. As a student, I also benefited from the devoted labor of many language lecturers at Columbia University and the University of California at Berkeley, who shared their learning without stint.

This project first took shape as an abridged *Three Kingdoms*, which Pantheon Books published in 1976 for use in college classes. The abridged version has its limitations and its mistakes, however, and I harbored the hope that some day the opportunity to translate the entire text would present itself. That opportunity came in 1982 when the late Luo Liang, deputy editor-in-chief at the Foreign Languages Press, proposed that I translate the whole novel for the Press. He and Israel Epstein arranged for me to spend the year 1983–84 at the FLP as a foreign expert. I arrived in Beijing and began work in September of 1983. At the FLP I enjoyed the friendship and benefited from the advice of a number of colleagues. I wish to thank the staff of the English section, in particular the senior staff, for the help and encouragement that made that first year of work so pleasantly memorable. I was also fortunate to have been awarded a National Endowment for the Arts fellowship for the translation.

In the middle stages of the project Xu Mingqiang, vice director at FLP, and his colleague Huang Youyi, deputy editor-in-chief, facilitated my work in many ways. I am particularly grateful that they arranged to have the late C. C. Yin (Ren Jiazhen) serve as the FLP's reader. Mr. Yin read the whole manuscript with painstaking care and his recommendations improved the translation considerably. I thank him for sharing his learning and experience with me. At the same time I benefited from the erudition of my life-long teacher, friend, and colleague C. N. Tay, now retired from New York University. Professor Tay served as my reader, and many of his suggestions have been incorporated into the translation.

During 1984 Brian George of the University of California Press visited the FLP and helped to prepare the way for joint FLP-UCP publication. I thank him for his interest in my work and his encouragement over the long years of this project. William McClung and James Clark of the UCP arranged the joint publication with the late Zhao Yihe of the FLP. Shortly thereafter, the UCP, the FLP, and I concluded that the Western reader would be best served by adding a full set of notes and an extended commentary on the text. This format was adopted, and the translation became eligible for support from the National Endowment for the Humanities; in 1985 and 1986 I was fortunate to hold a fifteen-month fellowship from the NEH that relieved me of half my teaching duties.

The translation owes much to the wisdom of John S. Service, whom the UCP engaged to serve as its reader when the manuscript was completed. His stylistic grace has refined many a phrase, and his pertinent and penetrating queries on both the text and the introduction were of great value to me. Having so demanding and knowledgeable a reader turned the arduous last years of the project into an energizing experience. I also wish to thank Deborah Rudolph for contributing her considerable sinological and proofreading skills. In the later stages of the project William McClung and Betsey Scheiner of the UCP were generous with their encouragement and good counsel, lightening my task and my spirits.

Another scholar I wish to thank is Robert Hegel, who read the first half of the manuscript for the UCP. I made use of a significant number of his suggestions. Chauncey S. Goodrich kindly read the introduction in draft and suggested useful changes; these too have been incorporated. I would like to thank as well my friend James Peck; although he did not work directly on the manuscript, his thoughtful comments have widened the view on many issues. Mr. Peck was the editor for the abridged version published by Pantheon, and his continued interest in the project has been encouraging.

The abovementioned, by giving so generously of their time and talent, have improved this project greatly. Errors and doubtful points surely remain, and for these I take full responsibility. A word of recognition is also due to C. H. Brewitt-Taylor, whose 1925 translation of *Three Kingdoms* I read long before gathering enough Chinese to confront the original.

To the students in my Chinese language and literature classes, my thanks for twenty years of challenge and excitement in what has been (at least for me) a learning experience; and to my colleagues in the East Asian Studies Program of Washington Square College, New York University, my appreciation for the years of sustaining companionship and critical interchange.

To my mother, Helen, who takes a loving interest in my work, my gratitude for years of support and encouragement. The translation is dedicated to my wife, Florence, who serves the poorer citizens of New York City as a Legal Services attorney in family law.

FOREWORD

John S. Service

In 1942, during China's war against Japan, I happened to be a solitary American traveling with a party of Chinese from Chengdu to Lanzhou and beyond. They were officials and engineers of the National Resources Commission, with a sprinkling of journalists. All were college graduates; many had advanced degrees from foreign study. We rode together intimately in a small bus, and our first main objective was Hanzhong in southern Shaanxi.

Almost from the start I noticed that my companions were having vigorous discussions that seemed to involve the old names of various towns that our road passed through. Changing place-names are one of the problems of Chinese history, and I paid little attention. About the third day the discussions could no longer be ignored. Our youngest member, the *Dagong bao* correspondent, excitedly announced that the walled town we were approaching was the site of Zhuge Liang's "Empty City Stratagem."[1] The whole area we were passing through, it turned out, had been the scene of many hard-fought campaigns during the wars of the Three Kingdoms.

Years before, as a boy in China, I had heard vaguely of the famous novel. Travel in Sichuan in those days was by sedan chair. About once an hour the bearers would set us down while they regained strength at a tea shop. Sometimes, sitting at a small raised table at the rear, there would be a storyteller. To my queries, my patient father usually replied: "Probably something from *Three Kingdoms.*" Also, we occasionally saw a snatch of Chinese opera. Again, it seemed to be "something from *Three Kingdoms.*" But the tea shop rests were brief, and missionary families did not spend much time at the Chinese opera. Having read about King Arthur and his knights of the round table, I decided that *Three Kingdoms* must be something of the same: romantic myths of a misty never-never land of long ago. It was startling to find that for these men of modern China it was fact and history. Furthermore, these tales of martial valor and deepest loyalty had special relevance for them in that time of foreign aggression—with Chinese resistance being based on the actual area of Liu Bei's old kingdom of Shu.

Eventually, of course, I read *Three Kingdoms.* It was like donning a special pair of glasses. Our family's life while I was growing up in Sichuan had been dominated by the cataclysmic ebb and flow of local warlord politics (having the misfortune to be both rich and populous, Sichuan perhaps surpassed all other provinces as a "warlord *tianxia*"). Now the dramatic posturings and righteous manifestoes, the unending intrigues and sudden changes of alliances, the forays and retreats and occasional battles, even the actual tactics used—all had a familiar ring. The whole cast of players, it seemed, had absorbed the stories and lessons of *Three Kingdoms* and could not forget them.

It was not only the warlords who found guidance and inspiration in *Three Kingdoms*. After the success of the Communists' Long March, the Guomindang spent the years from 1934 to 1937 in largely fruitless efforts to obliterate all traces of the remnants left behind. It is recorded that the military leader of the old Eyuwan base area "was an avid reader, though not apparently of Marxist books. His favorite works included . . . *The Romance of the Three Kingdoms*. [This] he carried with him always, while fighting or marching, and he consulted it as a military manual between battles."[2]

The Guomindang, too, was not immune. When Chiang Kai-shek commissioned Dai Li in 1932 to set up a military secret service, he is reported to have instructed Dai to look for an organizational ethos in the Chinese traditional novels. Thus Dai's organization adopted operational techniques from the KGB, the Gestapo, and eventually the FBI, but it was built as a sworn brotherhood devoted to benevolence and righteousness and held together by bonds of mutual loyalty and obligation—with a clear model in *Three Kingdoms*.[3]

One could go on. But perhaps I have sufficiently made the point that *Three Kingdoms* continues to have vitality in Chinese attitudes and behavior. That fact alone makes it important to us outsiders who seek to know and understand China.

There is another important reason, more general and nonutilitarian, why *Three Kingdoms* well merits a reading. For at least four hundred years it has continued to be a favorite of the world's largest public. The literate of China read and reread it; those who can not read learn it (perhaps even more intensely) from storytellers and opera and word of mouth. It is, simply, a terrific story. Every element is there: drama and suspense, valor and cowardice, loyalty and betrayal, power and subtlety, chivalry and statecraft, the obligations of ruler and subject, conflicts in the basic ties of brotherhood and lineage. By any criterion, I suggest, it is an important piece of world literature.

We are fortunate, therefore, to have this new complete and, for the first time, annotated translation by Moss Roberts. Professor Roberts has admirably preserved the vigor and flavor of the Chinese text. His erudition and patience have produced a clarity of language and yet enable us to enjoy the subtleties and wordplays of the original. His translations of the poems, important in the story, are often inspired.

Though urging the reader on, I cannot promise that it will be an easy read. The story, admittedly, is long and complex. We are doubly fortunate, then, that Professor Roberts has complemented his excellent translation with background information and the translated notes and commentary by the editor of the traditional Chinese version of the novel. With the help of his research and the guidance of the Chinese commentary, the way is greatly eased. Few, I hope, will falter and thus fail fully to enjoy this absorbing, rewarding, and majestic novel.

NOTES

1. See chapter 95.

2. My thanks to Gregor Benton of the University of Leeds, whose forthcoming history of the Three Year War will be published by the University of California Press.

3. Wen-hsin Yeh, "Dai Li and the Liu Geqing Affair: Heroism in the Chinese Secret Service During the War of Resistance," *Journal of Asian Studies* 48, (1989): 545–47.

THREE KINGDOMS

A Historical Novel

On and on the Great River rolls, racing east.
Of proud and gallant heroes its white-tops leave no trace,
As right and wrong, pride and fall turn all at once unreal.
Yet ever the green hills stay
To blaze in the west-waning day.

Fishers and woodsmen comb the river isles.
White-crowned, they've seen enough of spring and autumn tide
To make good company over the wine jar,
Where many a famed event
Provides their merriment.[1]

1

Three Bold Spirits Plight Mutual Faith in the Peach Garden;
Heroes and Champions Win First Honors Fighting the Yellow Scarves

HERE BEGINS OUR TALE. The empire, long divided, must unite; long united, must divide. Thus it has ever been. In the closing years of the Zhou dynasty,[1] seven kingdoms warred among themselves until the kingdom of Qin prevailed and absorbed the other six. But Qin soon fell, and on its ruins two opposing kingdoms, Chu and Han, fought for mastery until the kingdom of Han prevailed and absorbed its rival, as Qin had done before.[2] The Han court's rise to power began when the Supreme Ancestor slew a white serpent, inspiring an uprising that ended with Han's ruling a unified empire.

Two hundred years later, after Wang Mang's usurpation, Emperor Guang Wu restored the dynasty, and Han emperors ruled for another two hundred years down to the reign of Xian, after whom the realm split into three kingdoms.[3] The cause of Han's fall may be traced to the reigns of Xian's two predecessors, Huan and Ling. Huan drove from office and persecuted officials of integrity and ability, giving all his trust to his eunuchs.[4] After Ling succeeded Huan as emperor, Regent-Marshal Dou Wu and Imperial Guardian Chen Fan, joint sustainers of the throne, planned to execute the power-abusing eunuch Cao Jie and his cohorts.[5] But the plot came to light, and Dou Wu and Chen Fan were themselves put to death. From then on, the Minions of the Palace knew no restraint.

On the fifteenth day of the fourth month of the second year of the reign Established Calm (Jian Ning),[6] the Emperor arrived at the Great Hall of Benign Virtue for the full-moon ancestral rites. As he was about to seat himself, a strong wind began issuing out of a corner of the hall. From the same direction a green serpent appeared, slid down off a beam, and coiled itself on the throne. The Emperor fainted and was rushed to his private chambers. The assembled officials fled. The next moment the serpent vanished, and a sudden thunderstorm broke. Rain laced with hailstones pelted down for half the night, wrecking countless buildings.

In the second month of the fourth year of Established Calm an earthquake struck Luoyang, the capital, and tidal waves swept coastal dwellers out to sea. In the first year of Radiant Harmony (Guang He) hens were transformed into roosters.[7] And on the first day of the sixth month a murky cloud more than one hundred spans in length floated into the Great Hall of Benign Virtue.[8] The next month a secondary rainbow was observed in the Chamber of the Consorts. Finally, a part of the cliffs of the Yuan Mountains plunged to earth.[9] All these evil portents, and more, appeared—too many to be dismissed as isolated signs.

Emperor Ling called on his officials to explain these disasters and omens. A court counselor, Cai Yong, argued bluntly that the secondary rainbow and the transformation of the hens were the result of interference in government by empresses and eunuchs. The Emperor merely read the report, sighed, and withdrew.

The eunuch Cao Jie observed this session unseen and informed his associates. They framed Cai Yong in another matter, and he was dismissed from office and retired to his village. After that a vicious gang of eunuchs known as the Ten Regular Attendants—Zhang Rang, Zhao Zhong, Feng Xu, Duan Gui, Cao Jie, Hou Lan, Jian Shuo, Cheng Kuang, Xia Yun, and Guo Sheng—took charge.[10] Zhang Rang gained the confidence of the Emperor, who called him "Nuncle." Court administration became so corrupt that across the land men's thoughts turned to rebellion, and outlaws swarmed like hornets.

One rebel group, the Yellow Scarves, was organized by three brothers from the Julu district—Zhang Jue, Zhang Bao, and Zhang Liang. Zhang Jue had failed the official provincial-level examination and repaired to the hills where he gathered medicinal herbs.[11] One day he met an ancient mystic, emerald-eyed and with a youthful face, gripping a staff of goosefoot wood. The old man summoned Zhang Jue into a cave where he placed in his hands a sacred book in three volumes. "Here is the *Essential Arts for the Millennium*," he said. "Now that you have it, spread its teachings far and wide as Heaven's messenger for the salvation of our age. But think no seditious thoughts, or retribution will follow." Zhang Jue asked the old man's name, and he replied, "The Old Hermit From Mount Hua Summit—Zhuang Zi, the Taoist sage." Then he changed into a puff of pure breeze and was gone.

Zhang Jue applied himself to the text day and night. By acquiring such arts as summoning the wind and invoking the rain, he became known as the Master of the Millennium. During the first month of the first year of the reign Central Stability (Zhong Ping),[12] a pestilence spread through the land. Styling himself Great and Worthy Teacher, Zhang Jue distributed charms and potions to the afflicted. He had more than five hundred followers, each of whom could write the charms and recite the spells. They traveled widely, and wherever they passed, new recruits joined until Zhang Jue had established thirty-six commands—ranging in size from six or seven thousand to over ten thousand—under thirty-six chieftains titled general or commander.[13]

A seditious song began to circulate at this time:

> The pale sky is on the wane,
> Next, a yellow one shall reign;
> The calendar's rotation
> Spells fortune for the nation.

Jue ordered the words "new cycle" chalked on the front gate of every house, and soon the name Zhang Jue, Great and Worthy Teacher, was hailed throughout the eight provinces of the realm—Qingzhou, Youzhou, Xuzhou, Jizhou, Jingzhou, Yangzhou, Yanzhou, and Yuzhou. At this point Zhang Jue had his trusted follower Ma Yuanyi bribe the eunuch Feng Xu to work inside the court on behalf of the rebels. Then Zhang Jue made a proposal to his two brothers: "Popular support is the hardest thing to win. Today the people favor us. Why waste this chance to seize the realm for ourselves?"

Zhang Jue had yellow banners made ready, fixed the date for the uprising, and sent one of his followers, Tang Zhou, to inform the agent at court, the eunuch Feng Xu. Instead, Tang Zhou reported the imminent insurrection to the palace. The Emperor

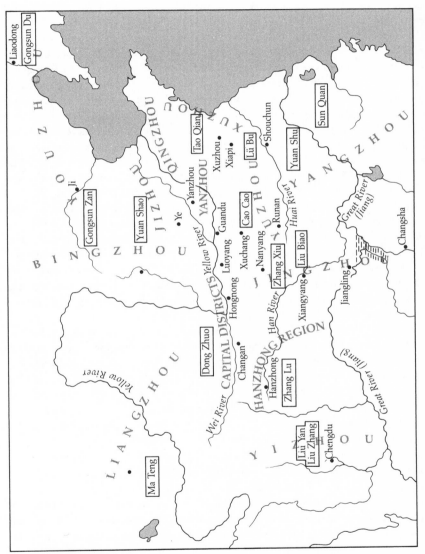

MAP. 1. Provinces (*zhou*), districts and towns, and military leaders at the end of the Han dynasty. The leaders' names appear in boxes. Source: Liu Chunfan, *Sanguo shihua* (Beijing: Beijing chubanshe, 1981), p. 21.

summoned Regent He Jin to arrest and behead Ma Yuanyi. This done, Feng Xu and his group were seized and jailed.

His plot exposed, Zhang Jue mustered his forces in great haste. Titling himself General of Heaven, his first brother General of the Earth, and his second brother General of Men, he addressed his massed followers: "Han's fated end is near. A new sage is due to appear. Let one and all obey Heaven and follow the true cause so that we may rejoice in the millennium."

From the four corners of the realm the common folk, nearly half a million strong, bound their heads with yellow scarves and followed Zhang Jue in rebellion, gathering such force that the government troops scattered on the rumor of their approach. Regent-Marshal He Jin appealed to the Emperor to order every district to defend itself and every warrior to render distinguished service in putting down the uprising. Meanwhile, the regent also gave three Imperial Corps commanders—Lu Zhi, Huangfu Song, and Zhu Jun—command of three elite field armies with orders to bring the rebels to justice.

As for Zhang Jue's army, it began advancing on Youzhou district. The governor, Liu Yan, was a native of Jingling county in Jiangxia and a descendant of Prince Gong of Lu of the imperial clan. Threatened by the approaching rebels, Liu Yan summoned Commandant Zou Jing for his estimate of the situation. "They are many," said Jing, "and we are few. The best course, Your Lordship, is to recruit an army quickly to deal with the enemy." The governor agreed and issued a call for volunteers loyal to the throne.

The call was posted in Zhuo county, where it drew the attention of a man of heroic mettle. This man, though no scholar, was gentle and generous by nature, taciturn and reserved. His one ambition was to cultivate the friendship of the boldest spirits of the empire. He stood seven and a half spans tall, with arms that reached below his knees. His ear lobes were elongated, his eyes widely set and able to see his own ears. His face was flawless as jade, and his lips like dabs of rouge.

This man was a descendant of Liu Sheng, Prince Jing of Zhongshan, a great-great-grandson of the fourth Han emperor, Jing. His name was Liu Bei; his style, Xuande.[14] Generations before, during the reign of Emperor Wu, Liu Sheng's son, Zhen, was made lord of Zhuolu precinct, but the fief and title were later forfeited when Zhen was accused of making an unsatisfactory offering at the eighth-month libation in the Emperor's ancestral temple.[15] Thus a branch of the Liu family came to settle in Zhuo county.

Xuande's grandfather was Liu Xiong; his father, Liu Hong. Local authorities had recommended Hong to the court for his filial devotion and personal integrity.[16] He received appointment and actually held a minor office; but he died young. Orphaned, Xuande served his widowed mother with unstinting affection. However, they had been left so poor that he had to sell sandals and weave mats to live.

The family resided in a county hamlet called Two-Story Mulberry after a tree of some fifty spans just southeast of their home. Seen from afar, the mulberry rose tall and spread broadly like a carriage canopy. "An eminent man will come from this house," a fortune-teller once predicted. While playing beneath the tree with the boys in the hamlet, young Xuande often boasted, "When I'm the Son of Heaven, my chariot will have a canopy like this." Impressed by these words, his uncle Liu Yuanqi remarked, "This is no ordinary child."[17] Yuanqi sympathized with the impoverished family and often helped out his nephew. At fifteen Xuande was sent away by his mother to study, and Zheng Xuan and Lu Zhi were among his teachers.[18] He also formed a close friendship with Gongsun Zan.

Xuande was twenty-eight when Governor Liu issued his call for volunteers. Reading the notice in Zhuo that day, Xuande sighed heavily. "Why such long sighs?" someone behind him asked brusquely. "A real man should be serving his emperor in the hour of peril." Xuande turned and faced a man eight spans tall, with a blunt head like a panther's, huge round eyes, a swallow's heavy jowls, a tiger's whiskers, a thunderous voice, and a stance like a dashing horse. Half in fear, half in admiration, Xuande asked his name.

"The surname," the man replied, "is Zhang; given name, Fei; style, Yide.[19] We've lived in this county for generations, farming our piece of land, selling wine, and slaughtering pigs. I seek to befriend men of bold spirit; when I saw you sighing and studying the recruitment call, I took the occasion to address you." "As a matter of fact," Xuande answered, "I am related to the imperial family. My surname is Liu; given name, Bei. Reading of the trouble the Yellow Scarves are stirring up, I had decided to help destroy the bandits and protect the people and was sighing for my inability to do so when you came by." "I have resources," said Zhang Fei, "that could be used to recruit in this area. Let's work together for the cause. What about it?"

Xuande was elated, and the two went to a tavern. As they drank, they watched a strapping fellow pushing a wheelbarrow stop to rest at the tavern entrance. "Some wine, and quickly—I'm off to the city to volunteer," the stranger said as he entered and took a seat. Xuande observed him: a man of enormous height, nine spans tall, with a two-foot-long beard flowing from his rich, ruddy cheeks. He had glistening lips, eyes sweeping sharply back like those of the crimson-faced phoenix, and brows like nestling silkworms.[20] His stature was imposing, his bearing awesome. Xuande invited him to share their table and asked who he was.

"My surname is Guan," the man replied. "My given name is Yu; my style, Changsheng, was later changed to Yunchang.[21] I am from Jieliang in Hedong, but I had to leave there after killing a local bully who was persecuting his neighbors and have been on the move these five or six years.[22] As soon as I heard about the recruitment, I came to sign up." Xuande then told of his own ambitions, to Lord Guan's great satisfaction.[23] Together the three left the tavern and went to Zhang Fei's farm to continue their discussion. "There's a peach garden behind my farm," said Zhang Fei. "The flowers are in full bloom. Tomorrow let us offer sacrifice there to Heaven and earth, and pledge to combine our strength and purpose as sworn brothers. Then we'll plan our course of action."[24] Xuande and Lord Guan agreed with one voice: "So be it."

The next day the three men had a black bull, a white horse, and other offerings brought to the peach garden.[25] Amid the smoke of incense they performed their ritual prostration and took their oath:

> We three, though of separate ancestry, join in brotherhood here, combining strength and purpose, to relieve the present crisis. We will perform our duty to the Emperor and protect the common folk of the land. We dare not hope to be together always but hereby vow to die the selfsame day. Let shining Heaven above and the fruitful land below bear witness to our resolve. May Heaven and man scourge whosoever fails this vow.

So swearing, Xuande became the eldest brother; Lord Guan, the second; and Zhang Fei, the youngest. After the ceremonies they butchered the bull and spread forth a feast in the peach garden for the three hundred local youths they had recruited; and all drank to their heart's content.

The next day they collected weapons, but they wanted for horses. Two visitors whose servants were driving a herd of horses toward Zhang Fei's farm provided the solution. "This must mean that Heaven is with us," said Xuande as the three brothers went forth to greet the men, Zhang Shiping and Su Shuang, two wealthy traders from Zhongshan. Every year, they said, they went north to sell horses; but this year they had had to turn back because of the Yellow Scarves. Xuande invited them to the farm, where he set out wine and entertained them before revealing his intention to hunt down the rebels and protect the people. The visitors were delighted to support the cause by supplying the brothers with fifty fine mounts, five hundred ounces of gold and silver, and one thousand *jin* of wrought iron to manufacture weapons.[26]

After bidding the traders a grateful farewell, Xuande had the finest smith forge for him a pair of matching double-edged swords; for Lord Guan a Green Dragon crescent-moon blade, also known as Frozen Glory, weighing eighty-two *jin*,[27] and for Zhang Fei, an eighteen-span spear of tempered steel. He also ordered full body armor for each of them.

At the head of five hundred local youths, the brothers presented themselves to Commandant Zou Jing. Jing brought them to Liu Yan, governor of Youzhou, before whom the brothers gave account of themselves. When Xuande mentioned his royal surname, the governor was delighted and acknowledged him as a nephew.

Some days later it was reported that the Yellow Scarves chieftain Cheng Yuanzhi was advancing on Zhuo district with fifty thousand men. The governor had Commandant Zou Jing lead the brothers and their five hundred against the enemy. Eagerly, Xuande took his company to the base of Daxing Mountain where he encountered the rebels, who as always appeared with hair unbound and yellow scarves across their foreheads.

The two forces stood opposed. Xuande rode out, Lord Guan to his left, Zhang Fei to his right. Raising his whip, Xuande cried out, "Traitors to the Emperor, surrender now!" Enraged, Cheng Yuanzhi sent his subordinate commander Deng Mao into the field. Zhang Fei sped out, leveled his eighteen-span serpent-headed spear and jabbed his adversary through the chest. Seeing Deng Mao tumble dead from his horse, Yuanzhi cut toward Zhang Fei, slapping his mount and flourishing his blade. Lord Guan swung out his mighty sword and, giving his horse free rein, rushed the foe. Cheng Yuanzhi gulped with fright and, before he could defend himself, was sliced in two with a stroke of Lord Guan's weapon. A poet of later times praised the two warriors:

> Oh, what a day for gallantry unveiled!
> One man proved his lance and one his blade.
> In maiden trial their martial force was shown.
> A thrice-torn land will see them gain renown.

Their leaders slain, the rebels dropped their spears and fled. Xuande pursued, taking more prisoners than could be counted, and the brothers returned triumphant. Governor Liu Yan met them personally and rewarded their soldiers. The next day Liu Yan received an appeal from Governor Gong Jing to relieve the rebel-besieged city of Qingzhou. Xuande volunteered to go there, and Liu Yan ordered Zou Jing to join him and his brothers with five thousand men.

As the rescue force approached Qingzhou, the Yellow Scarves divided their army and tied up the government troops in a tangled struggle. Xuande's fewer numbers could not prevail, and he had to retreat some thirty *li* where he pitched camp. "They are too many for us. We can win only by surprising them," Xuande told his brothers. He had Lord Guan and Zhang Fei march off with one thousand men each and conceal themselves along both sides of a hill.

The following day Xuande and Zou Jing advanced noisily but drew back when the enemy gave battle. The rebel horde eagerly pursued, but as they passed the hill the gongs rang out in unison. From left and right, troops poured down as Xuande swung his soldiers around to resume combat. Squeezed between three forces, the rebels broke up and were driven to the very walls of Qingzhou where an armed populace led by Governor Gong Jing met them. After a period of slaughter the Scarves were routed and the siege of Qingzhou was lifted. In later times a poet praised Xuande:

> Seasoned plans and master moves; all's divinely done.
> To one mighty dragon two tigers can't compare.
> At his first trial what victories are won!
> Poor orphan boy? The realm is his to share.

After the governor had feasted the troops, Commandant Zou Jing wanted to return to Youzhou. But Xuande said, "We have word that Imperial Corps Commander Lu Zhi has been battling the rebel chief Zhang Jue at Guangzong. Lu Zhi was once my teacher, and I'd like to help him." So Zou Jing returned to Youzhou with his men, and Xuande headed for Guangzong with his brothers and their five hundred men. They entered Lu Zhi's tent and, after the customary salutations, explained their purpose in coming.

Lu Zhi rejoiced at the arrival of this relief and took the brothers under his command. At this time Zhang Jue's one hundred and fifty thousand and Lu Zhi's fifty thousand were deadlocked at Guangzong. "We have them contained here," Lu Zhi said to Xuande, "but over in Yingchuan, Zhang Jue's two brothers, Zhang Liang and Zhang Bao, are holding out against our generals Huangfu Song and Zhu Jun. Let me add one thousand to your company. Then go and investigate the situation there and fix the time to sweep the rebels out." On Lu Zhi's order, Xuande rode through the night to Yingchuan.

Meanwhile, checked by Huangfu Song and Zhu Jun, the Yingchuan rebels had retreated to Changshe, where they hastily built a campsite near a field. "If they're by a field," General Huangfu Song said to Zhu Jun, "we should attack with fire." They ordered each soldier to lie in wait with unlit torches of straw. That night the wind rose. After the second watch the government soldiers burned the camp.[28] Huangfu Song and Zhu Jun attacked the rebels' stockade as flames stretched skyward. Without saddling their horses or buckling their armor, the rebels fled panic-stricken in every direction. The slaughter continued until morning.

Zhang Liang and Zhang Bao were in full flight when their fire-decimated forces were intercepted by a contingent of men with red flags flying. The leader of this new unit flashed into sight—tall, narrow-eyed, with a long beard. This man's rank was cavalry commander. His surname was Cao; his given name, Cao; his style, Mengde. Cao Cao's father, Cao Song, was originally not a Cao but a Xiahou. However, as the adopted son of the eunuch Cao Teng he assumed the surname Cao. Cao Song was Cao Cao's natural father. In addition, Cao Cao had the childhood nickname Ah Man and another given name, Jili.[29]

As a youth Cao had loved the hunt and delighted in song and dance. He was a boy with ingenious ideas for any situation, a regular storehouse of schemes and machinations. Once Cao's uncle, outraged by his nephew's wild antics, complained to Cao's father, who in turn reproached Cao. The next time the boy saw his uncle, he dropped to the ground and pretended to have a fit. The terrified uncle fetched the father, who rushed to his son's side only to find him perfectly sound. "Your uncle told me you'd had a fit," said Song. "Has it passed?" "Nothing of the sort ever happened," responded Cao. "My uncle accuses me of everything because I have lost favor with him." The father believed the son and thereafter ignored the uncle's complaints, leaving Cao free to indulge his whims.[30]

At about that time a man called Qiao Xuan said to Cao, "The empire is near ruin and can be saved only by a man capable of dominating the age. You could be the one." On another occasion He Yu of Nanyang said of Cao Cao, "The house of Han is going to fail. Yet I feel certain this is the man to steady the realm." In Runan a man named Xu Shao, known for his insight into human character, refused to give Cao a reading. But pressed repeatedly, the man finally spoke: "You could be an able statesman in a time of peace or a treacherous villain in a time of chaos." This prediction pleased Cao immensely.

At twenty, Cao received his district's recommendation for filial devotion and personal integrity, and this led to his initial appointment to the palace. Later, he was given command of security in the northern half of the district where the capital, Luoyang, was located. On assuming office he had a dozen decorated cudgels placed at the four gates of the city. They were to be a sign that any violator of the laws, however high or mighty, would be punished. One night the uncle of the eunuch Jian Shuo was seen going through the streets carrying a broadsword. Cao, making his nightly rounds, apprehended him and had one of the bludgeons applied. Thereafter no one dared to break the laws, and Cao Cao's prestige increased. Later he was made magistrate of Dunqiu.

During the Yellow Scarves uprisings the court elevated Cao to the rank of cavalry commander, and it was in this capacity that he led five thousand mounted warriors and foot soldiers to the Yingchuan district. He encountered the routed troops of Zhang Liang and Zhang Bao and cut off their retreat. In the ensuing fray his men took ten thousand heads as well as flags, banners, gongs, drums, and horses in large numbers. Zhang Liang and Zhang Bao, however, managed to escape after a desperate struggle. Cao presented himself to Huangfu Song and Zhu Jun, the imperial field generals, and then went after the two rebel leaders.[31]

· · · · ·

Meanwhile Xuande and his brothers neared Yingchuan, hurrying toward the roar of battle and the glowing night horizon. They reached the scene only to find the rebels already scattered. Xuande presented himself to Huangfu Song and Zhu Jun and explained why Lu Zhi had sent him. "Zhang Jue's two brothers are done for by now," said Huangfu Song. "They'll be taking refuge with Jue at Guangzong. That's where you are needed." Xuande accepted the order and led his men back. En route they came upon some soldiers escorting a cage-cart holding none other than Lu Zhi as prisoner. Amazed to find under arrest the commander whom he so recently had been serving, Xuande dismounted and asked what was the matter. "I had Zhang Jue surrounded and nearly defeated," Lu Zhi explained, "when he prevented our victory by some kind of magic. The court sent the eunuch Zuo Feng from the Inner Bureau to investigate. He was only looking to get paid off, but I told him that with supplies exhausted we had nothing to spare for the imperial envoy. My refusal only angered him. He bore the grudge back to court and reported that I was weakening morale by keeping on the defensive and not engaging the enemy. The court sent Imperial Corps Commander Dong Zhuo to relieve me and return me to the capital to face charges."

Outraged by this treatment of Xuande's former teacher, Zhang Fei moved to cut down the guard and rescue the prisoner. But Xuande checked him. "The court will see to it that justice is done" he said. "Better not act rashly." They let the escort pass. "With Lu Zhi arrested and replaced," said Lord Guan, "we have nowhere to go but back to Zhuo district." Xuande agreed and began marching north. But on the next day they heard a great tumult beyond a hill. Xuande and his brothers climbed to high ground. A beaten Han army came into their view. Behind it, hill and dale swarmed with Yellow Scarves bearing banners that read "Heavenly Commander." "Zhang Jue himself!" cried Xuande. "Let's attack at once."[32]

The three brothers swung their men into fighting position just as Zhang Jue was beating down the forces of Dong Zhuo, Lu Zhi's replacement as Imperial Corps commander. Carried by their momentum, the rebels drove hard until they ran up against the brothers. A murderous clash followed. Jue's men were thrown into confusion and had to retreat more than fifty *li*. The brothers rescued Dong Zhuo and saw him back to his camp. Zhuo inquired what offices they held but, upon learning that they were commoners without position, disdainfully refused to acknowledge their service.[33] The three started to leave the camp with Zhang Fei grumbling, "Is that how the wretch treats us for risking our lives to save him? Then I'll have another kind of satisfaction!" Bent on revenge, Zhang Fei turned and stamped back toward Dong Zhuo's headquarters, a sword in his hand. It was a case where, indeed:

> Status is what counts and always has!
> Who needs to honor heroes without rank?
> Oh, let me have a Zhang Fei straight and true,
> Who'll pay out every ingrate what he's due.

Did Zhang Fei kill the Imperial Corps commander?

READ ON.

2

Zhang Fei Whips the Government Inspector;
Imperial In-Law He Jin Plots Against the Eunuchs

GOVERNOR OF HEDONG DONG ZHUO (styled Zhongying), a native of Lintao in Longxi in the far northwest, was a man to whom arrogance came naturally. His rude treatment of Xuande had provoked Zhang Fei to turn back and seek satisfaction, but Xuande and Lord Guan warned their brother, "He holds the court's mandate. You cannot take the law into your own hands." "If we don't do away with the wretch," Fei retorted, "we'll be taking orders from him—the last thing I could stand. You two stay if you like. I'm leaving." "We three, sworn to live and die as one," said Xuande, "must not part. We'll go elsewhere." "We're all going, then?" responded Zhang Fei. "That's some consolation."

Riding all night, the three warriors reached the camp of Zhu Jun, the Imperial Corps commander, who welcomed them heartily and united their forces with his own. Together they advanced against the second rebel brother, Zhang Bao. (The third brother, Zhang Liang, was battling Cao Cao and Huangfu Song at Quyang at the time.) Zhang Bao had command of eighty or ninety thousand troops camped behind a mountain. Zhu Jun sent Xuande forward, and Zhang Bao dispatched his lieutenant Gao Sheng to taunt the government forces. Xuande waved Zhang Fei into combat, and he charged and ran Gao Sheng through after a few brief clashes. Sheng toppled from his horse as Xuande signaled his men to advance.

Zhang Bao, on horseback, unbound his hair and, sword in hand, began to work a magic formula. As throngs of Xuande's soldiers charged, a thunderstorm started to gather, and a black mist surrounded what seemed like an army of warriors in the sky. When the apparition plunged toward them, the men were thrown into confusion. Xuande hurried back to camp to report the defeat. "They were using shamanic tricks," said Zhu Jun. "Tomorrow we will slaughter a pig, a goat, and a dog and throw down on the rebels a mixture of the animals' blood, entrails, and excrement."[1] Xuande placed Lord Guan and Zhang Fei, each with a thousand men, in ambush high on a slope of the hill, ready to hurl down the abominable preparation when Zhang Bao's troops passed.

The next day, with banners waving and drums rolling, Zhang Bao arrived in force. Xuande rode out to face him. As the soldiers prepared to engage in battle, Bao used his powers and a storm sprang up as before. Sand and stones went flying, and a murky mist packed with men and horses began to descend from the sky. Xuande wheeled and fled, drawing Bao in pursuit past the hill. At the given signal Lord Guan and Zhang Fei dumped their concoction over the enemy. In front of everyone's eyes, the storm died away, and the mist dissolved as paper men and straw horses tumbled from the sky every which way. Sand and stone lay still. Seeing his craft undone, Bao retreated quickly, but Lord Guan came forth on his left and Zhang Fei on his right, while Xuande and Zhu Jun raced up behind. Between these converging forces the rebels were crushed.

Xuande spotted Bao's "General of the Earth"[2] banner some distance away and gave chase. Bao rode frantically for the brush, but Xuande shot an arrow through his left arm. The wounded rebel sought shelter in the city of Yang, to which Zhu Jun at once lay siege. Zhu Jun also sent for news of Huangfu Song's battle with Zhang Bao's brother, Liang, and received the following message:

> Huangfu Song won a great victory, and the court used him to replace the oft-defeated Dong Zhuo. Song arrived to find the chief rebel, Jue, dead, and Liang, who had taken over his command, locked in battle with our units. Song won seven battles in sucession; he killed Liang at Quyang. Then they opened up Jue's coffin, mutilated the corpse and impaled his head, which they later sent to the capital. The surviving rebels gave themselves up, and the court rewarded Song with the title of general of Chariots and Cavalry and appointed him protector of Jizhou.[3] Song then petitioned the Emperor, stating that Lu Zhi's conduct was meritorious, not blameworthy, and the court restored his former office. Cao Cao's service, too, was recognized, and he was awarded a fief at Jinan. When I left, they were about to return to the capital in triumph before assuming their new posts.

This was heartening news to Zhu Jun, and he pressed the siege harder. The rebels' position became critical. Finally, Zhang Bao was slain by Yan Zheng, one of his own commanders, who then surrendered with his leader's head. The battle won, Zhu Jun pacified several neighboring districts and reported to the throne.

•   •   •   •

Meanwhile, three other rebel leaders—Zhao Hong, Han Zhong, and Sun Zhong—had gathered tens of thousands of followers to avenge their fallen master, Zhang Jue, by new acts of plunder and destruction. The court summoned Zhu Jun to punish them with his victorious units. Bearing the imperial command, Zhu Jun advanced on the rebel-held city of Wancheng. Zhao Hong sent Han Zhong to engage Zhu Jun's army. Zhu Jun ordered Xuande and his brothers to attack the southwest corner of the city wall. Han Zhong rushed to its defense with seasoned troops. Zhu Jun personally led two thousand hardened cavalrymen directly to the northeast corner. Fearful of losing the city, the rebels quickly withdrew from their southwest position. Xuande beset their rear, and the horde, badly defeated, fled into the city. Zhu Jun responded by dividing his force and surrounding Wancheng. The city was short of food, and Han Zhong offered to surrender. But Zhu Jun refused his offer.

Xuande argued for accepting: "Gao Zu, founder of the Han, won the empire because he knew how to invite surrender and how to receive it. Why refuse their offer, my lord?" "That was then," Zhu Jun replied. "Now is now. Before Han, the empire was convulsed with uprisings against Qin, and there was no established sovereign for the people to acknowledge. To welcome submission and reward allegiance was no doubt the way to attract adherents. But this land of ours enjoys unity today. It is only the Yellow Scarves who have resorted to arms. If we accept their surrender, how will we encourage loyal and decent men? If we allow those who pillage at will when they win to give themselves up when they lose, we give an incentive to subversion. A rather poor idea, I'd say."

"You are right," Xuande conceded, "to deny an appeal from these criminals. And yet, trapped like this in an iron grip, they can only fight to the last. A myriad single-minded men cannot be withstood, let alone desperadoes several times that number. We could pull back from the southeast and concentrate on the northwest. The rebels will flee the city; and having lost their taste for combat, they can be quickly captured." Zhu Jun acted on Xuande's suggestion, and the rebel Han Zhong, as expected, led his soldiers in headlong flight from Wancheng. Zhu Jun, joined by Xuande and his two brothers, attacked them in full force. Han Zhong was killed with an arrow shot. The survivors scattered. But as the government forces were mopping up, the battle took another turn. Zhao Hong and Sun Zhong arrived and engaged Jun, who retreated before this unexpected show of strength. The Yellow Scarves retook Wancheng.

Zhu Jun removed ten *li* and was preparing to counterattack when he saw a mass of soldiers coming from the east. At their head was a man of broad forehead and wide face, with a body powerful as a tiger's and a torso thick as a bear's. This man from Fuchun in the imperial district of Wu was surnamed Sun.[4] His given name was Jian; his style Wentai; he was descended from the famous strategist Sunzi.

Years before, when Sun Jian was seventeen, he and his father watched a dozen pirates seize a merchant's goods and divide the spoils on the shore of the Qiantang River. Jian said to his father, "Let's take them prisoner." Sword bared, Jian leaped ashore and confronted the thieves, gesturing left and right as if signaling his followers. Fooled into thinking government troops were nearby, the thieves left their loot and fled, except for one whom Jian killed. This is how he made a name for himself in the region and was recommended for the post of commandant.

Some time after Sun Jian's appointment, one Xu Chang of Kuaiji revolted, titling himself the Sun Emperor and mobilizing tens of thousands of men. Jian and a district commanding officer recruited a thousand fighters and rallied the province's districts. Together they destroyed the rebels and killed Xu Chang and his son Shao. The imperial inspector of the province, Zang Min, reported Sun Jian's achievements to the Emperor, and Jian was promoted to deputy magistrate of Yandu, Xuyi, and Xiapi.

In response to the risings of the Yellow Scarves, Sun Jian gathered young men from his village, as well as many traders and experienced soldiers from the area of the Huai and Si rivers—some fifteen hundred in all—and went to aid the embattled Zhu Jun at Wancheng. Thus reinforced, Zhu Jun ordered Jian to attack the south gate and Xuande to attack the north. Zhu Jun himself lay siege on the west, giving the rebels a way out only on the east. Sun Jian was the first to gain the city wall, where he cut down twenty men and threw the rebels into confusion. Zhao Hong brandished his lance and made for Sun Jian, but Jian flung himself on his attacker, wrested away the lance, and ran him through. Then, taking Hong's horse, he charged the swarming rebels and slew many. Sun Zhong and his rebel force tried to break through the north gate, only to encounter Xuande, before whom Zhong fled in panic. Xuande felled him with a single arrow. Zhu Jun's main force then set upon the rebels from behind. Tens of thousands were beheaded, and untold numbers gave themselves up. Throughout the Nanyang area more than ten imperial districts were pacified.

Zhu Jun returned in triumph to the capital, where he was raised to the rank of general of Chariots and Cavalry and appointed governor of Henan. As governor, he reported to the throne the merits of Sun Jian and Xuande. Profiting from his connections,[5] Jian obtained a post as an auxiliary district commanding officer and went at once to assume his new office. Only Xuande was left waiting many days, receiving no word of an appointment.

•   •   •   •

Disheartened, the three brothers were walking in the capital when they came upon the carriage of the courtier Zhang Jun. Xuande presented himself and gave a brief account of his victories. Zhang Jun was surprised that the court had neglected such a man, and at his next audience with the Emperor said, "Sale of office and rank by the Ten Eunuchs is the fundamental cause of the recent uprisings. They have appointed only their own and punished only their enemies, and have thrown the realm into chaos in the process. For peace to prevail, it would behoove Your Majesty to execute the Ten, hang their severed heads outside the south gate of the capital, and proclaim to all the empire that hereafter merit will be well rewarded." The eunuchs counterattacked, accusing Zhang Jun of lese majesty. The Emperor resolved the dispute by ordering his guards to expel Zhang Jun from court.

The eunuchs continued discussing the matter: "This complaint," they agreed, "must have come from some deserving warriors who were passed over. It might be useful to have the central office review some of the lesser ones for appointment. We will have time enough to deal with them afterwards."[6] And so Xuande was appointed judicial officer of Anxi county in the Zhongshan jurisdiction of Dingzhou imperial district, with orders to depart on a specified date. Xuande disbanded his troops and set out with his brothers and some two dozen followers. In Anxi he avoided all injury to the interests of the local people, and civic morality improved within a month. While in office Xuande shared bed and board with his brothers, and they stood beside him throughout long public sessions.

In a few months' time, however, the court decreed a purge of leading officials whose posts had been awarded in recognition of military service, a measure Xuande suspected would lead to his removal. Just then a district inspector came to Anxi, one of the counties under his jurisdiction. Xuande received the official outside the city with full honors. But the inspector remained mounted, reciprocating Xuande's salutation with a faint flick of his whip. Zhang Fei and Lord Guan seethed with resentment. At the posthouse the inspector seated himself upon a raised platform and faced south like an emperor holding court, while Xuande stood respectfully at the foot of the platform. After an extended wait the official spoke: "Tell me about your background, Officer Liu." "I am a descendant of Prince Jing of Zhongshan," replied Xuande. "I began campaigning against the Yellow Scarves in Zhuo county and have destroyed many of them, achieving some slight merit in over thirty engagements, some small, some large. As a result, I was appointed to this post."

"Isn't your claim of imperial ancestry a lie?" roared the inspector. "Like those phony reports of your 'achievements'? I have here in hand the court's decree purging such undeserving officials and corrupt officers as you." Xuande could only back away, humbly voicing his agreement. "Yes, sir. Yes, sir," he said and returned to the *yamen* to consult with another officer. "The inspector is creating a scene," the latter suggested, "only because he wants a bribe." "But I have never taken advantage of the people here," Xuande argued, "and have acquired nothing of value to give him." The following day the inspector sent for this county officer and pressured him into accusing Officer Liu of abusing the people. Every time Xuande tried to see the inspector to justify himself, guards turned him away.

After comforting himself with a few cups of wine, Zhang Fei rode by the posthouse. At the door he saw dozens of elderly folk weeping and wailing. When Zhang Fei asked the reason, they said, "The inspector is forcing the county officer to make statements that will enable him to get rid of our Lord Liu. We have come to plead for him but cannot get inside. The guards beat us back for our pains."

Zhang Fei's eyes widened with anger. Jaw set, he slid from his saddle and went straight to the posthouse, broke through the guard, and dashed to the rear. He saw the inspector holding formal session and the county officer, bound, on the ground. "Plague to the people," thundered Zhang Fei, "do you know me?" Before the inspector could open his mouth, Zhang Fei had him by the hair, dragged him to the front of the posthouse, and tied him to the hitching post. Then with some light switches stripped from a nearby willow, he whipped the inspector across the legs so soundly that a dozen of the switches split.

Xuande, having been kept from the inspector's presence, could not tell what was going on. Then he heard the commotion outside the posthouse and was told, "Commander Zhang Fei is beating the life out of somebody there." Xuande found out who the victim was and, aghast, demanded an explanation of Zhang Fei. "This enemy of the people should be beaten to death," his brother said, "and the sooner the better." But the inspector pleaded, "Let me live, my good lord," and Xuande, a kindhearted sort when all was said and done, shouted to Zhang Fei to desist.

At this moment Lord Guan turned up. "Brother," he said, "your great service has been ill rewarded with this miserable post. Add to that this inspector's insults. Does a phoenix belong in a briar patch? Let's kill him, resign the office, and go home to plan for a better day." At these words Xuande took his seal and ribbon of office and hung them on the inspector's neck, saying, "For the harm you've caused the people we should have your life. However, we shall spare you. You may take these back, and I shall take my leave."[7]

The inspector returned to Dingzhou and reported the incident to the governor, who in turn notified higher central and regional authorities in order to have the brothers arrested. But the wanted men found refuge in Daizhou with Liu Hui, who hid them in his home in consideration of Xuande's imperial lineage.

· · · · ·

Meanwhile, at the court the Ten Eunuchs were using their great power to do away with anyone who went against them. Zhao Zhong and Zhang Rang demanded payment of gold and silk from all who had won distinction fighting the Yellow Scarves, and removed from office those who would not pay. In consequence, commanders Huangfu Song and Zhu Jun were deprived of office. The Emperor added the rank of general of Chariots and Cavalry to Zhao Zhong's other honors and awarded lordships to Zhang Rang and twelve others.

Administration worsened and the people grumbled. Ou Xing staged an uprising in Changsha. In Yuyang, Zhang Ju and Zhang Chun rebelled, Zhang Ju claiming to be emperor and Zhang Chun his marshal. The court was swamped with emergency appeals from every quarter of the land, but the Ten blithely filed them away and never informed the throne.

One day the Emperor and the Ten were feasting in the rear garden when Liu Tao, a court counselor, came before the sovereign and began weeping passionately. The Emperor requested an explanation, and Liu Tao replied, "With the empire in peril, how can Your Majesty continue feasting with these capons?" "Why, our nation is as peaceful as ever," the Emperor said. "What 'peril' do you have in mind?" "Bandits and rebels rise everywhere," responded Liu Tao, "plundering province and district—all because of the sale of office and the abuse of the people by the Ten Eunuchs, who have wronged and deceived Your Majesty. All upright men have fled your service. Disaster looms."

At this indictment, the Ten threw down their caps and prostrated themselves. "If Counselor Liu Tao cannot tolerate us," they cried, "we are done for. We beg only our lives and your permission to return to our farms. Everything we own will be donated to the army." Then they wept freely. The Emperor turned on the count counselor. "You," he said, "have your attendants. Should I not have mine?" He ordered the guards to march Liu Tao out and behead him. "I care not for my life," cried Tao, "but how my heart aches for the empire of Han—on the verge of extinction after four hundred years!" The guards had removed him and were about to execute him when a high official checked them with a shout: "Stay your hand until I make my plea!"

The assembly saw that it was Minister of the Interior Chen Dan, coming directly into the palace to place his objections before the Emperor. "What fault of Counselor Liu's deserves such punishment?" he asked. "He slanders our close attendants," said the Emperor, "and sullies our person." "These eunuchs whom you honor like parents," said the minister, "the people would eat alive if they could. They are raised to lordships without the least merit—to say nothing of the traitors among them like Feng Xu, who colluded with the Yellow Scarves. If Your Majesty will not consider this, the sacred shrines of the royal house could fall at any moment."

The Emperor said, "Feng Xu's role in the rebellion was never proven. As for the Ten Eunuchs, do you mean to tell me there isn't a single one who is loyal?" Chen Dan emphasized his protest by striking his head against the steps below the throne. The indignant Emperor had him dragged off and thrown into prison beside Liu Tao. That night the eunuchs had the two officials murdered. Then they forged an official decree making Sun Jian governor of Changsha with a commission to put down the rebellion of Ou Xing. Within fifty days Sun Jian reported victory and the Jiangxia region was secured.

A decree enfeoffed Sun Jian as lord of Wucheng and made Liu Yu protector of Youzhou.[8] Liu Yu launched a campaign against Zhang Ju and Zhang Chun in Yuyang; and Liu Hui of Daizhou wrote the new protector recommending Xuande, whom he had sheltered. Liu Yu was delighted and appointed Xuande district commander. Xuande took the battle straight to the bandits' lair. In several days' hard fighting Xuande beat down the impetuous spirit of the rebels, who then turned upon Zhang Chun, their violent and autocratic leader. He was killed by one of his own chieftains, who brought Chun's head to the government authorities and surrendered with his soldiers. Zhang Ju, his position collapsing, hanged himself. Now Yuyang, too, was fully pacified.

Protector Liu Yu reported Xuande's great service to the court. Not only was he forgiven for having flogged the inspector, but he was promoted to deputy magistrate of Xiami and made judicial officer of Gaotang. Gongsun Zan added his praise of Xuande's former service; on his recommendation Xuande was made an auxiliary corps commanding officer and assigned to Pingyuan county as magistrate. At Pingyuan, Xuande had considerable resources and manpower at his disposal and was able to reestablish the atmosphere of former days. Liu Yu, for his great service in quelling the bandits, was made grand commandant.

•   •   •   •   •

In the fourth month of the sixth year of the Zhong Ping reign (A.D. 189), Emperor Ling fell gravely ill and called for Regent He Jin to make plans for the succession. He Jin was from a butcher's family and had attained his powerful position only through the influence of his younger sister, Lady He, a royal concubine who on giving birth to a son, Bian, had become Empress He. Emperor Ling had a second favorite, Beauty Wang. Lady Wang too bore a son, and Empress He out of jealousy poisoned her. The child, Xie, was raised in the palace of the Emperor's mother, Dong.

Queen Mother Dong was the wife of Liu Chang, lord of Jiedu precinct. Because Huan, the previous emperor, had had no male issue, Liu Chang's son was made heir apparent and became Emperor Ling upon the death of Huan. When Ling succeeded to the throne, his mother was taken into the palace and honored as queen mother. In the matter of Ling's heir apparent, Queen Mother Dong urged the Emperor to name Xie, son of the murdered concubine Wang, over Bian, son of Empress He. The Emperor himself was disposed to make this change as he was partial to Prince Xie.

As Emperor Ling's end drew near, the eunuch Jian Shuo[9] advised him, "If it is Your Majesty's wish that Prince Xie, not Prince Bian, follow you on the throne, first get rid of Regent He Jin, Bian's uncle, to forestall countermeasures." Emperor Ling took his advice and commanded He Jin to appear. He Jin arrived at the palace gate but there was warned by the commanding officer, Pan Yin, not to enter because Jian Shuo meant to kill him. He Jin fled to his quarters and summoned the ministers and high officials to consider executing all the eunuchs. To this drastic step one man rose to object. "The influence of the eunuchs," he argued, "goes back to the reigns of emperors Chong and Zhi [A.D. 145–47]. Now they have overrun the court. How can we kill each and every one of them? If discovered, we will be killed and our clans exterminated. Pray consider this thoroughly."

Regent-Marshal He Jin regarded the man. It was Cao Cao, commandant for Military Standards. "What do you junior officers know of court matters?" said Jin, turning disdainfully to Cao. The problem was still under discussion when Commanding Officer Pan Yin brought the news of the Emperor's demise. "Jian Shuo and the eunuchs," he informed He Jin, "plan to keep the death secret. They have forged a decree summoning you to the palace and expect to have their way by eliminating you before declaring Prince Xie emperor." The group had not yet reached a decision when the court's messenger came commanding He Jin's immediate appearance to resolve all pending issues.

"Today before all else we must rectify the succession," cried Cao Cao. "Then we can take care of the traitors." "Who will join me," asked He Jin, "in supporting the legitimate heir, Prince Bian, and bringing the traitors to justice?" "Give me five thousand crack troops," one official spoke up, "and I will march into the palace, enthrone the rightful emperor, destroy the eunuchs, and purge the court, thus restoring peace in the land." He Jin eyed the speaker. It was Yuan Shao (styled Benchu), son of former Minister of the Interior Yuan Feng, nephew of Yuan Wei; at the time Shao was commander of the Capital Districts. He Jin, gratified by the offer, assigned five thousand of his Royal Guard to Yuan Shao's command.

Yuan Shao girded himself for battle. With He Jin in the lead, He Yu, Xun You, Zheng Tai, and some thirty other high officials filed into the palace. There before the coffin of Emperor Ling they placed He Jin's nephew, Prince Bian, on the throne as Ling's successor, Emperor Shao. When shouts of allegiance from the assembled officials died down, Yuan Shao entered the palace to arrest Jian Shuo. Jian Shuo fled to the royal garden and hid himself, but Guo Sheng, one of the Ten, found and killed him, and the Palace Guard, which Jian Shuo had commanded, all surrendered. Yuan Shao said to He Jin, "These eunuchs have organized their own gang. But today the tide runs with us. Let's kill every last one."

Zhang Rang and his group of Ten Eunuchs, realizing that their end was near, rushed to see the Empress He, sister of Regent-Marshal He Jin. "Jian Shuo and Jian Shuo alone," they assured her, "tried to kill your brother the regent. Not one of us was involved. But Yuan Shao has won the regent over and is bent on doing away with all of us. Have pity, Your Majesty." Empress He, whose son, Bian, had just been enthroned, said, "Have no fear. I shall protect you." She ordered He Jin before her and spoke to him privately: "You and I are humbly born and could not enjoy the wealth and status we have today except for Zhang Rang and the Ten. Jian Shuo has paid for his crime. Don't listen to those who want to kill them all." Thus admonished, He Jin came out and addressed the assembly: "Jian Shuo tried to murder me. Now he is dead, and his clan will be destroyed. There is no need to punish the rest." "If we don't root them out for good," objected Yuan Shao, "we will pay with our lives." "The decision is made," He Jin insisted. "Let no more be said." With that the assembly retired. The following day Empress He ordered He Jin to supervise the work of the Imperial Secretariat, which issues decrees, and the regent-marshal's associates were granted official positions. [10]

Now the rival empress, Dong (mother of the late Emperor Ling and guardian of Prince Xie), summoned Zhang Rang of the Ten Eunuchs. "I was the one," she told him, "who first helped Empress He. Now her son reigns over all officialdom, inside and outside the court. Her power is great. What are we to do?" "Your Majesty," replied Rang, "control the court from behind the scene; preside over administration; have the imperial son, Xie, enfeoffed as a prince; have high office conferred on your bother, the imperial uncle; see that he gets real military power; use us in important ways, and we can aim higher soon enough." Immensely pleased with this advice, Empress Dong held court the following day and issued a decree naming Xie as prince of Chenliu and Imperial Uncle Dong Chong as general of the Flying Cavalry. Zhang Rang and the eunuchs were again permitted to participate in court affairs.

Empress He, seeing her rival gather power, arranged a banquet in the palace for her. When the company was well warmed with wine, Empress He lifted her cup and kneeled respectfully as she addressed Empress Dong: "We two women should not concern ourselves with court affairs. In the founding reign of this dynasty Empress Lü wielded great power. [11] But in the end her clan, one thousand strong, was extinguished. You and I should seclude ourselves in the palace and leave court business to the great ministers and elder statesmen. The ruling house will benefit. I hope you will give this your consideration."

To this challenge Empress Dong rose angrily. "Your jealousy drove you to poison Beauty Wang," she accused. "Now you have the temerity to say any damned thing you please because your son rules and your brother is in power. But without lifting a finger I can have the general of the Flying Cavalry cut off He Jin's head." "I spoke in good faith," responded Empress He hotly. "What gives you the right to lash out at me?" "A lot you know" retorted Empress Dong, "you offspring of butchers and wine merchants!" The two queens quarreled back and forth until Zhang Rang persuaded them to return to their chambers. That night Empress He summoned her brother and described to him the scene at the banquet.

Regent He Jin then met with the three elder lords (grand commandant, minister of the interior, minister of works). And the following morning, in accordance with their decision, a courtier petitioned the Emperor not to allow Empress Dong to remain in the palace, on the grounds that she was originally a provincial princess, but to return her to Hejian, her original fief, without delay. The He faction assigned escorts for the rival empress and detailed the Palace Guard to surround the home of Flying Cavalry General Dong Chong and demand his insignia. Chong knew he was trapped and cut his throat in a rear chamber. The household raised the cry of mourning and the cordon was lifted. The eunuchs Zhang Rang and Duan Gui, foiled by the destruction of Empress Dong's faction, proceeded to cultivate He Jin's brother Miao and his mother, Lady Wuyang. Plying them with gifts of gold and pearls, the eunuchs had them visit Empress He day and night and gloss their deeds with fine phrases. In this way the Ten Eunuchs regained the privilege of waiting on the Emperor.

In the sixth month He Jin had Empress Dong poisoned at the government relay station in Hejian. Her coffin was brought to the capital and buried in the tombs at Wen. On the pretext of illness, Regent He Jin was absent from the ceremonies. The commander of the Capital Districts, Yuan Shao, visited He Jin and told him, "Zhang Rang and Duan Gui are spreading the rumor that you poisoned Empress Dong in order to usurp the throne. Unless you eliminate the eunuchs this time, the consequences will be unspeakable. Early in the last reign Dou Wu tried to destroy them, but they discovered his plans and killed him instead. Today you and your brother have the finest commanders and officers in your service. If they are with you, events can be kept in control. Do not let a Heaven-sent opportunity slip your grasp." He Jin responded, "This is a matter that bears further consideration."

Meanwhile, some of He Jin's men were secretly reporting to Zhang Rang, who in turn informed He Miao, Jin's brother, and also bribed him richly. Miao then went before Empress He and said, "The regent, mainstay of the new Emperor, has been guilty of cruel and inhuman conduct. Killing seems to be his sole concern. He has been trying to do away with the Ten Eunuchs for no good reason. It is going to lead to chaos." The Empress agreed, and when He Jin later declared his intention to liquidate the gelded attendants, she replied, "Supervision of palace affairs by these officials of the women's quarters is a long-standing practice of the Han. With the late sovereign so recently departed, your desire to put the old ministers to death does not show proper respect for the ancestral temple of the ruling house."

He Jin, by nature an indecisive man, feebly muttered his agreement as he left his sister's presence. And to Yuan Shao's question, "How fares our cause?" he could only answer, "The queen mother does not concur. What can we do?" "Indeed," said Yuan Shao sharply, "let us summon the gallants of the realm, march into the capital, and wipe out these capons. Now is the critical moment. Forget the queen mother's disapproval!" "A superb idea," He Jin exclaimed and issued a call to various military stations for troops.[12]

But Chen Lin, first secretary to He Jin, objected: "That's not going to work! You know the proverb, 'You can't catch a sparrow with your eyes shut.' Even trivial ends cannot be gained by self-deception; what of affairs of state? Now, General, you have the weight of the throne behind you and military authority in your hands. You can 'prance like a dragon and prowl like a tiger.' Whatever you wish is yours. You can execute the eunuchs as easily as you can burn a hair in a furnace. Act with lightning speed, with decision and expedition, and the whole world will go along. There's no need to call in outside forces and bring a mob of warriors down on the capital, each with his own ambitions. That is like handing someone a weapon pointed toward yourself! You will fail, and worse, you will create an upheaval." With a laugh, He Jin said, "This weak-kneed scholar understands nothing!" Another officer beside He Jin was laughing and applauding. "This really presents no problem," he said. "Why waste so much time discussing it?" The speaker was Cao Cao, and his advice was simple. Indeed:

> Wise counsel can undo the harm of vicious ministers—
> When and if it is heeded.

What did Cao Cao say?
READ ON.

3

In Wenming Garden, Dong Zhuo Denounces Ding Yuan;
With Gold and Pearls, Li Su Plies Lü Bu

"EUNUCHS," CAO CAO WENT ON, "have been a plague since ancient times. But the founder of the Eastern Han, Emperor Guang Wu, granted them excessive power and favor and sowed the seeds of the crisis that is upon us today. The remedy is to eliminate the ringleaders. A single bailiff could do it. Why involve regional forces? Any attempt to execute the lot of them is bound to get out and likely to fail for that reason." Angered, He Jin shot back, "You have your own view of the matter, Mengde, I see." "He Jin will be the one to undo the empire!" Cao Cao muttered as he left the meeting. Having disposed of his opponent, He Jin dispatched messengers bearing secret decrees to various regional garrisons.

•   •   •   •   •

Dong Zhuo, general of the Forward Army, lord of Aoxiang, and imperial inspector of the westernmost province of Xiliang, had escaped the court's penalties for his losses to the Yellow Scarves by bribing the Ten Eunuchs. After that, through the good offices of certain highly placed courtiers, he secured a notable appointment as the commander of two hundred thousand men farther west in Xizhou. But despite such favors, he had no loyalty to the Emperor.

When He Jin's secret summons came, he prepared to set out for the capital in full force. Zhuo ordered his son-in-law Imperial Corps Commander Niu Fu to remain and defend his western domains and arranged to take with him to Luoyang four commanders—Li Jue, Guo Si, Zhang Ji, and Fan Chou—and their men. Li Ru, another son-in-law and an adviser, said to Dong Zhuo, "The summons we have received contains much that is unclear. Let us present a statement to the throne legitimating our position. Then we can bid for higher stakes." Pleased with this counsel, Zhuo submitted a petition that said in essence:

It is our humble understanding that seditious opposition can no longer be controlled because Zhang Rang and the Constant Attendants of the Inner Bureau have perverted the fundamental order of things. In our view, a raging cauldron is best cooled by removing the fuel. Lancing a pustule, though painful, is preferable to harboring the infection. Your subject makes bold to sound the alarm and enter the capital, with your permission, to destroy Zhang Rang and his gang—for the benefit of the dynasty and the empire.[1]

He Jin put Dong Zhuo's request to enter the capital before the principal ministers. Zheng Tai, the court censor, objected: "Dong Zhuo's a jackal. Let him into the capital and he'll devour us." "Your indecisiveness," said He Jin, "renders you unfit to discuss major questions." Lu Zhi[2] also voiced opposition: "The Dong Zhuo I have known for many years hides a vicious mind beneath that benign exterior. We're courting disaster. Better keep him out." He Jin ignored all objections. The two critics resigned their offices, and more than half the court followed their example. He Jin had Dong Zhuo greeted at Mianchi.

Dong Zhuo restrained his troops and made no move. Zhang Rang and the eunuchs learned of the arrival of outside forces and said, "A plot of He Jin's. If we don't head it off, our clans will be exterminated." Planting fifty hatchetmen inside the Gate of Praiseworthy Virtue at the Palace of Lasting Happiness,[3] Zhang Rang went in and told the Empress, "The regent means to destroy us and has forged a decree summoning outside troops to the capital. We beg Your Majesty, have mercy and save us."[4] "Present yourselves at his headquarters and apologize for your offenses," was her reply. "If we go there," said Rang, "his men will beat us to a pulp. We appeal to Your Majesty to summon him to the palace and stop him. If he refuses, we prefer to die at your feet." Empress He ordered He Jin to appear.

Chen Lin, He Jin's first secretary, sought to dissuade the regent. "This," he argued, "is a plot of the Ten Eunuchs. Keep away. If you go we are ruined." "It is the Empress's own command," said He Jin. "Nothing can happen." "Our plans," Yuan Shao said, "have been leaked. Our cause is publicly known. Do you still want to enter the palace?" "Have the Ten come out before you go in," suggested Cao Cao. "How silly!" said He Jin with a laugh. "I am the master of the empire. What can those Ten do to me?" "If you insist," Yuan Shao said. "But let us bring an armed guard—just in case."

Yuan Shao and Cao Cao each selected five hundred of their finest and put them under the command of Yuan Shao's brother Shu. Fully armored, Yuan Shu drew his men around the ornate palace entrance. Yuan Shao and Cao Cao strapped on their swords and accompanied He Jin to the gate of the Palace of Lasting Happiness. But the Inner Bureau conveyed the Empress's wish: "The Empress has summoned only the regent. No one else may enter." Yuan Shao and Cao Cao stood barred beyond the outer gate as He Jin marched grandly on, straight into the palace.

Their henchmen in place, Zhang Rang and Duan Gui accosted He Jin from both sides at the Gate of Praiseworthy Virtue. In a stern tone Zhang Rang read out a list of charges to the astounded regent: "For what crime did you poison Empress Dong? How could you miss the services for the nation's mother on the pretext of illness? You came from a family of butchers; your recommendation to the throne came from us; and through us you rose to power and glory. But now you conspire against us, forgetting the duties and the thanks you owe. Who is so pure, tell me, if we are as corrupt as you say?"

He Jin searched frantically for a way to escape, but every gate was shut. The assassins closed in and cut He Jin in two at the waist. A poet of later times lamented his fate:

> The Han will fall, its star-told fate fulfilled,
> With feckless He Jin counseling the king.
> Deaf to honest words, he seals his doom:
> Quartered in the queen's receiving room.

Having waited for a long time, Yuan Shao shouted at the gate, "Regent, your carriage is ready!" In response Zhang Rang threw the victim's head down from the wall. "He Jin was executed for plotting to overthrow the dynasty," he cried. "Those who joined him under duress are pardoned, one and all!" "The geldings have murdered a great minister," Shao yelled fiercely. "Those who would destroy this evil faction—lend us your aid!" One of He Jin's commanders, Wu Kuang, set a fire outside the main gate, and Yuan Shu burst into the palace grounds. Every eunuch they caught, they killed. Yuan Shao and Cao Cao broke into the inner sanctum, drove the four eunuchs, Zhao Zhong, Cheng Kuang, Xia Yun, and Guo Sheng, to the House of Emerald Flowers, and hacked them to pieces. From the palace buildings flames sprang skyward.

Four of the Ten Eunuchs—Zhang Rang, Duan Gui, Cao Jie, and Hou Lan—forced Queen Mother He, the crown prince (Liu Bian, i.e., Emperor Shao), and the prince of Chenliu (Liu Xie) out of the main compound and along a rear path toward the north palace compound. Lu Zhi, though he had quit his office, had remained in the imperial complex. Seeing the coup in progress, he armed himself and stood under a second-story walkway. Catching a glimpse of Duan Gui threatening Empress He, Zhi shouted, "Traitor! To kidnap the queen mother!" Gui turned and ran. The queen mother jumped from a window, and Lu Zhi rushed her to safety. Wu Kuang cut his way into the courtyard, where he found He Miao with sword drawn. "Miao was part of the plot against his brother," shouted Kuang. "He must die!" The crowd around Kuang also demanded Miao's head. He Miao tried to flee but was encircled and hacked down. Yuan Shao ordered his men to spread out and kill the Ten Attendants and their families, regardless of age. Many who had no beard were killed by mistake. Cao Cao managed to quell the fires and appealed to the queen mother to assume temporary authority. At the same time he sent soldiers after Zhang Rang and his gang to find Emperor Shao (Prince Bian).

Earlier, Zhang Rang and Duan Gui had seized the two royal sons, Emperor Shao and the prince of Chenliu (Xie). Braving smoke and fire, the two eunuchs reached the Beimang Hills.[5] During the second watch they heard the clamor of soldiers charging up. In the front ranks was Min Gong, an aide in the Henan district. "Don't move, you traitors," he shouted. Zhang Rang saw he was done for and drowned himself in a nearby stream. Emperor Shao and the prince of Chenliu, unable to tell friend from foe, lay low in the tangled weeds by the water's edge, eluding the wide search.[6] Though famished, the two brothers stayed out of sight until the fourth watch. A chill early dew settled over them. They huddled together and started to sob but swallowed their cries for fear of discovery. "We can't stay here forever," said the prince, "we have to find a way out." They tied themselves together by their clothes and climbed the bank thick with thorny brambles. It was still too dark to see the path. The boys despaired. Suddenly thousands of fireflies gathered before them, emitting a beam of light as they swirled in front of the Emperor. "Heaven is helping us," said the prince. They followed the glow and soon found a road. By the fifth watch their feet ached, and they lay down beside some hay stacked on a hillside ridge.

Beyond the haystack was a manor whose master had dreamed of two red suns falling to earth behind his farm. Startled from his sleep, he went out and saw two red rays probing the sky. He hurried to the source and discovered the boys. "What family do you belong to?" he asked. The Emperor could not reply. "This is the reigning Emperor," said the prince. "We fled the violence caused by the eunuchs. I am his younger brother, the prince of Chenliu." The astonished lord of the manor saluted them repeatedly. "I am Cui Yi," he said, "brother of the late emperor's minister of the interior, Cui Lie. I retired here when I saw how the eunuchs were corrupting the government." Cui Yi helped the Emperor into his manor and humbly served his guests wine and food.

Meanwhile Min Gong had apprehended Duan Gui. "Where is the Emperor?" he demanded. "We became separated on the road," answered Gui, "and I don't know where he went." Gong killed Gui and tied his severed head around the neck of his horse. Gong's men continued searching in all directions, and Gong himself continued alone along the road. Chance brought him to the Cui manor. The lord received him and asked for an explanation of the gory trophy. In reply, Gong recounted the night's events. Cui Yi then led Min Gong to the Emperor. Sovereign and subject wept bitterly. "The realm," said Gong, "may not lack its lord, even for a single day. Return to the capital, Your Majesty, I pray." Cui Yi had but one feeble horse, which he gave to the Emperor. Gong shared his mount with the prince of Chenliu.

Some three *li* from the manor an array of hundreds of soldiers drew near, led by Minister of the Interior Wang Yun, Grand Commandant Yang Biao, Commandant of the Left Army Chunyu Qiong, Commandant of the Right Army Zhao Meng, Commandant of the Rear Army Bao Xin, and Commandant of the Central Army Yuan Shao.[7] The Emperor and his subjects wept together when they met. Duan Gui's severed head was sent to the capital as a warning. Fine horses were provided for the Emperor and the prince, and the whole troop escorted the Emperor to Luoyang. Prior to these events a child's ditty sung in Luoyang had foretold:

> A king who isn't a king,
> And a prince who is no prince.
> Together the prince and the king must fly
> To the Beimang graves,
> Where their ancestors lie.

Events had fulfilled this prognostication.

The imperial procession had advanced barely a few *li* when a host of banners darkened the sky. Spreading dust everywhere, a mass of soldiers and horsemen came into view. The officials paled. The Emperor panicked. Yuan Shao raced forward and demanded, "Who are you?" From the shadows of spangled pennons a general came forth and cried in a stern voice, "Where is the Emperor?" The Emperor was too frightened to speak, but the prince of Chenliu guided his horse forward and said tearfully, "Who comes here?" "Dong Zhuo, imperial inspector of Xiliang," was the reply. "Are you here to protect the Emperor or to seize him?" asked the prince. "Only to protect him," said Zhuo. "Then get off your horse," said the prince. "The Emperor is here!" The astonished Zhuo dismounted before the Emperor and prostrated himself at the left side of the road.

The prince graciously reassured Dong Zhuo, expressing himself from first to last with discretion and dignity. Dong Zhuo was deeply impressed but did not show it: the idea of deposing Emperor Shao and placing Prince Xie on the throne had already formed in his mind. That day the whole entourage returned to the palace, and the Emperor presented himself before Queen Mother He, as one and all wept freely. But the jade seal, whose possession confirms imperial authority, was not to be found. A search of the palace proved fruitless.

Dong Zhuo stationed his troops outside Luoyang, but his cavalry daily entered the city and ran riot through the streets, striking fear into the hearts of the people. Dong Zhuo himself went in and out of the imperial buildings, showing neither respect nor restraint. Bao Xin, commandant of the Rear Army, told Yuan Shao that Dong Zhuo's disloyalty was manifest and urged his removal. But Shao replied, "With the court but lately stabilized, this is no time for rashness." Bao Xin also raised the matter with Minister of the Interior

Wang Yun, who simply said, "This will have to be considered further." Thus rebuffed, Bao Xin led his own unit out of the capital and took refuge in the Mount Tai region.

Dong Zhuo skillfully gained the confidence of the troops of the He brothers, Jin and Miao, and brought them under his authority. Then he spoke privately to his adviser, Li Ru: "I want to depose the Emperor and enthrone the prince. What do you think?" "The court has no ruler," said Ru. "Act now before circumstances change. Tomorrow call the officials to the Garden of Benign Wisdom and inform them of your decision. This is the time to act upon your authority." Li Ru's answer delighted Dong Zhuo.

The next day Dong Zhuo laid a great banquet in the garden for the elder lords and nobles, all of whom he had intimidated into attending. He waited until all the court officials had arrived and then with studied slowness rode to the gate, dismounted, and entered the grounds without removing his sword.[8] After several rounds of wine he ordered the festivities to cease. "I have only one thing to say," he said, his voice loud and harsh. "Hear it in silence." The assembly was keenly attentive. "The Son of Heaven is sovereign lord of all," Dong Zhuo went on, "but without awe-inspiring dignity he cannot do honor to the ancestral temple or our sacred shrines. The present Emperor is timid and weak. For intellect and learning he cannot match the prince of Chenliu, who deserves to inherit the throne. Hence I shall depose the Emperor and instate the prince. What do the great ministers have to say?"

The assembly was struck speechless, save one man, who pushed forward his setting and stood up. "This is wrong, wrong!" he shouted. "Who are you to dictate such a thing? The Son of Heaven, lawful heir of true descent, is innocent of fault. To propose his removal is madness. Are you trying to overthrow the dynasty?" Dong Zhuo eyed the speaker, Ding Yuan, imperial inspector of Jingzhou.[9] "Those who obey me," Dong Zhuo rasped, "live; those who do not, die." Grasping his sword, he menaced Ding Yuan. At that moment Li Ru spotted a man standing behind Ding Yuan, a massive presence that inspired a shiver of awe. The man was clenching a figured halberd with two side blades, his eyes filled with anger. "Let us not speak of politics at the banquet," Ru said smoothly, hastening forward. "There will be time some other day for open discussion at the council hall." At the audience's urging, Ding Yuan mounted and left.

Again Dong Zhuo put the question. "Do you see reason in what I have said?" "Not altogether, my wise lord," responded Lu Zhi. "In ancient times Yi Yin, the sage minister of the Shang dynasty, immured Tai Jia, an unfit sovereign, in the Paulownia Palace; and during the Han Prime Minister Huo Guang indicted his sovereign, the prince of Changyi, in the ancestral temple for three thousand misdeeds committed in twenty-seven days after he came to the throne, and then dethroned him. However, in the present situation, although the Emperor has not reached maturity, he has demonstrated his receptive intelligence and humane wisdom. There is no blemish in him. You, my lord, an imperial inspector from the western border districts, have never been a part of court administration. Lacking the remarkable abilities of an Yi Yin or a Huo Guang, how can you arrogate to yourself the authority to alter the succession? As the sage has said, 'For the reasons of an Yi Yin it may be done; otherwise, it is treason.'"

Dong Zhuo, enraged by Lu Zhi's speech, advanced on him with bared sword. But Privy Counselor Cai Yong and Court Counselor Peng Bo voiced objection: "Secretary Lu Zhi is renowned throughout the land. Begin by killing him and the realm will soon succumb to terror." On this advice, Dong Zhuo desisted. "The banquet is no place for such questions," said Minister Wang Yun. "Let us consider them another day." With that, the assembly adjourned.

Standing at the garden gate looking out, Dong Zhuo saw a man leap on his horse, halberd in hand, and charge back and forth. "Who is that?" he asked Li Ru. "Ding Yuan's adopted son, Lü Bu, styled Fengxian," was the reply. "Avoid him for now, my lord." Dong Zhuo reentered the garden and kept out of sight. The next day word came that Ding Yuan was outside the city with his men spoiling for a fight. Dong Zhuo, joined by Li Ru, led his forces out to meet them. The two armies faced off. There for all to see was Lü Bu, his topknot bound in a golden crown, wearing a millefleurs battle robe, girded with armor and a belt bearing a motif of lions and reptiles.

Giving his horse free rein, his halberd poised, Lü Bu followed Ding Yuan to the front of the lines. Ding Yuan pointed at Dong Zhuo and cried out: "Power-hungry eunuchs, the curse of the dynasty, have thrown the masses of the people into the depths of misery. Now you, without a jot of merit, speak madly of meddling in the succession. Do you want to overthrow the dynasty yourself?" Before Dong Zhuo could reply Lü Bu was charging him; Dong Zhuo fled. Ding Yuan took a heavy toll of his forces, driving them back thirty *li*, where they pitched camp and took counsel. "Lü Bu is extraordinary!" said Zhuo. "If only I could win him to our side, the realm would be ours with little trouble!"

Someone stepped up to Dong Zhuo and said, "Your problem is solved, my lord. I come from Lü Bu's village and know him to be brave but shallow, and forgetful of honor when it's to his advantage. Let me try my powers of persuasion on him; I am sure I can get him to join us with his hands meekly folded." A delighted Dong Zhuo observed the speaker. It was Li Su, a commander of the Imperial Tiger Escort. "How do you plan to do it?" asked Zhuo. "I understand," Li Su replied, "that you, my lord, have a prize horse, called Red Hare, of extraordinary speed and stamina.[10] Let me offer it to him, together with gold and pearls, to engage his interest. I will add some arguments of my own, and I guarantee that Lü Bu will betray Ding Yuan and enter your service." "Is this feasible?" Dong Zhuo asked, turning to Li Ru. "If your ambition," responded Li Ru, "is to take possession of the empire, don't begrudge a single horse, my lord." Contented, Dong Zhuo gave Li Su the horse along with one thousand taels of gold, several dozen lustrous pearls, and a jade belt.

Li Su took the treasures and headed for Lü Bu's camp. When the sentries closed in on him, he said, "Call General Lü at once. An old friend is here." Shortly, Li Su was led into Bu's presence. "Have you been well, worthy brother, since we parted?" said Li Su after being received. "It has been many years," said Lü Bu, bowing with hands clasped. "What is your position now?" "I am presently a commander of the Imperial Tiger Escort," Su answered. "I am proud and pleased to hear that my worthy brother is acting in support of the sacred shrines. I have with me a superb horse. He can travel a thousand *li* a day, ford streams and climb hills as if riding on flat ground. He's called Red Hare. I especially want you to have him to enhance your formidable prestige." Lü Bu had the animal led over to him. True to his name, every hair of his hide was the color of glowing embers. He measured ten spans head to tail, and stood eight spans from hoof to neck. His whinnies and neighs expressed the power to vault up to the sky or plunge into the deep. A poet of later times left this description:

> Tearing, lunging a thousand *li*,
>   behind, a duststorm starts;
> Breasting rivers, scaling hills,
>   above, a dark mist parts.
> He snaps his reins and shakes

his jeweled gear,
A fiery dragon diving down
from Heaven's upper tier.

Lü Bu thanked Li Su enthusiastically. "How can I ever repay you for this dragon-steed?" he said. "I have come out of personal respect and look for no thanks," Li su re-plied. Lü Bu set out wine. When they had drunk to their heart's content, Li Su continued, "We see each other rarely enough, but your father often visits." "You must be drunk," Lü Bu responded. "My father died years ago. How could he visit you?" "No, no," said Li Su. "I actually meant Imperial Inspector Ding." Lü Bu responded uncertainly, "I have been Ding Yuan's man, it's true. But out of necessity more than choice."

"Worthy brother," Li Su went on, "you have the talent to prop up the heavens, to command the seas. Where in our land are you not looked up to? Success, fame, status, wealth—all yours for the asking. Do not say you are someone's underling 'out of ne-cessity.'" "If only I had the right master," Lü Bu sighed. Li Su replied, "'The wise bird chooses its branch, the wise servant his master.' Later you will regret missing this op-portunity." "Tell me, brother," Lü Bu pressed. "You are at court. Whom do you consider a hero of our time?" "Among the Emperor's servants," Li Su replied, "not one compares with Dong Zhuo, a man who instinctively shows respect to the worthy and receives the learned cordially, a man who rewards and punishes with unerring judgment. He will do great things!" "I would follow him," said Lü Bu, "but how?"

Li Su set the gold and pearls together with the jade belt in front of his host. "What are these for?" Lü Bu asked in surprise. Li Su had him dismiss his attendants. "His Ex-cellency Dong Zhuo himself," Su began, "commissioned me to offer these to you, tokens of his long-standing admiration for your reputation. The horse is also his gift." "How can I reciprocate such affection?" Lü Bu asked. "If someone as ordinary as myself," Li Su answered, "can rise to commander of the Imperial Tiger Escort, then there will be no bounds to the rewards for someone like you." "Alas," Lü Bu responded, "I haven't a speck of merit to offer as an introduction." "To the contrary," returned Li Su, "it lies in the slightest turn of your hand. But I fear you would be reluctant to . . ." Lü Bu mused a long while before saying, "I should like to kill Ding Yuan and take his men with me into Dong Zhuo's service. What do you think?" "Worthy brother," said Li Su, "there could be no greater service. But time is precious. Act without delay." They arranged for Lü Bu to join Dong Zhuo the next day. Then Li Su took his leave.

Late that night during the second watch Lü Bu, armed with a knife, stole into Ding Yuan's tent and found him reading by candlelight. "What brings you here, my son?" asked Ding Yuan. "I am my own man," answered Bu, "and proud of it. I am no 'son' of yours." "Why have you turned against me?" Ding Yuan pleaded. Lü Bu, already moving on him, cut off his head and shouted to the attendants, "Ding Yuan is dead! I have killed him for his inhumanity. Those for me, stay. Those opposed, leave." Most of the troops dispersed.

The next day Lü Bu brought Ding Yuan's head to Li Su, and Li Su brought Lü Bu to Dong Zhuo. With great satisfaction Dong Zhuo ordered wine and invited Lü Bu to drink. He said, kneeling, "To have you here is to me like rain to the parched seedling." Lü Bu then raised Dong Zhuo, urged him to his seat, and prostrated himself in turn. "If you will have me, I beg to honor you as a foster father." Dong Zhuo presented Lü Bu with gleaming metal armor and a richly damasked battle gown. After drinking heartily, the two parted.

Dong Zhuo's authority increased after Lü Bu's arrival. Zhuo took personal command of the Forward Army and conferred on his brother, Dong Min, the title general of the Left and made him lord of Hu. He appointed Lü Bu cavalry commander[11] and Imperial Corps commander, and enfeoffed him with a capital precinct.

Li Ru urged Dong Zhuo to arrange as quickly as possible for the deposing of Emperor Shao and the enthroning of the prince of Chenliu. Dong Zhuo convened a banquet in the imperial quarters for the lords and noblemen and ordered Lü Bu to stand by with one thousand soldiers. That day Imperial Guardian Yuan Wei and the entire official corps were in attendance. After several rounds of wine, Dong Zhuo, hand on sword, spoke: "The present sovereign is inept and feeble, unfit to serve the ancestral temple. I mean to follow the hallowed precedents of Yi Yin and Huo Guang and place the prince of Chenliu upon the throne of Han. The present Emperor will become the prince of Hongnong. Those who resist will be killed."

The officials were too astounded to respond. But Yuan Shao, commandant of the Central Army, rose to his feet and declared, "The present sovereign has held the throne but briefly. There are no defects in his character, no lapses in his conduct. Removing the Empress's son and enthroning a concubine's—what do you call that if not treason?" "This matter of state is mine to decide," Dong Zhuo said angrily. "Who dares defy me? Do you think this sword not sharp enough?" Yuan Shao, too, bared his sword. "This one may prove as sharp," he retorted. The two warriors confronted each other before the guests. Indeed:

> Ding Yuan stood for honor and lost his life;
> Yuan Shao challenged Dong Zhuo and stood in peril.

And what was Yuan Shao's fate?

READ ON.

4

The Installation of the Chenliu Prince; Emperor Shao Is Deposed;
A Plot Against Traitor Dong; Cao Cao Presents a Jeweled Knife

DONG ZHUO STARTED FOR YUAN SHAO, but Li Ru checked him: "Things are not yet under control. You must not kill rashly." Thus Yuan Shao left, sword still in hand, after bidding the assembled officials farewell. He hung his credentials on the east gate and fled to the province of Ji. "Your nephew has been most uncivil to us," Zhuo said to Imperial Guardian Yuan Wei, "but in deference to you I forgive him. Where do you stand on the succession?" "With you, Grand Commandant," was the reply. "Then let martial law deal with those who defy us!" Dong Zhuo declared. Shaken and fearful, the assembly responded, "We shall obey."

After the banquet Dong Zhuo asked Privy Counselor Zhou Bi and Commandant Wu Qiong how to deal with Yuan Shao. "He left in a terrible rage," said Zhou Bi. "But if you try to arrest him, the situation could turn against you. Don't forget, the Yuan clan has held high office for four generations. The empire abounds with their followers and former subordinates, powerful men who would gather their forces at his call. And then if other gallant heroes rally to his cause, the whole region east of Huashan Mountain will no longer be yours. Pardon Yuan Shao and give him an imperial district. He will be glad to be exonerated, and you will buy security." "Yuan Shao," added Wu Qiong, "loves to contemplate action but lacks resolution. He's not a problem. Do give him a governorship, if only to keep people's confidence." Dong Zhuo agreed and that same day had Shao appointed governor of Bohai.

On the first day of the ninth month the Emperor was invited to ascend the Hall of Praiseworthy Virtue before a grand convocation of civil and military officials. Dong Zhuo drew his sword and addressed them: "The Son of Heaven is too feeble in mind and in body to sustain his reign. I have a statement to make." At Zhuo's order Li Ru read it:

Although the late Majestic Emperor Ling the Filial departed all too soon, there were high expectations in the land when the present Emperor assumed the throne. But Heaven did not endow him with the steady and serious character, the deportment and demeanor to command respect. His inattention and nonchalance during the mourning period exhibit his meagre virtue. All this has been detrimental to the throne itself. Queen Mother He has failed to give proper guidance, leaving government administration untended and disordered. The violent death of Queen

Mother Dong has left public opinion confused. The mainstays of our social order, the very bonds between Heaven and earth, have fallen slack.

The prince of Chenliu is rich in sagely virtue and strictly devoted to proper rule. Throughout the mourning he was distraught with grief. His words were unfailingly apt, and all the world knows his excellent name. It is thus fitting and proper for him to receive the boundless patrimony of the Han as legitimate heir for all time. Thus: the sovereign is hereby deposed and reduced to prince of Hongnong. The queen mother will be relieved of all administrative duties. We enthrone the prince of Chenliu, in response to Heaven, in concurrence with men, and to satisfy the people's expectations.

When Li Ru had finished reading, Dong Zhuo sharply ordered the attendants to lead the Emperor down from the hall and to remove his seal and cord. They told him to face north and on bended knees declare his intention to serve and to obey. The queen mother was ordered to remove her royal costume and await instructions. Mother and son wept bitterly, and the assembly of officials moaned. But from below one official cried out indignantly, "Traitor Dong Zhuo. Dare you abuse Heaven itself? Then let my blood bear witness." He shook his pointed ivory tablet and attacked Dong Zhuo, at whose angry command the guards seized the man, Imperial Secretary Ding Guan. Dong Zhuo ordered him removed and beheaded. To the moment of his death his oaths streamed forth; neither his spirit nor his expression altered. In later times men still sighed for his sacrifice, as these lines attest:

> The traitor's plot to change a sovereign
> Would soon consign to dust the shrines of Han.
> A courtful of courtiers helpless in Dong Zhuo's hand,
> And no one but Ding Guan to take a stand!

Dong Zhuo invited the prince of Chenliu to ascend, and the assembly voiced its congratulations. Dong Zhuo ordered Queen Mother He and the former emperor, now prince of Hongnong, together with the imperial consort, Lady Tang, immured in the Palace of Eternal Peace. No access to them was permitted. Alas for the Emperor Shao, enthroned in the fourth month and deposed in the ninth.

The new Emperor, prince of Chenliu, Liu Xie (styled Bohe), second son of Emperor Ling, became known to history as Emperor Xian. He was nine years old, five years younger than his deposed brother. A new reign period, Beginning Peace (Chu Ping, A.D. 190–93), was proclaimed. Dong Zhuo became prime minister.[1] But he did not use his own name when saluting the sovereign nor comport himself reverently by scurrying in his presence, nor did he remove his boots and sword before the throne as required. The prestige and wealth he amassed raised him above all. Li Ru urged Dong Zhuo to broaden his support by elevating a few eminent men, Cai Yong in particular. Accordingly, Dong Zhuo summoned Cai Yong, but he refused to appear until threats of death to himself and his clan forced the scholar to present himself. Dong Zhuo was so pleased that he advanced Cai Yong three times within the month, finally making him privy counselor. Such was the kindness and generosity Cai Yong enjoyed.

· · · · ·

Meanwhile the former Emperor Shao, his mother, and his consort—all imprisoned in the Palace of Eternal Peace—were allotted but meagre shares of food and clothing.

Emperor Shao's tears were never dry. One day he happened to notice a pair of swallows flying in the courtyard and intoned these lines:

> Fresh vernal grasses tint the morning haze;
> Homing swallows lace the sky in pairs;
> The River Luo, a stretch of darker green—
> People cry in wonder at the scene.
>
> But out beyond the depths of yonder clouds
> Stand palaces and courts that once were ours.
> Who will stand for loyalty, take honor's part,
> And ease the heavy wrongs upon my heart?

A spy, who kept the deposed Emperor under constant surveillance, reported to Dong Zhuo the words he heard sung. "Well, if grievance is his theme, we have our excuse," said Dong Zhuo and commanded Li Ru to take ten armed men and murder the Emperor.

The Emperor, Empress He, and Consort Tang were in an upper story of the palace when Li Ru was announced. The Emperor panicked. Li Ru offered him a cup of poisoned wine.[2] The Emperor wanted to know the occasion for the toast. "The prime minister drinks your health to greet the spring season," replied Li Ru. "If it is 'our health,'" said the queen mother, "you may drink first." "You won't drink it?" Li Ru said impatiently and ordered his men to show their knives and silken cords. "If the toast is refused, these will have to do," he added. Consort Tang fell to her knees and said, "Let this humble woman drink instead. Only, my lord, preserve the mother and the son." "And who are you to offer yourself in a prince's place?" snarled Li Ru, holding out the wine to the queen mother. "You drink first," he said. She cursed He Jin for having ruined the family by letting traitors into the capital.[3] Li Ru pressed the cup on the Emperor. "Allow me to bid my mother good-bye," he said. Then he sang with deep feeling:

> Earth tops Heaven; sun and moon change places.
> Once I had a kingdom; now, a border town.
> Robbed of life; by subjects overthrown.
> All is lost; tears in vain flow on.

In turn the consort also sang:

> Majestic Heaven falls; mother earth sinks down.
> Given in marriage, I follow where he goes.
> Two different paths—life and death here part.
> So swift the course, and sorrow-filled my heart.

After the song the two embraced and wept. "The prime minister awaits our report," said Li Ru cruelly. "You are delaying things. Who do you think is coming to save you?" At that, the queen mother cried, "The traitor Dong drives us to our doom. But Heaven will never sanction it. Your entire clan will perish for aiding this criminal." Li Ru laid hands on the queen mother and thrust her out of a window. Then he barked the order to strangle the consort and force the wine down Emperor Shao's throat. His work finished, Li Ru reported to Dong Zhuo, who ordered the three buried outside the city wall.

Dong Zhuo now began to indulge himself freely, debauching the imperial concubines and sleeping in the Emperor's bed. One day he took some troops to the city of Yang, a place outside Luoyang. It was the second month when the villagers, men and women, were celebrating the spring thanksgiving festival in honor of their local god. Dong Zhuo ordered his troops to surround the crowd and behead all the men. He seized the women and the goods that the people had with them and loaded everything onto his carts, tying to the sides the severed heads—more than one thousand. As the train reentered the capital Dong Zhuo announced that he was returning from a great victory over some bandits. The heads were burned at the city gate; the women and valuables were distributed among the army.[4]

The commandant of the Exemplary Cavalry, Wu Fu (styled Deyu), indignant at Dong Zhuo's cruelties, put a vest of armor and a knife under his court dress in order to assassinate him. When Dong Zhuo entered the court, Wu Fu greeted him outside the ministerial chambers and then lunged at him with the knife. Dong Zhuo, a powerful man, caught Wu Fu with both hands, and Lü Bu stepped in at once and forced him to the ground. "Who is behind this treason?" cried Dong Zhuo. Wu Fu stared boldly and shouted: "You are not my sovereign. I am not your subject. What 'treason' are you talking about? Your crimes tower to Heaven, and the whole world longs to see you dead. My one regret is that I cannot have you pulled apart by horses—like any traitor—to satisfy the realm." In a fury Dong Zhuo had Wu Fu dragged out and carved up. The curses streamed from his lips till the moment of death. A verse of later times praised him:

> If you must tell of loyalty,
> Tell of Wu Fu's to the Han.
> His courage mounted to the skies
> When down below was none.
>
> He struck at Dong Zhuo in the court;
> His fame is with us still.
> Forever and ever he's won the name
> Of a man of iron will.

Thereafter armed guards constantly attended Dong Zhuo.

At this time Yuan Shao was governor of Bohai. Informed of Dong Zhuo's abuses, he wrote secretly to Minister of the Interior Wang Yun:

> This traitor wronged Heaven itself when he dethroned the Emperor, more than one can bear to say. Yet you have indulged his outrageous conduct as if you have heard nothing. Does this befit a subject who owes the dynasty his utmost loyalty? I am calling up and training soldiers to clear the royal house of villains, but I am not yet ready to act. If you share my views, be alert for any opportunity. I stand at your beck and call, awaiting your command.

After reading the letter, Wang Yun racked his brains for a plan. One day he came upon a group of former courtiers awaiting audience and said to them, "Today is my birthday. I should like to invite you to a little gathering at my humble home this evening." "We will come, of course, to wish you long life," the courtiers replied.

That evening the elder lords and ministers arrived for the banquet Wang Yun had prepared in the rear chamber. The wine had gone round several times when Wang Yun covered his face and burst into tears. "Why this show of sorrow on a day of celebration?" asked the startled guests. "Today is not really my birthday," answered Wang Yun. "I said so only because I had something to tell you and wanted to avoid suspicion. Dong Zhuo has wronged the Emperor and abused his power. The dynastic shrines stand in peril.

When I think how the founder of the Han overthrew the Qin, destroyed Chu, and gathered the empire into his hands, I cannot believe that the succession is to die out at the hands of a Dong Zhuo. That is why I cry!'' The officials wept with him.

One of the guests, however, was rubbing his hands and laughing loudly. ''This courtful of nobles can weep till morning and round to the next evening, too. But can you weep Dong Zhuo to death?'' Wang Yun eyed the speaker, Cao Cao, commandant of the Valiant Cavaliers. In a tone of annoyance, Wang Yun said, ''Your ancestors also held office under the Han. Why do you laugh when you should be thinking of how to settle the score for the dynasty?'' ''What makes me laugh,'' Cao went on, ''is simply that not one of you gentlemen seems to have any idea how to get rid of Dong Zhuo. Despite my lack of ability, I would like nothing better than to cut off his head and hang it at the gates to the capital—to redeem ourselves in the eyes of the empire.''

Rising from his mat in a gesture of respect, Wang Yun said, ''Mengde, what is your worthy plan?'' ''Recently,'' Cao replied, ''I demeaned myself and entered Dong Zhuo's service only for the chance to move against him. Since he has come to trust me, there are times I can get near him. I believe you have a knife with seven jewels. If you let me borrow it, I will go into his chamber and stab him—for I am prepared to die without regret.'' ''Mengde, if you really mean to do this, the empire will be in your debt,'' Wang Yun responded. He personally poured out and offered him wine, which Cao Cao drained as his pledge; then Wang Yun gave him the precious dagger. Cao concealed it on his person. When he had finished drinking, Cao took leave his leave. The courtiers adjourned soon afterwards.

The next day Cao Cao, the jeweled knife at his side, arrived at the prime minister's chambers and was shown into his private quarters. Dong Zhuo was seated on a platform, Lü Bu beside him. ''You're late today,'' said Zhuo. ''My horse was slow,'' Cao replied. ''We have some fine ones from my district,'' said Dong Zhuo. ''Fengxian will go and bring one in for you.'' Lü Bu went out and Cao Cao said to himself, ''How much this traitor deserves to die!'' But he resisted the impulse to stab him then and there, fearing Dong Zhuo's enormous physical strength.

Dong Zhuo, a large, heavy man, could not comfortably sit for long, so he stretched himself out facing the rear wall. Again Cao Cao thought, ''This traitor is done for,'' and was about to strike when Dong Zhuo suddenly looked into the metal reflector sewn on his clothing and saw the weapon drawn. ''What are you up to, Mengde?'' he asked, turning quickly round again. At that moment Lü Bu returned with the horse, and Cao dropped shakily to his knees, proffering the knife with both hands. ''I wanted to offer this treasure in gratitude to Your Excellency,'' he said.[5] Dong Zhuo took the knife. It was about a foot long and had seven jewels set in the handle and a finely honed point—truly a priceless gift. Dong Zhuo passed it to Lü Bu, as Cao Cao untied the scabbard and handed it over. Then Dong Zhuo led Cao out to see the horse. ''Let me ride,'' Cao proposed. Dong Zhuo gave him saddle and bridle. Cao guided the horse out of Dong Zhuo's quarters, laid on the whip and headed southeast.

''If you ask me,'' Lü Bu said to Dong Zhuo, ''Cao meant to murder you but got scared and made a show of presenting the knife.'' ''I had the same thought,'' said Dong Zhuo. As they were speaking Li Ru came in, and Dong Zhuo described to him what had happened. ''Cao has no family in the capital and lives alone. Call him back,'' Li Ru suggested. ''If he comes promptly, it was a gift. If not, your suspicions will be confirmed and you can have him arrested and questioned.'' On this advice Dong Zhuo sent out four bailiffs. They reported back: ''Cao never went home but raced out the eastern gate, claiming to be on urgent business for Your Excellency when the watchmen tried to question him." "So you see," Li Ru concluded, "the hypocritical traitor has slipped away. It was treachery." "And to think I placed such faith in a man who meant to murder me," said Dong Zhuo bitterly. "There have to be others in on it," said Li Ru. "We'll know more when we catch him." Dong Zhuo circulated warrants with a sketch of Cao Cao's face, offering a thousand pieces of gold and a fief of ten thousand households for his arrest; he appended a warning that anyone caught sheltering the fugitive would be punished as severely as Cao Cao himself.

Cao Cao fled the capital and headed for Qiao, his home district. Passing Zhongmou country he was apprehended by guards at the barrier and taken for questioning to the county magistrate. "I am a traveling merchant," said Cao. "My surname is Huangfu." The magistrate, however, recognized the prisoner and, after musing a long while, said, "I knew you as Cao Cao when I was in Luoyang seeking office. Why are you concealing your identity? You are under arrest. Tomorrow I will deliver you to the capital for the reward." The official then gave the guards wine and food and sent them away.

That night the magistrate had Cao secretly brought to his rear court and inquired further: "I have heard that the prime minister was more than generous to you. Why did you bring this on yourself?" "Does the sparrow know of the swan's ambition?" Cao responded. "You have me. Turn me in for the reward. Why bother with questions?" The magistrate sent his attendants away and went on, "Don't despise me. I am no ordinary officeholder. I simply haven't met a worthy master." "My forefathers," Cao said, "enjoyed the bounty of Han for generations. If I fail to honor the debt, I am no better than bird or beast. I demeaned myself to serve Dong Zhuo only for the chance of ridding the dynasty of the scourge, but fate has thwarted me."

"Mengde," the magistrate said, "where were you heading?" "Back to my village," answered Cao. "I mean to rally the lords of the realm in the name of the Emperor for unified military action against Dong Zhuo." After hearing Cao's plan, the magistrate personally removed Cao's bonds and helped him to a seat for honored guests. "You are truly the loyal and honorable man of the day!" he said, saluting Cao. Cao returned the salute and asked the magistrate's name. "My surname is Chen," he replied, "given name, Gong; style, Gongtai. My mother and family are in Dongjun. Your devotion to the Han moves me to abandon my office and follow you." Cao Cao was immensely pleased. Chen Gong put together some money for traveling and gave Cao a change of clothes. Each carrying a sword, they set out for Cao's village.

After three days' riding, they came to a place called Chenggao. The hour was late. Cao pointed with his whip to a deep grove and said, "Somewhere around here lives a man, Lü Boshe, who once swore an oath of brotherhood with my father. Let's go there and get news of my family and a night's rest." Chen Gong gladly agreed, and the two men rode to the farmhouse, where they found Lü Boshe. "They say the court circulated a warrant for your arrest," Lü Boshe said. "They applied so much pressure that your father left the Chenliu area. How did you get here?" Cao Cao related the recent events and continued, "If not for the magistrate, I would have been reduced to mincemeat." Boshe saluted Chen Gong and said, "Your Honor, the Caos would have been exterminated but for you. Here you may relax and sleep in the back cottage."

Lü Boshe rose and went inside. Eventually he returned and said he was out of wine and had to go to the next village to buy some. Then he hopped on his donkey and was off. Cao Cao and Chen Gong sat a good while. Suddenly behind the farmhouse they heard the sound of knives being whetted. "You know, Lü Boshe is not a close relative," Cao said.

"There's something suspicious about his leaving. Let's look into this." The two men stole behind the cottage and overheard someone mumble, "Let's tie'm up an' kill'm." "I thought so," Cao Cao whispered. "If we don't strike first, we'll be caught." Cao Cao and Chen Gong entered at once and killed everyone, women and men, eight in all; only then did they see the trussed pig waiting to be slaughtered.

"You were too suspicious," Chen Gong said. "We've killed good folk." The two men hurried from the farm, but before they had ridden half a mile they met their host on his donkey with two jars of wine suspended from the pommel and fruit and vegetables hanging from one hand. "Dear nephew and honorable sir," he cried, "why are you leaving so suddenly?" "Marked men can't remain anywhere for long," answered Cao Cao. "But I told my family to slaughter a pig for your dinner," Lü Boshe said earnestly. "Don't begrudge us the night, nephew, nor you, good sir. Turn back, I pray." But Cao spurred his horse on. Then he turned and dashed back, his sword drawn, calling to Lü Boshe, "Who's coming over there?" As Boshe looked away Cao Cao cut him down, and he fell from his donkey. Chen Gong was astounded. "What happened at the farm was a mistake—but why this?" "Had he gotten home and seen them he would never have let it lay. He'd have brought a mob after us and we would've been done for." "But you murdered him knowing he was innocent—a great wrong," Chen Gong asserted. "Better to wrong the world than have it wrong me!" Cao Cao retorted. Chen Gong said nothing.[6]

That night, after riding several *li* under a bright moon, they knocked at the door of an inn and found a night's shelter. Cao fed the horses and went to sleep, but Chen Gong lay awake. "I took Cao for a good man," he mused, "and left office to join him. Now I see he's a savage beast at heart. If I let him live, only trouble will come of it." Chen Gong drew his sword. Indeed:

> A good man cannot have a bane-filled mind.
> Dong Zhuo and Cao Cao proved two of a kind.

Was this the end of Cao Cao?

READ ON.

5

Cao Cao Rallies the Lords with a Forged Decree;
The Three Brothers Engage Lü Bu in Battle

HIS ARM RAISED TO STRIKE, Chen Gong reflected, "I followed Cao Cao for the good of the
Emperor. But killing him only adds another wrong. Better simply to leave." Having come
to that decision, he put away his sword and, without waiting for daybreak, rode toward
Dongjun, his family's home district.[1]

Cao Cao awoke to find Chen Gong gone. "He thought me inhumane," Cao reflected,
"for that comment I made about wronging the world before it wrongs me, so he left. But
I can't stay here, either." Later, home in Chenliu, Cao Cao related the recent events to his
father and urged him to contribute the family's property for the purpose of recruiting
troops. "Our means can't accomplish such a thing," said his father. "But Wei Hong lives
nearby. He was recommended for office as a man of filial devotion and personal integrity.
He is generous and supports men of worth. If you can enlist his aid, your plan may
succeed.

Accordingly, Cao Cao invited Wei Hong to a banquet at his home and used the occasion to make his appeal. "The dynasty no longer has a rightful ruler," Cao began.
"Dong Zhuo wields all power, betrays the sovereign, and plagues the people. Bitter resentment has spread through the realm, but I alone cannot protect the shrines of Han.
Therefore, I make bold, my lord, to seek the aid of a man as loyal and honorable as yourself." "I have long felt the way you do," replied Wei Hong, "but regrettably have yet to
meet a hero loyal and true. Mengde, since you have such ambition, allow me to put the
resources of my house at your disposal." Elated with the response to his appeal, Cao Cao
forged a decree in the Emperor's name, and swift messengers carried it to various points.
Next, he recruited volunteers for the cause and raised a white standard bearing the words
"Loyalty and Honor."[2] Within days, commitments of support came pouring in.

One day two men came to offer their services: Yue Jin (styled Wenqian) of Wei in
Yangping and Li Dian (styled Mancheng) of Julu in Shangyang. Cao Cao took both on as
guards in his headquarters. Another who came was Xiahou Dun (styled Yuanrang) from
Qiao in the fief at Pei.[3] Xiahou Dun was a descendant of Xiahou Ying. Since childhood
Dun had trained with spears and clubs and by fourteen was learning martial arts. He was
later forced to flee the district for killing someone who had insulted his teacher. Now,
hearing that Cao Cao was organizing an army, he and his clansman, Xiahou Yuan,
brought a thousand hardy warriors each to Cao's camp. In fact these two men were Cao's
own clansmen, as Cao's father, a Xiahou, had been adopted into the Cao family. Cao's

cousins from the Cao clan, Ren and Hong, also brought in over a thousand men each. Cao Ren's style was Zixiao, and Hong's was Zilian. Both were past masters of archery and horsemanship as well as other martial arts. Cao Cao was delighted with his gathering army, which he trained in the village. Wei Hong contributed all his wealth to provide clothing, armor, and banners. Countless others sent grain. When Yuan Shao[4] received Cao's forged decree, he gathered his officials and officers and led a body of thirty thousand from Bohai to form an alliance with Cao Cao.

At this time Cao Cao sent the following proclamation to the various imperial districts:

Cognizant of their grave responsibility, Cao and his confederates proclaim to the realm their loyalist cause. Dong Zhuo, violator of Heaven and earth, has destroyed the dynasty and murdered the Emperor, dishonored the palace's forbidden quarters, and grievously injured the common folk. The crimes of this ruthless, avaricious man mount high. Now we have in hand a secret decree from the Emperor, on which authority we are summoning soldiers to our cause. We vow to extirpate these evils and preserve the sacred heartland of our civilization. We aim to field a righteous host to satisfy the indignation of the people, support the royal house, and save the suffering millions. Let this proclamation be acted upon immediately when received.

In response to this call the lords of seventeen military townships mustered their forces. The roster read:

1. Yuan Shu, governor of Nanyang and general of the Rear
2. Han Fu, imperial inspector of Jizhou
3. Kong Zhou, imperial inspector of Yuzhou
4. Liu Dai, imperial inspector of Yanzhou
5. Wang Kuang, governor of Henei
6. Zhang Miao, governor of Chenliu
7. Qiao Mao, governor of Dongjun
8. Yuan Yi, governor of Shanyang
9. Bao Xin, lord of Jibei
10. Kong Rong, governor of Beihai
11. Zhang Chao, governor of Guangling
12. Tao Qian, imperial inspector of Xuzhou
13. Ma Teng, governor of Xiliang
14. Gongsun Zan, governor of Beiping
15. Zhang Yang, governor of Shangdang
16. Sun Jian, lord of Wucheng and governor of Changsha
17. Yuan Shao, lord of Qixiang and governor of Bohai

These contingents varied considerably in strength, some numbering as many as thirty thousand, others, ten or twenty thousand. Each leader, together with his civil and military personnel, headed for the capital.

Gongsun Zan, governor of Beiping, was marching fifteen thousand men through Pingyuan county in Dezhou when in a distant mulberry grove he saw a group of horsemen under a yellow banner riding toward him. The leader was Liu Xuande.[5] "What brings you here, good brother?" asked Gongsun Zan. "Some time ago," replied Xuande, "I had the good fortune to be appointed magistrate of Pingyuan, thanks to your recommendation. I heard you were passing through and came to offer my respects. Please come into the town to rest your horses." Pointing to Lord Guan and Zhang Fei, Gongsun Zan asked who they were. "My oath brothers," Xuande said. "They helped you against the Yellow Scarves?" queried Zan. "They did it all," was the reply. "What posts do they hold?" Zan wanted to know. "Lord Guan is a mounted archer," answered Xuande, "Zhang Fei a standing archer." "A waste of talent," sighed Zan. "Dong Zhuo has the court in thrall, and the lords of the realm are moving on Luoyang to punish him. Worthy brother, give up this humble post and join me in the campaign to support the house of Han. What do you say?" "I am willing," Xuande responded. "If you had let me kill the traitor that time," Zhang Fei interjected, "we wouldn't have all this trouble." "Deal with the present," Lord Guan urged. "Let's collect our things and be going."

Cao Cao welcomed Gongsun Zan, the three brothers, and the several riders accompanying them. The various lords were arriving one after another, pitching their camps over an area stretching for two hundred *li*. Cao Cao slaughtered cattle and horses, feasted the leaders, and convened a war council to consider the next step. Wang Kuang, governor of Henei, said, "In serving this great cause we must first establish a war-ruler and pledge him our strictest obedience. Only then can we march." In response Cao Cao proposed, "Yuan Shao's family has held highest office for four generations, and many former officers still serve them. As the descendant of distinguished ministers, Shao is most fit to lead our confederacy." This view prevailed among the lords, and Yuan Shao, after initially declining, consented to serve.[6]

The following day a three-tiered platform was built, and the flags of every garrison were planted round it. Above they set a yak-tail pennant, a gilded battle-axe, and the seal and tally of military authority. Then Yuan Shao, at the invitation of the lords, ascended grandly in full regalia, a sword at his side. He burned incense, saluted, and read out the pledge:

> Misfortune has struck the Han. The sacred continuity of the royal line is broken. The traitor Dong Zhuo exploits the lapse of rule to loose great evils upon us, sparing not even the sovereign, spreading suffering among the people. We fear for the sacred shrines and have rallied a righteous force to meet the crisis. All members of the covenant dedicate body and soul to the cause as conscientious subjects. Let no man harbor contrary ambitions, or fail his oath and debase our mandate, lest he lose his posterity. O august Heaven above, fruitful Mother Earth, and you sentient spirits of our ancestors, bear true witness to our vow.

After the declaration had been read, the leaders of the confederacy pledged their faith by touching the blood of the sacrifice to their lips. The assembly, inspired by the words spoken to them, shed tears freely. Yuan Shao descended, and the crowd raised him to the place of command in his tent, facing two rows of chieftains seated by age and rank.

Cao Cao sent round the wine. "Now that we have a war-ruler," he said, "all must serve as assigned and cooperate in our task regardless of minor inequities." Then Yuan Shao spoke: "My unworthiness notwithstanding, you have elected me your chief. In that role I shall reward merit and punish offenders. Governmental sanctions shall be strictly applied and military discipline strictly observed. Let there be no violation of either." The assembly shouted its assent: "Command, and we obey." "My younger brother, Shu," Shao continued, "will manage the food and fodder, providing for each camp and ensuring against shortages. We also need one man to lead the van to the Si River pass and challenge the foe to battle. The rest of us will hold the various strategic points and stand ready to reinforce." Sun Jian (styled Wentai), governor of Changsha, offered to take the forward unit.[7] "Wentai is a man," Yuan Shao said, "who has the fierce courage required for this task." Sun Jian marched to the pass, and the defenders reported the new threat to officials at the prime minister's residence.

After taking power, Dong Zhuo spent his days feasting. It was Li Ru who received word of the emergency. He hurried with the news to Dong Zhuo, who convened his commanders. Lü Bu, lord of Wen, rose to speak: "Father, have no fear. Those lords beyond the pass are so many weak reeds to me. With my stout warriors I'll string up their heads on the capital gates." Dong Zhuo, immensely pleased, said, "With Lü Bu on our side, I sleep easy." But even as he spoke someone stood up behind Lü Bu and cried, "It hardly takes an ox-cleaver to kill a chicken.[8] Why send Lü Bu when I can take their heads as easily as pulling something from a sack?" Dong Zhuo cast his glance on a man some nine spans tall, molded like a tiger, supple as a wolf, with a pantherine head and apelike arms. It was Hua Xiong of Guanxi. His brave words pleased Dong Zhuo, who appointed him a commandant of the Valiant Cavaliers and sent him off that night with fifty thousand picked foot soldiers and horsemen to meet the enemy at the pass. Three other generals, Li Su, Hu Zhen, and Zhao Cen, went with Hua Xiong.

Among the insurgent lords led by Yuan Shao was the lord of Jibei, Bao Xin. Anxious lest Sun Jian's vanguard win the highest honors, he secretly sent his brother Bao Zhong ahead to the pass. Taking side paths to avoid detection, Bao Zhong arrived with three thousand men and incited the enemy to battle. Hua Xiong responded quickly. Racing to the pass with five hundred armored shock cavalry, he shouted, "Rebel! Stand where you are!" Bao Zhong tried desperately to turn back but fell to a stroke of Hua Xiong's blade. Many of his commanders were taken alive. The victor sent Bao Zhong's head to the prime minister and reported the triumph. Dong Zhuo made Xiong his chief commander.

Unaware of this defeat, Sun Jian was advancing to the pass. He had four commanders: Cheng Pu (Demou) from Tuyin in Youbeiping, wielding a steel-spined spear with snake-headed blade; Huang Gai (Gongfu) of Lingling, wielding an iron whip; Han Dang (Yigong) from Lingzhi in Liaoxi, wielding a great backsword; and Zu Mao (Darong) from Fuchun in Wujun, wielding a pair of swords-of-war.[9] Sun Jian donned his silver-sheened armor and red hood, and belted on a well-tempered sword. From his crenelle-maned horse he pointed to the pass and shouted directly to Hua Xiong, "Surrender, you wretched slave to villainy."

Hua Xiong's lieutenant commander, Hu Zhen, led five thousand men out of the pass to do battle. Cheng Pu[10] came on with leveled spear and pierced Hu Zhen's throat. Down he went. Sun Jian waved his men on toward the heart of the pass, but they suffered a heavy pelting with stones and arrows and withdrew to Liangdong. Sun Jian sent one messenger to Yuan Shao to report the victory and another to Yuan Shu for grain.

Concerning Sun Jian's request someone advised Yuan Shu: "Sun Jian is the tiger of the east. If he takes the capital and kills Dong Zhuo, we'll be facing a tiger instead of a wolf. Deny the grain and watch his army fall apart." Yuan Shu, persuaded, sent no supplies. Sun Jian's men became uncontrollable, and word of it soon reached the government camp at the pass. Dong Zhuo's adviser, Li Su, plotted the next step with Hua Xiong. "Tonight," said Su, "I'll take a company of men by side paths down from the pass and strike from the rear. You attack their forward positions. Jian can surely be captured." Hua Xiong approved and ordered his men to be fed well in preparation for the action.

The moon was bright and the breeze refreshing when Hua Xiong reached Sun Jian's camp. At midnight his men stormed in, howling and shrieking. Sun Jian donned his armor, leaped to horse, and took on Hua Xiong. As they tangled, Li Su struck from the rear, ordering his men to set fires wherever they could. Sun Jian's army fled, though some commanders skirmished individually. Zu Mao alone stuck by Sun Jian. The two dashed from the battleground, pursued by Hua Xiong. Xiong dodged two arrows and kept pace. Sun Jian shot a third, but drew so hard his bow split. He threw it aside and rode for his life.

"Your red hood's a perfect target," cried Zu Mao. "I'll wear it." The men switched headgear and took flight by different roads. Xiong's soldiers spotted the bright color in the distance and gave chase. Sun Jian followed a side road and got away. Zu Mao, hard-pressed, hung the hood on a half-burned piece of timber and hid in a nearby copse. Catching the moonlight, the hood attracted Hua Xiong's men, and they circled it. No one dared advance, but after someone shot at it, they discovered the ruse and went for the head-dress. At that moment Zu Mao came slashing out of the wood, wielding both his swords. But his object, Hua Xiong, uttering fierce cries, delivered a single fatal swordstroke that dropped Zu Mao from his horse.

The slaughter continued until morning. Then Hua Xiong brought his men back to the pass. Sun Jian's remaining commanders, Cheng Pu, Huang Gai, and Han Dang, found their leader and rounded up their men. Sun Jian grieved over the loss of Zu Mao and sent a messenger to report to Yuan Shao.

Stunned at the defeat of Sun Jian by Hua Xiong, Yuan Shao called the lords into session. Gongsun Zan reached the meeting late, and Yuan Shao invited him to sit among the lords. "The other day," Yuan Shao began, "General Bao Xin's younger brother ignored orders and advanced without authority. He himself was killed, and we lost many men. Now Sun Jian has been beaten. Our edge is blunted, our mettle dulled. What is our next step to be?" Not one of the lords replied.

The war-ruler scanned the audience. Behind Gongsun Zan three extraordinary-looking strangers stood smiling grimly. Yuan Shao asked who they were. Gongsun Zan had Xuande step forward. "This is Liu Bei," he said, "magistrate at Pingyuan. We were fellow students and like brothers even then." "Not the one who helped break the Yellow Scarves?" asked Cao Cao. "The very one," answered Gongsun Zan. He told Xuande to salute Yuan Shao and Cao Cao and then proceeded to describe his protégé's origins and accomplishments. "Since he belongs to a branch of the imperial family," Yuan Shao concluded, "let him come forward and be seated." But Xuande modestly declined.[11] "It is not your name or rank I salute," insisted Shao, "but your lineage." With that, Xuande took his place at the end of the line. Lord Guan and Zhang Fei posted themselves behind him, hands folded on their chests.[12]

At this point a spy reported that Hua Xiong had brought his armored cavalry down from the pass, displaying Sun Jian's red headdress on the tip of a pole, and was at the camp's entrance mouthing taunts. "Who will go?" asked Yuan Shao. From behind Yuan Shu, Yu She, a commander known for bravery, stepped forward and volunteered. But Hua Xiong made short work of him. Alarm stirred the assembly. Governor Han Fu recommended his own champion commander, Pan Feng, and Yuan Shao urged him to the field. Pan Feng went forth with a huge axe, but the news came back swiftly of his death too at Hua Xiong's hands. The assembly began to panic. "It's a pity Yan Liang and Wen Chou, my own top generals, are not here," Yuan Shao said. "Either one could end our worries." At that, a voice from the back boomed, "I offer to present Hua Xiong's head to you personally."

The assembled lords turned to the speaker, a man over nine spans, with a great beard flowing from rich ruddy cheeks. His eyes were like those of the crimson-faced phoenix, his brows like nestling silkworms, his voice like a tolling bell. He fixed his eyes directly on the audience. "Who is this man?" demanded Shao. "Guan Yu, sworn brother of Xuande," answered Gongsun Zan. "His position?" asked Shao. "Mounted archer under Xuande," was the reply. At that, the war-ruler's brother, Yuan Shu, burst out, "Are you trying to insult us? A mere archer! Have we no more commanders? What nonsense! Get him out of here!" But Cao Cao checked Yuan Shu: "Pray, hold your temper. This man has made his boast. He can't be a coward. Now let him make it good. You'll have plenty of time to condemn him if he fails." "But to send out an archer!" Yuan Shao said. "Hua Xiong will laugh in his sleeve!" "He doesn't look like an ordinary soldier," Cao Cao replied. "How is Hua Xiong going to know?" Finally, Lord Guan spoke: "If I fail, my head is yours."

Cao Cao had a draft of wine heated for Lord Guan before he mounted. "Pour it," said the warrior, "and set it aside for me. I'll be back shortly." He leaped to his horse, gripped his weapon, and was gone. The assembly of lords heard the rolling of drums and the clamor of voices outside the pass, and it seemed as if the heavens would split open and the earth buckle, as if the hills were shaking and the mountains moving. The terror-struck assembly was about to make inquiry when the jingling of bridle bells announced Lord Guan's return. He entered the tent and tossed Hua Xiong's head, freshly severed, on the ground. His wine was still warm. A poet of later times sang Lord Guan's praises:

> His might sufficed to hold in place
>   the frames of sky and land.
> The painted war drums charged the air
>   at the chieftains' field command.
> The hero put the cup aside
>   to slake his combat lust:
> Before the wine had time to cool,
>   Hua Xiong lay in the dust.

Cao Cao was elated by Lord Guan's display of prowess.[13] "My brother has taken Hua Xiong's head," cried Zhang Fei, stepping forward. "What are we waiting for? Let's break through the pass and take Dong Zhuo alive!" But Yuan Shu was enraged. "Even I," he bellowed, "a district governor, do not presume upon my position. How dare this magistrate's underling flaunt his powers before us! Drive the lot of them from our presence!" "The meritorious must be rewarded without regard to status," Cao Cao cautioned Yuan Shu. "Since you are so impressed with a mere magistrate," Shu retorted, "I announce my withdrawal." "Are we going to jeopardize our cause," Cao asked, "on account of a few words?" He ordered Gongsun Zan to take Xuande and his brothers back to camp. The assembly adjourned. Cao quietly sent meat and wine to cheer the three heroes.

Hua Xiong's subordinates reported the defeat, and Li Su sent an emergency appeal to the capital. There an agitated Dong Zhuo consulted Li Ru, Lü Bu, and others. "Their position is now greatly strengthened," Li Ru commented. "Yuan Shao commands the confederates, and his uncle, Yuan Wei, remains imperial guardian. If they coordinate their efforts, we could be in serious trouble. Get rid of Yuan Wei first; then, Your Excellency, lead the army yourself and root out the rebels one by one." Dong Zhuo approved Li Ru's proposal. On the prime minister's order, generals Li Jue and Guo Si surrounded Yuan Wei's home with five hundred men, put every member of the household to death regardless of age, and sent the imperial guardian's head to the pass, where it was exhibited.[14] Then Dong Zhuo led two hundred thousand men in two field armies against the confederate lords. The first army, fifty thousand under Li Jue and Guo Si, was to hold the line at the Si River and not engage in combat. Dong Zhuo himself led the second, a force of one hundred and fifty thousand, to guard Tiger Trap Pass, located some fifty *li* from Luoyang. Among his chief counselors and commanders were Li Ru, Lü Bu, Fan Chou, and Zhang Ji. Dong Zhuo ordered Lü Bu to place thirty thousand in front of the pass, while he posted himself behind it.

Swift runners brought the news to Yuan Shao, who convened his council. "Dong Zhuo is positioned at Tiger Trap," said Cao Cao, "intersecting our central corps. We should move half our men to engage him." Shao accordingly ordered eight of the lords—Wang Kuang, Qiao Mao, Bao Xin, Yuan Yi, Kong Rong, Zhang Yang, Tao Qian, and Gongsun Zan—to the pass. Cao Cao moved between them in support activity.

The eight lords mustered their men as Yuan Shao had directed. Wang Kuang, governor of Henei, reached the pass first, and Lü Bu rode out with three thousand armored shock cavalry. Wang Kuang deployed horsemen and foot soldiers into line and guided his horse to the bannered front of the formation. He watched Lü Bu emerge from the opposing ranks. A three-pronged headpiece of dark gold held his hair in place. His wargown was of Xichuan red brocade with a millefleurs design. Armor wrought of interlocking animal heads protected his torso. A lion-and-reptile belt that clinked and sparkled girt his waist and secured his armor.[15] A quiver of arrows at his side, a figured halberd with two side-blades clenched in his hand, Lü Bu sat astride Red Hare as it neighed like the roaring wind. Truly was it said: "Among heroes, Lü Bu; among horses, Red Hare."

Wang Kuang turned to his line and shouted, "Who dares fight him?" From the rear a rider galloped forth, spear held high. It was Fang Yue, a celebrated general from Henei. The warriors clashed; the warriors closed. Lü Bu dropped Yue with a stroke of his halberd and charged ahead. Kuang's army scattered. Bu pressed the slaughter, moving freely as if unopposed. Only when Qiao Mao and Yuan Yi arrived in time to save Wang Kuang did Lü Bu pull back. The forces of the three lords withdrew thirty *li* and made camp. Then the remaining five contingents joined them. Everyone agreed Lü Bu was a hero no one could match.

The eight lords were deliberating their next move when it was reported that Lü Bu had come to provoke them to battle. Moving as one man, the eight lords mounted and with their host divided into eight fighting squadrons rode to high ground. They watched Lü Bu's massed force hurtling toward them under gorgeous multicolored flags rippling in the air. Mu Shun, a brigade leader under Zhang Yang, governor of Shangdang, hoisted his spear and went forth to give battle, only to be slain with a casual pass of Lü Bu's blade. A wave of consternation stirred the lords. Next Wu Anguo, a brigade leader under Kong Rong, governor of Beihai, charged out on horseback swinging an iron mace. Lü Bu flourished his weapon and urged his mount on. After ten bouts Lü Bu cut off Wu Anguo's hand, and the mace fell to the ground. Men from the eight armies saved Wu Anguo as Lü Bu retired to his line.

Regrouped at camp, the lords again took counsel. "Lü Bu has no match," said Cao Cao. "Let us assemble the whole body of eighteen lords to form a sound plan. If we can capture him, Dong Zhuo will be easily defeated." As they conferred, Lü Bu returned to sound the challenge, and the eight lords answered it. Gongsun Zan thrust his spear into the air and took on Lü Bu, only to flee after a brief clash. Lü Bu gave Red Hare free rein and came pounding after Gongsun Zan. The horse's great speed and stamina brought him close behind. Lü Bu leveled his halberd, aiming for the center of Gongsun Zan's back.

To the side of the action stood a single warrior, his eyes rounding, his whiskers bristling. Holding high his eighteen-span snake-headed spear, he flew at Lü Bu, shouting mightily, "Stay! Bastard with three fathers! Know me for Zhang Fei of Yan!" Lü Bu veered from Gongsun Zan to confront the new challenger. Zhang Fei's fighting spirit flashed at this welcome chance. The two crossed and tangled more than fifty times. Lord Guan, seeing that neither could best the other, urged his horse forward and, flourishing his crescent-moon blade, Green Dragon, attacked from another side. The three horsemen formed a triangle. They fought another thirty bouts, but Lü Bu was unconquerable.

Then Xuande, clenching his matching swords, angled into the field on his tawny-maned horse, and the three brothers circled Lü Bu like the figured shade of a revolving lamp. The warriors of the eight lords stood transfixed. Soon Lü Bu could no longer fend off his enemies. Eyeing Xuande squarely, he feinted at him with the halberd. In dodging the thrust, Xuande opened a corner of the trap, and Lü Bu made good his escape, letting his weapon hang behind him, but the brothers would not let up. They gave chase, and the warriors who were witnessing the spectacle swept after them onto the field with a roar that shook the ground. Lü Bu's army broke and ran for the pass with the three brothers still leading the pursuit. A poet of later times described the contest thus:

> The house of Han approached its Heaven-destined end;
> Deep in the west its fiery sun had bent.
> Dong Zhuo deposed the rightful Emperor
> And filled the feeble prince with dreams of fear.[16]
> So Cao Cao sent his writ to all the lords,
> Who summoned up ten thousand righteous swords,
> Elected Yuan Shao to their league's command,
> And swore to stay the house and calm the land.
> Dong Zhuo's man, Lü Bu, warrior without peer,
> Far surpassed the champions of his sphere:
> In armor clad, a dragon etched in scales,
> His headpiece fledged with gallant pheasant tails,
> His jagged jade belt scored with lion jaws,
> A phoenix spread in flight; his surcoat soars.
> His chafing charger stirred a fearsome wind,
> In every eye his halberd's piercing glint.
> No lord could face his call to brave the field:
> Their hearts went faint, their senses reeled.
> Then Zhang Fei made his way into the list,
> His giant snake-head lance fast in his fist.
> His beard stuck out, defiant strands of wire;
> The circles of his eyes shot angry fire.
> They fought their fill. The contest undecided,
> Before his line Lord Guan no more abided:
> His dragon blade as dazzling as fresh snow,
> His war coat, parrot-hued, aswirl below.
> His pounding horse aroused the dead to howl.
> Blood would flow before his dreadful scowl.
> With double swords Xuande now joins the fight.
> The crafty owl will show his zeal and might.
> The brothers circle Lü Bu round and round.
> He fends, he blocks, too skillful to be downed.

The hue and cry set sky and land ajar;
The bloodlust sent a shudder through the stars.
His power spent, Lü Bu found an out
And rode for safety to his own redoubt,
His mighty weapon trailing at his back,
His gilded five-hued streamers all awrack.
Riding hard, he snapped his horse's rein,
Hurtling up to Tiger Trap again.

The brothers chased Lü Bu to the gateway to the pass. There they saw the blue silk command canopy fluttering above. "Dong Zhuo himself!" cried Zhang Fei. "Why bother with Lü Bu now? Let's get the chief traitor and root out the whole faction." The brothers started toward Dong Zhuo. Indeed:

"To catch a thief, you have to catch his chief."
But who, in fact, had the genius to do so?

What was the outcome of the fight?

READ ON.

6

In Razing the Capital, Dong Zhuo Commits Heinous Crimes;
By Concealing the Jade Seal, Sun Jian Betrays the Confederation

ZHANG FEI RACED AHEAD to the pass, but volleys of stones and arrows forced him back. The eight lords hailed the victory of the three brothers and reported it to the war-ruler. Yuan Shao called on Sun Jian to renew the attack.

Before going into battle, Sun Jian, attended by Cheng Pu and Huang Gai, visited Yuan Shu in his camp. In a hostile gesture Jian traced a line on the ground with a stick and said to Yuan Shu, "Between Dong Zhuo and me there is no enmity. I have risked death by stone and arrow in this war, not only in the cause of the Han, but also to avenge your own house.[1] Yet you gave ear to slanders and denied me vital rations, causing me to suffer a grave defeat. Where is your conscience?" Yuan Shu, taken aback, made no reply, but by way of apology he executed the man who had urged him to hold back the supplies. At that point a messenger announced that an enemy commander had come to see Sun Jian.

Sun Jian took leave of Yuan Shu and returned to his quarters, where he received the visitor, Li Jue, one of Dong Zhuo's trusted commanders. "What is your business?" asked Sun Jian. "You are among those the prime minister most admires," began Li Jue. "He has sent me in hopes of forming a new relationship—by joining his daughter and your son, General, in marriage." "The renegade!" Sun Jian cried in outrage. "Violating Heaven's canons, he has wrought havoc on the royal house. I am determined to destroy the nine branches of his clan to satisfy the indignation of the empire. Do you think I would debase myself in such a relationship? I spare you only to speed you with my reply: surrender the pass in time and save your skins. Delay and I'll destroy you all."

Li Jue scurried, shamefaced, off to Dong Zhuo and reported Sun Jian's refusal. Incensed, Dong Zhuo turned to Li Ru, who said, "Lü Bu's recent defeat has demoralized the men. I suggest you recall them to Luoyang and move the Emperor to Chang'an. This would be in keeping with the children's song that has been going around lately:

> There once was a Han in the west,
> And now there is one in the east.
> If only the deer[2] will flee to Chang'an,
> The world will again be at peace.

I take it that the words 'a Han in the west' refer to the founder of our dynasty, the Supreme Ancestor,[3] who inaugurated the first of twelve consecutive reigns in Chang'an, the western capital. The words 'a Han in the east,' however, refer to the founder of the Later Han,[4] who inaugurated another twelve glorious reigns in Luoyang, the eastern capital. Now the spheres of Heaven which hold men's fortunes have circled back to their starting positions. Thus, Your Excellency, if you transfer the court to Chang'an, all will be well." Delighted with Li Ru's proposal, Dong Zhuo said, "You have shown me the way." Immediately, he led Lü Bu back to Luoyang to decide how to move the capital.

Dong Zhuo assembled the civil and military officials in the great hall of the palace and declared: "For Luoyang, eastern capital of the Han during the last two hundred years, the allotted span of time now draws to a close. But in Chang'an I can see a reviving spirit and thus shall convey the royal presence to the west. Let each of you make the necessary preparations." Minister of the Interior Yang Biao objected: "The whole Guanzhong region[5] is devastated. We will throw the common people into panic if we abandon the imperial family temples and mausoleums here for no good reason. It is easy enough to disturb the peace of the realm; nothing is harder than preserving it. I only hope that the prime minister will reflect carefully." Angrily, Dong Zhuo shot back, "Are you going to stand in the way of the dynasty's plan for survival?"

Grand Commandant Huang Wan said, "I agree with Minister of the Interior Yang. At the end of Wang Mang's usurpation, in the reign period Recommencement [Geng Shi, A.D. 23–25], the Red Eyebrow rebels burned Chang'an, reducing the city to rubble. After the exodus, of every hundred inhabitants only one or two remained. So I would question the wisdom of abandoning this city of palaces and dwellings for a wasteland." To this objection Dong Zhuo replied, "Here, east of the land within the passes, rebellion is rife. Anarchy is loose in the land. Chang'an, however, is well protected by the forbidding Yao Mountains and Hangu Pass. What's more, it is close to the region west of the Longyou Hills, where timber, stone, brick, and tile are readily obtainable. A new palace shouldn't take more than a month to construct—so enough of your absurd arguments." At this point Minister of Works[6] Xun Shuang also protested: "If the capital is moved, the population will be thrown into commotion." "I am planning for an empire!" Zhuo bellowed. "I can't be bothered about the ruck." That day he deprived the three critics of rank, reducing them to commoner status.

As Dong Zhuo left the palace in his carriage, he noticed Zhou Bi, now the imperial secretary, and Wu Qiong, commandant of the City Gates, saluting from the roadside. Dong Zhuo asked their business. "They say," responded Zhou Bi, "that the prime minister plans to move the capital to Chang'an, so we have come to state our objections." Outraged, Dong Zhuo retorted, "Once before I listened to you two, when you advised me to put Yuan Shao in office. Now he has rebelled! And you are part of his faction!" He had the two beheaded outside the city gates. The following day he ordered the transfer of the capital to begin.

Li Ru came to suggest a measure. "We are short of funds and food," he said to Dong Zhuo, "and Luoyang has many rich householders. Any that we can link to Yuan Shao and the other rebels should be executed along with their clans and factions. We'll reap a fortune from the property we confiscate." Dong Zhuo approved, and on his authority five thousand crack troops raided several thousand of the wealthiest houses. The soldiers put signs on the topknot of each captive reading "Traitor and Rebel." Then they executed whole families and seized their goods.

At the same time Li Jue and Guo Si began the forced evacuation of Luoyang's millions. Military squads interspersed among the people drove them, pushing and pulling, on toward Chang'an. Untold numbers fell by the wayside. The soldiers were free to rape and plunder. The cries and outcries of the people resounded between Heaven and earth. Stragglers were pressed forward or killed outright by an army unit of three thousand that followed behind.

When Dong Zhuo was ready to leave the city he ordered all dwellings—in addition to the ancestral temples and imperial quarters—burned to the ground. The northern and southern palaces went up in flames, and all the chambers of the Palace of Lasting Happiness were reduced to ashes. On Dong Zhuo's orders Lü Bu dug up the crypts of former emperors and empresses and looted their treasures. Dong Zhuo's soldiers despoiled the tombs of officials and civilians alike and loaded the gold and jewels, silks, and other valuables onto several thousand carts; then Zhuo forced the Emperor and his women to leave for Chang'an. (This occurred in April, A.D. 190.)

·   ·   ·   ·

As soon as Zhao Cen, Zhuo's commander, learned that Luoyang had been abandoned, he surrendered the barrier at the River Si. Sun Jian rushed in to occupy it. Xuande and his brothers cut through Tiger Trap Pass, and the lords followed. Sun Jian rode on ahead to Luoyang. He saw flames in the sky and thick smoke covering the ground—for two or three hundred *li* no fowl, no dogs, no sign of human life. Sun Jian ordered the fires put out and told the lords to pitch their camps in the wasteland.

Meanwhile Cao Cao came to Yuan Shao and said, "The traitors' flight offers a perfect opportunity to attack their rear. Why are you holding back?" "The men are fatigued," Yuan Shao replied, "I doubt it would be to our advantage." "Dong Zhuo has destroyed the imperial dwellings and abducted the Emperor," said Cao. "People everywhere are in shock, uncertain where their allegiances belong. It is the final hour for this criminal. We can gain control in a single battle. Why wait?" But the leaders of the confederation, too, were reluctant to act. "Who can work with such worthless men!" Cao cried angrily. Attended by only his six commanders—Xiahou Dun, Xiahou Yuan, Cao Ren, Cao Hong, Li Dian, and Yue Jin—he led some ten thousand men in pursuit of Dong Zhuo.

Dong Zhuo reached Yingyang, where Governor Xu Rong received him. Li Ru cautioned Dong Zhuo, "We are hardly out of Luoyang and must guard against pursuit. Have the governor place an ambush by that row of hills that screens the city. If Yuan Shao's men come, let them through. Wait till I strike, then cut them off and surprise them from behind. That way nobody will dare follow them." Dong Zhuo agreed and sent Lü Bu with his best men to cover the rear.

Lü Bu was moving into position when Cao Cao's troops arrived. "Just as Li Ru foresaw," said Lü Bu with a laugh and deployed his forces. Cao Cao rode into the open, shouting, "Traitor! You have violated the Emperor's person and driven the people from their homes. Where do you think you're going?" "Coward turncoat!" swore Lü Bu in reply. "How dare you!" Xiahou Dun raised his spear and charged Lü Bu. As the warriors came to grips, Li Jue swung his contingent in from the left. Cao Cao commanded Xiahou Yuan to counter Li Jue. To the right more yells rang out as Guo Si and his company joined the battle. Cao Cao answered by sending Cao Ren to check Guo Si. But the three armies overpowered Xiahou Dun and drove him back to his lines. Then Lü Bu's crack armored cavalry fell upon Cao Cao's force, inflicting a heavy defeat and beating it back toward Yingyang.

Near the second watch the fleeing soldiers reached a barren hill. The moon rose bright and full. The scattered forces had barely reorganized and begun digging holes in the ground to cook their evening meal when fierce shouts erupted on all sides of them. Governor Xu Rong's ambush was sprung. Cao Cao laid the whip to his horse and fled blindly, only to run into Xu Rong himself. Cao turned sharply away, but Xu Rong shot him in the upper arm. Cao rode for his life over the slopes of the hill, the arrow fixed in his flesh. Two soldiers lying in wait hurled their spears, hitting Cao's horse. Cao rolled off the stricken beast, and the two men seized him. But at that moment Cao Hong raced over, cut down the two captors, and helped Cao Cao to his feet.

"My fate is sealed," said Cao. "Save yourself, good brother." "Get on my horse," Cao Hong answered. "I can go by foot." "How will you manage when the rebels catch up?" asked Cao Cao. "The world can do without Cao Hong," was the reply, "but not without you, my lord."[7] "If I survive," said Cao, "it will only be by your sacrifice." So saying, Cao Cao mounted. Hong removed his armor and outer garments and let his sword hang behind him as he hurried after the escaping Cao Cao. Toward the fourth watch they came to a wide river. Hearing the harsh yells of the pursuers, Cao Cao said, "We will die here." Cao Hong helped him down, removed his war gown and helmet and waded across, bearing Cao Cao on his back. As they crawled ashore, Lü Bu's men arrived on the other side and fired arrows across the water.

Cao Cao, drenched, continued his flight. Dawn broke. He traveled another thirty *li* before stopping at the foot of a low hill. Suddenly a party of soldiers charged up. It was Governor Xu Rong again; he had crossed upstream and kept up the chase. Cao Cao was panic-stricken, but Xiahou Dun, Xiahou Yuan, and several dozen horsemen arrived at the same moment. "Hands off our lord!" Xiahou Dun cried. Xu Rong started to attack, but Xiahou Dun felled him with a stroke of his blade, and killed or scattered his men. Soon after, Cao Ren, Li Dian, and Yue Jin caught up with Cao Cao, a reunion that brought both joy and dismay. Some five hundred of them regrouped and returned to Henei district. Dong Zhuo's armies proceeded toward Chang'an.

• • • •

When the confederacy under Yuan Shao moved into the abandoned capital of Luoyang, Sun Jian, having put out the fires in the imperial grounds, established headquarters inside the city wall on the site of the Hall of Paragons. He ordered the rubble cleared from the palace precincts and all the sacred tombs that had been opened by Dong Zhuo resealed. Where the royal ancestral temple had stood Sun Jian had three crude halls built and then invited the lords to set up the tablets of the deceased emperors and to perform the grand sacrifice of three animals.[8] After the ceremony all dispersed, and Sun Jian returned to his camp. The moon shone and the stars sparkled as he sat in the open, his hand on his sword, studying the heavenly pattern. He saw a whitish aura enveloping the circumpolar stars. "The imperial star is dim," he sighed. "Traitors have wrecked the dynasty and cast the people into misery. The capital lies in ruin." As he spoke, tears crept from his eyes.

A soldier drew Sun Jian's attention to a rainbow-like light coming out of a well to the south of the Hall of Paragons. Sun Jian told his men to go down with a torch and find the source. They fished up a woman's body, still preserved. She was dressed as a lady of the palace, and round her neck hung a small brocade pouch. Inside the pouch they found a vermillion box with a gold lock, and inside the box a jade seal, three or four inches around. The top was formed of five intertwined dragons. A gold inlay filled a chip on one corner. Eight characters in ancient seal script read: "By Heaven's mandate: long life and everlasting prosperity."

Sun Jian asked his adviser, General Cheng Pu, about the stone treasure.

Cheng Pu replied, "This is the seal of state. It confirms the devolution of authority from ruler to ruler. Long ago Bian He spied a phoenix perched on a rock in the Jing Mountains. He presented the rock to the King of Chu. They broke it open and found this jade. In the twenty-sixth year of the Qin dynasty[9] the First Emperor ordered a jade cutter to carve the seal; and Li Si, the First Emperor's prime minister, personally inscribed those eight words in seal script on its bottom surface. Two years later, when the Emperor was touring the Dongting Lake, high waves nearly engulfed his boat. He threw the jade into the water, and the waves subsided. Eight years after the incident, while in Huayin the Emperor came upon someone on the road holding out the seal to the royal attendants. 'I am returning this to His Majesty,' the man said and then disappeared.

"The following year the First Emperor died. Later Ziying, grandson of the First Emperor, presented the seal to the Supreme Ancestor.[10] Two hundred years later, when Wang Mang usurped the dynasty, the mother of the dethroned ruler struck two of the rebels, Wang Xun and Su Xian, with the seal and chipped the corner. The break was later filled in with gold. Guang Wu[11] obtained the jade in Yiyang, and it has been transmitted through succeeding reigns until this day.

"Recently, the deposed Emperor Shao was forcibly taken to the Beimang burial grounds during the upheaval caused by the Ten Eunuchs, and on the way back home he lost the treasured seal. If Heaven has placed it in your hands, it means that the throne is destined to be yours. But now we must not remain in the north too long. Let us return to our homeland southeast of the Yangzi and set our course from there."

"My thinking exactly," responded Sun Jian. "Tomorrow I shall take my leave, pleading ill health." Having reached this decision, Sun Jian imposed a vow of silence on the soldiers who had recovered the seal.

One of those present, however, was a townsman of Yuan Shao's, who, anxious to advance himself, slipped away from Sun Jian's camp and reported what he had seen to the war-ruler. Shao rewarded the informer generously and hid him in the army. The next day, Sun Jian came before Yuan Shao to take his leave and said, "I have an ailment that requires my return to Changsha. I come, my lord, to bid goodbye." With a smile Yuan Shao responded, "I know all about your 'ailment.' A severe case of 'royal seal,' is it not?" Sun Jian turned pale. "What makes you say such a thing?" he said. "We mustered our armies," Yuan Shao went on, "to bring traitors to justice and to rid the ruling house of its scourge. To that house the seal belongs. If it has come into your hands, you should leave it with me as leader of the confederation, here in front of the whole body of lords. After Dong Zhuo has been duly executed, it shall be returned to the court. For what purpose would you want to carry it away?"

"How could the seal have come into my possession?" Sun Jian asked. "Where is the object you found in the well by the Hall of Paragons?" countered Yuan Shao. "I have no such object," Sun Jian insisted. "Why are you harassing me this way?" "Make haste and produce it," Yuan Shao said flatly, "or suffer consequences of your own making." Pointing to Heaven, Sun Jian declared, "If I am concealing this treasure, may I die by sword or arrow." The assembled lords said, "If he gives such an oath, surely he cannot have the seal."

Yuan Shao then had the soldier who witnessed the incident brought forward. "When you pulled the woman from the well," Yuan Shao demanded of Sun Jian, "was this man present?" Sun Jian angrily drew his sword, menacing the soldier. Yuan Shao drew also, saying, "If you kill him, you are deceiving me!" Behind Yuan Shao, generals Yan Liang and Wen Chou had bared their swords, while behind Sun Jian, generals Cheng Pu, Huang Gai, and Han Dang had their weapons out. The lords tried to stop the quarrel, but Sun Jian took to his horse and left Luoyang with his entire army. Still outraged, Yuan Shao dispatched a letter to Liu Biao, imperial inspector in Jingzhou,[12] requesting him to intercept Sun Jian and seize the seal.

The following day Yuan Shao was informed that Cao Cao had pursued Dong Zhuo, engaged his forces at Yingyang, and had returned in defeat. Shao's men met Cao, and Yuan Shao called the lords together and served wine, hoping to hearten Cao Cao. During the repast Cao Cao sighed and said to Yuan Shao, "When I first rose to our great cause, to which these loyal lords have rallied, I intended for Benchu [Yuan Shao's style] to keep watch over the Meng ford with his Henei troops; and for my commanders based at Suanzao to guard Chenggao, hold Aocang Mountain, and close the Huanyuan and Daigu passes, thus securing the entire capital region. I meant for Gonglu [Yuan Shu's style] to post his Nanyang army in Dan and Xi counties, enter the pass at Wu, and let the western capital districts know the might of our arms. My objective was not so much to give battle as to dig in and make a show of force with decoys, demonstrating that the situation was turning in our favor. As fighters in the Emperor's cause, we could have swiftly chastised those who rose against him. But immobilized by hesitation, we have lost the confidence of the realm, and it makes me deeply ashamed." There was no reply Yuan Shao could make, and the assembly adjourned.

The separate and conflicting ambitions of Yuan Shao and the various lords had shown Cao Cao that they would achieve nothing, so he took his troops to Yangzhou. Gongsun Zan, too, said to Xuande and his brothers, "Yuan Shao has no future; the lords will turn against him in the long run. We might as well go home." Gongsun Zan decamped and went north. When he came to Pingyuan, he enjoined Xuande to remain as lord of the fief, and he went on to secure his own territory and replenish his forces.

In Yuan Shao's camp dissension was evident. Qiao Mao, governor of Dongjun, refused Liu Dai, governor of Yanzhou, a loan of grain. In retaliation Liu Dai raided Qiao Mao's camp, killed him, and took over his troops. Yuan Shao, seeing the confederation breaking apart, pulled up his own camps and left the capital to go east.

Riding south to his fief in Changsha, Sun Jian had to pass through Jingzhou, the province under the jurisdiction of Imperial Inspector Liu Biao (Jingsheng), a native of Gaoping in Shanyang and a relative of the imperial family. From his youth, Liu Biao had had a wide circle of friends and was one of a group of outstanding men from the area, the Eight Paragons of Jiangxia. Who were the other seven?

1. Chen Xiang (Zhonglin), from Runan
2. Fan Pang (Mengbo), also from Runan
3. Kong Yu (Shiyuan), from the fief of Lu
4. Fan Kang (Zhongzhen), from Bohai
5. Tan Fu (Wenyou), from Shanyang
6. Zhang Jian (Yuanjie), also from Shanyang
7. Cen Zhi (Gongxiao), from Nanyang

In addition, Liu Biao was assisted by Kuai Liang and Kuai Yue of Yanping as well as Cai Mao of Xiangyang.

On receipt of Yuan Shao's letter, Liu Biao ordered Kuai Yue and Cai Mao to take ten thousand men and intercept Sun Jian. When the two forces met, Sun Jian demanded,

"Why do you prevent me from passing?" Kuai Yue responded, "Why are you, a subject of the Han, carrying off the imperial seal? Leave it with me and you may pass." Sun Jian was outraged and ordered Huang Gai into battle. Cai Mao, brandishing his sword, took to the field. After a few clashes Huang Gai scored a blow with his whip on the armor plate over Cai Mao's chest, forcing him to retreat. Carried by the momentum of the victory, Sun Jian pushed across the line. At that moment Liu Biao himself led his men out as gongs and drums resounded in unison behind a hill.

Sun Jian immediately extended his respects from horseback and said, "Why are you making things difficult for a neighbor merely on Yuan Shao's word?" "You are hiding the seal of state," said Liu Biao. "Are you going to rebel?" "May I die by sword or arrow if I have it," swore Sun Jian. "If you expect me to believe you," replied Liu Biao, "then let me search your gear." "Are you so mighty to demean me this way?" retorted Sun Jian. The two warriors stood there on the verge of blows when Liu Biao backed off. Sun Jian gave his horse free rein and pursued Liu Biao—right into the waiting ambush. Kuai Yue and Cai Mao emerged from behind, trapping Sun Jian on all sides.

> Thus the royal seal proved no blessing to its finder;
> It proved rather a cause of war.

Would Sun Jian escape with his life?
READ ON.

7

Yuan Shao Battles Gongsun Zan at the River Pan;
Sun Jian Attacks Liu Biao Across the Great River

BY DINT OF THE HEROIC EFFORTS of his three commanders, Cheng Pu, Huang Gai, and Han Dang, Sun Jian broke out of the trap. Half of his men were lost, however, as they struggled to get back to the land south of the Great River. Liu Biao and Sun Jian became mortal enemies.

•　　•　　•　　•

Yuan Shao had positioned troops at Henei. Food and fodder were scarce, but Han Fu, provincial protector of Jizhou, provided grain for Shao's men.[1] Yuan Shao's adviser, Peng Ji, proposed attacking Han Fu. "A brave and powerful leader like yourself, who can move where he will," Peng Ji argued, "should not have to depend on another for supplies. Jizhou is a productive and wealthy province. Why not seize it?" "Have you a sound plan?" asked Yuan Shao. "Write to Gongsun Zan," Peng Ji said. "Suggest that he join us in a two-fronted attack on Jizhou. Zan is sure to muster his army. And Han Fu, who lacks the ability to cope with such a challenge, will invite you to take charge of his province. Thus you can pluck the prize with no effort at all." This advice delighted Yuan Shao, and he wrote Gongsun Zan proposing military action against Jizhou.

Zan was pleased with the idea of dividing Jizhou with Yuan Shao and called up his army the day the letter came. Meanwhile, Yuan Shao quietly informed Han Fu of the threat to his province. Han Fu summoned Xun Chan and Xin Ping to counsel. "Gongsun Zan commands hardened troops from the northern border districts of Yan and Dai," said Xun Chan. "They are advancing rapidly and are too strong to oppose directly. If Xuande and his brothers join then, they will be irresistible. Now then, Yuan Shao is a leader of unsurpassed courage and wisdom. He can field a large number of outstanding commanders. Why not invite him to govern the province jointly with you? He will treat you well and we'll have nothing to fear from Gongsun Zan." Accordingly, Han Fu dispatched his deputy Guan Chun to deliver the invitation to Yuan Shao.

However, Geng Wu, a lieutenant to the provincial protector, protested: "Yuan Shao is isolated and hard-pressed. Like a babe in arms he needs us for the very breath he draws. Cut off his milk, and he soon starves. It makes no sense to entrust our province to him. It's like inviting a tiger into a sheepfold." "I used to be an officer under the Yuans," Han Fu argued back, "and Shao's ability is far greater than mine. In olden times princes yielded their rule to worthy men whom they had selected. Why are you all so jealous?"

"Jizhou is done for!" sighed Geng Wu. More than thirty officials resigned, but Geng Wu and Guan Chun decided to waylay Yuan Shao outside the city wall. Several days later, when Yuan Shao arrived at Jizhou, the two bared their knives and tried to murder him, but General Yan Liang cut Geng Wu down instantly, and General Wen Chou swiftly beheaded Guan Chun.

Yuan Shao entered Jizhou,[2] commissioned Han Fu as General Known for Vigor-in-Arms, and assigned his own men—Tian Feng, Ju Shou, Xu You, and Peng Ji—to take control of the province. Provincial Protector Han Fu, stripped of all power, now knew the futility of regret. He rode alone to Zhang Miao, governor of Chenliu, to seek refuge.

As soon as Gongsun Zan heard that Yuan Shao was master of Jizhou, he sent his brother, Yue, to claim his share of the territory. But Yuan Shao said to Gongsun Yue, "Have your elder brother come to me himself. We have things to discuss." Gongsun Yue took his leave and had traveled some fifty *li* homeward when a group of soldiers set upon him. "We are bodyguards for Prime Minister Dong Zhuo!" they cried. The next moment Gongsun Yue was cut down by a volley of arrows. His attendants, however, survived and reported the murder. The news infuriated Gongsun Zan. "Yuan Shao tricked me into raising an army," he railed, "and plucked the prize from behind. Then he killed my brother and tried to put the blame on Dong Zhuo. This injustice must be avenged!" Zan mustered his entire army and headed for Jizhou.

Yuan Shao learned of Gongsun Zan's approach and led his own army out. The two met at the River Pan, the former on the east, the latter on the west side of a bridge linking the two shores. Gongsun Zan guided his horse onto it and shouted, "Treacherous villain, so to play me false!" Yuan Shao urged his horse toward the bridge and shouted back, "Han Fu knew his limits and turned his province over to me voluntarily. What concern is that of yours?" "There was a time," answered Gongsun Zan, "when I regarded you as loyal and just, and supported you as leader of the confederation. Today I see that you think like a wolf and act like a dog. How can you stand up in the world of men without a shred of self-respect left?" Outraged, Yuan Shao cried, "Who will take him?"

Wen Chou sped forward and leveled his spear. He fought his way to the bridge and crossed points with Zan. After ten passes Zan gave way and retreated and his line broke. Wen Chou pursued headlong, riding on his momentum. Zan entered his own ranks, but Chou rushed the center and wrought havoc, charging back and forth. Four of Gongsun Zan's ablest commanders faced Wen Chou. He killed one with a single thrust, and the other three fled. With Wen Chou in hot pursuit, Zan headed into the hills for safety. Wen Chou, close behind, called out, "Dismount and surrender!" Gongsun Zan had already lost his bow and arrows. His helmet, too, had fallen to the ground. Disheveled, he rode for his life, veering and swerving over the slopes, but his horse slipped and threw him to the bottom of a hill. Wen Chou fingered his spear and moved in for the kill.

Suddenly a young commander, spear in hand, rode into view, racing toward Wen Chou. Gongsun Zan climbed the slope and observed his rescuer: a towering figure of eight spans, with thick eyebrows and enormous eyes, a broad face and heavy jaws. He made an awesome impression. The unfamiliar warrior engaged Wen Chou, and they clashed fifty or sixty times, but neither prevailed. In the meantime, a rescue force under Gongsun Zan's lieutenants arrived, and Wen Chou swung round and departed. The young warrior did not pursue him, and Zan hurried down to ask his name. Bowing low, the youth replied, "I come from Zhending in Changshan. My surname is Zhao; given name, Yun; and my style is Zilong. I was serving under Yuan Shao but soon realized he was neither loyal to the throne nor a savior of the people, so I left him to join your camp.

I never expected we would meet here!" Overjoyed, Gongsun Zan took Zhao Zilong back to camp with him and began reordering his forces.[3]

The following day Gongsun Zan divided his army into two wings. His force was primarily a mounted one, numbering more than five thousand horses, most of which were white. In his previous campaigns against the Qiang tribesmen Gongsun Zan had put white horses in the vanguard because the Qiang would flee at the sight of one.[4] Gongsun Zan thus kept a large supply of these animals and was known as the White Horse General. Yuan Shao ordered his generals, Yan Liang and Wen Chou, to take one thousand crossbowmen each and deploy into two wings at the front. Those on the left were to fire on Gongsun Zan's right wing, those on the right on Gongsun Zan's left. In addition, Yuan Shao ordered Qu Yi to deploy eight hundred archers and fifteen thousand foot soldiers between the crossbowmen. Yuan Shao himself brought up the rear with tens of thousands of troops, foot and horse.

Gongsun Zan was still not entirely sure of his rescuer, Zhao Zilong, so he gave him a rear unit to command. General Yan Gang had the van, and Gongsun Zan led the main army up to the bridge. There he reined in. In front of his horse he planted a banner with a large red circle enclosing the words "Commanding General" woven in gold. Through the morning hours the drums rolled incessantly, but Yuan Shao made no move. Qu Yi kept his archers behind their shields with orders not to shoot until the bombards roared. Then amid heavy drumming and the war cries of soldiers Yan Gang began the onslaught. Crouching low, Qu Yi's soldiers watched their attackers draw near. Then a bombard sounded, and eight hundred archers stood up and let fly.

Before Yan Gang could turn, Qu Yi charged and cut him down. Gongsun Zan's contingent was mauled, and his two wings were pinned down by Shao's crossbowmen when they tried to effect a rescue. Yuan Shao's forces advanced en masse and cut their way straight to the bridge separating the adversaries. The bridge once gained, Qu Yi struck down the standard-bearer, and the embroidered banner fell before Gongsun Zan's eyes. He backed off the bridge and fled. Qu Yi kept riding toward Zan's rear line until he met Zhao Zilong, who sprang to the challenge. In moments Zilong had pierced Qu Yi through with his lance and left him dead on the ground. He then ran unaided across Yuan Shao's line, slashing right and thrusting left as if moving through a no-man's-land. Gongsun Zan rejoined the battle, and the two warriors dealt their enemy a nasty defeat.

Yuan Shao was unprepared for the counterattack because his mounted scouts had informed him only of the initial victories—Qu Yi's killing of the standard-bearer, his capture of the standard, and his pursuit of the defeated troops. Yuan Shao was with General Tian Feng, a few hundred lancers, and a few dozen mounted archers, laughing pompously, exclaiming as he observed the scene, "How useless that Gongsun Zan is!" Even as he spoke, Zhao Zilong charged into view. Yuan Shao's archers scrambled for their weapons. Zilong stabbed several soldiers, and the others fled. More of Zan's troops swarmed round. Tian Feng cried anxiously, "My lord, hide inside this hollow wall." But Yuan Shao threw his helmet to the ground and shouted, "A worthy man of war must face death in battle, not seek safety in a wall." Heartened by his words, his men fought fiercely, holding off Zilong's advance. Yuan Shao's main army then arrived on the scene, followed by Yan Liang's troops, and the two units pressed the enemy back. Defeated again, Gongsun Zan, guarded by Zhao Zilong, forced a passage through the encircling soldiers and made his way back to the bridge.

In pursuit of Gongsun Zan, Yuan Shao's army crossed the bridge in full force. Many drowned in the river. Yuan Shao, in the lead, had advanced less than five *li* when he heard a great cry coming from behind a hill. A bank of soldiers flashed into view, led by Xuande, Lord Guan, and Zhang Fei. While in Pingyuan they had learned of the battle and had come to Zan's aid. Accosted by three fresh warriors with their various weapons, Shao took fright. His sword dropped from his hand, so he immediately swung round and rode back across the bridge to safety, with the help of many more who risked their lives. Gongsun Zan gathered up his men and returned to camp. The three brothers made courteous inquiry after Zan's condition. "If not for Xuande, coming so far to help us," Zan declared, "we would have been battered to pieces." Gongsun Zan introduced the brothers to Zhao Zilong; Xuande took an instant liking to him and secretly hoped the respected warrior would join him.

Though defeated, Yuan Shao clung to his position and did not retire; the two armies stayed locked in place for more than a month. The situation was reported to the court in Chang'an, and Li Ru advised Dong Zhuo: "Yuan Shao and Gongsun Zan, two outstanding men of the present day, are in mortal combat at the River Pan. It might be useful to arrange for an imperial order to settle their quarrel. Both sides will be grateful for your kindness and transfer their loyalties to you, Imperial Preceptor."[5] "Good!" responded Dong Zhuo and sent the imperial guardian, Ma Midi, and the court steward, Zhao Qi, to deliver the decree.

When the two men reached Hebei, Yuan Shao received them one hundred *li* from his camp and accepted the royal order with deep respect. The next day Dong Zhuo's two representatives entered Gongsun Zan's camp and read out the decree. In response, Gongsun Zan sent a letter to Yuan Shao suggesting peace talks. The officials returned to Chang'an and reported the success of their mission. Gongsun Zan withdrew his forces that same day and recommended to the court that Xuande be appointed governor of Pingyuan fief. For Xuande and Zilong parting was difficult, and they held onto one another tearfully in their reluctance to be separated. "I thought Gongsun Zan was a true hero," Zilong sighed, "but now I see I was wrong. His conduct today befits a Yuan Shao!" "Bear up and serve him well for now," Xuande said. "Time will bring us together again." They shed more tears and went their ways.

•   •   •   •   •

Back in the district of Nanyang, Yuan Shu learned that his brother had taken possession of Jizhou, and sent a messenger there requesting one thousand horses. Yuan Shao refused, and thereafter the brothers were on bad terms. Yuan Shu next tried to borrow a large amount of grain from Liu Biao, imperial inspector of Jingzhou. Biao also said no. Yuan Shu was so galled by these refusals that he wrote Sun Jian urging him to attack Jingzhou.[6] The note read as follows:

> When Liu Biao blocked your way south, he was acting in collusion with my brother Benchu [Yuan Shao]. Now the two of them are conspiring to attack your lands south of the Great River. You should raise an army as swiftly as possible and attack Liu Biao while I deal with Benchu for you. Two accounts will be settled. You will gain Jingzhou; I will gain Jizhou. Don't let the opportunity pass.

After reading the letter, Sun Jian said, "Oh, to be rid of Liu Biao! He cut me off that time. I may not get another chance at him." Jian called his generals—Cheng Pu, Huang Gai, and Han Dang—to counsel. "Yuan Shu is full of tricks," Cheng Pu said, "and not to be trusted." "I want revenge, with or without Yuan Shu," said Sun Jian and sent Huang Gai to prepare warships and load them at the Great River, most of them with weapons and provisions, the larger ones with war-horses.

Spies brought word of these preparations to Liu Biao, who hastily conferred with his advisers. Kuai Liang said, "No cause for alarm. Let Huang Zu lead the van with men from Jiangxia. You hold the rear with forces from the Xiangyang area. Once Sun Jian has crossed rivers and lakes to get here, how much strength will he have left for the battle?" Liu Biao approved these steps.

Sun Jian had four sons by Lady Wu. The eldest was Ce (Bofu); the next, Quan (Zhongmou); the third, Yi (Shubi); and the fourth, Kuang (Jizuo). Sun Jian had a second wife, Lady Wu's younger sister. She bore him a son, Lang (Zaoan), and a daughter, Ren. Sun Jian had also adopted a son—Shao (Gongli)—from the Yu family. Finally, he had a younger brother, Jing (Youtai).

As Sun Jian was about to set out against Liu Biao, his brother Jing led all six sons in front of his horse in an effort to stop him. "Dong Zhuo controls the throne," Jing argued. "The Emperor is powerless; the empire in disorder. Each region is really a separate domain, and ours here, south of the river, is at peace. It makes no sense to raise a major force for the sake of a trifling insult. Please reconsider." "Say no more, brother," Sun Jian answered. "I'll have my way in every part of the empire and will never leave unanswered an enemy like Liu Biao." "Father, if you insist on going," Sun Ce pleaded, "allow me to come." Sun Jian agreed and took his eldest son on board. They set out for the city of Fankou.

Liu Biao's general, Huang Zu, had posted archers and crossbowmen along the river. As Sun Jian's war-boats neared shore, Huang Zu's men shot heavy volleys. Sun Jian ordered his men not to fire back but to huddle down in the holds and let the enemy shoot. Over a three-day period the boats approached shore a dozen times, drawing fresh volleys each time. As Sun Jian had anticipated, Huang Zu's stock of arrows was finally depleted, while he had accumulated a supply of more than one hundred thousand from the enemy. The fourth day the wind favored the shipborne force. Sun Jian ordered his men to shoot. Waves of arrows drove the men on shore into retreat as Sun Jian's warriors landed. Cheng Pu and Huang Gai led their contingents directly to Huang Zu's camp. Han Dang, moving swiftly, joined them. Squeezed from three sides, Huang Zu abandoned Fankou for the town of Deng. Sun Jian had Huang Gai guard the boats while he personally gave chase. Huang Zu led his men into open country and there confronted his pursuer. Sun Jian formed his lines and rode out in front of his banners, accompanied by his son Ce in full military dress, spear at the ready.

With Huang Zu were two generals, Zhang Hu from Jiangxia and Chen Sheng from Xiangyang. Huang Zu raised his whip and shouted, "Vermin from the south! How dare you intrude on the territory of an imperial relative?" He sent Zhang Hu to taunt the opposing line. Han Dang came out to meet him. The two horsemen closed and fought some thirty passages-at-arms. Chen Sheng saw Zhang Hu tiring and rushed to his aid. Observing from a distance, Sun Ce set aside his spear, took up his bow, and let fly. The arrow hit Sheng squarely in the forehead, and he collapsed. Zhang Hu was distracted by the sight of Chen Sheng on the ground, and in that moment Han Dang cleaved his skull with a stroke of his sword. Cheng Pu galloped to the front, hunting for Huang Zu, who got rid of his helmet and his horse and saved himself by mingling with the foot soldiers. Sun Jian pressed the slaughter all the way to the Han River. Then he ordered Huang Gai to move the boats upriver and moor them.

Huang Zu regrouped his shattered force and went to tell Liu Biao that Sun Jian was too powerful to resist. Liu Biao conferred with Kuai Liang, who said, "After a defeat like this, our men will have no fighting spirit. All we can do now is hold our strongpoints, avoid the thrust of their attack, and try to get help from Yuan Shao. Then we can break their siege."[7] "That's a clumsy plan," said Cai Mao. "With the enemy at our very gates and moat, are we to tie our hands and await our end? However unfit I may be, I beg to take one contingent outside the walls and fight to the finish." With Liu Biao's approval, Cai Mao led more than ten thousand men out of Xiangyang and deployed his line at Xian Hill.

Sun Jian and his victorious troops advanced swiftly to meet the new challenger. Cai Mao rode out before his contingents. "There's the brother of Liu Biao's wife!" cried Sun Jian.[8] "Who will seize him for me?" Cheng Pu raised his iron-spined spear and engaged Cai Mao, driving him off in defeat after several encounters. Sun Jian pursued with his main army and did great slaughter. Cai Mao retreated to Xiangyang for safety. Kuai Liang demanded that Cai Mao be executed for ignoring sound strategy and causing a major defeat, but Liu Biao was loath to punish the brother of his new wife.

Meanwhile, Sun Jian had placed men on all sides of Xiangyang and was mounting an attack when a storm sprang up and broke the shaft bearing the banner inscribed "Commanding General." "An ill omen," declared Han Dang. "Let us withdraw for now." "I have fought and won every battle," said Sun Jian. "Xiangyang is about to fall to us. I can't turn back because the wind has broken a flagpole." And so Sun Jian attacked the city all the harder, ignoring Han Dang's warning.

Inside the city Kuai Liang said to Liu Biao, "The other night I saw a 'general's star' that seemed about to fall in that portion of the sky corresponding to Sun Jian's territory. The star must be a sign of his fate. Get a message to Yuan Shao as quickly as you can." Accordingly, Liu Biao wrote the letter and asked for a volunteer to run the blockade and deliver it. Lü Gong, one of his ablest generals, answered the call. Kuai Liang said to him, "Complement your courage with a little strategy. We are giving you five hundred soldiers. Take enough marksmen, and when you penetrate Sun Jian's line head for Xian Hill. They will pursue. Assign one hundred to the hilltop and have them collect plenty of rocks. Post another hundred, archers and crossbowmen, in the woods nearby. When Sun's men give chase, don't flee directly. Wind round the hills and valleys until they follow you into the ambush. Then hit them with stones and arrows all at once. If you get the upper hand, sound the bombards in rapid succession, and we'll know to reinforce you. If they do not pursue, fire no shots but go on to Yuan Shao with our message. The moon will be dim tonight, so you can leave at dusk."

After he had absorbed the plan, Lü Gong tethered the horses he would need. At sunset the east gate was eased open and Gong slipped out. Sun Jian, in his tent, detected the sound and rode out with thirty horsemen to investigate. A scout reported that a group of warriors had left the city in the direction of Xian Hill. Sun Jian did not wait to summon his commanders but gave chase with his thirty riders. Lü Gong had already reached the thicker section of the woods and set his ambush in place. Sun Jian rode fast, pulling away from his cohort, and came up alone. Lü Gong was only a little ahead. "Halt!" Sun Jian shouted. Lü Gong swung around to engage. They came to grips but once, then Lü Gong darted away onto a mountain path. Sun Jian kept close but lost sight of his man. He was starting up the hill when a sudden beating of gongs was followed by a cascade of rocks and volleys of arrows. The missiles found their mark, and the brains were dashed from his head; man and horse perished on Xian Hill. Sun Jian was only thirty-seven years old.

Lü Gong intercepted Sun Jian's thirty followers and slaughtered them to a man. Then he signaled the city with a string of bombards. Huang Zu, Kuai Yue, and Cai Mao came forth to do their deadly work. The army from the south fell into confusion. Huang Gai heard the clamor and joined the fighting with his marines. He quickly captured Huang

Zu. At the same time, Cheng Pu, who was guarding Sun Jian's eldest son Ce, encountered Lü Gong. Cheng Pu raced ahead and unhorsed Lü Gong with a fatal blow. The two sides battled on till morning, when each was called back.[9] Then Liu Biao's men entered the city.

Only when Sun Ce returned to the River Han did he learn that his father had been killed and his body removed to the enemy city. Sun Ce wailed loud and long, and the army mourned. "We cannot leave my father's body in their hands," said Sun Ce. "We took Huang Zu alive," responded Huang Gai. "Have someone go into the city and negotiate a truce and an exchange." "I have a long-standing relationship with Liu Biao," Huan Jie, an army officer, volunteered. "Let me represent our side." With Sun Ce's agreement, Huan Jie came before Liu Biao with the proposal. Liu Biao said, "Sun Jian's corpse rests in its coffin. Return Huang Zu to us, and we can end our hostilities—as long as you never attempt another invasion." Huan Jie expressed respectful gratitude and was about to leave when Kuai Liang appeared below Liu Biao's platform and cried, "No! No! I have a plan to wipe out the enemy to the last man! But first we have to kill this messenger." Indeed:

> Sun Jian lost his life pursuing his foe,
> And Huan Jie risked his life in search of peace.

The outcome lay in Liu Biao's hands.[10]

READ ON.

8

Wang Yun Shrewdly Sets a Double Snare;
Dong Zhuo Starts a Brawl at Phoenix Pavilion

"SUN JIAN IS DEAD," Kuai Liang continued, "and his sons are still young. The south is vulnerable, and if we strike swiftly it will fall with a roll of the drums! Returning the body and making a truce will only give them time to renew their strength, and it will sacrifice our safety." "That means sacrificing Huang Zu," was Liu Biao's answer, "but I don't have the heart to do it." "Is one muddleheaded Huang Zu worth the whole southern region?" retorted Kuai Liang. "Huang Zu and I are the closest friends," replied Liu Biao. "I cannot break faith and let him die." So Liu Biao sent Huan Jie back to implement the exchange.

After Sun Ce received the coffin, he canceled military operations and went home to bury his father in the plains of Qu'e. Then he led his army to Jiangdu and enlisted the services of the wise and talented men of the region. By humbling himself and treating others generously he gradually attracted many outstanding men to his court.

•　•　•　•

In Chang'an, Dong Zhuo learned of Sun Jian's death and said, "I am well rid of a mortal enemy. But how old is his first son?" "Seventeen," someone said. This answer persuaded Dong Zhuo he need not fear the south.

Dong Zhou's behavior became more arbitrary and arrogant than ever. He had himself addressed as Honorary Father,[1] and in his public appearances usurped the regalia of the Emperor. He appointed his brother, Min, general of the left and lord of Hu, and his nephew, Huang, privy counselor with overall command of the Palace Guard. All members of the Dong clan—whether young or old—were honored with titles. Preceptor Dong put a quarter of a million people to hard labor building a large structure, called Mei, two hundred and fifty *li* from Chang'an. The walls, which enclosed palaces and granaries, were modeled in height and thickness after those of the capital. Twenty years' supply of grain was placed in store. From among the commoners Dong Zhuo chose eight hundred beauties to adorn the palace rooms, where gold and jade, colored silks and rare pearls were hoarded. The Dong family lived amidst this wealth and splendor while Dong Zhuo himself traveled to the capital once or twice a month. Each time he left or returned to Chang'an all ranking court officials saw him off or greeted him outside the city's northwest gate, the Heng. Usually, Dong Zhuo set up tents on the wayside to feast these high officials.

On one such occasion, with all of officialdom present, several hundred enemy troops from the north who had voluntarily surrendered were brought in. Then and there Dong Zhuo ordered his guards to mutilate them: some had their limbs lopped off; some, their eyes gouged out; some, their tongues cut; some were boiled in vats. The howls of the victims shook the officials so that they could not hold their chopsticks. But Dong Zhuo kept drinking, chatting, and laughing away, utterly unperturbed, as was his wont.[2]

Another day Dong Zhuo convened the officials in front of the ceremonial platform. The assembly was seated in two long rows according to rank. As the wine was going round, Lü Bu stepped over to Dong Zhuo and whispered a few words. "So that's how it is!" said Dong Zhuo, smiling, and he had Lü Bu haul out the minister of public works, Zhang Wen. The other officials paled. Moments later Zhang Wen's head was carried in on a red platter. Dong Zhuo laughed at the terrified assembly, saying, "Nothing to fear, my lords. My son, Fengxian [Lü Bu], came upon a letter Yuan Shu had written to Zhang Wen. The two were conspiring against me; but no one here was implicated, so don't worry." "Of course not, of course not," the officials chimed in obsequiously. With that the banquet ended.[3]

Minister of the Interior Wang Yun returned home despondent over the day's events. Late that night, strolling in his garden under a high moon, he stopped by a rose trellis and gazed at the sky. His eyes filled with tears. In the silence he heard moans and sighs near the Peony Pavilion. Stealing over, he discovered the singing girl, Diaochan, a child he had taken in and trained in the arts of dance and song. She was now sixteen and possessed unearthly beauty and skill. Wang Yun regarded her as his own daughter.

After listening a good while, Wang Yun called her to him. "Wretched girl, is there someone you pine for?" he asked sharply. Diaochan dropped to her knees and replied, "Would this humble maid dare?" "Then why," Wang Yun continued, "are you sighing here deep into the night?" "Allow me to open my innermost thoughts to you," the girl replied. "Keep nothing back," Wang Yun said. "Tell me the whole truth." "My lord," Diaochan began, "I am obliged to you for your unstinting care, for having me instructed in the arts of music and dancing, and for treating me with the utmost kindness and generosity. No sacrifice on my part could repay even one ten-thousandth of what I owe you. Recently you have been looking terribly sad, as if burdened by some great affair of state,[4] but how could I inquire into such matters? This evening again I saw you pacing uneasily, and it brought a sigh to my lips. I never thought my lord would take notice. But if there is any way I can serve you, I would welcome death ten thousand times before declining." At these words Wang Yun struck the ground with his walking stick and cried out, "It never occurred to me that you could be the one to save the Han! Come with me to the gallery of murals." Diaochan followed Wang Yun to the room. Impatiently he dismissed the waiting maids and servants and conducted Diaochan to a seat. Then he touched his head and hands to the floor in front of her. At once Diaochan prostrated herself in astonishment. "My lord," she said, "what is the meaning of this?"

"Have pity," Wang Yun pleaded, weeping openly, "on those who live under the Han!" "I can only repeat what I have just said," the girl replied. "Ten thousand deaths would not deter me from doing whatever it is you wish me to do." "The common folk," Wang Yun went on, still kneeling, "are in dire peril. The sovereign and his officials are balanced on the edge of disaster. You may be the only one who can save us. Here is how matters stand: the traitor Dong Zhuo is preparing to seize the throne, and our civil and military officials have no means to prevent him. Now then, Dong Zhuo has an adopted son, Lü Bu, a man of extraordinary courage and might, but, like his stepfather, a slave to his passions.

I would like to catch them in a double snare by first promising you in marriage to Lü Bu and then offering you to Dong Zhuo, thus putting you in a perfect position to turn them against one another. Drive Lü Bu to kill Dong Zhuo, and you will have eliminated a great evil, stabilized the dynastic shrines, and restored our ruling house. It lies in your power. But are you willing?" "I have already agreed to serve," said Diaochan. "I am eager to be presented to them. Leave all the rest to me." "If this gets out," Wang Yun cautioned her, "my house will be destroyed." "Have no fear, my lord," she said. "If I cannot live up to my duty, may I die by ten thousand cuts." Wang Yun saluted her in gratitude.

The next day Wang Yun had a smith fashion a golden headpiece studded with priceless pearls from his family's treasure chest. When the helmet was finished, he sent a man to present it secretly to Lü Bu. Delighted with the gift, Lü Bu came to Wang Yun's home to express his appreciation. The minister received him outside the main gate and ushered him into his private apartment, where he prepared a feast of choice delicacies. Then Wang Yun led Lü Bu to the seat of honor. "I am merely one of the prime minister's generals," the guest said, "but you are a great minister. I am not worthy of such courtesy." "In this day and age," Wang Yun replied, "the world has no heroes save you, General. It is not your office but your great ability to which I pay homage." These words gave Lü Bu immense pleasure. Wang Yun toasted him with solicitous hospitality, never ceasing to extol the virtue of Imperial Preceptor Dong Zhuo[5] and General Lü Bu. Lü Bu laughed broadly and imbibed freely.

Wang Yun dismissed the attendants, keeping a few serving girls to pour the wine. Both men were well warmed when Yun called for his "daughter." Two maids led out Diaochan, dressed most alluringly. Lü Bu, startled, asked who she was. "My daughter, Diaochan," was the reply. "You have favored me, General, with more kindness than I could possibly deserve, as if we were closely related. That's why I would like to present her to you." He ordered Diaochan to offer a cup to Lü Bu. As she held out the wine with both hands a subtle interest crept into their glances. Wang Yun, feigning intoxication, said, "My child, invite the general to drink deeply. He is the mainstay of our household."

Lü Bu offered Diaochan a seat, but she feigned a move to withdraw. "The general is my closest friend," Wang Yun admonished her, "there is no reason not to sit with him." Diaochan seated herself beside Yun. Lü Bu's eyes never left her.[6] A few more cups and Wang Yun said, "I would like to offer my daughter to you—if you would be willing to have her as your concubine." Lü Bu rose to express his appreciation: "For that I would be bound to you in loyalty even as a horse or a dog." "Then," said Yun, "we will select an auspicious day to deliver her." Lü Bu's delight knew no bounds. His glance clung to her, and she reciprocated with her own suggestive signs. The party came to an end. "I would have asked you to stay the night," said Wang Yun, "but was afraid the imperial preceptor would become suspicious." Lü Bu saluted his host repeatedly and departed.

Several days later at court, choosing a time when Lü Bu was out of sight, Wang Yun knelt before Dong Zhuo, hands touching the floor, and said, "Would the imperial preceptor deign to dine at my humble home?" "The invitation from the minister of the interior is accepted with pleasure," was the response. Wang Yun expressed his thanks and returned home.

Delicacies of land and sea furnished Wang Yun's feast. The setting was placed at the center of the main hall. Exquisitely embroidered cloths were spread over the ground, and drapes hung inside and outside the dining chamber.

Toward noon Dong Zhuo arrived by carriage. Dressed in court attire, bowing and tendering his respects, Wang Yun received his guest as he descended. One hundred hal-berdiers escorted him into the room and ranged themselves at either side. At the dais Wang Yun prostrated himself again. Dong Zhuo ordered his men to help his host to a seat beside him. "Imperial Preceptor," Wang Yun said, "your magnificent virtue towers above us. The greatest sages of antiquity—Preceptor Yi Yin and Regent Zhougong[7]—cannot approach you in virtue." These words pleased Zhuo enormously. The wine was served and the entertainment began. Wang Yun continued to shower his guest with gracious compliments.

The day waned. The wine warmed them well. Wang Yun invited Dong Zhuo to his private apartment. Zhuo dismissed his guard. Yun proffered a goblet and congratulated the preceptor. "Since my youth," said Wang Yun, "I have been studying the patterns of the heavens. The signs I see at night say that the Han has completed its allotted span. The whole realm is moved by your achievements and virtue. The wish of Heaven and the hopes of men would be well fulfilled if you followed the example of the ancient worthies Shun and Yu, who accepted their sovereigns' abdication on the strength of their own merit."

"That," Dong Zhuo exclaimed, "is more than I dare hope for." Wang Yun continued, "Since earliest times those who would govern rightly have taken action against those who govern ill, and those without virtue have yielded power to those with virtue. In the present circumstances there would not be the slightest question of your exceeding your proper place."[8] Dong Zhuo smiled and said, "If the Mandate of Heaven should actually settle upon me, you would be honored as a founder of the house." Wang Yun bowed deeply to show his gratitude.

In the chamber decorated candles were lit. Only the serving maids stayed behind, tendering wine and food. "Our regular musicians," Wang Yun said, "are too ordinary for such an occasion as this. But there happens to be a performer here whom I beg leave to have appear before you." "A wonderful and ingenious thought!" exclaimed Dong Zhuo. Wang Yun ordered the curtain lowered and outside it, encircled by an ensemble of pipe and reed, Diaochan began her dance. Admiration of her art is expressed in this lyric:

> Like Flying-Swallow of Zhaoyang Palace,
> The swan-sprite turns in an opened palm—
> Is she fresh from Dongting's vernal lake?[9]
>
> Her graceful step keeps the Liangzhou air:
> As the tender scent a flowering branch exhales
> Fills the paneled room with springtime warmth.

Another poem describes her performance:

> To the quickening beat the swallow now takes wing,
> Reaching the gorgeous room still trailing mist:
> Those black brows caused the rover's heart to ache,
> Those looks have pierced the souls of all who sued.[10]
>
> No elmseed coin could buy those golden smiles;
> No gem or jewel need gild her willow waist.
> Now done and screened again, she glances to discover
> Who next will play the goddess's royal lover.[11]

Dong Zhuo ordered the dancer to approach him. Diaochan entered from behind the curtain, making profound salutations. Dong Zhuo took in the expressive beauty of her

face and asked, "Who is this girl?" "The songstress Diaochan," answered Wang Yun.
"Then she can sing as well?" Dong Zhuo inquired. Wang Yun had Diaochan take up the
sandalwood blocks and tap the rhythm as she sang. This poem describes the moment
well:

> Her parting lips were like the cherry bud.
> Across two rows of jade an air of spring flowed forth.
> But her clove-sweet tongue proved a steely sword
> That put to death a base, betraying lord.

Dong Zhuo could not stop marveling at her voice. Wang yun ordered Diaochan to
serve more wine. Dong Zhuo lifted his cup and asked, "How many springs have you
passed?" "Your servant is just sixteen," she replied. "You must have come from a land
of fairies," Dong Zhuo said. At that moment Wang Yun rose from his mat and declared,
"I would like to present this girl to the imperial preceptor, if it would be agreeable." "I
would be at a loss to repay such a boon," Dong Zhuo responded. "To serve the imperial
preceptor would be splendid luck for her," Wang Yun added. Again Dong Zhuo voiced his
thanks. Wang Yun immediately ordered a felt-lined closed carriage to carry Diaochan
ahead to the prime minister's residence. Then Dong Zhuo rose and bade his host good-
bye. Wang Yun escorted his guest home before taking his leave.

Wang Yun was halfway home again when he saw two lines of red lanterns on the road
ahead; in their light stood Lü Bu, armed and mounted. Lü Bu reined in and reached over,
taking hold of Yun's upper garment. "You promised Diaochan to me," he snarled. "Now
you give her to the imperial preceptor. What kind of game are you trying to play?" "This
is not the place to talk," Wang Yun responded. "Come to my house. Please." Lü Bu accompanied Wang Yun home. They dismounted and went to the private apartment. After
the amenities Wang Yun asked, "What grounds do you have for such an accusation, General?" "It was reported to me," Lü Bu answered, "that you delivered Diaochan to the
prime minister's residence in a felt-lined closed carriage. What is the meaning of this?"

"Then you really do not know! Yesterday," Wang Yun explained, "the preceptor said
to me at court, 'There is something I wish to discuss. I will visit you tomorrow.' So I
prepared a small banquet. As we were dining, he said, 'I understand you have a daughter,
Diaochan, whom you have promised to my son, Fengxian. Lest the agreement seem less
than official, I have come especially to confirm it and to meet your daughter as well.' I
could hardly disobey, so I led her out to pay her respects to her future father-in-law. The
preceptor said, 'Today is an auspicious day. I shall take Diaochan back with me for my
son.' A moment's reflection, General, and you will realize that I could hardly refuse the
preceptor's personal request." "Then you must forgive me, Your Honor," Lü Bu said. "I
was mistaken and will come another time to apologize properly." "My daughter," Wang
Yun added, "has a sizable trousseau. I will deliver it as soon as she joins you at your
residence." The general thanked the minister and left.

The next day Lü Bu made inquiries at Dong Zhuo's residence but was unable to learn
anything. He went directly into the ministerial quarters and questioned the serving
maids. "Last night," they informed him, "the imperial preceptor had a new girl with him.
They have not yet arisen." Lü Bu felt great anger swell within him. He stole close to the
outside of Dong Zhuo's bedroom and peered in. Diaochan was combing her hair by the
window. Suddenly she saw a reflection in the pool outside, that of a huge man with a
headpiece that caught his hair in a knot. Assuming it was Lü Bu, she puckered her brows,

feigning sorrow and dabbing at her eyes with a filmy scarf. Lü Bu observed her a good while before moving away. Moments later he reentered the main hall where Dong Zhuo was seated.

Dong Zhuo saw Lü Bu come in and asked, "Is everything all right outside?" "No problems," answered Lü Bu and stood in attendance beside the preceptor. Dong Zhuo was eating. Lü Bu glanced around. He spotted a young woman moving back and forth behind a damask curtain, peeking out now and then and letting a corner of her face show. Her eyes bespoke her affection. Lü Bu knew her to be Diaochan, and the soul within him fluttered. Dong Zhuo noticed Lü Bu's distraction and, pricked by jealousy and suspicion, said, "If there is nothing else, you may go." Sullenly, Lü Bu left.

Enthralled by Diaochan's charms, Dong Zhuo let official business lapse for more than a month. Once he fell ill, and Diaochan stayed up every night catering to his needs and wishes. On one occasion Lü Bu entered the private apartments to see him. Dong Zhuo was sleeping. Behind the bed Diaochan tilted her shoulders toward Lü Bu and pointed first to her heart and then to Dong Zhuo. Her cheeks were moist. Lü Bu felt his own heart crumble within him. Dong Zhuo opened his eyes and slowly focused on Lü Bu, who was staring at the rear of the bed. Dong Zhuo swung around and spied Diaochan behind him. "Have you been flirting with my favorite concubine?" he screamed and ordered Lü Bu thrust from the room. "Never enter here again!" he shouted.

Rage and hatred struck deep in Lü Bu. On the way home he met Li Ru and told him what had happened in the bedroom. Li Ru rushed to see Dong Zhuo. "Imperial Preceptor," he pleaded, "if you hope to make the realm your own, there's no point in blaming Lü Bu for so trifling an offense. Our cause is lost if he turns against us." "What shall I do?" asked Dong Zhuo. "Summon him tomorrow morning," Li Ru counseled, "and honor him with presents of gold and silk. Mollify him with gentle phrases. There should be no further problems." Dong Zhuo agreed and the next day had Lü Bu called before him. "Yesterday," Dong Zhuo began, "I was unwell and not at all myself. I said the wrong thing and did you injury. Do not hold it against me." Dong Zhuo conferred on his general a bounty of ten catties of gold and twenty rolls of silk. Lü Bu thanked him and went home. But from then on, though his body remained with Dong Zhuo, his mind dwelled on Diaochan.

After Dong Zhuo got over his illness, he held court once again. Lü Bu, armed as always, attended him. One day he saw the preceptor in conference with Emperor Xian and slipped away to Dong Zhuo's residence. He tied his horse at the front entrance and went into the rear chambers, halberd in hand, where he found Diaochan. "Wait for me," she said, "in the back garden by the Phoenix Pavilion." Lü Bu went where he was told and stood by the curved railing that surrounded the little belvedere. After a long while he saw her coming, parting the flowers and brushing aside the willows—truly, to any mortal eye, a celestial being from the Palace on the Moon. Weeping, she joined him and said, "Though I am not his real daughter, Minister Wang Yun treats me as his own flesh and blood. The moment he presented me to you, my lifelong prayers were answered. I can't believe that the preceptor's conscience could permit him to stain my purity, so that I now despair of life itself. I have borne my shame and prolonged my worthless existence only for the chance to say good-bye to you. Our fortunate meeting today answers my wish. But never again, disgraced as I am now, could I serve a hero such as you. I shall die before your eyes to show my earnest heart." With that, she grasped the curved railing and started into the lotus pool.

Lü Bu lunged forward and caught her. Through his tears he said, "I have long known your real feelings, but alas, we could never speak." Diaochan reached out and clutched Lü Bu's clothing. "Since I can never be your wife in this world," she said, "I want to arrange to meet you in the next." "If I cannot have you as my wife in this world," answered Lü Bu, "then I am no hero worthy of the name." "I count my days as years. Pity me, my lord, and save me," the girl implored. "I had to slip away or else the old villain would suspect something," Lü Bu said. "Now I must go back." Diaochan would not let go of him. "If you are so afraid of the 'old villain,'" she cried, "then I will never see the light of day again, for I am lost." Lü Bu stood still. "Give me time to think," he said finally, as he took his halberd and turned to leave. "Oh, General!" cried Diaochan, "even in the seclusion of my boudoir your name resounded like thunder. I thought you the foremost man of the age and never imagined another could subjugate you." Her tears rained down. Shame covered Lü Bu's face as he leaned on his halberd, listening. Then he turned and embraced Diaochan, comforting her with tender words. The pair clung together fondly.

Dong Zhuo, who was still at court, began to wonder where Lü Bu had gone. He bid the Emperor a hasty good-bye and returned home in his carriage. Seeing Lü Bu's horse tied at his front gate, he questioned the gateman and was told that the general was in the rear chamber. Dong Zhuo dismissed his servants roughly and went looking for Lü Bu. Not finding him in the rear chamber, he called for Diaochan. She too was not to be found. "She is in the back garden viewing the blossoms," the maidservants told him. Dong Zhuo rushed there and saw the amorous pair tête-à-tête at the Phoenix Pavilion. The halberd had been set aside. Dong Zhuo's anger flared and he let out a dreadful shout. Lü Bu spotted him, panicked, and fled. Dong Zhuo picked up the great halberd and gave chase. Lü Bu was swift. Dong Zhuo, too fat to catch up, heaved the weapon. Lü Bu knocked it aside. Dong Zhuo retrieved it and continued running, but Lü Bu was already out of range. Dong Zhuo dashed out the garden gate, collided head on with another man running in, and fell to the ground. Indeed:

> His fury mounted to the sky,
> But his heavy frame sprawled upon the ground.

Who had knocked him down?

READ ON.

9

Lü Bu Kills the Tyrant for Wang Yun;
Li Jue Invades the Capital on Jia Xu's Advice

THE MAN WHO PLOWED INTO DONG ZHUO was none other than his most trusted adviser, Li Ru. Horrified, Li Ru scrambled to help Dong Zhuo into the library, where the preceptor sat down and composed himself. "Whatever brought *you* here?" gasped Dong Zhuo. "I came in through the main gate," Li Ru replied. "They told me you'd charged off into the rear garden looking for Lü Bu. I rushed over, too, and saw him bounding away, crying, 'The preceptor's after me!' So I headed into the garden to try and smooth things over, but I have only offended Your Worship and made things worse. I deserve to die." "Oh, to be rid of that scoundrel!" Dong Zhuo said fiercely. "He was flirting with my darling. I'll have his head for it." "That would be most unwise, Your Worship," Li Ru responded. "In ancient times at the famous banquet where all guests were told to tear the tassels from their hats, King Zhuang of Chu overlooked an amorous gesture toward his queen from Jiang Xiong, the very man who later saved the king from Qin soldiers.[1] Now, this Diaochan is just another woman; but Lü Bu is a fierce and trusted general. Give her to him now, and he will risk life and limb to requite your generosity. I entreat you, consider it carefully." After absorbing this advice, Dong Zhuo said, "You have a point. I shall think it over." Li Ru thanked him and left.

Dong Zhuo returned to his private apartments and asked Diaochan, "Are you having an affair with Lü Bu?" Diaochan burst into tears before replying, "I was enjoying the flowers in the back garden when he accosted me. I was frightened and tried to slip away. He said, 'I am the imperial preceptor's son. You don't have to avoid *me*.' Then he chased me with that halberd of his over to the Phoenix Pavilion. I could see he meant no good. What if he forced himself on me? I tried to throw myself into the pool, but the brute wrapped his arms around me. My life was hanging there in the balance when you came— just in time to save me."

"I have made a decision," Dong Zhuo declared. "I am going to give you into Lü Bu's service. What do you think of that?" Panicked, Diaochan pleaded through tears:[2] "Having had the honor of serving Your Worship, I could not bear the shame of being handed down to an underling." She took hold of a sword hanging against the wall and pressed it to her throat. Dong Zhuo snatched it away and embraced her. "I spoke in jest," he said. Diaochan collapsed in his arms. "I know this is Li Ru's doing," she murmured as she hid her face and sobbed. "He and Lü Bu are fast friends and must have worked this out between them without giving the slightest consideration to the dignity of the Imperial Preceptor or to my own life. Oh, I could eat him alive!'' ''I will never give you up,'' said Dong Zhuo, comforting her. ''Though I enjoy the favor of your attention,'' Diaochan went on, ''I don't think I should remain here too long. Lü Bu will find a way to ruin me.'' ''Tomorrow,'' said Dong Zhuo, ''you and I shall repair to the new palace at Mei and take our pleasure there together. Try not to worry.'' Diaochan mastered her fears and thanked Dong Zhuo.

The following day Li Ru appeared before Dong Zhuo and said, ''Today is an auspicious day for presenting Diaochan to Lü Bu.'' ''Lü Bu and I,'' Dong Zhuo replied, ''are father and son. It would be unseemly for me to present her to him. Despite his offense, however, I will take no action against him. Convey my wishes—and speak gently to comfort him.'' ''Preceptor,'' Li Ru urged, ''you should not let a woman beguile you.'' Dong Zhuo's expression turned ugly. ''Would you care,'' he asked, ''to give your wife to Lü Bu? Let us hear no more of this, or the sword will speak for me.'' Li Ru left Dong Zhuo's presence and, raising his eyes to Heaven, sighed, ''We are all doomed, and at a woman's hands.'' A reader of later times was moved to write this verse:

> Wang Yun staked the empire's fate
>   on a gentle maiden's charm.
> Spear and shield were set aside,
>   no soldier came to harm.
> In the fray at Tiger Pass
>   three heroes fought in vain.
> Instead the victory song was sung
>   at Phoenix Pavilion.

That same day Dong Zhuo prepared to return to Mei. The whole assembly of officials came to see him off. From her carriage Diaochan picked out Lü Bu in the throng, staring at her. She covered her face as if weeping. The carriage began to move. Lü Bu led his horse to a knoll and watched the dust rising behind the wheels. A sigh of remorse escaped from his lips. ''Why are you staring into the distance and sighing?'' someone asked from behind. ''Why aren't you with the preceptor?'' It was Minister of the Interior Wang Yun.

After they had exchanged greetings, Wang Yun said, ''A slight indisposition has kept me indoors the past few days—that's why we haven't seen each other—but I felt I had to get myself out for the preceptor's departure. And now I have the added pleasure of meeting you. Forgive my question, General, but is something the matter?'' ''Your daughter, that's all,'' was the reply. ''You mean, he's kept her all this time?'' Wang Yun asked, affecting surprise. ''That old villain made her his favorite long ago,'' answered Lü Bu. ''I don't believe it!'' Wang Yun exclaimed. Lü Bu then related what had happened to Diaochan as Wang Yun looked skyward and stamped his feet. Finally he spoke: ''It amazes me that the preceptor could do such a beastly thing.'' He took Lü Bu's hand and said, ''Why don't we discuss this further at my home?''

Lü Bu returned with Wang Yun, who ushered him into a private room. Given wine and treated cordially, Lü Bu narrated in full his confrontation with Dong Zhuo at the pavilion. ''Then the preceptor has violated my daughter!'' responded Wang Yun, ''and snatched your wife. We stand shamed and mocked before the world. *He* is not mocked—only you and I. I am nothing but a useless old man, and I suppose I will have to swallow the insult. What a pity, though, for you, General—for a hero, head and shoulders above them all, to suffer such disgrace!''

Lü Bu's anger could have lifted him to the heavens. He struck the table and roared. "I should never have said what I did," Wang Yun said immediately. "Please compose your-self." "The villain's life will clear my name," Lü Bu shouted. "Do not say so, General," Wang Yun admonished, hastily touching Lü Bu's mouth. "I'm afraid I shall be impli-cated." "As a man of honor standing before Heaven and earth," Lü Bu went on, "I will not be his underling forever." "A man with your abilities," Wang Yun agreed, "should not be subject to the authority of someone like Preceptor Dong." "I would love to be rid of the old villain," confided Lü Bu, "but history would brand me an unfilial son." Smil-ing faintly, Wang Yun said, "You are a Lü. He is a Dong. Where was his fatherly feeling when he threw that halberd?" Lü Bu's temper flared again. "I nearly overlooked that!" he cried. "Thank you for reminding me."

As his suggestions took hold, Wang Yun continued working on Lü Bu: "Your service to the Han will secure your reputation for loyalty, and historians will preserve your good name for posterity. But support for Dong Zhuo is disloyal and will earn you an eternity of condemnation." Lü Bu shifted off his seat and bowed to the ground to show his re-spect. "My mind is made up," said Lü Bu. "Do not doubt it." "But failure means disas-ter," Wang Yun cautioned. With his knife Bu pricked blood from his arm to seal his pledge. In response Wang Yun dropped to his knees and said, "Your gracious favor en-ables the temple services of the Han to continue.[3] But you must disclose nothing. A plan of action will be ready in due time, and you will be informed." Lü Bu assented and took his leave.[4]

Next, Wang Yun summoned Shisun Rui, a superviser in the Secretariat, and Huang Wan, commander of the Capital Districts, to try to work out a plan. "The Emperor," Rui began, "has recently recovered from an illness. Send a smooth talker to the new palace in Mei requesting Dong Zhuo's presence in the capital. At the same time have the Emperor secretly authorize Lü Bu to place an ambush at the court gates. Escort Dong Zhuo in and kill him there. That's the best way." "Who will take the message?" asked Huang Wan. "Cavalry Commander Li Su," suggested Rui, "comes from Lü Bu's own district. He has resented Dong Zhuo ever since he was passed over for promotion, but Dong Zhuo is un-likely to suspect him." "A good choice," said Wang Yun.

Wang Yun presented the plan to Lü Bu, who said, "Li Su! He talked me into killing Ding Yuan! He'll go all right, or I'll have his head." Li Su was secretly brought in, and Lü Bu confronted him: "Once you convinced me to kill my benefactor and stepfather Ding Yuan and go over to Dong Zhuo. Now he has wronged the Emperor and caused the people to suffer. His foul crimes have roused the indignation of men and gods alike. We want you to carry the Emperor's edict to Mei, commanding Dong Zhuo to appear at court, where soldiers in hiding will be ready to kill him. We must work for the house of Han as loyal subjects. Do we have your consent?" "I, too," replied Li Su, "have longed to be rid of him, but I despaired of finding allies. If *you*, General, are so minded, then Heaven itself favors our cause. I am with you, heart and soul." He broke an arrow to confirm his oath. "If your mission succeeds," said Wang Yun, "a handsome commission awaits you."

Li Su and a dozen riders went to Mei the following day. The arrival of the imperial edict was announced, and Dong Zhuo received the bearer. Li Su paid his respects. "What edict from the Emperor?" asked Dong Zhuo. "His Majesty," began Li Su, "has recovered from his illness and desires to call together the full assembly in the Weiyang Hall. This edict was issued in connection with a decision to yield the throne to the preceptor." "What is Wang Yun's view?" asked Dong Zhuo. "The minister of the interior," Li Su replied, "has already arranged for the construction of a platform for the ceremony of abdication. Only your presence is awaited, my lord." Delighted, Dong Zhuo said, "Last night I dreamed that a dragon was encircling me; today these auspicious tidings arrive. My time has come. I must not miss it." Dong Zhuo ordered four trusted generals—Li Jue, Guo Si, Zhang Ji, and Fan Chou—to guard Mei with three thousand men from his Flying Bear Corps.[5] Then he made ready to return to Chang'an. "When I am emperor," he said, turning to Li Su, "you will bear the gilded mace as chief of the Capital Guard." Li Su gave thanks, speaking as a subject addressing his sovereign.

Dong Zhuo went to take leave of his mother, a woman more than ninety years old. "Where are you going, son?" she asked. "I am going to accept the succession from the Han," he replied. "Shortly you will be made Queen Mother." "These few days," she said, "I have been feeling unsteady, and my heart won't quiet down. Could it be an ill omen?" "Mother," Dong Zhuo answered, "you are going to be Mother of the Realm. That's what these little premonitions mean." He took his leave. Before departing, he told Diaochan, "When I am emperor, you will be made Precious Consort." Diaochan, who realized he was falling into the trap, feigned great pleasure and expressed profound gratitude.

Surrounded by his adherents, Dong Zhuo ascended his carriage and set out for Chang'-an. He had traveled less than thirty *li* when a wheel broke. Dong Zhuo switched to horseback. After another ten *li* the horse began snorting wildly and snapped its reins. Dong Zhuo said to Li Su, "First the wheel, now the horse—what do these signs mean?" "Simply," Li Su answered smoothly, "that the preceptor will be replacing the Han, discarding the old for the new, and should soon be riding in the imperial carriage with its jewels and golden gear!" Dong Zhuo found this answer delightful and convincing.

The next day the journey continued. A fierce storm sprang up, and a dark mist spread over the heavens. "What does *this* signify?" Dong Zhuo asked. "When you ascend the dragon throne," answered Li Su, "there will be red streaks of light through purple mists demonstrating the heavenly power of Your Majesty." Dong Zhuo's doubts were again satisfied by this interpretation.

Dong Zhuo's carriage reached the capital gate. The assembly of officials welcomed him. Only Li Ru had absented himself for reasons of health. Dong Zhuo entered his official residence, followed by Lü Bu, who extended his congratulations. "I shall be ascending the imperial throne," Dong Zhuo said, "and you will become the head of all military forces." Lü Bu thanked his patron and spent the night outside his sleeping quarters. That night a dozen boys were singing in the outskirts of the city, and the wind carried their melancholy voices into the bed chamber:

> A thousand *li* of green, green grass
> Beyond the tenth day, one can't last.

"What is the meaning of the rhyme?" asked Zhuo.[6] "It only means," Li Su replied, "that the house of Liu will fall, and the house of Dong will rise."

At dawn the following day Dong Zhuo arrayed his honor guard. As his sedan chair reached court, he was surprised to see a Taoist priest in a dark gown and white headdress, holding a long staff. Tied to the top was a strip of cloth about ten feet long with the word "mouth" written on either end.[7] "What is this priest trying to say?" asked Dong Zhuo. "He is deranged," Li Su replied and had him chased away.

Dong Zhuo went into the main court area. The assembled officials, splendid in their formal robes and caps, greeted him from the sides. Sword in hand, Li Su followed the carriage. They came to a side gate on the north. Only twenty of Dong Zhuo's charioteers were let through. Further ahead at the entrance to the main hall Dong Zhuo could see a group with drawn swords standing around Wang Yun. Perturbed, Dong Zhuo asked, "What is the meaning of these swords?" Li Su made no reply as he helped push the carriage straight on in.

"The traitor is here!" shouted Wang Yun. "Where are my men?" On either side a hundred weapons appeared. Halberd and lance were thrust against Dong Zhuo, but his armor prevented injury. Then, wounded in the arm, he fell from the carriage. "Where is my son?" he screamed. Lü Bu stepped out from behind the carriage. "Here is the edict to punish the traitor!" he cried and cut Dong Zhuo's throat with his halberd. Li Su severed the head and held it aloft.[8] Lü Bu produced the edict, shouting, "This is the Emperor's writ. Only the traitor Dong Zhuo is to answer for his crime."[9] Officers and men hailed the Emperor. Dong Zhuo's fate moved someone to write these lines:

> Success would have placed him on the throne itself;
> Failing that, he meant to have an easy life of wealth.
> What he forgot is that the gods ordain a path so strict:
> His palace newly done, his enterprise lay wrecked.

At once Lü Bu said, "Li Ru abetted Dong Zhuo in all his brutal crimes. Who will seize him?" Li Su volunteered to go. Suddenly there was a commotion at the gate. Li Ru's household servants had already tied him up and brought him in. Wang Yun ordered Li Ru executed in the marketplace. Dong Zhuo's corpse was displayed on the main thoroughfare. There was so much fat in his body that the guards lit a fire in his navel; as it burned, grease from the corpse ran over the ground. Passing commoners knocked Dong Zhuo's severed head with their fists and trampled his body. Wang Yun ordered Lü Bu, Huangfu Song, and Li Su to march fifty thousand men to the new palace complex at Mei and take custody of all property and residents.[10]

Meanwhile the four generals Dong Zhuo left in charge of Mei—Li Jue, Guo Si, Zhang Ji, and Fan Chou—hearing that their master was dead and that Lü Bu was on his way, led their Flying Bears west to Liangzhou by rapid night marches. At Mei, Lü Bu first took Diaochan into his charge, while Huangfu Song freed the sons and daughters of the good Chang'an families. All members of Dong Zhuo's family, including his aged mother,[11] were put to death. The heads of Dong Zhuo's brother Min and his nephew Huang were publicly displayed. The entire wealth of the new complex was confiscated: several hundred thousand taels of gold, millions of silver coins, fine sheer silks, pearls, precious implements, grain stores—a vast treasure.[12] When the results were reported back to Wang Yun, he feasted the troops and held a grand celebration at the Office of the Secretariat.

The festivities were interrupted by a report that someone had kneeled and wept beside Dong Zhuo's body. "Everyone cheered his execution. Who dares mourn?" Wang Yun said angrily and ordered the man arrested. Brought before the astonished officials was none other than Privy Counselor Cai Yong. Wang Yun denounced the offender: "For what reason do you, a subject of the Han, mourn a traitor whose death benefits the dynasty, instead of joining our celebration?" Cai Yong acknowledged his offense: "Despite my meagre abilities," he said, "I can tell right from wrong and would never honor Dong Zhuo instead of the Han. Yet I could not help shedding a tear out of gratitude for the favor he has shown me. I know I should not have done it. I only pray that if my face is branded and my feet cut off, I may nonetheless be permitted to continue my work on the history of the Han as a form of atonement. I seek no other mercy."[13]

The court officials, who esteemed Cai Yong's ability, pleaded for him strenuously. Imperial Guardian Ma Midi also urged Wang Yun privately, "It would be a boon to let so unique a talent complete the history. Moreover, his filial devotion is widely respected. If you condemn him without due consideration, we may forfeit people's confidence." "Centuries ago," responded Wang Yun, "Emperor Wu spared Sima Qian and let him write his history, with the result that we have a slanderous account whose ill effects are felt to this day. At a time when our destiny is uncertain and court administration faltering, how can we permit a toady like Cai Yong to wield the pen by the side of a junior emperor? He will defame us."[14] To these words the imperial guardian made no reply; but privately he told officials, "May Wang Yun leave no posterity. Able men of character are the mainstay of the ruling house, institutions its legal basis. Destroy the mainstay, discard the basis, and the Han cannot long endure." Wang Yun rejected Ma Midi's appeal and had Cai Yong taken to prison and strangled. The news moved many scholars to tears. Later, many held that Cai Yong was wrong to mourn Dong Zhuo but that Wang Yun went too far when he had him killed. A poet voiced these feelings:

> Power was Dong Zhuo's means to tyranny;
> And Cai Yong's death, his own ignominy.
> Kongming lay low in Longzhong and every hero weighed.[15]
> Would *he* waste his talents on a renegade?[16]

• • • •

The four generals Dong Zhuo left guarding Mei—Li Jue, Guo Si, Zhang Ji, and Fan Chou—had fled west to Shanxi; from there they sent to Chang'an a petition for clemency. "Those four abetted the tyranny of Dong Zhuo," Wang Yun said. "Our general amnesty will exclude them."[17] Learning of this decision, Li Jue said, "We are denied. Let each man fend for himself." But their adviser, Jia Xu, recommended a different course: "If you abandon your armies and go it alone, a single constable will be enough to arrest you. Shouldn't we recruit local people, march back into Chang'an, and avenge Dong Zhuo? If we prevail, we can set the realm to rights in the name of the court. If we fail, we'll have time enough to escape."

Li Jue approved this plan and spread rumors throughout Liangzhou to the effect that Wang Yun was plotting a massacre in this locality. When he had sufficiently terrified the population, he issued the call, "Why die for nothing? Follow me and rebel!" Many volunteered, and the four generals divided more than one hundred thousand men into four field armies and descended on the capital. On the way they met Dong Zhuo's son-in-law, Niu Fu, an Imperial Corps commander leading a force of five thousand. Niu Fu was thirsty for vengeance, and Li Jue put him in the vanguard. The four generals continued their advance.

Wang Yun learned of the new invasion by Liangzhou troops and conferred with Lü Bu. "Have no fear, Minister," Lü Bu assured him, "of that contemptible pack of scoundrels." Lü Bu sent Li Su to engage the invaders. Li Su and Niu Fu clashed, and a period of bloodshed ensued. Niu Fu fell back in defeat, then rallied and counterattacked that night at the second watch. He caught Li Su by surprise and sacked his camp. Li Su's army fled in all directions, sustaining major losses. The defeat so enraged Lü Bu that he shrieked at Li Su, "You have ruined our fighting spirit!" and had him executed. Li Su's head was impaled at the entrance to the camp.

The following day Lü Bu himself went forth to confront Niu Fu and overwhelmed him. That night the badly defeated Niu Fu said to his most trusted man, Hu Chi'er: "Lü

Bu is more than a match for us. We might as well run off with some treasure and quit, taking a few lackeys along without letting Li Jue and the others know." Hu Chi'er concurred. The conspirators scooped up the spoils and quit camp, accompanied by three or four men. As they were preparing to cross a river, Hu Chi'er turned on Niu Fu and killed him. He stashed away the stolen treasure and presented Niu Fu's head to Lü Bu. Lü Bu soon learned the truth from the accomplices, however, and executed Hu Chi'er.[18]

Lü Bu advanced and engaged Li Jue. Before Jue could organize his line, Lü Bu—spear couched, steed rearing—waved his soldiers on. From this frontal assault Li Jue fell back fifty *li* and camped by a hillside, where he conferred with his three partners. "Lü Bu is brave, to be sure," Li Jue said, "but not smart enough to pose any real problem. I will take a detachment to the mouth of the gorge and provoke him to fight. When he does, General Guo Si can harry his rear, using the reverse signaling tactics Peng Yue used to harass Chu,[19] advancing at the gong and retreating at the drum. At the same time I want you two, Zhang Ji and Fan Chou, to attack Chang'an directly with your two armies. A two-fronted assault like this will keep Lü Bu and Wang Yun from coming to each other's aid, and we can defeat them." All agreed with Li Jue's plan.

Lü Bu's army halted near the hillside camp. Li Jue emerged to draw him into combat. Lü Bu's temper took control and he charged headlong. Li Jue retreated up the hill, blocking pursuit with a shower of boulders and arrows. Suddenly Guo Si attacked Lü Bu from the rear, forcing him to turn around. Lü Bu attempted to come to grips with Guo Si's force, but Guo Si also retreated when the drum sounded. Lü Bu was preparing to draw back, when gongs rang out on the other end, and Li Jue resumed the offensive. As Lü Bu turned to meet this new threat, Guo Si struck again and withdrew immediately.

For several days the two generals worked Lü Bu's army back and forth until he was too exasperated to fight or rest. To add to Lü Bu's great vexation, word came that the other two enemy generals, Zhang Ji and Fan Chou, had advanced on the capital and that its fall was imminent. Frantically, Lü Bu wheeled his army round toward Chang'an as Li Jue and Guo Si together savaged his rear ranks. Rushing to the capital, Lü Bu abandoned the struggle; he had suffered heavy loses. At Chang'an he found a living sea of warriors surrounding the walls and moat. With defeat following defeat, many of his men, dreading his tyrannical temper, deserted. Lü Bu sank into despair.

Several days later two adherents of Dong Zhuo's who had remained in the capital, Li Meng and Wang Fang, stealthily opened the city gates to the invaders, who poured in from all directions. Lü Bu fought hard but could not hold them off. He led several hundred horsemen to the palace gate. "It's all over," he called to Wang Yun. "Ride with me. We'll find a better way out." But Wang Yun refused, saying, "If the spirits dwelling in the sacred shrines of Han favor me, I will restore peace for the ruling family. If I fail, I die. But I cannot steal away in the heat of the crisis. Give this message to the lords beyond the pass: 'Strive to keep the Han foremost in your thoughts.'" Lü Bu could not change Wang Yun's mind. The city gates were on fire. Leaving his own family behind, Lü Bu dashed away with one hundred horsemen to seek refuge with Yuan Shu.

Li Jue and Guo Si let their soldiers plunder Chang'an at will. Minister of Ritual Chong Fu, Court Steward Lu Kui, Minister of Protocol Zhou Huan, Commandant of the Capital Gates Cui Lie, and Commandant of the Exemplary Cavalry Wang Qi all perished in the fighting. The rebels drew a tight ring around the court, and the courtiers pleaded with the Emperor to appear above the Declaring Peace Gate and calm the tumult. The Emperor came forth. When Li Jue and the others saw the yellow canopy sheltering the imperial person, they instantly called on their armies to desist and cried out, "Long live the

Emperor!" Emperor Xian, speaking from the gate tower, demanded, "Why have you generals entered the capital without my permission?" Li Jue and Guo Si raised their faces toward their sovereign and appealed to him: "Imperial Preceptor Dong Zhuo, the guardian of your royal shrines, was wrongly slain by Wang Yun. We have come to avenge him and have no disloyal thoughts. We will withdraw once we have seen the murderer."

Wang Yun, standing beside the Emperor, heard the accusation. "I acted only for the sake of the royal shrines," he said to the Emperor. "Under present conditions Your Majesty must think only of the safety of the imperial house. Permit me to go down to see the two traitors." The Emperor hesitated, but Wang Yun leaped to the ground and shouted, "Here stands Wang Yun!" Li Jue and Guo Si drew their swords and denounced him: "For what crime did the imperial preceptor deserve to die?" "Dong Zhuo's unspeakable crimes," Wang Yun responded, "filled Heaven and earth. On the day of his execution all Chang'an rejoiced, though you may not know it." "Even so," replied the two generals, "what was our crime that you excluded us from the amnesty?" In response Wang Yun swore: "Hold your tongues, treasonous villains! Wang Yun has come to die and that is all." The two outlaws cut him down in front of the gate tower. A historian has left this remembrance:

> Wang Yun spun an artful scheme
> That ended Dong Zhuo's evil dream.
> His heart ached for the ruling line,
> His brow was knitted for its shrine.
> His noble spirit reached the skies,
> His heart has joined the guiding stars.
> Down below his souls remain
> And haunt the Phoenix Pavilion.

The rebels put Wang Yun's entire clan to the sword. The people of the city mourned. In fact, Li Jue and Guo Si had further ambitions. "Now that we are here, what better opportunity will we have to kill the Emperor and create a new dynasty?" they shouted. Swords bared, they charged into the palace. Indeed:

> The execution of Dong Zhuo had barely eased the crisis,
> When rebels running amok brought fresh woes.

The life of the Emperor was now at stake.

READ ON.

10

Ma Teng Takes Up Arms to Save the Throne;
Cao Cao Musters an Army to Avenge His Father

LI JUE AND GUO SI WOULD HAVE TAKEN the sovereign's life, but the other two generals, Zhang Ji and Fan Chou, demurred: "The people will never accept the authority of regicides. Rather, uphold the Emperor and lure the lords of the realm into the region Chang'an controls. That way we can pare down the Emperor's support and prepare to take over at the proper time." On this counsel Li Jue and Guo Si refrained from acting.

The Emperor, meanwhile, speaking from the palace tower, issued a statement to those below: "Wang Yun has been executed. On what grounds have you not withdrawn your forces?" Li Jue and Guo Si responded, "Our service to the royal house has not yet been requited by titles from Your Majesty. That is what we are waiting for." The Emperor said, "Which titles do you want?" Each of the four generals wrote on a piece of paper the offices and fiefs he required and submitted it to the Emperor; having no choice, he made the following awards:

> Li Jue, appointed general of Chariots and Cavalry and enfeoffed as lord of Chiyang; also named commandant of the Capital Districts and granted insignia and battle-axe confirming military authority
> Guo Si, appointed general of the Rear and lord of Meiyang and granted insignia and battle-axe; both generals to control court administration
> Fan Chou, appointed general of the Right and lord of Wannian
> Zhang Ji, appointed Flying Cavalry general and lord of Pingyan, with his garrison stationed at Hongnong
> Li Meng and Wang Fang (who had opened the city gates to the rebels) were assigned commands.

Generals Li Jue and Guo Si thanked the Emperor and led their armies out of the city. Then they ordered Dong Zhuo's corpse recovered. Since only bits of skin and bone could be found, they ordered a sculptor to make a statue of their fallen leader out of fragrant wood. When the work was done, they dressed the statue in royal robes and placed it in a royal coffin. They chose an auspicious day and led a funeral procession to Mei. At the burial, however, a tremendous cloudburst flooded the area, and the force of the thunder shook the coffin open, knocking the statue out. Li Jue waited for the skies to clear, but the storm raged on and interment had to be postponed again and again until the fragments of Dong Zhuo's corpse had been consumed by lightning. Great indeed was Heaven's wrath.

Now that they dominated the government, Li Jue and Guo Si terrorized the capital. Their henchmen infiltrated the palace staff and kept the Emperor under close watch, a virtual prisoner. Officials were promoted and demoted as the two villains saw fit. To restore some degree of public confidence, they made the gesture of appointing Zhu Jun to be court steward and invited him to participate in court affairs.[1]

One day it was reported that Ma Teng, governor of Xiliang, and Han Sui, imperial inspector of Bingzhou, were advancing on the capital with an army of one hundred thousand, proclaiming their intention to punish the rebels in the name of the Emperor. In preparation for this mission, Ma Teng and Han Sui had secured the collaboration of three important men inside Chang'an: Privy Counselor Ma Yu, Court Counselor Chong Shao, and Left Imperial Corps Commander Liu Fan. These three had secretly persuaded the Emperor to appoint Ma Teng and Han Sui to the rank of general—the former, Conqueror of the West, the latter, Queller of the West—and to authorize them to unite against the party of traitors.

In response to these developments Li Jue and the other three generals put their heads together to work out a plan of resistance. Their adviser, Jia Xu, said, "Ma Teng and Han Sui are coming a great distance. All we need do is to dig in and defend ourselves resolutely. Their food will be gone in a few months; they'll have to withdraw. Then we can pursue and capture them easily." The two commanders Li Meng and Wang Fang objected. "A poor idea!" they said. "Give us ten thousand men, and we will deliver the heads of Ma Teng and Han Sui in short order." "If you engage them now," Jia Xu warned, "you will lose." "If we fail, we will offer our own heads," Li Meng and Wang Fang said, "and if we succeed, we'll demand yours!" So Jia Xu made a suggestion to Li Jue and Guo Si: "Let generals Zhang Ji and Fan Chou guard the Zhouzhi Hills two hundred *li* west of Chang'an. The terrain there is quite difficult. Then Li Meng and Wang Fang may go forth." Li Jue and Guo Si followed his advice, placing fifteen thousand men under the two volunteers. They set out in high spirits and camped two hundred and eighty *li* west of the capital.

The two commanders confronted the loyalist troops from the west. Ma Teng and Han Sui rode out together in front of their lines and roadblocks. Pointing to Li Meng and Wang Fang, they cried, "There are the rebels. Who will seize them?" Before they had finished speaking, a young general was already in the field. His face was like flawless jade; his eyes gleamed like shooting stars. He had a powerful torso, brawny arms, a lusty stomach, and a supple waist. On a splendid charger he sped forward, gripping a long spear. It was Ma Chao (Mengqi), the seventeen-year-old son of Ma Teng, a lad of supreme courage.

Wang Fang scorned the youthful challenger and engaged him proudly. But Ma Chao slew Wang Fang handily and wheeled his horse about. Li Meng galloped after the victor. Ma Chao kept riding for his line seemingly unaware of the danger. Ma Teng shouted a warning, but his son already had Li Meng prisoner. Ma Chao had allowed Li Meng to pull close enough to attempt a thrust, and then artfully dodged so that Li Meng speared thin air as his horse carried him abreast of Ma Chao's. At that moment Ma Chao scooped Li Meng up with a supple sweep of his brawny arm. Now leaderless, the troops from the capital broke formation. Ma Teng and Han Sui pursued them hotly and turned their advantage into a great victory. The western army pitched camp at one of the passes outside the capital. Li Meng was beheaded and his severed head publicly displayed.

Li Jue and Guo Si had new respect for Jia Xu's foresight after hearing of the death of Li Meng and Wang Fang. They reverted to his original strategy, keeping the passes tightly guarded and refusing all challenges. As Jia Xu had predicted, within two months the western army had to retreat for lack of supplies. At the same time Ma Teng and Han Sui's three collaborators within Chang'an were betrayed by a household servant. Li Jue and Guo Si executed the three and set their heads on the front gate of the capital. Then they extinguished the plotters' entire clans, young and old, noble and commoner. With all hope gone of ousting the clique of four generals, the Xiliang force withdrew. Li Jue and Guo Si ordered Zhang Ji to pursue Ma Teng, and Fan Chou to pursue Han Sui. Though the western forces were in disarray, Ma Chao managed to drive off Zhang Ji. But near Chencang, Fan Chou caught up with Han Sui, who turned and faced his enemy. "You and I are townsmen," he cried. "How can you hunt me down like this?" "I act in the service of the Emperor," said Fan Chou. "I too fight for the ruling house," Sui protested, "why press me so hard?" Without another word, Fan Chou swung his horse round and led his men back to camp, allowing Han Sui to escape.

Fan Chou's act of mercy did not go unnoticed. A nephew of Li Jue's reported it to the general, who wanted to send out the army to punish Fan Chou. But Jia Xu restrained him: "When the people are so unsettled, there is nothing to be gained by constant resort to war. It would be much simpler to hold a celebration for the two generals, seize Fan Chou, and execute him then and there." This advice satisfied Li Jue. He invited the victorious generals to a banquet, and they attended with pleasure. Midway through the toasts Li Jue suddenly dropped his cordiality and demanded, "Why was Fan Chou plotting with Han Sui? Is he going to rebel?" Fan Chou panicked; before he could defend himself, swords and axes hemmed him in, and his head was quickly taken. Zhang Ji prostrated himself in terror. But Li Jue lifted him up, saying, "Fan Chou conspired against me—that is why I killed him. In you I have complete trust. Have no fear." Fan Chou's forces were then placed under Zhang Ji, who returned to his base in Hongnong.

. . . . .

After Li Jue and Guo Si had defeated the Xiliang army, no other leaders dared challenge them. At Jia Xu's insistence, they took measures to benefit the population and attract worthy and outstanding men. As a result, the court began to reassert its authority. Unexpectedly, the Yellow Scarves in Qingzhou staged another uprising.[2] Hundreds of thousands of rebels under numerous chieftains ravaged the region. The recently appointed court steward Zhu Jun recommended to Li Jue someone who he was sure could put down the Scarves. The man he named was Cao Cao. "Where is Mengde [Cao Cao] now?" asked Li Jue. "At present he is governor of Dongjun," replied Zhu Jun, "and he has a massive army. If we authorize him to act, the rebellion will be crushed swiftly." Li Jue accepted the suggestion and penned an edict authorizing Cao Cao to join forces with Bao Xin, lord of Jibei, for that purpose.

Cao Cao accepted the commission and joined forces with Bao Xin. They attacked the Yellow Scarves at Shouyang. Bao Xin forced his way into a strongpoint and was killed. Cao pursued the rebels to Jibei, where tens of thousands surrendered to him. Cao placed these former rebels in his vanguard. Wherever he went, the rebels transferred their allegiance to him. In one hundred days Cao Cao had induced the surrender of over three hundred thousand troops and one million noncombatants. He picked the finest of the Yellow Scarves troops and organized them into the Qingzhou army. The remainder he sent back to their farms. In consequence, Cao Cao's prestige rose steadily, and the court recognized his triumphs by naming him General Garrisoning the East.

Back in Yanzhou, Cao Cao summoned worthy and capable men to build his administration. First came the Xun family of Yingyin in Yingchuan, uncle and nephew. Xun Yu (Wenruo), the son of Xun Gun, had once served Yuan Shao but had shifted his allegiance to Cao Cao. Cao took great delight in Xun Wenruo's opinions and referred to him as "my Zifang."[3] He was appointed military counselor. Wenruo's nephew, Xun You (Gongda), a renowned scholar and an attendant in the Inner Bureau when the court was still in Luo-yang, had left his office and retired to his village. Cao made him a military instructional superviser. Xun Wenruo recommended to Cao Cao the scholar Cheng Yu (Zhongde), who came from Dong'e in Dongjun. "A name long known to me," Cao commented and sent an emissary, who found Cheng Yu studying in a mountain retreat and persuaded him to enter Cao's service. Cheng Yu said to his patron Xun Wenruo, "I am a foolish, poorly informed man, of little note, undeserving of the honor of your recommendation. But your fellow townsman, Guo Jia (Fengxiao), is a true and worthy scholar of our day. Why not recruit him?" "He nearly escaped my mind!" exclaimed Xun Wenruo, and he urged Cao to invite Guo Jia to Yanzhou to consult with him on the state of the realm. Guo Jia arrived and in turn recommended Liu Ye (Ziyang) from Chengde in Huainan, a descendant of the principal branch of the first imperial family of the Eastern Han. Liu Ye recommended two more notables: Man Chong (Boning) of Changyi in Shanyang, and Lü Qian (Zike) of Wucheng. These two men were also known to Cao Cao, and he gave them positions as military aides. Man Chong and Lü Qian recommended Mao Jie (Xiaoxian) of Pingqiu in Chenliu, and Cao also appointed him military aide.

Cao Cao made further additions to his newly formed staff: Yu Jin (Wenze) from Ju-ping in Taishan arrived with several hundred troops and was accepted. Cao Cao saw that Yu Jin was a seasoned mounted archer and outstanding in the martial arts. He appointed him captain of the roll. One day Xiahou Dun brought in Dian Wei of Chenliu, a big fellow of almost supernatural strength. Dun introduced him to Cao Cao: "Dian Wei previously served with Zhang Miao. During a quarrel with Zhang Miao's other followers, Dian Wei killed several dozen men with his own hands and then fled into the hills. Some time later while hunting, I spotted Dian Wei chasing a tiger across a stream. It was then that I recruited him, and now I present him to you." "The man is a colossus," said Cao Cao. "He must be extremely powerful." "Once he killed a man to avenge a friend," said Xiahou Dun, "then he marched off with the victim's head. Out of a crowd of hundreds of witnesses, not one dared approach him. He has two steel spears, each weighing eighty catties, and on horseback he wields them like the wind." Cao Cao ordered Dian Wei to demonstrate his skill. Dian Wei grasped his weapons and was dashing back and forth when he noticed that the main pennant above Cao Cao's headquarters was about to blow over despite the attempt of many soldiers to steady it. Dian Wei shouted the soldiers out of his way and held the pole with one hand, immobile against the wind, a tower of strength. Cao Cao exclaimed: "He's certainly another Elai!" and assigned him to guard his headquarters.[4] He also presented him with the brocade shortcoat he was wearing, as well as a fine horse and a tooled saddle.

Thus Cao Cao, aided by wise counselors and fierce fighters, made his prestige felt east of the pass. He now wanted to be reunited with his father, Cao Song, and so sent Ying Shao, governor of Taishan, to Langye to fetch him.[5] Song had been living there quietly since leaving Chenliu, the Cao clan's home area, when Cao Cao became a fugitive.[6] As soon as Cao Song received his son's message, he and his younger brother Cao De loaded the entire clan—more than forty relatives and one hundred attendants—onto one hundred carts and headed for Yanzhou.

En route the Cao clan passed through Xuzhou, whose imperial inspector was Tao Qian (Gongzu), a warm and sincere man who had always wanted to be associated with Cao Cao. Now, learning that Cao Cao's father was passing through his province, Tao Qian meant to treat him royally. He received the procession at the border, paid his highest respects, and led it to the capital where he spread forth a splendid banquet that lasted two days. When Cao Song insisted on resuming the journey, Tao Qian personally escorted him out of the city. He then assigned Commander Zhang Kai and five hundred men to escort the family.

The procession reached the area around Hua and Fei counties. It was late summer, and a sudden storm blew up. The travelers sought shelter in an ancient temple, where the resident monk received them. Cao Song settled the family in and told Zhang Kai to quarter his men in the corridors. The soldiers, drenched from the storm, began grumbling. Zhang Kai called some of his lieutenants to a private conference at which he said, "We were once Yellow Scarves and surrendered to Tao Qian out of compulsion. What good has it done us? The Caos' freight and wagons are enough to make us all rich. We strike at the third watch, kill the whole family, and go into hiding with the goods. What do you say?" The lieutenants agreed.

That night as the storm raged, Cao Song heard the clamor of voices; his brother, Cao De, took his sword and went out to find the cause. He was cut down immediately. Cao Song tried to help one of his concubines over the wall behind the abbot's quarters, but she was too heavy to climb it. Cao Song hid with her in a toilet, where the guards found them and slew them. Ying Shao, the man Cao Cao had originally sent to fetch his father, escaped and fled to the camp of Yuan Shao. His bloody work completed, Zhang Kai burned down the temple and fled south to Huainan with his five hundred followers. A poet of later times wrote:

> Cao Cao in all his vaunted cunning,
> Slew his hosts and kept on running.
> Now that *his* whole clan's been slain,
> The scales of Heaven are level again.

One of Ying Shao's soldiers got away and reported the massacre to Cao Cao, who fell to the ground weeping. As his attendants helped him up, Cao Cao gnashed his teeth and swore: "Tao Qian allowed his men to kill my father! The two of us cannot share the same sky. First I will put his city[7] to the sword to quench my wrath." Cao ordered a full-scale invasion of Xuzhou, leaving only Xun Wenruo and Cheng Yu with thirty thousand men to guard the three counties of Juancheng, Fanxian, and Dong'e. Xiahou Dun, Yu Jin, and Dian Wei led the invasion—under orders to slaughter the inhabitants as soon as the capital was taken—to avenge Cao Cao's father.

Governor of Jiujiang Bian Rang, a close friend of Tao Qian's, learned of the trouble and brought five thousand troops to aid Xuzhou. Angered by this move, Cao sent Xiahou Dun to intercept Bian Rang and kill him. Another friend of Tao Qian's was Chen Gong,[8] who held a position in Cao's district, Dongjun. When Chen Gong learned that Cao Cao intended to exterminate the populace of Xuzhou in his thirst for vengeance, he sought an audience. At first Cao Cao refused to see any man coming to plead for Tao Qian, but sentiment prompted him to hear out his former benefactor. Chen Gong appealed to Cao Cao: "They are saying that you are about to invade Xuzhou and avenge your father's murder by wholesale bloodshed. Let me attempt to dissuade you. Tao Qian is a humane and honorable gentleman and would never seek improper gain. Your father's death was Zhang Kai's crime, not Tao Qian's. Moreover, what enmity is there between the people of Xuzhou and yourself? Taking their lives would augur ill for your larger ambitions. I pray you, reflect on this." "Didn't you once abandon me?" Cao asked angrily. "How can you face me again? Tao Qian slew my whole family, and I mean to pluck out his entrails to satisfy my hatred. What you say in his behalf will not sway me." Taking his leave, Chen Gong thought sadly, "Then I cannot face Tao Qian again myself," and he went to Chenliu to serve Governor Zhang Miao.[9]

Cao's army invaded Xuzhou. Wherever it struck, multitudes were slaughtered and graves were despoiled. When Tao Qian learned of the toll taken by Cao's army of vengeance, he lifted his eyes and cried bitterly, "I have offended Heaven and brought this on my people." He called his advisers to counsel. One of them, Cao Bao, said, "Let us not meekly turn ourselves over to them. I would like to help you defeat them, my lord." Reluctantly, Tao Qian led his army forth to battle. In the distance he could see Cao Cao's forces spread out over the earth like a vast blanket of snow. Above the central force two huge white banners read "Vengeance and Satisfaction."

The invaders began assuming battle formations as Cao Cao himself—dressed in mourning white—rode out from the lines, cursing at the enemy as he gestured with his whip. Tao Qian rode forward, bowed low, and tendered his respects. "At first, my lord, I sought your friendship," he said, "and that is why I sent Zhang Kai to guarantee your father's safety. Little did I realize the rebel's criminal nature had never changed. That is the cause of this misfortune. I had nothing to do with it. I pray you, examine the facts." "Despised wretch," Cao swore. "You slew my father and dare to lie about it! Who will take this old scoundrel for me?" Xiahou Dun answered the call. Tao Qian fled back to his lines, and his commander, Cao Bao, came out. The two warriors grappled with one another. Suddenly a violent storm blew up and sent sand and stones flying about, throwing both armies into disorderly retreat.

Tao Qian reentered his city and addressed his followers: "Considering the size of Cao Cao's army, I have decided to put myself at his mercy and spare the population further suffering." But someone made a countersuggestion: "Xuzhou has long benefited from your protection. The enemy may be numerous, but they cannot take this city quite so easily. Let us dig in and defend it. Though I possess little talent, I beg to try something that should cause Cao Cao to die without hope of decent burial." This boast astonished one and all. What was his plan? Indeed:

> In Cao Cao, Tao Qian sought a friend and found a foe;
> Now in his extremity, would destiny surprise him again?

Who had spoken up?

READ ON.

11

Liu Xuande Rescues Kong Rong at Beihai;
Lü Bu Defeats Cao Cao near Puyang

THE MAN WHO PROPOSED TO RESIST Cao Cao's siege was Mi Zhu (Zizhong), from an old and wealthy family in the county of Qu in the district of Donghai. Mi Zhu had once had an extraordinary experience. On the way home after doing business in Luoyang, he met a beautiful woman who requested a ride. Mi Zhu offered the woman his seat and proceeded on foot, but the woman insisted that they share the carriage. So Zhu climbed back up, but he sat stiffly, holding his gaze away from the passenger. Several *li* farther on the woman said good-bye, adding, "I am the deity of solar fire, sent by the Supreme God to destroy your household. Your commendable gentility has moved me to give you this warning: rush home and remove your valuables. I am due tonight." With that she disappeared. Mi Zhu raced home in shock and cleared out his goods. True to the prediction, a fire broke out in the kitchen that night and burned down his house. Thereafter Mi Zhu became known for showing generosity and concern to those in need. Thus, Tao Qian, imperial inspector of Xuzhou, invited him to serve as an aide to the inspector's lieutenant.

Mi Zhu now submitted a plan to hold off Cao Cao: "I will go to Beihai and apply to Governor Kong Rong for help. Someone else should make a similar appeal to Tian Kai in Qingzhou. If both send troops, we can drive Cao Cao away." Tao Qian approved and prepared two letters. Chen Deng (Yuanlong) of Guangling volunteered to carry the second to Qingzhou. After Mi Zhu and Chen Deng had left, Tao Qian organized the city's defenses.

Kong Rong (Wenju), governor of Beihai, was originally from Qufu in the fief of Lu, Confucius' native place,[1] and was a descendant twenty generations removed from the great master. Kong Rong was the son of the military commander of Taishan and had been a precocious child. At age ten he presented himself at the gate of Li Ying, governor of Henan. Challenged by the guard, he asserted that he was a family friend of the governor's. The guard allowed him to see the governor, who asked, "What relationship do your ancestors have with mine?" "In ancient times," the boy replied, "Confucius is said to have questioned the Taoist sage Laozi[2] about the rites. How could our two lineages not be connected?" Li Ying was impressed by this unexpected response. Presently one of the governor's advisers, Chen Wei, came into the room. The governor, pointing to Kong Rong, said, "This is an extraordinary lad." "Not all clever youths," Chen Wei responded, "stay clever when they are grown." "I take it," Kong Rong quipped promptly,

83

"you were quite brilliant as a child." Chen Wei and the governor laughed. "When this child grows up," they agreed, "he will do great things." Kong Rong's rise to fame began at that time. Later named an Imperial Corps commander, he rose to be governor of Beihai. Kong Rong loved to receive guests and often said, "How I like to see my house full of friends and the cups full of wine!" During his six-year tenure as governor he had enjoyed the people's love and respect.

Governor Kong Rong was in the company of some guests the day Mi Zhu arrived. He asked him in to find out the purpose of his visit. Mi Zhu produced Tao Qian's letter and said, "Cao Cao is laying siege to Xuzhou. We need your help." "I have long been a friend of Imperial Inspector Tao," Kong Rong said. "And with your personal endorsement of his request, how could I refuse? The problem is, I bear Cao Cao no grudge, so I would rather try first to mediate an end to the quarrel. If that fails, I will levy troops." Mi Zhu replied, "Cao Cao is too confident of his power to agree to a settlement." Kong Rong began military preparations and sent out his letter.

Kong Rong was still deliberating the matter when he received an emergency report that tens of thousands of Yellow Scarves, led by Guan Hai, were rapidly approaching, killing everyone in their path. Kong Rong mobilized his forces at once and met the rebels outside of his city. Guan Hai rode forth and shouted, "We know how much grain you have in there. Give us ten thousand piculs, or we'll sack the city and kill you all, young and old alike." "I am a servant of the Han!" Kong Rong answered defiantly, "and I govern this territory for the Han. We give no grain to outlaws." Stung to fury, Guan Hai slapped his horse and, carving the air with his sword, lunged for Kong Rong. General Zong Bao, his spear leveled, rushed to intervene but was struck down swiftly. Kong Rong's troops panicked and stampeded back inside the gates. Guan Hai sealed all four sides of the city. Kong Rong expected the worst, and Mi Zhu despaired of securing aid for Tao Qian.

From the city wall the next day Kong Rong surveyed the Scarves' overwhelming advantage with a growing sense of futility. Suddenly, an armed rider plunged through the enemy ranks, striking left and thrusting right—as if unopposed—until he reached the base of the wall. "Open up," he shouted. Not recognizing the man, Kong Rong hesitated. Throngs of rebels overtook the rider at the moat. He turned and dispatched a dozen with his spear. The rebels pulled back. At last Kong Rong ordered the gate opened. The stranger entered, dismounted, and set aside his weapon. Then he climbed the wall to pay his respects to Kong Rong. "I have the double surname Taishi," he said. "My given name is Ci, my style Ziyi. I come from Huang county in Donglai. My mother has often benefited from your generosity. When I came home yesterday from Liaodong to see her, I heard the city was besieged. She told me to offer my assistance to show our gratitude to you. That's why I've come."[3]

Kong Rong had never met Taishi Ci, but he knew his reputation as a warrior. The governor, while Taishi Ci was away, had often sent grain and cloth to his mother, who lived a mere twenty li from the city. To show her gratitude she now sent her son to him. Kong Rong received the young warrior handsomely and presented him with armor, horse, and saddle. "I need one thousand picked men," Taishi Ci said, "to tackle the rebels." "Brave as you are," responded Kong Rong, "I would caution against it in view of their numbers." "My mother is indebted to you," Taishi Ci insisted. "She sent me here, and I will have failed her if I cannot break the siege. I would rather fight to the death here." "People tell me Liu Xuande is one of the heroes of our time," said Kong Rong. "If we could get his help, the siege could be lifted. But I have no one to send." "Compose the letter, Your Honor," said Taishi Ci, "and I will deliver it posthaste."[4]

Kong Rong wrote to Liu Xuande and entrusted the letter to Taishi Ci, who strapped on his armor and mounted his horse, bow and arrow at his waist, iron spear in hand. Having eaten heartily and armed himself to the hilt, he burst out of the city gate. A rebel captain spotted him by the moat and led his forces toward him, but Taishi Ci speared several of the captain's squad and broke through. Guan Hai realized Taishi Ci was going for help and pursued him with a few hundred men. Guan Hai tried to hedge Taishi Ci in, but putting by his spear, Taishi Ci felled pursuers on all sides with arrows shot in quick succession. The rebels gave up the chase.

Taishi Ci rode on to Pingyuan, where he extended his formal respects to Liu Xuande. He then explained Kong Rong's plight and presented the governor's appeal. Liu Xuande read it through and asked, "And who are you, sir?" "Taishi Ci," replied the envoy, "from an out-of-the-way place in Donghai. Though Kong Rong and I have no common ties of blood or birth, our thoughts are congenial, and I feel obliged to share his burden out of personal loyalty.[5] Just now, Guan Hai has Beihai surrounded, and his rebellion is roiling the region. Tao Qian has no one to turn to and may succumb at any moment. He knows of your reputation for humanity and honor, and of your willingness to aid people in distress. He has therefore sent me to brave the rebels' spears in hopes of gaining your help." Looking serious but apparently pleased, Xuande replied, "So the governor of Beihai knows there's a Liu Bei in this world?" and set out for Beihai with Lord Guan, Zhang Fei, and three thousand select fighters.

Guan Hai chose to deal with Xuande's relief force himself, hardly concerned by the little army. The three brothers and Taishi Ci halted in front of their line as a snarling Guan Hai came straight for them. Taishi Ci was riding out to engage him, but Lord Guan was already in the field, tangling with him as the troops clamored. Guan Hai was no match for Lord Guan.[6] After a few dozen clashes the dragon blade found its mark. Then Taishi Ci and Zhang Fei came out together and, working their spears in coordination, tore into the enemy line. At this point Xuande sent his soldiers in for the kill. Atop the wall Kong Rong watched the rebels run like sheep before tigers. The brothers overbore all opposition. The governor now fielded his own troops, and the rebels, hit from all sides, broke. Many surrendered and the horde was scattered.

Kong Rong welcomed Xuande into the city. After the formalities, the governor spread a banquet to celebrate the victory. He also introduced Mi Zhu to Liu Xuande. Zhu told him how Cao Cao's father had died at the hands of Zhang Kai. "Cao Cao," said Mi Zhu, "has let his armies run wild in the province, and the city is under siege. I am here in Beihai to seek aid for Imperial Inspector Tao Qian." "Tao Qian," replied Xuande, "is a kind and honorable man. It's hard to believe an innocent man is being wronged in this way." "Xuande," said Kong Rong, "you are connected to the royal house. Cao Cao's bullying is causing the people terrible suffering. Why don't we both go to Tao Qian's aid?" "I would not shirk the task," answered Xuande, "but my forces are small and my commanders few. I don't think I am ready for such an action."[7] "My desire to save Tao Qian," replied Kong Rong, "is based on justice as well as friendship. I doubt that you, of all people, could be indifferent to such a cause." "In that case," Xuande responded, "you set out first while I approach my patron Gongsun Zan for another three or five thousand men. I'll follow you directly to Xuzhou." "Whatever you do, do not fail us!" Kong Rong said. "What kind of a man do you take me for?" Xuande asked. "As the sage has said,

'Death comes to all men; but one who does not keep his word will fall.' Whether or not I succeed in borrowing troops, I will come myself.''[8]

Kong Rong, persuaded, sent Mi Zhu back to Tao Qian with the news; then Kong Rong made his own preparations and marched south. At this point Taishi Ci took his leave, saying, "I came to your assistance at my mother's behest. Now, fortunately, the danger has passed. Imperial Inspector Liu Yao of Yangzhou, originally from my district, has called for me. I feel I must go, but hope that we may meet again." The governor offered Taishi Ci generous gifts of gold and silk, but Ci declined them and went home. His mother was delighted to see him back and said, "I'm glad you have done something to repay the governor of Beihai's kindness," and sent him off to Yangzhou.

•   •   •   •

Liu Xuande put before Gongsun Zan his proposal for rescuing Tao Qian. "There is no hatred between you and Cao Cao," said Gongsun Zan. "Why trouble yourself for another man's cause?" "I have given my word," Xuande replied. "How can I go back on it?" "I can let you have two thousand foot and horse," Gongsun Zan said. "One other thing," Xuande continued. "I would like to have Zhao Zilong with me." Gongsun Zan granted this request. So Xuande, with his brothers and his own three thousand men, left for Xuzhou as the advance party, backed by Zhao Zilong and two thousand more.

Meanwhile, Mi Zhu reported to Tao Qian that Kong Rong had asked Liu Xuande to reinforce him. And Chen Deng returned from Qingzhou with news that Tian Kai too was coming to the defense of Xuzhou, so the hopes of the imperial inspector were raised. Both Kong Rong and Tian Kai, however, wary of the power and ferocity of Cao Cao's army, camped in the shelter of hills a comfortable distance from the city. Cao Cao divided his forces to meet the two relief armies and refrained from attacking the city.

Liu Xuande arrived soon after and went directly to Kong Rong. "Cao Cao's army is immense," said Kong Rong, "and he is an expert strategist. We must consider carefully before giving battle. Let us see how things develop before we advance." "What worries me," Xuande said, "is the food situation. The city may not be able to hold out. I am going to place Lord Guan and Zhao Zilong, with four thousand men, under your command while Zhang Fei and I attack Cao Cao's base camp. Then I will cut over to Xuzhou to consult with Tao Qian." Kong Rong happily agreed and worked out a strategy with Tian Kai for a two-pronged attack, which Lord Guan and Zhao Zilong stood ready to support.

Xuande and Zhang Fei were leading one thousand warriors to break through Cao Cao's perimeter, when drums rolled within and soldiers and horsemen, led by General Yu Jin, poured out. Jin reined in his horse and shouted, "Fools! Where do you think you're going?" Zhang Fei wasted no words but took on Yu Jin headlong. The two riders came to grips and fought several bouts. Then Xuande, wielding his twin swords, signaled for a general advance. Yu Jin broke off and ran. Zhang Fei, in the lead, pursued Yu Jin's men to the wall of Xuzhou city. The fighting was heavy. Tao Qian, seeing a red banner inscribed "Liu Xuande of Pingyuan" in white, ordered the gates opened and received Xuande in his headquarters.

After the formalities the host feasted Xuande and his men. Tao Qian secretly rejoiced at finding in Liu Xuande a man of dignified bearing and high-minded speech, and instructed Mi Zhu to hand him the provincial seal and other tokens of authority. "What is the meaning of this?" Xuande exclaimed. "With the world in turmoil," replied the inspector, "the mainstays of kingly rule have weakened. But as a kinsman of the royal house of Han, you will serve its shrines devotedly. This worthless old man would prefer to entrust the province to your governance. Please do not refuse me. I will personally petition for the throne's approval."

Xuande rose from his seat, making the ritual gesture of respect and gratitude. "It is true," he said, "that I am descended from the royal house. But my merit has little weight, my virtue little substance. I fear myself unworthy even of the fief of Pingyuan that I now hold. I am here today only for the sake of a principle. Your proposal suggests suspicion of my motives. If I have any designs on your province, may Heaven disown me forever." "I have spoken my sincere and heartfelt wish," responded Tao Qian. But Liu Xuande was steadfast in his refusal.[9] At this point Mi Zhu offered a suggestion: "The enemy is virtually upon us. Let's concentrate on driving them back before we consider this other matter." "I am going to write to Cao Cao," said Xuande, "to urge him to settle this peacefully. If he says no, there'll be time enough for battle." Xuande confined all units to their camps while his messenger went to Cao Cao.

Cao Cao was conferring with his generals when the letter from Xuzhou arrived. He opened it and saw that it was from Xuande. The text read in part:

> Since I came to know you in our campaign outside the pass, destiny has carried us to different corners of the realm, and I have had no opportunity to pay my respects. Recently your esteemed father met his death at the ruthless hands of Zhang Kai. Tao Qian had nothing to do with this crime. At present subversive remnants of the Scarves are disturbing the realm, while Dong Zhuo's adherents hold the court at their mercy. I would urge, my lord, that you place the exigencies of the dynasty before your private feud and withdraw from Xuzhou in order to address the emergency in the empire. This would be a great blessing for the realm as well as for this province.

On reading the letter, Cao exploded in rage. "Who is Liu Bei to teach me lessons?" he roared. "And with such sarcasm in the lines!" He ordered the messenger executed and the city attacked with full force. But Guo Jia remonstrated with him: "Liu Bei has come from afar to rescue Tao Qian. He has tried peaceful means before resorting to force. A civil answer, my lord, will allay his suspicions; then we may advance and take the city." Cao Cao accepted Guo Jia's advice and treated the messenger handsomely. But even as they were formulating the reply, a fast courier brought word that Lü Bu had taken Yanzhou and was holding Puyang. Cao Cao's own province was about to fall.

•   •   •   •   •

After fleeing Chang'an during the invasion of Dong Zhuo's two generals, Li Jue and Guo Si, Lü Bu had turned to Yuan Shu. But Yuan Shu mistrusted the turncoat warrior and refused his service; however, Yuan Shu's brother Shao welcomed Lü Bu, and together they defeated Zhang Yan in Changshan. Impressed with his own success, Lü Bu snubbed Yuan Shao's officers and men, and Yuan Shao tried to kill him. Thereupon, Lü Bu took refuge with Zhang Yang. At that time one Pang Shu, who had been hiding Lü Bu's family in Chang'an, sent the members on to rejoin him. In Chang'an Li Jue and Guo Si learned of this and put Pang Shu to death. They also asked Zhang Yang to kill Lü Bu. Lü Bu had to move on; he left Zhang Yang and found another protector in Zhang Miao.

By coincidence Chen Gong had already been introduced to Zhang Miao by his brother Zhang Chao. Having failed to talk Cao Cao out of invading Xuzhou, Chen Gong urged Zhang Miao to invade Cao Cao's territory. "The empire is breaking apart," he said, "and heroes are rising all over. It is demeaning for someone with the territory and population you have here to be subject to another's control. Cao Cao's province of Yanzhou is vulnerable while he is occupied with his eastern campaign against Tao Qian. Lü Bu, who has just applied for your protection, is a renowned warrior. If you and he could conquer Yanzhou, you would be in a position to establish independent rule."

Chen Gong's proposal excited Zhang Miao. He ordered Lü Bu to attack Yanzhou and to occupy Puyang. As a result, all of Cao Cao's territory was seized, except the three counties of Juancheng, Dong'e, and Fanxian—saved by the concerted and spirited defense put up by Xun Wenruo and Cheng Yu. Cao Cao's cousin, Cao Ren, shaken by these repeated defeats, now reported the emergency.

●   ●   ●   ●

"If I lose Yanzhou," said Cao Cao, "I lose my home. We must act." "This," suggested Guo Jia, "is the perfect time for a friendly turn. Accept Xuande's offer of peace so we can recover Yanzhou." Cao Cao wrote Xuande at once, agreeing to lift the siege, then he left the field.[10] Tao Qian rejoiced at Cao Cao's concession. He invited Kong Rong, Tian Kai, Lord Guan, and Zhao Zilong to a grand assembly in the city.

After banqueting, Tao Qian led Liu Xuande to the seat of honor and, saluting the audience with clasped hands, said, "I am advanced in years now, and my two sons are unfit for the heavy responsibility of governing Xuzhou for the dynasty. Lord Liu, a scion of the royal house, a man of broad virtue and high ability, is fit to govern. It is therefore my wish to retire as imperial inspector and to care for my declining health." "Governor Kong Rong brought me here," responded Xuande, "to relieve Xuzhou as a matter of honor. There can be no justification for my taking possession of this land, and the world will call me dishonorable if I do so."

Mi Zhu pressed the issue. "The house of Han is faltering," he said. "The world we know is turning upside down. It is a time to stake one's claim to fame and fortune. Xuzhou is a prosperous province of one million souls. You must not refuse the rule of such a place." "I cannot give you an affirmative reply," Xuande insisted. "Inspector Tao," Chen Deng added, "is in poor health and cannot attend to official business. Please do not decline, my lord." "Yuan Shu," Xuande suggested, "comes from a family that has held the highest office for the last four generations. The world esteems him. He is nearby in Shouchun. Why not offer the province to him?" "Yuan Shu is like a buried skeleton," burst out Kong Rong, "not worth a second thought. You will regret declining this Heaven-sent opportunity when it's too late." None of these arguments and appeals changed Xuande's mind.

"If you abandon me like this," Tao Qian pleaded in tears, "I will lie unquiet in my grave with eyes unclosed." "Why not accept the inspector's offer on a trial basis, brother?" Lord Guan suggested. And Zhang Fei added, "It's not as if we were demanding his territory. He makes the offer of his own free will. What's the point of this stubborn refusal?" "Shall I dishonor myself for you?" Xuande asked adamantly.[11] Tao Qian, seeing that no amount of persuasion would soften Xuande's determination, said, "Since you are set against my proposal, would you consider stationing your army nearby in Xiaopei? The place should suffice for your army's needs, and you can protect the province from there."[12] Urged by the whole assembly, Xuande consented.

The feasting ended. Zhao Zilong took his leave, and Xuande held the warrior's hands as he tearfully said good-bye. Governor Kong Rong and Tian Kai also left. Xuande and his brothers went to Xiaopei, where they repaired the fortifications and reassured the inhabitants.

•　　•　　•　　•

Returning from the siege of Xuzhou, Cao Cao was welcomed by Cao Ren, who told him that Lü Bu had grown powerful; that, assisted by Chen Gong, he had seized every strongpoint; that Juanzhou and Puyang were both lost; and that only Xun Wenruo and Cheng Yu's fierce and concerted resistance had saved the three counties, Juancheng, Dong'e, and Fanxian. "Lü Bu is all valor and no brain," remarked Cao. "I fear him not." He pitched camp and planned his counterattack.

Lü Bu learned that Cao Cao and his troops had passed Tengxian on their way back; he discussed tactics with his two captains, Xue Lan and Li Feng. "I have been hoping to put your talents to use," said Lü Bu. "Now I want you to stay and defend Yanzhou with ten thousand men. I will go ahead and destroy Cao Cao myself." The two captains accepted the assignment, but Chen Gong tried to dissuade Lü Bu: "General, if you leave Yanzhou, where will you go?" "I will place my army at Puyang," replied Lü Bu, "to give us control of two legs of the tripod." "A serious error," Chen Gong argued. "Xue Lan will never hold Yanzhou. One hundred eighty *li* due south, in the treacherous roads of the Taishan district, we can set an ambush with as many as ten thousand troops. Now, Cao Cao knows Yanzhou is lost and will redouble his efforts to get here. If we wait until half his troops have passed, we can spring the ambush and capture him in one strike." But Lü Bu ignored Chen Gong's advice, saying, "I have a better plan for moving the army to Puyang. What do you know about it?" And he set out, leaving Xue Lan in charge of Yanzhou.

When Cao Cao came to the Taishan district, Guo Jia warned him not to advance in case of ambush. Cao Cao smiled. "Lü Bu hasn't a plan in his head. Didn't he leave Xue Lan in Yanzhou and head for Puyang? He wouldn't think of setting an ambush," he said and sent Cao Ren ahead to surround Yanzhou city while he himself marched to Puyang to attack Lü Bu. In Puyang, Chen Gong, hearing of the approach of Cao Cao's troops, advised Lü Bu: "Cao Cao has come a long way; his men must be exhausted. Attack at once, before they regain their strength." "On this horse," retorted Lü Bu, "I have covered the length and breadth of the land. I'm not about to start worrying about Cao Cao! Let them pitch their camp—then I'll take care of him myself."

Cao Cao camped near Puyang. The following day he arrayed his forces in the open field and surveyed those of Lü Bu. As the opposing lines filled out their positions, Lü Bu emerged, flanked by eight of his ablest generals: Zhang Liao (Wenyuan), a native of Mayi in Yanmen, backed by Hao Meng, Cao Xing, and Cheng Lian; and Zang Ba (Xuangao), a native of Huayin in the district of Taishan, backed by Wei Xu, Song Xian, and Hou Cheng. Above the troops, fifty thousand strong, drumbeats charged the air. Cao Cao shouted across to Lü Bu, "We have never been enemies. Why have you taken my land?" "The walled towns of Han," Lü Bu replied, "belong to all. Why to you alone?"[13] Then he sent Zang Ba to give battle.

From Cao Cao's side Yue Jin came forth. The riders tangled; their spears rose and locked. The warriors had reached the thirtieth bout when Xiahou Dun sped out to assist Yue Jin. Zhang Liao, eager for the kill, intercepted Dun. Lü Bu himself, in the heat of anger, galloped into the fray, his halberd poised. Cao Cao's generals, Xiahou Dun and Yue Jin, fled. Lü Bu pressed the slaughter, forcing Cao Cao's army to retreat some thirty to forty *li*. Lü Bu regathered his men, and Cao Cao returned to his camp to confer with his generals. "Today," said Yu Jin, "I noticed while surveying from a hilltop that their position west of Puyang is lightly guarded. Their leaders should be unprepared tonight after our defeat. If we can take that camp, Lü Bu's army will lose courage. This is our best chance." Cao Cao approved and led six generals—Cao Hong, Li Dian, Mao Jie, Lü Qian, Yu Jin, and Dian Wei—with twenty thousand picked cavalry and foot soldiers toward Lü Bu's camp.

Under cover of night Cao Cao approached by side roads. Lü Bu was feasting his troops when Chen Gong said to him, "The west camp is a key position; what if Cao Cao attacks there?" "We taught him a lesson today," Lü Bu replied. "He won't be back that soon." "Cao Cao knows something of the art of war," Chen Gong answered. "We must guard against surprises." Convinced by Chen Gong's argument, Lü Bu selected Gao Shun, Wei Xu, and Hou Cheng to defend the western camp.

At dusk, before the reinforcements from Lü Bu arrived, Cao Cao hit the camp from all sides and overran it. The defenders fled and Cao Cao occupied it. Toward the fourth watch Gao Shun's relief force fought its way in, and the two armies fell upon one another in a melee. Toward dawn drums rolled in the west as Lü Bu joined the fight, forcing Cao Cao to flee the camp. Gao Shun, Wei Xu, and Hou Cheng pursued him. From the front Lü Bu was closing in; Yu Jin and Yue Jin could not stop him. Cao Cao turned and headed north. Suddenly, generals Zhang Liao and Zang Ba emerged from behind a hill and attacked. Cao Cao had generals Lü Qian and Cao Hong offer battle, but they were defeated. Cao Cao changed course and fled west, but he was checked by four more of Lü Bu's commanders, Hao Meng, Cao Xing, Cheng Lian, and Song Xian. Cao Cao's commanders fought desperately. Cao Cao took the lead and charged the line as arrows, following a signal of beating sticks, pelted down around him. He could neither advance nor escape. "Who will save me?" he cried.

From the body of his attendants Dian Wei rode up, an iron halberd in each hand. "Have no fear, master!" he shouted. Dian Wei dismounted and after putting away the two giant weapons, took a dozen small battle-axes and told his followers to warn him when the enemy was at ten paces. Then he strode ahead, braving the arrows. A score of Lü Bu's horsemen started after him. "Ten paces!" someone cried. "At five," said Dian Wei. "Five paces!" came the reply. Hurling his battle-axes rhythmically, Dian Wei brought down rider after rider. The pursuers scattered. Dian Wei remounted and slashed away with his halberds, and Lü Bu's generals broke before his charge. Dian Wei dispersed the enemy troops and rescued Cao Cao.[14] The rest of Cao Cao's commanders, catching up, accompanied him back to camp. Suddenly, from behind, Lü Bu's shout rent the evening air: "Cao! You villain! Stop!" Cao Cao's men, completely exhausted, looked at one another helplessly, each hoping to run and save his neck. Indeed:

> No sooner had Cao Cao broken through the enemy lines,
> Than he was pursued again by a powerful foe.

Had Cao Cao escaped only to be hunted down in flight?

READ ON.

12

Tao Qian Yields Xuzhou Three Times;
Cao Cao Overwhelms Lü Bu in Battle

THE PANICKED CAO CAO WAS SAVED by Xiahou Dun, who had rushed to the southern front, intercepted Lü Bu, and engaged him. As night fell, a rainstorm finally forced them apart. Later, at camp, Cao Cao rewarded Dian Wei amply and gave him a command.

Lü Bu returned to his base. "Here in Puyang," said his adviser Chen Gong, "lives the wealthy householder Tian. He heads the district's most influential house and has hundreds of servants. Have him write something like this to Cao: 'Lü Bu's cruelty has outraged our people. He will be moving the army to Liyang, leaving only Gao Shun behind. Waste no time getting here, and I shall work with you from within.' If Cao Cao takes the bait and enters the city, burn the gates. With an ambush outside, even if Cao Cao were strategist enough to plot the course of Heaven and earth, he couldn't escape us." Lü Bu approved and set the plan in motion, telling Tian to send a man to Cao Cao's camp.

Cao Cao was recovering from the defeat and pondering his next step when Lord Tian's message arrived:

Lü Bu has gone to Liyang. The city is defenseless. We pray you, come as quickly as possible. We will be working from within. Look on the wall for a white flag bearing the word "Honor."

"Heaven delivers Puyang into our hands," Cao Cao exclaimed. He rewarded the messenger and readied his army. Liu Ye, however, urged caution: "Lü Bu is foolish, all right. But Chen Gong is full of tricks. We must prepare for a trap. If you go, my lord, leave two-thirds of your men hidden outside the city and take the other third along. Otherwise . . . " Following this advice, Cao Cao divided his forces into three and made his way to the wall around Puyang.[1]

Cao was glad to see the white flag flying over the west gate among the other pennants. The gate opened at midday, and two generals, Hou Cheng of the rear army and Gao Shun of the forward army, came out to fight. Cao Cao sent Dian Wei against Hou Cheng, who, unable to resist, fled back toward the city. Dian Wei pursued him to the drawbridge. Gao Shun, too, fell back before Dian Wei and followed Hou Cheng into the city. In the confusion someone from Lü Bu's side slipped through to present Cao Cao a letter from the householder Tian. "At the first watch tonight," it read, "when gongs sound from the wall, advance. I will surrender the gate."

Cao Cao directed Xiahou Dun to advance to the left and Cao Hong to the right, while he led Xiahou Yuan, Li Dian, Yue Jin, and Dian Wei into the city. "Let *us* go in first," said Li Dian. "I have to go myself," Cao Cao shouted, "or no one will advance." He led the army forward. It was near the first watch; the moon had not risen. Above the gate a conch began to blow amid a swelling clamor. Torches appeared on top of the gate as it opened, and the bridge was lowered over the moat. Cao galloped across and headed for the *yamen*. The streets were deserted. Cao sensed a trap and wheeled round, shouting to his men, "Pull out!" From the government building[2] the bombards boomed as flames shot up by the four gates to the city. Gongs banged and drums sounded, and voices roared like a raging river or a storm-tossed sea.

Lü Bu's generals—Zhang Liao from the east, Zang Ba from the west—caught Cao Cao in a deadly vise. With his men Cao made for the north gate, harassed on the way by more of Bu's commanders, Hao Meng and Cao Xing. Cao Cao turned and tried for the south gate, but Gao Shun and Hou Cheng blocked him. Cao Cao's faithful commander Dian Wei, gaze fixed and jaw set, pushed Gao Shun and Hou Cheng back through the south gate to the bridge but lost sight of Cao Cao. Dian Wei then turned and fought his way to the wall, where he discovered Li Dian. "Where is our lord?" asked Dian Wei. "I can't find him either," Li Dian answered. "Go out and rally a rescue force," Dian Wei said, "while I search further." Li Dian left. Bearing up against fierce opposition, Dian Wei looked on either side of the city wall. He came upon Yue Jin, who said, "Where is our master?" "I've looked all over," Dian Wei said. "Let's go in again," Yue Jin replied. The two men approached the gate. From the wall fiery missiles rained down. Yue Jin's horse balked, but Dian Wei, braving smoke and fire, forced his way in again and continued the search.

Cao Cao, in fact, had seen Dian Wei battling through the south gate. Cut off by converging enemies, however, Cao Cao could not go out by the south gate and headed north once more. Through the blaze he saw Lü Bu riding from the opposite direction, his halberd pointed outward. Cao raised his hand to cover his face and laid on the whip. The horses passed each other closely. Lü Bu swung around and knocked his halberd against Cao's helmet. "Have you seen Cao Cao?" Lü Bu shouted. Cao pointed behind him. "There he goes. On the bay." And Lü Bu dashed in the direction Cao had indicated. Cao Cao turned round and fled east, finally meeting up with Dian Wei, who protected his lord and slashed a bloody path toward the east gate.

By the gate the flames were intense. Lü Bu's men were throwing down clumps of bramble and straw, which were burning everywhere. Dian Wei used his halberd to sweep aside the burning piles as he plowed through the smoke and flame, followed by Cao Cao. But when they reached the gate, a fiery beam fell and struck the haunch of Cao's horse, causing the horse to fall. Cao pushed the beam away, singeing his arm, hair, and beard. Dian Wei rushed to the rescue, and Xiahou Yuan came on the scene. Together they lifted Cao up and got him through the gate. Dian Wei hacked out a route for their flight, Cao Cao rode behind Xiahou Yuan, and after heavy fighting the three made it back to camp by dawn.

The generals at the base prostrated themselves before Cao Cao, solicitously expressing their concern, but Cao Cao only threw back his head and laughed. "I fell for that lowdown trick!" he said. "But I'll make Lü Bu pay for it!" "The sooner the better," Guo Jia urged. "Let's give him a taste of his own medicine," Cao Cao said. "Spread the rumor that I died of my burns. Lü Bu will attack immediately. We'll ambush him in the Maling Hills when his troops are halfway across, and capture him then and there." "An excellent plan," Guo Jia replied.

Accordingly, the troops put on mourning and made funeral preparations as if Cao Cao had died, and Lü Bu was duly informed that Cao Cao had perished in his camp of burns sustained during the battle at Puyang. Lü Bu lost no time assembling a force. He marched to the Maling Hills and near Cao Cao's camp was ambushed from all sides as the rolling drums echoed in the valleys. Lü Bu struggled free but lost many men. After this defeat he shut himself up in Puyang. Food was scarce: the harvest had been devoured by locusts, and throughout the northeast the price of grain rose to five thousand strings of cash per bushel.[3] People were reduced to eating human flesh. Cao Cao removed to Juancheng to find food, and Lü Bu withdrew to Shanyang for the same reason. Both sides suspended hostilities.

.   .   .   .   .

During the truce between Cao Cao and Lü Bu, Tao Qian, the sixty-two-year-old imperial inspector of Xuzhou, fell gravely ill. He summoned Mi Zhu and Chen Deng to discuss the province's future. "Cao Cao left us in peace," Mi Zhu said, "only because Lü Bu attacked his home base at Yanzhou. The fighting has died down with the famine, but Cao Cao will be back after the winter. Your Lordship twice offered Xuzhou to Liu Xuande, but he did not accept because you were still in good health. Under the present circumstances I doubt he will refuse again." On this advice Tao Qian called Xuande from Xiaopei to discuss the military situation. Xuande and his two brothers arrived and were shown into the inspector's bedchamber.

Xuande expressed concern for the inspector's health. "I asked for you," Tao Qian began, "for only one reason. My condition is critical. I remain hopeful that you will demonstrate your concern for the districts of the Han by accepting the position of inspector here so that I may die in peace." "My lord," responded Xuande, "you have two sons. Shouldn't you hand on your office to them?" "Neither the elder, Shang, nor the younger, Ying," replied Tao Qian, "has the ability to assume the responsibility; they would require your guidance after my death in any event. Please do not leave the affairs of the province to them." "How could I alone," Xuande said, "undertake such a task?" "Sun Qian, styled Gongyou, from Beihai can serve as your lieutenant," Tao Qian answered. "And Mi Zhu," the inspector continued, turning to him, "you must serve Lord Liu well. He is an eminent man." Even after this appeal Xuande would not agree, but Tao Qian passed away before his eyes, his finger to his heart.

After the mourning rituals, the seal and other tokens of authority were presented to Liu Xuande, but he declined them. The next day the common folk of Xuzhou crowded around the entrance to the inspector's residence and pleaded, "Lord Liu, unless you take charge, we can't live in peace." Xuande's brothers added their own exhortations. Finally Xuande consented to serve temporarily. He appointed Sun Qian and Mi Zhu his lieutenants and made Chen Deng a member of his staff. Xuande moved his army from Xiaopei to Xuzhou and issued a proclamation to calm the populace. Then he and his men donned mourning garb and completed the rituals for Tao Qian, who was interred somewhere on the plains of the Yellow River. His testament was forwarded to the court in Chang'an.

.   .   .   .   .

In Juancheng, Cao Cao learned that Tao Qian had died and that Liu Xuande had succeeded him as inspector. "My father's death not answered for," he cried bitterly, "and he takes Xuzhou without effort, without spending half an arrow! I will kill the undeserving Liu Xuande first and then avenge my father by scourging Tao Qian's corpse." He ordered a date set for the invasion of Xuzhou, but his adviser, Xun Wenruo, remonstrated with him: "The Supreme Ancestor, founder of the Han, controlled the region within the passes. Guang Wu[4] based himself in the region within the rivers. Both emperors struck deep roots in their respective base regions before expanding their rule over the realm so that when they advanced they could overpower their enemy and when they retreated they could defend themselves. Thus they eventually came to power. My lord, your original base was Yanzhou, by the Yellow and Ji rivers, a strategic part of the empire. This is your 'region within the passes,' your 'region within the rivers.' If you try to take Xuzhou, you will have to divide your forces. Leave too many behind and your attack must fail. Take too many along and Lü Bu will attack here. How will we ever get Yanzhou back? And where will you go, my lord, if you fail to capture Xuzhou? Tao Qian is dead, and Xuande holds Xuzhou. The people have accepted him and will fight for him. To risk Yanzhou for Xuzhou is to sacrifice what is important for what is not, the fundamental for the peripheral, something sure for something uncertain. Please reconsider."[5]

"We can't have the army idling here," said Cao, "in a year of dearth." "Why not raid the Chen area to the east?" suggested Xun Wenruo. "The army can find food in Yingchuan and Runan, where those remnants of the Yellow Scarves, He Yi and Huang Shao, have stuffed their sacks with gold, silk, and grain. Those rebels are easy prey. If we can seize their grain to feed our army, the court will approve, the people will cheer, and Heaven will be served." Cao Cao took Wenruo's advice. He left Xiahou Dun and Cao Ren in Juancheng, first attacked the Chen area, and then went on to Runan and Yingchuan.[6] The rebel leaders, He Yi and Huang Shao, confronted Cao's army at Goat Hill. The Scarves, though numerous, had no more discipline than a pack of dogs. Cao Cao ordered his archers and crossbowmen to shoot and Dian Wei to ride forth. He Yi sent his second-in-command to oppose, but Dian Wei did away with him in a brief skirmish. On the momentum of the victory Cao stormed past Goat Hill and pitched camp.

On the second day Huang Shao took command of the rebels. From the front line a solitary general strode out, a yellow scarf wound around his head. He wore a green jacket and held an iron staff. "I am He Man," he cried, "the devil who defies Heaven! Who dares test me?" Cao Hong, blade in hand, dismounted and raced out shouting hotly. After forty or fifty fierce exchanges Cao Hong feigned defeat and fled, drawing He Man after him. Cao Hong let his sword hang behind, then swung around, surprising his pursuer with one stroke and dispatching him with another. Li Dian galloped at once into the rebel line, seized Huang Shao and brought him back to camp. Cao's army overwhelmed the horde and seized their wealth and grain.

Isolated, the rebel He Yi fled toward Kudzu Hill with a few hundred riders, but their escape was cut off by a mighty warrior, a powerfully built man well over eight spans tall. Wielding a large sword, he handily captured He Yi and penned up the surrendering rebels near Kudzu Hill. The warrior then confronted Dian Wei, who had been leading the pursuit. "Are you one of the Scarves?" Dian Wei demanded. "I have just taken several hundred of them prisoner," replied the man. "Then hand them over," Dian Wei ordered. "That I'll do," answered the man, "if you can take this sword from me." In a fury Dian Wei charged, his two halberds raised. The warriors grappled from morning until noon, neither overcoming the other, before separating to recover their strength. Soon the stranger returned to taunt Dian Wei. The fight resumed and lasted until nightfall. Then they stopped again to rest their horses. Meanwhile, someone had informed Cao Cao, who rushed to the scene.

The following day the warrior came forth for combat. Cao Cao observed his presence with a secret delight and ordered Dian Wei to feign defeat. After some thirty exchanges on the field, Dian Wei ran for his line as instructed. The warrior gave chase but was driven off by archers. Cao retreated five *li*, where he had a pit dug and men armed with hooks placed nearby. The next day Dian Wei, leading a hundred riders, sought out the stranger. "The loser returns," the warrior taunted as he rode up. Dian Wei fought a few rounds, then turned and ran. The warrior pursued recklessly and unescorted, and plunged—man and horse—into the pit. He was tied up and taken to Cao Cao.

Cao Cao dismissed his attendants and personally untied the man's bonds, gave him clothes, and bade him sit down. "What is your name and native place?" Cao asked. "I am Xu Chu, styled Zhongkang, from the county of Qiao in the fief of Qiao," was the stranger's reply. "When some outlaws came, we organized our clan of several hundred and sealed ourselves up in defense. We were ready for their attack. I myself brought down a good many of them with well-aimed stones. When they next appeared, our fortress was out of grain, and we agreed to trade our oxen for some of their grain. They delivered the food and took our oxen away, but the beasts bolted and ran for home. I myself grabbed two by the tail and dragged them backward, perhaps a hundred feet. But the outlaws got scared and ran off without the oxen. Since then, things have been quiet around here." "I have long heard of you," Cao said. "Are you willing to come over to us?" "That's really what I want," Xu Chu said. Thus his whole clan joined Cao Cao, who made Xu Chu a commander and rewarded him bountifully. The rebel leaders, He Yi and Huang Shao, were executed, and the Runan-Yingchuan area returned to normal.

· · · · ·

Cao Cao, back in Juancheng, met with his commanders, Xiahou Dun and Cao Ren. They told Cao that Lü Bu's generals, Xue Lan and Li Feng, had let their troops scavenge the area, leaving Yanzhou virtually unguarded—an easy target. Cao Cao marched straight to the city, surprising Xue Lan and Li Feng, who had to come out and fight. Xu Chu said to Cao Cao, "Let me take on those two for you as my 'presentation' gift." Cao sent him forward. Li Feng came out, wielding his figured halberd. The two horsemen crossed, and Li Feng fell. Xue Lan raced back to his line, but Li Dian was already at the drawbridge, barring his entrance. Xue Lan tried to take his men toward Juye, but Lü Qian, pursuing like the wind, finished him off with an arrow. His troops scattered.

Having recovered Yanzhou, Cheng Yu proposed retaking Puyang.[7] Cao Cao mobilized his forces at once. He put Dian Wei and Xu Chu in the vanguard, Xiahou Dun and Xiahou Yuan on the left flank, and Li Dian and Yue Jin on the right flank. Cao Cao himself took the center. Yu Jin and Lü Qian brought up the rear.

In Puyang, Lü Bu wanted to oppose Cao Cao personally, but Chen Gong advised him to wait until all his commanders had gathered. "I fear no man," Lü Bu said and led his men out of the city to confront the attackers. Resting his giant halberd across his horse, Lü Bu reviled Cao Cao. Xu Chu rode forth and fought twenty passes with Bu, but neither prevailed. "No man can defeat Lü Bu alone," Cao Cao said and ordered Dian Wei to assist Xu Chu by attacking Bu from another side. Next, Xiahou Dun and Xiahou Yuan arrived on the left, and Li Dian and Yue Jin arrived on the right. Lü Bu, unable to withstand the combined attack of Cao's six commanders, retreated to Puyang. But the head of the Tian family (who had previously helped Lü Bu by luring Cao Cao into the city) now ordered the drawbridge raised. "Let me in!" Lü Bu demanded. "I have already surrendered Puyang to Cao Cao,'' cried Tian.[8] Enraged, Lü Bu raced to Dingtao as Chen Gong rushed Lü Bu's family out through Puyang's east gate.[9]

Cao Cao took possession of Puyang and forgave Tian for his deception. "Lü Bu is a wild beast,'' Liu Ye advised Cao Cao. "Don't let up on him in his hour of difficulty.'' Cao ordered Liu Ye to guard Puyang while he pursued Lü Bu to Dingtao.

Lü Bu, Zhang Miao, and Zhang Chao were all in Dingtao; Gao Shun and the other generals—Zhang Liao, Zang Ba, and Hou Cheng—were patrolling the seacoast or gathering crops. Cao Cao reached Dingtao but did not offer battle, camping instead forty *li* away. He told his soldiers to cut for themselves the wheat ripening just then in the area. A spy described these movements to Lü Bu, who rushed to the scene with troops; but, reaching a wood near Cao's camp, he turned back, fearing ambush. Informed of Bu's movements, Cao said, "He suspected an ambush in the woods. Plant banners in there to strengthen his suspicions, and hide our troops west of the camp, behind that dike above the dry streambed. He'll come back tomorrow to burn the woods; we can cut him off then and capture him.'' Cao Cao placed his best men in ambush, leaving only fifty behind to beat the drums and get the captive villagers shouting at the right moment.

Lü Bu told what he had found to Chen Gong, who said, "Cao Cao is full of tricks. Don't take chances.'' "I am going to burn out his ambush,'' said Lü Bu. He left Chen Gong and Gao Shun guarding the city and approached Cao's camp the next day. He saw the pennants in the woods and set fires on all sides. But the woods were empty, and no one came out. As Lü Bu started for the camp, loud drums broke the silence. He wavered. Suddenly a body of troops flashed into view. Lü Bu charged. To the peals of bombards, Cao's six generals—Xiahou Dun, Xiahou Yuan, Xu Chu, Dian Wei, Li Dian, and Yue Jin—attacked and drove Lü Bu from the field in confusion. His general Cheng Lian was shot to death by Yue Jin. Two-thirds of Lü Bu's men were lost.

The survivors reported to Chen Gong, who said, "An empty city is difficult to defend. We must leave at once.'' Chen Gong and Gao Shun gathered Lü Bu's family together and left. Cao Cao took the city as easily as a knife splits bamboo. Zhang Chao slit his own throat; Zhang Miao went over to Yuan Shu; and the entire northeast came under Cao Cao's control. He immediately set to work calming the populace and improving the defenses.

Lü Bu met up with his generals, and Chen Gong also caught up with them. "Despite my losses,'' Lü Bu said, "I can still defeat Cao Cao.'' He started turning his troops back. Indeed:

> To the military man defeat is commonplace.
> Who knows when the loser will rise to fight again?

Would Lü Bu emerge the victor?
READ ON.

13

Li Jue and Guo Si Cross Swords;
Yang Feng and Dong Cheng Rescue the Emperor

BADLY BEATEN AT DINGTAO BY CAO CAO, Lü Bu collected his battered units at points near the coast; his commanders rallied, eager for a showdown with Cao Cao. "Cao Cao has the upper hand now," objected Chen Gong. "This is no time to take him on. Once we have a base of our own, there will be time enough for another battle." "What about turning to Yuan Shao as we did before?" Lü Bu suggested. "Send someone to Jizhou to sound him out," replied Chen Gong, and Lü Bu did so.

Informed of the standoff between Cao Cao and Lü Bu, Yuan Shao considered his options. "Lü Bu is a ravenous beast," Shen Pei advised Yuan Shao. "If he takes Yanzhou, our Jizhou will be next. It's safer to help Cao." Thus Yuan Shao sent Yan Liang, commanding some fifty thousand, to aid Cao Cao. The news astounded Lü Bu, and he turned to Chen Gong for advice. Chen Gong said, "I hear that Liu Xuande has recently taken over Xuzhou. Let's try him." Lü Bu agreed and headed for Xuzhou. On hearing of his approach, Xuande said, "Lü Bu is a hero of our time. Let us receive him." But Mi Zhu objected: "He is a beast, a brute. We will suffer for it in the end." "Don't forget," Xuande replied, "that we owe our present position to his attack on Yanzhou: that caused Cao to lift the siege of Xuzhou. He comes to us now in desperation. I can see no other motive." "Eldest brother is too kindhearted," Zhang Fei put in. "Under the circumstances we had better be on guard."

Liu Xuande and others received Lü Bu with full honors thirty *li* from the city wall, and the two rode in side by side. They came to the provincial headquarters and, after the formalities, conferred together. "After Minister of the Interior Wang Yun and I had Dong Zhuo killed," Lü Bu began, "his generals Li Jue and Guo Si staged a coup against me. Since then I have been moving from place to place, but none of the lords in the region east of Huashan will have me. Recently that scoundrel Cao Cao, whose ruthless ambition is all too well known, invaded Xuzhou. Imperial Inspector Tao Qian was fortunate indeed to have had Your Lordship's help, and I, for my part, attacked Cao's base in Yanzhou in order to divide his forces. But Cao Cao trapped me and killed my officers and men. Now I turn to Your Lordship that we may plan for the dynasty together. What is your esteemed view?"

"Imperial Inspector Tao Qian," Xuande responded, "died only recently. He had no one to manage the province, and so I agreed, at his behest, to take charge for the time being. Your arrival suits me well as it is only proper for me to stand down and let you fill the office." Xuande moved to hand over the seal and tokens of authority. Lü Bu was reaching out for them when, behind his host, he saw wrath written on the faces of Lord Guan and Zhang Fei. Lü Bu forced a laugh and said, "I am but a warrior, hardly capable of serving as the inspector of an entire province." Xuande repeated his offer, but Chen Gong interjected, "'A stronger guest should not coerce his host,' as they say. I pray, Lord Liu, do not doubt us." At that Xuande dropped the matter. He spread a banquet for Lü Bu and had quarters prepared for him and his men.

The next day Lü Bu hosted a return banquet for Xuande and his brothers. When all were warmed with wine, Lü Bu invited Xuande to his private chambers. Followed by his brothers, Xuande accompanied his host. Lü Bu called for his wife and daughter to pay their respects to the guest, but Xuande politely declined the honor. "Worthy younger brother," Lü Bu said, "*do* accept their compliments." The moment Zhang Fei heard this, his eyes widened and he shouted, "Our eldest brother is a prince of the blood, a jade leaf on the golden branch. Who are you to call him 'younger brother'? Come out now and fight three hundred rounds with me." Xuande cut Zhang Fei short with a word, and Lord Guan hustled him out of the room.

"My unruly brother," Xuande said apologetically, "says the wrong thing when he's had a drop too much. Do not take offense, elder brother." Lü Bu remained silent, and the banquet soon ended. When Lü Bu saw Xuande to the gate, Zhang Fei was there on his prancing steed, his spear couched for action. "Three hundred rounds, Lü Bu!" he cried. "You and me!" Again Xuande had Lord Guan take Zhang Fei away.

The next day Lü Bu came to take leave of Xuande. "I am grateful that you have not rejected me, Your Lordship," he said, "but I fear your brother has. I shall find refuge elsewhere." "If you leave, General," replied Xuande, "I must bear the blame. My unruly brother has offended you. Let me have him make it up. Previously I stationed my army at Xiaopei. I know it is small; but if you can overlook its limitations, please use it as a place to rest and recover. What do you say? We shall see to all the provisions for your men." Lü Bu thanked Xuande and settled down in Xiaopei. And Xuande went to Zhang Fei to express his displeasure.

•   •   •   •   •

Cao Cao advised the court in Chang'an that he had brought major sections of the northeast under control. The government appointed him General Who Establishes Virtue and lord of Feiting. At this time the court was in the hands of Li Jue, who had made himself regent-general, and Guo Si, the self-styled regent.[1] These two generals rode roughshod over everyone. Who at court could protest? Grand Commandant Yang Biao and Treasurer Zhu Jun secretly petitioned Emperor Xian: "Cao Cao now has command of two hundred thousand troops and scores of able advisers and generals. If he would uphold the dynasty and clean out this faction of traitors, the whole realm would benefit."

Weeping, the Emperor said, "How long those two traitors have mistreated me! What a blessing it would be if they could be done away with!" Yang Biao then addressed the sovereign: "Your humble servant has a plan to turn the two traitors against each other and then summon Cao Cao to purge their faction and secure the court." "What kind of plan?" the Emperor asked. "Your servant has heard," Biao continued, "that Guo Si has a jealous wife. We can use her to sow dissension between Li Jue and her husband." The Emperor secretly authorized Yang Biao to put his plan into action.

Availing himself of some pretext, Yang Biao arranged for his wife to visit Guo Si's home. There Lady Yang found occasion to say to Lady Guo, "I have heard that your husband is involved in an intimate relationship with the wife of Regent-General Li Jue. If General Li finds out, he will murder your husband. Madame would be well advised to prevent him from meeting Lady Li again." "That explains why he's been away nights," Guo Si's wife, taken aback, exclaimed. "He has actually been engaged in a scandal! If not for you, Lady Yang, I would never have found out. But I shall surely put an end to it." Lady Yang rose to take her leave, and Lady Guo again expressed her thanks.

A few days later as Guo Si was preparing to go to Li Jue's home for his usual evening visit, Lady Guo said to him, "There's no telling about Li Jue, you know. Now, especially, there may not be room for two ambitious men in one court. If he were to poison you, what would become of me?" Guo Si dismissed his wife's objections; but she persisted, and he remained at home. Li Jue had the banquet delivered to Guo's home instead. Lady Guo slipped some poison into the food before it was served. As Guo Si began to eat, his wife stopped him, saying, "One cannot simply take what comes in from outside." She gave a little to their dog, who fell over dead. After that incident Guo Si never trusted Li Jue.

Another day, Li Jue persuaded Guo Si to come home with him after court. They ate and drank until late. Guo Si went home drunk and coincidentally was seized with stomach cramps. "You've been poisoned!" cried Lady Guo, and she forced an emetic on him. He felt better after vomiting. "I collaborated with Li Jue in the takeover; what cause has he to do me in? If I don't act first, however, I'll be the loser," Guo Si said and quietly readied his army for an attack on Li Jue. Li Jue, informed of Guo Si's moves, said, "How dare he!" and sent his own forces against his collaborator. The two armies, tens of thousands in all, fought in a free-for-all just outside the capital, at the same time availing themselves of the opportunity to plunder the populace.

Li Jue's nephew, Li Xian, surrounded the palace with his men. He put the sovereign in one carriage, the Empress in another, and assigned Jia Xu and Zuo. Ling to escort them out of the capital. The rest of the palace staff and the women followed on foot. As they crowded through the rear gate of the ministerial house, Guo Si's soldiers accosted them and killed many with volleys of arrows. At that moment Li Jue rode up and forced Guo Si's men to give way. The imperial party thus got out of the city, but then Li Jue without explanation hustled them into his camp.

Guo Si and his men entered the palace and removed all the female attendants to his own camp. Then he put the palace halls to the torch. On the morrow Guo Si learned that Li Jue had abducted the Emperor, so he marched straight to Li Jue's base camp to do battle. The royal couple feared for their lives.[2] A poet of later times lamented their plight:

> The Later Han revived the line of Liu:
> Twelve sovereigns in succession ruled the realm.
> But Huan and Ling—the downfall of their shrines—
> Let their eunuchs rule and doomed the house.
> Feckless He Jin, raised to guide the state,
> Called tigers into court to clear the rats.
> Vicious vermin out! Savage killers in!
> Then Zhuo, the western rebel, spread new bane.
> But loyal Wang Yun deployed a subtle maid,
> Who turned Lü Bu against his master Zhuo.
> Dong Zhuo cut down, the realm again knew peace,
> Till Li Jue and Guo Si avenged their lord
> And plunged our hallowed realm in misery.

Their civil strife brought king and queen to grief.
Allegiance broken, Heaven's Mandate failed:
Ambitious heroes carved our hills and streams.
Let every future king keep vigil keen
For our nation's precious harmony,
Lest living souls be ground into the earth
And stain our soil with blood unjustly shed.
To read these pages must break every heart,
As men once sighed for great Zhou's glory gone.
They warn the prince to stabilize his rule,
And watch who holds the sword that guards the laws.

Li Jue fought off Guo Si's attack and moved the royal pair to the palace at Mei, placing them in the custody of his nephew Li Xian. Li Xian dismissed the imperial staff and reduced the provisions for the attendants, who went wan from hunger. The Emperor sent someone to beg five bushels of grain and some ox bones for his servants, but Li Jue said angrily, "We send up food morning and night. What else does he want?" Finally he delivered some spoiled meat and moldy grain. The Emperor said, reproachfully, "How these traitors bully us!" "Your Majesty," Privy Counselor Yang Qi urged, "Li Jue is a cruel and violent man. Try to bear things as they are and not cross him." The Emperor lowered his head and kept silent. Tears soaked his sleeves.

Suddenly a new message came: "A band of soldiers, spears and swords gleaming in the sun, gongs and drums shaking the heavens, is coming to save the Emperor." But when the Emperor learned it was Guo Si, he despaired again. Outside the wall at Mei fearful shouts rang out as Li Jue confronted Guo Si. "I have treated you most generously," swore Li Jue, pointing his whip at Guo Si. "How could you plot to kill me?" "Traitor!" cried Si, "I have every reason to kill you." "I am guarding the Emperor," retorted Li Jue. "Is that treason?" "You are abducting the Emperor," countered Guo Si, "not protecting him." "Let's not waste words," Li Jue said, "or men. Let's settle it between ourselves. The winner takes the Emperor."

In front of their lines the two generals went at each other. Ten passages-at-arms produced no victor. Grand Commandant Yang Biao rode up and parted the combatants. "I have invited the court to settle your quarrel," he announced. Generals Li Jue and Guo Si withdrew to their respective camps.

Yang Biao and Zhu Jun convened more than sixty courtiers and officials. The body first presented themselves at Guo Si's camp to urge compromise, but Guo Si took them all captive. "We came," they protested, "in a spirit of good will. Why treat us like this?" "If Li Jue can seize the Emperor," Guo Si replied, "why can't I seize you?" "One holds the Emperor, the other the court. What do you want?" cried Yang Biao. Guo Si threatened Yang Biao with his sword. An Imperial Corps commander, Yang Mi, pleaded with Guo Si, who released Yang Biao and Zhu Jun but detained the senior lords and ministers. Yang Biao turned to Zhu Jun and said, "We two servants of the court can neither protect nor rescue our liege. We have lived in vain." The two high ministers wrapped their arms around each other and wept until they fell faint upon the ground. Zhu Jun took ill and soon passed away.[3] For two more months the killing continued day after day as Li Jue and Guo Si fought on. The loss of life was beyond reckoning.

Now Regent-General Li Jue, having a penchant for the occult, often summoned sorceresses to his camp. These women communicated with the gods by beating a drum and

going into a trance. Jia Xu had often protested the practice, but in vain. Mindful of Jia
Xu's attitude, Privy Counselor Yang Qi secretly appealed to the Emperor: "Your servant
has observed that Jia Xu, though enjoying Li Jue's confidence, has not forgotten his duty
to his liege. Your Majesty should consult with him." As Yang Qi was speaking, Jia Xu
himself arrived. The Emperor dismissed his attendants and, weeping, addressed the man:
"My lord, can you feel pity for the Han court and protect our safety?" Jia Xu prostrated
himself. "Such has ever been my desire," he responded. "Let Your Majesty say no more.
I shall devise a plan." The Emperor mastered his tears and thanked Jia Xu.

Shortly after, Li Jue entered the royal presence, a sword buckled to his waist. The
Emperor paled. "Guo Si has proved disloyal," Jue said. "He has detained the senior lords
and ministers and meant to abduct Your Majesty. But for me, you would have been their
captive." The Emperor raised his folded hands to his forehead in salute and thanked him.
Li Jue left, and Huangfu Li entered. The Emperor received him in audience.

The Emperor knew that Huangfu Li was a skillful talker and a townsman of Jue's, so
he instructed him to arrange a truce between the two generals. Huangfu Li took his mandate to Guo Si's camp. "If Li Jue will deliver the sovereign," Guo Si said, "I will release
the court." Huangfu Li then went to see Li Jue and said, "His Majesty has directed me
to settle your quarrel with Guo Si because I am from Xiliang and also your townsman.
Guo Si has already complied. What do you say?" "I was responsible for defeating Lü
Bu," said Li Jue. "And I have upheld the court for four years, a signal service which the
world recognizes. Guo Si is no more than a horse thief who takes it upon himself to defy
me by holding the court captive. For this I am sworn to execute him. Observe our ample
forces, my lord, and tell me if I can't defeat him."

"I cannot agree," replied Huangfu Li. "Let me remind you of the legend of Hou Yi of
the Youqiong.[4] He relied only on his marksmanship to govern and ignored all else. As a
result he was wiped out. More recently we have had the example of Imperial Preceptor
Dong Zhuo, whose power you yourself witnessed. Lü Bu was well loved by Dong Zhuo,
yet he turned against him, and in no time Dong Zhuo's head was on display at the capital
gate. Thus power alone counts for little. Now you hold the highest military office as well
as the seals of authority. Your kinsmen and descendants occupy illustrious positions. The
dynasty has not been stingy with its favor. Guo Si has detained the court, but you have
detained the Most Honored. Whose offense is graver?" Li Jue angrily drew his sword and
said, "Has the Son of Heaven sent you here to slander me? I'll have your head to begin
with!" Cavalry Commander Yang Feng pleaded, "If you kill the Emperor's messenger,
Guo Si will have good cause to mobilize against us, and the lords of the realm will support him." Jia Xu added his own admonition, and Li Jue relented.

Jia Xu next urged the messenger, Huangfu Li, to depart. But the moment he was out
of Li Jue's presence, the messenger began screaming, "Li Jue refuses the decree. He wants
to kill the Emperor and take the throne!" "How can you say such things?" cried Privy
Counselor Hu Miao. "You will suffer for it." Huangfu Li retorted, "Hu Miao, are you
not a servant of the Han as well as I? You have fallen in with traitors. 'When the liege
is wronged, the vassal dies'—that's the code we live by. If Li Jue kills me, it is only my
due." Huangfu Li continued to revile Li Jue. When the Emperor learned of it, he sent the
messenger back to Xiliang.

Li Jue's army was composed largely of Xiliang men, with the support of the Qiang
tribesmen.[5] When Huangfu Li returned to Xiliang, he spread the rumor that anyone aiding Li Jue's rebellion would suffer the consequences. As a result, many soldiers became
disaffected, and Li Jue began to lose control of his army. Li Jue sent Wang Chang of the

Imperial Tiger Escort to bring Huangfu Li back, but Wan Chang regarded Huangfu Li as a loyal and honorable man and simply reported that he could not be found. At this time Jia Xu secretly informed the Qiang: "The Son of Heaven is aware of your loyal devotion and of your sufferings through these long wars. He authorizes you to return to your home districts. Rewards will follow." The Qiang, who had resented Li Jue's refusal to confer rank and reward, took this opportunity and defected.

Jia Xu next appealed to the Emperor: "Li Jue is greedy and reckless. His army is falling apart, and he is losing heart. It is time to tempt him with an important post." The Emperor issued a decree appointing him regent-general. Li Jue exclaimed in delight, "This is due to the prayers of the sorceresses," and rewarded them—but not his soldiers. Li Jue's cavalry commander Yang Feng complained to Song Guo, "We face death every day from arrow and missile. Are those witches' services greater than ours?" "Why not kill the traitor and save the sovereign?" Song Guo suggested. "Set a fire in the main army base as a signal," said Yang Feng. "I will be ready outside." The two men agreed to act on the second watch. However, someone informed Li Jue of the conspiracy, and he executed Song Guo; so when Yang Feng arrived at Li Jue's camp, no signal was given. Instead, he was met by Li Jue himself. The two armies fell upon each other and battled wildly until the fourth watch. Unable to defeat Li Jue, Yang Feng took off with his troops to Xi'an.

Li Jue's position was crumbling under Guo Si's continuing attacks when the report of a new intervention startled all parties: Zhang Ji[6] had arrived from Shanxi with a large army to conciliate the two generals, vowing to strike down whichever one refused. Li Jue tried to impress Zhang Ji with his good will by agreeing at once to a settlement. Guo Si could only do the same. Zhang Ji then petitioned the Emperor to move to Hongnong.[7] Delighted, the Emperor said, "We have long been thinking of our eastern capital. This opportunity to return is a boundless blessing." He appointed Zhang Ji general of the Flying Cavalry, and Zhang Ji provided grain, wine, and meat for the entire court. Guo Si released the elder lords and ministers he was holding. Li Jue organized the imperial entourage, sending a few hundred of the original Royal Guard to escort the Emperor.

The imperial procession passed Xinfeng and reached the Baling bridge. It was autumn, and a sharp west wind was blowing. Hundreds of troops clattered onto the bridge, blocking the carriages. "Who wants to pass?" a harsh voice demanded. Privy Counselor Yang Qi rode onto the bridge and answered, "The Emperor. Who dares prevent us?" Two generals stepped up to Yang Qi. "We are here," they said, "at the order of General Guo Si, to guard against spies. We will have to verify your claim." Yang Qi lifted the bead curtain and revealed the sovereign, who said, "We are here. You may retire." "Long live the Emperor!" the soldiers cried and made way for his party.

The two generals reported the incident to Guo Si, who said, "I meant to fool Zhang Ji and take the Emperor back to Mei myself. Who gave you the authority to release him?" He promptly executed the two and pursued the Emperor with his own men. As the procession reached Huayin county, Guo Si overtook it. "Halt the train!" someone shouted. The Emperor was distraught. "Out of the wolf's lair," he lamented, "and into the tiger's mouth. What can we do?" His whole entourage trembled. Guo Si's rebels edged closer. Then, to the blast of drums another general appeared from behind a hill, unfurling a giant banner reading "Yang Feng of the Great Han." He had one thousand soldiers ready for combat.

After fleeing from Li Jue, Yang Feng had moved his army to the foothills of the Zhongnan Mountains and, hearing that the Emperor was passing, had come to offer his services. Now his army stood opposite Guo Si's. Guo Si's general, Cui Yong, rode before the two lines and denounced Yang Feng. Feng turned to his line and called for Xu Huang, who charged out, battle-axe in hand, on a superb steed. Huang went straight for Cui Yong and cut him down in a quick exchange. Yang Feng then overpowered Guo Si's forces and drove them off some twenty *li*.

The Emperor received the victor and said in a tone of solicitous appreciation, "You performed no small service in saving us." Yang Feng knocked his head on the ground and expressed his gratitude. The Emperor spoke again: "Which of your commanders has distinguished himself?" Yang Feng introduced the warrior. "This is Xu Huang, styled Gongming," he said, "from Yangjun in Hedong." The Emperor indicated his recognition of the achievement. Yang Feng then escorted the procession while runners cleared the roadway. Thus the Emperor reached Huayin, where the party rested for the night. General Duan Wei provided food and clothing, and the Emperor was quartered in Yang Feng's camp.

Undaunted by defeat, Guo Si returned in force the following day. Xu Huang rushed out for combat, but Guo Si's men, coming from all directions, encircled the Emperor and Yang Feng. Moments later, another general emerged from the southeast and, in a riotous assault, dispersed the rebels. Xu Huang seized his advantage and rode down Guo Si's men once again. The rescuer was Dong Cheng, an imperial in-law.[8] The Emperor described the recent events to him in bitter tones. "Your Majesty need worry no more," Dong Cheng said. "General Yang Feng and I have sworn to execute both Guo Si and Li Jue to restore calm in the realm." The Emperor ordered the procession to hurry toward the eastern capital, and that very night the imperial party set out for Hongnong.

Meanwhile, Guo Si, returning in defeat, met up with Li Jue and said, "Yang Feng and Dong Cheng have escorted the Emperor to Hongnong. If the court is reestablished in the east, they will broadcast their cause to the realm and rally the lords against us. Our clans will perish." "Zhang Ji holds Chang'an now," replied Li Jue. "We must proceed with care. But what's to stop us from joining forces, killing the Emperor in Hongnong, and taking the realm for ourselves?" Guo Si agreed. The two generals, reconciled again, combined their armies and looted their way to Hongnong, leaving devastation wherever they passed.

Yang Feng and Dong Cheng, the Emperor's new protectors, now had to meet the threat from the two generals. They turned back and confronted the rebels at Dongjian. Li Jue and Guo Si, with a much larger force, led a wild assault on both flanks of the Emperor's guard, intent on overwhelming it. Yang Feng and Dong Cheng mounted a desperate defense and managed to get the royal carriage safely out of the city, but the courtiers and palace women as well as the records of appointment, the archives, and the Emperor's household goods had to be abandoned. Guo Si entered Hongnong and looted it. The Emperor fled to Shanbei with Li Jue and Guo Si in hot pursuit.

To keep the Emperor from harm, Yang Feng and Dong Cheng adopted a twofold strategy: they sent men to arrange a truce with Li Jue and Guo Si and at the same time secretly enlisted the three leaders of the White Wave rebels (an offshoot of the Yellow Scarves), Han Xian, Li Yue, and Hu Cai, in the imperial cause. This urgent call unavoidably included Li Yue, who had inspired rebels from hill and wood. The prospect of amnesty and awards induced the rebels to rouse themselves from their camps and join Dong

Cheng in a counterattack on Hongnong. Li Jue and Guo Si had already begun to attack the city. They killed the old and feeble and put the strong into the army, forcing their new conscripts into the front ranks as suicide squads. The augmented forces of the two rebel generals were overwhelming.

Led by Li Yue, the White Wave troops gathered at Weiyang. Guo Si responded by ordering that clothing and other articles be scattered on the roads, so that the White Waves broke ranks to scramble for them. The armies of Li Jue and Guo Si then fell upon them, inflicting heavy casualties. Yang Feng and Dong Cheng had to flee north with the Emperor, the rebels close behind. "The situation is desperate," Li Yue, the White Wave leader warned. "Have His Majesty mount and go on." "No," the Emperor responded. "I cannot leave my courtiers." His weeping retinue struggled after him. The pursuers drew closer. One White Wave leader, Hu Cai, was killed. The sovereign abandoned his carriage, and Yang Feng and Dong Cheng escorted him on foot to the south bank of the Yellow River.

Li Yue found a small boat to take the Emperor and Empress across. The cold was fierce. The royal couple struggled to the bank but found it too high to board the boat. The pursuers were almost upon them. Yang Feng said, "Tie the reins together and with them lower the Emperor down by the waist." Fu De, the Empress's brother, stepped forward, proffering ten bolts of plain silk. "I picked these up from the rampaging soldiers," he said. "Tie them together to use as a sling instead." A military aide wound the silk around the royal pair. The Emperor was lowered into the boat, followed by the Empress, whom Fu De carried aboard. Those at the water's edge who could not get on clutched at the rope anchoring the boat. Li Yue slashed away at them, and many dropped into the river. The boat came back for the courtiers after the imperial pair was ferried to the north shore. As the courtiers fought to get on, their fingers were severed. Cries of pain filled the air.

The Emperor was left with barely a dozen of his adherents. Yang Feng found an ox cart to carry the royal couple into Dayang, but there was no food. They stopped for the night in a tile-roofed hut, where some elderly folk from the open country offered them millet, but it was too coarse for them to swallow. The next day the Emperor appointed the White Wave leaders as generals—Li Yue, Conqueror of the North, and Han Xian, Conqueror of the East. The procession resumed.

Two ministers—Grand Commandant Yang Biao and Court Steward Han Rong—came and prostrated themselves before the carriage, weeping profusely. The Emperor and Empress wept too. Han Rong said, "The rebel generals have some confidence in me. I am willing to risk my life to get them to desist. I pray for Your Majesty's well-being." Han Rong then left. Li Yue asked the Emperor to rest in Yang Feng's camp, but Yang Biao urged him to proceed to Anyi and establish his capital there. The procession entered Anyi, but finding no building with an upper story, the royal couple had to stay beneath the thatched roof of a simple farmhouse without a gate. A screen of brambles on all sides took the place of an outer wall. In the farmhouse the Emperor conferred with his ministers while the generals stood guard outside.

Li Yue controlled the court and played the tyrant, beating the courtiers and denouncing them before the throne for the slightest opposition. He purposely presented to the Emperor unpalatable wine and food, which he knew better than to decline. Together with the other White Wave leader, Han Xian, Li Yue handed the Emperor a list of nominees for high civil and military positions that included outcasts, common soldiers, sorcerers, and errand-runners—some two hundred all told. These new appointments of commandants, censors, and others were so hurried that there was no time to engrave seals; fresh ones were simply cut with chisels. Never had the decencies of court procedure been so scanted.

Meanwhile, Han Rong's mission of conciliation to Li Jue and Guo Si bore fruit. After strenuous arguments he persuaded them to release the courtiers and the palace women. But it was a year of dearth. People were reduced to eating the leaves of jujube trees. Corpses were seen everywhere in the countryside. Zhang Yang, governor of Henei, presented grain and meat to the Emperor. Wang Yi, governor of Hedong, submitted silk and cloth. As a result, the Emperor's distress was eased.

Yang Feng and Dong Cheng decided to have the Luoyang palace grounds restored in preparation for the Emperor's return, but Li Yue opposed them. "Luoyang," Dong Cheng argued, "is the original capital. Anyi is too small for his needs. The Emperor must be delivered to Luoyang." "Then you do it," Li Yue retorted, "I'm staying here." Dong Cheng and Yang Feng set out for Luoyang with the Emperor. But Li Yue now decided to join the rebels and sent someone to Li Jue and Guo Si with a plan for seizing the Emperor. Dong Cheng, Yang Feng, and Han Xian had been warned, however, and deployed troops to speed the Emperor to the pass in the Winnow Basket Hills. Li Yue did not wait for the rebel generals. Alone, he overtook the Emperor in the Winnow Basket Hills slightly before the fourth watch. "Go no further!" he shouted. "This is Li Jue and Guo Si!" The Emperor trembled with fear; his entrails quivered. The surrounding hills lit up with torches. Indeed:

> What was begun with two rebels falling out
> Was ending with three rebels joining forces,

placing the Emperor in greater peril than ever.[9] What was his fate?

READ ON.

14

Cao Cao Moves the Emperor to Xuchang;
Lü Bu Attacks Xuzhou by Night

FEAR OVERCAME THE EMPEROR at the thought that Li Yue now had Li Jue and Guo Si's backing. But Yang Feng said, "It's only Li Yue!" and sent out Xu Huang, who cut the rebel down in a single exchange. The White Wave gang dispersed, and Yang Feng guided the Emperor safely through Winnow Basket Pass. Zhang Yang, governor of Henei, provided grain and silk as he welcomed the sovereign at Zhidao. The Emperor elevated the governor to regent-general, and Yang Feng moved his troops to Yewang, northeast of Luoyang.

The Emperor entered Luoyang and saw the ruin of his former capital—the palace buildings burned out, the streets and markets desolate. Everything was overgrown with weeds. The walls of the palaces were crumbling.[1] Emperor Xian ordered Yang Feng to build a small dwelling to serve as a provisional palace. In the meantime court was held in the open woods.

The Emperor mandated that the reign year be changed from Stability Restored (Xing Ping) to Reestablished Peace (Jian An), year 1.[2] But it was another year of famine. The few hundred families remaining in Luoyang survived on tree bark and grass roots foraged outside the city. Even members of the Secretariat had to gather their own fuel there too, and many simply perished beside falling walls or within crumbling houses. Never was the dynasty at lower ebb, as these lines lament:

> Slain by Liu in the Mang-Dang Hills,
>   The white snake bled;[3]
> The fire-red flag triumphant
>   Toured the realm of Han.
> They chased and downed the deer of Qin
>   To raise a newer shrine;
> They brought Chu's warrior steed to earth
>   To mark the limes of Han.
>
> If the Son of Heaven has no power,
>   Vice and error rise.
> Once his prime is past,
>   Crime and treason thrive.
> Two cities lie in ruin,

Luoyang and Chang'an:
Even tearless men of iron
Cannot but despond.

Grand Commandant Yang Biao appealed to the Emperor: "The decree with which you honored me has yet to be dispatched. At present Cao Cao has the most powerful army in the northeast. He should be summoned to support the royal house." "I have so ordered," said the Emperor. "A second petition is not necessary. Send someone and be done with it." In accordance with the imperial will, an envoy was sent.[4]

Cao Cao, on learning of the Emperor's return to Luoyang, called together his advisers. "More than eight hundred years ago," Xun Wenruo said, "Lord-Patriarch Wen of the state of Jin protected King Xiang of the failing Zhou dynasty, and the lords of the realm accepted Wen's leadership. The founder of the Han conducted the mourning services for Chu's Emperor Yi, and the realm tendered it allegiance.[5] Today the Son of Heaven, evicted from his capitals, roams the land, an exile. This is the moment, General, to answer the expectations of all by calling for loyalist forces to uphold the imperial honor. It is a stroke to define the age. But if you delay, someone else may act first." Cao Cao reacted with enthusiasm to Xun Wenruo's advice and was preparing to muster his army when the imperial summons arrived. On the appointed day Cao Cao was ready to march.

In Luoyang the Emperor found all in ruin. Even the walls were beyond repair. Moreover, reports of new threats from Li Jue and Guo Si alarmed him. To Yang Feng the Emperor said, "Our messenger has not returned. Our enemies could come at any time. What can we do?" Yang Feng and Han Xian replied, "We will fight to the death to protect Your Majesty." But Dong Cheng said, "Look at our walls and how few soldiers we have! What if we fail? I recommend that Your Majesty proceed to Cao Cao's camp." The Emperor approved, and that day the court set out for the region east of Huashan. Horses were so scarce that the officials followed the Emperor's carriage on foot.

The procession was hardly under way when clouds of dust darkened the sky ahead, and the air throbbed with drums and gongs. Masses of troops loomed in the distance. Emperor and Empress were too frightened to speak. A single rider approached. It was the imperial envoy. "General Cao Cao," he reported, "has called up every soldier in the northeast and is coming in response to your decree. He has sent Xiahou Dun on ahead with ten top generals and fifty thousand picked men to deal with the threat to Luoyang from Li Jue and Guo Si." At last the Emperor felt safe.

Xiahou Dun, flanked by Xu Chu and Dian Wei, presented himself before the Emperor with due military etiquette. As the sovereign was making his will known to the three generals, Cao Cao's infantry arrived and commanders Cao Hong, Li Dian, and Yue Jin were also granted audience. Cao Hong petitioned the Emperor: "Your Majesty, my brother, Cao Cao, has sent us by rapid marches to assist Xiahou Dun against Li Jue and Guo Si." "General Cao is a true servant of our shrines," the Emperor replied. Cao Hong escorted the sovereign forward.

Mounted scouts reported the approach of Li Jue and Guo Si at a forced march. The Emperor ordered Xiahou Dun to divide his force and meet the enemy. Xiahou Dun and Cao Hong deployed their men in two wings. The cavalry went out first; the infantry followed behind. They attacked in full force, and the army of Li Jue and Guo Si was severely defeated, losing more than ten thousand.

At the suggestion of Cao's generals, the Emperor returned to his former palace in Luoyang. Xiahou Dun stationed his army outside the city. The next day Cao Cao arrived with the main force, established camp, and was received. Prostrating himself below the stairs to the imperial dais, Cao Cao acknowledged his sovereign. The Emperor bade him stand and commended him for his service. "My debt to the dynasty," Cao said, "is foremost in my thoughts. The crimes of the two traitors, Li and Guo, have exceeded all bounds. My army of more than two hundred thousand stands ready to crush the renegades in Your Majesty's behalf. Guard well Your Dragon-self for the sake of the sacred shrines." The Emperor appointed Cao Cao commander of the Capital Districts, granted him the insignia and battle-axe empowering him to conduct all military operations, and gave him control of the Secretariat, where decrees originated.

When Li Jue and Guo Si heard of Cao Cao's arrival, they wanted to fight at once. But Jia Xu objected: "You will fail. His men are too good, and his leaders too brave. Better to surrender and beg amnesty." "Are you trying to thwart us?" Li Jue demanded, drawing his sword. But all who were present stopped him. That night Jia Xu slipped away to his home village.

On the morrow Li and Guo engaged the forces of Cao Cao. Cao sent forth Xu Chu, Cao Ren, and Dian Wei at the head of three hundred armored cavalry. The three commanders made three quick strikes through the enemy lines before positioning their own soldiers. Li Jue's nephews, Xian and Bie, sallied forth in the semicircle of their line. Before taunts could be exchanged, Xu Chu raced out and felled Li Xian with one stroke. Li Bie panicked and lurched out of his saddle. Xu Chu killed him too and took both men's heads back to his line. "My own Fan Kuai!" exclaimed Cao, patting Xu Chu's back.[6] Then Cao Cao sent Xiahou Dun with a force to the left and Cao Ren with a force to the right, while he led the assault through the center. Signaled by drums, the three corps advanced. The traitors broke and fled. Wielding his sword, Cao Cao bore down on the enemy line, pressing the slaughter through the night. Thousands were flushed out and killed. Countless more surrendered.

Desperate as homeless dogs, Li and Guo headed west for the mountains to live as bandits—for who would receive them now? Cao Cao returned to Luoyang and stationed his army outside the city.[7] Yang Feng and Han Xian,[8] who had seen the Emperor all the way from Chang'an to Luoyang, realized that Cao Cao had no place for them and arranged for the Emperor to authorize them to pursue Li and Guo. Thus they were able to move their troops to Daliang.

One day the Emperor summoned Cao Cao to the palace. Receiving the messenger, Cao noticed that his eye was clear and his manner energetic. "After a year of dearth," mused Cao, "even the officials and the army, not to mention the people, look faint from hunger. How come this fellow is looking so well fed?" Cao said to him, "You at least are plump enough. How do you take care of yourself?" "No special method," replied the man. "I have fared hard and simply for thirty years." Cao nodded and continued, "And what office do you hold?" "I was recommended for filial devotion and honesty," the messenger replied, "and have served Yuan Shao, as well as Zhang Yang. When I heard the Emperor was back in the eastern capital, I came to pay my respects and was appointed court counselor. I am Dong Zhao (styled Gongren), a native of Dingtao in Jiyin."

Cao Cao raised himself from his mat and said, "A name long known to me. How fortunate to meet with you here." Cao Cao called for wine and introduced his chief adviser Xun Wenruo. Suddenly the passage of a contingent of troops headed east was announced. Cao Cao sent someone to investigate, but Dong Zhao said, "It's only Yang Feng and Han Xian leaving to take refuge in Daliang now that you're here." "Do you mean they mistrust me?'' asked Cao. ''Let's say they are too inept to be of concern,'' responded the Emperor's envoy. ''What about Li Jue and Guo Si?'' Cao pressed. ''Tigers with no claws,'' answered Dong Zhao. ''Birds with no wings. They'll be your prisoners soon enough.''

Cao Cao admired the aptness of Dong Zhao's replies and proceeded to ask him about the condition of the royal house. ''My lord,'' he answered, ''the loyal army you command has saved the court from chaos and rescued the Son of Heaven. For this you rank with the Five Protectors of antiquity, who safeguarded the sovereigns of the Zhou dynasty. In the present instance, however, we have many generals with many ambitions; they may not always obey you. Therefore it might be more advantageous to move the Emperor from Luoyang to Xuchang.⁹ On the other hand, the court is newly installed here in the former capital after a period of shuttling about, and men near and far yearn for stability. Another move will be widely resented. Still and all, extraordinary acts win extraordinary merit. The choice is yours.''

Cao Cao took Dong Zhao's hand and smiled. ''I really want to move the court,'' he said, ''but with Yang Feng loose in Daliang and the high ministers opposed, things could turn against me.'' ''That's easy,'' responded Dong Zhao. ''Write Yang Feng and put his mind at rest. Next, tell the high ministers that the food shortage in and around Luoyang imposes the necessity of moving the Emperor to Xuchang, where regular grain shipments from nearby Luyang can be virtually guaranteed. The ministers should be only too glad to cooperate.'' Cao Cao was delighted with Dong Zhao's advice. The envoy excused himself, but Cao took his hand again and said, ''Let me benefit from your advice whenever an important decision is pending.'' Dong Zhao thanked the general and left. That day Cao Cao conferred with his counselors on the question of transferring the capital.¹⁰

Privy Counselor and Historian-Astrologer Wang Li said privately to Liu Ai, director of the Imperial Clan, ''Since last spring Venus, associated with metal, had stood opposed to Saturn, associated with earth, at the same degree in the first two sectors of the northern sky, Ox and Dipper. Venus then crossed the star cluster Ford of Heaven in the adjacent sector, Woman, as Mars, associated with fire,¹¹ that flickering, disobedient planet, again reversed course to rendezvous with Venus in the Pass of Heaven cluster of the sector called Net. This conjunction of metal and fire means that a new sovereign will ascend. The sum of Han is told. In the central regions, the area of ancient Jin and Wei, another house will arise.''¹²

After speaking to Liu Ai, Wang Li petitioned the Emperor: ''The Mandate of Heaven does not permanently empower any dynasty, nor does any one of the five agents—water, fire, earth, wood, metal—remain ascendant forever. Fire, symbol of the Han, will be replaced by earth, symbol of the Wei.'' Apprised of this petition, Cao Cao sent a message to Wang Li: ''I know you speak out of devotion to the Han. But the ways of Heaven are too profound for man to follow. I would rather you said less about them.'' Cao Cao also discussed the matter with Xun Wenruo, who said, ''Han reigns by the strength of the element fire. You, my lord, are under the mandate of earth, with which the city of Xuchang is associated. If you move there, your fortunes should prosper, for fire yields ash, which is earth, and earth produces vegetation, which is wood: exactly as Dong Zhao and Wang Li have said, the future will see a new power arise.''

These arguments persuaded Cao Cao to petition the Emperor: ''Luoyang is ruined and cannot be restored. The grain shortage has caused severe hardship. Xuchang, close to Luyang's grain, has walls, buildings, riches, and resources more than sufficient for our needs. I propose removing there if it is acceptable to Your Majesty.'' The Emperor could only agree, for none of his officials dared oppose Cao Cao. On a chosen day Cao led the imperial escort, and the courtiers followed their sovereign to the new capital.

The procession had traveled but a few stages when it was stopped at a high hill by Yang Feng and Han Xian, backed by a noisy multitude. "Where are you taking the Emperor?" Xu Huang demanded. Cao Cao quietly admired Xu Huang's commanding appearance. Then he sent Xu Chu to engage him. Sword met battle-axe in a struggle of more than fifty exchanges that produced no victor. Cao Cao sounded the gong, and the soldiers retreated. "Yang Feng and Han Xian are not worth our breath," Cao told his advisers, "but Xu Huang is a fine general. It hurts me to have to take him by force. Couldn't we win him over?" Acting Military Aide Man Chong said, "My lord, perhaps I can be of use. I was once acquainted with Xu Huang. Let me slip into his camp tonight dressed as an ordinary soldier and persuade him that he can do no better than to join with us." Cao Cao gladly sent Man Chong to try his plan.

That night Man Chong slipped undetected into Xu Huang's tent. The warrior was sitting in full armor in the candlelight when Man Chong stepped suddenly before him, saluted, and said, "Have you been well since we parted, honored friend?" Startled, Xu Huang squinted and replied, "Is that Man Chong of Shanyang there? What brings you?" "I am now in the service of General Cao," was the response. "Today we had a glimpse of your prowess in the field and hope to put a suggestion before you. That is why I risked my life coming here." Xu Huang offered him a seat. "Your bravery and strategic sense," Man Chong continued, "are all too rare. Why lower yourself serving the likes of Yang Feng and Han Xian? General Cao is a true hero of our age; his respect for the worthy, his courtesy toward the able are widely known. Today because of his deep admiration for your ability, he refrained from sending his best generals to finish the fight and sent me instead to extend this invitation. Why not abandon a lost cause for a part in our promising enterprise?"

After pondering this offer, Xu Huang said with a heartfelt sigh, "I know full well these two men will accomplish nothing, but I can't bear to abandon them after serving them so long." "You must know the saying, 'The wise bird chooses its branch, the wise servant his master.' To let this chance to serve a worthy lord slip away shows lack of mettle." Thus Man Chong responded. Xu Huang rose and said gratefully, "I would like to accept your proposal." "Then," suggested Man Chong, "why not kill Yang Feng and Han Xian outright as your 'presentation' gift?" "I cannot do something so dishonorable as murder the lords I have served," was the reply. "Truly, you are a man of honor," Man Chong said. Taking a few dozen comrades, Xu Huang rode nightlong for Cao Cao's camp.

The next morning Yang Feng discovered the defection and pursued Xu Huang furiously with one thousand horsemen. Drawing close, he called out, "Xu Huang, you turncoat. Go no further!" But as he spoke, bombards resounded and torches appeared on a nearby hill, high and low, signaling an ambush that took Yang Feng from four directions. "Finally he's come!" Cao Cao cried out, leading the charge. "Don't let him escape." Panicked, Yang Feng tried to maneuver a retreat, but Cao's troops walled him in—until Han Xian rode up and broke through, enabling Yang Feng to escape in the ensuing melee. The battle, however, was not over. Cao overwhelmed both armies, taking more than half the troops prisoner; and Yang Feng and Han Xian, stripped of military force, found refuge with Yuan Shu. [13]

Back at camp Man Chong introduced Xu Huang to Cao Cao, who received the warrior warmly and generously. Cao then escorted the imperial procession to Xuchang. Royal dwellings and temples were erected; the ancestral sanctum and soil shrine established;

the court, administrative departments, and garrisons set up; and the city walls and store-houses built. Dong Cheng and thirteen others were awarded lordships of the first rank. Cao Cao assumed complete authority over all benefits and penalties and had himself appointed regent-marshal and honored as lord of Wuping.[14] His chief adviser, Xun Wenruo, was named privy counselor and executor of the Secretariat. Xun You was made military director; Guo Jia, chief of sacrifices; Liu Ye, chief of the Ministry of Public Works; and Mao Jie and Ren Jun, Imperial Corps commanders for the farmer-soldier colonies,[15] supervising taxes in money and kind. Cheng Yu became lord of the fief of Dongping; Fan Cheng and Dong Zhao became prefects of Luoyang; Man Chong, prefect of Xuchang, the new capital. Xiahou Dun, Xiahou Yuan, Cao Ren, and Cao Hong were appointed generals; Lü Qian, Li Dian, Yue Jin, Yu Jin, and Xu Huang, commandants; Xu Chu and Dian Wei, district military commanders. The other captains and officers were given minor positions. Power was concentrated in Cao Cao's hands to such a degree that all important issues at court were first proposed by petition to him and then presented to the Son of Heaven.

Having established the new government, Cao Cao invited all his advisers to a banquet in his private quarters. There he announced:[16] "Liu Bei has posted his army in Xuzhou and controls the province. Recently Lü Bu went over to him after suffering a major defeat at Chang'an, and Bei has installed him in Xiaopei. What can we do to prevent them from combining against us? That would be a dire threat indeed!" Xu Chu responded promptly, "Give me fifty thousand of our finest, Your Excellency,[17] and I'll deliver their heads!" But Xun Wenruo took a different approach. "No one," he said to Xu Chu, "questions your bravery. But the possibilities of intrigue must also be considered. We cannot rush headlong into war, having hardly settled into Xuchang. I have an idea, though, which I'll call 'Two Tigers Fight for Food.' Now, Liu Bei's position is still unofficial. Why not petition the Emperor to confirm Liu Bei as protector of Xuzhou, and secretly instruct him to get rid of Lü Bu? If Bei succeeds, he should be manageable enough without that fierce warrior—when the time comes. And if he fails, Lü Bu will kill him. This is my 'two tigers trick.'" Cao Cao approved the plan and petitioned the Emperor, who accordingly sent his envoy to Xuzhou to appoint Liu Xuande as General Who Brings Justice to the East, to honor him with a fief as lord of Yicheng precinct, and to empower him as protector of Xuzhou. The envoy also carried the secret instructions.

In Xuzhou, Liu Xuande was preparing to felicitate the Emperor on his move to Xuchang when the envoy arrived. Xuande received him outside the city walls, accepted the imperial honors, and hosted the envoy at a grand banquet. "My lord," the envoy began, "we grant this gracious decree by virtue of General Cao's earnest recommendation to the throne." Xuande expressed thanks, and the envoy delivered the special communication. Xuande read it and said, "This requires further deliberation." The banquet adjourned, and the envoy was entertained in the guesthouse.

Xuande spent the night conferring over the Emperor's instructions.[18] "Lü Bu," Zhang Fei said, "is a faithless and unscrupulous fellow. There's no reason not to kill him." "He came to us in desperation," Xuande replied. "It would dishonor us to kill him." "He'll only bite the hand," Zhang Fei said. But Xuande would not give his consent.

The next day Lü Bu visited his host and said, "I hear you have received an imperial appointment, and I have come to congratulate you." Xuande thanked him modestly. At that moment Zhang Fei entered with drawn sword, but Xuande swiftly blocked him. "Why does he always want my life?" Bu cried. "Cao Cao says you have no honor and told my brother to kill you!" Zhang Fei said grimly, but Xuande shouted Zhang Fei out of the room. Then he led Lü Bu to his private chambers and showed him Cao Cao's confidential letter. "So," said Lü Bu after reading it, "the villain would like to turn us against each other." "Have no fear," Xuande assured him, "I will never do so dishonorable a deed." Lü Bu thanked his host repeatedly, and the two continued drinking for some time.

Later, Lord Guan and Zhang Fei demanded, "Why did you spare him?" "Because," replied Xuande, "Cao Cao expects Lü Bu and me to combine forces and attack him—unless he can get us to devour each other. I can't let him use me like that!" Lord Guan saw the point, but Zhang Fei said, "I wanted to kill him and prevent trouble, that's all." "That would not be an honorable act," responded Xuande.

The next day Xuande sent the envoy back to the capital to thank the Emperor and to inform Cao Cao that his special instructions would require time to plan and execute. The envoy told Cao Cao that Xuande had not killed Lü Bu. Cao Cao consulted Xun Wenruo. "Your plan didn't work," Cao said. "What next?" "I have another," Wenruo answered, "called 'Drive the Tiger to Swallow the Wolf.' Have Yuan Shu notified that Liu Bei has secretly petitioned the throne for authority to take control of his district Nanjun. Yuan Shu should attack Bei. When that happens, openly mandate Liu Bei to subdue Yuan Shu. With Shu and Bei locked in struggle, Lü Bu will waver." Cao Cao agreed to the plan and sent a man to Yuan Shu as well as a forged decree to Xuande.

Xuande received this second envoy with the fullest courtesies and accepted the command to march against Yuan Shu. "Another of Cao Cao's tricks," warned Mi Zhu. "I know," Xuande said, "but the Emperor must be obeyed." Xuande readied his forces for the appointed day. Sun Qian advised, "Before we leave, let's assign someone to defend the city." "Which of my brothers will take that responsibility?" Xuande asked. Lord Guan volunteered. "No," said Xuande, "I need you with me at all times." Zhang Fei then offered to do it. "You cannot protect Xuzhou properly," chided Xuande. "First of all, you lose your judgment after drinking and start beating the soldiers. Second, you are careless about responsibility and ignore sound advice. I would never breathe easy." "I will neither drink nor beat the men from now on," Zhang Fei vowed humbly. "And I will take advice to heart." "If you mean what you say," said Mi Zhu caustically. "In all these years I have never broken a promise to elder brother," Zhang Fei retorted. "Do I really deserve such scorn?" "I appreciate your pledge," responded Xuande. "But I could not help expressing my misgivings. Let us leave Xuzhou in Chen Deng's hands. He can see to it that our younger brother moderate his drinking in the interest of security." Chen Deng accepted the assignment. Xuande gave final instructions and set out for Nanyang with thirty thousand men.

Yuan Shu[19] reacted hotly when informed that Liu Xuande had sought imperial sanction for an invasion of his region. "That miserable mat-weaver and sandal-maker!" he cried. "An upstart who took over a province and thrust himself into the ranks of the lords of the realm! I'm going to attack him! Let him scheme all he wants! I'll show that vile schemer!" So saying, Yuan Shu sent his top general, Ji Ling, and one hundred thousand men against Xuzhou. The two armies met at Xuyi.

Xuande, with far fewer troops, camped close to water and hills. Ji Ling, wielding a trident of some fifty pounds, paraded before his ranks cursing Xuande. "You country bumpkin," he shouted. "How dare you trespass on my territory?" "I hold an imperial decree," Xuande retorted, "to punish your insubordination. To resist me is a crime that not even your life could pay for." Striking his horse and brandishing his weapon, Ji Ling made for Xuande. Lord Guan dashed out first, shouting, "Save your show of strength, bastard!'' After thirty bouts Ji Ling called it off, and Lord Guan rejoined his line. Ji Ling then sent Xun Zheng into the fight, but Lord Guan cried, ''Let's have Ji Ling alone out here so we can all tell the cock from the chicken.'' To this Xun Zheng retorted, ''You are an underling, known to no one—no match for General Ji!'' Lord Guan closed with Xun Zheng and cut him down. Following up, Xuande sent his men in for the kill. Yuan Shu's army sustained a heavy defeat and retreated to the mouth of the river at Huaiyin. Ji Ling refused to fight again but sent soldiers to harass Xuande's camp. These were slain, and the two armies were at a standoff.

• • • • •

After seeing his elder brother off, Zhang Fei left Xuzhou's administrative responsibilities to Chen Deng and concerned himself only with military matters. One day he held a banquet for the various officials, at which he declared, ''When my brother set out, he warned me to limit my drinking for fear of trouble. Today is our last revel: drink your fill, for starting tomorrow wine is forbidden. I need your help in guarding this city.'' So saying, he rose and began to toast the guests.

When Zheng Fei reached Cao Bao, Bao said, ''I have always abstained.'' ''What man of war refrains from drink!'' cried Zheng Fei. ''Down your wine!'' Cowed, Cao Bao took the cup. Zhang Fei continued his tour, quaffing great goblets as he toasted each official. Full drunk after scores of drafts, Zhang Fei nonetheless rose to repeat the round. For the second time he stood before Cao Bao, who said, ''I really cannot.'' ''You did before,'' Zhang Fei urged. ''Why refuse now?'' But Bao stood his ground, and Fei, drunk beyond all reasoning, exploded, ''You disobey my command? One hundred lashes!'' The guards came for Cao Bao.

''Isn't this what Lord Xuande cautioned you against?'' objected Chen Deng. ''Civil officials,'' Zhang Fei replied, ''need concern themselves only with civic affairs—and not with mine.'' Cao Bao made a last appeal to the drunken general: ''Lord Yide—Zhang Fei—for the sake of my son-in-law, I beg forgiveness this once.'' ''And who might your 'son-in-law' be?'' inquired Zhang Fei. ''Lü Bu,'' was the reply. ''I was going to spare you,'' Zhang Fei cried, ''but if you think dragging Lü Bu into this is going to scare me, I will beat you, and in so doing I am beating him as well.'' The guests could not calm Zhang Fei down. He gave Cao Bao fifty lashes, stopping only after agonized protests from his guests.

After the banquet Cao Bao went home with pent-up hatred for Zhang Fei. That night he sent a message to Lü Bu in Xiaopei describing Zhang Fei's barbarous behavior and adding, ''Xuande has left for Huainan with his army to fight Yuan Shu; Zhang Fei is dead drunk: Xuzhou can be taken. Don't let the moment pass.'' Lü Bu showed the letter to Chen Gong, who said, ''Our stay in Xiaopei was not meant to be permanent. A chance like this won't come again.'' Lü Bu agreed. Armed and mounted, he took five hundred horsemen to Xuzhou. Chen Gong and Gao Shun followed with the main army. From Xiaopei to Xuzhou was barely forty li. Lü Bu reached the city in the fourth watch. The moon was bright; the sentries on the wall suspected nothing. ''I come on a secret mission for Protector Liu,'' Lü Bu shouted up, and a guard who was in on the conspiracy rushed word to Cao Bao, who ordered the gate opened. Lü Bu gave the signal, and his five hundred riders crashed into the city.

Zhang Fei's frantic attendants tried to shake their master out of his stupor. ''Lü Bu has tricked us into opening the gate,'' they shouted, ''and there's fighting in the city.'' Zhang Fei shouldered his armor, took up his eighteen-span snake-headed spear, and had scarcely mounted when Lü Bu confronted him. Zhang Fei was still unsteady, but Lü Bu feared his power and failed to press him. Eighteen cavalry commanders from Fei's home district, Yan, formed a guard around their lord and got him out of the city. But in the fighting there was no time to see to Xuande's family, and they were left behind in their quarters.

Cao Bao saw that Zhang Fei was lightly guarded and gave chase, but Zhang Fei turned on his pursuer, drove him back to the river's edge, and speared him in the back. Man and horse tumbled into the water. Zhang Fei then scraped together what soldiers he could find and headed south for Huainan. Lü Bu entered Xuzhou and calmed the populace. He kept Xuande's family secluded under guard, allowing no one to see them without permission.

Zhang Fei overtook Xuande in Xuyi and recounted his sorry tale to an appalled audience. "Is gain worth celebrating, or loss worth mourning?" Xuande responded with a sigh. "Where are our sisters-in-law?" Lord Guan demanded.[20] "In Xuzhou city," Zhang Fei replied. Xuande held his peace, but Lord Guan could not suppress his accusing questions: "What did you say when we gave you the city to protect? What did elder brother caution you about? Now the city and our sisters as well are lost. What are we going to do?" In the clutches of anxiety and despair, Zhang Fei set his sword to his throat, for indeed:

> Drink had driven him to acts
> Which his very life could no longer redeem.

Would he take his life?
READ ON.

15

Taishi Ci and Sun Ce Fight Their Hearts Out;
Sun Ce Plants His Kingdom South of the River

ZHANG FEI WAS ABOUT TO SLIT HIS OWN THROAT when Xuande seized the weapon and flung it down. Then he admonished Zhang Fei: "There's an old saying, 'Brothers are like arms and legs; wives and children are merely garments that can always be mended. But who can mend a broken limb?' We three swore in the peach garden to die together however fate might keep us apart in life. Now despite the loss of city and family, do you think I could let death part us midway in our course? In any event, the city was not mine to begin with, and Lü Bu is unlikely to harm my family. They can still be rescued. I will not let you throw your life away, good brother, for this momentary slip." So saying, Liu Xuande cried bitterly, and his two brothers, moved as well, wept with him.

Meanwhile, Yuan Shu (the object of Xuande's southern expedition) had learned of Lü Bu's coup in Xuzhou and promised him fifty thousand bushels of grain, five hundred horses, ten thousand ounces of gold and silver, and one thousand rolls of varicolored silk.[1] Lü Bu, encouraged by this offer, eagerly sent General Gao Shun and fifty thousand men to attack Xuande from the rear. Xuande, however, was informed in time and under cover of foul weather managed to flee east to Guangling. Gao Shun, arriving too late, demanded the promised gifts. "You may withdraw now," was General Ji Ling's reply, "while I arrange it with my lord." Gao Shun reported the conversation to Lü Bu, who also received a letter from Yuan Shu saying, "Your general, Gao Shun, reached Xuyi, but Xuande is still at large. When he is taken, I will deliver all I promised." Lü Bu cursed Yuan Shu for bad faith and intended to attack him, but Chen Gong objected: "Yuan Shu holds Shouchun. His army is large, his supplies ample. Do not take him lightly. Instead, invite Xuande back to Xiaopei to enter our service.[2] Soon we can put him in the vanguard and defeat not only Yuan Shu to the south but Yuan Shao to the north. That would give us the run of the realm." Lü Bu agreed and sent a messenger to Xuande.

Yuan Shu had raided Guangling, Xuande's refuge, and killed half the defenders, so Lü Bu's offer of Xiaopei was most welcome to Xuande, but not to his brothers. "A man so dishonorable cannot be trusted," they protested. Xuande replied, "He makes us a fair offer in good will. Why question his motives?" And so they returned to Xuzhou. To dispel Xuande's doubts, Lü Bu sent his wives ahead to meet him. Lady Gan and Lady Mi told Xuande how Lü Bu had protected their home and provided for their needs. "You see," Xuande said to his brothers, "no harm has come to them." But Zhang Fei's hatred for Lü Bu was unabated. He refused to go with Xuande to thank Lü Bu and instead escorted Lady Gan and Lady Mi to Xiaopei.

Xuande expressed his appreciation to Lü Bu. "I did not intend to take over your city," Lü Bu said, "but because your brother went into a drunken rage, I had to take charge or risk losing the province." "I had intended to yield it to you all along," replied Xuande. Lü Bu then offered to step aside, but Xuande strenuously refused and took his men to Xiaopei, where they entrenched themselves. His brothers were not reconciled to the turnabout. "Bending when one must," Xuande said to them, "and accepting one's lot makes it possible to await a more favorable time. Who can contest fate?" Lü Bu had foodstuffs and cloth sent to Liu Xuande, and amity was restored between the two.

•   •   •   •

Now at Shouchun, Yuan Shu was feasting his officers when a report came in on the triumphant return of Sun Ce after his conquest of Lujiang district, which was under Governor Lu Kang. Yuan Shu summoned Sun Ce, who saluted him in the hall. After commending Sun Ce for his success in battle, Yuan Shu invited him to join the banquet.[3]

(Since his father's death, Sun Ce had withdrawn to the region below the Great River, gathering around him men of ability.[4] Later, because Tao Qian, imperial inspector of Xuzhou, and his uncle Wu Jing, governor of Danyang, had a falling out, Sun Ce moved his mother and the whole family to Qu'e and entered Yuan Shu's service.[5] Yuan Shu greatly admired Sun Ce and often exclaimed, "If I had such a son, I could die without regret." Yuan Shu appointed him Commandant Who Cherishes Loyalty. In this capacity Sun Ce had made his mark by defeating Zu Lang, governor of Jingxian, after which Yuan Shu sent him to attack Lujiang. Sun Ce was coming back fresh from his victory there.)

After the banquet Sun Ce returned to his camp feeling that Yuan Shu had been condescending to him during the festivities. He spent the moonlit night pacing the inner courtyard, brooding over the memory of his heroic father and the insignificance of his own accomplishments. A heartfelt cry broke from his lips. "What is troubling you?" asked a man who entered the yard. "When your honored father was alive, he often turned to me. If there's something on your mind, you can tell me instead of crying your heart out." The speaker was Zhu Zhi (Junli), a native of Guzhang in Danyang, who had served Sun Jian.

Mastering himself, Sun Ce offered Zhu Zhi a seat and said, "I despair of fulfilling my father's ambition." "Why not ask Yuan Shu for troops to rescue Wu Jing?" Zhu Zhi suggested. "That will give you a chance to bring the Danyang region under your control, instead of remaining cooped up here under Yuan Shu."[6] At that moment another man unexpectedly entered the courtyard. "I am sympathetic to your plan," he said, "and I would like to contribute one hundred able-bodied men." The speaker was Lü Fan (Ziheng) from Xiyang in Runan, an adviser to Yuan Shu. The three men talked on. "But I fear only that Yuan Shu will deny you the troops," Lü Fan said. "I still have the royal seal passed on to me by my late father," Sun Ce pointed out, "to offer as my pledge." "How long Yuan Shu has wanted that!" exclaimed Lü Fan. "He will supply you the troops without doubt." Thus the three men settled their plan.

The next day in audience with Yuan Shu, Sun Ce said, "My father's death remains unavenged. Liu Yao, inspector of Yangzhou, threatens my uncle Wu Jing, and I fear for the lives of my mother and family in Qu'e. I come, therefore, to beg a few thousand soldiers to take across the river in order to save my family and visit with them again. I have here the imperial seal left me by my father; I offer it to you as security." Yuan Shu had long known of this treasure. Examining it with great interest, he said, "I have no wish for your seal; however, you may leave it with me temporarily, and I will lend you three thousand men and five hundred horses. After you have pacified the region, hurry back. As your rank is still too low to wield authority, I shall propose that the court appoint you General Who Annihilates Outlaws and Commandant Who Breaks the Enemy. Set out on the designated day."

Sun Ce thanked Yuan Shu and took command of his men. With him were Zhu Zhi and Lü Fan as well as generals Cheng Pu, Huang Gai, Han Dang, and others who had served his father.[7] They marched first to Liyang, where they were met by another army whose commander—a man of gallant bearing and striking appearance—dismounted and saluted Sun Ce. It was Zhou Yu, from Shucheng in Lujiang.

When Ce's father, Sun Jian, was a member of Yuan Shao's alliance against Dong Zhuo, he moved his family to Shucheng. Zhou Yu and Sun Ce, born in the same year, had become close friends and bound themselves in brotherhood. Zhou Yu, two months junior, looked upon Sun Ce as an elder brother. Now on his way to visit his uncle Zhou Shang, governor of Danyang, Zhou Yu found himself face-to-face with his dear friend. Sun Ce was delighted and proceeded to share his innermost ambitions with Zhou Yu, who said, "If I could serve you, I would toil loyally and unremittingly so that together we might reach our goal." "If you are with me, success is assured," exclaimed Sun Ce and introduced Zhou Yu to Zhu Zhi, Lü Fan, and the other leaders.

"Elder brother," Zhou Yu said, "to further your plans you should meet the two Zhangs, Zhang Zhao (styled Zibu) of Pengcheng and Zhang Hong (styled Ziwang) of Guangling. Both men have the talent to chart the course of Heaven and earth. They live here in obscurity, avoiding the chaos around them. I suggest you invite them to serve you." Pleased with this recommendation, Sun Ce sent for them, but they politely declined. Sun Ce then visited them personally and found their views inspiring. They consented to serve after much persuading on Sun Ce's part. Sun Ce appointed Zhang Zhao his senior adviser with the title Imperial Corps Commander Who Cheers the Army, and he made Zhang Hong his counselor with the title Commandant of Sound Judgment. Together they began to plan the attack on Liu Yao.

Liu Yao (Zhengli) from Mouping in Donglai was an imperial relation and the nephew of Grand Commandant Liu Chong. His elder brother, Liu Dai, was imperial inspector of Yanzhou. Previously, Liu Yao had been imperial inspector of Yangzhou, stationed at Shouchun. After Yuan Shu drove him southeast across the Great River, he came to Qu'e, where he eventually threatened Sun Ce's mother and her brother Wu Jing. On hearing that Sun Ce was coming to rescue his relatives, Liu Yao met with his advisers. A brigade leader, Zhang Ying, volunteered, "Let me take a company to Ox Landing, and he won't get through—not even with a million men!" Another seconded Zhang Ying. "I will take the van!" he cried. It was Taishi Ci from Huangxian in Donglai.

After rescuing Kong Rong, Taishi Ci had entered the service of Liu Yao.[8] "You are too young for a command," Liu Yao had said, "stay by me and await orders." Taishi Ci retired discontented.[9]

Liu Yao sent Zhang Ying to defend Ox Landing where one hundred thousand bushels of grain were stored. Sun Ce arrived, and the two armies met at the water's edge. Sun Ce took personal command of his force. His general Huang Gai engaged Zhang Ying, but before the battle was fully under way, a fire in Zhang Ying's camp forced him to retreat. Sun Ce pressed his advantage, killing many. Zhang Ying fled toward the hills.

The fire had been set by Jiang Qin (Gongyi) of Shouchun and Zhou Tai (Youping) of Xiacai—two counties in Jiujiang district. Jiang Qin and Zhou Tai, who lived by brigandage in these times of turmoil, had heard that Sun Ce was a powerful warrior receptive to the able and talented. They therefore brought three hundred of their adherents into Sun Ce's service and were made vanguard commanders for their contribution. After the fire had routed Zhang Ying, Sun Ce gathered up the stores and weapons at Ox Landing, reorganized thousands more who had surrendered, and advanced to Shenting.[10]

Liu Yao wanted to execute Zhang Ying for losing Ox Landing, but his advisers dissuaded him. He then ordered Zhang Ying to garrison the city of Lingling and hold back Sun Ce's advance. Liu Yao himself occupied the ground south of the Shenting Hills. Sun Ce stationed his army north of the hills. He asked one of the local people, "Is there a temple to the founder of the Later Han near here?" "On a hilltop to the south," was the reply. Later Sun Ce told his followers: "Last night I dreamed that the founder was calling me to audience. I wish to pray to him." But Zhang Zhao opposed the trip, arguing, "Liu Yao is camped on the southern side. What if there is an ambush?" "The gods will protect me," Sun Ce replied.

Fully armed, he rode with a dozen men to the shrine where, kneeling, he prayed, "If it be granted me to establish our patrimony in this land below the Great River, building on the foundation my late father set down, I shall restore this shrine and offer service here every season." Then Sun Ce rose and told his commanders he wanted to scan Liu Yao's positions. They objected, but Sun Ce insisted, so they climbed a high ridge and surveyed the groves and villages below.

Sentries had already reported Sun Ce's moves to Liu Yao. "He is only trying to lure us into the open," said Liu Yao. "Do not pursue." But Taishi Ci, spoiling for a fight, argued, "If we don't catch him now, when will we?" And without receiving an order, he rode out of the camp, shouting, "Those who dare, follow me!" But only one minor leader joined him, saying, "Taishi Ci has real courage!" The rest laughed and did not move.

Having observed the enemy, Sun Ce was starting back north over the ridge when he saw two horsemen racing down toward him. Sun Ce and his commanders, thirteen all told, formed a line, and he prepared to do battle. "Which one is Sun Ce?" Taishi Ci shouted. "Who are you?" Sun Ce demanded back. "I am Taishi Ci of Donglai, here to arrest Sun Ce." "Here I am!" Sun Ce retorted. "Two of you cannot scare one of me! If I feared you, I would not be Sun Ce!" Taishi Ci responded, "Nor do I fear you! Not even if all of you come!" He galloped out with leveled spear straight toward Sun Ce, who raised his own spear and met the attack. On horseback the two heroes fought mightily, exchanging some fifty blows, but neither could prevail. Sun Ce's general Cheng Pu marveled quietly at Taishi Ci's skill.

Taishi Ci, seeing that Sun Ce's spear work was flawless, feigned defeat and ran, luring his opponent to follow. Taishi Ci took an unexpected route up the hill and then turned behind it. Sun Ce, striving to overtake him, shouted, "The coward flees!" Taishi Ci reckoned, "This bastard has a dozen men with him. I have one. Even if I capture him, his men will free him. But if I can take him another stretch to where he can't be found, I'll do him in." So Taishi Ci kept on, occasionally turning back to fight.

Since Sun Ce was hardly the sort to abandon a chase, he pursued Taishi Ci to level ground. There Taishi Ci swung his horse around and the two champions exchanged another fifty blows. Taishi Ci dodged each thrust of Sun Ce's spear and caught the shaft under his arm; Sun Ce likewise snatched each thrust of Taishi Ci's spear. The two men closed and grappled, pulling each other down from their saddles. The horses ran off. The warriors threw down their spears and wrestled wildly, tearing each other's battle dress to shreds. With a lightning grab Sun Ce ripped away the short halberd on Taishi Ci's back; and Taishi Ci tore off Sun Ce's helmet. Sun Ce thrust with Taishi Ci's weapon; Taishi Ci blocked with Sun Ce's helmet. Suddenly, new voices filled the air. Liu Yao had arrived with a thousand men to aid Taishi Ci, and Cheng Pu and the other twelve commanders also charged up. The combatants finally parted.

Taishi Ci, freshly armed and mounted, returned to the field. Cheng Pu had found Sun Ce's runaway horse, so Sun Ce, too, took his spear and remounted. Liu Yao's force and Cheng Pu's twelve cavalry joined in a bloody free-for-all that worked its way back to the Shenting Hills. There another outburst of shouting accompanied the entry of Zhou Yu's men into the fray. The day ended with a thunderstorm lashing the field, and each side recalling its troops.

The next day Sun Ce rode to the front of Liu Yao's camp with Taishi Ci's short halberd held high on the tip of his spear. "Only quick feet saved Taishi Ci!" Sun Ce's men shouted. Taishi Ci appeared and displayed the helmet he had seized. His men shouted, "And Sun Ce's head would have been here!" Amid noisy boasts and taunts from both lines Taishi Ci sallied forth, but Sun Ce's general Cheng Pu said, "No need for you, my lord, to bother with him. I will take him." Cheng Pu rode to the front of the camp. "You're not my man!" cried Taishi Ci. "Let's have Sun Ce!" Cheng Pu went for Taishi Ci with leveled spear. Their horses crossed and they fought thirty exchanges, after which Liu Yao recalled Taishi Ci. "I was about to capture the bastard," he complained. "Why did you sound the gong?" "Zhou Yu has surprised Qu'e with the support of Chen Wu (styled Zilie) of Lujiang," Liu Yao answered. "Our home base is lost, and we cannot remain here. I must go at once to Moling and get Xue Li and Ze Rong's men to rescue Qu'e." Taishi Ci withdrew with Liu Yao, and Sun Ce recalled his troops.

Zhang Zhao, Sun Ce's senior adviser, said, "Zhou Yu has taken Qu'e, and Liu Yao has no heart for battle. Sack their camp tonight." Accordingly, Sun Ce divided his forces into five units and overran Liu Yao's positions. Taishi Ci could not thwart this attack alone and fled for his life with a score of riders to Jingxian county.

In Chen Wu, Sun Ce had a new ally. He was a man seven spans tall, with a sallow complexion and reddish eyes. His general appearance was somewhat peculiar. But Sun Ce admired him, appointed him commandant, and put him in the vanguard of the attack against Xue Li. Chen Wu, accompanied by a dozen or so cavalry, charged into Xue Li's ranks and took more than fifty heads. In response Xue Li shut the gates of Moling and refused to come out. Sun Ce continued the siege until informed that Liu Yao and Ze Rong had joined forces to attack Ox Landing. In great anger Sun Ce led the bulk of his force there, and Liu Yao and Ze Rong rode forth to meet him.

Sun Ce said, "Surrender to me now!" From behind Liu Yao, Lieutenant Commander Yu Mi galloped out, spear held high. They clashed briefly; Sun Ce captured him alive and dashed back to his line. Another of Liu Yao's commanders, Fan Neng, seeing Yu Mi's capture, gave chase. He was about to deliver a fatal spearthrust when Ce's men shouted, "Ambush behind you!" Sun Ce turned on Fan Neng and bellowed thunderously; the pursuer lost control and was thrown from his mount and killed. Reaching the entrance to his position, Sun Ce threw down Yu Mi's body; he had been squeezed to death. For these feats of strength Sun Ce was given the nickname the Young Hegemon.[11] It was a day of defeat for Liu Yao. More than half his force surrendered to Sun Ce; over ten thousand were beheaded. Liu Yao and Ze Rong took refuge in Yuzhang with Liu Biao.

Sun Ce, returning to the siege at Moling, rode to the foot of the city wall to demand surrender, but he was shot in the left thigh. He fell from his horse and had to be carried back to camp, where the arrowhead was removed and the wound treated. Sun Ce ordered his men to spread the rumor that he had died. His army went into mourning and decamped. The news lured Xue Li, Liu Yao's general, out of the city. Together with the general of the Valiant Chargers, Zhang Ying, and Chen Heng, Xue Li rode forth to give chase. Suddenly, they found themselves in an ambush. Sun Ce, in the lead, shouted, "Master Sun has come!" The soldiers panicked, flung down their weapons, and prostrated themselves. Sun Ce ordered them spared. Zhang Ying, however, had tried to escape and was speared by Chen Wu; Chen Heng fell to Jiang Qin's arrow; and Xue Li died in the turmoil of battle. Sun Ce entered Moling and calmed the inhabitants. Then he moved his army to Jingxian to capture Taishi Ci.

Taishi Ci had recruited some two thousand hardy warriors into his army in order to avenge Liu Yao. Sun Ce and Zhou Yu laid plans for taking Taishi Ci alive. Zhou Yu ordered Jingxian attacked on three sides, leaving the east gate free for the enemy to escape. On the east, twenty-five *li* from the town, Zhou Yu placed in ambush one detachment from each of the three attacking forces. He expected that Taishi Ci, his men fatigued and his horses spent, would be easy to capture there.

Now Taishi Ci's raw recruits were mostly mountain folk who knew nothing about discipline. And the Jingxian wall was not especially high. That night Sun Ce ordered Chen Wu, wearing a short jacket and carrying a dagger, to climb up and start a fire. When Taishi Ci saw the flames, he rode through the east gate, and Sun Ce sped after him. He pursued Ci for thirty *li* and then broke off. After fleeing for fifty *li*, Taishi Ci's men were exhausted. Suddenly from the reeds shouts rang out. Before Ci could get away, his horse was snared from both sides and pulled down. Taishi Ci was taken alive and delivered to Sun Ce's headquarters. Sun Ce came out from his tent, dismissed the escort, and personally untied the prisoner's bonds. Then he placed his own brocade surcoat over him and invited him to enter the camp. "I know you for a man of true fighting spirit," Sun Ce said to Taishi Ci. "You were defeated only because that useless fool Liu Yao did not give you a high command." Moved by Sun Ce's generosity, Taishi Ci begged to surrender.

Sun Ce took Taishi Ci's hand and said, "If you had captured me at Shenting, would you have killed me?" "It is hard to say," Taishi Ci replied. Sun Ce laughed, invited him into the headquarters, and bade him be seated in the place of honor at a sumptuous dinner. Taishi Ci said, "Liu Yao's defeated troops have no unity now. I would like to go myself and recruit them for Your Lordship. Are you willing to trust me?" "It's exactly what I was hoping for," said Sun Ce, rising to express his thanks. "I will expect your return by noon tomorrow." Taishi Ci agreed and left. Sun Ce's commanders expressed doubt that the warrior would ever return, but Sun Ce answered them, "He is a trustworthy and honorable warrior and would never betray me." The commanders were unconvinced.

The next day Sun Ce had a gnomon set in the ground in front of the camp to measure the shadow cast by the sun. Just before noon Taishi Ci returned with more than one thousand soldiers. Sun Ce was delighted, and his commanders praised him as a fine judge of character. After these events Sun Ce gathered tens of thousands more. When he crossed the river into the Southland to encourage the population, another wave of followers joined him. The people of the Southland hailed Sun Ce as Young Master Sun. The moment his armies approached, his foes lost heart and fled. But when his armies arrived, they were forbidden to abduct anyone or even disturb the livestock. Thus they enjoyed great popularity, and the common people brought meat and wine to their camps. Sun Ce always responded with gifts of gold and silk, and the rejoicing of the people spread wide. As for Liu Yao's former troops, those who wanted to join him were welcome; those who did not were rewarded and sent home to their farms. Sun Ce was universally acclaimed, and his military power grew great. Sun Ce settled his uncle and cousins in Qu'e, leaving his younger brother Sun Quan and Zhou Tai guarding the walled town of Xuan. Next, Sun Ce led his troops south to capture Wujun.

·   ·   ·   ·   ·

Wujun was a district controlled by Yan Baihu, who called himself the Virtuous King of Eastern Wu. His lieutenants were guarding Wucheng and Jiaxing. On learning that Sun Ce's army was coming, Yan Baihu ordered his younger brother Yan Yu to check Sun Ce at Maple Bridge. The news made Sun Ce eager to fight, but Zhang Hong objected: "My lord, the entire army depends on you for direction. Why risk your life fighting a minor enemy? Take yourself more seriously, General." "Your view is a worthy one," Sun Ce replied, "but unless I myself take the forefront in battle, braving arrow and stone, I will lose authority over my officers and men." Nevertheless, he sent Han Dang out first.

By the time Han Dang reached the bridge, Jiang Qin and Chen Wu had already crossed the river in a small boat to support him. They sprayed the bank with arrows, taking a heavy toll, and then leaped ashore swinging their swords. Yan Yu retreated before Han Dang, who advanced to the west gate, driving the enemy into the city. Sun Ce now moved up by land and water and laid siege to the city of Wu. For three days no one came out to fight. Sun Ce led his men to the west gate to induce Yan Baihu to submit. A minor commander was on the wall, his left hand braced against a beam, his right pointing downward as he shouted taunts. Taishi Ci took up his bow and set an arrow in place. Turning to the men around him, he said, "Watch me hit that bastard's left hand!" No sooner said than done! At the twang of the bowstring the arrow found its mark, piercing the commander's left hand and fixing it to the beam—a shot hailed by all who saw it. The injured commander was helped down by his men.

Amazed, Yan Baihu said, "How can we resist such warriors?" He decided to sue for peace and the next day sent his brother Yan Yu to negotiate with Sun Ce. Sun Ce invited Yan Yu into his tent; wine was poured. After they had drunk well, Sun Ce asked, "What does your honorable brother have in mind?" "He wants to share the rule of the Southland with you, General," was the reply. "That skulking rat rates himself my equal?" Sun Ce cried angrily and ordered Yan Yu executed. Yan Yu drew his sword, but Sun Ce made short work of him, severed his head, and sent it back into the city. Yan Baihu understood the futility of further resistance and fled the city of Wujun.

Sun Ce set out in pursuit. Huang Gai stormed Jiaxing, and Taishi Ci captured Wucheng. Several other cities fell into Sun Ce's hands. Yan Baihu, on his way to Yuhang, looted the places he passed through, and so a native called Ling Cao led the local people to attack him. Consequently, Yan Baihu turned in the direction of Kuaiji. Ling Cao and his son meanwhile welcomed Sun Ce, who appointed them commandants of the march. Together they led their forces across the Great River. Yan Baihu mustered his forces and deployed them around a ford. Cheng Pu engaged him and routed him again, so he hastened on toward Kuaiji.

Wang Lang, governor of Kuaiji, was minded to go to Yan Baihu's rescue. A district official from Yuyao in Kuaiji named Yu Fan (Zhongxiang) stopped him, saying, "Sun Ce wages war for principles humane and honorable; Yan Baihu represents brute force. You would be better advised to deliver the latter to the former." Wang Lang angrily dismissed this counsel, and Yu Fan left deeply saddened. Wang Lang joined forces with Yan Baihu, and the two deployed their men in the fields near Shanyin. Both sides assumed battle formation. Sun Ce then rode forth and said to Wang Lang, "My army is dedicated to humanity and justice and will bring peace to this region. Why aid the traitor Yan Baihu?" Wang Lang denounced Sun Ce: "Are you so greedy that even Wujun is not enough for you? Do you have to take our district as well? Today I avenge Yan Baihu!"

In great anger Sun Ce was preparing to engage Wang Lang when Taishi Ci came forth. Wang Lang urged his horse forward and swung out his sword. He battled Taishi Ci briefly, then his commander Zhou Xin joined the fray. From Sun Ce's side Huang Gai raced out and met Zhou Xin. A mutual slaughter ensued; drums and shouts echoed and reechoed. Suddenly, Wang Lang's rear ranks began to break as a band of soldiers struck them from behind. Wang Lang turned in alarm to confront this threat: it was Zhou Yu and Cheng Pu, who had led their force in from the side, catching the enemy in a two-front struggle. Wang Lang had too few men to resist. With Yan Baihu and Zhou Xin he cut a bloody path into the city, pulled up the drawbridge, and sealed the gates.

Sun Ce's main force arrived and circled the city, laying siege to the four gates. Wang Lang realized the situation was critical and wanted a showdown battle, but Yan Baihu said, "Sun Ce has a powerful force. All you need do is dig in and fortify the walls. Inside of a month they will run out of grain and withdraw; then we can surprise them and defeat them without a major battle." On this advice Wang Lang defended Kuaiji and refused to come out. After several days of fruitless assault, Sun Ce consulted his commanders. His uncle Sun Jing said, "Wang Lang has the city too well defended for a quick victory. But most of Kuaiji's coin and grain are stored in Chadu, only a few dozen *li* from here. Our best chance is to occupy Chadu in accordance with the maxim 'Attack where they are least prepared; do what is least expected.'"

Delighted with this plan, Sun Ce said, "Uncle, this brilliant plan will destroy the foe." Immediately he ordered fires set at each gate, flags and banners ostentatiously displayed, and decoy troops positioned to cover his withdrawal south. Zhou Yu made a proposal: "My lord, the moment we decamp, Wang Lang will come out and pursue us. A surprise attack should suffice to defeat him." Sun Ce replied, "Everything is ready. The city falls tonight." He then ordered the army to begin moving out.

On learning of the retreat of Sun Ce's army, Wang Lang climbed the watchtower with his companions to observe. Below he saw the usual fires and smoke, the flags and banners in proper order, and became suspicious. His chief aide, Zhou Xin, said "Sun Ce is gone. He left this display to confuse us. We should strike!" But Yan Baihu cautioned, "Sun Ce's next move may well be Chadu! I'll have my own troops and General Zhou Xin pursue them." Wang Lang responded, "Chadu is where I store my grain. It needs to be well guarded. You and your men go first, and I will follow." Yan Baihu and Zhou Xin led five thousand soldiers in pursuit of Sun Ce's army.

Close to the first watch, when the pursuers were some twenty *li* from the city, drums and voices rang out from a dense wood, and torches turned dusk to daylight. Panicked, Yan Baihu turned his mount to flee, but a single general barred his way; in the glare of the fires he recognized Sun Ce himself! Zhou Xin brandished his blade and sallied forth, but Sun Ce killed him with a single spear thrust. Zhou Xin's men surrendered. Yan Baihu fought his way out of the fray and fled toward Yuhang. Wang Lang, learning of the defeat of the advance force, did not dare return to the city. He and his force hurried on to a remote point on the coast.

Sun Ce and his army then turned back, captured the city, and restored order. A day later someone came to Sun Ce's camp with Yan Baihu's head. Sun Ce studied the man. He was eight spans tall with a square face and broad mouth and answered to the name of Dong Xi (Yuandai) of Yuyao in Kuaiji. Sun Ce was pleased and appointed him auxiliary commanding officer. Thereafter the eastern region was pacified; Sun Ce left his uncle Sun Jing to garrison it and had Zhu Zhi serve as governor of Wujun. He then returned in triumph to the region below the Great River.

• • • • •

Now Sun Quan, Sun Ce's brother, and Zhou Tai were defending Xuancheng when they were set upon from all sides by mountain bandits. It was late at night; resistance was impossible. Zhou Tai helped Sun Quan to a horse as scores of bandits descended on the two with swords swinging. Proceeding on foot, Zhou Tai, stark naked, killed ten or more bandits. From behind, a mounted bandit attacked him, but Zhou Tai seized his spear and yanked the rider to the ground. He mounted the attacker's horse and, cutting his way through the confusion, rescued Sun Quan. The remaining bandits fled.

Zhou Tai had more than twelve major wounds. They were festering, and his life hung in the balance. Sun Ce was alarmed. Dong Xi said, "Once I received many spear wounds while fighting the coastal bandits. In Kuaiji a rather capable official, Yu Fan, recommended a surgeon who cured me in a fortnight." "Yu Fan is none other than Yu Zhongxiang, I take it?" Sun Ce asked. "Yes," Dong Xi replied. "He is a worthy scholar. I should employ him." Accordingly, Sun Ce had Zhang Zhao and Dong Xi go to solicit the services of Yu Fan.

Yu Fan came, and Sun Ce treated him handsomely, appointing him to the Bureau of Merit. Then he mentioned his interest in finding a physician. Yu Fan replied, "The man you want is a native of the Qiao district in the fief at Pei, Hua Tuo (styled Yuanhua), perhaps the most marvelous physician of our time. You should invite him here." That day the invitation went out, and the doctor arrived. Sun Ce observed the man: young of face with hair like the feathers of a crane. He had the light and easy manner of one who no longer belongs to this world. He was treated as an honored guest and ushered in to see the patient. "Not a difficult case," Hua Tuo pronounced. He applied certain medicines, and the wounds healed in a month. Sun Ce was delighted and rewarded the doctor richly.

Next he eliminated the mountain bandits, and the region returned to normal. Sun Ce then took four steps: he dispatched men and officers to the several strongpoints; he presented a memorial to the court detailing his victories; he established relations with Cao Cao; and he sent a messenger to Yuan Shu to demand the return of the imperial seal.

Yuan Shu had been biding his time until he could declare himself emperor, so he made excuses to Sun Ce and did not return the seal. He then gathered his council of more than thirty. Among them were: Senior Adviser Yang Dajiang, field commanders Zhang Xun, Ji Ling, and Qiao Rui, and the ranking generals Lei Bo and Chen Lan. Yuan Shu said to them, "Sun Ce started his campaigns with forces borrowed from me. Today he is master of the Southland. He seems to have no thought of repaying us but simply demands the return of the royal seal. His conduct is outrageous. How shall we deal with him?" Senior Adviser Yang Dajiang said, "Sun Ce controls the strategic points along the river. His troops are excellent and his supplies ample. We can do nothing now. Rather, we should first attack Liu Xuande for his treacherous invasion. Victory there would put us in a better position to take on Sun Ce, and I have a scheme that should made Xuande ours immediately." Thus:

> Instead of tackling the young tiger to the south,
> Yuan Shu moved to fight the dragon in the north.[12]

What plan was presented to Yuan Shu?
READ ON.

16

Lü Bu Demonstrates His Marksmanship Before His Camp;
Cao Cao Suffers Defeat at the River Yu

SENIOR ADVISER YANG DAJIANG had a plan for attacking Liu Bei. "How will it work?"
Yuan Shu asked. Yang Dajiang replied, "Liu Bei, stationed in Xiaopei, is easily taken; but
Lü Bu has firm control of Xuzhou. We held back the goods we promised Lü Bu—gold,
silk, grain, and horses—so he could not aid Liu Bei. Now is the time to send the grain—
though not the gold and silk—to win back his good will and to keep him from going to
Liu Bei's aid when we attack. Once we take Liu Bei, we can attack Lü Bu and the province
is ours." Yuan Shu approved and sent Lü Bu two hundred thousand bushels of grain and
a secret letter describing the plan.[1] Lü Bu accepted the proposal and the gifts and treated
the envoy, Han Yin, royally. Han Yin reported the success of his mission back to Yuan
Shu, who commanded Ji Ling, with Lei Bo and Chen Lan as deputies, to lead tens of thousands of troops against Xiaopei.

Liu Xuande summoned his advisers and commanders to discuss the emergency. Zhang
Fei was for giving battle, but Sun Qian said, "We have neither the manpower nor the
wherewithal to defend ourselves.[2] We'd better write Lü Bu at once." "Is that bastard
going to help us?" Zhang Fei cried. But Xuande approved Sun Qian's suggestions and
wrote as follows:

> My thanks for your kind concern and boundless favor in granting us refuge in
> Xiaopei. Yuan Shu now seeks private revenge and has sent Ji Ling with an army.
> My fate hangs in the balance. Only you can save me. I entreat you to relieve our
> plight. I will be eternally grateful.

Lü Bu read the letter and conferred with Chen Gong. Lü Bu reasoned, "Yuan Shu has
sent grain to keep us from aiding Xuande. Now Xuande seeks our help. In my view
Xuande at Xiaopei is no threat to us; but if Yuan Shu swallowed him up and then allied
with the Mount Tai commanders to the north, our position could become untenable.
We'd better give Xuande what he needs."[3] Lü Bu led a force to Xiaopei.

Ji Ling, Yuan Shu's general, had already pitched camp southeast of Xiaopei. By day his
banners spangled the hills. By night his camp fires lit the sky and his drums shook the
earth. Xuande's five thousand could hardly maintain a defense line around the town. Ji
Ling was soon informed that Lü Bu was camped to the southwest only a *li* away and
intended to rescue Xuande. Ji Ling wrote Lü Bu accusing him of bad faith. The letter only
made Lü Bu laugh. "I think I have a way to satisfy both sides," he said and summoned

the two antagonists—Ji Ling and Xuande—to a banquet. Xuande was willing to attend despite his brothers' fear of Lü Bu's treachery. "I have treated him fairly and doubt he would harm me," he said and went on horseback, accompanied by Lord Guan and Zhang Fei.

Receiving Xuande, Lü Bu said, "Today I act solely to help you through this crisis. If someday you gain power or high position, please do not forget it." Xuande gave thanks and, at Lü Bu's invitation, was seated. Lord Guan and Zhang Fei remained standing behind their brother, hands on their swords. At that moment Ji Ling was announced. Xuande rose to leave, but Lü Bu checked him. "I have made a point," he explained, "of bringing you two together. Trust me in this." Xuande remained puzzled and ill at ease.

Ji Ling entered the tent, saw Xuande in his seat, and pulled back in fright, breaking free of Lü Bu's attendants. Lü Bu stepped forward and dragged him back as if he were lifting a child. "You're going to kill me?" asked Ji Ling. "Of course not," Lü Bu replied. "Then you must be going to kill the big-eared one?"[4] Ji Ling responded. "Wrong again," said Lü Bu. "What is all this for?" Ji Ling asked. "Xuande and I are brothers," Bu explained. "You threatened him, and I have come to save him." "So you will kill me!" Ji Ling exclaimed. "Certainly not!" said Lü Bu. "I have always preferred resolving conflicts to fighting, and that's what I intend doing now." "By what method, may I ask?" Ji Ling said. "We shall let Heaven decide your quarrel!" Lü Bu declared as he hauled Ji Ling back into the tent. He placed Ji Ling on his left, Xuande on his right, and proceeded to call for wine and food. The two warriors kept a wary eye on one another.

After several rounds of wine Lü Bu said, "For goodness' sake call this off." Xuande sat silent. Ji Ling responded, "I have a mandate from my lord Yuan Shu, who gave me an army of one hundred thousand to capture Liu Bei. This cannot be 'called off.'" Zhang Fei drew his sword and said grimly, "Our men are fewer, but you look like child's play compared to a million Yellow Scarves! Just try and do something to my elder brother!" Lord Guan restrained Zhang Fei, saying, "Let's see what General Lü Bu has in mind before we start the bloodletting."

"I called you here," Lü Bu continued, "to settle things. I cannot allow you to slaughter one another." But Ji Ling expressed discontent; and Zhang Fei welcomed war. Letting his anger show, Lü Bu shouted, "Bring me my halberd!" Ji Ling and Xuande paled as he wrapped his huge hands around the shaft. "I insist you cease this quarrel," Lü Bu cried. "It is in Heaven's hands." He handed his weapon to his attendants and had it planted in the ground, well in front of the entrance to his camp. Then, turning to his guests, he said, "The entrance is one hundred fifty paces away. If I hit the small side blade with one shot, you will call off your war. If I miss, you are free to return to your camps and prepare for battle. If either of you refuses these terms, I will join the other against him." Ji Ling reckoned to himself, "A shot like that is impossible. I might as well agree and complete my mission when he fails." He gave his consent, and Xuande was pleased to concur.

Lü Bu bade them remain seated for a last round of wine. Then he called for his bow. Xuande secretly prayed for his success. Lü Bu threw back his sleeve, fitted an arrow to the string, and drew the bow full stretch. "Hit!" he cried as he shot. From a bow drawn wide as the full-orbed moon an arrow sped like a shooting star. A perfect hit! Round the camp the commanders cheered. A poet has left these lines of admiration:

> With an immortal shot, one rarely seen on earth,
> Lü Bu saved the day at the war camp gates:
> A marksman to shame Hou Yi, downer of nine suns,

And bidding fair to outclass Yang Youji.
Tiger-thewed, he drew till the bowstring groaned.
Hawk-feathered, the flying dart struck home.
The leopard-tail quivered on the halberd haft:
One hundred thousand men untied their gear.[5]

Lü Bu laughed heartily, threw his bow aside, and took his guests by the hand. "Thus Heaven commands you to desist!" he said, calling for more wine. Each man quaffed a great flagonful. Xuande was thankful for a lucky escape, and Ji Ling held his peace. Presently he said, "General, I dare not disobey. But my master will never believe this!" "I'll write him," said Lü Bu. More wine was passed round. After Ji Ling departed with the letter, Lü Bu reminded Xuande, "If not for me, you would have been done for." Xuande thanked Lü Bu and left with his brothers. The next day the war camps were disbanded.

Ji Ling returned to Huainan, presented Lü Bu's letter to Yuan Shu, and described the outcome of his campaign. "Is that how Lü Bu repays me for the grain I sent," Yuan Shu ranted, "saving Liu Bei with a child's trick? I am going to march on the two of them!" "Do not be so impetuous, my lord," Ji Ling urged. "Lü Bu is a powerful warrior, and he controls Xuzhou. He and Liu Bei may prove too strong for us. I hear, though, that Lü Bu's wife, Lady Yan, has a daughter ready for marriage; and you have a son who has come of age—that's a way to ally your two houses. If Lü Bu agrees, he'll have to kill Xuande because 'Strangers never come before relatives.'" Yuan Shu agreed and sent Han Yin with appropriate gifts to arrange it.

Han Yin presented himself to Lü Bu, saying, "My master, long your admirer, seeks your treasured daughter's hand in behalf of his son in order to bind the two houses in marriage as the states of Qin and Jin did in ancient times."[6] Lü Bu took up the proposal with Lady Yan, the girl's mother.

Lü Bu had three wives. His principal wife was Lady Yan; Diaochan was his concubine; and later he had married a daughter of Cao Bao's when he was Xuande's guest in Xiaopei. His second wife died young and without issue; Diaochan had never borne a child. Lady Yan's daughter was Lü Bu's only child and the dearest object of his affections. In response to Han Yin's offer Lady Yan said to Lü Bu, "Yuan Shu has dominated the region below the River Huai for a long time. From such a powerful base he should become emperor sooner or later. Our daughter could be empress. But how many sons does he have?" "Only the one," Lü Bu replied. "Then give your consent at once!" she said. "Empress or no empress, our hold on Xuzhou will be strengthened." His course decided, Lü Bu treated Han Yin royally and agreed to the marriage. Han Yin reported to Yuan Shu, who sent the envoy back to Xuzhou with betrothal gifts. Lü Bu accepted them with pleasure. He feasted Han Yin and lodged him in the guesthouse.

The next day Lü Bu's chief adviser, Chen Gong, paid call on Han Yin. The formalities concluded, Chen Gong dismissed the attendants and asked, "Who proposed this marriage alliance? Is the purpose to take Xuande's head?" Han Yin shuddered. He then rose and said, "I beg you, do not breathe a word of it." "Of course not," Chen Gong assured him. "Only, if things are delayed, someone else may see the point and interfere." "What can be done?" asked Han Yin. "I'll try to get Lü Bu to send his daughter off today," said Chen Gong. "That will seal the marriage." "Then Lord Yuan will be all the more deeply in your debt," Han Yin said appreciatively.

Chen Gong went directly to Lü Bu and said, "I was delighted to hear that your daughter is promised to Yuan Shu. When is the wedding?" "The arrangements will be made in due course with due deliberation," was the reply. "In ancient times," Chen Gong went on, "the time interval between the engagement and the nuptial ceremony was strictly defined: for the emperor, one year; for the fief-lords, six months; for the noble houses, one season; for commoners, one month." "Heaven," said Lü Bu, "has bestowed the royal seal on Yuan Shu, and in time he is bound to become emperor. Doesn't it seem right to observe the one-year waiting period?" "No," answered Chen Gong. "Six months, then?" asked Lü Bu. "Not that long either," Chen Gong said. "Then it will have to be one season," said Lü Bu, "as stipulated for a noble house." "I'm afraid not," was Chen Gong's answer. "Do you really expect me to follow the precedent set for commoners?" Lü Bu demanded. "By no means," said Chen Gong. "Well then," Lü Bu rejoined, "what do you have in mind?"

"The lords of the realm," Chen Gong explained, "are striving for supremacy. Won't an alliance with Yuan Shu arouse jealousy? Selecting an auspicious day in the remote future will only give someone the opportunity to ambush the bridal procession. Where would that leave us? If you had not already consented, the matter could be dropped. But since you have, we must act before the lords hear of it. That is my advice. Send your daughter to Shouchun and sequester her; then select the day and conclude the marriage. Nothing can go wrong."

Lü Bu took this advice gladly. He informed his wife of the change in plan, prepared the trousseau, put horses and carriage in order, and sent the girl off the same night. Han Yin, together with Lü Bu's generals Song Xian and Wei Xu, rode escort. Gongs and drums sounded as the marchers left the city. Chen Deng's (i.e., Yuanlong's) father, Gui, an elderly gentleman living at home in retirement, heard the noise of the procession and, learning the reason, said, "The 'family before strangers' scheme! Liu Xuande is done for!"

Despite his ailment, the old man took himself to see Lü Bu.[7] "What brings you, venerable sir?" asked Lü Bu. "I hear your death is imminent, General," answered Chen Gui, "and I have come to condole." "What are you talking about?" Lü Bu snapped. "Some time ago," replied Chen Gui, "Yuan Shu sent presents, hoping you would kill Xuande. But your marksmanship got Xuande out of that. Now he's back again seeking an alliance through marriage. He must want your daughter as a hostage so he can attack Xuande. Once Xiaopei falls to him, Xuzhou is no longer safe. After the marriage they will come to borrow food or soldiers. If you meet their demands, you will be wearing yourself out for nothing and making enemies into the bargain. If you refuse, you will lose your daughter and find yourself at war with Yuan Shu. Or else, since Yuan Shu has seditious intentions and may declare himself emperor, you could be treated as a relative of the traitor, guilty of high treason, and have to face the world's wrath."

Realizing the sense of Chen Gui's argument, Lü Bu panicked. "So Chen Gong has led me astray!" he cried and ordered Zhang Liao to overtake the bridal carriage—it was already thirty *li* away—force it to return, and seize Han Yin. At the same time he told Yuan Shu to expect his daughter when her trousseau was ready. Chen Gui also wanted Lü Bu to deliver the prisoner, Han Yin, to Cao Cao in the capital at Xuchang, but Lü Bu delayed deciding.[8]

At this point Lü Bu was informed that Liu Xuande was recruiting troops and buying horses for undetermined reasons. "Isn't that what a general normally does?" Lü Bu responded. Then two of his officers, Song Xian and Wei Xu, reported, "At your command we went east of the mountains and bought three hundred splendid mounts, but near Xiaopei thieves took half of them. We found out later their chief was Zhang Fei claiming to be an outlaw." Lü Bu marched at once to Xiaopei. Xuande, bewildered by this turn of events, mustered a force to meet him.

As the opposing lines formed, Xuande rode out. "Elder brother," he said to Lü Bu, "what is the cause of this?" Lü Bu replied angrily, "My bowshot saved you from grave danger. Why are you stealing my horses?" "We're short here," Xuande answered. "I sent all over to buy some. My men would never steal from you." "Can you deny," Lü Bu cried, "that Zhang Fei has stolen one hundred and fifty of my best?" "Yes, I stole them! So what?" Zhang Fei cried, dashing out with spear poised. "Round-eyed rogue," Lü Bu retorted, "this is the final insult!" "You mind my stealing your horses?" Zhang Fei taunted him. "What about your stealing Xuzhou from my brother?" The two warriors said no more. They fought on the field like madmen, exchanging more than one hundred blows. But there was no victor. Xuande, fearful that Zhang Fei might slip, rang the gong recalling all men to Xiaopei. Lü Bu laid siege to the town.

Back inside, Xuande was furious at Zhang Fei. "This is your doing," he said. "Where are their horses?" "At various Buddhist temples," Fei replied. Xuande sent a man to Lü Bu offering to return the horses and make peace. Lü Bu was inclined to accept the offer, but Chen Gong argued, "Liu Bei is your nemesis. Kill him now." Lü Bu accordingly attacked Xiaopei with renewed ferocity.

Xuande consulted Mi Zhu and Sun Qian. "Cao Cao's worst enemy is Lü Bu," Sun Qian said. "Let's flee to the capital and place our fate in Cao's hands. Perhaps he'll even give us some troops to fight Bu. This is our best chance." "Who can take us through the blockade?" Xuande asked. "Let me try," answered Zhang Fei.

Under a bright moon, with Zhang Fei in the lead, Lord Guan bringing up the rear, and Xuande in between, they left Xiaopei by the north gate in the dead of night. Song Xian and Wei Xu accosted them, but Zhang Fei swept Lü Bu's two officers aside in a brief and bloody exchange. Thus the brothers broke through the encirclement. Zhang Liao tried to attack the rear, but Lord Guan checked him. Lü Bu, instead of pursuing, entered Xiaopei, calmed the populace, and then returned to Xuzhou, leaving General Gao Shun in command of the conquered town.[9]

Xuande pitched camp outside the capital and sent Sun Qian ahead to appeal to Cao Cao for refuge. "Xuande and I are brothers," Cao Cao said and declared him welcome. The following day Xuande left his two brothers outside the walls and, accompanied by Mi Zhu and Sun Qian, presented himself to Cao Cao, who received him as an honored guest. To Xuande's account of Lü Bu's conduct Cao Cao responded, "Lü Bu is no man of honor. Let's work together to get rid of him, worthy brother." Xuande expressed thanks. Cao Cao feasted his guest until a late hour and then saw him off.

Afterward Xun Wenruo said, "Liu Bei is someone who should be dealt with now, before he becomes a threat." Cao Cao said nothing. Xun Wenruo left and Guo Jia entered. "Wenruo advised me to kill Xuande," Cao said to him. "What should I do?" "I oppose it," Guo Jia replied. "Your Lordship has raised an army to uphold the house of Han and rid the people of oppression. Your reputation for good faith has attracted many outstanding men. Still, we worry that more may not come and lend their support. To kill a renowned hero like Liu Bei in his moment of distress will earn us a reputation for harming the worthy, and many capable men throughout the realm will choose not to join us. Who will help you restore order in the empire then? Eliminating this one threat will alienate many. In this situation you must weigh the pros and cons." "Your advice suits me well," said Cao Cao, pleased.[10]

The next day Cao Cao prepared a memorial to the Emperor recommending Xuande as protector of Yuzhou. But Cheng Yu advised, "Liu Bei will not remain long under anybody. You'd better deal with him before it is too late." "At a time," Cao Cao replied, "when we are calling for outstanding men to serve us, we cannot afford to lose the world by killing one person. Guo Jia agrees with me on this." Thus Cao Cao rejected Cheng Yu's advice. He gave Xuande three thousand men and ten thousand bushels of grain and sent him off to his new post with instructions to round up any soldiers near Xiaopei and continue the war against Lü Bu. After arriving in Yuzhou, Xuande maintained liaison with Cao Cao.

Cao Cao himself had mustered a force to march against Lü Bu when an urgent message came: "Zhang Ji marched east through the pass to attack Nanyang and was killed by a stray arrow; his nephew Zhang Xiu assumed command of his army and has Jia Xu for an adviser; Zhang Xiu has allied with Liu Biao and occupied Wancheng in order to enter the capital and seize the Emperor." Cao Cao wanted to take action against the invader from the west but feared Lü Bu would attack his capital. Xun Wenruo said, "The problem is not difficult. Lü Bu is no strategist and lives only for gain. Appoint him to high office and send gifts, ordering him at the same time to settle his differences with Liu Bei. Lü Bu will be content and stay put. He has no larger ambitions." "Well said," replied Cao Cao and sent Imperial Envoy Wang Ze to Xuzhou to carry out the plan.

Free of danger from the south, Cao Cao fielded an army of one hundred and fifty thousand to chastise Zhang Xiu in the name of the Emperor. The force consisted of three field armies; Xiahou Dun had the vanguard. They camped at the River Yu.[11] Jia Xu advised Zhang Xiu: "We are outnumbered. Surrender and deliver your soldiers to Cao Cao." Zhang Xiu saw the wisdom of the suggestion and sent Jia Xu to make the offer.

Cao Cao admired Jia Xu and was struck by his apt answer to every question. He offered to employ him as a counselor, but Jia Xu declined. "In the past," Jia Xu answered, "I committed a grave mistake by serving Li Jue, who rebelled against His Majesty. Now I am in the service of Zhang Xiu. He considers my views and follows my plans. I cannot cast him aside." The next day Jia Xu introduced Zhang Xiu to Cao Cao, who treated him generously. Cao Cao allowed Xiu to station some of his troops in Wancheng itself and the remainder outside the city. The encampments with their palisades stretched for more than ten li.

During this time Zhang Xiu feasted Cao Cao in Wancheng every day. Once Cao Cao retired drunk and discreetly asked his chamber attendants if there were any courtesans in the town. Cao Cao's nephew Anmin whispered obligingly, "I noticed a rare beauty yesterday near the local inn, the widow of Zhang Ji, Xiu's uncle." On Cao Cao's orders Anmin took fifty armed guards and brought her back. She proved as attractive as Cao Cao had anticipated. He asked her name. "Your servant," she replied, "is from the Zou family and was married to the late Zhang Ji." "Do you know who I am, my lady?" Cao Cao inquired. "Your prestigious name, Your Excellency, has been long known to me," she responded, "and I am honored this evening to be able to pay my respects in person." "It was in your behalf," Cao Cao said, "that I accepted Zhang Xiu's surrender. Otherwise, the entire clan would have been executed." Prostrating herself, Lady Zou replied, "I am truly grateful for your gracious reprieve." "To have met you today," Cao Cao went on, "is a blessing from Heaven. I would like you to share my mat and pillow this evening and then accompany me back to the capital where you will enjoy luxury in tranquility. What is your answer?"

Lady Zou accepted gladly and spent the night in Cao Cao's quarters. "I must not stay too long in town," she said. "My nephew Zhang Xiu will suspect something and others will talk." "Tomorrow, then," said Cao, "we will go to my camp." The next day Cao Cao moved his quarters to the central army camp and had Dian Wei stand guard. No one was allowed to enter unless summoned. Thus protected, Cao Cao took his pleasure day after day and gave no thought to returning to Xuchang.

The romance was reported to Zhang Xiu. "The scoundrel!" he cried in anger. "His insolence is unbearable!" He turned to Jia Xu for counsel. "Keep it absolutely secret," Jia Xu cautioned. "When Cao Cao shows up for talks, then . . ." And he whispered in Zhang Xiu's ear.

The following day Zhang Xiu went to Cao Cao's tent and said, "Many of the newly surrendered troops have run away. I request permission to station my men inside your camp lest more flee." Cao approved, and Xiu moved into the encampment, divided his forces into four groups, and bided his time. But the fierce courage of Dian Wei, Cao's personal guard, daunted Zhang Xiu. Seeing no easy way to get near him, Zhang Xiu spoke to Hu Juer, one of the four group commanders.

Hu Juer was a man with the physical strength to lift a weight of five hundred *jin* or to ride seven hundred *li* in a single day. He offered the following plan: "Dian Wei is to be feared only for his two iron halberds. My lord, invite him to dine tomorrow and send him home drunk. I will slip in among his men and find a way to remove the weapons. That should draw his sting." Zhang Xiu approved and prepared his archers and armored men. The other three groups were alerted. Zhang Xiu then hosted Dian Wei at the banquet, entertained him attentively, and sent him home late and drunk. Meanwhile, Hu Juer had slipped into the camp where Cao Cao and Lady Zou were carousing.

Cao Cao was the first to hear voices and the sound of restless horses. He sent a guard outside who reported that Zhang Xiu's men were making night rounds. Cao Cao suspected nothing. Toward the second watch there was an outcry: a cartload of hay had caught fire. "It's only an accident!" Cao Cao shouted. "Don't panic!" Moments later fire broke out on all sides. Cao Cao called for Dian Wei, but the mighty warrior was in a drunken stupor. Wakening to the clamor, he leaped to his feet groping for the halberds.

Zhang Xiu's men were at the front gate, mounted and brandishing lances. Grabbing a sword from a nearby soldier as the enemy poured in, Dian Wei advanced and cut down twenty men. The horsemen drew back, but the foot soldiers came forward. On either side spears poked up like reeds. Armorless, Dian Wei fought on valiantly, taking scores of cuts. Then his sword cracked and he threw it aside. He picked up two of the enemy bodily and wielded them as weapons, felling eight or nine. Zhang Xiu's rebels kept their distance and shot at him, but Dian Wei held the gate despite the pelting arrows. Another group of soldiers burst in from behind and speared him through the back. Three or four howls broke from Dian Wei's lips. Then he expired, his blood soaking the ground where he fell. Even after he was dead, no one dared pass through the front gate.

Dian Wei's heroic defense had enabled Cao Cao to ride out by the rear gate. Cao Anmin followed on foot. Cao Cao had an arrow in his right shoulder; his horse was also wounded. Luckily the powerful Fergana steed could run despite great pain and carried Cao Cao to the edge of the River Yu. But the pursuers overtook Cao Anmin and cut him to pieces. Cao Cao urged his mount through the waves; it was climbing the far shore when an arrow pierced its eye. The horse collapsed under its rider. Cao's eldest son, Ang, gave his horse to his father, and Cao Cao escaped; but Cao Ang fell in a fresh hail of arrows.[12] On the road Cao Cao met up with his commanders and they regrouped.

Taking advantage of the confusion, some Qingzhou soldiers under Xiahou Dun began raiding nearby villages.[13] Commandant Yu Jin, Queller of Bandits, tried to protect the villagers, leading his own men in wiping out the plunderers. The Qingzhou troops then ran back to Cao Cao, flung themselves to the ground, and tearfully reported the "rebellion." Indignant at Yu Jin's "betrayal," Cao Cao ordered generals Xiahou Dun, Xu Chu, Li Dian, and Yue Jin to prepare to fight the "traitor."[14]

In the distance, Yu Jin saw Cao Cao and his followers approaching and entrenched himself behind a moat. Someone said, "The Qingzhou troops told Cao you rebelled. Now that he's coming, why are you digging in instead of going to him to clear yourself?" "Those thugs could get here at any moment. I have to be ready. Preparedness counts for much more than explanations." No sooner were Yu Jin's defenses in place than Zhang Xiu attacked. Yu Jin met the enemy personally in front of his fortifications and drove them back. Inspired by his courage, Yu Jin's commanders dealt Zhang Xiu such a devastating defeat that he fled and threw himself on the mercy of Liu Biao.[15]

After the battle Yu Jin came before Cao Cao and explained that he had attacked the Qingzhou troops for despoiling the peasants. "Then why," Cao asked him, "did you fortify before coming to me?" Yu Jin explained his reasons, and Cao Cao concluded, "A commander who can array his men and construct his defenses in the heat of battle, unmoved by slander, undaunted by toil, and then carry the day—even the great generals of old hardly surpass that!" Cao Cao rewarded Yu Jin with a pair of gold vessels and appointed him lord of Yishou precinct. And he criticized Xiahou Dun for not disciplining his men. Then he performed sacrifice for his fallen comrade, Dian Wei, personally leading the lamentations and presenting the wine. At the ceremony he turned to his commanders and said, "I have lost my eldest son and my dear nephew. But the loss of Dian Wei hurts most." The assembly was deeply moved. The next day Cao Cao gave the order to return to the capital.[16]

•   •   •   •

Meanwhile Wang Ze, bearing Cao Cao's gifts, reached Xuzhou. Lü Bu received him, unsealed the edict appointing him General Who Calms the East, and accepted the seal and cord of office. Wang Ze also handed him Cao Cao's own letter instructing him to settle his differences with Xuande. Lü Bu listened with relish as the envoy described Cao Cao's profound regard for him. At that moment a messenger from Yuan Shu told Lü Bu, "Yuan Shu will eventually become emperor and establish his heir apparent. He expects the consort of the crown prince to proceed at once to her destination." "How dare that traitor!" Lü Bu cried. He killed Yuan Shu's envoy and clapped Han Yin, Yuan Shu's representative, into a cangue. He then dispatched Chen Deng with a letter to the Emperor acknowledging his appointment; he also sent the prisoner under guard along with Wang Ze to the capital as an indication of his gratitude. At the same time he wrote to Cao Cao expressing his interest in being advanced to protector of Xuzhou.

Cao Cao was delighted to learn that the planned marriage between Lü Bu's daughter and Yuan Shu's son had been canceled. He publicly put Han Yin to death. Chen Deng confided to Cao Cao, "Lü Bu is a jackal, fierce but foolhardy, and fickle in his loyalties. Do not wait too long to deal with him." "I am well aware," Cao Cao replied, "of his wolfish ambition. No one can keep his support for long. But only you and your father really understand the situation. I shall need your help against him." "Should you choose to act, Your Excellency," Chen Deng responded, "I shall work with you from within." To show his appreciation Cao Cao appointed Chen Deng governor of Guangling and awarded Chen Gui, Deng's father, a sinecure that paid a governor's salary of two thousand piculs of grain annually. As Chen Deng took his leave, Cao Cao touched his arm and said, "The situation in the east is now in your hands." Chen Deng nodded, confirming his intention to serve Cao Cao.

Chen Deng returned to Xuzhou, and Lü Bu questioned him on the outcome of his visit. "My father was given a free income," Chen Deng said, "and I was made governor of Guangling." Lü Bu was infuriated. "You solicited rank and emolument for yourself without mentioning my confirmation as protector of Xuzhou? It was your own father who convinced me to make peace with Cao Cao and break off the nuptials with Yuan Shu's son. You have achieved eminence, all right, but what have I got out of it? You've sold me out!"

Lü Bu drew his sword, but Chen Deng only laughed as he said, "How foolish can you be, General?" "What do you mean?" asked Lü Bu. "When I saw Cao Cao," Chen Deng said, "I told him to provide for you as for a tiger that needs his fill of meat lest hunger drive him to bite someone. 'No, my friend,' Cao answered me, smiling. 'We'll provide for Lü Bu as if he were a hunting hawk that must be kept hungry when hares and foxes are running about. Well fed, he'll just soar off contented.' 'Who are the hares and foxes?' I asked, and he replied, 'Yuan Shu of Huainan, Sun Ce of the Southland, Yuan Shao of Jizhou, Liu Biao of Jingzhou, Liu Zhang of Yizhou, and Zhang Lu of Hanzhong—every one of them fair game.'" Tossing his sword aside, Lü Bu laughed and said, "Cao Cao knows me well!" As they spoke, news of Yuan Shu's invading army was brought in. Lü Bu was alarmed. Indeed:

> The alliance fell through and war followed;
> Marriage plans had brought not peace but another trial by arms.

Lü Bu was facing many dangers. Could he survive them?
READ ON.

17

Yuan Shu Fields Seven Armies;
Cao Cao Joins Forces with Three Generals

YUAN SHU, POSSESSOR OF HUAINAN'S EXTENSIVE DOMINIONS and ample wealth as well as the royal seal Sun Ce had left as a pledge, now wanted to usurp the throne of Han. To his followers he declared: "The Supreme Ancestor of the Han, Gao Zu, started as a precinct head; yet the realm came into his hands. Now, four hundred years later, the allotted span of the dynasty is ending and the world seethes with rebellion. We Yuans, holders of highest office for four generations, enjoy the people's confidence. It would accord with the will of Heaven and satisfy the hopes of men for me to assume the dragon throne."

First Secretary Yan Xiang said, "That cannot be done! Hou Ji, high ancestor of the Zhou house, had great virtue and merit. Yet even in the last years of the Shang dynasty the Zhou remained loyal to the ruling house—though King Wen had the allegiance of two-thirds of the realm and could have overthrown the Shang. Your Lordship, the Yuan family, though noble for many generations, lacks the distinction of the Zhou ruling family; while the house of Han, however feeble, is guilty of no tyranny resembling the Shang's when the Zhou finally overthrew it. Your elevation is therefore unthinkable."

Yuan Shu, profoundly angered, replied, "The Yuan line springs from the Chen; the Chen descends from Shun.[1] The sequence of the elements dictates that the earth sign of the Chen will supplant the fire sign of the Han. Moreover, it has been predicted that whoever follows the Han will 'take the high road': my style, Gonglu, or Lord's Way, fits the prognostication. Finally, we hold the imperial seal. Thus for me to decline the leadership of the realm would be to turn against Heaven. My decision stands. Whoever says more, dies."

Yuan Shu then established the reign period Zhong Shi[2] and created a secretariat and other state offices. Borne in a dragon-and-phoenix carriage, he performed the imperial rituals at the northern and southern limits of the city.[3] He made Feng Fang's daughter his empress, his son crown prince, and sent an envoy to Xuzhou to speed the wedding with Lü Bu's daughter. At that point he learned that Lü Bu had already delivered the go-between, Han Yin, to the capital, where Cao Cao had had him executed.

In great anger Yuan Shu organized an army of over two hundred thousand under the leadership of Regent-Marshal Zhang Xun: his object, to conquer Xuzhou. There were seven field armies: the first, led by Zhang Xun, in the center; the second, led by Senior General Qiao Rui, on the left flank; the third, under Senior General Chen Ji, on the right; the fourth, under Deputy General Lei Bo, on the left; the fifth, under Deputy General Chen Lan, on the right; the sixth, led by Han Xian, a general who had surrendered, on the left; and the seventh, led by another general who had surrendered, Yang Feng, on the right.[4] Able commanders served each leader.

The army began marching north on the appointed day. Yuan Shu elevated Jin Shang, imperial inspector of Yanzhou, to the position of grand commandant so that he could supervise the supply of the seven field armies; but Jin Shang refused the promotion, and Yuan Shu had him executed. Ji Ling was put in charge of support for the army. Yuan Shu himself took command of thirty thousand men and assigned Li Feng, Liang Gang, and Yue Jiu to drive the lines forward and to direct reinforcement operations.

Lü Bu's scouts brought word that Zhang Xun was advancing on the main road to Xuzhou; Qiao Rui, toward Xiaopei; Chen Ji, toward Yidu; Lei Bo, toward Langye; Chen Lan, toward Jieshi; Han Xian, toward Xiapi; and Yang Feng, toward Junshan. The seven field armies made some fifty li per day and plundered the towns and villages along the way. Lü Bu called upon his counselors. Chen Gui and his son, Deng (now in league with Cao Cao), were present. Chen Gong, Lü Bu's chief adviser, said, "Chen Gui and Chen Deng are responsible for Xuzhou's present troubles, currying favor with the court for their own ends and leaving you to face the consequences, General. Deliver their heads to Yuan Shu, and his armies should retreat." Lü Bu agreed and ordered father and son, Chen Gui and Chen Deng, arrested.

Chen Deng scoffed aloud. "What are you afraid of?" he cried. "Those seven armies look like seven piles of rotten straw to me—beneath contempt!" "If you think you can defeat them," Lü Bu responded, "I will spare you." "General," Chen Deng asserted, "I have a plan to preserve Xuzhou and guarantee its future." "We are listening," Lü Bu said. "Yuan Shu's army," Chen Deng went on, "though large, is a motley mass with no bonds of mutual trust. If we defend the city straightforwardly while conducting surprise raids, we can defeat them easily. And I have something else up my sleeve which will keep Xuzhou safe and even allow us to capture Yuan Shu himself."

"How will you proceed?" Lü Bu asked. "Two of the generals, Yang Feng and Han Xian," Chen Deng replied, "who had long been faithful to the Han, went over to Yuan Shu only from fear of Cao Cao. They had no choice. Yuan Shu shows them no respect, and they are unhappy in his service. A letter should be enough to secure their collaboration. If you arrange for Liu Bei's support as well, Yuan Shu is yours!" "You will have to take the letter yourself," Lü Bu said, and Chen Deng agreed. After petitioning the Emperor and communicating with Liu Bei in Xuzhou, Lü Bu sent Chen Deng to Xiapi.

Han Xian arrived and camped. Chen Deng went to see him. Han Xian asked, "You are Lü Bu's man, are you not? What brings you here?" "I am a courtier in the service of the mighty Han," Deng replied with a smile. "How can you call me 'Lü Bu's man'? You yourself, General, once served the Han but now serve a rebel, wiping out the devotion to the Emperor you once showed when you helped him escape from Chang'an.[5] I should choose a different course if I were you, General. Besides, in Yuan Shu you will find a most mistrustful master, and he will do you in—unless you act first." Han Xian sighed. "I want to be loyal to the Han, but there's no way back." Chen Deng then produced Lü Bu's letter soliciting his cooperation. "I am not surprised," Han Xian said. "You return first. Yang Feng and I will move on Yuan Shu together. Look for a signal fire. Lü Bu should then attack in force." Chen Deng took leave of Han Xian and reported to Lü Bu.

Lü Bu deployed his troops in five field armies. Gao Shun marched to Xiaopei against Qiao Rui; Chen Gong to Yidu against Chen Ji; Zhang Liao and Zang Ba to Langye against Lei Bo; Song Xian and Wei Xu to Jieshi against Chen Lan. Lü Bu himself led a force on to the main road to confront Zhang Xun. Each army comprised ten thousand men. Other troops were left guarding the city.

Lü Bu advanced and camped thirty *li* from the city. Zhang Xun saw he could not prevail and camped twenty *li* away to await reinforcements. It was night. As the second watch began, Han Xian and Yang Feng had their men set fires and guide Lü Bu's soldiers into the camp. Zhang Xun's army quickly became disorganized. Lü Bu attacked in full force, and Zhang Xun fled. Lü Bu chased him until daybreak. He then met up with Ji Ling's reinforcements, and the two armies prepared to engage. But Han Xian and Yang Feng attacked and drove off Ji Ling's army. Lü Bu in pursuit took a heavy toll of the fleeing enemy.

At that moment Lü Bu saw a band of warriors approaching from behind a hill, marking out with flags and banners a detachment of horsemen holding high the imperial regalia. There were streamers showing the dragon and phoenix, and the sun and moon; feathered standards with the key stars of the four quadrants as well as the five directions of earth; and there were the gold mace and the silver battle-axe, the gilded axe and the white yak-tail command banner. Beneath a golden parasol draped with thin buff silk Yuan Shu rode in imperial yellow armor, a knife swinging from each wrist.[6]

Yuan Shu came before his battle line and swore, "Lü Bu! Traitor and slave!" Lü Bu raised his halberd and advanced. Yuan Shu's commander Li Feng engaged him. In a brief clash Lü Bu speared Li Feng's hand; he dropped his weapon and fled. Lü Bu's army, in a massive onslaught, dealt Yuan Shu a devastating defeat, capturing countless horses and pieces of armor. Yuan Shu had fled several *li* when a fresh detachment led by Lord Guan came from behind a hill and intercepted him. "Renegade!" Guan shouted defiantly. "Prepare to die!" Yuan Shu panicked. His remaining ranks broke under Guan's assault. Finally Yuan Shu escaped to his home region below the River Huai, accompanied by a remnant of his army.[7]

To celebrate the victory Lü Bu invited Lord Guan, Han Xian, Yang Feng, and a number of other leaders to a feast in Xuzhou. He also rewarded the soldiers of his five armies. The next day Lord Guan took leave. Lü Bu recommended Han Xian as protector of Yidu, and Yang Feng as protector of Langye. Lü Bu had wanted to keep the two generals in Xuzhou, but Chen Gui opposed it, arguing, "Establishing them east of the mountains will make all the towns there acknowledge your authority." Convinced, Lü Bu dispatched the two generals. But Chen Deng was puzzled by his father's maneuver. "Why didn't you want them here to support us against Lü Bu?" he asked. "If they sided with him," Chen Gui replied, "we would only be sharpening the tiger's claws." Chen Deng bowed to his father's wisdom.

Back in Huainan, Yuan Shu asked Sun Ce for troops to avenge his defeat. Sun Ce refused the request outright. "With *my* royal seal," he ranted, "Yuan Shu has arrogated the name of emperor, breaking his allegiance to the ruling house. It is high treason! And I mean to wage war and bring him to justice. Does the traitor expect my help?" Yuan Shu exploded with rage on receiving Sun Ce's rejection. "That milksop!" he cried. "How dare he! I will strike first!" Only Senior Adviser Yang Dajiang's strenuous opposition persuaded Shu to desist.

•   •   •   •   •

After sending his reply to Yuan Shu, Sun Ce defended the strategic points on the Great River as a precaution. At this juncture Cao Cao's envoy arrived in the Southland appointing Sun Ce governor of Kuaiji and authorizing him to chastise Yuan Shu by force of arms. Sun Ce and his advisers were eager for action, but Senior Adviser Zhang Zhao argued, "Despite his recent defeat, Yuan Shu has too many men and supplies for us to risk attack. Why not write back to Cao Cao urging *him* to march south against Yuan Shu, while we coordinate from the rear? Between the two armies Yuan Shu will be crushed; if we miscalculate, we can look to Cao for help." Sun Ce put this proposition in his reply to Cao Cao.

Back in the capital after being routed by Zhang Xiu, Cao Cao built a shrine to honor the memory of the late lamented warrior Dian Wei. He appointed Dian Wei's son Man to the Imperial Corps and took the lad into his own home. Cao Cao received Sun Ce's letter at the same time as a report that Yuan Shu, pressed by shortages, was plundering Chenliu, Cao's home district. Cao mustered an army and marched south, hoping to profit from Yuan Shu's difficulties. Cao Ren stayed behind to protect the capital; all other generals joined the campaign. Cao Cao's force came to one hundred and seventy thousand, and he had over one thousand wagons loaded with grain and supplies. As he set out, he informed Sun Ce, Liu Xuande, and Lü Bu of his intentions.[8]

Protector Liu Xuande greeted Cao Cao at the boundary of his province, Yuzhou, and was invited into the prime minister's camp. After the amenities, Xuande presented Cao Cao with two severed heads. "Who were these men?" Cao asked in astonishment. "Han Xian and Yang Feng," Xuande answered. "Why did you kill them?" Cao asked. "Lü Bu's orders," was the reply. "They let their soldiers run riot in the villages of Yidu and Langye, counties they were sent to govern, so I invited them to a banquet to discuss matters. While the wine was circulating, I dropped my cup as a signal, and Lord Guan and Zhang Fei killed them. We have accepted the surrender of their men. Today I come to beg forgiveness."

"You have rid the dynasty of a great evil," Cao Cao said, "and thus rendered a great service. There is no offense to forgive." He rewarded Xuande richly, and both armies proceeded to the boundary of Xuzhou, where Lü Bu met them. Cao Cao consoled Lü Bu and appointed him general of the Left, promising to send the seal of office after returning to Xuchang. Lü Bu was gratified. Cao Cao then assigned Lü Bu to the left and Xuande to the right, while he directed the center. Xiahou Dun and Yu Jin formed the vanguard.

On learning of Cao Cao's arrival, Yuan Shu sent his senior general, Qiao Rui, with fifty thousand men to counter the invaders. The two armies met near Shouchun.[9] Qiao Rui rode out first but was speared and killed by Xiahou Dun; Yuan Shu's army retreated to Shouchun. Sun Ce's boats attacked from the west bank of the river, and Lü Bu struck from the east. Xuande attacked from the south, and Cao Cao, at the head of one hundred and seventy thousand, from the north. Yang Dajiang advised Yuan Shu, "The Shouchun region has suffered flood and drought for the past several years. Food is short everywhere. The people will not tolerate another call to arms, and so the enemy cannot easily be thrown back. We had better stay inside the city and refuse battle. When the enemy's food runs out, they will revolt. In the interim, Your Majesty, take your Royal Guard across the Huai to familiar terrain, and you can avoid their thrust."

On this advice Yuan Shu took the rest of his army and the entire contents of his treasury across the Huai, leaving Li Feng, Yue Jiu, Liang Gang, and Chen Ji defending Shouchun with one hundred thousand troops. Meanwhile, maintaining the siege was proving a heavy burden for Cao Cao's army; it required vast stores of grain, but the surrounding districts, stricken by dearth, could offer no aid. Cao pressed for battle, but General Li Feng kept within the walls. After another month Cao Cao, faced with dwindling supplies, borrowed one hundred thousand bushels of grain from Sun Ce. But he did not distribute it.

During the emergency Granary Officer Wang Hou, who served under Ren Jun, administrator of rations, petitioned Cao Cao: "There is too little to feed so many. What shall we do?" "Distribute short rations," Cao Cao commanded him, "to tide us over." "And if they complain?" asked Wang Hou. "I have provided for that," Cao assured him. The officer gave out reduced rations as ordered. Meanwhile, Cao Cao sent his men around to the camps. From them he learned that soldiers were accusing him of cheating them. Cao Cao then summoned Wang Hou and said, "You have something I would like to borrow to quiet the soldiers. I hope you will not begrudge it." "What do I have," Wang Hou answered, "of use to Your Excellency?" "Your head," Cao replied, "to show the men." "But I have committed no fault!" the officer cried in fright. "I know that," Cao said. "I must act, or the army will revolt. I will see after your family personally, so have no concern on their account." Before Wang Hou could say more, the executioners were already pushing him out. They cut off his head and hung it from a pole with a signboard reading, "Wang Hou: Duly Punished by Military Law for Purposefully Assigning Short Rations and Stealing from the Granary." This measure improved the troops' morale.[10]

The next day Cao Cao ordered all camp commanders, "Work together and destroy the city in three days' time, or I will have you all put to death." Cao Cao went personally to the wall of Shouchun and supervised the filling of the moat with earth and stones. Rocks and arrows rained down from the walls. Two lieutenants tried to get away, but Cao cut them down himself. He then dismounted and joined in the earth-moving work, stirring officers and men to greater efforts. The moat got filled; the troops advanced, overcoming Shouchun's defenders, and gained the wall. Once inside, they killed the guards and opened the gates. Troops swarmed into Shouchun. Yuan Shu's generals were executed publicly. Every building fashioned in the imperial style and all prohibited fascimilies of the royal regalia were burned. The city was then stripped bare.

Cao Cao wanted to pursue Yuan Shu across the Huai, but Xun Wenruo objected: "It's not in our interest to impoverish the farmers and soldiers with further marches when food is as scarce as it has been these past years. I suggest returning to Xuchang until the winter wheat is ripe. We can try again in spring when rations should be dependable." The sudden appearance of a messenger dissuaded Cao Cao from chasing Yuan Shu: "Zhang Xiu has thrown in with Liu Biao and is mounting new attacks. Nanyang and Jiangling are again in revolt. Cao Hong, after losing several battles, cannot control the situation and has begged me to report the emergency." Cao Cao ordered Sun Ce to deploy his troops across the Great River to keep Liu Biao off balance while he hurried back to the capital to plan the battle against Zhang Xiu.

Before leaving, Cao gave Xuande special instructions: he had him station troops in Xiaopei and reestablish fraternal ties and cooperative relations with Lü Bu. After Lü Bu had departed for Xuzhou, Cao took Xuande aside. "I ordered you to Xiaopei," he said, "to 'dig the tiger's pit.' Keep in touch with Chen Gui and Chen Deng, and things should proceed smoothly. I will assist from without."[11]

•   •   •   •   •

Back in Xuchang, Cao Cao learned that Duan Wei had killed Li Jue and that Wu Xi had killed Guo Si, bringing the severed heads to the capital. In addition, Duan Wei was holding two hundred members of Li Jue's household. Cao Cao ordered the whole clan executed in groups at each of the gates and the severed heads posted as a warning. The people cheered the punishment of the two generals who had attacked the western capital and forced Emperor Xian to flee.

The restoration of order and tranquility was celebrated at a grand court banquet. Emperor Xian ascended the ceremonial hall and presided. Duan Wei was made General Who Purges Sedition and Wu Xi was made General Who Destroys Villainy. Both thanked Cao Cao for his favor and were sent to secure Chang'an. In a memorial to the throne Cao Cao reported Zhang Xiu's rebellion and declared his intent to suppress it. The Son of Heaven personally saw Cao Cao off with the army in a grand procession to the outskirts of the capital. It was the fourth month of the third year of Jian An (A.D. 198).

Leaving Xun Wenruo in the capital to supervise military operations, Cao Cao directed the main army's advance. The wheat was ripe along the way, but the peasants, frightened by the soldiers, would not work in the fields. Cao Cao circulated a formal letter of assurance to the village elders and local officials: "I hold the Emperor's decree to chastise the rebels and protect the people; for reasons beyond our control we have to march in a harvest season. We shall execute any officer high or low who tramples crops while crossing a field, enforcing military law without mercy or exception. Let no one fear or doubt us." The peasants welcomed the order with open praise and crowded round the approaching armies to pay their respects. Passing through the fields, the officers dismounted and carefully held aside the wheat stalks with their hands.

One day a turtledove flew up and caught the eye of Cao Cao's horse. The horse bolted onto a field and ruined a swath of crop. Cao Cao summoned his first secretary and proposed that his crime be punished. The officer said, "How can we condemn Your Excellency?" "If I violate a law I myself made," Cao Cao declared, "how can I hold my men to it?" He raised his sword to his throat. Soldiers and officers stopped him. Guo Jia said, "According to Confucius' *Spring and Autumn Annals*, 'the law shall not apply to those in the highest positions.'" Cao Cao brooded silently; then he said, "Since the *Spring and Autumn* so specifies, we may waive the death penalty. Let this stand for my head." He cut off his hair with his sword and threw it down for all to see. "The prime minister," messengers explained, displaying Cao's hair, "deserved to die as an example to all for destroying the wheat. In this case his hair has been cut off instead." The entire army was stricken with fear, and regulations were meticulously observed. A poet of later times wrote:

> Ten myriad silver wolves, ten myriad warrior hearts—[12]
> Can one man's voiced command rule this vast army?
> He sheared his locks in lieu of his own head.
> The depths of Cao Man's craft are plain to see.

• • • •

Zhang Xiu learned that Cao Cao was advancing west and requested Liu Biao's support on the southern front. He then went forth to meet Cao Cao, aided by two generals, Lei Xu and Zhang Xian. The opposing battle lines consolidated their ranks as Zhang Xiu rode forth and reviled Cao Cao: "False in virtue, false in loyalty; man of no shame, no integrity! Are you anything more than a beast?" Enraged, Cao Cao sent Xu Chu into battle, and Zhang Xiu sent Zhang Xian to meet him.

In a brief exchange Xu Chu thrust Zhang Xian from his horse and killed him. Zhang Xiu's army went quickly down to defeat, and Cao Cao chased him to the walls of Nanyang. Zhang Xiu entered and sealed the city. Cao Cao laid siege, but the wide moat kept him from approaching. He ordered it filled and then used sacks of soil mixed with straw, sticks, and twigs to make a crude ramp against the wall. He also erected a scaling ladder for spying into the city. Cao Cao himself rode around the wall for three days overseeing the preparations. Finally he ordered earth and brambles piled up at a corner near the west gate, assembled his commanders, and ordered them to climb up. Inside Nanyang, Jia Xu told Zhang Xiu: "I can see what Cao Cao is up to. Let's match his tricks with some of our own." Indeed:

> The strongest to the strong shall yield;
> And schemers to counter-schemers shall fall prey!

Would Jia Xu outsmart Cao Cao a second time?
READ ON.

18

Jia Xu Outwits the Enemy and Carries the Day;
Xiahou Dun Plucks Out and Swallows His Wounded Eye

JIA XU SAW THROUGH CAO CAO'S PLAN and prepared countermeasures. "For three days I have been watching Cao Cao circling and examining the wall," he told Zhang Xiu. "I'm sure he noted those crudely built sections of rammed earth at the southeast corner, as well as the half-wrecked 'antler' barrier of spikes and branches. He knows the southeast corner is vulnerable and has conspicuously piled up wood and grass on the northwest, hoping we'll move our men there so that he can get in over the southeast corner at night." "What do we do?" Zhang Xiu asked. "That's easy enough," Jia Xu replied. "Call up your best men tomorrow. Feed them well, equip them lightly, and hide them in the dwellings near the southeast. Then on the northwest, station civilians disguised as soldiers. Come nightfall, let Cao Cao climb the southeast corner. When his men are all inside, sound the bombard and spring the ambush. Cao Cao will be captured." The plan pleased Zhang Xiu.

The next morning scouts told Cao Cao that Zhang Xiu had rallied his men to defend the northwest, leaving the southeast open. "So they've fallen for it," Cao Cao said. He ordered equipment for digging and climbing readied under cover. During the day he maintained pressure on the northwest, but as night deepened he brought his best troops to the southeast, got across the moat, and broke down the "antler" barrier.

The city was still when Cao Cao's men poured in. The bombard sounded and the ambush commenced. The invaders struggled to retreat, but Zhang Xiu's stalwarts took a bloody toll. Cao Cao's army, shattered, fled dozens of *li*. Zhang Xiu pressed the slaughter until dawn; then he pulled back into the city. Cao Cao's army had lost over fifty thousand men and vast quantities of supplies. Moreover, Lü Qian and Yu Jin were wounded.

The victorious Zhang Xiu, at Jia Xu's insistence, urged Liu Biao by letter to cut off Cao Cao's retreat. Liu Biao wanted to meet the request at once, but scouts informed him that Sun Ce had moved troops into Hukou. Kuai Liang advised Liu Biao: "Sun Ce's deployment around the river is part of Cao Cao's plan. If we don't follow up Zhang Xiu's victory, we will pay for it later." Liu Biao agreed. He assigned Huang Zu to secure Jingzhou's points of entry while he marched to Anzhong to intercept Cao Cao. Zhang Xiu, on getting word that Liu Biao was joining the fight, began harassing Cao Cao's rear.

Cao Cao's army moved slowly. At the River Yu beyond Xiangyang, Cao Cao groaned impulsively. "I couldn't help crying out," he explained to his startled followers. "It was here that I lost General Dian Wei last year." He called a halt and spread a sacrificial feast to mourn the soul of Dian Wei. Cao Cao personally offered incense, weeping as he paid homage. The entire army was profoundly stirred. After the memorial service Cao Cao made offerings for his nephew Cao Anmin and for his son Cao Ang as well as for the soldiers who had fallen in the battle. Even the gallant Fergana horse, shot dead from under Cao, was ritually honored.

The following day Xun Wenruo sent a messenger to inform Cao Cao that Liu Biao, aiding Zhang Xiu, had taken Anzhong to block the retreat. Cao Cao replied in a letter, "We are making only a few *li* each day, and I know Zhang Xiu is close behind. But I have not overlooked him, as you shall see. I will destroy him at Anzhong, rest assured." Then, quickening his pace, Cao Cao came to the outskirts of Anzhong county.

Liu Biao already controlled the strategic points around the city, and Zhang Xiu was closing in rapidly. Cao Cao ordered his men to work all night cutting passages through the strongpoints and placing ambushes there. As dawn broke, Liu Biao and Zhang Xiu linked up. By the small number of Cao Cao's troops they deduced that he had run away; so they rushed into the newly fortified positions, springing Cao's ambushes. Liu Biao and Zhang Xiu suffered a severe defeat. Cao Cao's men now broke through Anzhong's points of access and made camp as Liu Biao and Zhang Xiu strove to reorganize their ranks. "Who expected so treacherous a trap?" said Liu Biao. "We'll have another chance at him," Zhang Xiu answered. They regrouped at Anzhong.

At this point Xun Wenruo relayed an urgent report concerning Yuan Shao's impending attack on the capital, forcing Cao Cao to rush his army home. Zhang Xiu wanted to pursue Cao, but Jia Xu said, "If you do, you will fail." Liu Biao also favored pursuit, arguing, "This is an opportunity not to be lost"; and so the two generals took after Cao Cao with ten thousand men. They overtook Cao's rear guard some ten *li* from Anzhong, where Cao's soldiers dealt them a resounding defeat. After returning, Zhang Xiu said to Jia Xu, "I should have listened to you." "Now," responded Jia Xu, "you can regroup and pursue." "We've just been badly beaten," the two generals said. "How can we go and chase him again?" "This time you will win," was the adviser's reply. "If I prove wrong, my head is yours." Zhang Xiu was persuaded; Liu Biao remained behind. Zhang Xiu defeated Cao's troops and dispersed his supply train, but he could not exploit his advantage: a group of soldiers swarmed out from behind a hill and blocked his advance. Zhang Xiu returned to Anzhong.

Liu Biao questioned Jia Xu: "The first time we lost with our best troops, as you predicted. The second time we sent defeated troops against victorious ones and, as you predicted, won the battle. You proved right twice in opposite circumstances. What was your reasoning?" "It was simple," replied Jia Xu. "You are a fine strategist, but no match for Cao Cao. Though defeated, he would make sure to have crack troops in the rear in case of pursuit: our troops, however excellent, had no chance. I knew we would lose. Cao Cao's sudden retreat, however, must have been caused by a threat to the capital; so, after spoiling our attack, he would have had to get back as quickly as possible and not bother any longer with the rear defense. That's why the second attack succeeded." Liu Biao and Zhang Xiu acknowledged Jia Xu's wisdom. Jia Xu persuaded Liu Biao to return to Jingzhou and Xiu to defend Xiangyang, so that the two could reinforce each other. Thus the two armies parted (it was the summer of A.D. 198).

•   •   •   •   •

As Cao Cao was racing to Xuchang to head off Yuan Shao's invasion, he heard of Zhang Xiu's second pursuit. He dashed to the rear only to find that Zhang Xiu's army had already withdrawn. Harried survivors told Cao, "We were saved when some troops came from behind the hill and blocked the enemy's advance." Cao Cao wanted to meet the rescuer. Spear in hand, the man dismounted, saluting Cao Cao and kneeling. It was Imperial Corps Commander Li Tong (Wenda) from Pingchun in Jiangxia. "I was guarding Runan," Li Tong explained to Cao Cao, "when I heard you were battling Liu Biao and Zhang Xiu; so I've come to help." The grateful Cao Cao awarded him the title Lord of Proven Merit and ordered him to defend the western side of Runan against Liu Biao and Zhang Xiu. Li Tong thanked Cao Cao and went to carry out his mission.

Cao Cao returned to Xuchang, where he apprised the Emperor of Sun Ce's service; the Emperor honored him as General Who Brings Renegades to Justice and awarded him the rank of lord of Wu. Cao Cao sent the imperial decree bestowing these honors to the Southland and directed Sun Ce to harass Liu Biao's positions. Cao Cao returned to his ministerial residence and received all the officials. Afterward Xun Wenruo asked, "Your Excellency went to Anzhong with deliberate slowness. How did you know you would defeat the enemy?" "They had no avenue of retreat," Cao Cao replied, "and were sure to fight to the death, so I took my time and lured them into my traps. The outcome was no surprise." Xun Wenruo saluted Cao's ingenuity.

At this point Guo Jia entered. "Why are you late?" Cao Cao asked. Guo Jia handed him a letter conveying Yuan Shao's request for food and men for his campaign against Gongsun Zan. "I thought Yuan Shao was going to attack us!" Cao Cao exclaimed. "He's come up with another scheme now that I've returned." The arrogant tone of the letter outraged Cao Cao. "I'd love to teach him a lesson," he went on. "But do you think we're strong enough?"

Guo Jia replied, "As you know, Liu Bang, founder of the Han, and his archrival, Xiang Yu, were hardly an even match. But the Supreme Ancestor, Liu Bang, prevailed through superior intelligence, and Xiang Yu, though the stronger, was eventually hunted down. Now then, Yuan Shao has ten weak points, and you have ten advantages. The size of his forces should not intimidate us. Consider. First, Yuan Shao governs with a profusion of rules and regulations; your order is simple and not constraining. Thus, you excel in principles of government. Second, Yuan Shao acts without legitimacy; you lead with the imperial sanction. Thus, your cause is true and honorable. Third, since the reigns of Huan and Ling, court rule has suffered from laxity, and Yuan Shao, too, has the same habit; you require strict discipline. Thus, you excel in administration. Fourth, Yuan Shao is ostensibly tolerant but inwardly envious and awards appointments mainly to his relatives; you are outwardly direct and inwardly understanding and employ men according to their ability. Thus, you excel in judgment. Fifth, Yuan Shao makes many plans but rarely a decision; you formulate a plan and act on it. Thus, you excel in strategy. Sixth, Yuan Shao seeks only to enhance his reputation; you treat others with utter sincerity. Thus, you excel in morality. Seventh, Yuan Shao is solicitous of those close to him, indifferent to those farther away; you have an all-embracing concern. Thus, you excel in humanity. Eighth, Yuan Shao is often misled by petty slander; you are impervious to gossip. Thus, you excel in discretion. Ninth, Yuan Shao does not distinguish right and wrong; you have rules and regulations that are strict and clear. Thus, you excel in civil administration. Tenth, Yuan Shao is inclined to take empty stances but is ignorant of the essentials of warfare; you have won battles even when outnumbered, waging war with uncanny skill. Thus, you excel in arms. You will prevail over Yuan Shao by virtue of these ten points of excellence."

Cao Cao smiled appreciatively. "I don't think," he said, "I am adequate to live up to such a description." "I fully agree with Guo Jia's evaluation," said Xun Wenruo.

"Though Yuan Shao has many troops, need we fear them?" "The most immediate threat," Guo Jia went on, "is Lü Bu, so Yuan Shao's present campaign in the northeast against Gongsun Zan frees us to take care of Lü Bu and clean up the southeast. This done, we can turn our attention to Yuan Shao. That makes the most sense. Otherwise, the minute we attack Yuan Shao, Lü Bu will move against us, creating serious trouble." Cao Cao accepted his advice and began making plans. At Xun Wenruo's suggestion he alerted Liu Xuande. At the same time he sent Yuan Shao's envoy back, granting in the name of the Emperor the highest titles for Yuan Shao: regent, grand commandant, and concurrently chief commander of the four northeastern provinces, Jizhou, Qingzhou, Youzhou, and Bingzhou. Cao Cao also secretly informed Yuan Shao that he would assist him in the campaign against Gongsun Zan. Delighted with Cao Cao's response, Yuan Shao commenced operations.

•   •   •   •

Meanwhile in Xuzhou, Chen Gui and his son Deng, Cao Cao's allies in Lü Bu's camp, praised Lü Bu's virtues fulsomely at every ceremonial occasion. Lü Bu's chief adviser, Chen Gong, disturbed by their blatant flattery, cautioned, "Chen Gui and Chen Deng have been fawning on you, General. Who knows what they're really up to? Be on your guard." "You slander good men for no reason," Lü Bu retorted. Chen Gong left Lü Bu's presence. "If loyal counsel is refused," he said with a sigh, "we're all doomed." It occurred to Chen Gong to seek a new master, but fearing ridicule, he simply marked time in silent discontent.

One day, hunting in the Xiaopei area to dispel his depression, Chen Gong spotted a courier speeding down the main road. His curiosity piqued, Chen Gong and a few of his attendants chased him down. "Whose message do you carry?" he shouted. The man, recognizing Chen Gong, fumbled for an answer, so Chen Gong ordered him searched. He discovered Liu Xuande's reply to Cao Cao's letter. Chen Gong brought message and messenger to Lü Bu, who demanded an explanation. "His Excellency, Cao Cao," the courier said, "had me carry a letter to Inspector Liu of Yuzhou, and this is his answer. I have no idea what it says." Lü Bu unsealed it and read.[1]

> I have your order to prepare to attack Lü Bu, and have wasted no time. But with so few troops and a bare handful of commanders, what I can do is limited. If you field a large force, I will gladly serve as the vanguard. I am diligently training my men and preparing equipment as I await your command.

"How could that swine Cao Cao do this to me?" swore Lü Bu. He had the courier executed and then mobilized for war. First, he sent Chen Gong and Zang Ba to link up with the Mount Tai rebels—Sun Guan, Wu Dun, Yin Li, and Chang Xi—in order to secure the districts of Yanzhou and the region east of the mountains. Second, he ordered Gao Shun and Zhang Liao[2] to capture Xiaopei from Liu Xuande. Third, he dispatched Song Xian and Wei Xu to seize Runan and Yingchuan to the west. Lü Bu himself commanded the main army, which would reinforce the three expeditions.

Gao Shun's approach was reported to Xuande, who quickly called a meeting. Sun Qian advised an emergency appeal to Cao Cao. Jian Yong (Xianhe), a man from Xuande's home region who was serving as his personal assistant, volunteered to go to the capital with a letter. Xuande saw to the city's defenses, taking command of the south gate himself, assigning Sun Qian to the north, Lord Guan to the west, and Zhang Fei to the east.

Mi Zhu and his younger brother Mi Fang were dispatched to command the troops in the center. (Mi Zhu's sister had become Xuande's new wife,[3] making Xuande brother-in-law to both. That is why he could leave the command of the center and the care of his family in the hands of Mi Zhu and Mi Fang.)[4]

Gao Shun's army arrived. Xuande climbed the watchtower and shouted to him, "Lü Bu and I have no quarrel. Why have you brought troops here?" "You and Cao Cao conspired to kill my lord—the whole thing has come out. You can turn yourself in," Gao Shun shouted back and signaled the attack. Xuande sealed the city. The next day Zhang Liao attacked the west gate. Lord Guan hailed him from the wall: "Why should a man of distinction waste himself on a traitor?" Zhang Liao lowered his head and made no reply. Lord Guan knew Zhang Liao for a man of devotion and loyalty and refrained from defaming him; nor did he come out and fight.

Zhang Liao shifted his men to the east gate. Zhang Fei met him in the field. Zhang Liao was already pulling back when Lord Guan reached the scene. Zhang Fei wanted to give chase, but Lord Guan recalled him to Xiaopei. "He was on the run," Fei said. "Why not pursue him?" "He's our equal in arms," Lord Guan answered, "and backed off only because I had urged him to repent." Satisfied with this explanation, Zhang Fei held the gate and did not seek battle.[5]

Meanwhile Jian Yong, Xuande's envoy, informed Cao Cao of Lü Bu's attack. Cao Cao took counsel with his advisers. "I want to move on Lü Bu," he told them. "Yuan Shao can't hamper us now, but Liu Biao and Zhang Xiu threaten the rear." Xun You, nephew of Xun Wenruo, said, "Liu Biao and Zhang Xiu are unlikely to act after their recent defeats. But Lü Bu has to be reckoned with. How will we deal with him if he links up with Yuan Shu and the two of them overrun the Huai and Si River region?" "Lü Bu's revolt against the throne," Guo Jia said, "has yet to win popular support. We should strike swiftly." Cao Cao approved a campaign against Lü Bu and sent Xiahou Dun, Xiahou Yuan, Lü Qian, and Li Dian ahead with fifty thousand soldiers. The main units, under Cao Cao himself, set out in succession. Jian Yong accompanied him.

Spies reported Cao Cao's moves to Gao Shun, who in turn informed Lü Bu. Lü Bu first sent Hou Cheng, He Meng, and Cao Xing to reinforce Gao Shun with two hundred cavalry; this enabled Gao Shun to move his forces thirty *li* from Xiaopei and meet the invaders. Lü Bu himself followed with the main army. Gao Shun's withdrawal told Xuande that Cao Cao would be coming. Leaving Sun Qian guarding the city and the Mi brothers guarding his household, Xuande and his brothers camped outside the wall, ready to aid Cao Cao.

Cao Cao's general Xiahou Dun spotted Gao Shun, raised his spear, and rode out to challenge him. The two horsemen tangled, closing and breaking some forty or fifty times. Then Gao Shun yielded and made for his line; Xiahou Dun galloped after. Gao Shun began circling round his formation; Xiahou Dun would not let up. From a point of vantage, Cao Xing drew his bow and, sighting true, shot Xiahou Dun in his left eye. Bellowing in pain, Xiahou Dun plucked out the arrow; the eyeball had stuck fast to the point. "The essence of my parents cannot be thrown away," he cried, and swallowed the eye. Then he went for Cao Xing and speared him in the face before he could defend himself. Cao Xing fell dead from his horse. The spectacle left both sides aghast.

Xiahou Dun rode back to his men. Now Gao Shun gave chase, waving his troops on. Cao Cao's army was defeated. Xiahou Yuan covered his brother as they fled the field. Lü Qian and Li Dian led the retreat to Jibei, where they camped. The victorious Gao Shun then turned to attack Xuande as Lü Bu arrived with the main army. Lü Bu, Zhang Liao, and Gao Shun split their forces into three to destroy the brothers' three camps.

Indeed:

> Swallowing his eye, the valiant Xiahou Dun fought on;
> But Cao Cao's vanguard, its commander wounded, could not hold out for long.

And Xuande's fate—what would that be?[6]

READ ON.

19

Cao Cao Battles Fiercely at Xiapi;
Lü Bu Falls at White Gate Tower

GAO SHUN LED ZHANG LIAO to attack Lord Guan's camp; Lü Bu attacked Zhang Fei's. The brothers met the enemy, and Xuande formed two columns to back them up. Lü Bu split his force into squads that hit Lord Guan and Zhang Fei from behind and shattered their companies. Xuande and a few dozen riders dashed back to Xiaopei, Lü Bu close behind. Urgently, Xuande called down the drawbridge, but Lü Bu rode up as it descended. The defenders could not shoot for fear of hitting Xuande, and Lü Bu crashed through the gate, scattering the guard. Behind him more troops stormed into the city. Xuande was desperate. Alone on horseback, he fled by the west gate, abandoning his family.[1]

When Lü Bu approached Xuande's house, Mi Zhu met him and said, "A true hero will not destroy a man's family. It is Cao Cao and Cao Cao alone who contends with you for the empire. Xuande will never forget how you saved his life when your arrow hit your halberd's side blade. He is a true friend and has joined Cao Cao because he had to. If only you could sympathize with his position." "Xuande and I have been friends many years. I will do no harm to his family," Lü Bu replied and told Mi Zhu to find a safe place for Xuande's wives in Xuzhou. Lü Bu then headed for Yanzhou and the districts east of the mountains, leaving Gao Shun and Zhang Liao to guard Xiaopei. Xuande's adviser Sun Qian had already left the city; Lord Guan and Zhang Fei had made for the hills with some horsemen.[2]

On the road outside the town of Xiaopei, Sun Qian overtook Xuande riding alone. "I do not know what has happened to my brothers, and my family is lost, too.[3] What am I to do?" Xuande asked. "Go to Cao Cao," Sun Qian replied, "then plan further." Xuande agreed and headed for the capital. Peasants in the villages Xuande entered looking for food along the way outdid one another in serving him as soon as they learned he was Inspector Liu of Yuzhou.[4]

Once he asked for lodging at a household, and a young man came to pay his respects. The lad turned out to be a hunter named Liu An. He wanted to offer the inspector fresh game but, unable to find any, butchered his wife.[5] At dinner Xuande asked, "What kind of meat is this?" "Wolf," replied Liu An. Suspecting nothing, Xuande ate his fill and retired. Toward dawn he went to the rear to fetch his horse and noticed a woman's corpse in the kitchen. Her arms had been carved away. Then Xuande realized what he had eaten and tears of gratitude streamed from his eyes. As Xuande mounted, Liu An said, "I wish

I could accompany you, Inspector, but with my elderly mother to care for, I cannot travel.'' Xuande expressed his thanks and rode out of the district.[6]

Suddenly, the road ahead was darkened by dust. In the distance Xuande recognized Cao Cao's men. Xuande and Sun Qian rode to the central command, where Cao Cao received them. Xuande told him of the fall of Xiaopei, his separation from his brothers, and the capture of his family. Cao Cao shed tears of sympathy. Xuande also related how Liu An had slaughtered his wife to feed him. Cao Cao ordered Sun Qian to reward the hunter with one hundred taels of silver.[7]

Cao Cao marched to Jibei, where Xiahou Yuan greeted him and explained that his brother was still recovering from the loss of his eye. Cao Cao went to see Xiahou Dun and subsequently sent him to the capital to recuperate. He also ordered a search made for Lü Bu. The report came back: ''Lü Bu, Chen Gong, and Zang Ba have joined with the Mount Tai bandits in attacks on the districts around Yanzhou.'' Cao Cao dispatched Cao Ren with three thousand soldiers to take Xiaopei, while he and Xuande marched to fight Lü Bu. They advanced east of the Mang-Dang Hills near Xiao Pass. There they were confronted by a force of thirty thousand bandits led by Sun Guan, Wu Dun, Yin Li, and Chang Xi. Cao Cao ordered Xu Chu into battle. The four bandit leaders fell back as Xu Chu threw himself into the combat. Cao Cao pressed the slaughter all the way to the pass.

Lü Bu waited in Xuzhou and kept himself informed. He decided to leave Chen Gui guarding the city and proceed to Xiaopei with Chen Deng to relieve the siege. Before the departure, Chen Gui told his son, ''You remember Cao Cao's saying that the situation in the east is in your hands? Lü Bu is on the verge of ruin. The time to act has come.'' ''I can handle things outside,'' Chen Deng replied. ''If Lü Bu returns here defeated, Mi Zhu will help you hold the city. Do not let him in. I will see to my own safety.'' ''But,'' countered Chen Gui, ''Lü Bu's whole family is here and plenty of his followers.'' ''I have provided for that, too,'' Chen Deng said.

Chen Deng advised Lü Bu, ''Xuzhou is beset by enemies; Cao Cao will soon attack in force. We must have a fallback position. Let's move food and money to Xiapi. If Xuzhou is besieged, Xiapi can still supply it. My lord, we must plan ahead.'' ''That makes sense,'' Lü Bu said. ''I will move my wives and daughter there, too.''[8] Lü Bu had Song Xian and Wei Xu transfer his family, grain stores, and cash to Xiapi; then he and Chen Deng started out for Xiao Pass to help his confederates withstand Cao Cao's assault.

Halfway there, Chen Deng said, ''Let me go ahead and probe Cao's positions.'' Lü Bu agreed, and Chen Deng went to the pass, where Chen Gong met him. ''Lü Bu is deeply disturbed at your reluctance to advance,'' Chen Deng said, ''and is coming to reprove you.'' ''Cao Cao's forces are overwhelming,'' Chen Gong argued. ''We cannot risk doing more. The entry points are secure. Urge our lord to protect Xiaopei at all costs—that is the best plan.''[9] ''Yes, yes, of course,'' responded Chen Deng.

That night Chen Deng climbed the pass and surveyed Cao Cao's army, which was bearing down on the strongpoint. Unseen in the dark, he shot three arrows—carrying notes he had prepared—into the area below the pass. The next day he took leave of Chen Gong and raced back to Lü Bu. ''Sun Guan and the other bandits,'' he reported, ''are ready to surrender the pass to Cao Cao. Chen Gong was still holding this vital point when I left, but you must reinforce him after sundown.'' ''You have saved the pass,'' Lü Bu replied gratefully and sent Deng hurrying back to Chen Gong with instructions to signal by fire when he wanted Lü Bu to attack.

Next, Deng informed Gong, ''Cao's men have already taken the small roads and penetrated our side of the pass. Xuzhou may fall. You must get back there as quickly as you can.'' Chen Gong abandoned Xiao Pass to rescue Xuzhou. Chen Deng then set the signal fire atop the pass calling for Lü Bu to strike. Thinking himself protected by the night, Lü Bu commenced a fierce attack. Chen Gong met the attack in the darkness; the soldiers cut each other to pieces. Cao Cao, responding to the same signal, made a coordinated strike under the most favorable circumstances. Sun Guan and the other bandits fled in every direction. Lü Bu battled on until morning before he saw through the trick Chen Deng had played. Finally, he met up with Gong and they hurried back to Xuzhou.

A shower of crossbow bolts greeted Lü Bu and Chen Gong at the city gate. Mi Zhu cried to them from the watchtower, "You stole Xuande's city. Now it returns to my lord. You may not enter again." "Give me Chen Gui!" Lü Bu ranted. "I've killed him," Mi Zhu answered. Lü Bu turned to Chen Gong and asked, "Where is Chen Deng?" "Are you still so bound to illusions, General," he asked, "as to call for this depraved traitor?" Lü Bu ordered a general search, but Chen Deng was not to be found.

Chen Gong persuaded Lü Bu to go to Xiaopei. En route they met up with their generals, Gao Shun and Zhang Liao. Lü Bu asked what had happened. "Chen Deng told us," the generals explained, "you were surrounded and had to be rescued." "Another of the traitor's tricks," Gong observed. "I will kill the villain," Lü Bu cried. When he arrived at Xiaopei he found the city already in Cao Ren's hands and Cao Cao's colors flying on the wall.

Standing below, Lü Bu reviled Chen Deng, who appeared above and shouted back, "I am loyal to the Han. I would never serve a traitor like you!" Lü Bu was about to attack when Zhang Fei appeared at the head of an armed contingent. Gao Shun rode forth but fell back before Zhang Fei's assault. Then Lü Bu himself took the field, and the two warriors fought fiercely as another roar of voices announced the arrival of Cao Cao's main army. Overpowered, Lü Bu fled east. Cao's men gave chase. Lü Bu felt himself and his horse failing. More soldiers darted out and blocked his way. Mounted, sword leveled, the commander shouted, "Stand your ground, Lü Bu! I am Lord Guan." Lü Bu made a confused attempt to engage him, but Zhang Fei was too close behind. Unwilling to go on, Lü Bu abandoned the field and fled to Xiapi with Chen Gong. General Hou Cheng came forth with troops and received them.

• • • • •

Reunited after the rout at Xiaopei, Lord Guan and Zhang Fei shed tears as they spoke of their separation. "I was camping on the Haizhou Road when I got word and rushed here," Lord Guan said. "I stayed around the Mang-Dang Hills. What a stroke of fortune to meet like this!" After exchanging tales, they went to Xuande, before whom they knelt and touched their hands to the ground. Torn between grief and joy, Xuande led his brothers before Cao Cao. Then all followed the victorious Cao Cao back to Xuzhou, where Mi Zhu received them and reported that Xuande's family was safe. Chen Deng and Chen Gui came to pay their respects.

Cao Cao feasted the commanders. At the banquet he sat in the center, Chen Gui to his right, Xuande to his left, other leaders according to rank. After the festivities Cao Cao showed his appreciation for the contribution made by Chen Gui and his son, Deng, by awarding them a fief of ten counties and appointing Chen Deng General Who Tames the Deep.

• • • • •

The acquisition of Xuzhou was a great satisfaction to Cao Cao. He began at once to plan the attack on Xiapi. Cheng Yu advised him: "Lü Bu holds this one town and will fight to the death to keep it; he might join Yuan Shu below the River Huai—an alliance that would present quite a problem. For now, have some capable person contain Lü Bu and keep Yuan Shu in check by covering the roads running south. Remember that we still have Zang Ba and Sun Guan and their Mount Tai bandits—that's another danger." "I'll take care of the mountain region," Cao Cao said. "Let Xuande cover the area between Lü Bu and Yuan Shu." "Your Excellency's command is mine to obey," Xuande answered.

The next day Xuande left Mi Zhu and Jian Yong in Xuzhou and took Sun Qian and his brothers to guard the roads leading south. Cao Cao attacked Xiapi, where Lü Bu, with his reserves of grain and the protection of the River Si, was content to remain on the defensive. His chief adviser, Chen Gong, urged, "Cao Cao's troops have just come. Before they build their camps, let's attack while they are still exhausted and we are rested. We can overcome them." "I've been beaten too often to risk another battle now," Lü Bu replied. "Let them attack. We'll drown them in the Si!"

In a few days Cao Cao's camps were ready. He marched to the city wall and called, "Lü Bu! Answer for yourself!" Lü Bu appeared, standing on the wall. "They say," Cao Cao shouted, "you are trying again to marry into Yuan Shu's family. That's what brings me here. Yuan Shu is a notorious imposter, while you have the elimination of Dong Zhuo to your credit. Why forsake your previous service to the Han to follow a traitor like Yuan Shu? Once this town falls, it will be too late to repent. If, however, you choose to surrender and join with me in supporting the royal house, your present rank and status can be preserved." "Your Excellency," Lü Bu replied, "please hold off while I consider." But Chen Gong shouted, "Traitor!" and released an arrow that pierced the parasol above Cao Cao's head. "I'll have your life, then," Cao Cao swore, and commenced the attack.[10]

Chen Gong advised Lü Bu: "Cao Cao has come too far to mount a sustained assault. Station cavalry and soldiers outside, General, while I hole up inside. If he attacks you, I will strike from behind. If he attacks the city, you rescue me from his rear. In ten days their food should be gone, and we can catch them between us." "Absolutely right!" Lü Bu said and prepared his armor. It was the coldest time of year; Lü Bu warned his men to take plenty of padding.

Lady Yan, Lü Bu's principal wife, asked, "Where are you going, my lord?" Lü Bu explained the plan. "You are entrusting the city wholly to Chen Gong," she said, "abandoning your wife to venture out alone? What if he seizes power? How could I remain true to my marriage vow?" Lü Bu, torn by indecision, remained in the city three days more.

"General," Chen Gong urged, " we are surrounded. The enemy will box us in if you don't move outside." "I prefer a tight defense," Lü Bu countered. "The latest news," Gong pressed, "is that Cao Cao has sent to Xuchang for more food. Sooner or later he'll have to be resupplied. Take our best troops and intercept the delivery."

Lü Bu, convinced by Chen Gong's argument, again went to Lady Yan to explain. But she wept and pleaded, "Once you go, how will Chen Gong and General Gao Shun hold the city? If anything goes wrong, what use will there be for regrets? You abandoned me once before in Chang'an. Luckily, we were reunited—only because Pang Shu hid me. I never thought you would do it again. But you must not give your wife a second thought. You have a great future before you." She cried more bitterly.

Lü Bu despaired of reaching a decision and took the dilemma to his concubine Diaochan, who said, "My life depends on yours. Do not risk it." "You need not worry," Lü Bu assured her. "With my halberd and my fleet Red Hare, who dares approach me?" But to Chen Gong he said, "That story about Cao's running out of food is typical of his tricks. I'm not budging." Chen Gong left Lü Bu and sighed, "We're done for! And there will be no decent burial for us, either!" After this, Lü Bu stayed indoors all day drinking with Lady Yan and Diaochan to dispel his sorrows.

Counselors Xu Si and Wang Kai came before Lü Bu and presented a plan: "Yuan Shu is in Huainan; his influence is great. Why not renew the attempt to form an alliance by marriage with him, General? If he sends troops to relieve us, we will be able to defeat Cao Cao with a two-sided attack." Lü Bu approved the plan and ordered the two to take a letter to Yuan Shu. Xu Si said, "We will need a company of troops to clear a way for us." Lü Bu accordingly ordered Zhang Liao and He Meng to take one thousand men and conduct the envoys through the enemy checkpoint.

At the second watch Zhang Liao and He Meng, the one in the van and the other in the rearguard, fought their way out from Xiapi. In their two charges, they skirted Xuande's vast stockade, outracing some commanders who tried to pursue them, and made it through the checkpoint. He Meng, in command of five hundred men, continued on with Xu Si and Wang Kai; Zhang Liao led the other five hundred back. Approaching the checkpoint, however, Liao found Lord Guan blocking his way. A skirmish was avoided when Gao Shun rode out from the city and escorted Zhang Liao back into Xiapi.

Lü Bu's envoys, Xu Si and Wang Kai, reached Shouchun; there Yuan Shu received them in audience, and they delivered Lü Bu's letter. Yuan Shu said, "The last time, Lü Bu killed my envoy and reneged on the marriage. What is this inquiry about?" Xu Si replied, "He was duped by Cao Cao's treacherous scheme. I beseech Your Majesty to consider this with great care."[11] "If your master were not at Cao Cao's mercy," Yuan Shu said, "he would never be offering his daughter to us." "If you do not save him, Your Majesty," Wang Kai responded, "the protection you afford one another will be gone—to Your Majesty's own disadvantage." "How fickle and faithless Lü Bu is," Yuan Shu said; but he added, "Send the girl first; then I'll send troops." The two envoys departed with due ceremony and started back to Xiapi guarded by He Meng.

As they reached the perimeter of Xuande's encampment, Xu Si said, "We cannot pass in daylight. When night falls, Wang Kai and I will go first; He Meng can guard the rear." The three agreed to this plan. That night Xu Si and Wang Kai managed to get by the encampment, but as He Meng started to follow them, he was stopped by Zhang Fei. After a brief clash, Zhang Fei captured He Meng and put his guard to bloody flight. The prisoner was first brought to Xuande, who then had him delivered to Cao Cao in the main camp. He Meng related in detail the nature of his mission for Lü Bu. Enraged, Cao Cao had him beheaded at the entrance to the camp and had messengers warn all stations to maintain vigilance. He ordered the maximum punishment for anyone letting Lü Bu or his men slip through. A shiver of fear ran through the army.

Xuande returned to his position and instructed his brothers: "We sit squarely on the key route in Huainan. You must take the greatest care not to permit the least violation of Cao Cao's command." "Didn't we just capture one of Lü Bu's rebel commanders?" Zhang Fei demanded. "I don't see any reward coming from Cao Cao—only an attempt to scare us. What for?" "That's not so," Xuande replied. "He commands the entire army. Is there a better way to ensure obedience? Do not violate his order." The brothers assented and withdrew.[12]

Meanwhile, Xu Si and Wang Kai returned from their mission and conveyed Yuan Shu's agreement to send troops after the delivery of Lü Bu's daughter. "And how am I to send her?" Lü Bu asked. "They've captured He Meng," Xu Si responded, "so Cao Cao knows our plan and will try to thwart it. You are the only one, General, who can get her safely through their lines." "What about today?" Lü Bu said. "An inauspicious day,"

Xu Si replied. "Tomorrow should be favorable, but only between sundown and midnight." Lü Bu told Gao Shun and Zhang Liao, "Take three thousand men and ready a small carriage. I will go the first two hundred *li*; you finish the journey without me."

The next night, during the second watch, Lü Bu wrapped his daughter in cotton wadding, outfitted her in armor, and set her on his back. Weapon in hand, he mounted and slipped out of the city, attended by Gao Shun and Zhang Liao. They were headed toward Xuande's camps when the drums rolled: Lord Guan and Zhang Fei barred the way, shouting, "Halt!" Lü Bu had little heart for combat but wanted to force his way out; just then Xuande arrived ready for the kill. The two companies battled hotly. Lü Bu, though a warrior of boundless courage, would not rush the enemy lines lest the girl come to harm. But Xu Huang and Xu Chu were menacing him from the rear, and all around men were shouting, "Don't let Lü Bu get away." Finally he was forced back into Xiapi, and Xuande recalled his fighters. Xu Huang and the others returned to Cao Cao's camp. Not one of Lü Bu's men had succeeded in getting through Xuande's blockade. In despair Lü Bu drank heavily.

•   •   •   •   •

Cao Cao's offensive against Xiapi, after two months, had stalled. Besides, he had news requiring his return to the capital: "Governor of Henei, Zhang Yang, had wanted to send Lü Bu troops, but his lieutenant Yang Chou killed him. Yang Chou had wanted to present the governor's head to Your Excellency but was killed in turn by one of the governor's henchmen. Their relief force is now moving toward Quan city." Cao Cao sent Shi Huan to kill the henchmen. He then assembled his commanders and said, "Governor Zhang Yang is fortunately out of the way; but we still have Yuan Shao in the north to worry about, not to mention Liu Biao and Zhang Xiu. This siege has gone on too long without results. I want to call a truce and return to the capital. What do you say?"

Xun You was swift to oppose: "Lü Bu's fighting spirit is low after many defeats. An army is only as good as its leader: when the leader fails, the men flag. His adviser Chen Gong is shrewd enough but sluggish. Now—before Lü Bu's morale revives and before Gong can decide on a plan—strike and take him." "I have a plan for taking the city," Guo Jia added, "a plan far more effective than an army of two hundred thousand." "Don't tell me," Xun Wenruo broke in, "that you want to divert water from the rivers Yi and Si into the city?" "Exactly," replied Guo Jia. Cao Cao was delighted and ordered his men to carry out the project.

Cao Cao's army watched from high ground as the waters flooded Xiapi. Only the area near the east gate remained dry. Soldiers raced to Lü Bu with the news. "I have a champion horse," Lü Bu said, "that crosses water as if it were land, flat and dry. We have nothing to fear." Joined by his wives, Lü Bu went on sating himself with choice wines. His face grew wasted from his excesses. Once he stared into the mirror and exclaimed, "How wine and lust have ruined me! Starting today I shall ban them." Lü Bu sent an order around the city that anyone caught drinking would be executed.

The prohibition was broken by Hou Cheng, one of Lü Bu's top generals. The general's stableman had stolen fifteen horses, meaning to deliver them to Xuande. Hou Cheng pursued and killed the thief and brought back the horses. When his commanders came to congratulate him, Hou Cheng fermented five or six vats of wine to celebrate the recovery of the horses. At the same time, lest Lü Bu take the celebration amiss, Hou Cheng took five jars to Lü Bu's residence, saying, "It was thanks to your awesome prestige that we recovered our horses. All the commanders are celebrating, and we have brewed this wine, which we offer first to you for your permission to drink." But Lü Bu retorted, "You brew wine for a party on the heels of my ban? You must be planning to attack me!" He ordered Hou Cheng removed and executed. Song Xian and Wei Xu pleaded for him, but Lü Bu said, "Purposeful violation of my order will be met with the most severe penalty. However, in consideration of the commanders, I will let him go with one hundred lashes." The appeals continued, and so Lü Bu dismissed Hou Cheng with fifty cuts. The commanders were deeply disheartened.

Song Xian and Wei Xu comforted Hou Cheng, who said tearfully, "You saved my life." "Lü Bu loves only his family," Xian said. "We are chaff to him," added Wei Xu. "The city is besieged; the towers are flooded round—we are done for." "He has no humanity, no honor. Why not leave him to his fate?" suggested Xian. "That's not a hero's part," replied Wei Xu. "Let's deliver him to Cao Cao instead." At this point Hou Cheng spoke up: "I suffered for recapturing the horses, yet it is Red Hare that he depends on. If you two seize Lü Bu and deliver the city, I will steal his horse and present it to Cao Cao myself." Thus the three men set their course.

That night Hou Cheng entered the stable, removed the renowned horse, and fled the city. Wei Xu let him through the gate, then feigned pursuit. When Hou Cheng reached Cao Cao's camp, he presented the horse to his lieutenants. He told them a white flag on the city wall would be their signal to attack Xiapi. Accordingly, Cao Cao ordered copies of the following proclamation tied to arrows and shot over the wall:

> Regent-Marshal Cao Cao, empowered by the sovereign's illustrious mandate, has taken up arms against Lü Bu. Whoever opposes himself to this great undertaking will fall to the sword, together with his entire clan, on the day of conquest. Whoever delivers Lü Bu—dead or alive—be he commander or commoner, will gain rank and wealth. Let all be cognizant of these instructions.

The next day at dawn the walls seemed to shake from the tumult the besiegers raised. Alarmed, Lü Bu picked up his halberd and ascended the wall, checking each gate. He vowed to punish Wei Xu for letting Hou Cheng get away with his prize steed. Beyond the wall Cao's soldiers saw the white flag and launched their attack. Lü Bu, virtually alone, resisted the assault, which went on from dawn to midday before abating slightly. Giving way to fatigue, Lü Bu dozed off in the city tower. Song Xian dismissed the guards, removed the halberd, and, with Wei Xu's help, tied up Lü Bu. Jerking awake, Lü Bu called for his guard, but the captors cut them down and waved the signal flag. Cao Cao's men stormed the wall. "We have Lü Bu alive!" shouted Wei Xu. General Xiahou Dun refused to believe it until Song Xian threw down Lü Bu's famed halberd and opened the city gate. Cao Cao's soldiers poured through. Gao Shun and Zhang Liao were trapped by the flood at the western gate and captured; Chen Gong was taken by Xu Huang at the southern gate.

After entering Xiapi, Cao Cao ordered the river restored to its normal course and a placard hung assuring the people of their safety. Together with Liu Xuande, whose two brothers stood beside him, Cao Cao sat in the tower at the White Gate examining the captives. Lü Bu, a tall, powerful man now trussed into a ball, continually pleaded for the ropes to be loosened. "A tiger needs to be tightly bound," Cao Cao said to him. Lü Bu saw Song Xian, Wei Xu, and Hou Cheng standing free and cried, "Did I not treat you well? How could you betray me?" "You listened only to your women," Song Xian answered, "not to your commanders. Is that what you mean by 'treat well'?" Lü Bu was silent.

When Gao Shun was hustled in, Cao Cao asked him, "Anything to say?" Gao Shun made no reply, and Cao Cao dispatched him to his death. Then Xu Huang delivered Chen Gong. "I trust you have been well since we parted," Cao Cao said.[13] "Your mind is depraved," Chen Gong retorted. "Does that explain why you had to serve Lü Bu?" Cao Cao asked. "He may have been incapable at strategy," Chen Gong answered defiantly, "but he was equally incapable of treachery." "And you, with all of your shrewdness and strategy, how are you going to get out of this?" Cao Cao demanded. Chen Gong looked toward Lü Bu and said, "Alas! Had he taken my advice we might never have been captured." "And now," said Cao Cao, "what shall we do?" "Today," Chen Gong replied, "I look only for death." "And what of your mother," asked Cao, "your wife and your children?" "It is said," Gong responded, "that he who governs with filial duty will never injure another's parents; that he who rules humanely will never cut off the sacrifices from a man's descendants. My lord, their fate lies with you. I am your captive and ask only for execution; I have no misgivings."[14]

Cao Cao felt a lingering affection for his former companion, but Chen Gong strode brusquely down from the tower, shaking off the guards who tried to stop him. Cao Cao rose from his seat and wept to see him go, but Chen Gong never turned back. Cao Cao said to his men, "Take his family to the capital and see to their needs as long as they live. Anyone mistreating them will die." Though he heard Cao Cao, Chen Gong said nothing as he offered his neck to the executioner. The assembly wept. Cao Cao had the corpse placed in a double coffin and buried in Xuchang.[15] A later poet lamented Chen Gong:

> In life, in death, an undivided will—
> A hero staunch and doughty!
> But only to a lord of rarest worth
> Should a vassal pledge his fealty.
> All homage for upholding his liege lord.
> We sorrow as he bids his kin farewell.
> At White Gate Tower he met his death unbowed:
> The conduct of Chen Gong none can excel.

After Cao Cao had left to escort Chen Gong to his execution, Lü Bu appealed to Xuande: "Now you sit in honor, and I sit, a prisoner, at your feet. Won't you spare a word in my behalf?" Xuande nodded. When Cao Cao returned, Lü Bu shouted, "I was your chief foe, but now I submit. With you as commander in chief and me as your lieutenant, the world can be easily conquered." Cao Cao looked over to Xuande and asked, "What do you say?" "Have you forgotten what happened to his former patrons, Ding Yuan and Dong Zhuo?" was the reply. Lü Bu eyed Xuande and cried, "You! Most faithless of all!" Cao Cao ordered Lü Bu removed and put to death by strangulation. "Long-eared one," Lü Bu pleaded, looking back at Xuande, "have you forgotten how I saved you with a shot of my bow?" Suddenly someone shouted, "Lü Bu you coward! Die and be done with it! What are you afraid of?" Everyone turned to the speaker, Zhang Liao, who was surrounded by armed guards. Cao Cao ordered Bu's execution to proceed. Afterward his head was displayed. A poet has described his final hour at Xiapi:

> The flood tide surged and swamped his last stronghold;
> His own men led him bound before his foes.
> What use now, his thousand-*li* steed?
> And where was his many-bladed halberd?

Coward now, the tiger looks for mercy:
"Never give the hunting hawk its fill."
Fooled by Cao's words, woman-doting,
Spurning Chen Gong's warning plea—
What right had he to blame
The long-ear'd one's bad faith?

Another poet wrote of Liu Xuande:

No mercy for the tiger when he's tied:
Of Yuan and Zhuo the bloody memory's fresh.
Though, why not spare Bu as a "son" for Cao,
Knowing of his taste for father-flesh![16]

Zhang Liao, the one who had told Lü Bu to die like a man, was marched under guard up to Cao. "This man looks familiar," Cao Cao remarked. "We met once—at Puyang. Have you forgotten?" Zhang Liao said. "So, you remember," Cao Cao said. "Only to regret," was the reply. "Regret what?" asked Cao Cao. "That our fires failed to burn out a traitor like you," he shot back. "No fallen general abuses me!" Cao Cao cried, raising his sword. Zhang Liao remained calm, awaiting death. But someone seized Cao Cao's arm from behind, and another knelt before him, pleading, "Your Excellency, desist."

Indeed:

Lü Bu begged mercy and was refused.
Zhang Liao denounced the traitor and was spared.

Who pleaded for his life?

READ ON.

20

Cao Cao Leads the Royal Hunt near the Capital;
Dong Cheng Receives a Mandate in the Palace

LIU XUANDE CAUGHT CAO CAO'S ARM in midair, and Lord Guan kneeled before the prime minister. "Zhang Liao has a true and guileless heart," Xuande pleaded. "We need more like him." "I know him for a man of loyalty and honor," Lord Guan added, "and I will vouch for him with my life."[1] Cao Cao tossed his sword aside and said, smiling, "And I think so too! I acted in jest!" Untying Zhang Liao's bonds himself, Cao wrapped a garment of his own around the prisoner and invited him to a seat of honor. Zhang Liao, moved by Cao Cao's earnestness, swore his allegiance to Cao. Cao Cao then appointed Liao Imperial Corps commander and an honorary lord[2] and sent him to demand the submission of Zang Ba, leader of the Mount Tai bandits.

Zang Ba, however, had already heard of Lü Bu's death and Zhang Liao's surrender; with his men he promptly went over to Cao Cao. Richly rewarded, Zang Ba was able to secure the surrender of the other bandit leaders—Sun Guan, Wu Dun, and Yin Li. Only Chang Xi held out. Cao Cao appointed Zang Ba governor of Langye fief. He gave Sun Guan and the others appointments and ordered them to protect the coastal region of Qingzhou and Xuzhou.

Lü Bu's wives and daughters were transported to the capital. The imperial army was feasted; then all units decamped and the army marched back to the capital. As they passed through Xuzhou (the province Lü Bu had taken over from Xuande), the people lined the road, burning incense and appealing to Cao Cao to restore Xuande as protector. But Cao Cao said, "Protector Liu has rendered great service. Let him first come before the Emperor for his enfeoffment." The common folk touched their heads to the ground in appreciation.[3] Meanwhile, Cao Cao appointed General of Cavalry and Chariots Che Zhou provisional protector of Xuzhou. Back in Xuchang, Cao Cao rewarded all who had joined his campaign and assigned Xuande comfortable quarters near his ministerial residence.[4]

The next day Emperor Xian held court. Cao Cao hailed Xuande's feats of arms and presented him. Attired in court apparel, Xuande paid homage at the base of the steps to the throne. The Emperor then instructed him to ascend. "Tell me of your lineage," the Emperor said.[5] "I can trace my ancestry through Prince Jing of Zhongshan," Xuande replied, "back to his father, Jing, the fourth emperor. My grandfather was Liu Xiong, my father Liu Hong." Emperor Xian ordered the director of the Imperial Clan to recite from the clan registry.

"Emperor Jing had fourteen sons," the official intoned, "the seventh of whom was Prince Jing of Zhongshan, Liu Sheng by name. Sheng begat Zhen, precinct master of Lu; Zhen begat Ang, lord of Pei; Ang begat Lu, lord of Zhang; Lu begat Lian, lord of Yishui; Lian begat Ying, lord of Qinyang; Ying begat Jian, lord of Anguo; Jian begat Ai, lord of Guangling; Ai begat Xian, lord of Jiaoshui; Xian begat Shu, lord of Zuyi; Shu begat Yi, lord of Qiyang; Yi begat Bi, lord of Yuanze; Bi begat Da, lord of Yingchuan; Da begat Buyi, lord of Fengling; Buyi begat Hui, lord of Jichuan; Hui begat Xiong, prefect of Fan, a county of Dongjun; Xiong begat Hong, who held no office; Xuande is the son of Hong."

The Emperor checked the order of the lineage and found that Xuande was indeed an imperial uncle. Elated, Emperor Xian summoned him to an adjoining room, where they enacted the formalities befitting uncle and nephew. The Emperor mused, "Cao Cao abuses his authority to the point that state affairs are out of our control. But now we may have a remedy in this heroic uncle of mine." He made Xuande general of the Left and precinct master of Yi. After a grand banquet to mark the occasion, Xuande thanked the sovereign for his generosity and left the court. He was known thereafter as Imperial Uncle Liu.

Returning to his quarters, Cao Cao was confronted by his advisers. "You have nothing to gain, Your Excellency," Xun Wenruo argued, "from this new relationship between Liu Bei and the Emperor." "Although he has been recognized as an imperial uncle," Cao Cao replied, "I still command him by imperial decree. He is thus doubly bound. Don't forget: so long as he's here in Xuchang, we have him well in hand—however near the Emperor he may be.[6] There's nothing to fear. What really worries me is that Yang Biao, our grand commandant, is a member of Yuan Shu's clan and could do us great harm if he decided to work for the Yuan brothers. I want him eliminated at once."[7] Accordingly, Cao Cao had Yang Biao incarcerated for alleged connivance with Yuan Shu. Man Chong was assigned to the case.

At this time Kong Rong, governor of Beihai,[8] was in the capital; he protested to Cao, "Yang Biao comes from a family that has exhibited the purest virtue for four generations. You can't prosecute him for his ties to the Yuans." "It is His Majesty's wish," Cao Cao replied. "Suppose," Kong Rong retorted, "that at the beginning of the Zhou dynasty the child emperor Cheng had had Duke Shao killed. Who would believe a protestation of innocence from the regent, the Duke of Zhou?" On the strength of this argument Cao Cao released Yang Biao and sent him home to his village. But when Court Counselor Zhao Yan, indignant at Cao Cao's high-handed rule, accused the prime minister of lese majesty in arbitrarily arresting high ministers, Cao Cao arrested Zhao Yan and had him killed. The whole court trembled at this demonstration of Cao's temper.

Cheng Yu advised Cao Cao, "Sir, your prestige increases day by day. Perhaps the time is ripe for preparing to ascend the throne yourself?" "The court," Cao Cao replied, "has too many loyal ministers for us to move imprudently. I plan to invite the Emperor to a grand hunt. We'll see what the reaction is then."

Prime horses, pedigreed hunting hawks, and champion hounds were selected; the bows and arrows were made ready. Cao Cao assembled his soldiers outside the city and then entered the palace to invite the Emperor to lead the hunt. "This appears somewhat unorthodox," the sovereign commented. "The kings and emperors of ancient times," Cao explained, "held four grand hunts yearly, riding forth from the capital each season to show the world their prowess. Now with the empire in commotion, a hunt should provide an ideal occasion for us to demonstrate our skill at arms." Unable to refuse, the Emperor mounted his easy-gaited horse and, armed with jeweled bow and gold-tipped arrows, led the procession out of the city.[9]

Liu Xuande, Lord Guan, and Zhang Fei, bows and blades at the ready, breastplates under their dress, led several dozen horsemen in the cavalcade. On a rich chestnut horse, a "flying spark," Cao Cao rode at the head of one hundred thousand men. Arriving at Xutian, they fanned out and enclosed the field in a ring of some two hundred *li*. Cao Cao kept his horse parallel to the Emperor's, never more than a head apart. His trusted commanders and officers massed behind him. The regular imperial officials, civil and military, trailed in the rear, none daring to draw close.

As the Emperor galloped toward the field, Xuande saluted him from the roadside. "I look forward to admiring the imperial uncle's marksmanship today," the Emperor said. As if receiving a command, Xuande took to his horse. That moment a hare sprang from the bushes. Xuande felled it with one shot from his bow. The Emperor complimented him and rode on. The procession turned and was crossing a low hill when a stag charged from the wood. The Emperor shot three arrows but missed. "Try for it, my lord," the Emperor cried to Cao Cao. Impudently, Cao asked for the Emperor's jeweled bow and gold-tipped arrows. Drawing the bow to the full, he released an arrow that pierced the deer's back; the animal toppled in the grass.

The crowd of ministers and generals, seeing the royal arrow, assumed that the Emperor had scored the hit and surged forward to congratulate him, crying, "Long life to the Emperor!" But it was Cao Cao, guiding his horse ahead of the Son of Heaven, who acknowledged the cheers. All who saw it blanched. Behind Xuande, Lord Guan seethed. Brows arching, eyes glaring, he raised his sword and rode forward to cut Cao Cao down. A sharp look with a motion of the head from Xuande changed his mind, and he reined in.

Xuande bowed to Cao Cao and congratulated him: "Your Excellency shoots with more than human skill. Few in this age can equal you." "It was the largess of the Emperor, really," Cao replied, laughing as he rode his horse round to express his compliments to the sovereign. But instead of returning the jeweled bow, he simply hung it at his side. When the hunt was over, the multitude feasted in Xutian. Afterward the Emperor led the procession back to the capital, and it dispersed.[10]

Later Lord Guan asked Xuande, "Why did you stop me? I could have rid the dynasty of a traitor at whose hands the Emperor suffers personally." "'If you aim for the mouse,'" Xuande warned, "'don't bring down the house!' Cao Cao was at the Emperor's side, and his lieutenants were thick around him. Dear brother, had you accidentally injured the Emperor in a moment of foolish wrath, we would be the ones accused of the very crimes you denounce." "Spared today—a plague tomorrow," Lord Guan retorted. "Say no more," said Xuande. "We cannot speak freely."

•   •   •   •

Inside the palace the Emperor spoke tearfully to Empress Fu: "Since I first assumed the throne, treacherous pretenders have multiplied. First we suffered the disaster of Dong Zhuo, followed immediately by the sedition of generals Li Jue and Guo Si. We have faced griefs unknown to most. Then came Cao Cao, whom we thought a loyal servant of the dynasty, never dreaming he would usurp the government and abuse his authority by arbitrary exercise of fear and favor. I wince to see him. Today in the hunting field he impudently acknowledged the cheers meant for his sovereign. Before long there will be a usurpation, and you and I shall not die natural deaths." Empress Fu replied, "In this court full of lords and peers—not a one of whom but eats and lives at the pleasure of the Han—is there none to assist the dynasty in distress?"

As the Empress was speaking, her father, Fu Wan, entered. "Your Majesties," he said, "do not despair. I have the man who can remove the scourge of the royal house." The Emperor wiped his tears as he replied, "Then you too can see how imperious Cao Cao is?" "Who could have missed the incident at the deer hunt?" Fu Wan responded. "But the whole court consists of either his clansmen or his followers. Except for the imperial in-laws, who will demonstrate loyalty by bringing the traitor to justice? I don't have the power to do it, but why can't we turn to Dong Cheng, brother of the imperial concubine, general of Cavalry and Chariots?" "He has stepped into the breach more than once," the Emperor agreed. "Have him summoned."

"All Your Majesty's attendants," Fu Wan went on, "are Cao Cao's confidants. If they find out, the consequences will be serious." "What can we do?" the Emperor asked. "I have an idea," Fu Wan responded. "Fashion a garment and obtain a jade girdle, both of which you can privately bestow on Dong Cheng. Sew a secret decree into the girdle lining. When he reaches home and discovers the decree, he will devote himself to devising a strategy, and not even the spirits will know." The Emperor approved and Fu Wan withdrew.

Emperor Xian prepared to write the mandate. He bit his finger, transcribed his words in blood, and instructed the Empress to sew the mandate into the purple embroidered lining of the girdle. The Emperor then slipped on the brocade robe he had had made, tied the girdle, and ordered a palace officer to command Dong Cheng's appearance. The formalities of audience concluded, the Emperor spoke: "Last night the Empress and I were recalling the loyal service you tendered us when we fled from Chang'an across the River Ba, and decided to send for you to express our gratitude." Dong Cheng touched his head to the ground and disclaimed the honor.

The Emperor guided Dong Cheng to the ancestral temple and then into the Gallery of Meritorious Officials, in whose honor the Emperor burned incense before walking on with Dong Cheng to admire the portraits. "Tell me," the Emperor said, stopping before a portrait of the Supreme Ancestor, "where did the founder of the Han commence his career, and how did he create the heritage we enjoy?" "You mock me," Dong Cheng responded, astonished. "How could I forget the deeds of our sacred ancestor? He began as a precinct master in Sishang. From there he went on to slay the white serpent with his three-span sword, marking the rising against the Qin dynasty. Traversing the land, he annihilated Qin in three years and Chu in five. Thus he took possession of the empire and established this enduring patrimony."

"So splendid, so heroic the forefather," sighed the Emperor, "so fainthearted and feeble the progeny. One can't help sighing." As he spoke, he directed Dong Cheng's attention to the portraits of the two officials on either side of the Supreme Ancestor. "Is this not Zhang Liang," he went on, "lord of Liu? And this, Xiao He, lord of Cuo?" "Indeed," replied Dong Cheng, "the Supreme Ancestor relied greatly on them in founding the dynasty." The Emperor observed that no one was near and whispered, "So should you, uncle, stand by us." "I have no merit," Dong Cheng answered, "to serve as they served." "We remember well," the Emperor continued, "your service at the western capital, for which no reward could suffice." Then, pointing to his garments, he added, "Won't you wear this robe of mine and tie it with this girdle so that you will always seem to be by my side?"

Dong Cheng touched his forehead to the ground. The Emperor undid the robe and girdle, whispering, "Examine these carefully when you get home. Do not fail me." Perceiving the Emperor's intention, Dong Cheng put on the garment and, taking leave, quit the gallery.

Informed of this audience, Cao Cao intercepted Dong Cheng outside the palace gate. Where could he hide? Alarmed but helpless, he stood at the roadside and offered a ritual greeting. "What is the imperial in-law here for?" asked Cao. "The Emperor summoned me to present this brocade robe and jade girdle," replied Dong Cheng. "For what reason were you so honored?" Cao Cao asked again. "In recognition of my service at the western capital," was the answer. "Show me the girdle," Cao demanded. Believing the girdle to contain a secret decree concerning the prime minister, Dong Cheng demurred until Cao Cao barked to his attendants, "Strip it off him!"

Cao Cao examined the girdle closely. "A beautiful belt," he said. "Now take off the robe." Dong Cheng dared not refuse. Cao Cao held the garment up to the sun and scrutinized it. Then he slipped it on, tied the girdle and turned to his men, saying, "Fits me well, doesn't it?" "Perfectly," was the reply. "Would the imperial in-law," Cao Cao suggested, "consider turning these over to me as a gift?" "What the sovereign bestows of his generosity," Dong Cheng protested, "may never be given away. Let me have others fashioned to present to you." "These clothes," Cao Cao snapped, "must be connected with some intrigue." "How could one dare!" Dong Cheng gasped. "If Your Excellency insists, of course I shall leave them with you." "Sire," Cao Cao reassured him, "would I seize what the sovereign vouchsafes? Bear with my facetiousness." He returned the garment and the girdle to Dong Cheng, who took his leave and went home.

Alone in his library that night, Dong Cheng went over the robe inch by inch. Finding nothing, he mused, "When the Son of Heaven instructed me to examine these clothes, he must have had something in mind. But there's no sign of anything. Why?" He inspected the girdle: white jade tesserae wrought into a miniature dragon snaking through a floral design; the underside was lined with purple brocade. The stitching was flawless. Nothing was visible. He placed the girdle on his desk and puzzled over it until he grew drowsy.

Dong Cheng was on the verge of falling asleep, his head on the desk, when a spark from the lamp's smoldering snuff flew onto the material and burned through the lining. He brushed it out, but the spark had already eaten away a bit of the brocade, revealing the white silk and traces of blood. He slit open the girdle: there was the decree, bloodscript in the Emperor's hand:

> We believe that in the human order the bond of father and son is foremost, and that in the social order the obligation between sovereign and servant is paramount. Of late the treasonous Cao Cao, abusing his authority, insulting and degrading his sovereign, has connived with his cohorts to the detriment of our dynasty's rule. Instructions, rewards, land grants, and punishments now fall outside the imperial jurisdiction. Day and night we brood on this, dreading the peril to the realm. General, you are a prominent public servant and our nearest relative. Think of the obstacles and hardships the Supreme Ancestor faced when he founded this dynasty: forge a union of stouthearted men, stalwarts of unimpaired integrity and unimpeachable loyalty; exterminate this perfidious faction and restore the security of our holy shrines for our ancestors' sake. I have cut my finger and shed this blood to compose this decree confided to you. Remain vigilant. Do not fail our hopes. Decree of the third month, spring, Jian An 4 [A.D. 199].

Dong Cheng read the edict through his tears. He could not sleep that night and in the morning returned to the library to reread the document. But no concrete plan occurred to him. Finally he fell asleep against his desk pondering the means to get rid of Cao Cao.

The courtier Wang Zifu arrived. Recognizing his master's intimate friend, the gateman did not stop him, and he went straight into the library. Wang Zifu saw Dong Cheng dozing at his desk, a silk scroll under his sleeve. The imperial "we" was barely visible on it. Becoming curious, Wang Zifu quietly took up the document. After reading it, he stowed it in his own sleeve. "Imperial In-law Dong," he cried, "are you not ashamed? How carefree to be sleeping so!" Dong Cheng came to immediately. Missing the decree, he felt his senses swim and his limbs fail. "You plan to murder the prime minister, then?" Zifu demanded. "I shall have to denounce you." "Brother," Dong Cheng wept, "if that is your intention, the house of Han expires."

"I was simply playing a part," Wang Zifu reassured Dong Cheng. "Our clan has enjoyed the fruits of service to the Han for many generations. Far from failing in loyalty, I mean to lend my all to the task of destroying the traitor." "The dynasty is fortunate indeed if you are so minded," Dong Cheng responded. "Let us retire, then," Wang Zifu suggested, "and draw up a loyalist pledge to do our duty to the Emperor whatever the risk to ourselves and our clans."

In great excitement Dong Cheng fetched a length of white silk and wrote his name at the head. Wang Zifu added his, saying, "My trusted friend General Wu Zilan should make cause with us." "Within the court," Dong Cheng said, "only Changshui Commandant Chong Ji and Court Counselor Wu Shi are trusted friends who will join us."[11] At that moment a servant announced the two officials. "Thus Heaven aids us!" Dong Cheng exclaimed and sent Wang Zifu behind a screen to observe while he received the two in his library. After tea Chong Ji said, "The incident at the hunt must have infuriated you." "Yes," replied Dong Cheng, "but what could I do?" "I'd vow to do away with the traitor," Wu Shi added, "but I despair of finding allies." "To rid the dynasty of evil," Chong Ji said, "I would die without regret."

At these words, Wang Zifu emerged from behind the screen and cried, "So! The two of you would assassinate the prime minister! I mean to turn you in, and the imperial in-law will corroborate my charge." "A loyal subject does not fear death!" Chong Ji shot back angrily. "I'd rather be a ghost of the Han than a traitor's lackey like you!" Dong Cheng smiled. "We staged this to test you both. Wang Zifu did not speak in earnest," he explained as he drew the edict from his sleeve and showed it to them. The two men wept copiously as they read. Dong Cheng then asked for their signatures. "Will you gentlemen stay here a while," Wang Zifu said, "while I see if Wu Zilan will join us?" He returned shortly with the general, who added his name. Dong Cheng invited the four to dine in a rear chamber.

The unexpected arrival of Ma Teng, governor of Xiliang, was announced. "Say I am not well and cannot receive him," Dong Cheng instructed the gateman. But when this answer was brought, Ma Teng shouted angrily, "I saw him only yesterday at the Donghua Gate in a new robe and girdle. Why is he giving me excuses? I have important business. He must let me in." After hearing the gateman's report, Dong Cheng excused himself and received his latest guest.

"I am on my way home after an audience with His Majesty," Ma Teng said, "and have come to take leave. Why refuse to see me?" "I had a sudden illness," Dong Cheng said, "and failed my duty as a host. Forgive the offense." "You look in the pink of health to me," Ma Teng remarked. Dong Cheng could not bring himself to speak. Flicking his sleeves, Ma Teng rose to leave. "And no one to save the dynasty!" he said with a sigh. Dong Cheng caught his words and held him back, saying, "What do you mean, 'no one to save the dynasty'?" "I am still fuming over the incident at the deer hunt," Ma Teng said. "Even you, it seems, the closest relative of the ruling house, are sunk in dissipation and give no thought to punishing the traitor. How could you be one to relieve the dynasty's distress?"

Wary of deception, Dong Cheng feigned surprise and said, "His Excellency Cao Cao is a high minister, the mainstay of the court. How can you say such a thing?" Enraged, Ma Teng cried, "You still believe that traitor is a decent man?" "There are eyes and ears everywhere," Dong Cheng cautioned. "You must lower your voice." "Those who crave life above all," Ma Teng retorted, "are unfit to discuss serious matters." He rose to leave. Convinced of Ma Teng's loyalty, Dong Cheng said at last, "Restrain yourself a moment, my lord. I have something to show you." He drew the governor into his chamber and handed him the imperial edict.

As he read, Ma Teng's hair stood on end; he bit his lips until blood covered his mouth. "If you plan to act," he said, "my Xiliang troops will help." Then Dong Cheng led the governor to meet the other supporters of the indictment against the prime minister. At Dong Cheng's request, Ma Teng affixed his signature, confirming his oath with a swallow of wine and some drops of blood. "What we swear here we will never disavow," he said, and pointing to the five men, he added, "If five more will join us, our cause will succeed." "Loyal and stalwart men," Dong Cheng warned, "are all too few. If we take in the wrong ones, we will only ruin ourselves." Ma Teng asked to see the register of current office-holders. Coming to the names of the house of Liu, he clapped his hands and cried, "Here is the man we must talk to!"[12] The group asked who. Calmly and deliberately, Ma Teng spoke the name. Indeed:

> Because an in-law received the Emperor's call,
> An imperial kinsman came to the dynasty's aid.

Whom did Ma Teng name?
READ ON.

21

Cao Cao Warms Wine and Rates the Heroes of the Realm;
Lord Guan Takes Xuzhou by Stratagem and Beheads Che Zhou

"Whom do you recommend?" Dong Cheng had asked Ma Teng. "I see here the name of Liu Xuande, protector of Yuzhou. Why not try him?" was the reply. "True, he's the Emperor's uncle," Dong Cheng said thoughtfully, "but he is too close to Cao.[1] He can't get involved in this." "I saw what happened on the hunting field," Ma Teng responded, "when Cao Cao accepted the public accolade meant for the Emperor. Lord Guan was right behind Xuande and would have struck Cao Cao down had not Xuande stopped him with an angry glance. Xuande is more than willing to organize against Cao, but he feels thwarted, unequal to Cao's many guards. Try to enlist his help—I know he will respond eagerly." The group dispersed with Wu Shi cautioning, "Let's not be too hasty. This requires careful consideration."

The next night Dong Cheng pocketed the imperial decree and paid a quiet call on Xuande. Flanked by his brothers, Xuande received him in a small chamber. After host and guest were seated, Xuande said, "Only a most serious occasion would bring the imperial in-law in the dead of night." "I couldn't risk coming by day," Dong Cheng replied. "Cao would have suspected something." Xuande called for wine, and Dong Cheng went on, "The other day at the hunt Lord Guan seemed set to kill Cao Cao, but you motioned him off. Why?" Taken by surprise, Xuande parried the question, asking, "How do you know that?" "No one else noticed," Dong Cheng said, "but I did." Unable to maintain his pose of indifference, Xuande answered, "My brother, outraged by Cao's insolent ambition, acted impulsively."

Dong Cheng hid his face and wept. "If only the vassals at court compared with Lord Guan," he cried, "the peace of the land would be assured." Wondering if Cao Cao had sent the imperial brother-in-law to sound him out, Xuande said, "With His Excellency Cao Cao in power, is not the peace of the land already well assured?" Dong Cheng's face stiffened as he rose. "It is only because you are the Emperor's uncle that I opened my heart and soul to you. Why have you played me false?" he asked. "Lest *you* play *me* false, Imperial Brother-in-law," Xuande admitted at last, "I had to test you." Dong Cheng then produced the secret edict. Dismay and indignation welled up in Xuande as he read the Emperor's sacred words.

Next, Dong Cheng handed him the loyalists' pledge bearing six signatures: Dong Cheng, general of Cavalry and Chariots; Wang Zifu, an official[2] in the Ministry of Works; Chong Ji, commandant of the Changshui command; Wu Shi, court counselor;

Wu Zilan, General of Manifest Trust; and Ma Teng, governor of Xiliang. "Since the Emperor has charged you with the task of punishing the traitor," Xuande said, "I commit myself to the cause and offer my fullest devotion." Dong Cheng thanked him, and Xuande placed his name and title, general of the Left, on the silk roll.[3] "There are three more we should approach," Dong Cheng said. "If they join, we will have ten righteous men confronting the traitor." But Xuande warned Dong Cheng to act with the utmost caution and secrecy. The two men continued talking until the fifth watch; then they parted.

To avoid arousing Cao Cao's suspicions, Xuande took to his back garden, planting and tending vegetables, keeping his purposes hidden. Lord Guan and Zhang Fei asked, "Brother, why have you lost interest in the great issues of the realm and given yourself to a commoner's toil?" "This is something you might not appreciate," responded Xuande, and his brothers did not ask again.[4]

One day when Lord Guan and Zhang Fei were away and Xuande was watering his plants, two of Cao's generals, Xu Chu and Zhang Liao, led a score of men into the garden. "His Excellency," they announced, "requests that Your Lordship come at once." Alarmed, Xuande asked, "An emergency?" "I don't know," Xu Chu answered. "I was told to request your presence." Xuande could only follow the two men to Cao Cao's residence.

A smiling Cao Cao greeted Xuande. "That's quite a project you have under way at home," he said in a tone that turned Xuande's face pale as dust. Taking Xuande's hand, Cao led him to his own garden. "You have taken up a most difficult occupation in horticulture," Cao continued. "Just to while away the time," Xuande answered, relieved. "There is nothing else to occupy me."

"I was admiring the plums on the branch," Cao remarked. "The new green ones called to mind last year's campaign against Zhang Xiu, when we ran short of water on the march. How parched the men were! Then something occurred to me. 'There's a plum grove ahead,' I cried and pretended to locate it with my whip. When the troops heard me, their mouths watered and their thirst was gone. Seeing these plums now, I can't help enjoying the sight;[5] and having some wine just heated, I decided to invite Your Lordship[6] for a drink at this little pavilion." Regaining possession of himself, Xuande went along with Cao Cao. Delicacies had already been set out: a plate piled with new green plums and a jar brimming with warmed wine. Sitting opposite one another, the two men drank freely and enjoyed themselves without constraint.

The wine had enlivened their spirits when dark clouds appeared and overspread the heavens: a flash storm was threatening. An attendant pointed to what seemed like a distant dragon suspended on the horizon. The two men leaned against the balcony and watched it. Cao turned to Xuande and asked, "Does my lord understand the dragon's multiform manifestations?"[7] "Not in great detail," Xuande replied. "The dragon," Cao continued, "can enlarge and diminish itself, surge aloft or lie beneath the surface of the water. Enlarged, it creates clouds and spews mist. Diminished, it can veil its scaly form from view. Aloft, it prances triumphant in the upper realm of space. Under the surface, it lurks among the surging breakers. Now in the fullness of spring it mounts the season, like men who would fulfill an ambition to dominate the length and breadth of the land. In this respect the dragon can well be compared to the heroes of the age. You yourself have traveled widely and surely must be familiar with the great heroes of our time. Please try to point them out for me."

"How can these eyes of mine sight heroes?" Xuande said. "Set your modesty aside," Cao urged. "Thanks to Your Excellency's gracious benefaction," Xuande responded, "I have succeeded in serving the dynasty. But as for the heroes of the realm, such things are more than I would know of." "Even if you do not know any personally," Cao Cao persisted, "you should at least have heard of some." "Yuan Shu of Huainan?" Xuande ventured.[8] "His warriors are first rate, his provisions abundant. Would he be one?" "Dry bones," Cao laughed, "rattling in the grave. Sooner or later I will have him." "Yuan Shao, then," Xuande suggested. "For four generations the Yuans have held highest office, and many officials served under them. Shao has a firm grip on Jizhou, where he is supported by capable men. Would you count him?" "His expression is fierce enough," Cao said. "But his courage is thin. He enjoys conniving but lacks decision. He plays for high stakes but begrudges personal sacrifice, spots a minor gain and risks his life. No hero he!"

Xuande asked, "And how would you rate Liu Biao, a paragon whose reputation stretches across the realm?" "Liu Biao?" Cao answered. "A name without substance, and no hero either." "There is Sun Ce," Xuande suggested. "The leader of the Southland is in his prime." "Sun Ce," Cao replied, "stands on his father's reputation. He's no hero." "Liu Zhang, then," Xuande said, "perhaps he could be considered." "Though connected to the royal house," Cao Cao said, "he is nothing but a watchdog by the gate and hardly deserves the name of hero." "Then," Xuande continued "what about Zhang Xiu, Zhang Lu, Han Sui, and the other warlords?" Cao Cao clapped his hands and laughed. "Petty mediocrities," he said, "beneath our notice." "Truly," said Xuande, "I can think of no one else."

"Now," Cao Cao went on, "what defines a hero is this: a determination to conquer, a mine of marvelous schemes, an ability to encompass the realm, and the will to make it his." "Who merits such a description?" Xuande asked. Cao pointed first to Xuande, then to himself. "The heroes of the present day," he said, "number but two—you, my lord, and myself." Xuande gulped in panic. Before he realized it, his chopsticks had slipped to the ground. Then the storm came on. A peal of thunder gave him the chance to bend down casually and retrieve them. "See what a clap of thunder has made me do?" he remarked. "A great man afraid of thunder?" Cao asked. "Confucius himself became agitated in thunderstorms," Xuande reminded him.[9] "How could I not fear them?" In this way he succeeded in glossing over the cause of his anxiety. Later a poet left these lines in admiration:

> Xuande sheltered in the tiger's lair:
> Cao betrayed two names that made him quake.
> He seizes on the thunder as the cause—
> A perfect ploy negotiates the pause.

The rain stopped. Two men burst into the garden. Swords in hand, they dashed to the pavilion, shoving aside the guards. There before Cao's eyes stood Lord Guan and Zhang Fei! The two warriors, after returning from archery practice, were told that Xu Chu and Zhang Liao had escorted Xuande to see Cao Cao. Anxious for their elder brother's safety, the two had rushed to the prime minister's residence and pushed their way into the rear garden, only to find Cao Cao and Xuande calmly drinking together. Lord Guan and Zhang Fei stood still, hands resting on their weapons. Cao asked the reason for the visit, and Lord Guan replied, "We heard Your Excellency was carousing with our brother and have come to present a sword dance for your amusement." "Not another Hongmen, I hope," Cao said, smiling. "We hardly need a repeat of that performance."[10] Xuande smiled too. "Two more cups," ordered Cao, "to take the edge off these would-be Fan Kuais!" But the brothers respectfully declined and the party broke up. Xuande bid Cao Cao good-bye and returned to his quarters.

"We thought it was the end," Lord Guan said. Xuande told them how he had dropped his chopsticks, and his brothers asked what that meant. "I work in the garden," Xuande explained, "to show Cao Cao I have no ambition. But he caught me off guard by calling me a hero, and the chopsticks slipped from my hand. I told him it was the thunder to put him off the track." The brothers marveled at Xuande's quickness.

The following day found Xuande a guest of Cao's once again. While they were together, Man Chong reported that Yuan Shao had defeated Gongson Zan. Xuande, anxious about his longtime friend, asked for details.

Man Chong replied, "Zan could not cope with Yuan Shao in the field, so he walled in his position, built a hundred-span tower above it called Yijing Tower, and laid in three hundred thousand measures of grain. His soldiers, however, kept passing in and out of the fortified area, and some were caught outside. Zan's followers wanted to rescue them, but Zan said, 'Rescue one, and others who will have to fight will be looking for help instead of fighting to the death.' Zan's denial of help only prompted many of his men to surrender to Yuan Shao. Isolated now, Zan sent to the capital for help. Unfortunately, Shao captured his messenger. Next, Zan tried to get Zhang Yan to cooperate inside of Shao's camp by setting a fire as a signal. Again, Shao intercepted the letter and used the information to draw Zan into an ambush. Zan lost more than half his men before retreating into the city. Shao then tunneled under the Yijing Tower and set it ablaze. Trapped, Zan killed his wife and children and hanged himself. The rest of his family was consumed in the flames.

"Consequently, Yuan Shao is now vastly strengthened by the new forces he has acquired. Meanwhile, Yuan Shu, Shao's brother, lives a dissipated life, scorning the needs of his army and his people—many of whom have already turned against him. Shu has proposed transferring to Yuan Shao the imperial title he usurped, and Shao for his part wants the royal seal more than anything.[11] Shu has promised to deliver it personally and is now moving from south of the Huai to north of the Yellow River. If the Yuan brothers overcome their former enmity and join forces, we may not be able to handle them. I beg Your Excellency to deal with this emergency."

Xuande grieved for the loss of Gongsun Zan, who had once so kindly recommended him. And where, he worried, could his dear friend General Zhao Zilong be? The time had come, Xuande calculated, to make his break with Cao Cao. Xuande stood up and faced the prime minister. "For Yuan Shu to join his brother, Shao," Xuande declared, "he will have to pass through Xuzhou. Grant me an army to attack him en route, and I will capture Yuan Shu." Cao Cao smiled and said, "Shall we submit your proposal to the Emperor? We can take action after that."[12]

The following day, after formal request to the Emperor, Cao Cao gave Xuande command of fifty thousand men and sent two generals, Zhu Ling and Lu Zhao, to accompany him. The Emperor was distraught as Xuande begged his leave, and wept in parting with his uncle. Back at his quarters, Xuande spent the night preparing weapons and gear; then he took his general's seal and set out. Dong Cheng rushed to the wayside pavilion ten *li* beyond the city to see him off. "You must bear with this," Xuande said to him. "I will find a way to fulfill the decree." "Take care and remain loyal to the Emperor's purpose," Dong Cheng pleaded. The two men parted. Lord Guan and Zhang Fei, riding beside Xuande, asked, "Brother, what made you so eager to fight this battle?" "Here I am a caged bird, a trapped fish," Xuande replied. "With this move I gain the sea, the lofty space, free of cage or net." He told his brothers to have Zhu Ling and Lu Zhao hurry the troops along.[13]

Cao Cao's advisers, Guo Jia and Cheng Yu, who had just returned to the capital from checking the treasury and granary, opposed Cao Cao's decision to send Xuande to Xuzhou. "How could you give him a military command?" they asked. "I wanted to cut off Yuan Shu," Cao explained, "that's all." "When Xuande was protector of Yuzhou," Cheng Yu said, "we urged you to kill him. You ignored the advice. Now by giving him troops you have let the dragon into the sea, the tiger into the hills. You can never again dominate him." "Even if you could not bring yourself to kill him," Guo Jia added, "what was the point of letting him leave? The ancients warned that 'endless difficulties ensue when you let the enemy escape.' I hope Your Excellency will consider what we say." Persuaded by this advice, Cao Cao sent Xu Chu ahead with five hundred men to bring Xuande back. Xu Chu took up his orders and left.

Xuande spotted the pursuers and told his brothers, "Cao must have sent men after us." He stopped the march, camped, and posted Lord Guan and Zhang Fei, weapons in hand, at either side of the entrance. Xu Chu arrived to find Xuande's company in perfect formation, completely armed. Cao's general dismounted and entered the camp. Xuande received him, asking, "What brings you here?" "I have an order from the prime minister," Xu Chu said. "You are to return for further consultation." "You know the custom," Xuande answered, "'A general in the field may refuse his lord's command.' I have appeared before the Emperor and have been duly assigned by His Excellency. What remains to be discussed? Ride back to him with my answer."[14]

Xu Chu thought, "The prime minister has always been close to Xuande. And I was told not to use force. What can I do but report what he says? Any action against him will have to wait." Thus, Xu Chu took his leave and gave Cao Cao an account of his mission. Cao was of two minds about his next step. "If he won't return," Cheng Yu and Guo Jia argued, "clearly he has turned against us." But Cao rejoined, "Two of our generals are with him. My guess is he won't rebel. Anyway, we have sent him. Regrets are useless." The idea of bringing Xuande back was dropped. Admiration of Xuande is expressed in these lines of later times:

> The soldiers packed, the horses fed, the hero dashed away;
> But ever sacred to his mind was what Xian had decreed.
> He broke from an iron cage, a tiger loose again;
> He sprung the metal lock, a dragon newly freed.

Now that Xuande was gone, Ma Teng returned west to Xiliang to calm a disturbance on his border.

At Xuzhou, Xuande was greeted by Che Zhou, the acting imperial inspector Cao Cao had appointed after defeating Lü Bu.[15] The welcoming feast concluded, Xuande's men, Sun Qian and Mi Zhu, paid their respects to him. Then Xuande went home to see his family. He also had agents investigate Yuan Shu's situation. The scouts reported back, "Yuan Shu has sunk into a life of excess. Lei Bo and Chen Lan have left him and gone to Mount Song. Shu's position is now so weak that he has offered the imperial title to his brother Yuan Shao. At Shao's summons, Shu got together men, horses, and articles of the sacred regalia and set off. But he will first have to come through Xuzhou."[16]

In command of fifty thousand men, Xuande, Lord Guan, and Zhang Fei—joined by Cao's generals Zhu Ling and Lu Zhao—marched forth. They met Yuan Shu's advance guard, led by Ji Ling. Wasting no words, Zhang Fei went for Ji Ling. Before ten thrusts had been exchanged, Zhang Fei gave an ear-splitting shout and ran his opponent through. Ji Ling tumbled from his horse; his army fled. Yuan Shu advanced and offered battle.

Xuande divided his men into three units: Zhu Ling and Lu Zhao to the left, Lord Guan and Zhang Fei to the right, Xuande himself holding the center. As Yuan Shu came into view, Xuande stood beneath his colors and denounced him. "Treasonous renegade!" he cried. "I hold here a mandate to bring you to judgment. Bind your hands and surrender, and your crimes will be excused." "Miserable mat-weaver! Sandal-maker!" Yuan Shu answered. "Will *you* insult *me?*" He waved his soldiers forward.

Xuande held back to allow his flanks to strike first. Their fierce onslaught took its toll: Yuan Shu's slain soldiers were strewn over the blood-soaked field. Thousands more fled. Yuan Shu's former commanders, Lei Bo and Chen Lan of Mount Song, plundered his treasure, grain, and fodder. Bandits kept Shu from returning to his base city, Shouchun, and he was forced to remain at Jiangting with barely a thousand men, most of them old and weak. It was midsummer. He had thirty pecks of wheat to feed his followers. Many of his own family had already starved to death. Shu could not swallow the coarse meal and asked the cook to find some honeyed water to ease his thirst. "We have bloody water," the cook said, "no honey." Suddenly Shu, who had been seated on his couch, groaned and toppled over. He spit up mouthfuls of blood and died. It was the sixth month of the fourth year of Jian An (A.D. 199).[17] Later this verse was written:

> The end of Han saw all the realm in arms:
> What grounds had Yuan Shu for his mad ambition?
> From family high in service all these years,
> He alone craved the royal throne.
>
> Having seized the precious seal of state,
> He claimed by Heaven's signs to be elected.
> Denied a little honey at the end,
> Alone he died, spitting blood, in bed.

After Yuan Shu's death, his nephew Yin fled to Lujiang, accompanied by the surviving relatives and Shu's coffin. En route they were captured and killed by Xu Liu, who brought the seal to Cao Cao in Xuchang. Cao expressed his satisfaction by appointing Xu Liu governor of Gaoling.[18]

Xuande officially informed the court of Yuan Shu's death. He also reported the fact to Cao Cao. Then he sent Cao's generals, Zhu Ling and Lu Zhao, back to the capital— but without their troops, whom he detailed to guard Xuzhou. At this time Xuande left the city to exhort the people who had scattered during the fighting to return to their occupations.

Back in Xuchang, Zhu Ling and Lu Zhao told Cao Cao how Xuande had kept their troops. Cao wanted to execute the two generals at once, but Xun Wenruo opposed it. "Xuande had the authority," he argued. "Your generals were obliged to obey." Cao therefore released them. Then Xun Wenruo advised him, "Write to the protector of Xuzhou, Che Zhou, and have him work against Xuande from within." Cao Cao adopted this plan and sent instructions to Che Zhou. Che Zhou turned to Chen Deng for advice. "I have a simple solution," Chen Deng said.[19] "While Xuande is out of the city urging people to return to work, place men in ambush by the city's outer wall. When he comes back, they can cut him down as you go out to welcome him. I will have archers placed on the walls to hold off his supporting forces. This plan will work." Che Zhou approved.

Chen Deng then explained the plan to his father, Gui.[20] Gui wanted no part of it and ordered his son to inform Xuande. Obediently, Chen Deng raced off and met up with

Lord Guan and Zhang Fei, who were returning ahead of Xuande. After Chen Deng had disclosed the plot to them, Zhang Fei wanted to attack the concealed troops, but Lord Guan cautioned him, "They are waiting for us at the outer wall. If we attack, we will lose. I have a better plan. Tonight, let's pretend to be an army of Cao Cao's arriving in Xuzhou. Che Zhou will have to come out and welcome us—then we kill him." Zhang Fei agreed.

In the dead of night the brothers led a company of men to the gates of Xuzhou, flying the flags and clad in the dress and armor of Cao's army.[21] To the guard's challenge they answered that they were Zhang Liao's soldiers, marching on orders from Prime Minister Cao Cao. Their demand for entry was taken to Che Zhou, who consulted Chen Deng. "If we don't receive them," Zhou said, "we could arouse suspicion; but it could be a trap."

Che Zhou climbed the wall and shouted, "We cannot tell who you are in the dark. We will receive you at dawn." Below the gate someone shouted back, "What if Xuande sees us here? Open at once!" Che Zhou still hesitated. Then, unable to resist the clamor of the troops outside, he rode out in full armor with one thousand men. As they crossed the lowered drawbridge, Che Zhou shouted, "Where is Zhang Liao?" In the glare of torches he saw Lord Guan bearing down on him, sword held high. "How dare a wretch like you plot to kill our brother?" he cried. Che Zhou took fright. The warriors tangled and fought, but Che Zhou soon fell back. He swung his horse round and raced for the drawbridge, only to be met with volleys of bolts shot on Chen Deng's order. Che Zhou fled, riding close to the wall. Lord Guan overtook him and cut off his head. "The traitor is dead," he shouted. "All others are forgiven. Give up and be spared." Che Zhou's men downed their weapons and surrendered. The army and the people were assured that peace was restored.[22]

Lord Guan carried Che Zhou's head to Xuande and explained the plot against his life. "What will we do if Cao Cao comes now?" he asked. "Zhang Fei and I will deal with him," was Lord Guan's answer. But Xuande remained remorseful.[23] Then he reentered Xuzhou to a warm welcome from the people and the elders of the city. He went to the protector's residence looking for Zhang Fei, only to find that his brother had exterminated Che Zhou's entire family. "We've killed Cao Cao's trusted official. Do you think he is not going to act?" he asked Chen Deng. "I think I know how to keep him away," Deng replied. Indeed:

> No sooner was Xuande out of the tiger's lair
> Than he needed a plan to stop a brewing war.

Chen Deng's cunning had delivered Lü Bu to Cao Cao; could he now save Xuande from Cao Cao?

READ ON.

22

Cao Cao Takes the Field Against Yuan Shao;
Lord Guan and Zhang Fei Capture Two Generals

CHEN DENG OFFERED THE FOLLOWING PLAN to Xuande: "Cao Cao fears no man more than Yuan Shao, for Shao holds firmly the four northern provinces of Ji, Qing, You, and Bing. He commands a million men, and civil and military officials in ample numbers. Why not send to him for help?" "Yuan Shao and I have had no dealings with one another," Xuande responded. "And now that I have just defeated his younger brother, how could he possibly aid us?" "Here in Xuzhou," Chen Deng said, "is a scholar whose family has been intimate with the Yuans for three generations. If he wrote in our behalf, Shao would aid us, I am certain." Xuande asked the man's name. "Someone you have always held in great esteem. Have you forgotten?" Chen Deng said. "Not Zheng Xuan?" Xuande replied, suddenly having a thought. "But of course!" Chen Deng answered.

Zheng Xuan (Kangcheng) was a scholar of many talents who had once studied under Ma Rong, famed for his knowledge of the classic *Book of Odes*. Ma Rong himself was in the habit of lecturing to students before a crimson curtain behind which sat singing girls. Around the room maids stood in waiting. But during the three years that Zheng Xuan studied there, his glance never strayed from the books before him—an act of self-discipline that Ma Rong admired. After Zheng Xuan had completed his studies and returned home, Ma Rong sighed and said, "Xuan is the only one who has grasped the essence of my teachings."

In Zheng Xuan's own household all the serving girls were versed in the *Odes*. Once a maidservant displeased Zheng Xuan, and he had her kneel for a long time at the steps before the main hall. Another maidservant teased her, quoting from the *Odes:* "'What hast thou done to land in the mire?'" The punished maid, quoting back, replied, "'I voiced my plaint and met with wrath.'"[1] This shows the refinement of Zheng Xuan's household. Under Emperor Huan, Zheng Xuan advanced to chief of the Secretariat. Afterward, during the upheaval caused by the eunuchs, he resigned and went home to his farm in Xuzhou. When Xuande was in Zhuo county, he studied under Zheng Xuan.[2] After he became protector of Xuzhou, Xuande often visited this former teacher whom he revered, and sought his advice. Thus Xuande was delighted to be reminded of Zheng Xuan and went with Chen Deng to solicit the scholar's help. Zheng Xuan consented wholeheartedly and wrote a letter, which he gave to Xuande; Xuande delegated Sun Qian to deliver it immediately to Yuan Shao.

Reading the renowned scholar's recommendation, Yuan Shao mused, "I should not be helping the man who caused my younger brother's death, but this letter in his behalf from the former chief of the Secretariat obliges me to act." Shao put the question of attacking Cao Cao to his officers and officials. Adviser Tian Feng said, "These long years of war have wearied the common people. We lack the grain to supply a large force. This is the time not to make war but to report our victory over Gongsun Zan to the Emperor. If they deny us access to him, we can protest formally—and then we can take up arms and plant ourselves at Liyang, enlarge our fleet on the Yellow River, repair and deploy our weapons, and assign crack troops to dig in along the borders. Inside of three years we can take power."

Adviser Shen Pei, however, opposed Tian Feng. "Sire," he began, "your marvelous martial prowess and your splendid might have calmed the entire north; we can bring Cao Cao to justice with a wave of the hand. Why keep putting it off?" A third adviser, Ju Shou, said, "It is not 'splendid might' that determines victory. Cao Cao has kept civil order in his realm. His army, steeled and seasoned, is not the easy target Gongsun Zan's was when you encircled it. I beg you not to start an unjustified war but rather to follow the sound strategy of formally announcing the recent victory to the Emperor."

Adviser Guo Tu joined the argument. "Not at all!" he cried. "Who says we have no right to move against Cao Cao? It is high time to set our enterprise in motion. I urge following the course Zheng Xuan's letter recommends—joining with Xuande in loyalty to the throne and sweeping the criminal Cao from his haven! This would correspond to the mind of Heaven and coincide with the mood of the people, an action doubly felicitous." The four counselors disputed back and forth without coming to an agreement. Yuan Shao hesitated to make the decision himself.

Unexpectedly, Xu You and Xun Shen entered, and Yuan Shao thought, "Here are two men of wide experience. Let me hear what they favor." After the exchange of courtesies, Yuan Shao said to them, "I have a letter from Zheng Xuan urging me to help Liu Bei attack Cao Cao. Should I do it, or not?" "Most enlightened lord," they replied, "you have the numbers and the strength to prevail. We, too, favor calling up the army to uphold the royal house and punish the traitor." "My view exactly," Yuan Shao said.[3]

Yuan Shao began to make preparations. First, he sent Xuande's representative, Sun Qian, to inform Zheng Xuan of his decision; then he coordinated arrangements with Xuande. He appointed Shen Pei and Pang Ji to overall command; Tian Feng, Xun Shen, and Xu You as military advisers; Yan Liang and Wen Chou as generals. Yuan Shao mustered a total of one hundred and fifty thousand cavalry and an equal number of infantry and deployed them at Liyang.[4] At this point Guo Tu said, "Since Your Lordship resorts to arms in the name of the highest allegiance, it behooves us to spell out Cao's crimes and circulate the indictment through all districts in order to publish his offenses and secure his punishment. Our claim thus will be valid and our position lawful." Yuan Shao took this advice and had Master of Documents Chen Lin draft a bill of charges.

Chen Lin (Kongzhang) was a renowned literary genius. He had served as first secretary during the reign of Emperor Ling. But when his admonitions to Regent-Marshal He Jin went unheeded and the Dong Zhuo calamity overtook him, he fled to safety to Jizhou. There Yuan Shao employed him as documents officer. In response to the command to prepare an indictment of Cao Cao, Chen Lin wrote the following:

All men know that a wise lord anticipates danger in order to master the unexpected, and a devoted subject stands vigilant against any eventuality. Verily, the extraordinary mission requires extraordinary men, and the extraordinary mission will lead to extraordinary merit. But the extraordinary is far from what ordinary men aspire to.

Of old, when a weakling ruled the mighty house of Qin, Prime Minister Zhao Gao concentrated control in his hands, making himself the sole source of authority and favor. In that time of fear and oppression no one in the court dared to speak out for what was right. The Emperor finally committed suicide in the Wangyi Palace, and the royal clan was consumed in the ensuing conflagration—a disgrace remembered even today and an object lesson for all time.

After the death of the Supreme Ancestor, Empress Lü took power. Toward the end of her reign, she allowed her two nephews Lü Chan and Lü Lu to monopolize the administration. They held military authority in the capital, while the lords of Liang and Zhao did their bidding outside. In the secrecy of the imperial chambers they summarily decided all questions, abusing those below, intending to supplant the One above, until the hearts of all froze in despair. At that point the lords of Jiang and Zhuxu raised an army and displayed their wrath.[5] They punished the traitors and enthroned Emperor Wen, a son of the Supreme Ancestor, enabling the kingly principle of true descent to flourish once again, and the imperial luster to shine with new brilliance. What a splendid instance of great ministers standing ready to prevent usurpation.

Turning to the present case of Minister of Works[6] Cao Cao, his grandfather, Teng, was a palace eunuch who joined with other eunuchs like Zuo Guan and Xu Huang to commit unspeakable crimes.[7] His rampant avarice injured the imperial leadership and ruined the common people. Cao Song, Teng's adopted son and the father of Cao Cao, wheedled his way into Teng's family and bribed his way to advancement. Conveying precious metals and jade to the gates of the mighty, he crept into the highest public office and then subverted the instruments of government. Cao Cao, vile legacy of this eunuch, an unnatural child, a man without integrity or virtue, quickly found his advantage in sedition and calamity.[8]

The valiant warriors of the military command under Yuan Shao swept out the vicious, usurping eunuchs. Alas, the next crisis swiftly followed: Dong Zhuo laid violent hands on officialdom and even on the throne. That was when we took up our swords and flourished our war drums, issuing word to the east of the realm: gather and pick the finest heroes to serve our cause. Thus we came to accept Cao Cao's cooperation and assigned him a supporting command, thinking to put this bird of prey's fierce claws to our good use.

Cao Cao proved himself to be ignorant and frivolous—shortsighted in strategy, hasty in advance, capricious in retreat—and his troops were decimated time after time.[9] Yet our command again and again parceled out the finest men to make his losses good, his strength whole. Then, on our recommendation, he was put in charge of Hedong district and made imperial inspector of Yanzhou.[10] We cloaked him in the tiger colors of military authority in hopes of gaining the full fruit of his vengefulness against Dong Zhuo, as the state of Qin did when it used Meng Ming against Jin.[11]

But now Cao Cao has run wild with what we have provided him. By his unbridled conduct and malignant excesses he has bloodied the common people, ruined the worthy, and injured the innocent. Was not Bian Rang, governor of Jiujiang, known across the land for his splendid talents and exalted name, his frank views and forthright expression? Was he not honored as a man whose views were free of craven flattery? And was he not decapitated, his head piked, his harmless wife and babes snuffed out?[12] Since that time, the community of scholars has been sore with indignation. And as the grievances of the people grew heavier, one man rose in opposition and a whole province responded. Was not Cao Cao crushed near Xuzhou and his territory seized by Lü Bu, leaving him to roam the eastern fringe with nowhere to tread or hold?[13]

But this command, affirming the principle of "strong trunk, weak branches," sanctioned no revolt of the disaffected Lü Bu against central authority. Hoisting our standards and donning our armor, we again set out in force to commence the campaign. Gong and drum echoed and shuddered. Lü Bu's hosts melted away as we plucked Cao Cao from sure disaster and restored his position in Yanzhou—though this was more fortunate for Cao than for the people of that province.[14]

After Cao was installed in Yanzhou, the royal entourage was attacked by criminal remnants of Dong Zhuo's faction. Preoccupied by a military emergency in the northern reaches of our home province, Jizhou, we had Xu Xun, an imperial corpsman, dispatch Cao Cao to restore the temples and sacrificial sites and to protect the young sovereign.[15] But Cao seized the occasion to give full rein to his ambition. Like a domineering bully, he moved the capital by force and took charge of the inner life of the court; he demeaned the royal house and destroyed its laws and standards. Taking the three highest offices under his control, he monopolized administrative power, dictating according to his whim appointments, conferments, punishments, and executions. Those who held his favor won prestige for their entire clan. Those he held in disfavor were exterminated to the last kinsman. Those who objected openly were publicly executed. Those who objected privately were secretly done away with. Officialdom sealed its lips. Men in the streets communicated with glances. The Secretariat confined itself to recording court sessions. The ministers were reduced to bureaucratic ciphers.

The former grand commandant Yang Biao, who once had served as minister of works and later as minister of the interior, enjoyed the highest station in the land. But once he became an object of Cao's jealous fury, he was smeared with calumny, beaten mercilessly, and tortured. Indeed, Cao Cao punished capriciously anyone who offended him, heedless of the requirements of law.[16] Take the case of Court Counselor Zhao Yan, whose devoted admonitions and forthright criticisms could not be dismissed. The Emperor received his counsel with delight and approval. But Cao was determined to deprive the Emperor of all wise judgment. He terminated the counselor's access and then arrested him and had him killed, without bothering even to inform the court.

Then there was the incident of Prince Xiao's tomb. Prince Xiao of Liang, son of Emperor Wen, was the brother of Emperor Jing. His sepulcher and the trees planted there by his ancestors—the mulberry and the lindera, the pine and the cypress—should have been held in most sacred reverence. Yet Cao Cao personally directed his officers in the exhumation of the tomb. Breaking open the coffin, they exposed the remains and seized all the buried treasure. To this day the Emperor weeps for it, and the people grieve.

Next, Cao Cao set up new offices—Imperial Corps Commander for Exhumations, Commandant for Uncovering Valuables—with agents who made havoc with everything they came upon, exhuming corpses to the last bone. Thus Cao held highest office but brutally played the tyrant's part, corrupting the government and injuring the people; the poison has touched the spirits of the dead as well as living men.

On top of that came the suffering caused by trivial regulations and augmented by mutual surveillance, hedging men's activities with hidden dangers. Lift a hand and catch it in a net; move a foot and spring a trap. That is why the people of Cao's own provinces, Yanzhou and Yuzhou, have lost all spirit, and why the groans of wronged men fill the capital. Search through the annals for renegade ministers who surpass Cao Cao for blatant avarice and cruel malice!

This command, occupied with the punishment of external sedition, had no time to confront the problem at court. More recently we have refrained from taking action in the hope that the situation could be rectified. But the rapacious jackal Cao harbors dire designs. He seeks to destroy the pillars of the dynasty, weaken the house of Han, and remove all righteous and devoted men so that he can play the potentate unopposed.

When we marched north to chastise Gongsun Zan, those stubborn rebels held off our siege for a whole year thanks to the aid Cao quietly gave them while he was overtly supporting our royal forces. But Cao's envoy was discovered. Gongsun Zan was executed and his forces eliminated. We had blunted Cao's thrust, and his scheme came to naught. [17] At present, though Cao Cao holds the Ao granary and enjoys the protection the Yellow River affords, he resembles the mantis that stands against the oncoming chariot wheel with its forelegs upraised.

This command, imbued with the sacred spirit of Han's majesty, will fend off any thrust from any quarter. Our long spears number in the millions, our mounted nomad hordes are in the thousands. We have rallied warriors who are the equal of heroes of myth, and summoned the strength of crack archers and crossbowmen. We shall cross the Taihangs in Bingzhou and ford the Ji and the Ta in Qingzhou to descend in force on the Yellow River and pierce Cao Cao's front; from Jingzhou Liu Biao will sweep up through Wancheng and Ye and block him from the rear. We shall overpower and overwhelm Cao as surely as seawater quenches embers, as the torch fires the kindling.

Those of Cao's officers and men who can fight come from the northern provinces, Ji or You, or from units of former legions—all of whom chafe at their long service and yearn to go home, tearfully gazing northward. The rest are men of Yan and Yu, or remnants of Lü Bu's and Zhang Yang's troops who, vanquished and coerced, follow him out of mere expedience. Scathed in many battles, all nurse grievances and enmities. If they turn their banners against Cao, mounting the high ground and sounding the drum and fife, and we wave the white to offer an avenue of surrender, Cao's host will break apart like clods of clay, without waiting for a decision by blood and blade.

Now the house of Han is dying a slow death. The social fabric hangs slack and torn. The court stands without a shred of support. The top administration is defenseless. In the imperial estates the elite look downcast, heads bowed, wings furled, having lost all hope of succor. Though loyal liegemen remain, how can they manifest their integrity when they are menaced by so cruel and violent a vassal!

Cao Cao controls a picked force of seven hundred that surrounds the palace. It poses as the residential guard, but in reality detains the sovereign, a sign of im-

pending usurpation that we find all too alarming. The time is ripe for those loyal
to the dynasty to splash the ground with their life's blood, for upright men to make
their mark. Let no one fail to rise to the occasion.[18]

Cao Cao has counterfeited an edict empowering him to dispatch envoys and
soldiers. We are concerned lest remote regions provide for the renegade out of a
mistaken sense of obedience. Whoever aids him will lose imperial sanction and be
ridiculed by all. No sensible man will follow such a course.

On this day we are advancing from four provinces—You, Bing, Qing, and Ji.
When this proclamation reaches Jingzhou, Liu Biao will coordinate his forces with
those of the General of Established Loyalty [Zhang Xiu, stationed at Wancheng].
Let every region and district mobilize its loyal forces, stake out its borders, and
display its might to join us in protecting our dynasty's shrines to the gods of soil
and grain. Thus will we accomplish our extraordinary mission in full view of the
realm.

Whoever takes Cao Cao's head will be made lord of five thousand households
and awarded fifty million cash. Any commander of a unit, subordinate commander,
military or civil official who surrenders to us will be welcomed without question.
Let our generosity and bounty be widely published, together with announced rewards, so that by this proclamation the empire will know of the grave crisis facing
the sacred court.

This order has the force of law.

Yuan Shao read Chen Lin's draft proclamation with great satisfaction and ordered it
circulated through all regions, and hung at key passes, fords, and other points of entry.
The document reached the capital at a time when Cao Cao was stricken with migraine and
confined to bed. As he read it, he began quaking to his marrow and broke into an icy
sweat. Suddenly his migraine passed, and he leaped out of bed. He found Cao Hong and
demanded, "Who wrote this?" When Hong replied that it was said to be from the brush
of Chen Lin, Cao laughed and commented, "Such literary style won't work very well
without military strategy. However exquisitely Chen Lin writes, what can he do for Yuan
Shao's failings in the field?" So saying, Cao Cao summoned his counselors to discuss
ways of dealing with Yuan Shao.

The scholar Kong Rong argued, "Yuan Shao's power is immense; we cannot fight him:
let us come to terms." "Yuan Shao is incompetent," Xun Wenruo countered. "Nothing
compels us to consider a peace." "Shao's territory is broad, and his people are hardy,"
Kong Rong said. "He has shrewd planners like Xu You, Guo Tu, Shen Pei, and Pang Ji;
loyal servants like Tian Feng and Ju Shou; and brave generals such as Yan Liang and Wen
Chou; while his other military leaders—Gao Lan, Zhang He, Chunyu Qiong, for example—are known to all. What do you mean, calling Shao incompetent?"

With a laugh Xun Wenruo replied, "His troops are numerous but disorderly. Tian
Feng is rigid and insubordinate; Xu You, greedy and unseeing; Shen Pei, arbitrary and
inept at planning; and Pang Ji, resolute but ineffective. These men have little tolerance for
one another and are therefore bound to quarrel. His generals, Yan Liang and Wen Chou,
are brave but reckless. They will be ours in a single battle. And the rest of his misbe-
gotten host, even though a million strong, aren't worth worrying about." Kong Rong
fell silent, but Cao Cao burst out laughing. "Wenruo has certainly sized them up!" he
exclaimed.

Cao Cao named General Liu Dai to lead the forward army and General Wang Zhong
to lead the rear army, a force numbering fifty thousand. They marched east and attacked

Xuande in Xuzhou. Cao Cao assigned them the colors of the prime minister to create
the impression that he personally was in command. Liu Dai had been imperial inspector of Yanzhou when Cao Cao seized the province and, after submitting to Cao, was
appointed auxiliary commander. Thus Liu Dai, joined by Wang Zhong, came to receive
the assignment.

Cao Cao himself marched north toward Liyang with two hundred thousand to oppose
Yuan Shao. Adviser Cheng Yu said to Cao, "What if Liu Dai and Wang Zhong fail their
mission?" "You know as well as I do," Cao Cao replied, "that they are no match for
Xuande. Their function is to divert the enemy." He then ordered the two commanders:
"Do not advance until I have defeated Yuan Shao. Then I will turn my attention to Liu
Bei." Liu Dai and Wang Zhong set out.

Cao Cao led his army toward Liyang. Yuan Shao's army was eighty *li* away. Both sides
dug in and held their ground through the autumn. Disputes in Shao's camp undermined
morale: Xu You was unhappy that Shen Pei had a command; Ju Shou resented Shao for
rejecting his plans. Commanders and advisers were at odds with one another, and no one
thought of taking the initiative. Shao himself, plagued by doubts, chose not to attack.
Under the circumstances, Cao Cao ordered Zang Ba (formerly Lü Bu's deputy commander) to maintain pressure on Qingzhou and Xuzhou; Yu Jin and Li Dian to fortify
points on the Yellow River; and Cao Ren to station the main army at Guandu. Cao Cao
himself took one army back to the capital at Xuchang.

•   •   •   •   •

Liu Dai and Wang Zhong camped one hundred *li* from Xuzhou. At the command
headquarters they raised the prime minister's ensign but did not advance. They sent men
north of the river for word of Cao Cao's progress. Xuande knew nothing of the actual
situation and hesitated to act; he, too, tried to keep informed of developments to the
north.

Suddenly the order to attack reached Liu Dai and Wang Zhong. "His Excellency," Dai
said, "has commanded us to strike Xuzhou. You should go first." "His Excellency ordered *you*," Wang Zhong replied. "I am the general in charge," Dai said, "it is not for me
to begin the action." "Then we'll go together," Wang Zhong proposed. "We'll draw lots,
rather," Liu Dai said. Zhong drew and lost. He took half of the men to attack the city.

Xuande said to his adviser Chen Deng, "Yuan Shao is well positioned at Liyang, but
frustrated by conflicts on his staff, he takes no initiative. Cao Cao's whereabouts meanwhile remain unknown. They say his personal banner is not with the force near Liyang,
but it seems to have turned up here. I wonder why." "Cao Cao's cunning is manifold,"
Chen Deng said. "His main concern lies north of the river, where he takes command himself. But he has his banner raised here instead of there in order to deceive us. I doubt if
he is really here." "Which of you will go and find out?" Xuande asked his two brothers.
Zhang Fei volunteered, but Xuande demurred. "Your temper's too hot," he said. "If Cao
Cao is there," Zhang Fei pleaded, "I'll bring him here." "Let me go and find out what is
happening," Lord Guan said. "If you are going," Xuande said, "I am at ease." So, Lord
Guan set out from Xuzhou with three thousand men.

It was early winter. Under a heavy sky snowflakes swirled lightly. Braving the snow,
Lord Guan's men positioned themselves for battle as Guan charged up, blade bared, and
hailed Wang Zhong. "The prime minister is here!" Zhong shouted. "Therefore, surrender." "Please have him come out," Lord Guan responded. "I have a few things to tell
him." "Would His Excellency receive the likes of you?" Zhong demanded. Lord Guan
charged; Wang Zhong poised his spear. Their horses crossed. Lord Guan whipped his

mount and galloped off; Wang Zhong pursued. After rounding a hillside, Lord Guan spun around and with a single short cry, his blade dancing, rushed his pursuer. Unable to defend himself, Wang Zhong tried to bolt, but Lord Guan, passing his sword to his left hand, snatched Zhong's armor straps in his right and dragged him out of the saddle and sideways onto his own mount. Lord Guan rode back to camp as Wang Zhong's soldiers scattered.

Lord Guan took his prisoner to Xuande, who demanded, "Who are you and what office do you hold that you dare counterfeit the colors of the prime minister?" "Would I dare?" was the reply. "They told me to create a false impression as a decoy. In fact, the prime minister is not here." Xuande had the captive provided for and guarded until Liu Dai could be taken and a final disposition made. "I knew you wanted no bloodshed," Lord Guan said to Xuande, "so I took him alive." "I was uneasy about our brother's temper," Xuande said. "He might have slain Wang Zhong. There's no point in killing someone who can be detained and used in negotiations."

Then Zhang Fei spoke up: "Now that second brother has captured Wang Zhong, let me go for Liu Dai." "Dai used to be imperial inspector of Yanzhou," Xuande warned. "In the struggle against Dong Zhuo at Tiger Trap Pass he was one of the lords of the alliance. Today he heads Cao's vanguard. Do not slight his abilities." "Is he really worth all this talk?" Zhang Fei asked. "I'll take him alive the same as second brother took Wang Zhong. That's all there is to it!" "Be sure not to kill him and ruin my plans," Xuande cautioned. "I'll answer with my life if I do," was Fei's reply. Xuande gave him three thousand men, and he set out.

After Wang Zhong's capture, Liu Dai refused to show himself. Day after day Zhang Fei came before the camp to try to taunt him into appearing, but Liu Dai was only the more determined to remain inside. Several days passed. Zhang Fei decided to try a stratagem: first he issued an order to raid Dai's camp at the second watch, and then he spent the day in his tent, drinking heavily and feigning intoxication. Next, he found fault with a soldier and had him beaten and tied up. "Tonight," he declared, "I will sacrifice this man to my banners." But he arranged to have the man quietly freed. As anticipated, the soldier fled to Liu Dai's camp and reported the impending raid. The dreadful bruises on his flesh dispelled Dai's doubts. Liu Dai evacuated his camp and posted his forces outside it to await Zhang Fei's attack.

That night Zhang Fei divided his men into three groups. From the center a team of thirty was to raid the camp and burn it. The flanking units were to circle behind the base, watch for the fire signal, and attack from both sides. At the third watch Zhang Fei led his best men to cut off Liu Dai's retreat; then the team of thirty burst into the empty camp and set it ablaze. Liu Dai's waiting troops were about to strike when they themselves were struck from both sides. Dai's army fell into disarray, unable to gauge the size of the enemy it faced. Liu Dai fled with some remnant troops. Zhang Fei was ready for him. Confronted head on, Dai had no time to turn off, and he was seized in a single encounter. The small force with him surrendered.

Zhang Fei reported his victory to Xuande, and Xuande remarked to Lord Guan, "I'm glad to hear our normally rash and reckless brother is starting to use his head." Then Xuande went to greet Zhang Fei outside the walls of Xuzhou. "Well," Fei said to him, "do you still think me impetuous?" "I harped on your failings so you'd learn some tricks," Xuande said, and Zhang Fei roared with delight.

Liu Dai was brought in bonds to Xuande, who hastened to free him. "My younger brother," Xuande said to the prisoner, "has been most disrespectful! I hope you will forgive him." Xuande led Liu Dai into the city and had Wang Zhong released; he treated them with civility. Then Xuande said to them, "Cao Cao's imperial inspector, Che Zhou, tried to kill me, so I was forced to defend myself. His Excellency wrongly suspected me of rebellion, and he sent you to make me answer for it. But I wish nothing more than to requite with my devotion His Excellency's grace and generosity, and never meant to betray him. If you two would speak well of me to him when you get back to the capital, I would be most grateful." "We owe you our lives," the commanders replied, "and shall plead your cause to the prime minister on the security of our families." Xuande expressed his thanks.

The following day Xuande returned the two commanders' men and horses and escorted them out of the city. They had traveled some ten *li* when they heard a great rolling of drums. Zhang Fei was blocking the way. "My elder brother did not know what he was doing when he let you go," Fei shouted. "How can enemy commanders in custody simply be released?" Liu Dai and Wang Zhong began to tremble. Eyes round with anger, Zhang Fei rushed forward, his spear raised. But at that moment another rider appeared, shouting, "You can't abuse them like that!" It was Lord Guan; Dai and Zhong knew they were saved. "Elder brother has released them," Lord Guan insisted. "You cannot violate his command." "Free them now," Zhang Fei said, "and they'll return." "We'll take care of them then," was Guan's reply. The two commanders reassured the brothers, "Even if the prime minister kills off our entire clans, we will not return. We beg forgiveness." "Even if Cao Cao himself comes here," Zhang Fei retorted, "we'll hit him so hard not a piece of armor will go back. This time the two live heads will do!" The commanders scurried off, grateful to be spared.

But returning to Xuande, Lord Guan and Zhang Fei said, "Cao Cao will be coming." "Xuzhou is too exposed to hold for long," Sun Qian advised. "We'd better fortify Xiaopei and the town of Xiapi, giving us a two-pronged deployment against Cao Cao." Xuande approved the suggestion. He sent Lord Guan to Xiapi and placed his wives, Lady Gan and Lady Mi, in his care. (Lady Gan was from Xiaopei, and Lady Mi was Mi Zhu's younger sister.) Sun Qian, Jian Yong, Mi Zhu, and Mi Fang remained to guard Xuzhou. Xuande and Zhang Fei went to Xiaopei.

In the capital Liu Dai and Wang Zhong defended Xuande's conduct to Cao Cao. But the prime minister swore angrily, "You have disgraced our government. Why should I spare you?" Cao ordered them to be marched out and executed. Indeed:

> Can dogs and pigs with tigers share the field?
> Can shrimp and fish with dragons vie below the waves?

Would Cao Cao kill the men Xuande had shrewdly spared?

READ ON.

23

Mi Heng Strips, Denouncing the Traitor;
Ji Ping Is Executed for Threatening Cao's Life

CAO CAO WANTED TO EXECUTE the two commanders, but Kong Rong pleaded for them. "They were no match for Xuande," he said. "Killing them would only demoralize your officers and men." So Cao Cao contented himself with depriving them of rank and pay. Then he began planning his campaign against Xuande. Again Kong Rong sought to dissuade him. "We cannot mobilize in the winter cold," he argued. "We must wait until spring comes. If we can get the support of Zhang Xiu and Liu Biao first, we'll be in a better position to attack Xuzhou." Cao Cao accepted this advice and dispatched Liu Ye to Zhang Xiu in Xiangcheng.

The envoy sang Cao Cao's praises to Zhang Xiu's adviser, Jia Xu.[1] Jia Xu welcomed Liu Ye as his personal guest and the following day brought him before Zhang Xiu, explaining that Cao's envoy was offering amnesty. During this discussion an envoy from Yuan Shao was announced. Shao too, according to the documents the envoy bore, was seeking Zhang Xiu's allegiance. Jia Xu said to Yuan Shao's representative, "Your master has taken the field against Cao Cao. How do things stand now?" "We have suspended operations for the winter," he replied. "My lord is making the offer to General Zhang Xiu and Liu Biao because he regards both as leaders of the land." Jia Xu said with a laugh, "Go back and tell Yuan Shao that if he couldn't make common cause with his own brother, how can he expect to do so with the 'leaders of the land'?" Then and there Jia Xu destroyed Yuan Shao's letter in the presence of the envoy and dismissed him harshly.

"Yuan Shao is stronger than Cao Cao," Zhang Xiu complained. "You have torn up his letter and offended his envoy. What if Shao attacks?" "Cao Cao's the surer ally," Jia Xu answered. "But we are enemies," Zhang Xiu said. "How can we work together?" "There are three advantages to allying with Cao," Jia Xu said. "First, by controlling imperial edicts Cao legitimizes his campaigns throughout the realm. Second, precisely because Shao is the more powerful, as you say, he is unlikely to appreciate your small contingent, while the weaker Cao will receive it with enthusiasm. Third, Cao aspires to mastery of the realm and therefore must eschew all personal enmities so that he can manifest his virtue across the land. Do not doubt it, General."

Jia Xu's arguments convinced Zhang Xiu to receive Cao's envoy. At the audience Liu Ye praised Cao Cao's abundant virtues and then added, "If the prime minister carried grudges, General, would he be sending me to seek your friendship?" Delighted with the offer, Zhang Xiu went with Jia Xu to the capital to tender his allegiance. At the steps leading up to the main hall of the palace, Zhang Xiu prostrated himself before Cao Cao, who hastened to help the general to his feet. Taking Zhang Xiu's hand, Cao Cao said, "It was I who offended. Do not hold it against me." He appointed Zhang Xiu General of Manifest Might and Jia Xu an officer in the Capital Guard. Then Cao Cao asked Zhang Xiu to write to Liu Biao urging him to come to terms.

"Liu Biao likes to befriend the luminaries of our day," Jia Xu told Cao Cao. "What we need is a noted man of letters to persuade him to join us." On Xun You's advice, Cao Cao sent for Kong Rong. "His Excellency," Xun You explained to Kong Rong, "seeks a distinguished scholar to represent his views to Liu Biao. Would you consider it, sire?" "I have a friend, Mi Heng (styled Zhengping)," Kong Rong replied, "who is ten times more talented than I. He belongs in the Emperor's personal service, not just handling a minor matter like this. Let me recommend him to the Son of Heaven." Kong Rong submitted the following petition to the court in Mi Heng's behalf:

> When floods overran the land, the Emperor provided for their control, searching every corner of the realm for able men. When Shi Zong took the throne,[2] he meant to expand the patrimony, and toward that end sought out men who would shed luster on his enterprise. Thus he attracted exceptional talent to his service. With profound sagacity, Your Majesty, heir to the great tradition of Han, has met with an unfortunate situation and spends the days in anguish. But spirits are descending from the sacred hills; and remarkable men are coming to the fore.
>
> I know of one such worthy, presently still a commoner. His name is Mi Heng (styled Zhengping); his age, twenty-four. He is a clean and simple man of shining integrity and outstanding ability. He became conversant with literature first, and later was initiated into the secrets of the arts. What he sees but once he can recite in full. What he hears in passing he can commit to memory. His nature is at one with the true way. His power of thought has something divine in it. It would not surprise me if he proved the equal of Sang Hongyang in calculation and Zhang Anshi in comprehensive recall.[3] Moreover, his loyalty is unswerving and his intentions pure as snow. The good inspires him, and evil disgusts him. He would risk his life to defend useful criticism as promptly as he would protect Your Majesty from unscrupulous counsel in the manner of a Ren Zuo or a Shi Yu.[4] A hundred eagles cannot compare to one wise osprey: Mi Heng would have a wonderful effect if placed at court. His quick thinking and elegant rhetoric are never wanting. He can work out problems and resolve dilemmas with absolute mastery, and will never be at a loss in dealing with the enemy.
>
> In the early years of the Han, Jia Yi petitioned the Emperor to establish frontier colonies as a means for controlling the Xiongnu, and Zhong Jun, sent to placate the kingdom of Nanyue, was ready to haul its king to Chang'an to pay homage to the Emperor. Former generations celebrated these two high-spirited youths.
>
> In more recent times Lu Cui and Yan Xiang have been appointed at court because of their unusual ability. Such treatment should be accorded Mi Heng. A dragon like him aloft in the heavenly court, beating his wings among the constellations, raising his voice among the circumpolar stars,[5] and sending down the rainbow's beams will lend glory to the newly appointed officials and magnify the dignity of Your Majesty's house. The imperial music festivals are for rare and wonderful performers; the imperial chambers, for preserving extraordinary treasures. Men like Mi Heng are all too rare. The song and dance "Ji Chu" and the

composition "Yang E" are the music master's first choice for performance par excellence. Fei Tu and Yao Niao, those fleet gallopers, are what the trainer Bo Le and the charioteer Wang Liang were ever eager to obtain. Though but a humble servant of little note, I feel obliged to call this man to Your Majesty's attention. Your Majesty's earnest caution in selecting men to serve you requires comparison and trial. Now I appeal for an audience for this commoner. If you find in him nothing useful, I will accept the blame for leading you astray.

The Emperor read Kong Rong's petition and passed it on to Cao Cao, who summoned Mi Heng. But at his audience with the prime minister, Mi Heng suffered the indignity of not being commanded to take a seat; and so the scholar looked skyward and said with a sigh, "In this wide, wide world I see not one real man!" Cao snapped back, "I have dozens in my service who rate as heroes of our time. What's your point?" "Name them," Mi Heng responded. Cao Cao answered, "Xun Wenruo, Xun You, Guo Jia, and Cheng Yu are all men of depth and vision, far superior to Xiao He and Chen Ping.[6] I have Zhang Liao, Xu Chu, Li Dian, and Yue Jin, whose valor surpasses Cen Peng's and Ma Wu's.[7] Then there are the military aides Lü Qian and Man Chong, and the vanguard leaders Yu Jin and Xu Huang. Xiahou Dun, moreover, is a rare field commander, and Cao Ren one of fortune's favorite generals. What, then, is your point?"

"I beg to differ," Mi Heng said, scoffing. "These men you mention are known to me—all too well. Xun Wenruo is good for attending funerals and visiting the bedridden. Xun You will do for guarding grave sites. Cheng Yu would make a superb gatekeeper. Guo Jia's real talent is for reading prose and reciting verse. Zhang Liao would serve well tapping the chimes and drums, and Xu Chu belongs tending cattle and horses. Yue Jin is good for receiving petitions and reading edicts, Li Dian for transmitting documents and delivering instructions, Lü Qian for sharpening blades and forging swords. Man Chong consumes wine and dregs. Yu Jin can work at lugging blocks and raising walls. Xu Huang would be best employed slaughtering pigs and dogs. Xiahou Dun deserves the title 'Unscathed General'; Cao Ren, 'Well-bribed Governor.' The rest of the lot are so many clothes racks, rice bags, wine casks, meat sacks. . . . "

"And what is your specialty?" Cao asked, cold with fury. "I," was Mi Heng's reply, "have mastered the patterns of the heavens and the contours of the land. I have knowledge of the three great teachings and the nine minor traditions. With virtue equal to Confucius' and his dearest disciple Yan Yuan's, I can make a king into as sage a sovereign as Yao or Shun. And you rate me with those mediocrities!" Zhang Liao, who was standing nearby, drew his sword and moved toward Mi Heng, but Cao Cao said, "It so happens, I am short a drum master for our ceremonies and banquets. Let Mi Heng have that job." Mi Heng did not refuse and left as soon as Cao Cao had finished speaking. "Why spare this vulgar fellow?" Zhang Liao asked. "He has something of a name," Cao Cao answered. "Why, I don't know. Everyone seems to have heard of him, though. If I killed him, the world would call me mean and intolerant. Since he thinks so highly of himself, I made him a drummer—to humiliate him."

A few days later Cao Cao summoned Mi Heng to perform for his guests at a palace banquet.[8] The previous drum master had warned Mi Heng to put on fresh attire before touching the instruments, but he entered shabbily dressed and proceeded to sound out the "Triple Tolling of Yuyang." The tone and rhythm were superb and the notes resounded with the richness of pealing bells and shining stones. Every guest was moved to tears. But in the midst of the performance Cao's attendants shouted to him rudely, "Why haven't you changed your clothes?'' A moment later Mi Heng had stripped himself stark naked before the assembly. The guests hastily shielded their eyes. Then, his expression unchanged, Mi Heng nonchalantly drew his trousers back on.

"How dare you commit such an outrage," Cao cried, "in the hallowed hall of the imperial court?'' "To abuse one's lord," Mi Heng shot back, "to deceive the sovereign, is what I call an 'outrage.' Let everyone see that I have kept the form my parents gave me free of blemish." "If you are so pure," Cao demanded, "who is corrupt?" Mi Heng responded, "That you cannot distinguish between the able and the incompetent shows that your eyes are corrupt. Your failure to chant the *Odes* and the *Documents*[9] shows that your mouth is corrupt. Your rejection of loyal advice shows that your ears are corrupt. Your ignorance of past and present shows that your whole being is corrupt. Your conflicts with the lords of the realm show that your stomach is corrupt. Your dream of usurpation shows that your mind is corrupt. To make a renowned scholar like me serve as drum master is a poor imitation of the tricks of such villains of old as Yang Huo who slighted Confucius, or Zang Cang who tried to ruin Mencius. Do you think you can hold men in such contempt and still become the leader of the lords of the realm?"

Kong Rong, witnessing the scene, feared for the life of the man he had recommended. Approaching Cao, he said calmly, "For this crime let him be sent to do hard labor as a convict. He will never be another Fu Yue!"[10] Cao Cao pointed to Mi Heng and said, "I am sending you to Jingzhou as my envoy. Win Liu Biao to our side, and you may return as a high official." But Mi Heng refused to go. Cao Cao ordered three horses made ready and had Mi Heng escorted away. Cao also arranged a departure feast at the Eastern Gates to be attended by his officials and commanders. Mi Heng appeared, but on instructions from Xun Wenruo, the assembly did not rise. Suddenly, the guest of honor gave a mournful cry.

"What are you wailing for?" Xun Wenruo asked Mi Heng. "I'm walking among dead men waiting to be buried—why shouldn't I wail?" was the reply. "If we are in our coffins," the officials responded, "you are a headless demon." "I," Mi Heng declared, "am not of Cao's clique. I serve the Han. I have my head!"[11] The officials wished to kill him on the spot, but Xun Wenruo said, "Don't dirty your blades on a rat." "I may be a rat," Mi Heng retorted, "but I have my human nature. The likes of you can only be called parasitic wasps." The exchange of insults ended, and the officials dispersed in an angry mood.

Under duress Mi Heng went to Jingzhou where Liu Biao received him. He sang his host's praises, but in a tone so ironic that Liu Biao took offense and sent him off to Huang Zu in Jiangxia. Someone said to Liu Biao, "Mi Heng has mocked Your Lordship and should die for it." But Liu Biao replied, "He slandered Cao Cao more than once and has survived because Cao couldn't risk killing a noted scholar. He sent him here, hoping we would save him the trouble—and take the blame. I've sent Mi Heng on to Huang Zu to show Cao that two can play that game." Liu Biao's advisers were impressed with his shrewdness.

At this time Yuan Shao's envoy also arrived in Jingzhou. "Now," Liu Biao said, "we have envoys from Shao as well as Cao. Which of them can do more for us?" Han Song, an Imperial Corps commander assigned to Liu Biao,[12] said, "Two rivals are locked in struggle. General, if you have serious ambitions, you have a chance now to destroy your enemies. The alternative is to go with the better man. Cao Cao is adept at warfare. Many able men have joined him. Judging from the situation, he will conquer Yuan Shao first and then move against the Southland. I don't see how we can hold Cao off. But if you commit your province to him now, he should treat you well." "I'd rather you went to the capital and looked things over before I decide," Liu Biao responded.

"Sovereign and subject have their inescapable duties," Han Song said. "Now I serve you, General, and am bound to obey you at whatever risk. So long as you fully intend to follow the Emperor and cooperate with Lord Cao, I can represent you. But if, when I enter the capital, you are still undecided, should the Emperor offer me an office, I will have to become his loyal subject instead of Your Lordship's pledged servant." "Go and find out what you can," Liu Biao said. "I have plans of my own." And so Han Song took leave of Liu Biao and went to Xuchang. Cao Cao made him a privy counselor and governor of Lingling. Xun Wenruo said to Cao Cao, "Han Song came to spy on us, yet you have richly rewarded him before he has made the slightest contribution to our cause. At the same time you have sent Mi Heng to Liu Biao, though the outcome of his mission seems to be of no interest to you." "He went too far," Cao said. "I meant for Liu Biao to kill him. The matter is closed." He sent Han Song back to Jingzhou to enlist Liu Biao's support.

Han Song returned, praised the virtues of the new court, and urged Liu Biao to send a son into the imperial service. But Liu Biao, in a burst of rage, cried, "Death for your double-dealing!" "It is you, my lord," Han Song replied, "who betrays me, not I you." Biao's adviser Kuai Liang agreed, reminding the protector that Han Song had anticipated what would happen before he left. Liu Biao therefore relented and pardoned him.

At this time Liu Biao learned that Huang Zu had executed Mi Heng. "They were drinking together," a messenger reported, "and both of them became drunk. Huang Zu asked Mi Heng, 'Tell me, who are the great men at the capital?' Heng answered, 'There's that big child Kong Rong and a smaller one, Yang Xiu. No one else.' 'And what do you think of me?' Huang Zu asked him. 'You?' Mi Heng replied. 'A deity in a temple, who receives the fragrant offerings but is lifeless and impotent!' 'So you take me for an idol of wood or clay?' Huang Zu cried, and ordered him put to death. Curses streamed from Mi Heng's lips until the last moment." Liu Biao openly lamented the death of Mi Heng and ordered his body recovered and interred on Yingwu Isle. A poet of later times wrote:

> Huang Zu was not a man of charity;
> Upon his shores Mi Heng died, yet worthily.
> Now his body lies on Yingwu Isle:
> Who visits, but the river flowing by?

The news of Mi Heng's death made Cao Cao smile. "A rotten pedant," he remarked, "done in by his own sharp tongue." Cao Cao was impatient for Liu Biao's submission and prepared to send the army. But Xun Wenruo cautioned, "Yuan Shao remains to be conquered, Xuande to be eliminated, and you want to wage war in the great river region of the Yangzi and the Han. Go for the vital organs, not the limbs. Do away with Yuan Shao and Xuande first, then sweep the central river region." Cao Cao agreed.

• • • •

After Liu Xuande left the capital, Dong Cheng continued to meet night and day with Wang Zifu and other members of his cabal, but they were unable to concert any action against Cao Cao. At the New Year's court ceremonies for the fifth year of Jian An (A.D. 200), Dong Cheng watched Cao Cao's arrogant and ruthless behavior with growing indignation until his health was affected. The Emperor noticed that the imperial brother-in-law looked unwell and ordered the noted court physician Ji Ping of Luoyang to treat him. Ping called on Dong Cheng at his residence and applied various remedies. He stayed with his patient day and night, noting his mournful sighs but refraining from expressing his concern.

On the fifteenth of the first month, the time of the first full moon festival, the physician was ready to take his leave, but Dong Cheng detained him, and the two men began drinking. After several hours Dong Cheng felt fatigue; loosening his clothes, he drifted into a dream in which Wang Zifu and three other comrades were announced. As Dong Cheng received them, Wang Zifu said "Everything is going smoothly." "Let me hear the details," Cheng answered. "Liu Biao," Zifu began, "has joined with Yuan Shao. They have half a million men marching here in ten field armies. In the northwest Ma Teng and Han Sui have mobilized seven hundred thousand Xiliang troops; they are advancing now. Cao Cao has mustered his last man and horse, dividing his fronts to meet his enemies. The capital is undefended. If we marshal a thousand servants and young attendants from our five households, we can surround the prime minister's residence this evening while the full moon festival is being held, and charge in and kill him. We have a unique opportunity." Enthusiastically Dong Cheng gathered the men of the household. Arms were collected. Dong Cheng was mounted and dressed for battle, spear couched for action. They were to assemble at Cao's inner gate and storm his quarters. Night, the second watch: all advanced. Dong Cheng raised his jeweled sword and strode into the banquet hall, where Cao was presiding. "Don't move, traitor!" Dong Cheng cried to Cao, chopping at him with his blade. Cao crumpled in the wake of the blow, as Cheng repeated the words "traitor, traitor," until he had awoken from the empty dream.

The physician leaned forward. "So you intend to murder Lord Cao?" he asked. Dong Cheng was too stunned to reply. "Calm yourself," Ji Ping went on. "Though a mere physician myself, I have never forgotten how much I owe the Han. Day after day I have listened to your deep-drawn sighs but hesitated to question you. Now, by chance, the words you spoke in your dreams have disclosed the actual situation. Please do not keep the truth from me. If there is any way I can help, even if it means clan-wide extermination, I shall do it without regret." Then, as a pledge, Ji Ping bit off the tip of his finger.[13]

"I only hope you are sincere," Dong Cheng said, covering his face; then he handed Ji Ping the Emperor's secret edict, adding, "Our prospects are poor now, with Xuande and Ma Teng gone. My worries over our inability to act have made me ill." "You have nothing to worry about," the physician replied. "The traitor's life is in these hands. He suffers from chronic headaches, with pain that pierces his marrow. The moment one comes on, he calls for me; and the next time he does, I will administer a treatment sure to kill him. Why bother with weapons?" "If we succeed in this," Dong Cheng answered, "the sacred shrines of the Han will owe their salvation to you." Ji Ping then took his leave.

Dong Cheng suppressed his excitement and was walking to his room when he came upon a house servant, Qin Qingtong, whispering in a secluded corner with the concubine Yunying. Dong Cheng had them seized. Only on his wife's appeal did he spare their lives. Each was given forty strokes with a staff, and the man was locked in an empty room. During the night Qin Qingtong, burning with resentment, forced open the metal lock and bounded over the wall. He went straight to Cao's residence, offering valuable information. Questioned in a side room, the man said, "Wang Zifu, Wu Zilan, Chong Ji, Wu Shi, and Ma Teng held a secret talk with my master[14]—I am sure there is a plot against you— and my master brought out a roll of silk with something written on it. And yesterday Ji

Ping bit off his fingertip to seal an oath. That much I saw myself." Cao Cao kept the man in his house. Dong Cheng thought he had simply run away and made no attempt to locate him.

The next day Cao Cao feigned headache and called for Ji Ping. "A traitor meets his end," the physician thought, entering Cao's residence with the poison. From his bed Cao ordered Ji Ping to prepare the drug. "One dose and you'll be over it," Ping said. He called for a pot and decocted the brew in front of Cao. When the contents were half boiled down, he added the poison and handed the drink to Cao. But Cao, knowing the truth, was slow to drink it. "Take it while it is hot," Ji Ping urged. "A brief sweat and your headache will pass." Cao sat up and said, "You are versed in the Confucian texts and familiar with the proprieties. The servant must taste the lord's medicine; the son, the father's. As one of my closest, most trusted servants, shouldn't you taste the medicine before offering it?"

"Medicine is for the sick," the physician responded. "What's the use of my tasting it?" But Ji Ping knew he had been exposed and yanked Cao's ear in an attempt to pour the potion into him. Cao forced it aside, and the liquid spattered on the ground, causing the bricks to crack and split. Before Cao could give the order, his guards had pinned Ji Ping to the ground. "You really thought I was ill?" Cao said. "It was all arranged to test you, to see if you actually meant to do me harm." Twenty husky jailers whisked Ji Ping to a rear yard for interrogation. He lay bound on the ground, impassive, showing no fear; Cao Cao sat on a raised platform. "A mere physician," he said, "wouldn't have the nerve to poison me. Who put you up to it? Talk and you'll be spared." "Traitor who has wronged the sovereign!" Ji Ping retorted. "The entire realm would see you dead—not I alone." Cao hammered him with questions, but Ji Ping replied vehemently, "I meant to kill you for myself alone. No one sent me. My mission has failed. I'm ready to die." Cao Cao ordered Ji Ping beaten without mercy. After several hours his skin split open and the stairs before Cao Cao were covered with blood. Finally, rather than lose the man and his testimony, Cao Cao ordered a respite.

The next day Cao invited all the eminent court officials to a banquet. Only Dong Cheng declined, pleading illness. Wang Zifu and the rest felt compelled to attend so as not to arouse Cao's suspicions. The banquet was laid in Cao's private apartment. After several rounds of wine Cao said, "Our feast wants entertainment. We do have one man, though, who may sober you all up." At Cao's command the twenty jailers dragged in Ji Ping, secured in movable stocks. "You officials," Cao cried, "may not be aware that this fellow is associated with an evil faction that tried to rebel against the court and kill me. But today Heaven has ruined him. Please hear it in his own words." Cao had the prisoner struck. Ji Ping collapsed on the ground in a faint. Revived by a few splashes of water to the face, he opened his eyes. Then, grinding his teeth, he said, "Traitor! Is there a better time to kill me?"

"Initially there were six conspirators," Cao said. "You made the seventh. Right?"[15] Ji Ping renewed his denunciation. Wang Zifu and his three comrades stared helplessly at one another in torment, as if on a bed of needles. Cao ordered the jailers to continue alternately beating and reviving the prisoner. But Ji Ping had no thought of seeking mercy, and Cao had him dragged off, realizing he would never testify. The assemblage dispersed. Cao detained only Wang Zifu and the other three for an evening banquet. They could feel their souls take flight in fear but had to stay on.

"I had not intended to hold you," Cao said, "but I've been meaning to ask you about your discussions with Dong Cheng." "Nothing of any importance," Wang Zifu replied.

"What is written on the white silk roll?" Cao pressed. No clear answer forthcoming, Cao had the servant who had betrayed them brought in. "Well, where did you see it?" Wang Zifu demanded. "Six of you, in private, together, put down your names. You deny it?" the servant responded. "This wretched runaway," Wang Zifu said, "was punished for illicit involvement with the imperial brother-in-law's concubine. Now he slanders his master. He cannot be credited." "Ji Ping tried to poison me," Cao Cao said sharply. "If it was not at Dong Cheng's bidding, then at whose was it?" The four men denied any knowledge of the act. "If you own up here and now, there will still be time for leniency," Cao said. "If you wait until the whole affair is exposed, it will be difficult to make allowances." But the four men insistently denied everything. Cao harshly ordered them confined.

The next day Cao Cao led his men to Dong Cheng's home to inquire after his health. Dong Cheng had no choice but to receive his guests. "What kept you from last night's banquet?" Cao asked him. "An ailment that continues to trouble me," Dong Cheng replied. "I do not go out unless absolutely necessary." "Probably just a touch of 'concern for the Han,'" Cao said. Dong Cheng quailed. Cao continued, "You are aware of the Ji Ping affair? No? How could the imperial brother-in-law not know?" Cao turned and said to his guards, "Bring him in to ease the imperial brother-in-law's ailment." Dong Cheng stood helplessly. Moments later twenty jailers dragged in a swearing Ji Ping and threw him down. "This man," Cao said to Dong Cheng, "has implicated Wang Zifu and the other three in a scheme to poison me; I have them in custody. Only one remains to be apprehended. Now, Ji Ping, who instructed you to kill me? Testify quickly."

"Heaven," the prisoner cried, "sent me to kill a rebel traitor." Cao ordered him beaten, but his body had no skin left to flay. Watching, Dong Cheng felt as if his heart were being crushed. Again Cao turned to Ji Ping and said, "You were born with ten fingers. Why is one missing?" "I chewed it off to mark an oath to kill a traitor!" Ji Ping shot back. Cao called for a knife and cut off the other nine. "Done in one stroke," he said. "Now make your oath." "I still have a mouth to devour a traitor, a tongue to curse him!" Ji Ping responded. Cao ordered his tongue cut out. "Stay your hand," Ji Ping cried. "I can bear it no longer. I am resigned to giving evidence. Release the bonds." When it was done, Ji Ping stood up; then he kneeled, facing the palace gate. "That I failed to rid the land of this traitor is but the design of Heaven." With those words Ji Ping dashed his head against the stair and died. Cao Cao gave a public order for his dismemberment. It was still the first month of the fifth year of Jian An. The records keeper left the following verses:

> The ailing court of Han in deep decline,
> The court physician worked to save the crown.
> Pledging to purge the traitor's clique,
> He gave his life for the sacred throne.
>
> Cruelly scourged, he spoke with stronger passion;
> Through death's agony his spirit will live on:
> For those ten bloody stumps,
> A name revered across a thousand autumns.

Now that Ji Ping was dead, Cao Cao confronted Dong Cheng with the informer. "Does the imperial brother-in-law recognize this man?" Cao demanded. "That runaway! Here?" was the angry reply. "He should be put to death at once." "He has volunteered information concerning the conspiracy," Cao said. "He is here to give evidence. Who dares to threaten him?" "Why should the prime minister give credence to the tales of a runaway slave?" Dong Cheng said sharply. "Wang Zifu and the others have already been taken," Cao retorted. "They have confessed. Do you still deny your guilt?" Dong Cheng was held while Cao's followers entered his sleeping quarters. There they discovered the decree in the girdle and the loyalists' oath. Cao Cao read them and laughed, saying, "How could such a pack of rats expect to get away with this?[16] I want every member of Dong Cheng's clan seized, bar none!" Cao Cao brought the documents to his counselors and advisers, intending to depose Emperor Xian and enthrone another.[17] Indeed:

> A few columns of vermillion ink lead to naught,
> And a loyalist oath leads to a tragic end.

Once again, the Emperor's life hung in the balance.[18]
READ ON.

24

The Traitor Cao Murders the Consort Dong;
The Imperial Uncle Liu Flees to Yuan Shao

HAVING DISCOVERED THE SECRET DECREE, Cao Cao consulted his advisers. He was determined to depose Emperor Xian and find a man of virtue to reign in his stead. But Cheng
Yu opposed it. "Your illustrious Lordship," he argued, "makes his influence felt and his
commands effective throughout the kingdom by invoking the cause of the Han. If you
rush to depose the Emperor now, while the lords of the realm remain unpacified, it will
end in civil war." Cao Cao agreed, contenting himself with the execution of Dong Cheng,
his fellow conspirators, and their entire households, adults and children alike.[1] All told,
over seven hundred died in executions conducted at every gate of the capital. The spectators, both officials and commoners, wept freely. In later times these lines mourning
Dong Cheng were written:

> By secret edict sewn into his sash,
> He bore the word of Heaven through the gate.
> This man, who guarded once the fleeing king,
> Had earned again his sovereign's gratitude.
> In anguish for the safety of the throne,
> "Kill the traitor!" filled his dreaming soul.
> Loyalty in memoriam a thousand ages hence—
> Success or failure? Loyalty past all doubt!

Another verse honored the memory of Wang Zifu and the other three:

> Life and loyalty pledged on a foot-long silk;
> They yearned to redeem the sovereign sire.
> Mourn their sheer courage; hundreds fell.
> Fire-tried hearts outlast a thousand autumns.

Cao Cao's rage was not allayed. The Emperor's beloved high consort, Dong Cheng's
younger sister, now five months with child, was his next target. Armed with a sword, Cao
Cao went to the palace. The Emperor was in the rear. He had been telling the Empress Fu
that he had heard nothing from Dong Cheng concerning the task entrusted to him. Without warning, Cao entered, all fury. The Emperor lost his composure.

"Was Your Majesty aware or not," Cao Cao said, "that Dong Cheng was conspiring to
rebel?" "Dong Zhuo was duly punished long ago," the Emperor responded. "I said Dong

Cheng," Cao snapped, "not Dong Zhuo!"[2] The Emperor quivered. "We had no knowledge of this—really," he said. "I suppose," Cao Cao continued, "you have forgotten the pierced finger and the decree drawn in blood." All reply failed the Emperor. Cao ordered his lieutenants to bring in the high consort. "She is in her fifth month," the Emperor pleaded. "We hope the prime minister will show compassion." "Had Heaven not spoiled things for you," Cao replied, "I would have been murdered. Why should I spare a future nemesis?" "Demote her, then," the Empress Fu appealed, "to the cold palace[3] and wait until she has delivered. There will be time enough to get rid of her." "And spare the rebel seed to avenge the mother?" Cao Cao retorted.

The consort sobbed. "Then let me die," she begged, "with my corpse intact—and no exposure." Cao Cao had the white cord shown to her. The Emperor wept, saying to his consort, "In the netherworld below the Nine Springs, Beloved, hold no grievance against us." His tears poured forth. The Empress Fu sobbed heavily. "Still these carryings on!" Cao cried. At his curt command the soldiers bore the consort off and strangled her outside the palace gate. Later these lines were written lamenting her death:

> The Majesty that graced her could not save her.
> Grieve for the dragon seed aborted with her life.
> The Royal One, stern and stately, lifted his hand
> To screen from welling eyes his undefended wife.

Cao Cao commanded the palace security officer, "Hereafter no kin or member of the imperial clan by marriage may enter without my decree. Execute anyone attempting or permitting entry." Cao Cao also assigned three thousand trusted followers to fill the ranks of the Royal Guard and then placed it in Cao Hong's charge.

Cao Cao said to Cheng Yu, "Dong Cheng and his cohorts are out of the way, but two remain: Ma Teng and Liu Bei. They too must be eliminated." "Ma Teng leads the garrison army in Xiliang," Cheng Yu said. "He cannot be easily taken. Send our greetings to him; let's not arouse his suspicions. Afterward, entice him to the capital and deal with him. As for Liu Bei, his force in Xuzhou, deployed in pincer formation, is not to be slighted. Then there is Yuan Shao, posted at Guandu and ever aiming at our capital. An attack eastward on Liu Bei will drive him to seek aid from Yuan Shao, who will surely exploit the capital's exposure. How will you meet that?"

"I don't agree," Cao said. "Xuande is a figure of great importance. If we hold back until his wings are full spread, we are going to have a hard time coping with him. Yuan Shao, despite his strength, is rarely able to make up his mind. He is really not worth worrying about." At this moment Guo Jia came in and joined the discussion. "I want to march on Liu Bei," Cao said to him. "How much of a threat is Yuan Shao?" "By nature," Guo Jia replied, "Yuan Shao is slow to move, and he frets about everything. His counselors are jealous of each other. I don't see much danger. Liu Bei has just revamped his forces, and they are not yet completely loyal. If Your Excellency leads an eastern campaign, a single battle should give you control." "This coincides with my own thinking," Cao Cao exclaimed. He mobilized two hundred thousand troops and led them out in five field armies to subdue Xuzhou.[4]

Spies brought the news to Sun Qian, who first informed Lord Guan in Xiapi and then Xuande in Xiaopei. In counsel with Sun Qian, Xuande said, "Help from Yuan Shao is our only hope." He composed a note to Shao, which Sun Qian took north of the Yellow River.

Sun Qian was received by Tian Feng, to whom he described the situation in detail; then Sun Qian requested an audience with Yuan Shao. Tian Feng introduced Xuande's representative, who presented the letter to Yuan Shao. When Yuan Shao appeared, he was emaciated, his attire in disarray. "What's wrong, my lord?" Tian Feng asked. "My life is over," he cried. "What does Your Lordship mean?" Tian Feng inquired. "Of the five sons born to me," Yuan Shao explained, "the youngest is the one I dote on. Now he is on the brink of death, afflicted with scabies, and I have no heart to think about anything else."

Tian Feng said to Yuan Shao, "Cao Cao's march against Xuande leaves the capital vulnerable. This is the moment to invade with a loyalist force to preserve the Emperor and save the populace—a rare opportunity for Your Lordship." "That is true," Yuan Shao replied. "But my mind is distracted—something might go wrong." "What," asked Tian Feng, "is it that distracts you?" "Of my five sons only this one has great promise. If something should happen to him, my fate is sealed," Yuan Shao replied. And so he resolved not to strike; he asked Sun Qian to convey his reasons to Xuande and to assure him that if things went badly, he would find refuge north of the river. Tian Feng beat the ground with his staff and cried in despair, "A godsend! And for the sake of an infant's illness to let it slip! Our cause is lost. What a shame!" With protracted sighs he staggered out.[5]

Sun Qian rode nonstop back to Xuande with the disappointing news. "What do we do?" Xuande asked in alarm. "No need to worry, elder brother," Zhang Fei said. "Cao's force, coming so far, is bound to be fatigued. If we storm their camp the moment they arrive, we will demolish them!" "I used to think you a mere warrior," Xuande said to Zhang Fei. "But you showed great command of tactics when you captured Liu Dai. And your present plan agrees well with the logic of warfare." Thus Zhang Fei's proposal was adopted, and troops were readied for attack.

Cao Cao led his army toward Xiaopei. On the march a gale sprang up, and something cracked loudly. One of the leading banner poles had snapped. Cao Cao halted and called a conference to consider the omen. Xun Wenruo asked the direction of the wind and the color of the banner. "The wind came from the southeast," Cao answered, "and broke one of the banners at the side of our formation. It was two-colored, blue and red." "It must signify a night raid by Liu Bei," Xun Wenruo announced. Cao Cao nodded in agreement. A later poet expressed his chagrin in these lines:

> Alas for this scion of kings, isolate, outspent,
> Staking his all on a night foray.
> The broken-banner sign betrayed his plan.
> Old Man Heaven! Why let that villain free?

"Heaven answers our prayers," Cao Cao said. "Prepare defenses." Cao divided his men into nine contingents. One was placed forward, simulating encampment. The other eight lay in ambush all around.

That night the moon was dim. Xuande and Zhang Fei led two groups forward. Sun Qian stayed in Xiaopei. Confident of his plan, Zhang Fei rode ahead and burst into the camp with his small cavalry force. He found here and there a few men and horses. Even as he realized he was caught, flames surrounded him and voices resounded everywhere. Escape seemed impossible. To the east, Zhang Liao; to the west Xu Chu! To the south, Yu Jin; to the north, Li Dian! To the southeast, Xu Huang; to the southwest, Yue Jin! To the northeast, Xiahou Dun; to the northwest, Xiahou Yuan! From eight sides Cao's commanders closed in. Zhang Fei thrust left and charged right, blocked front and fended rear. But his men, mostly soldiers captured from Cao's army, defected in the heat of combat.[6]

Zhang Fei, striving mightily, clashed with Xu Huang; Yue Jin threatened him from behind. Zhang Fei barely escaped with a few dozen riders, slashing a bloody trail. The road back to Xiaopei was blocked, and the way to Xiapi or to Xuzhou was sure to be closed. The region of the Mang-Dang Hills was his only hope.

Unaware of Zhang Fei's fate, Xuande was still moving toward Cao's camp when he heard the noise and cries of war. Suddenly behind him an enemy force cut off half his unit. Ahead, Xiahou Dun came fully into view. Xuande struggled free and fled, Xiahou Yuan in hot pursuit. Xuande had only some thirty men. Xiaopei was in flames; he could not return there. And Cao's soldiers had blanketed the approaches to Xiapi and Xuzhou. Xuande thought he was doomed; then he remembered a line from Yuan Shao's letter—"If things go badly, I will shelter you"—and decided to seek refuge in Qingzhou until he could make new plans. He started north only to be checked, this time by Li Dian. In the confusion Xuande managed to slip away, but his all his followers were taken.

Alone, Xuande rode north, making three hundred *li* a day. When he reached Qingzhou, the gate guards reported his name to the imperial inspector, Yuan Tan, Shao's eldest son. Yuan Tan had always respected Xuande. He admitted him at once and conducted him to his official quarters. Xuande recounted the details of his defeat and his hopes for Yuan Shao's protection. Yuan Tan provided for him in the guesthouse and sent a letter to his father. He then had Xuande escorted to the border of Pingyuan district. Leading a crowd of retainers, Yuan Shao came out of the city of Ye thirty *li* to welcome Xuande. Xuande expressed his appreciation, and Yuan Shao promptly returned the courtesy, saying, "Our son's recent illness has caused us to neglect your needs—to our sincere regret. But now fortune brings us together, fulfilling a lifelong expectation."

"Here is a poor and helpless Liu Bei," Xuande replied, "who has long desired to serve in your ranks, though by fate or circumstance it has never come to pass. Now I am under attack by Cao Cao; my family is lost. I believe that you, General, are willing to welcome warriors from round the realm, so in all humility I have come straight to you. If I may enter your service, I will be sworn to repay your kindness." Well pleased with these words, Yuan Shao treated Xuande with great generosity and allowed him to remain in his home province, Ji.[7]

On the night of Xuande's abortive raid Cao Cao seized Xiaopei and attacked Xuzhou. Mi Zhu and Jian Yong fled, unable to defend the city; and Chen Deng delivered it to Cao Cao. Cao entered in force and, after calming the populace, summoned his advisers to plan the capture of Xiapi. "Lord Guan is there," said Xun Wenruo, "keeping Xuande's family. He will defend it to the death. If you don't strike quickly, Yuan Shao will!"[8] "I have always admired Lord Guan's military competence and personal ability," Cao Cao said, "and would be delighted to have him in my service. Could someone persuade him to submit to us?" "His loyalty is too deep," Guo Jia said. "He would never do it, and the envoy could well lose his life." But Zhang Liao stepped forward and said, "I am acquainted with the man and would like to attempt it." Cheng Yu said to Cao Cao, "Though Zhang Liao and Lord Guan are on familiar terms, as I read the man, no words will persuade him. But consider—if we can corner him first and then use Zhang Liao to work on him, he should transfer his allegiance to the prime minister." Indeed:

> The hidden arrow fells the savage tiger,
> But it takes some tasty bait to land a fish or turtle.

With Xuande lost, how would Lord Guan act?
READ ON.

25

Trapped on a Hill, Lord Guan Sets Three Conditions;
At Baima, Cao Cao Breaks the Heavy Siege

CHENG YU'S PLAN WAS THIS: "Lord Guan can stand off a myriad of men. To take him we need a stratagem. Now suppose we send some of the soldiers we've just captured back to Xiapi posing as escapees but remaining in covert contact with us. Next, we draw Lord Guan out to battle, feign defeat, and lure him to a prearranged point while crack troops cut off his way back. Then you can begin to negotiate with him." Cao Cao approved and put Cheng Yu's plan into action by sending a few score of Xuzhou troops to Xiapi to surrender. Lord Guan took the men back in good faith.

The next day Xiahou Dun spearheaded Cao Cao's attack. With five thousand in his command he tried to provoke Lord Guan to battle, but it was in vain. Finally, he sent a man to the base of the city wall to denounce Lord Guan personally. And Lord Guan, incensed, rode forth with three thousand. The two warriors clashed, but after ten bouts Dun wheeled and fled. As Lord Guan pursued, Dun fought and ran in turn until he had drawn his man some twenty *li* from the city. Fearing that Cao's army might seize Xiapi, Lord Guan turned back—only to hear the peal of bombards. To his left, Xu Huang; to his right, Xu Chu—their squadrons checked his retreat. Lord Guan moved to force a path. Ambushers concentrated their crossbow shots from two sides, and bolts whizzed down like locusts. Lord Guan could not pass. He pulled his men back, but Xu Huang and Xu Chu were ready for him. With a supreme effort Lord Guan pushed them back, making a valiant last attempt to fight his way through to Xiapi, but Xiahou Dun barred the way. The battle raged into the night. Finding no way home, Lord Guan struggled to a hilltop with his followers. There he rested.

Cao Cao's men clustered around the base of the hill, sealing all avenues of escape.[1] In the distance Lord Guan could see flames rising from the city. (In fact, the false defectors sent by Cao Cao had quietly opened the gates, and Cao, after battling his way into Xiapi, had told his men to set some harmless fires to weaken Lord Guan's will.) Distraught at the sight, Lord Guan charged down the hill again and again throughout the night, only to be driven back by volleys of arrows. At dawn he marshaled his men for a breakthrough when he saw a single rider—as if from nowhere—racing toward him. He recognized Zhang Liao.[2]

"You come as an adversary, I presume," Lord Guan called to him as he approached. "No," Liao replied. "I come in respect of our long-standing friendship." The envoy threw down his sword and dismounted. The formalities concluded, the two men sat together at the summit. "You must have come to win me over," Lord Guan began. "Not so," Zhang Liao responded. "Brother, you once saved my life. How could I not try to return the favor?" "Then you come to lend us aid!" Lord Guan exclaimed. "Not that, either," Zhang Liao said. "Then why have you come?" Lord Guan asked.[3] "Xuande's survival is in doubt," Zhang Liao went on, "as is Zhang Fei's. Last night Lord Cao took Xiapi, without injury to soldier or civilian. A special detail guards Xuande's family for their safety and peace of mind. I come first of all to tell you this."

"You will not succeed in influencing me," Lord Guan said angrily. "Bad as things look, death means no more to me than a welcome homecoming. You'd better leave at once. I will be riding down to do battle." Zhang Liao laughed loudly. "Brother," he said, "do you want to be the laughingstock of the empire?" "I will die," Lord Guan said, "devoted to my duty. I don't think the world will take it as a joke." "Dying here," Zhang Liao said, "you commit three offenses."[4] "Well then," Lord Guan replied, "what are they?"

"In the beginning," Zhang Liao said, "when you, brother, and Protector Liu[5] bound yourselves in fraternal allegiance, you swore to share life or death. Now your brother has been defeated, and you are about to die in combat. If Xuande survives and seeks your aid in vain, won't you have betrayed your oath? That is your first offense. Protector Liu's immediate family was placed in your care. If you die now, his two wives will have no one to defend them, and you will have betrayed his trust.[6] That is your second offense. And third, not only is your martial skill incomparable, you are learned in the classics and the histories. You joined with the protector to uphold the house of Han. If you lapse in your determination and achieve a fool's valor instead by vainly rushing to certain death, how have you fulfilled your 'duty'? This is the statement, brother, I felt obliged to make."

Lord Guan pondered. "Well," he said at last, "you have explained the three offenses. What would you have me do?" "Lord Cao's troops," Zhang Liao replied, "are on four sides. If you refuse to submit, you will die. To die in vain avails nothing. It makes more sense to submit, for now, while you seek news of the protector. When you learn where he is, you may go to him immediately. That way you will ensure the safety of the two ladies, you will remain true to the peach garden oath, and you will preserve your own most useful life. These, brother, are the advantages for you to weigh." "Brother," Lord Guan replied, "you speak of three advantages. I have three conditions. If His Excellency agrees, I will lay down my arms at once. If not, I am content to die with the three offenses upon my head." "His Excellency is magnanimous and accomodating and has always shown forebearance. I beg to hear your conditions," answered Zhang Liao.

"First," Lord Guan said, "the imperial uncle, Liu Xuande, and I have sworn to uphold the house of Han. I shall surrender to the Emperor, not to Cao Cao.[7] Second, I request for my two sisters-in-law the consideration befitting an imperial uncle's wives. No one, however high his station, is to approach their gate. And third, the moment we learn of Imperial Uncle Liu's whereabouts, no matter how far away he may be, I shall depart forthwith. Denied any of these conditions, I shall not surrender. Please return to Cao Cao with my terms."

Zhang Liao communicated Lord Guan's terms to Cao Cao. Told of Lord Guan's insistence on yielding to the Emperor and not to the prime minister, Cao Cao laughed and said, "I am the prime minister of the Han. The Han and I are one. This then may be granted." To the second condition, protection of the women, Cao Cao responded, "To the income of an imperial uncle I will add a like amount, thus doubling it. As for prohibiting outsiders from entering the residence of Xuande's wives, that is the rule of any decent house and a matter of course here." But at Lord Guan's third condition, rejoining Xuande if he was located, Cao Cao demurred. "In that case," he said, "I would be feeding him for nothing. It is difficult to grant." Zhang Liao asked Cao Cao, "Have you forgotten Yurang's saying?[8] Liu Xuande treats Lord Guan with generosity and consideration—no more. If Your Excellency extends a greater largess to bind his love, need we fear his leaving us?" "Apt words," Cao replied. "I agree to his three conditions."[9]

Zhang Liao returned to the hilltop and announced Cao Cao's acceptance. "Nevertheless," Lord Guan said, "I shall have to request that His Excellency withdraw temporarily so that, before formally surrendering, I may reenter the city and inform my two sisters of the arrangements." Zhang Liao carried this new request back to Cao Cao, who ordered the army to remove thirty *li*. Xun Wenruo opposed it, saying, "It could be a trap." But Cao Cao answered, "Lord Guan's word is his bond. He would never break faith." The pullback was implemented.

Escorted by his own soldiers, Lord Guan entered Xiapi. He found public order undisturbed. At Xuande's residence Lady Gan and Lady Mi received him eagerly. Lord Guan saluted them from below the stair. "The distress you have suffered," he said, "is my fault." "Where is the imperial uncle?" they asked. "I do not know," Lord Guan replied. "What are we to do now, brother-in law?" they asked. "When I left the city," he replied, "I fought as hard as I could but was trapped on a hill. Cao Cao sent Zhang Liao to talk me into surrendering, and I agreed—but on three conditions, which Cao Cao has already accepted. Then, at my request, he withdrew his troops, enabling me to enter the city and consult you two first."

"What are the three conditions?" the ladies asked. Lord Guan recounted the terms of his agreement with Cao Cao. Lady Gan said, "Yesterday, when Cao's army entered the city, we thought we were doomed.[10] To our surprise we have enjoyed security. Not a single soldier has dared come through our gate. Brother-in-law, since you have already given your word, why bother asking us? But I do fear Cao Cao will prevent you from finding the imperial uncle." "Rest assured, sisters," he said. "I will handle that in my own way." "Brother," they said, "make all these decisions yourself. It is not necessary to consult us womenfolk."

Lord Guan took his leave and rode to Cao Cao's camp with a few dozen horsemen. Cao greeted him before the entrance as Lord Guan dismounted and made obeisance. Cao rushed forward to reciprocate. "As the general of a defeated army," Lord Guan began, "I am obliged by your mercy in sparing me." "Having long esteemed your loyalty and sense of honor," Cao responded, "I am favored today with a meeting which fulfills a lifelong desire." Lord Guan said, "Zhang Liao has conveyed to you on my behalf the three conditions of my surrender. I am honored by your consent and trust there will be no retraction." "My word, once given, is honored," was Cao's reply. "Should I learn of the imperial uncle's whereabouts," Lord Guan went on, "I must go to join him, whatever the dangers or obstacles. In that event, I may not have time even to take formal leave, so I humbly beg your pardon against that time." "If Liu Xuande still lives," Cao Cao said, "you are free to join him. But he may have perished unnoticed in the confusion of battle. For the time being you might as well content yourself while we gather more information." Lord Guan expressed his respectful appreciation. Cao Cao held a banquet in his honor.

The following day Cao Cao began withdrawing the imperial army from the newly conquered Xiapi for the march back to the capital. Lord Guan prepared for the journey, provided the carriage guard, and bade his sisters-in-law ascend. En route he rode along-side in attendance.

They broke their trip at a hostel, where Cao Cao, aiming to disrupt the proprieties between lord and liege man, assigned Lord Guan and his sisters-in-law to a single chamber. But Lord Guan never entered the chamber; he remained at attention outside the door, holding a candle that burned through the night until dawn. His eyes showed no trace of fatigue. Cao Cao's respect for him grew.[11] In the capital Cao Cao provided official quarters for Lord Guan and Xuande's wives. Lord Guan had the dwelling divided into two compounds. At the inner gate he posted ten elderly guards. He occupied the outer compound himself.

Cao Cao conducted Lord Guan into the presence of the Emperor, who conferred on him the title adjutant general. Lord Guan gave thanks for the sovereign's grace and returned to his quarters. The next day Cao Cao held a grand banquet, assembling his entire corps of advisers and officers and treating Lord Guan as an honored guest. Cao invited him to take the seat of honor and presented him with brocade silks as well as gold and silver utensils—all of which Lord Guan gave over to his sisters-in-law for safekeeping. Cao Cao showed unusual generosity, giving him small banquets every third day, large ones every fifth. Ten handsome women were given to Lord Guan, but he sent them on to serve his two sisters-in-law. Every three days he would appear at their door to perform the proper formalities and inquire about their condition. They in turn would ask for news of the imperial uncle. Only when the ladies had excused him would he retire. Learning of this high courtesy, Cao Cao inwardly honored Lord Guan more than ever.

One day Cao Cao noticed that Lord Guan's green embroidered combat garb was badly worn. He had the warrior's measure taken and presented him with battle dress of the rarest brocade. Lord Guan accepted it, but he wore it underneath the old one. Cao Cao teased him for being frugal, and Lord Guan said, "It is not frugality. The old dress was a gift from Imperial Uncle Liu. I feel near him when I wear it. I could never forget my elder brother's gift on account of Your Excellency's new one. That is why I wear it underneath." "Truly, a man of honor," Cao Cao exclaimed. But inwardly he was troubled.

One day a message was brought to Lord Guan: "The ladies have collapsed in tears. No one knows why. Pray go to their chamber soon." Lord Guan, formally attired, kneeled before their door and asked the cause of their distress. "Last night," Lady Gan began, "I dreamed the imperial uncle was trapped in a pit. I woke and told Lady Mi, and we believe he is now in the netherworld. That is why we have lost our composure." "Dreams of the night bear no credence," Lord Guan responded. "This is from excessive worry. Please do not let such matters vex you."

At this time Cao Cao invited Lord Guan to a banquet. Lord Guan took leave of his sisters and came before Cao Cao, who asked the reason for his sorrowful look. "My sisters-in-law, " Lord Guan replied, "yearn for my elder brother and cry so pitifully that I grieve despite myself." Cao Cao smiled and tried to console him, urging him to drink. Lord Guan became intoxicated and, stroking his beard, said, "I have lived in vain, having neglected my responsibility to the imperial house and my duty to my elder brother." "Have you ever counted the hairs in your beard?" Cao asked. "There are several hundred," Lord Guan replied. "In autumn I lose a few. In winter I wrap it in a black silk sack so the hairs don't break." Cao Cao had a gorgeous silk sack made to protect Lord Guan's beard.

Early the next morning they were received by the Emperor, who asked the purpose of the sack that hung on Lord Guan's chest. "As my beard is rather long," Lord Guan informed the sovereign, "the prime minister bestowed this sack on me to keep it safe." At the Emperor's request he unfurled it in the royal sanctum, and it reached below his stomach. The Emperor called him the Man of the Magnificent Beard—and so he was known thereafter.

One day after a banquet Cao Cao was escorting Lord Guan from the ministerial residence when he noticed that his mount was emaciated. "Why is your horse so skinny?" Cao inquired. "My worthless carcass has grown heavy," Lord Guan replied. "The horse is worn out from bearing me." Cao had his aides bring in a horse. Its color was like fiery coal, its stature magnificent. Pointing to it, Cao asked, "Do you recognize this horse?" "Isn't it Red Hare," Lord Guan answered, "the horse Lü Bu once rode?"[12] Cao Cao nodded and presented the mount, completely equipped, to Lord Guan, who bowed repeatedly and declared his gratitude. Piqued, Cao Cao asked, "I have sent you beautiful women, gold, rolls of silk, one after the other, and never did you condescend to bow. Now for this horse you keep bowing and bowing. Do you value a beast above humans?" "I admire this horse," Lord Guan said. "It can cover a thousand *li* in a single day. It is a gift that will enable me to reach my brother in a single day should his whereabouts become known." Cao Cao swallowed his astonishment and regretted the gift. Later a poet wrote:

> Upon a realm divided shines this hero's fame;
> Staying by his sisters, he kept his honor clean.
> The cunning chancellor showed false courtesy,
> Little knowing Guan would never bend the knee.

Cao Cao asked Zhang Liao, "Why is Lord Guan so determined to leave us when I have treated him with the greatest generosity?" "Let me look into it," Zhang Liao replied. The next day he visited Lord Guan. After greetings were exchanged, Zhang Liao said, "Since I recommended you to the prime minister, has anyone been favored over you?" "I am deeply grateful," Lord Guan answered, "for the prime minister's generosity. But though my body is here, my heart is still with the imperial uncle. He never leaves my thoughts." "I believe your attitude is incorrect," Zhang Liao said. "In this world a real man must be able to establish correct priorities. Xuande could not have treated you better than His Excellency has. Why are you bent on leaving?" "I know only too well," Lord Guan continued, "how lavishly Lord Cao honors me. But I have received Xuande's favor. We are sworn to die for each other. Bound by that oath, I cannot remain here. Nonetheless, before I leave, I am determined to perform some act of merit to requite Lord Cao's kindness." "And if Xuande is no longer alive?" Zhang Liao asked. "I am bound to follow him to the world below."[13] Seeing Lord Guan immune to persuasion, Zhang Liao took his leave and went to report the results of his conversation to Cao Cao. "To follow one's lord, always true to the first oath," the prime minister said with a sigh, "that is the meaning of loyalty in this world." Then Xun Wenruo added, "He said he would not leave until he had done us a major service. If we deny him the opportunity to do so, it will be difficult for him to go." Cao Cao indicated his approval.

·   ·   ·   ·   ·

Meanwhile, having joined Yuan Shao, Liu Xuande was in a state of constant fretfulness. "What troubles you?" Yuan Shao asked him. "Not a shred of news of my two brothers," Xuande answered. "My family is in the traitor Cao's hands. I have neither served the Han nor kept my loved ones from harm. How can I help grieving?" "I have long wanted," Yuan Shao said, "to move against the capital. The spring thaw has arrived—the ideal time for marshaling the army." The two men discussed strategies for defeating Cao Cao. But Tian Feng objected. "Last time," he said, "when Cao attacked Xuzhou and left the capital undefended, you did not respond to the opportunity. Now Xuzhou has fallen, and Cao's troops are keen. He is formidable now. Shouldn't we hold fast here until some weakness shows itself in Cao's army?" "Give me time to think it over," Yuan Shao said.

Yuan Shao asked Xuande's view of Tian Feng's conservative tactics. "Cao Cao," Xuande said, "is a traitor to the sovereign. If Your Lordship fails to bring him to justice, I fear that in the eyes of the world you will forfeit our claim on the great principle of allegiance." "Your position is well taken," Yuan Shao replied and ordered the mobilization. To Tian Feng's repeated protests he said angrily, "Those like you, addicted to civil procedures, despise the military side of things. Do you want us to renege on our allegiance to the Han?" Tian Feng bowed low and knocked his head on the ground. "Ignore my words," he cried, "and you will march into disaster." Yuan Shao wanted Tian Feng executed, but agreed to have him simply incarcerated after Xuande's strenuous appeals.

Tian Feng's fate prompted Ju Shou to gather his clan, distribute his property among them, and say farewell. "I am off to war," he explained. "If we win, there will be no limit to my wealth and influence. If we lose, not even my life can be saved." Tearfully, his people saw him off.

Yuan Shao sent General Yan Liang in the lead; his first target, Baima. Ju Shou protested: "Yan Liang, though brave and spirited, is too narrow to assume command alone." "He is my best general," Yuan Shao replied. "The likes of you cannot take his measure." Yuan Shao's army advanced to Liyang. Liu Yan, governor of Dongjun, reported the invasion to the capital, and Cao Cao called his advisers into conference to work out tactics. Lord Guan went to see the prime minister. "I understand Your Excellency is calling up the army," he said. "I volunteer for the vanguard." "I don't think I should trouble you, General," Cao Cao replied. "But sooner or later we will require your services, and I shall come to you then." Lord Guan withdrew.

Cao Cao had command of a force of one hundred and fifty thousand divided into three armies. As they marched, bulletins from Liu Yan kept arriving. Cao Cao took one army of fifty thousand to Baima and pitched camp there with the hills to his back. In the distance he could see Yan Liang's one hundred thousand deployed over the open fields and the flats near the river. Uneasily Cao said to Song Xian, formerly in Lü Bu's service, "You are known as one of Lü Bu's fiercest fighters. I want you to go against Yan Liang." As ordered, Song Xian galloped out in front of his line, spear couched for combat. Yan Liang, sword leveled, horse poised, waited beneath the bannered entrance to his formation. When he spotted Song Xian, a roar burst from his throat, and he raced forth. The clash was brief. A hand rose, a sword struck, and Song Xian fell. "What a warrior!" Cao Cao exclaimed in consternation.

Wei Xu volunteered to avenge his comrade, and Cao Cao sent him out. Lance set, Wei Xu galloped to the front where he loudly cursed Yan Liang. Liang wasted no words. On the first exchange he cleaved Wei Xu's forehead. "Who have we left to oppose him?" Cao asked. In response Xu Huang took the field and fought twenty bouts with Yan Liang, only to be driven back to his line. Cao's commanders began to tremble. Cao recalled the army, and Yan Liang withdrew also.

The spectacle of his fallen generals left Cao Cao depressed. Cheng Yu said to him, "I can suggest a match for Yan Liang—Lord Guan." "I fear that if he scores such a victory," Cao replied, "he will leave." "If Xuande lives," Cheng Yu said, "he must be with Yuan Shao. If Lord Guan destroys Yuan Shao's troops, Shao is sure to turn against Xuande and kill him. With Xuande dead, where can Lord Guan turn?" Satisfied, Cao Cao sent for Lord Guan to request his help. Lord Guan went first to bid his sisters-in-law farewell. "This is your chance," they said, "to get news of the imperial uncle." Lord Guan accepted the call.

Armed with his blade Green Dragon, mounted on Red Hare, and accompanied by a handful of men in train, Lord Guan rode to Cao Cao at Baima. Cao described to him the exploits and ferocity of Yan Liang and asked his opinion. "Let me have a look at him," Lord Guan said. Cao ordered wine for the warrior. While drinking, they were told that Yan Liang was issuing his challenge. Cao Cao led Lord Guan to a hilltop to observe. They sat together, ringed by the chief commanders, and Cao pointed to the foot of the hill, where Yan Liang's forces had camped. Their banners and standards were fresh and brilliant, and their spears stood tall like a stand of trees, impressive in their strict array. "How strong and valiant, this army from north of the river!" Cao Cao exclaimed. "Mud hens and clay dogs to me!" was Lord Guan's response. Cao Cao pointed again. "Under the command canopy," he said, "with the brocade robe and gold-trimmed armor, armed with a sword, erect on his horse—that's Yan Liang." Lord Guan glanced over the scene. "His head is ours for the asking," he said. "Do not underrate him," Cao Cao warned. "With as little merit as I have," Lord Guan answered, "I beg permission to present his head to Your Excellency. I will seize it from under their very noses!" "We do not make sport in the army," Zhang Liao commented. "Take care."

With a thrust Lord Guan mounted. Pointing his blade to the ground, he raced downhill, his phoenix eyes round and fixed, his silkworm eyebrows bristling. He dashed into the enemy line. The northern army parted like a wake as Lord Guan charged straight for Yan Liang, who was still under his canopy. Before Liang could identify the figure crashing toward him, the speed of Red Hare had already brought them face-to-face. Yan Liang was too slow, and with a stroke of the blade Lord Guan pierced him. Before the stunned enemy Lord Guan dismounted and cut off the head, strapped it to the neck of his horse, remounted, and sped away, sword raised in warning. All the while it seemed as if Lord Guan was moving across an empty plain. The men and leaders of the northern force were thrown into tumult, routed without having fought. Cao's troops seized their chance and struck, taking a toll in lives beyond numbering. The booty in weapons and horses was enormous.[14]

Lord Guan reascended the hill to the acclaim of Cao's generals, and placed the head before the prime minister, who said, "General, this is more than any mortal could do!" "Not worth mentioning," Lord Guan replied. "My brother Zhang Fei could snatch the head of the chief general of an army ten times that size." Cao Cao turned in astonishment to his aides, saying, "Hereafter, should we encounter Zhang Fei, we must not risk engaging him!" And he had them write down the warning under their lapels.

·   ·   ·   ·

Yan Liang's defeated force fled homeward. Meeting Yuan Shao on the way, the soldiers described all that had happened. Yuan Shao asked in amazement who the warrior could be. "It must have been Lord Guan, Liu Xuande's younger brother," Ju Shou answered. Angrily, Yuan Shao turned to Xuande and said, "Your brother has killed my beloved commander. I am certain you were involved. What am I keeping you for?'' He had the axemen take Xuande to be executed. Indeed:

> Moments ago an honored guest;
> Now a prisoner awaiting death.

Would Xuande meet his doom?[15]
READ ON.

26

Yuan Shao Loses a Battle and Another General;
Lord Guan Returns His Official Seal

UNPERTURBED BY YUAN SHAO'S THREAT, Liu Xuande said, "My lord, do you really mean to sever an old friendship on the basis of an uncorroborated report? Since my brothers and I were separated at Xuzhou, we have had no reliable information regarding Lord Guan's fate. Many men in this world look alike: not every ruddy-faced, long-bearded man can be Lord Guan. Why not try and verify the report before anything else?" Yuan Shao, who was basically a man with little mind of his own, reacted by rebuking Ju Shou. "You nearly misled me into killing my good friend," he said and invited Xuande to resume his privileged place in his council.

Discussion on avenging Yan Liang was in progress. One man stepped forward and spoke: "Yan Liang and I were like brothers. That villain Cao has killed him, and I have to avenge him." Xuande observed the man. He was eight spans tall, with a long, flat face that reminded him of the mythical wild goat that butted down wrongdoers. The volunteer was Wen Chou, the renowned general from north of the river. Gratified by the offer, Yuan Shao said, "You are the one who can avenge Yan Liang. I am giving you one hundred thousand men. Cross the river and rout those villains now." Ju Shou protested: "It won't work. This is the time to remain entrenched in Yanjin while sending a corps over to Guandu. It is no time to risk a general crossing. Our army could never get back in the event of a surprise." "The likes of you," Yuan Shao said irately, "dull my men's spirits, backing away from the tasks at hand and spoiling our chances. Don't you know that in warfare 'the moment matters most'?" Ju Shou sighed and withdrew, saying, "The leader is willful; the followers ambitious; the Yellow River flows on and on. What power have I to change things?" Pleading ill health, Ju Shou attended no more councils.

Xuande said to Yuan Shao, "You have honored me with great favor, and I have not reciprocated. I want to go along with Wen Chou, both to requite your kindness and to find out whatever I can about Lord Guan." Delighted to oblige, Yuan Shao ordered Wen Chou and Xuande to lead the vanguard. But Wen Chou complained, "Xuande has lost one battle after another. He will bring bad luck. Since you insist on his going, I am assigning him thirty thousand men to bring up the rear." Thus, Wen Chou advanced with his seventy thousand.

• • • •

Lord Guan's stunning victory over Yan Liang prompted Cao Cao to recommend that
the Emperor enfeoff him as lord of Hanshou precinct.[1] The seal was cast and presented to
Lord Guan. At this time it was reported that Wen Chou had crossed the river and reached
Yanjin. Cao took action at once. First he had the residents west of the river evacuated;
then he moved his forces up but ordered the rear guard to the front and the vanguard to
the rear, so that the grain and fodder preceded the main army. Lü Qian asked, "What is
Your Excellency's purpose?" "Our supplies," Cao replied, "have been raided a number of
times. Now I want them in the front." "What if the enemy makes off with them?" Lü
Qian asked. "I'll think of something," Cao said. But Lü Qian thought the plan dubious.

Cao Cao sent the supply train ahead along the riverbank to Yanjin. Soon shouts of
panic arose from the van. A runner reported back, "General Wen Chou appeared from
the north, and the supply guards scattered. The provisions are lost. Our main force is too
far behind to help. What shall we do?" Cao Cao pointed south. "Take shelter on that
small hill," he ordered. The soldiers rushed up the hill in response. Cao Cao had them
remove their armor and let all the horses run free while the men rested, even as Wen
Chou's army was drawing near. "The enemy is coming," Cao's commanders reported.
"We have to round up the horses and retreat to Baima." But Xun You quickly stopped
them. "These horses," he told them, "make the perfect bait for the enemy. Why retreat?" Cao Cao smiled meaningfully at Xun You, who, having perceived Cao's intent,
said no more.

After capturing Cao Cao's supplies and wagons, Wen Chou's men began swarming
over the field, eager to plunder the horses. At Cao's signal his commanders descended the
hill and attacked in well-coordinated assaults that threw Wen Chou's army into chaos.
Ringed by Cao's soldiers, Wen Chou's men trampled over each other. Wen Chou, powerless to control his men and unable to fight on alone, tried to escape. From the hilltop
Cao Cao singled him out. "There!" he cried, "the famed general from the north! Who
will take him?" Zhang Liao and Xu Huang rode swiftly down together, shouting to Wen
Chou, "You can't escape!"

Wen Chou turned and saw two warriors charging. He put his spear aside and aimed
an arrow at Zhang Liao. Xu Huang shouted a warning: "The devil's about to shoot."
Zhang Liao ducked, and the arrow pierced his helmet, shooting away its ornamental tuft.
Liao resumed his charge. Wen Chou's second shot hit his horse in the face. Down it went,
its knees folding, tossing Liao forward into the dirt.

Wen Chou was turning back for the kill. Xu Huang, twirling his great axe, intercepted
him only to take flight at the sight of fresh forces coming up behind Wen Chou. Chou
pursued, galloping along the river. Suddenly he saw a dozen riders, pennants flying
bravely. Their leader, sword held high, came at him. It was Lord Guan. "Halt, rebel commander!" he shouted. The two tangled, but after a few moments Wen Chou lost heart
and fled. Lord Guan gave chase, overtook his man, and felled him with a stroke to the
back of the head. Observing from the hilltop, Cao Cao ordered another wave of attacks.
Half of Yuan Shao's northern army perished in the river, and Cao Cao recovered all his
supplies and horses.[2]

During the fighting Lord Guan's cohort attacked savagely on all sides. Xuande meanwhile arrived on the opposite shore with his contingent of thirty thousand. Spies informed him that Wen Chou had been killed by a red-faced, long-bearded warrior, so he
rode to the river's edge. Xuande looked across and saw a group of men and horses moving
back and forth as if they were flying. In their midst was a banner that read "Lord Guan,
Lord of Hanshou Precinct." Xuande silently thanked Heaven and earth. "So my brother

is with Cao Cao," he murmured to himself. He looked for a way to hail Lord Guan, but a mass of Cao's men swallowed him up, and Xuande pulled back.

Yuan Shao next reinforced Guandu with fresh camps and barricades. Guo Tu and Shen Pei came before Yuan Shao and said, "Once again that Guan has killed our general, and Liu Bei feigns ignorance." "Long-eared devil! How dare he!" Yuan Shao railed and ordered Xuande seized for execution once again. "What have I done?" Xuande asked him. "You sent your brother to defeat my top general again," Shao answered. "You claim you are innocent?" "Allow me one last statement," Xuande pleaded. "Cao Cao has always been bitterly jealous of me. He knows I am with Your Lordship and dreads my helping you. That's why he sent Lord Guan to cut down your generals—to provoke Your Lordship and then use you to do me in. I beg you to consider this." "There is truth in what you say," Yuan Shao conceded. Then, turning to his advisers, he said, "You almost ruined my reputation, having me kill a worthy man!" Roughly he dismissed the two and invited Xuande to the seat of honor in his tent.

Xuande said gratefully, "I am indebted for Your Lordship's magnanimous consideration, which I could never repay. But let me have someone you trust carry a secret letter to Lord Guan. Once he knows where I am, he will come at once to lend his support, and together we may punish Cao Cao and avenge Yan Liang and Wen Chou. What do you say?" Delighted, Yuan Shao said, "Getting Lord Guan would be worth more to me than ten Yan Liangs or Wen Chous."[3] Xuande drew up a letter, but there was no one to deliver it.

Yuan Shao ordered his army back to Wuyang, where he set up a string of encampments scores of *li* long and suspended all military operations. Cao Cao sent Xiahou Dun to guard the entry points to Guandu and took the main army back to the capital. At a great feast of the court he hailed Lord Guan's victories, then he turned to Lü Qian and declared, "Remember how I trapped the enemy by shifting provisions to the front? Only Xun You read my mind." The assembly voiced its admiration.

During the banquet Cao Cao received an urgent report: "Yellow Scarves, led by Liu Pi and Gong Du, are spreading havoc in Runan. Cao Hong, unable to suppress them, wants troops." Lord Guan volunteered. "Let me do my best to break the rebels," he said. "You have rendered distinguished service time and again," Cao Cao said, "and have yet to receive your due. How can we let you serve?" "If I remain inactive too long," Lord Guan replied, "I will lose my health. Let me go." Impressed by his zeal, Cao Cao detailed fifty thousand men to follow him, assigning Yu Jin and Yue Jin as his deputy commanders.

The next day after Lord Guan's army had set out, Xun Wenruo quietly warned Cao Cao, "His allegiance to Xuande is firm as ever. If he gets word of his brother, he will leave us. I wouldn't keep sending him out on these campaigns." "After this," Cao Cao responded, "I won't let him fight again."

Lord Guan pitched camp close to Runan. His men seized two spies in the night. Lord Guan recognized one of them as Sun Qian, an adviser to Xuande. Dismissing his attendants, Lord Guan said to him, "After the debacle at Xuzhou I lost all trace of you. What are you doing here?" "After the defeat," Sun Qian replied, "chance brought me to Runan, and Liu Pi gave me refuge. What are you, General, doing on Cao Cao's side? Are Lady Gan and Lady Mi safe?" Lord Guan then related the intervening events. "I have heard," Sun Qian said, "that our lord is with Yuan Shao. I have wanted to join him but have found no chance to. At the moment Liu Pi and Gong Du, the two Yellow Scarves leaders, have pledged to help Yuan Shao against Cao Cao. We learned that providence had led you to Runan, and so they arranged to have me brought here in disguise to tell you they will feign defeat tomorrow. You will then be able to bring the two ladies to Yuan Shao and be reunited with our lord."

"Since my elder brother is with Yuan Shao," Lord Guan said, "I must go to him at once. If only I had not killed Yuan Shao's two generals—now anything could happen." "I'll sound things out for you," Sun Qian said, "and report back." "I am ready to die ten thousand times," Lord Guan declared, "for one look at my brother. I am returning to the capital now to bid Cao Cao good-bye." That night Lord Guan sent Sun Qian north on his mission to Yuan Shao.[4]

The next day Lord Guan went into battle against Gong Du. Clad for combat, Gong Du appeared before his lines. Lord Guan cried to him, "Why have you turned against the court?" Gong Du retorted, "As one who has turned against his lord, you are in no position to reproach me." "I, betray my lord?" Lord Guan demanded. "What are you doing in Cao Cao's service," Gong Du went on, "when Liu Xuande is with Yuan Shao?" Lord Guan said no more. He swung his sword and charged. Gong Du fled. Lord Guan pursued. Du shouted back, "Remember your former lord's kindness. Advance swiftly—we will yield Runan." Lord Guan knew what he meant and sent his army forward. Feigning defeat, Liu Pi and Gong Du abandoned the field. Lord Guan took control of the district, reassured the populace, and returned to the capital. Cao Cao welcomed him outside the city walls and rewarded the troops.

After the celebration Lord Guan went home and paid his respects to his sisters-in-law. From behind her screen Lady Gan asked, "Brother, after two expeditions, is there still no news of the imperial uncle?" "Not yet," Lord Guan answered and left. The two ladies cried bitterly. "The imperial uncle is probably no more, and second brother is sparing us from the truth." But just then an old soldier long in their service heard them sobbing and whispered through the screen, "Dry your tears, ladies, your lord is with Yuan Shao north of the river." "How do you know that?" they asked. "I was on campaign with General Guan," the soldier replied. "Someone at the front told me."

The two ladies summoned Lord Guan and demanded an explanation. "The imperial uncle has never wronged you," they said. "But now that you have Cao Cao's favor, you have promptly forgotten your duty to your former liege. Why have you kept the truth from us?" Lord Guan touched his head to the floor. "It is true," he replied, "that elder brother is north of the river. I kept it from you to ensure secrecy.[5] We have to plan carefully now; haste will accomplish nothing."[6] "Do not delay," Lady Gan pleaded. Lord Guan retired again but knew no peace, racking his brains for a plan.

In fact, Yu Jin had already informed Cao Cao of Xuande's whereabouts, and Cao Cao had sent Zhang Liao to learn Lord Guan's intentions. Zhang Liao found his friend sitting, depressed. "I hear you had news of your brother on the last campaign," Zhang Liao said, "and come especially to congratulate you." "My former lord may be alive," Lord Guan replied, "but I have yet to see him. There is no cause for rejoicing." Zhang Liao asked, "How does your relation with me differ from that between you and Xuande?" "You and I," Lord Guan replied, "are just friends. Xuande and I are friends to begin with, brothers in the second place, and, finally, lord and vassal. The relationships are not comparable."[7] "Xuande is with Yuan Shao," Zhang Liao continued. "Are you going to join him?" "I must stand by my pledge," Lord Guan replied. "Please convey my best wishes to the prime minister." Zhang Liao reported the conversation to Cao Cao, who said, "I have a way to detain him."

Lord Guan was mulling over the situation when an old friend was announced. But it turned out to be someone Lord Guan did not recognize. "Who are you, sir?" he asked. "Actually," the man replied, "I am in the service of Yuan Shao—Chen Zhen of Nanyang."

Astounded, Lord Guan dismissed his attendants and said, "What have you come for, sir?" The man handed him the letter from Liu Xuande. It read in part:

> In the peach garden you and I once swore to share a single fate. Why have you swerved from that course, severing the bond of grace and allegiance? If you seek recognition for your deeds or aspire to wealth and status, I will gladly offer up my head to make your accomplishment complete. Who can write all he wishes to say? Unto death I will abide by your instruction.

Lord Guan wept bitterly reading Xuande's words. "Would I not have sought out my brother," he cried, "had I known where to seek him? Would I break our original covenant for the sake of wealth and status?"[8] "Xuande's anxiety to see you is most keen," the messenger said. "If you remain true to the oath, you should go to him as soon as possible." "In this life," Lord Guan said, "man stands between Heaven and earth. He who fails to finish as he starts is no man of honor. I came to Cao Cao open and aboveboard and can leave him no other way. I shall compose a letter for you to carry to my brother. This will give me time to take leave of Cao and bring my sisters-in-law to Xuande." "What if Cao Cao refuses?" the messenger asked. "I am content to die rather than remain here," Lord Guan declared. "Then draft it quickly," the messenger said, "for Lord Liu despairs." Lord Guan sent the following reply:

> In my humble view, honor brooks no reservation, nor does loyalty respect death. In my youth I came to know the classics and to appreciate something of our traditions and code of honor. When I reflect on the fraternal devotion and sacrifice of such ancient models as Yangjue Ai and Zuo Botao, I cannot help sighing over and over through my tears.[9] At Xiapi, which you assigned me to guard, we had no stores and no reinforcements. My own wish was to fight to the death, but with the heavy responsibility of my two sisters-in-law, could I sacrifice myself and thus abandon those entrusted to me? So I assumed a temporary obligation in hopes of rejoining you later. Only recently at Runan did I first receive reliable information about you. Now I shall go at once in person to bid Lord Cao good-bye. I will then deliver the two ladies to you. May the gods and man scourge me if I harbor any undutiful intent. I open my bosom to you, but pen and silk cannot convey my loyalty, my sincerity. Humbly awaiting the time when I can bow before you, I offer this for your examination.

The messenger took the letter. After informing the ladies of what he had done, Lord Guan went to the ministerial residence. But Cao Cao knew why he was coming and had a sign saying "Absent" hung at his gate. Lord Guan left, perturbed. He next ordered his original followers to prepare the carriages and horses for departure at a moment's notice. Finally he instructed the members of his household to leave all gifts from Cao—even the least trifle—in place. Nothing was to be taken away.

The following day Lord Guan went to the prime minister's residence. The same sign greeted him. He returned several more times but never succeeded in seeing Cao Cao. Lord Guan then sought out Zhang Liao at his home, but he would not appear, pleading ill health. Realizing that the prime minister would not formally let him leave and yet resolved to do so, Lord Guan wrote this farewell message:

> In my youth I undertook to serve the imperial uncle, vowing to share with him both life and death. Radiant Heaven and fertile earth bore witness to the oath.

When I lost my command at Xiapi, I received your gracious consent to my three demands. Now I have discovered that my first liege is in the army of Yuan Shao. Our covenant is ever in my thoughts; to betray it is unthinkable. Despite the great favor you have bestowed on me of late, this original bond must be honored. I hereby deliver this letter to announce my departure, presuming to hope that you may consider it. For whatever benefaction I may yet remain in your debt, kindly defer the accounting until some future day.

Transcribed and sealed, the letter was taken to the prime minister's residence.

Lord Guan locked away all valuables received during his stay and left his seal of office, lord of Hanshou precinct, hanging in the hall. Next he had his sisters-in-law mount the carriage readied for them. Astride Red Hare, the sword Green Dragon in hand, and ringed by his original followers, Lord Guan, with menacing eye and leveled blade, pushed straight out of the north city gate, past the objecting gate warden. Lord Guan then dropped back to deal with any pursuers as the retinue hastened along the highroad.

Cao Cao was still considering his next move when Lord Guan's letter was brought to him. Stunned, Cao said, "So he has left!" Next, the warden of the north gate reported: "Lord Guan burst out of the gate. One carriage and some twenty riders are heading north." Lord Guan's house staff also reported, "He locked up all Your Lordship's gifts; the ten ladies-in-waiting are in a separate room. His seal of office was left hanging in the hall. He took none of the servants assigned to him, only his followers from former days and some personal belongings. They left by the north gate." Cao Cao's entire council was shocked. But one general stood boldly forth and said, "Give me three thousand horsemen and I will deliver him alive!" It was Cai Yang. Indeed:

> Lord Guan exchanged the dragon's lair
> For a pack of wolves in hot pursuit.

Would Cao Cao send Cai Yang to seize Lord Guan?[10]
    READ ON.

27

The Man of the Magnificent Beard Rides Alone a Thousand Li;
The Lord of Hanshou Slays Six Generals and Breaches Five Passes

LORD GUAN HAD TWO FRIENDS in Cao Cao's camp, Zhang Liao and Xu Huang. Moreover, he was generally respected by the other generals, with one exception—Cai Yang. But Cai Yang's offer to bring him back drew an angry rebuke from Cao Cao: "Lord Guan is a man of highest honor, for his loyalty to his lord and for leaving as aboveboard as he came. All of you would do well to emulate him." "Your Excellency," Cheng Yu declared, "you treated that fellow with the utmost generosity, yet he departed without taking leave. That scrap of nonsense he wrote insolently sullies your prestige—a great offense. If you permit him to give his allegiance to Yuan Shao, you lend your enemy new strength. Pursue and dispatch him, and spare yourself future troubles." "At the beginning," Cao said, "I granted his demands. Can I break my own promises? He acts for his own lord. Let him go!"[1]

Turning to Zhang Liao, Cao continued, "Lord Guan locked away his valuables and left his seal. Rich bribes seem not to move him, nor do dignities and emoluments deflect his purpose. We cannot esteem such men too highly. He must still be within range. We might as well make one last effort to cultivate him. Ride ahead and beg him to stop until I can escort him off properly—provide some money for the journey and a battle dress—so he will remember me in future times." Zhang Liao raced off, followed by Cao Cao and a few dozen riders.

Lord Guan, on Red Hare, could not normally have been overtaken. But he was keeping to the rear to guard the carriage. Hearing a shout, he turned. Zhang Liao was pounding toward him. Lord Guan ordered the carriage guard to press on while he reined in and, hand on sword, said, "I trust you are not coming in pursuit?" "I am not," Zhang Liao replied. "The prime minister, in consideration of the long road ahead of you, wishes to see you off personally and has sent me to request that you delay for a few moments. I have no other intent." "Even if he comes in force," Lord Guan replied, "I will do battle to the death." He poised his horse on a bridge, surveying their approach. Cao Cao himself, surrounded by a small contingent, was racing up, trailed by Xu Chu, Xu Huang, Yu Jin, and Li Dian. Before the bridge Cao Cao told his commanders to rein in and spread out. Seeing they carried no weapons, Lord Guan became easier.

"Why do you go in such haste?" Cao Cao asked. Remaining mounted, Lord Guan bent forward to show respect and replied, "It is as I petitioned on arriving:[2] now that my original lord is north of the river, I must not delay. Time after time I presented myself at your quarters but never succeeded in seeing you, so in all humility I wrote to announce my departure, stored away your valuable gifts, and hung up my seal for return to Your Excellency, who, I am confident, will not forget what we agreed to." "I seek the trust of all the world," Cao Cao said. "Would I renege on my word? I was only concerned that you might run short on your journey, General, and so I have made a point of coming to see you off with something for your expenses." At this point one of Cao Cao's commanders extended toward Lord Guan a plate heaped with gold.

"Time and again," Lord Guan said, "I have benefited from your considerable bounty, of which much yet remains. Reserve this treasure to reward your officers." "This trifling recompense for your magnificent services," Cao Cao responded, "is but one ten-thousandth of what I owe you. Why decline it?" "My paltry efforts," Lord Guan answered, "are not worth the mention." "You are the model of the honorable man," Cao Cao exclaimed. "I only regret that destiny deprives me of the opportunity to keep you. This damask robe is an expression of my good will." One of Cao Cao's captains dismounted, carried the robe to Lord Guan, and offered it up to him with two hands. Cautiously, Lord Guan leaned down, lifted the garment on the tip of his sword, and draped it over his body. "I am indebted," he said, "for Your Excellency's gift. Another day we may meet again." Turning, Lord Guan rode off the bridge and headed north.

"Insolent barbarian!" Xu Chu cried. "Why not seize him?" "He was outnumbered, more than ten to one," Cao Cao replied. "He had to be on his guard. I gave my word. Do not pursue him." Cao Cao led his men back to the capital, but the loss of Lord Guan weighed on him.

·   ·   ·   ·   ·

Lord Guan rode on for thirty *li* but found no trace of the carriage. He was anxiously searching in all directions when a rider hailed him from a hilltop. Lord Guan looked up at a young man in a brocade garment and yellow scarf, holding a spear. A human head swung from his horse's neck. He raced down with a hundred men on foot. "Who are you?" Lord Guan demanded. The young man threw down his lance, dismounted, and touched the ground before Lord Guan, who said again, "Tell me your name, young warrior!"

"I come from Xiangyang," he began. "My surname is Liao; my given name Hua, my style Yuanjian. In these troubled times I've turned to a roving life. My five hundred men and I survive by plunder. My partner, Du Yuan, patrolling the foot of the hill, seized the two ladies by mistake. Their attendants mentioned they were the wives of Imperial Uncle Liu and under your protection. I wanted to deliver them to you right away, but Du Yuan was outraged; so I killed him and have brought his head to atone for our offense." "Where are the ladies now?" Lord Guan asked. "At the moment, on the hill," Liao Hua replied. On Lord Guan's demand they were brought forth.

Lord Guan approached the carriage. Standing with hands clasped to show respect, he inquired, "Did these men frighten you, sisters-in-law?" "If not for Commander Liao," they answered, "we would have lost our honor to Du Yuan." "How so?" Lord Guan asked. The attendants explained, "Du Yuan abducted the ladies. He wanted to wed one and offered the other to Liao Hua. But once Liao Hua discovered who they were, he treated them with due respect and killed Du Yuan for objecting to their return." Lord Guan thanked Liao Hua, who volunteered to serve him. But Lord Guan was reluctant to associate with a Yellow Scarves bandit and declined the offer as well as the gold and silk Liao Hua proferred. They parted, therefore, and Liao Hua went back to the hills. Lord

Guan described to the ladies his last encounter with Cao Cao. He then told the carriage guard to push on.[3]

At nightfall they stopped at a farmstead. The elder of the household, hair and beard all white, greeted them and asked Lord Guan, "Who are you, General?" "A brother of Liu Xuande, known as Guan," he replied, bowing. "Not the warrior who cut down Yan Liang and Wen Chou?" the old man asked. Lord Guan nodded, and the delighted host invited him into the farmstead. "There are still two ladies in the carriage," Lord Guan said, so the host had his wife and daughter escort the ladies to their thatched grange. Lord Guan stayed beside the ladies, standing, hands clasped, and declined the offer to be seated. "Not in the presence of my sisters-in-law," he said. The elder had his wife and daughter provide for them in the inner chamber, while he entertained Lord Guan in the main hall. "I am Hu Hua," the elder said, "a court counselor in the reign of Emperor Huan. I retired to tend my farm. At present my son, Hu Ban, is serving as an aide to Wang Zhi, governor of Yingyang. Do you expect to pass that way, General? I have a letter for him." Lord Guan agreed to carry it.

The next morning after breakfast Lord Guan escorted his sisters-in-law to the carriage. He took the letter for Hu Ban, bid his host good-bye, and set out for Luoyang. Soon he reached Dongling Pass, which was guarded by Commander Kong Xiu and five hundred men. Lord Guan guided the coach toward the pass. Kong Xiu stepped forward to meet Lord Guan, who dismounted and extended the ritual courtesies. "Where are you bound, General?" Kong Xiu asked. "I have bid the prime minister good-bye," Lord Guan replied, "and am going north of the river to find my brother." "Into Yuan Shao's territory?" Kong Xiu said. "He's the prime minister's enemy. No doubt you have his authority for your trip?"[4] "I don't have it. Our departure was rushed," Lord Guan replied. "In that case," Kong Xiu said, "I cannot let you pass until I send for the prime minister's approval." "That would delay us," Lord Guan remarked. "I am bound by regulations," Kong Xiu explained, "there is no alternative." "You will not let us through, then?" Lord Guan asked. "Not unless you leave the imperial uncle's kinfolk as security," he said.

Lord Guan drew his sword. Kong Xiu went into the pass and returned mounted and in battle regalia, summoning his men with drums. "I dare you to come through," he shouted. Lord Guan had the carriage and escort removed to safe ground; then he charged. Kong Xiu raised his lance. The two riders clashed. Lord Guan's steel blade struck but once, and Kong Xiu slumped, dead, from his mount. The soldiers fled. "Stay!" Lord Guan shouted to them. "Kong Xiu forced my hand, but you are blameless. Inform Prime Minister Cao that Kong Xiu left me no choice." The pass guards prostrated themselves before Lord Guan.

Lord Guan had the ladies' carriage guard pass through and resume the journey toward Luoyang. Han Fu, the district governor, learned of their approach and gathered his commanders. Captain Meng Tan said, "If he has no papers from the prime minister, he is a fugitive, and we will be held to account unless we stop him." "Lord Guan," Han Fu said, "is a powerful and ferocious fighter. He has killed Yan Liang and Wen Chou. I think he can be taken by strategy better than by force." "In that case," Meng Tan replied, "we should block the pass with an 'antler' barricade of sharpened sticks and branches. When he arrives, let me engage him. I will feign defeat and draw him in pursuit. Your Lordship, in hiding, can fell him with an arrow and we will all be well rewarded back in the capital." The governor approved this plan.

Soon they sighted the carriage. Han Fu took his bow and deployed a thousand men; he challenged the approaching party, "Who comes here?" Lord Guan leaned forward to show respect. "The lord of Hanshou, known as Guan, begs leave to pass." "Have you the necessary documents from the prime minister?" Han Fu asked. "I neglected to obtain them in the rush of departure," Lord Guan answered. "The prime minister," Han Fu declared, "has charged me with the responsibility of guarding this point—above all, to check for spies. If you have no papers, you are a runaway." "At Dongling," Lord Guan said testily, "I killed Kong Xiu. Do you want to die too?" "Who will take him?" Han Fu cried.

Meng Tan rode forth, twirling two swords; he made for Lord Guan. Lord Guan had the carriage moved away and met his opponent. After two exchanges Meng Tan wheeled and fled, expecting to be pursued but not overtaken. But Lord Guan caught up and cut him in half. He then reined in and rode back. Hiding on horseback by the gate, Han Fu got off a powerful shot, and the arrow struck Lord Guan's left arm. Lord Guan pulled the bolt out with his teeth and, despite the bleeding wound, raced for Han Fu. Plowing through the pass guards before Han Fu could escape, Lord Guan knocked him from his horse with a blow that cleaved his head and shoulder. Han Fu's guard scattered, and Lord Guan returned to his charges.

Lord Guan delayed only long enough to cut a piece of his robe and dress his wound. Then, fearful of more foul play, he led his party through the pass toward the Si River. They traveled through the night and by morning had reached the next pass. The commander in charge was Bian Xi from Bing province, a warrior who specialized in hurling irons. Originally a Yellow Scarves adherent, Bian Xi had been posted at this checkpoint after giving himself up to Cao Cao. The moment he learned Lord Guan was arriving, Bian Xi decided to place an ambush in the Zhenguo Temple on his side of the pass. Inside, two hundred men armed with hatchets waited to strike the moment Bian Xi tapped his wine-cup. His preparations made, Bian Xi received Lord Guan as he dismounted.

"General," Bian Xi said, "the realm reveres your name. Your return to the imperial uncle demonstrates true loyalty and a most honorable sense of duty." Lord Guan described his difficulties at the previous pass, and Bian Xi said, "Your action was entirely justified. When I see the prime minister, I shall petition in your behalf." Lord Guan was delighted. The two men rode through the pass and dismsounted in front of the temple. A crowd of monks surged forth to welcome them as bells chimed. This temple, where Emperor Ming, second ruler of the Later Han, once worshiped, now housed more than thirty monks.

One of the monks, whose name in religion was Pujing, or Universal Purity, turned out to be from Lord Guan's home area. Knowing what was afoot, the monk said to Lord Guan, "How many years has it been since you left Pudong?" "Nearly twenty," Lord Guan replied. "Don't you recognize this poor monk anymore?" he asked.[5] "After so many years," Lord Guan responded, "I'm afraid not." "Our homes," the monk reminded him, "were separated only by a stream." As the monk went on about their native place, Bian Xi, fearful he might give away the plot, said sharply, "I have invited the general to a banquet. Why are you going on so?" "Please! Please!" Lord Guan interjected. "When fellow townsmen meet by chance, why shouldn't they catch up on old times?" The monk invited Lord Guan to the abbot's quarters for tea. "I have the ladies in the carriage," Lord Guan said. The monk served them first and walked Lord Guan to his chamber. Signaling with his eyes, he raised the monastic knife symbolizing the sacred renunciations. Lord Guan caught his suggestion and ordered his followers to stick close with ready swords.

Bian Xi came to escort Lord Guan to the banquet in the temple's main hall. "My friend, is this invitation well intentioned?" Lord Guan asked. He had already spotted the henchmen behind the arras. Without waiting for a reply, Lord Guan turned and bellowed, "I took you for a decent man. How dare you!" Bian Xi called out his men, but Lord Guan swept them down with his sword before they could act. Bian Xi fled around a corridor. Lord Guan changed his sword for his dragon blade and gave chase. Bian Xi hurled one of his iron missiles at Lord Guan, but Lord Guan brushed it aside with his sword, overtook the commander, and cut him in two. He then rescued his sisters-in-law from the guards who had surrounded their carriage.

When it was over, he thanked the monk, saying, "If not for you, master, we would have fallen to those villains." "I cannot remain here," he responded. "I shall gather my robe and alms bowl and go wherever my steps may lead me. Perhaps we shall meet hereafter.[6] Pray care for yourself, General." Lord Guan again voiced his appreciation and, positioning himself by the carriage, set off for Yingyang.

Wang Zhi, governor of Yingyang, was related to Han Fu, commander of the second pass, by their children's marriage. On learning that Lord Guan had killed Han Fu, Wang Zhi and his advisers planned to assassinate him. Their first step was to reinforce the pass. When Lord Guan arrived, Wang Zhi greeted him heartily. Lord Guan explained that he was searching for his brother. "The ladies," Wang Zhi said, "must be exhausted from such hard travel. They should spend the night in the city and resume their journey tomorrow." Wang Zhi seemed so sincere and thoughtful that Lord Guan agreed. In the guesthouse everything had been perfectly arranged. Wang Zhi invited Lord Guan to a banquet, but he declined, so Wang Zhi had a grand dinner sent to his quarters. Afterwards, at Lord Guan's urging, the ladies retired to the master room. He let his attendants off, had the horses fed, removed his armor, and tried to get some rest himself.

Wang Zhi, meanwhile, secretly instructed his lieutenant, Hu Ban, "This Guan is a fugitive, an enemy of the prime minister. What's more, he killed a district governor and several commanders and captains at the passes. Death is better than he deserves! But he is a brave and invincible warrior. Tonight I want you to put a thousand men around his quarters, each with an unlit torch. At the third watch burn the place down. I don't care who dies in there. I'll back you up with troops."

As ordered, Hu Ban organized the men and had kindling moved to the gate of the guesthouse. But all the while he was thinking, "I have heard about Lord Guan. I wonder what he looks like. Let me see if I can get a peek." He entered the building and found out from the keeper that Lord Guan was reading in the main hall. Hu Ban stole up to the doorway and observed the warrior at a desk, stroking his long beard with his left hand while he read by lamplight. "Truly like a god!" The words escaped Hu Ban and attracted Lord Guan's attention. "Who's there?" he called.

Hu Ban entered and saluted. "Hu Ban, lieutenant to Governor Wang Zhi," he announced. "Not the son of Hu Hua who lives outside the capital?" Lord Guan asked. "The same," he replied. Lord Guan had an aide fetch the letter he was carrying. Hu Ban read it and sighed. "We almost killed a worthy man!" he said. "Wang Zhi is a schemer. He plans to kill you. They're going to surround the guesthouse and burn it down at the third watch. But I'm going to open the city gate now. Get everything ready." Lord Guan rearmed himself and mounted his horse. He placed the ladies in the coach and left. Outside he saw soldiers waiting with torches. He hurried to the wall and, finding the open gate, motioned the carriage ahead. Quickening his pace, he followed it out of the city. Hu Ban went back to set the fire.

After riding several li, Lord Guan saw the glow of torches behind him and a body of men approaching. "Halt where you are!" cried Wang Zhi. "Do not proceed!" Lord Guan reined in and cursed him, "You cur! For what grudge would you burn us to death?" Wang Zhi charged, lance ready, but a thrust of Lord Guan's blade severed him at the waist. Wang Zhi's men bolted. Lord Guan continued on his way, silently thanking Hu Ban.

Lord Guan's arrival at the boundary of Huazhou was reported to Liu Yan, who met them outside the city wall with a contingent of horsemen. Lord Guan bent low over his horse and asked, "Governor, have you been well since we parted?" "Where are you bound?" Liu Yan inquired. "I have taken leave of the prime minister," Lord Guan explained, "to rejoin my brother." "Liu Xuande is with Yuan Shao, the prime minister's enemy," said the governor. "How could Lord Cao allow you to go there?" "It was agreed to long ago," Lord Guan explained. "The strategic crossing at the river," Liu Yan warned, "is guarded by Qin Qi, a deputy general to Xiahou Dun. I don't think he'll let you cross." "Governor," Lord Guan asked, "could you accommodate me with a boat?" "I have boats," he replied, "but cannot accommodate you." "When I killed Yan Liang and Wen Chou," Lord Guan reminded him, "I saved you a lot of trouble. Why refuse me a single boat?" "Xiahou Dun would hold me responsible if he found out," was the reply.

Lord Guan knew that Governor Liu Yan would be of no use, so he left him alone and headed for the crossing. Qin Qi met him. "Who comes here?" he demanded. "Lord Guan of Hanshou," was the reply. "Where bound?" Qin Qi asked next. "I'm trying to find my brother, Liu Xuande, on the other side," Lord Guan said, "and respectfully request passage." "Where is your approval from the prime minister?" Qin Qi demanded. "I am not subject to his authority," Lord Guan answered. "Why should I need documents?" "I have orders from General Xiahou Dun to guard this point. A pair of wings couldn't get you through," Qin Qi said. A powerful anger took hold of Lord Guan. "You know," he said, "I have killed those who tried to block my way." "Try and kill me!" Qin Qi taunted him. "You think you're as good as Yan Liang and Wen Chou?" Lord Guan cried.

Qin Qi charged, sword held high. The two riders crossed but once. Lord Guan's blade rose and fell, beheading Qin Qi. Lord Guan shouted to Qin Qi's troops, "Your commander opposed me; now he's dead. No one else will be hurt. Do not run. Prepare a boat for us." A soldier promptly poled a craft to shore, and Lord Guan escorted the ladies onto it. Once across, they were in Yuan Shao's territory. In all Lord Guan had forced five checkpoints and slain six commanders. A later poet wrote:

> Nor rank nor gift could tempt Lord Guan to stay.
> Seeking his brother by long and winding road,
> He covered the ground on a thousand-*li* horse;
> With dragon blade he took each pass by force.
>
> He thrust loyalty and honor high into the spheres,
> A manly model who kept the world in awe.
> This single knight, before whom each foe fell,
> Left the world a story that men will ever tell.

Riding on, Lord Guan sighed. "Circumstances have forced me to kill Cao's guards," he mused. "It was not my wish. But Cao Cao will only consider me ungrateful for his kindness." His thoughts were interrupted by a single rider coming toward him from the north. "Lord Guan, go no farther!" he shouted. Lord Guan reined in. Liu Xuande's adviser Sun Qian was before him. "What has happened since we parted at Runan?" Lord Guan asked. "Liu Pi and Gong Du have retaken Runan," Sun Qian replied. "They sent me to work out an alliance with Yuan Shao and to coordinate Xuande's plans to move against Cao Cao. But I found Yuan Shao's leadership torn by rivalries. Tian Feng remains in jail and Ju Shou in disgrace. Shen Pei and Guo Tu compete for power. Yuan Shao himself is sunk in misgivings and wavers on every issue. I convinced the imperial uncle to clear out, and he has already gone to join Liu Pi in Runan. Had you gone on to Yuan Shao unaware of the change, you would have come to harm. That is why my lord, Liu Pi, sent me to find you—luckily I did! Make haste for Runan!"

Lord Guan had Sun Qian salute the two ladies. Sun Qian then told them, "On two occasions Yuan Shao wanted to kill the imperial uncle. Fortunately he has escaped to Runan; you can meet him there." They covered their faces and wept.

Lord Guan took the road to Runan. But he had hardly set out when a squad of men, obscured by dust, accosted them from behind. It was Xiahou Dun. "Do not advance!" he cried. Indeed:

> Six pass commanders fell, but Lord Guan rode through;
> Now a fresh squad blocked his way, spoiling for a fight.

Could Lord Guan make good his escape?
READ ON.

28

Lord Guan Slays Cai Yang, Dispelling His Brothers' Doubts;
Liege and Liege Men Unite Again at Gucheng

LORD GUAN AND SUN QIAN, escorting the two ladies on to Runan, found themselves pursued without warning by Xiahou Dun and three hundred riders. Sun Qian went along with the carriage guard, while Lord Guan turned, reined in, and, resting his hand on his sword, said to Cao Cao's general, "Are you trying to compromise the prime minister's reputation for magnanimity?" "I have no specific orders," Xiahou Dun responded. "But you have murdered people and killed my commander. And that's an outrage! I have come to arrest you and deliver you to the prime minister, who will make the final disposition."

So saying, Xiahou Dun urged his mount on and pointed his lance. But behind him a single rider called out, "Hold off! Do not fight Lord Guan!" The warriors stood still as the messenger drew a paper from inside his upper garment and proclaimed, "His Excellency holds Lord Guan's fealty and honor in highest esteem and, to ensure his passage, authorizes his safe-conduct in our territory. He has sent me with documents to notify all concerned." "Does the prime minister know," Xiahou Dun replied, "that Guan has killed our commanders and pass guards?" "He does not," the messenger replied. "I merely want to take him alive to the prime minister," Xiahou Dun explained. "His Excellency can release Guan if he sees fit."

Lord Guan broke in, "You think I fear you?" And gripping his weapon, he started toward the general. Xiahou Dun parried with his lance. The two exchanged ten blows. Another messenger then arrived, shouting, "Generals! Cease fighting!" Xiahou Dun put up his lance and demanded, "Does the prime minister want me to capture this fellow Guan?" "No!" came the answer. "The prime minister has sent me with a safe-conduct pass. He was afraid the commanders at the checkpoints might stop General Guan." Xiahou Dun said, "Does His Excellency know Guan has killed people on his way?" "No," the messenger replied. "In that case, I cannot release him," Xiahou Dun said and signaled his men to surround Lord Guan. The antagonists were about to resume combat for the third time when a third rider appeared, demanding that the fighting stop. It was Zhang Liao.

The warriors halted. Zhang Liao approached. "I have here," he declared, "the prime minister's command. He has heard of the incidents at the checkpoints and, hoping to prevent any further conflict, has sent me to instruct all stations to let Lord Guan pass." "Qin Qi," Xiahou Dun cried, "was the nephew of Cai Yang, and Cai Yang entrusted the lad to me. How can I let his killer go?" "I will explain things to Cai Yang," Zhang Liao said.

"Since the prime minister in his generosity grants Lord Guan freedom to pass, you gen-tlemen should not disregard his wishes." Confronted with this order, Xiahou Dun had to pull back.

"Where are you headed, brother?" Zhang Liao asked Lord Guan. "It seems that my brother is not with Yuan Shao after all," Lord Guan replied. "I shall have to keep looking." "Since his whereabouts are uncertain," Zhang Liao said, "why not return to the prime minister for the time being?" "That is impossible," Lord Guan said, smiling. "My friend, do me a kindness. When you see the prime minister, offer my apologies." Lord Guan saluted Zhang Liao and left. Zhang Liao and Xiahou Dun led their contin-gents homeward.

·   ·   ·   ·

Catching up with the carriage, Lord Guan described the incident to Sun Qian. The party continued on for several days. They were forced to stop by a sudden rainstorm that drenched the baggage. A manor house stood beside a hill ahead of them. Lord Guan steered them toward it to put up for the night. An old man came out, and Lord Guan explained to him who they were and why they had come. "I am Guo Chang," the old man said. "We have lived here for generations. Your great name has been long known to us. It is an honor to pay my respects to you." He butchered a lamb for them and served wine. After inviting the two women to rest in a rear apartment, he joined Lord Guan and Sun Qian in the hall, where they drank freely while the luggage was dried and the horses fed.

At dusk a young man burst into the hall with a few companions. Guo Chang called him over. "My son," he said, "pay your respects to the general." Turning to Lord Guan, the old man added, "My humble son." "What was he doing?" Lord Guan asked. "Hunt-ing," was the reply. After the lad left, Guo Chang said in tears, "For generations we have lived tilling the land and studying the classics, but my only son cares for nothing but hunting. Misfortune is sure to visit our house." "These are times of great disorder," Lord Guan remarked. "If he is accomplished in the military arts, he may yet make a name for himself that way. Why speak of 'misfortune'?" "If only he were willing to devote himself to such a discipline," the father said, "it would show a sense of responsibility. But all he does is roam around, getting himself into all sorts of trouble. That's what worries me." Lord Guan sighed sympathetically.

Late that night Lord Guan and Sun Qian were preparing to retire when they heard a horse neighing and men's angry voices. They went out with drawn swords and found Guo Chang's son groaning on the ground and their own followers brawling with the ser-vants of the manor. One of Lord Guan's men said, "This fellow tried to steal Red Hare, but the horse kicked him. His cries brought us out. Then these servants started a row." "Little rat of a thief!" Lord Guan exclaimed, raising his hand. But Guo Chang flung him-self before the warrior and pleaded, "My unfilial son deserves to die for this, but his old mother dotes on him so—I beg your mercy, General. Spare him." "He really is a bad son, as you said yourself a moment ago," Lord Guan responded. "Who knows a son better than his father? I spare him only out of respect for you, sir." He had his men see to the animal, dispersed the servants, and returned with Sun Qian to his quarters.

The next day Guo Chang and his wife bowed in front of Lord Guan's lodging. "Our son dared to affront you, esteemed General," they said. "We are deeply grateful for your mercy." "Call him," Lord Guan said. "I want a word with him." "He dashed off again during the fourth watch," the father said, "with those worthless companions of his. Who knows where he is now?'' So Lord Guan bid his host good-bye, saw the women into the carriage, and set out. They had traveled some thirty *li* over hilly paths when they saw more than one hundred men rushing toward them. The horsemen were in the lead. The first wore a yellow scarf and a battle gown. Right behind him was Guo Chang's son.

"I was a commander,'' the leader cried, "under General of Heaven Zhang Jue! You there, leave the red horse and I'll let you pass.'' "Ignorant villain!'' Lord Guan mocked him. "You followed the bandit Zhang Jue? Then you ought to know of the three brothers, Liu, Guan, and Zhang!'' "I've only heard of a red-faced long-beard known as Guan, but I've never seen his face,'' the rider replied. "Who are you?'' Lord Guan set his weapon to one side and steadied his horse; then he opened the sack protecting his beard and let it show full length. Instantly the bandit chief jumped down, pulled Guo Chang's son down by his hair, and thrust him before Lord Guan. "I am Pei Yuanshao,'' he announced. "We've had no master since Zhang Jue. We rendezvous in the hills and were lying low here. This morning this good-for-nothing fool told us that a guest with a splendid horse was staying at his house; he wanted me to steal it. What a surprise to find you, General!'' Meanwhile, Guo Chang's son lay on the ground, begging for mercy. "I spare you,'' Lord Guan growled, "only for your father's sake.'' The young man took to his heels.

"You didn't know my face,'' Lord Guan said to Pei Yuanshao, "how did you know my name?'' "Twenty *li* from here,'' he replied, "on Sleeping Ox Hill lives a Guanxi[1] man, Zhou Cang, with the strength to lift a thousand pounds. He has a striking face with a wiry, curled beard—used to be a commander under the Yellow Scarves leader Zhang Bao. When Bao died, Zhou Cang became an outlaw. He's often told me about you, but what hope had I of ever meeting you?'' Lord Guan replied, "A life of banditry is not for a gallant man like you. Better get back on the right track and not fall into the mire.'' Pei Yuanshao thanked him for his advice. Behind them a body of men flashed into view. "It must be Zhou Cang!'' Pei Yuanshao cried. Lord Guan held his horse still, waiting.

A tall, dark-faced man, armed with a spear, rode up with his followers and exclaimed, "General Guan!'' Prostrating himself at the roadside, he continued, "Zhou Cang pays his humble respects.'' "Where did a stout warrior like yourself hear of me?'' Lord Guan asked. "Following Zhang Bao,'' he replied, "I once saw your esteemed face. If only I had joined you, General, instead of losing myself with a pack of bandits! How thankful I am for this meeting. Give me the chance, General, and I will serve you as a common foot soldier or personal attendant. What wouldn't I give for that!'' Moved by the man's earnest appeal, Lord Guan said, "What would you do about your own followers, then?'' "Those who wish to join me may,'' he answered. "The rest are free to leave.'' All the men were for staying.

Lord Guan put the request to his sisters. "Brother,'' Lady Gan said, "since leaving the capital we have come through many an ordeal, but we've never heard you suggest taking on men. You turned down Liao Hua before. Why make an exception now? But the views of women matter little. Brother, you decide.'' "I think you are right,'' Lord Guan said. Then he told Zhou Cang, "Do not think me lacking in friendly feeling, but the ladies I serve, I regret to say, do not agree to your proposal. You should all return to the hills, and when I have found my elder brother, I will call for you.''

Touching his head to the ground, Zhou Cang replied, "I am but a rough and vulgar fellow who has wasted his life. This meeting, General, is like seeing the sun after living in darkness. I cannot bear to lose the opportunity. If it is inconvenient for my men to accompany you, let them follow Pei Yuanshao, and I will join you alone on foot. A journey of ten thousand *li* could not deter me!'' Zhou Cang's second offer was presented to the ladies. "There's no harm in one or two coming with us," Lady Gan said. Lord Guan had Zhou Cang assign his men to Pei Yuanshao, but Pei himself wanted to follow Lord Guan. "If you and I both leave," Zhou Cang argued, "our men will disband. Better for you to lead them for the time being. Let me go first with General Guan. I will come for you after we are settled." Disconsolate, Pei Yuanshao took his leave.

·   ·   ·   ·   ·

Lord Guan and Zhou Cang proceeded in the direction of Runan. As they neared a city in the hills, a local resident told them, "This is Gucheng. Some months back a general named Zhang Fei rode in with a few dozen horsemen, threw out the county officer, and established himself. He recruited troops, purchased horses, gathered fodder, and stored grain. Now he has a few thousand men, and no one dares oppose him in this area." "This is the first I've heard about my younger brother since the debacle at Xuzhou," Lord Guan cried joyfully. "Who would have thought he'd turn up here!" Sun Qian was sent into the city to talk with Zhang Fei and arrange for him to come and receive his two sisters-in-law.

After fleeing Xuzhou, Zhang Fei had lain low in the Mang-Dang Hills for more than a month. Once, coming into the open in hopes of getting word of Liu Xuande, he had chanced upon Gucheng and entered the town to borrow grain. The county officer refused him, however; so Zhang Fei drove him off, took his seal, and occupied the city. Thus things stood when Sun Qian arrived.

After the formal greeting Sun Qian said to Zhang Fei, "Xuande left Yuan Shao and went to Runan. Lord Guan is here from the capital with Lady Gan and Lady Mi and requests that you receive them." Zhang Fei made no response. Arming himself, he mounted and led one thousand men out of the north gate. Lord Guan saw his brother approaching and, excitedly handing his sword to Zhou Cang, raced forward. Moments later he was confronting Zhang Fei's steady, menacing gaze and bristling tiger whiskers. With a thundering shout Zhang Fei brandished his spear. Lord Guan, aghast, dodged the taunting thrusts and cried, "What does this mean, worthy brother? Can you have forgotten our pact in the peach garden?"

Zhang Fei shouted, "You have the face to confront me after dishonoring yourself!" "Have I dishonored myself?" Lord Guan demanded. "You betrayed our elder brother," Zhang Fei cried, "by submitting to Cao Cao and accepting rank and title under him. Now it looks as if you've come back to trick me. Let's settle things here once and for all." "Can you actually not know?" Lord Guan continued. "How can I explain myself? You see our two sisters. Question them yourself, worthy brother."

Raising their screen, the ladies spoke: "Third Brother, what is the reason for this?" "Sisters," Zhang Fei replied, "watch me dispatch a faithless man before I escort you into the city." "Second brother did not know where you were," Lady Gan pleaded, "so we lodged temporarily with Cao Cao. Then we learned that eldest brother was in Runan. Second brother has borne great hardship attempting to bring us to him. Do not misjudge him!" "Second brother's sojourn in the capital," Lady Mi added, "was beyond his control." "Be deceived no longer, sisters," Zhang Fei went on. "A loyal vassal[2] prefers death to disgrace. What self-respecting man serves two masters?"

"Worthy brother," Lord Guan pleaded, "you do me wrong." Sun Qian interjected, "Lord Guan has been looking for you. That's why he is here." "You too speak like a fool," Zhang Fei snapped. "Don't tell me of his good intentions. He's here to capture me." "Wouldn't I have needed an army?" Lord Guan asked. "And what is that?" Zhang

Fei cried, pointing at an armed cohort approaching in a haze of dust: Cao Cao's troops, the windblown banners proclaimed. "Still trying to keep up the act?" Zhang Fei shouted, moving toward Lord Guan with his eighteen-span snake-headed spear. "Brother," Lord Guan protested, "hold on. Let me kill their leader to show my true feelings." "If you have 'true feelings,'" Zhang Fei said, "get him before the third drum roll." Lord Guan agreed.

Cai Yang, in the lead, galloped toward Lord Guan. "You killed my nephew Qin Qi," he shouted, "yet expect to escape me here? I have the prime minister's warrant to take you prisoner." Lord Guan did not trouble to respond. He lifted his blade and aimed his blow. Zhang Fei himself sounded the drum. Before the first roll had ended, Cai Yang's head was tumbling on the ground in the wake of Lord Guan's stroke.

Cai Yang's cohort fled. Lord Guan captured the flag-bearer and demanded an explanation. "Cai Yang was furious over his nephew's death," the soldier said, "and wanted to cross the river to attack you. The prime minister would not allow it and sent him instead to Runan to destroy Liu Pi. We ran into you by accident." Lord Guan had the soldier tell his story to Zhang Fei, who questioned him carefully concerning Lord Guan's conduct in the capital. The soldier's answers confirmed Lord Guan's account, and so Zhang Fei's faith in his brother was restored.

At this moment a report came from the city that a dozen unfamiliar horsemen were riding hard toward the south gate. Zhang Fei rode to the scene and found a small contingent with light bows and short arrows. They dismounted at once when Zhang Fei appeared. Recognizing Mi Zhu and Mi Fang, Zhang Fei also jumped down and welcomed them. "After the rout at Xuzhou," Mi Zhu said, "my brother and I fled to our native place. We inquired high and low and finally heard that Lord Guan had submitted to Cao Cao and that Lord Liu—and Jian Yong too—were with Yuan Shao. We had no idea you were here, General. Yesterday a group of travelers told us that a General Zhang, whom they described briefly, was occupying Gucheng. We thought it must be you and came to find you. How fortunate that we have met!" Zhang Fei replied, "Lord Guan and Sun Qian have just brought my sisters-in-law. Eldest brother too has been located." Overjoyed at the reunion, the brothers Mi presented themselves to Lord Guan and then to the two ladies. Zhang Fei led his sisters to his headquarters in the city. At their description of the ordeal Zhang Fei wept and bowed deeply to Lord Guan. The brothers Mi were profoundly moved as well. Later Zhang Fei recounted his own adventures at a grand feast.

•   •   •   •   •

The following day Zhang Fei was for going at once to Runan to see Xuande. "Not yet, brother," Lord Guan said. "Better stay and guard the ladies while Sun Qian and I seek news of our brother." Zhang Fei consented. Lightly attended, Lord Guan and Sun rode to Runan, where Liu Pi and Gong Du informed them, "The imperial uncle remained here only a few days; then he went back to Yuan Shao to see if he could work things out since we simply had too few troops here." Lord Guan looked downcast. "Do not lose heart," Sun Qian said. "One more hard ride will take us to him, and we can all go back to Gucheng together."

The two returned and told Zhang Fei what they had found out. Once again they had to persuade him to stay behind. "This city," they said, "is our only retreat. We can't afford to lose it. Qian and I will bring our elder brother here. Please stay to defend it." "Brother," Zhang Fei argued, "you have killed Yuan Shao's finest generals. How can you go there?" "It's all right," Lord Guan assured him. "When I get there, I'll do whatever's called for." Then he asked Zhou Cang, "How many troops does Pei Yuanshao have on

Sleeping Ox Hill?'' ''Four or five hundred,'' was the reply. ''I'll take a short cut to my elder brother,'' Lord Guan said. ''You go to the hill, assemble the men, and meet me on the main road.'' Zhou Cang left to carry out the order.

Lord Guan and Sun Qian headed north of the Yellow River with two dozen followers. At the boundary Sun Qian advised, ''Let's not rush in. You stay here while I talk to the imperial uncle.'' Sun Qian rode on, and Lord Guan headed for a nearby farm to spend the night. He was met by an old man who steadied himself on a cane. After an exchange of courtesies Lord Guan gave an account of himself. ''I too am surnamed Guan,'' the old man said. ''My given name is Ding. I am most gratified by this unexpected meeting with one I have long admired.'' He called out his sons, and they welcomed Lord Guan and his men warmly.

Meanwhile, Sun Qian had entered Yuan Shao's base, Jizhou city, capital of Jizhou province, and had described the multiple reunion to Xuande. Xuande called in Jian Yong, and the three considered ways and means of escape. ''My lord,'' Jian Yong suggested, ''when you see Yuan Shao tomorrow, tell him you want to go to Jingzhou to convince Liu Biao to join our struggle against Cao Cao.[3] That will be your excuse for leaving.'' ''Ingenious!'' Xuande exclaimed. ''But can you come too?'' ''I have my own plan for escape,'' Jian Yong replied.

The next day Xuande said to Yuan Shao, ''Liu Biao keeps guard over the nine districts of Jingzhou and Xiangyang. He has keen soldiers and ample grain. We should cooperate in a joint attack on Cao Cao.'' ''I have tried to arrange it,'' Yuan Shao responded, ''but he is unwilling.'' ''Liu Biao is my clansman,'' Xuande said. ''If I go to him now, I know he will not turn us down.'' ''Liu Biao could be worth far more to us than that Liu Pi,'' Yuan Shao said and approved Xuande's mission. He then added, ''There's been a report that Guan has left Cao Cao and wants to come here. If he does, I mean to avenge Yan Liang and Wen Chou.'' ''My lord,'' Xuande replied, ''once you desired his service, so I summoned him. Now you want to kill him? Those two generals were but stags. Guan is a tiger. You've traded two stags for a tiger; how have you been wronged?'' Yuan Shao smiled and said, ''A jest, a jest! Indeed I do prize the man. Have him sent for at once.'' ''Sun Qian will take care of it,'' Xuande said. Yuan Shao was content.

After Xuande had set out for Jingzhou, Jian Yong came before Yuan Shao. ''Liu Bei,'' he said, ''is unlikely to return. I think I should accompany him—to help him work on Liu Biao and also to keep an eye on him.'' Persuaded by this argument, Yuan Shao directed Jian Yong to go with Xuande. The adviser Guo Tu cautioned Yuan Shao, however, ''Liu Xuande has just returned after failing to win Liu Pi to our side. Now you are sending him and Jian Yong to Jingzhou. I can tell you, they will never come back.'' ''You are too mistrustful,'' Yuan Shao replied. ''Jian Yong is experienced and knowledgeable.'' Guo Tu left in despair.

Sun Qian was sent ahead to join Lord Guan. Xuande and Jian Yong took their leave and rode to the border, where Sun Qian picked them up and took them to Guan Ding's farm. Lord Guan was waiting at the entrance. He bowed low, then took his brother by both hands, unable to master his tears. Guan Ding led out his two sons to pay their respects, and Lord Guan introduced the father to Xuande. ''This man is named Guan too,'' he said, ''and these are his sons, Guan Ning, a student of letters, and Guan Ping, the junior, a student of martial arts.'' Guan Ding said, ''I wish my second son could enter General Guan's service. I wonder if it would be possible.'' ''How old is he?'' Xuande asked. ''Eighteen,'' the father replied. ''Since you have been so generous,'' Xuande said, ''and since my brother has no son, your son may become his. What do you say?'' Guan

Ding was delighted and had Guan Ping honor Lord Guan as his father and address Xuande as uncle. Then, fearful of pursuit, Xuande quickly organized their departure. Guan Ping followed Lord Guan, and Guan Ding escorted them a good stretch before returning to his farm.

Xuande, Lord Guan, and their party headed for Sleeping Ox Hill to join Zhou Cang, whom Lord Guan had sent to rally his five hundred followers. But Zhou Cang rode up with only a few score of men, many badly wounded. "Before I reached the hill," Zhou Cang said, "a lone rider had killed Pei Yuanshao and all the men had surrendered. He took over our fortress. I could persuade only these few to join us; the rest were too afraid. I tried to put up a fight, but that warrior overpowered me. I took three wounds. I was just on my way to inform you, master." "What did he look like?" Xuande asked. "Do you know his name?" "He was formidable!" Zhou Cang answered. "His name I don't know." Lord Guan and Xuande headed for the hill, and Zhou Cang hurled curses at his conqueror from the bottom of the slope. The warrior emerged, fully armored, a spear in his fist. He rode downhill like the wind with his newly acquired followers. Xuande pointed with his whip. "It's Zhao Zilong!" he cried.

The warrior leaped from the saddle and prostrated himself by the roadside. It was Zhao Zilong indeed. Xuande and Lord Guan dismounted and asked him how he came to be here. "I rejoined Gongsun Zan after leaving Your Lordship," Zhao Zilong began, "but Zan was too headstrong to accept good advice. Yuan Shao defeated him, and he burned himself to death. Yuan Shao made many offers to me, but he couldn't seem to make good use of those serving him, either. So I stayed away. I went to join you in Xuzhou but heard that you had lost it and that Lord Guan had gone over to Cao Cao. When I learned Your Lordship was with Yuan Shao, I often thought of coming to you but doubted Shao would accept me now. I was still at loose ends, roaming the realm, when I passed by here and Pei Yuanshao tried to steal my horse. After I killed him, I decided to settle here. Next I heard that Zhang Fei was in Gucheng, so I decided to join him if it was true. What a miracle, meeting Your Lordship like this!"

Xuande excitedly recounted for Zhao Zilong the recent events, and Lord Guan filled it in with his story. "Since our first meeting," Xuande said, "I have hoped you would remain with us. I too rejoice in this reunion." Zhao Zilong replied, "I have covered this land in search of a lord to serve, and have not found your like. To follow you now satisfies my lifelong aspiration. Though my heart's blood stain the ground in your service, I shall never regret my choice." He destroyed his fortifications on Sleeping Ox Hill and led the men into Gucheng with Xuande.

Zhang Fei, Mi Zhu, and Mi Fang welcomed the party. Amid ritual bows and salutes they exchanged their stories. Xuande sighed over and over as the two ladies described Lord Guan's trials. Then they slaughtered an ox and a horse, gave thanks to Heaven and earth, and feasted their men.[4] Reunited with his brothers, Xuande rejoiced at having his commanders and advisers back uninjured and Zhao Zilong added to his service. Lord Guan too was delighted beyond measure with his newly adopted son, Guan Ping, as well as with Zhou Cang. For several days they all caroused exuberantly. Later a poet left these lines:

> Like severed limbs, three brothers torn apart:
> Doubtful news, scant word, a fading into silence.
> But when the liege and liege men renewed their brother-tie,
> Tiger winds joined dragon clouds, masters of the sky.

At this time Xuande, Lord Guan, Zhang Fei, Zhao Zilong, Sun Qian, Jian Yong, Mi Zhu, Mi Fang, Guan Ping, and Zhou Cang commanded an army of some four or five thousand, including infantry and cavalry. Xuande proposed leaving Gucheng to protect Runan, and, as luck would have it, Liu Pi and Gong Du sent an envoy requesting their aid. Thus Xuande and his followers set out, recruiting men and buying horses along the way and planning for their campaign.

•   •   •   •

When Yuan Shao realized Xuande would not return, he wanted to attack him. But Guo Tu said, "Xuande need not concern you. Cao Cao is a more formidable opponent. He must be eliminated. And Liu Biao, even though he holds the province of Jingzhou, will never become a power. On the other hand, Sun Ce dominates the land below the Great River, the Southland, an area that includes six districts. His counselors and commanders are numerous. Ally with him to attack Cao!" Yuan Shao accepted his advice and sent Chen Zhen to represent him. Indeed:

> Having lost Xuande, hero of the north,
> Yuan Shao sought a champion from the south.[5]

What happened next?
READ ON.

29

The Overlord of the Southland Executes a Sorcerer;
The Rule of the South Passes to Green-eyed Sun Quan

NOW SUN CE HAD BECOME RULER of the Southland. His army was well trained, his granaries well stocked. By the fourth year of Jian An (A.D. 199) he had taken Lujiang district from Governor Liu Xun and had sent his adviser Yu Fan to Yuzhang to accept the surrender of Governor Hua Xin.[1] Having made his name and power felt, Sun Ce dispatched Zhang Hong to the capital with a memorial to the throne detailing his victories. Cao Cao sighed and said, "We cannot take the lion head on," and arranged for Cao Ren's daughter to marry Sun Ce's youngest brother, Sun Kuang, thus binding the two houses. The emissary Zhang Hong he detained in the capital.

Sun Ce next sought the post of grand marshal, but Cao Cao refused him. The resentful Sun Ce plotted to surprise the capital.[2] But Xu Gong, governor of the Southland district Wujun, secretly wrote to Cao Cao. His letter said in part:

Sun Ce is bold and ambitious, another Xiang Yu in the making.[3] It might be appropriate for the court to show its ostensible appreciation by recalling him to the capital, rather than let him remain in a remote military area where he may become a serious problem.

A messenger was carrying this letter across the river when a border guard seized him and turned him over to Sun Ce. After reading the letter, Sun Ce beheaded the messenger. He then found a pretext for summoning the author of the document and showed it to him. "You would have sent me to my death," he said harshly and had Xu Gong strangled.[4] The governor's family took flight.

Among Xu Gong's retainers were three who wished to avenge him but despaired of finding any opportunity. One day Sun Ce was leading some troops in a hunt by Xishan in Dantu. They had a large deer on the run. Sun Ce's horse, given free rein, had chased it up a hillside. Sun Ce found himself among some trees, where three men with spears and bows appeared. They claimed to be Han Dang's men, also out hunting deer. Sun Ce was about to pass by, when on of them hefted his lance and slashed Sun Ce's left thigh. Sun Ce cut desperately at the man with his waist sword, but suddenly the blade snapped off, leaving him with only the hilt in his hand. Another of the men had raised his bow and positioned an arrow. He shot Sun Ce in the cheek. Sun Ce pulled the arrow out, took his own bow, and shot back. The man fell as the bowstring sang. The remaining two forced Sun Ce back, jabbing wildly with their lances. "We are Xu Gong's men, here to avenge our lord," they cried. Practically disarmed, Sun Ce tried to fend them off with his bow as he moved away, but the attackers were relentless. It was a struggle to the death. Sun Ce was stabbed in several places, and his horse was maimed. His life was hanging in the balance when Chen Pu rode up with a small party and at Sun Ce's command hacked the two assailants to pieces. Seeing his lord's bloody face and massive wounds, one of the rescuers bound Sun Ce with cloth cut from his own robe and took him to safety in Wu-jun. A poet of later times praised Xu Gong's avengers:

> Sun Ce, fearless cunning dynast of the south,
> Was trapped and scathed while hunting in the hills
> By three bold knights who paid what honor owed—
> Loyal in death, Yurang would have been proud.[5]

Once home, Sun Ce sought the services of the healer Hua Tuo, but the physician had gone to the north, leaving behind a disciple. He was summoned to treat Sun Ce's wounds. "The arrow," the doctor observed, "was tipped with a poison that has penetrated the bone. You need a hundred days' quiet convalescence before the danger will pass—and don't let moods of anger affect you, or the wounds will not heal." Sun Ce, it so happened, had a most irascible nature and was frustrated that he could not be cured that very day.

After some twenty days of resting, the patient heard that a messenger had returned from the capital, and he called him for questioning. "Cao Cao," the messenger began, "is quite wary of you, my lord, and his counselors respect your prestige. The only exception is Guo Jia." "And what does he have to say?" Sun Ce asked. The messenger hesitated, angering Sun Ce, who pressed him to convey the facts. "Guo Jia told Cao Cao," the envoy finally admitted, "that you were not a serious concern because you are reckless and always ill prepared, hasty and deficient in strategy, a foolhardy man[6] sure to die by a scoundrel's hand." "That fool dares to rate me![7] I'll take his capital!" Sun Ce swore. He wanted to begin planning the campaign without further delay, but Zhang Zhao objected. "The physician has cautioned my lord," he said, "against any activity for one hundred days. How can you risk your invaluable person to satisfy a moment's rage?"

At this point Yuan Shao's messenger, Chen Zhen, arrived with the news that his master wanted to ally with the south and attack Cao Cao. Delighted, Sun Ce called his commanders to the city tower for a banquet to honor Yuan Shao's envoy. But during the ceremonies the commanders suddenly began whispering to each other and then streamed down from the tower. Sun Ce was amazed at the disruption. His attendants told him, "The immortal Yu has passed below us. The commanders simply wanted to go out to honor him." Sun Ce rose and looked down over the railing at a Taoist priest cloaked in crane feathers, a staff of goosefoot wood in his hand. He was standing in the middle of the road while a group of commoners burned incense and prostrated themselves in veneration. "Who is this sorcerer?" Sun Ce demanded. "Bring him here at once!"[8]

"The man's name is Yu Ji," Sun Ce was informed. "He resides in the east and has traveled here distributing potions that have relieved an unusual number of ailments. He is widely known as an immortal. Pray do not abuse him." "I want him seized and brought here instantly," Sun Ce bellowed. "Obey me or die." As commanded, Sun Ce's men hustled the holy man in to see their master. "Lunatic priest!" Sun Ce growled. "You dare to fan the flames of men's ignorance?" Yu Ji replied, "This poor priest is a Taoist divine from Langye who, during the reign of Emperor Shun, found a sacred text near a spring in Yangqu while gathering herbs in the hills. Called *The Millennium: Purification and Guidance*, it had one hundred volumes, all concerned with techniques for curing pain and disease. Since obtaining it, I have devoted myself to spreading its influence on behalf of Heaven and for the salvation of mankind, never accepting the smallest gift from anyone nor stirring up the people's hearts."[9]

Sun Ce replied, "If that is true, how do you get food and clothing? Don't you really belong to the Yellow Scarves, Zhang Jue and his ilk? We will execute you now, or else you'll plague us later!" He delivered the order, but Zhang Zhao protested, saying, "The priest has been living in the Southland for decades guiltless of any offense. You can't put him to death!" "I can kill these sorcerers," Sun Ce responded, "the way a butcher kills pigs or dogs." The assembly of officials, including Yuan Shao's messenger, implored him to relent, but Sun Ce's wrath could not be assuaged. He ordered the priest imprisoned until he could decide what to do with him. The officials dispersed, and Chen Zhen retired to the guesthouse.

Even before Sun Ce had returned to his quarters, a palace attendant had notified his mother of the incident. Lady Wu promptly summoned her son to her private apartments. "They tell me you have imprisoned the immortal Yu," she said. "He has worked many cures and is revered by the army and the people alike. You must not cause him injury." "The man is a sorcerer," Sun Ce replied. "He uses his arts to mislead the multitude and must be eliminated." To Lady Wu's repeated pleas Sun Ce finally said, "Mother, you must not give credence to the absurd statements of outsiders. I will handle this my own way." He had Yu Ji summoned for interrogation.[10]

When Yu Ji was first arrested, the jailers removed his cangue and fetters out of respect for their prisoner, replacing them only when he was called out for questioning. On discovering how Yu Ji was treated, Sun Ce punished the jailers and sent the immortal back to prison bound hand and foot. Zhang Zhao and a large group of courtiers appealed for clemency, but Sun Ce said, "For men of learning you seem uninformed. Many years ago the imperial inspector of Jiaozhou, Zhang Jin, subscribed to false doctrine, strummed the zither, and burned incense. He bound his head with a red kerchief, claiming it stimulated his troops, yet he perished at the enemy's hands all the same. Such doings avail nothing, though you have yet to awaken to the fact. I am going to kill Yu Ji because I am determined to prevent such perversities and to alert the people to such deceptions."

Lü Fan said to Sun Ce, "It is well known that Yu Ji can invoke the wind and supplicate the rain. Since there is a drought, why not let him pray for rain to redeem his crimes?" "Very well," Sun Ce said, "let us see what this sorcerer can do." He had Yu Ji brought from prison, freed of his cangue and fetters, and told him to call for rain.

Yu Ji bathed and changed his clothes. Then he bound himself upon an altar under a blazing sun. The commoners thronged the streets and choked the lanes to witness the spectacle. Yu Ji spoke to them. "I will pray," he said, "for three spans of timely rainfall to succor the myriad people. But in the end I will not escape death." "If your rain-summoning craft proves itself," voices from the crowd called back, "our ruler will have to honor you." "My allotted time is up," Yu Ji answered. "Unfortunately there is no escape."

Soon Sun Ce himself arrived at the altar. "If no rain falls by noon," he decreed, "burn Yu Ji to death." In anticipation he had kindling heaped up. A little before noon wild winds claimed the skies, and dense clouds converged from all sides. "It is nearly noon," Sun Ce proclaimed. "The sky is black, but there is no rain. This proves he is a sorcerer." He had Yu Ji carried to the top of the kindling pile and ordered fires started all around it. The flames licked up in the wake of the wind; a trail of black smoke appeared and rose into the sky; then a crackling peal announced the storm. Thunder and lightning issued together, and the rain coursed down in currents. Moments later the main street was a river, and the streams were overflowing with—three spans of rain!

Flat upon the pyre, Yu Ji stared at the heavens and cried out. The clouds withdrew. The rains were stayed. The sun reappeared. Officials and commoners helped Yu Ji down from the pyre, bowing and voicing their thanks as they undid his ropes. But when Sun Ce saw the crowd around Yu Ji in knee-deep water paying tribute, he could not contain himself. "Fair weather and storms are natural phenomena," he cried. "The sorcerer has simply taken advantage of a lucky coincidence. What are all of you doing in such a mindless uproar?" Gripping his sword, Sun Ce ordered a soldier to execute Yu Ji on the spot. To all who protested he said, "Will you follow him in rebellion?" A single stroke left Yu Ji's head upon the ground. From it a trail of bluish vapor rose to the northeast. Sun Ce had the corpse displayed in the marketplace as a censure against sins of the supernatural.

Wind and rain thrashed through the night. By dawn the corpse was gone. Those assigned to watch the corpse reported this to Sun Ce, who threatened to kill them. Suddenly, from nowhere a man appeared, walking slowly in front of the main hall. It was Yu Ji. Sun Ce moved back and drew his sword to hack at the apparition; then he fainted and was carried to his bedroom. When he recovered, Lady Wu came to him. "My son," she began, "you have provoked disaster by killing an immortal." "From my earliest days," Sun Ce replied with a smile, "I accompanied my father on military campaigns, and we cut men down like stalks of hemp. There was no such thing as provoking disaster. Today we have killed a demon precisely to put an end to a great disaster. How can you say it will bring disaster upon us?" "It is your lack of belief that has brought you to this," she said. "Now you must perform some worthy deed to appease the spirits." "My destiny rests with Heaven," he answered. "No sorcerer can do me harm. Whom should I appease?" Her exhortation unavailing, Lady Wu privately arranged for good works to be done in order to win forgiveness from the spirits and thus ward off retribution.

That night during the second watch, as Sun Ce lay in his chamber, a chill wind sprang up. The lamp went dark, then flamed again. In the shadows it cast Sun Ce saw Yu Ji standing in front of his bed. Sun Ce screamed, "I am dedicated to destroying the supernatural and purging it from the world of men. You ghost from the shades, dare you approach?" He threw his sword toward the vision, and the ghost disappeared. A report of this incident caused Lady Wu great anxiety, and so Sun Ce, despite his condition, went to allay her fears.

Lady Wu said to her son, "Confucius claimed that 'ghostly spirits manifest inexhaustible potency.' He also said, 'Pray ye to the spirits dispersed above and concentrated below.' We may not doubt such things as ghostly spirits. The murder of Master Yu will be punished. I have ordered services for your health in the Temple of Precious Clarity. Go there yourself and pray. Perhaps things will settle themselves."

Unable to refuse his mother's command, Sun Ce went in a sedan chair to the temple. He burned incense at the priests' behest but offered no apology for what he had done. The fumes hung undispersed in the air, taking the form of a canopy with Yu Ji sitting erect atop it. Sputtering and cursing, Sun Ce quit the sanctuary, but Yu Ji appeared again perched on the temple gate, glaring down at Sun Ce. Sun Ce asked his followers if they had seen the sorcerer's ghost. None had. He aimed his sword at Yu Ji and threw it, felling a man. His followers saw the soldier who had killed Yu Ji the day before now lying dead himself, his skull cracked, blood running from his orifices. Sun Ce ordered the corpse removed and buried.

As Sun Ce left the temple grounds, Yu Ji appeared again, strolling toward him. "This temple harbors demons!" Sun Ce cried, and seating himself facing the building, he ordered five hundred warriors to tear it down. As they started pulling apart the tilework, Yu Ji appeared on the rooftop, hurling tiles to the ground. Sun Ce ordered the priests evicted, and had his men set fire to the sanctuary; but Yu Ji was visible at the heart of the flames.

Returning to his residence, Sun Ce found Yu Ji standing at his gates. Instead of entering, Sun Ce mustered the entire army and camped outside the city wall, calling his generals together to discuss joining Yuan Shao in a combined attack on Cao Cao. The generals said, "Your Lordship should not risk action while your health remains impaired. After you recover, there will be sufficient time." That night again Yu Ji appeared in the camp, his hair disheveled. In his tent Sun Ce emitted a stream of curses.

The next day Lady Wu came to him and, seeing him emaciated, sobbed, "Your natural self is no more!" Sun Ce reached for a mirror, which reflected a face utterly wasted. "What can I do, ravaged like this?" he cried to his attendants in desperation. Even as he spoke, Yu Ji was hovering in the mirror. A shout burst from Sun Ce as he struck at the mirror. His wounds reopened and he fainted. His mother had him carried to a bedchamber, where after a spell he regained consciousness. "I cannot live on," he said and summoned to his bedside the adviser Zhang Zhao, his brother Sun Quan, and others.

"In this period of upheaval the Southland has great possibilities. We have a substantial population and the natural defense of the rivers. I now ask Zhang Zhao and all of you to aid my younger brother." So saying, Sun Ce conferred his seal and ribbon on Sun Quan, adding, "For mobilizing our people, for the instantaneous decision on the battlefield, for contending with puissant adversaries for dominion, you are not my equal. But for selecting and employing worthy and capable men who will give their all to protect the south, I am not your equal. Always bear in mind the hardships and difficulties that our father and your elder brother suffered in founding this heritage, and be vigilant in guarding it." Sun Quan wept and bowed as he accepted the seal.

Sun Ce turned to his mother and declared, "Heaven allots me no more time to serve my dear, devoted mother. I hereby transfer the seal to my brother and pray, Mother, that you may guide him and instruct him never to neglect those who have served his father and elder brother." Weeping, Lady Wu said, "Your brother is yet immature. What if he proves unable to undertake affairs of state?" "He is ten times more able than I," Sun Ce replied. "He is fully capable of the highest responsibility. If there is an internal problem you cannot solve, however, take it to Zhang Zhao; for an external one, go to Zhou Yu. I only wish Zhou Yu were here to accept these instructions himself."

Next, Sun Ce summoned his remaining brothers. "After I die," he told them, "you must lend Sun Quan your full support. And you must join together in destroying anyone in our clan who may contemplate treason. No renegade of our flesh and bone is to be buried in the ancestral grave." Receiving this charge, his brothers wept. Sun Ce then summoned his wife, Lady Qiao. "Alas," he said to her, "you and I must part halfway through life. Honor my mother with your filial love; and when your sister visits, have her tell her husband to give Sun Quan his full support—for the sake of our friendship."[11] With that Sun Ce passed away peacefully at the age of twenty-six. Later a poet wrote in eulogy:

> His triumphs in the land below the Jiang
> Made men declare "Xiang Yu lives again!"
> He had the cunning of a tiger set to lunge,
> The decision of an eagle poised to plunge.
>
> His dominion made the south secure
> And carried his fair name across the realm.

He left behind an unfulfilled ambition
And charged Zhou Yu to bring it to fruition.

Sun Quan cast himself to the ground before his brother's bed. But Zhang Zhao reproached him. "This is no time for you to weep, General," he said. "You must arrange
the funeral and take charge of the army and the country." Sun Quan regained his self-
control. Zhang Zhao instructed Sun Jing to see to Sun Ce's burial rites and urged Sun
Quan to receive the acclamation of the officials in the great hall.

Sun Quan had a square jaw and a broad mouth, jade green eyes and a purplish beard.
Many years ago Liu Wan, a Han envoy on a mission to the south, had met all the sons
of the house of Sun. "In my view," he had remarked, "though these brothers have splendid talent, none is fated to live long—with the exception of Sun Quan. His striking and
heroic looks and massive frame betoken great nobility as well as long life."

• • • • •

Ordained Sun Ce's heir, Sun Quan undertook the governing of the Southland. He was
still organizing the court when Zhou Yu returned to Wujun with a body of troops. "My
worries are over," Sun Quan said, "now that Zhou Yu is here." Zhou Yu had been guarding Baqiu when he heard that assassins had wounded Sun Ce. On his way back he
learned, even before reaching Wujun, that his close friend had died. He hurried to the
funeral and was wailing at the coffin when Lady Wu appeared and delivered Sun Ce's
deathbed charge. Zhou Yu bowed to the ground and said, "I will discharge my duty with
the loyalty of a dog or a horse until I die." Sun Quan entered. After Zhou Yu had paid
his respects, Sun Quan said to him, "It is my heartfelt hope that you will never forget my
brother's dying words." Zhou Yu touched his head to the floor and declared, "I would
strew the very ground with my liver and brains to requite my dear friend's love."

"Now that I have taken possession of this patrimony," Sun Quan continued, "what
strategy shall I use to preserve it?" "One enduring rule," Zhou Yu began, "is that he
who finds good men will prosper, and he who does not will perish. To shape plans for the
present and to consolidate the Southland you must seek the support of high-minded, far-
seeing intellects." Sun Quan said, "My brother's last words were, 'Trust internal matters
to Zhang Zhao, external ones to Zhou Yu.'" Zhou Yu replied, "Zhang Zhao is a worthy
and accomplished scholar, fit for great tasks. But I am not, and I hesitate to shoulder the
burden consigned to me. Let me recommend a man to assist you, General—Lu Su (styled
Zijing) from Dongchuan in Linhuai. He is a mine of strategies, a storehouse of machinations. Early in life he lost his father and has served his mother since with utter devotion. Lu Su's family is extremely wealthy, and he is known for his generosity to the poor.

"When I was a precinct leader in Juchao, I was taking several hundred men through
Linhuai when we ran short of grain. People told us that the Lu family had two granaries,
each holding three thousand bushels. At our urgent request Lu Su put one of the granaries at our disposal. That's an example of his largess. In addition, he has a strong interest in swordsmanship and horseback archery. His home is in Qu'e, but he has returned
to Dongcheng for his grandmother's funeral. A friend of his, Liu Ziyang, is trying to get
him to go to Chaohu and join Zheng Bao, but Lu Su has not yet reached a decision. My
lord, call him to you without delay."

Sun Quan was pleased with Zhou Yu's recommendation and sent Zhou Yu to engage
Lu Su's services. After the formalities Zhou Yu respectfully relayed Sun Quan's intentions, but Lu Su replied, "Liu Ziyang has arranged for me to go to Chaohu and accept a

position there." "Remember," Zhou Yu said, "the words of Ma Yuan to Emperor Guang Wu: 'In times like these not only does the lord choose the man, but the man chooses the lord.' General Sun nurtures men of merit and receives scholars well. He has given support to remarkable and even extraordinary men, something all too rare. Do not heed the other commitment; come with me to the Southland. This is the right course for you." Lu Su accepted Zhou Yu's invitation.

Sun Quan received Lu Su with the greatest respect, and they held daylong discussions. One day, after court had adjourned, Sun Quan kept Lu Su behind to share a simple repast; then they went to bed at opposite ends of the same couch. In the middle of the night Sun Quan asked, "Now the house of Han totters precariously, and the four quarters of the empire are in turmoil. I have taken up an unfinished task left to me by my late father and elder brother. I yearn to emulate those ancient hegemons, patriarchs Huan and Wen, who took the Son of Heaven under their protection.[12] How should I proceed?"

"When the Han was founded," Lu Su began, "the Supreme Ancestor sought to give devoted service to the Righteous Emperor, but Xiang Yu frustrated his every effort.[13] Now Cao Cao may be compared to Xiang Yu. It is he who holds the Emperor in thrall. It is not within your power to play a lord protector's role. In my judgment, the Han is past recovery; and Cao Cao cannot be finally removed. Therefore the best plan for you, General, is to make the Southland the firm foot of the tripod, consolidate your region, and look for opportunities to take action. You can exploit the many preoccupations of the north: knock out Huang Zu's position, attack Liu Biao in Jingzhou, and take control of the Great River in its entirety. This done, establish your imperial title and turn your ambitions toward the rest of the realm, as the founder of the Han once did." Lu Su's analysis made Sun Quan exuberant. He slipped on a garment and got up to thank his guest. The next day he sent rich gifts to Lu Su, and fine clothes, curtains, and other items of value to Lu Su's mother.

At this time Lu Su recommended to Sun Quan another man of great learning, talent, and filial devotion, Zhuge Jin (Ziyu) from Nanyang in Langye. Sun Quan treated Zhuge Jin too as an honored guest.[14] On Zhuge Jin's advice Sun Quan decided not to associate himself with Yuan Shao, but rather to follow Cao Cao's lead for the time being until he could maneuver against him more easily. Consequently, Sun Quan sent Yuan Shao's envoy home with a letter declining the offer of an alliance against Cao Cao.

When Cao Cao heard that Sun Ce had died, he wanted to muster his forces and descend upon the Southland. But the censor Zhang Hong dissuaded him, saying, "To attack when the land is in mourning is dishonorable. If you fail, you will have thrown away whatever amity still exists and created instead a profound enmity. I would suggest you take the opportunity to treat the southerners handsomely." Cao Cao took this advice and recommended to the Emperor that Sun Quan be appointed general and governor of Kuaiji.[15] At the same time Zhang Hong was made military commander of Kuaiji and given the seal of office to deliver to Sun Quan. Sun Quan was elated to have Zhang Hong released from the capital,[16] and instructed him to work closely with Zhang Zhao in administering his kingdom.

At this time Zhang Hong recommended another man to Sun Quan, Gu Yong (Yuantan), a disciple of Court Counselor Cai Yong. Gu Yong was a man chary of speech, not given to drink, both severe and correct. Sun Quan employed him as a governor's deputy and acting governor. Throughout the Southland Sun Quan's prestige was recognized, and the people became deeply devoted to him.

Chen Zhen returned to Yuan Shao and delivered this message: "Sun Ce is dead, and Sun Quan has succeeded him. Cao Cao has made Sun Quan a general, thus securing his support." Yuan Shao was furious and summoned the armies of the four provinces he controlled, Ji, Qing, You and Bing. He called up some seven hundred thousand men in preparation for another attack on Xuchang, the capital. Indeed:

> No sooner did the wars in the south subside
> Than the battle cry was heard afresh in the north.

Which of the two great rivals would emerge supreme, Cao Cao or Yuan Shao?[17]
READ ON.

30

Yuan Shao Suffers Defeat at Guandu;
Cao Cao Burns the Stores at Wuchao

As Yuan Shao's vast army moved toward Guandu, Xiahou Dun called for help: Cao Cao mobilized seventy thousand men, leaving Xun Wenruo to hold the capital.

Before Yuan Shao ordered his northern army to advance, Tian Feng had sent him a warning from jail. "Now it is better," he wrote, "to sit tight and let the ways of Heaven run their course than to launch a general offensive that may well end in failure." But Pang Ji said critically, "My lord, we go forward in the name of the highest virtue and duty. Feng's ominous predictions are groundless." Yuan Shao ordered Tian Feng executed, but vigorous intercession by the officials won him a reprieve. "After we crush Cao Cao," Yuan Shao said, "his offense will be duly punished." With that, he commanded the army to march without delay.

Flags and banners covering the field, blades thickly clustered like a forest, the northern army pitched camp at Yangwu. Ju Shou said, "We outnumber Cao, but our troops don't have their courage and ferocity. On the other hand, despite the quality of their forces they are low on grain and fodder, while we have more than enough. Thus, their interest is to force a fight; ours, to delay and defend. If we can outwait them, we will win without having to fight." To this advice Yuan Shao retorted angrily, "First Tian Feng tries to undermine morale—the day I return he dies—now you advocate delay." He shouted to his attendants, "Arrest Ju Shou. After Cao's defeat I will take care of him and Tian Feng together!" He then ordered his force seven hundred thousand men to post themselves along the ninety *li* perimeter of the camp.

Spies returning to Guandu described Yuan Shao's order of battle, sending a shiver of fear through Cao Cao's newly arrived army. Cao Cao consulted his advisers. Xun You said, "Though Yuan Shao's army is large, we need not fear it. Our men are at their keenest. Any one of ours could take on ten of theirs. But we need to engage quickly. Our provisions will not last if this drags on." "My thought, exactly," Cao Cao said. He ordered the commanders to advance with much noise of drums and shouting. Yuan Shao's army encountered them, and the battle lines took shape. Shen Pei, one of Yuan Shao's generals, placed five thousand crossbowmen out of view at either wing and five thousand archers near the front entrance to the camp. All were to shoot on hearing the bombard sound.

The triple drumroll finished. Poised on horseback, Yuan Shao stood before his line in golden helmet and armor, fine surcoat and studded belt. His generals grouped around him, Zhang He, Gao Lan, Han Meng, and Chunyu Qiong. The flags and banners and instruments of command stood in perfect order.

Cao Cao rode forth from the bannered entrance to his line. Around him were Xu Chu, Zhang Liao, Xu Huang, Li Dian, and others, all fully armed. Pointing at Yuan Shao with his whip, Cao Cao cried, "I petitioned the Son of Heaven to appoint you regent-marshal. What justifies this rebellion?" Yuan Shao retorted, "You who pass yourself off as prime minister to the Han are the real traitor. Your crimes mount to the skies, higher than those of the usurpers Wang Mang and Dong Zhuo. Yet you slander others as rebels!" Cao Cao replied, "I bear an imperial decree to punish you." "And I," Yuan Shao countered, "have the decree the Emperor hid in the girdle as authority to bring a traitor to justice!"

Too angry to speak further, Cao Cao sent Zhang Liao into the field. From Yuan Shao's side Zhang He sprang to the challenge. The two commanders clashed some fifty times: it was an even match. Cao Cao watched Zhang He, secretly awed. Flourishing a blade, Xu Chu joined the battle to assist Zhang Liao, and Gao Lan, spear raised, took him on. The four grappled, hewing and slashing at one another.

Cao Cao ordered Xiahou Dun and Cao Hong to charge the enemy line with three thousand fighters each. To counter this move Shen Pei released the bombard, signaling the crossbowmen to commence shooting. At the same time the archers near the front stepped in order through the first line of soldiers, letting fly volleys that drove Cao Cao's troops back toward the south. Yuan Shao directed the infantry in a swift and murderous follow-up, turning Cao Cao's rout to defeat and driving all his troops back to Guandu.

Yuan Shao moved his camps closer to Guandu, Cao's strategic strongpoint. Shen Pei said, "Have a hundred thousand men raise mounds directly facing Cao's camp. Then our archers can control their positions. If Cao retreats, we gain the key point of entry to the capital area, and the capital will fall." Yuan Shao approved the plan. He had his brawniest fighters ply their shovels and carriers, and soon heaps of earth were rising. Cao Cao's men wanted to attack at once, but Shen Pei's archers, commanding the routes of access, deterred all advance. Within ten days more than fifty hills, topped with lookout posts and manned by crossbowmen, loomed over Cao's camp.

Fear gripped Cao's army. The soldiers crouched behind shields as bolts rained down periodically at the signal of wooden clappers. Yuan Shao's men howled with laughter at the sight of the cowering enemy. Confusion spread in the ranks, and Cao Cao convened his counselors. Liu Ye suggested building ballistas to stone the northerners and presented a model he had designed. Over the next several nights hundreds of frames were manufactured, then placed against the camp barricades and aimed at the scaling ladders by the mounds. The next time the archers let fly, Cao Cao's men discharged the first massed battery. Missiles filled the air and demolished the enemy stations. Unable to hide, the crossbowmen perished in great numbers. Yuan Shao's men termed the ballistas "thunder machines" and stopped climbing the mounds to stage attacks.

Shen Pei next proposed tunneling into Cao's camp. Yuan Shao approved the plan, and a corps of sappers went to work. Informed of the threat, Cao Cao again consulted Liu Ye. "Since they can't attack openly," he said, "they are trying to bore into our positions from under the ground." "How can we stop them?" Cao Cao asked. "A trench circling the camp will make their tunnel useless," was the reply. Cao Cao had one cut, and Yuan Shao's effort was wasted.

•   •   •   •   •

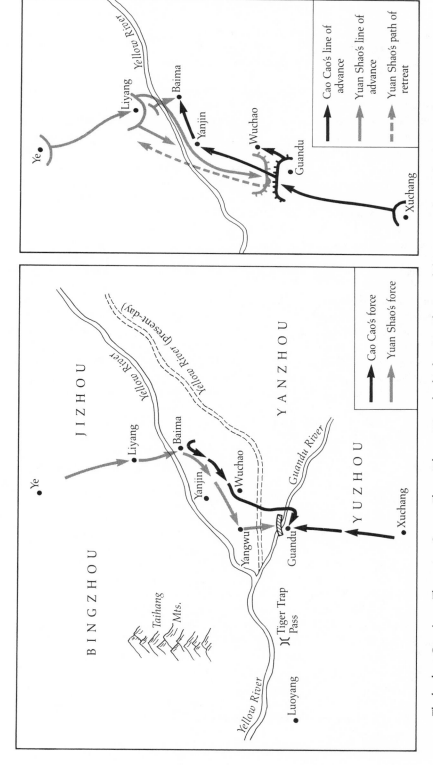

MAP 2. The battle at Guandu. *a*. The region. Source: Zhang Xikong, "Guandu zhi zhan," in Zhongguo lishi xiao congshu, *Gudai zhuming zhanyi* (Beijing: Zhonghua shuju, 1982), p. 132. *b*. The battleground. Source: Liu Chunfan, *Sanguo shihua* (Beijing: Beijing chubanshe, 1981), p. 57.

Cao Cao had held at Guandu from the beginning of the eighth month to the end of the ninth (A.D. 200). His men weary, his rations spent, he began thinking about retreating to the capital and wrote Xun Wenruo for advice. The reply that came back said in part:

> I have your esteemed letter instructing me to advise whether or not we should withdraw. In my humble view Yuan Shao has concentrated his forces at Guandu in order to seek a decision. Your weaker force is up against his stronger one. If you cannot dominate the enemy, prepare to have them dominate you. This is a fateful moment for the empire. Yuan Shao has many troops but cannot use them well. Your superb mastery of warfare and clear judgment should carry the day, whatever the circumstances. Though your numbers are few, you are still better off than Liu Bang when he divided the realm with Xiang Yu at Xingyang and Chenggao. Holding your ground at a crucial spot has blocked the enemy. The situation is critical, and at a turning point. It is time for an ingenious move. Do not let it pass. Pray consider my humble suggestion.

Heartened by Xun Wenruo's letter, Cao Cao ordered officers and men to hold firm with renewed effort.[1]

Yuan Shao's army pulled back thirty *li*, and Cao Cao sent scouts to reconnoitre. Shi Huan, one of Xu Huang's corps commanders, captured a northern spy. Under interrogation the man told Xu Huang, "Yuan Shao expects General Han Meng with a shipment of grain. They had me out to check the roads." Xu Huang informed Cao Cao. Xun You said to Cao, "Han Meng is a foolhardy warrior. One commander with a few thousand cavalry could knock him out, and the loss of supplies would throw their army into chaos. Xu Huang is the man to do it!" Cao Cao approved the plan, sending Xu Huang and Shi Huan first, with Zhang Liao and Xu Chu as reinforcements.

That night as Han Meng was escorting the several thousand supply wagons, Xu Huang and Shi Huan attacked. Han Meng struggled to defend the stores, but Xu Huang locked him in combat while Shi Huan and his squad put the carters to flight and set the carts afire. Han Meng turned and fled. Xu Huang urged his men on; they burned the whole train and its cargoes. From his base Yuan Shao saw flames to the northwest and in rising alarm learned of the loss from one of the routed guards. Yuan Shao sent Zhang He and Gao Lan to block the main road, but they crossed paths with Xu Huang coming back from the raid. Fighting began as Zhang Liao and Xu Chu arrived, driving off Yuan Shao's generals in a two-sided assault. Cao Cao's four generals returned together to Guandu. Cao Cao, elated by the victory, rewarded his officers and men handsomely. He then had defense points in the form of pincers constructed in front of his camp.

Han Meng returned defeated to an enraged Yuan Shao. Only the intercession of the entire body of officials saved him from execution. Shen Pei advised Yuan Shao, "Food is most vital to an army on the march. It must be protected at all costs. Wuchao is our main depot and should be heavily guarded." "I have formulated a strategy," Yuan Shao said to Shen Pei. "I want you to return to the capital[2] to assure that we have adequate supplies." Shen Pei went to implement the command, and Yuan Shao sent twenty thousand under General Chunyu Qiong to protect Wuchao. Assisting him were army inspectors Gui Yuanjin, Han Juzi, Lü Weihuang, Zhao Rui, and others. Chunyu Qiong was a hot-tempered drinker feared by his men. After reaching the depot, he passed his time carousing with the commanders.

•   •   •   •   •

Meanwhile, Cao Cao was almost out of food and had written to Xun Wenruo in the capital to arrange for a shipment of provisions. The messenger was captured barely thirty *li* from Guandu, however, and brought in bonds to Xu You. Xu You (Ziyuan), a companion of Cao Cao's in his youth but now in Yuan Shao's service, took Cao's intercepted letter to Yuan Shao and offered a suggestion. "Cao Cao has been holding Guandu for a long time," he said. "It's a stalemate. But his capital at Xuchang is vulnerable. A surprise attack will give us the capital, and then we can take Cao Cao. Now that their grain is nearly gone, we can strike twice." "Cao Cao is wily," Yuan Shao replied, "that letter leads to a trap." "Unless we act on this plan," Xu You argued, "we will suffer for it."

At this moment a messenger from Ye arrived with a letter from Shen Pei saying that grain was on its way. In addition, he mentioned Xu You's conduct in Jizhou—how he had taken bribes and how his sons and nephews had been jailed for raising tax rates for personal profit. "You thieving upstart!" Yuan Shao thundered. "You have the face to make proposals? You and Cao Cao go back a long way. I'm beginning to think you're in his service, here to stir up trouble in our ranks. You deserve to die, but we will leave your head where it is for the time being. Now get out and never come before me again."[3]

Turning his eyes to Heaven, Xu You left. With a sigh he said to his attendants, "What's the use of serving a fool who takes offense at loyal counsel? Shen Pei is persecuting my relatives. How can I go back to Jizhou and face my people?" He reached for his sword, but his men snatched it from him. "My lord," they pleaded, "do you hold your life so lightly? If Yuan Shao rejects honest counsel, he will surely fall to Cao. Once you were Cao's friend—why not foresake this hopeless cause for a brighter prospect?" These words opened Xu You's eyes, and he decided to offer his services to Cao Cao. Later a poet wrote:

> Yuan Shao's proud spirit towered o'er the realm.
> How foolish to despair at the stalemate at Guandu!
> If he had taken Xu You's sound advice,
> How could Cao have made the north his prize?

And so Xu You quietly approached Cao Cao's outposts. Sentries arrested him. "I am an old friend of the prime minister's," he told them, "Xu You of Nanyang. Please inform him at once." Cao Cao had already undressed when he was told Xu You had come. Without bothering even with footgear, he went to meet Xu You, rubbing his hands and laughing with pleasure the moment he laid eyes on him. Cao Cao took You's hand and led him back to his own quarters. Then he prostrated himself before his visitor. Xu You rushed to help Cao Cao up, saying, "You are the prime minister of the Han. I, a commoner, cannot accept such homage." "You are one of my oldest friends," Cao Cao said, "and friends need not stand on ceremony or be affected by considerations of status." "I chose my lord unwisely," Xu You went on. "I lowered myself to serve Yuan Shao. He ignored all my ideas, my plans. Now I have left him and only hope that you will accept my service."

Cao Cao said, "Now that you have done us this honor, our cause is served. Now tell me, I pray, how to defeat Yuan Shao." Xu You replied, "I urged Yuan Shao to surprise the capital with light cavalry while hitting Guandu with his main army." "That would have finished us," Cao Cao said, shaken. "How much grain have you got?" Xu You asked. "A year's worth," Cao replied. "Perhaps not," Xu You suggested, smiling. "Actually, enough for six months," said Cao. Xu You rose to leave, flicked his sleeves, and strode out of the tent, saying, "I came to you in all sincerity, little expecting to be deceived." "Don't be angry, old friend," Cao said to detain him. "The truth is, our grain will last three months." Xu You smiled again, saying, "The world calls you 'villain.' I see how true it is." Cao Cao was smiling too. "As you should know," he said, "there's no end of tricks in warfare." Whispering, he added, "We have enough for the month, and that's it." "Stop fooling around!" Xu You retorted abruptly. "Your grain is finished." "How did you know?" Cao asked, stunned.

Xu You then handed Cao Cao his own letter to Xun Wenruo asking for food. "Who wrote this?" Xu You inquired. "How did you get hold of it?" Cao Cao demanded. Xu You explained that Cao's messenger had been captured. Cao Cao took Xu You's hand and said earnestly, "Advise me what to do, old friend, I pray you." "My lord," Xu You began, "you face a vastly larger adversary: without a quick victory you are doomed. But I have a way to cause his million-strong multitude to destroy itself inside of three days. Will you give me a hearing, my lord?" "Yes," Cao Cao responded with great interest. Xu You continued, "Yuan Shao's rations and supplies are concentrated in Wuchao and guarded by Chunyu Qiong, a commander fond of liquor and ill prepared for an attack. Go there with picked troops, pretending to be Yuan Shao's general Jiang Qi, who has been detailed to help guard the grain. If you can burn the place down, Yuan Shao's army will fall apart in three days." Elated with this plan, Cao Cao treated Xu You royally and kept him in his camp.

The next day Cao Cao selected five thousand horsemen and soldiers for the mission. Zhang Liao warned the prime minister, "Their depot can't be altogether unguarded. You are running a great risk. What if it's a trap?" "I don't think it is," Cao replied. "Heaven has sent me Xu You to defeat Yuan Shao. We don't have the food to sustain our positions. Unless we use Xu You's plan, we'll be squeezed sitting here. Would he agree to remain here if it were a trap? Anyway, I've wanted to take this step for some time. We have to do it. Set aside your doubts." "We still have to defend this point while you're leading the operation," Zhang Liao said. "I have thought of everything," Cao answered, smiling.

Cao Cao had Xun You, Jia Xu, and Cao Hong guard his main camp, where the defector Xu You remained. Xiahou Dun and Xiahou Yuan were positioned to the left, Cao Ren and Li Dian to the right, in case of surprise. Then, with Zhang Liao and Xu Chu in front, Xu Huang and Yu Jin behind, Cao Cao led forth his commanders and captains and a force of five thousand under the false colors of his enemy. Each soldier carried bundles of straw and kindling, and kept a stick clamped in his mouth. The horses, too, were gagged. At dusk they moved out silently. Soon the night sky was crowded with stars.

Imprisoned by Yuan Shao for his unwelcome advice, Ju Shou could see a corner of the starry designs and persuaded the jailer to take him outside. Looking up, he noticed Venus moving retrograde into the zone of Ox and Dipper, the first two sections of the northern quadrant. Startled, he cried out, "Disaster looms!" and demanded an audience with Yuan Shao.[4]

Though drunk in bed, Yuan Shao granted the request. Ju Shou said to Yuan Shao, "I have been observing the sky. Venus was moving in the opposite direction between the lunar lodgings Willow and Ghost, as streaks of light shot into the zone of Ox and Dipper. I fear the enemy is going to strike. Alert the guards at Wuchao. Send your best men to patrol the roads nearby, or Cao will outmaneuver you." "You are an offender now," Yuan Shao scoffed irritably, "how dare you try to fool my people with nonsense!" Harshly he said to the jailer, "You were ordered to keep him confined. How dare you release him?" Yuan Shao called for a soldier to take the prisoner away and had the jailer executed. As Ju Shou was led out, he wept, saying, "Our army is doomed. My bones will have no resting place." A poet of later times lamented Ju Shou's fate:

Ju Shou's counsel earned his ruler's hate,
And Yuan Shao proved that he was tactics' fool.
He lost his grain, his base was sacked;
Still he hoped to hold Jizhou intact.[5]

Through the darkness Cao Cao advanced on Yuan Shao's outposts. Challenged by sentries, he had his men answer, "Jiang Qi here, on orders to proceed to Wuchao to guard the grain." Seeing their own colors, Yuan Shao's troops suspected nothing. Cao got through several outposts the same way and reached Wuchao at the fourth watch. He had his men encircle the depot with lit torches. Then his officers burst in making an uproar. Chunyu Qiong, sleeping off a drinking bout in the command tent, was roused by the din. "What's going on?" he shouted. Before he could say more, Cao's men had attacked him with staves and pulled him down.

Gui Yuanjin and Zhao Rui, officers of Yuan Shao's who were returning with a grain delivery, saw the flaming bins and raced to the rescue. Cao Cao was told of the officers' arrival: "They're almost upon us—to the rear. Send men to stop them." "The front," Cao shouted back, "give everything to the front. When they're at our backs, we'll deal with them." His commanders pressed forward, redoubling their blows. In moments fire was everywhere; smoke blotted out the sky. Yuan Shao's officers, Gui and Zhao, set upon the raiders from behind. Cao Cao turned on them, overpowering and killing both and burning the grain they were delivering. Next, Chunyu Qiong was brought before Cao Cao, who ordered his ears, nose, and fingers cut off, had him tied onto a horse, and sent him back in this manner to humiliate Yuan Shao.

In his tent Yuan Shao heard reports of the great fire to the north. He realized Wuchao was lost and summoned his advisers. Zhang He said, "Let me go with Gao Lan and save Wuchao." "Not a good idea," Guo Tu responded. "If they have plundered the stores, then Cao is there and Guandu is undefended. Strike Guandu first, and Cao will retreat swiftly. This is exactly how Sun Bin relieved Wei's siege of Zhao and went on to defeat Wei's army."[6] But Zhang He disagreed. "Cao Cao," he argued, "is full of schemes. He would never undertake such an operation and leave his base vulnerable. If we attack Guandu and fail, Chunyu Qiong will be captured and so will we." Guo Tu, however, insisted that Cao Cao, intent only on the supplies, had left no forces behind. Guo Tu's view prevailed. Yuan Shao sent Zhang He and Gao Lan with five thousand against Guandu, and Jiang Qi with ten thousand to relieve Wuchao.

Cao Cao's men decimated Chunyu Qiong's units and took possession of their battle dress, armor, and banners; then they disguised themselves as remnants of Chunyu Qiong's guards struggling back to camp. When they met up with Jiang Qi, the commander Yuan Shao had sent to relieve the depot, Cao's men said they were Wuchao guards fleeing Cao's attack. Unsuspecting, Jiang Qi rode on toward Wuchao. Suddenly, the backup contingents led by Zhang Liao and Xu Chu challenged Jiang Qi. "Halt!" they shouted; and before Jiang Qi could respond, Zhang Liao had cut him down and slaughtered his troops to a man. Meanwhile, Cao Cao arranged for a report to reach Yuan Shao saying that Jiang Qi had chased off the raiders. As a result, Yuan Shao sent more men on to Guandu and none to Wuchao.

Zhang He and Gao Lan had already begun their attack on Guandu. The three-sided defense—Xiahou Dun on the left, Cao Ren on the right, Cao Hong in the center—was concerted. By the time Yuan Shao's reinforcement arrived, Cao Cao was in striking position behind them, sealing shut the fourth side. During the ensuing slaughter Zhang He and Gao Lan managed to break away.

The defeated Wuchao guards straggled back to Yuan Shao with the mutilated Chunyu Qiong. Yuan Shao demanded to know how Wuchao was lost. "Chunyu Qiong was drunk," the guardsmen replied, "we couldn't fight them off." Yuan Shao had Chunyu Qiong beheaded.

Guo Tu realized that Zhang He and Gao Lan would testify to the folly of his advice to Yuan Shao, so he acted to prevent their return from Guandu. He began by slandering them. "I think, my lord," he told Yuan Shao, "that our defeat will be most gratifying to Zhang He and Gao Lan." "What are you talking about?" Yuan Shao asked. "Those two have been meaning to defect for some time," Guo Tu asserted. "By not exerting themselves on this mission they have caused us heavy losses." At once Yuan Shao sent for the two commanders to answer to their crime.

Guo Tu, however, had informed Zhang He and Gao Lan that Yuan Shao was going to execute them for the defeat at Guandu. Thus, when Yuan Shao's messenger delivered his summons, Gao Lan asked bluntly, "Why is our lord recalling us?" "I do not know," he replied. Without further ado Gao Lan slew the messenger and told the startled Zhang He, "Yuan Shao believes any slander. Sooner or later Cao Cao is going to take him. Why sit and wait to die? Let's join Cao Cao." Zhang He responded, "I have wanted to do it for a long time."

Yuan Shao's two commanders surrendered to Cao Cao with their troops. Xiahou Dun asked Cao Cao, "Is this genuine?" Cao Cao replied, "If I treat them well, they will come around in any event." The two commanders received permission to enter the camp. Coming before Cao Cao, they dropped their weapons and prostrated themselves. "Had Yuan Shao listened to you," Cao Cao said, "he could have spared himself this defeat. Now you two have come to us like Weizi, who quit the dying Shang dynasty, or Han Xin, who left Xiang Yu to serve the house of Han." Cao Cao appointed them adjutant generals and, respectively, lord of a higher precinct and lord of Donglai. The two defectors were completely satisfied.

Yuan Shao had now lost the services of Xu You, Zhang He, and Gao Lan, as well as his supply depot at Wuchao. His army was confused and demoralized. Xu You urged Cao Cao to strike quickly. Zhang He and Gao Lan offered to take the lead. Cao Cao approved and sent them to raid the northern army's main camp. At the third watch the attackers divided into three units and struck. Fighting raged until dawn; then the raiders withdrew, having inflicted casualties on half of Yuan Shao's army.

Xun You proposed the next step: "Spread rumors that you are sending one force to take Suanzao and attack Ye, and another to take Liyang and cut off their return to Jizhou. Yuan Shao will panic and divide his troops, and we can wipe him out." Cao Cao adopted the plan and ordered the army to noise about the new strategy. The rumors reached Yuan Shao and in alarm he dispatched Yuan Tan with fifty thousand men to Ye, and Xin Ming with fifty thousand to Liyang that very night. As soon as Cao Cao learned that Yuan Shao had made his move, he divided his army into eight units and descended on the enemy camp.

Having lost all taste for combat with Cao Cao's forces, Yuan Shao's troops broke and ran. The army disintegrated. With no time even to don his armor, Yuan Shao fled on horseback, wearing an unlined tunic and a headband. His youngest son, Shang, followed him. The attackers, Zhang Liao, Xu Chu, Xu Huang, and Yu Jin, swept after him. Yuan Shao, in his anxiety to cross the river, had left behind maps, documents, chariots, gold, and silk. Accompanied by a mere eight hundred riders, he outraced his pursuers.

Cao Cao gathered up all that Yuan Shao had abandoned. Eighty thousand of the northern army had perished. The earth ran red, and the drowned were past numbering. Cao Cao's victory was total; he rewarded his men with the captured valuables. Among the official papers he found a packet of letters written by those in his capital who had secretly communicated with Yuan Shao. Some of his advisers urged Cao Cao to round up the unreliable elements and kill them. But Cao Cao replied, "When Yuan Shao was powerful, my own safety stood in doubt—not to speak of others'." He ordered the letters burned and the matter dropped.

During the debacle Yuan Shao's imprisoned adviser, Ju Shou, had not been able to escape. Taken before Cao Cao, who had known the man in former times, he declared, "I shall not submit!"[7] "Yuan Shao," Cao Cao said, "was a fool to ignore your counsel. Why cling to folly? With you to advise me, the empire would know peace." Cao Cao treated Ju Shou handsomely and kept him in the army, but he stole a horse in an attempt to flee to Yuan Shao. He was consequently executed. Ju Shou maintained an unperturbed demeanor to the moment of his death. "I should not have killed so loyal and honorable a man," Cao Cao sighed and ordered that Ju Shou's body lie in state. He was interred at a crossing point of the Yellow River. A tumulus raised over the grave bore the inscription "Tomb of Master Ju, Who Died Gloriously for Loyalty." Later a poet expressed his admiration in these lines:

> Men of note abounded in the north:
> "Loyalty uncompromised" made Ju Shou's fame.
> His steady eye could gauge the turns of war.
> His upturned gaze could read a moving star.
>
> Iron-hearted to the very last;
> His spirit facing death was light and free.
> His splendid conduct led him to his doom;
> Cao Cao in tribute raised a lonely tomb.

Cao Cao gave the order to attack Jizhou. Indeed:

> The weaker prevailed by cunning calculation;
> The stronger failed for want of strategy.

Would Cao Cao become the master of the north?

READ ON.

31

Cao Cao Defeats Yuan Shao at Cangting;
Liu Xuande Turns to Liu Biao in Jingzhou

TO EXPLOIT YUAN SHAO'S DEFEAT, Cao Cao regrouped and tracked his fleeing enemy. But Yuan Shao reached Liyang on the north shore safely. He was wearing an unlined tunic and a headband. Eight hundred horsemen remained in his command. Jiang Yiqu, the general in charge, welcomed the defeated leader to Liyang and, after receiving an account of the battles at Guandu, publicly announced his arrival. Yuan Shao's scattered forces rallied in a vast multitude, and their morale revived. Yuan Shao ordered the newly assembled army to begin marching to his home province, Jizhou.

One night, bivouacked in the wilds, Yuan Shao heard faint cries. Investigating, he found stragglers from his army clutching one another, moaning for the loss of brothers, comrades, and kinsmen. "If only he had taken Tian Feng's advice," they cried, weeping and beating their breasts, "we would not have known these sorrows." Yuan Shao said remorsefully, "I doomed my own cause when I ignored Tian Feng's advice. How can I face him at home?"

The next day Pang Ji greeted Yuan Shao as he was setting out with a party of soldiers. Yuan Shao said to him, "This defeat was my doing. I ignored Tian Feng's counsel, and now I cannot face him." "My lord, when he heard of your defeat in the prison," Pang Ji lied, "he clapped his hands and smirked, saying, 'Just as I anticipated.'" Rage mounted in Yuan Shao. "Mocked by that idiot? He dies!" he roared, and sent his sword to the jail.

Meanwhile, a guard visiting Tian Feng in his cell said, "Congratulations, Assistant Inspector!" "The occasion?" Tian Feng asked. The guard responded, "When General Yuan returns, you are sure to be acclaimed for predicting his defeat." "I am done for," Tian Feng replied with a smile. "Everyone is so happy for you," the guard went on, "why speak of death?" "General Yuan," Tian Feng explained, "may appear broad-minded but is in fact deeply suspicious. Loyalty and sincerity count for little with him. In the rejoicing after a victory he might have been inclined to be lenient, but after a humiliation like this there is no hope." The guard shook his head doubtfully. At that moment the envoy arrived with Yuan Shao's sword and the order to behead Tian Feng. "It is no surprise," Tian Feng remarked to the astounded guard. All the jailers wept. "A man of honor," Tian Feng said, "takes his stand in the wide world between Heaven and earth. If he chooses the wrong lord, he is responsible for his ignorance. I can face death today. Despair is pointless." Then he slit his throat. In the words of a later poet,

> First Ju Shou fell, a captive of the foe;
> Then Tian Feng died, a prisoner of his lord.
> Breaking thus the pillars of his state,
> Yuan Shao sealed his northern country's fate.

Many grieved for Tian Feng.

Yuan Shao arrived in Jizhou too agitated to administer his province. His wife, Lady Liu, who had replaced Shao's principal wife after her death, urged him to name an heir. Of his three sons, the eldest, Tan (Xiansi), ruled Qingzhou, and the second, Xi (Xianyi), ruled Youzhou. The third son, Shang (Xianfu), was the son of Lady Liu and had grown to magnificent manhood. His father doted on him and kept him near home.

Since the battle of Guandu, Lady Liu had been pressing Yuan Shao to name Shang his heir. Yuan Shao took counsel with Shen Pei, Pang Ji, Xin Ping, and Guo Tu. Shen Pei and Pang Ji were in Shang's service and favored him; Xin Ping and Guo Tu served Tan and favored him. At the meeting each supported his master's cause. Yuan Shao said, "With continuing external threats, it is urgent that we establish the succession. My eldest, Tan, is hot-tempered and prone to violence. The second, Xi, is a weak sort, unlikely to amount to much. The third, however, has the makings of a true hero: he attracts the worthy and respects the able. He is my choice. What are your views?"

"Of the three," Guo Tu began, "the eldest, Tan, has priority. Moreover, he is ruling a province. My lord, to reject the elder and elevate the younger will cause strife. Now with our prestige somewhat tarnished and our enemies at our borders, we must not disturb the vital relation of father to son, brother to brother. My lord might better devote himself to coping with the threats we face and give less attention to the other matter." Yuan Shao wavered and took no action.

Suddenly Yuan Shao had a report that Yuan Xi was coming from Youzhou with sixty thousand men; Yuan Tan, from Qingzhou with fifty thousand; and Gao Gan, Shao's nephew, from Bingzhou with another fifty thousand to help Shao fight the enemy. Delighted, Yuan Shao consolidated his army and prepared to face Cao Cao.

Cao Cao pitched his triumphant forces along the river, where people greeted them with food and wine. The white-headed village elders were invited into Cao Cao's tent. He asked them, "How old are you gentlemen?" "Nearly a hundred, each of us," they responded. "Our troops have disrupted your communities, and it troubles me," Cao Cao said. "In the time of Emperor Huan," one of them responded, "a yellow star shone in the region above this ground, once the boundary between the ancient states of Song and Chu.[1] Yin Kui of Liaodong, the star-teller, stayed here one night. He told us that the yellow star foretold that in fifty years' time a true king would arise here between Liang and Pei. It is now fifty years since Yin Kui spoke those words. The people here have suffered from Yuan Shao's taxes, but you, Prime Minister, march in the name of the highest virtue and duty to succor the people and punish the guilty. Yuan Shao's defeat at Guandu confirms Yin Kui's prediction. Now the millions inhabiting this region can look forward to an era of just peace."

Cao Cao replied to the elder, "How can I live up to such claims?" He gave the elders gifts of food and drink and bade them good-bye. He then issued an order saying, "Any soldier who kills even a chicken or a dog in these villages will be punished as if he had taken human life." This command shocked the troops, but they complied and thereby won popular support, to Cao Cao's quiet satisfaction.

It was reported to Cao Cao that Yuan Shao had mobilized from his four provinces an army of two to three hundred thousand, which was now camped at Cangting. Cao Cao advanced and deployed his troops in opposition. The next day, when each side had consolidated its order of battle, Cao Cao showed himself before the formation with his generals. Yuan Shao also appeared, surrounded by his three sons, his nephew, and his civil and military officials. Cao Cao spoke first. "Yuan Shao," he cried, "your plans have come to naught, your strength is spent. Why hold out? Will there be time for regret when the sword is on your neck?"

Furiously Yuan Shao looked back at his generals. "Who will begin?" he said. His youngest son, Shang, anxious to impress his father, dashed forward, two blades dancing in the air. "Who's that?" Cao Cao asked. "Yuan Shao's third son," someone replied. Shi Huan, Xu Huang's lieutenant, was already in the field, spear couched for action. The horsemen tangled. After a few exchanges, Yuan Shang wheeled and reversed direction, parrying with his blade. Shi Huan pursued. Yuan Shang fitted an arrow to his bow and, twisting back, shot Shi Huan through the left eye. Down he went. Witnessing his son's triumph, Yuan Shao flourished his whip toward the enemy and his troops flocked forward. In the moil and ruck of battle great slaughter was done; then gongs from both sides recalled the troops.

Cao Cao convened his generals. Cheng Yu offered a plan for a "ten-part ambush." He advised withdrawing to the river and placing ten units in five pairs along either side of the route to the river and then enticing Yuan Shao to pursue. "Our troops," Cheng Yu explained, "backed against the water, will fight to the death and defeat Yuan Shao." Cao Cao approved the plan, and the men were assigned to the following squads: on the left, squad one, Xiahou Dun; squad two, Zhang Liao; squad three, Li Dian; squad four, Yue Jin; squad five, Xiahou Yuan; on the right, squad one, Cao Hong; squad two, Zhang He; squad three, Xu Huang; squad four, Yu Jin; squad five, Gao Lan. The center force was under Xu Chu in the van. Next day the ten squads assumed their positions. At midnight Xu Chu feigned a raid on Yuan Shao's camp, and as Cao Cao had expected, Yuan Shao's troops responded in force.

Xu Chu's raiding party reversed course at once, drawing Yuan Shao in pursuit, his men yelling steadily. By dawn they had crowded Cao Cao's men against the river. "There's no way out! Each man fights to the finish!" Cao Cao shouted to his troops, and they turned on the enemy with new vigor. Xu Chu now moved swiftly forward and slew ten of Yuan Shao's commanders, causing disorder in his ranks. Yuan Shao scrambled to retreat. Cao Cao harried his rear guard. Drums began beating, and the first ambush was sprung—a lightning squeeze on Yuan Shao from Xiahou Yuan to the left, Gao Lan to the right. Ringed by his sons and nephew, Yuan Shao hacked his way free. But they had retreated barely ten *li* from the river when Yue Jin and Yu Jin attacked from both sides, taking a bloody toll. The ground ran with gore. Yuan Shao advanced another few *li*; then Li Dian and Xu Huang gripped him in another murderous pincer.

Stricken with fear, Yuan Shao and his sons fled back to their original camp. Yuan Shao ordered a meal, but there was no time to prepare it: Zhang Liao and Zhang He had charged the camp. Yuan Shao took to his horse and sped to Cangting. His men and mounts were nearly spent. From behind, Cao Cao's main force came on. Yuan Shao fled for his life, but his escape was cut off by Cao Hong and Xiahou Dun. "Fight or fall!" Yuan Shao screamed to his followers. With a final burst of energy he broke out of the fifth trap. Yuan Xi and Gao Gan had been wounded by arrows; few troops survived. Yuan Shao embraced his sons and wept. Then he fainted. His men crowded around trying to revive him, but he kept vomiting blood. Finally he came round and said brokenly, "I never expected to be ruined like this after dozens of battles. Return to your own provinces. We'll settle with the traitor Cao yet!"[2]

Yuan Shao instructed Xin Ping and Guo Tu to follow Yuan Tan back to Qingzhou to reorganize and prevent Cao Cao from crossing the border there. He sent Yuan Xi back to Youzhou and Gao Gan back to Bingzhou. The three were to gather men and horses and await the next call to action. Yuan Shao and his third son, Shang, returned to Jizhou, where Yuan Shao recuperated. He placed Shang in charge of military affairs and assigned Shen Pei and Pang Ji to assist him.

*   *   *   *

After the victory at Cangting, Cao Cao rewarded his soldiers. Spies informed him that Yuan Shao was confined to bed and that Yuan Shang and Shen Pei were guarding the city of Jizhou tightly, while Yuan Tan, Yuan Xi, and Gao Gan had returned to their provinces. Cao Cao resisted arguments for an immediate attack, saying, "Jizhou is well stocked, and Shen Pei is an able adviser. The city will not fall easily. Now the crops are in the field, and we must protect the harvest. Wait for late autumn."

During the discussion Cao Cao had an urgent report from Xun Wenruo in the capital: "Liu Xuande has taken in tens of thousands in Runan, men who had been under Liu Pi and Gong Du.[3] When Xuande heard of your campaign in the north, he left Liu Pi holding Runan and marched toward the capital. Your Lordship must go back and head him off." Cao Cao assigned Cao Hong to maintain a presence along the river in Yuan Shao's domain; then he moved south toward the capital.[4]

Bent on surprising Xuchang, Liu Xuande with his two brothers and Zhao Zilong had reached the Rang Mountains when they encountered Cao Cao's troops marching toward them. Xuande pitched camp and divided his force into three units: Lord Guan at the northeast point; Zhang Fei at the southwest; and Xuande and Zhao Zilong due south, where they built a fortification. Amid a fearful din Cao Cao came into view, formed his line, and called Xuande out.

From beneath his banners Xuande rode forward. Leveling his whip at Xuande, Cao Cao cried out, "As my honored guest, you once received much kindness. Will you dishonor our friendship now?" Xuande replied, "You claim to be prime minister to the Han. In fact you are a traitor to the Han, whom I, a kinsman of the Han, am authorized by imperial decree to punish." Before the two armies Xuande read out loud and clear the secret decree from the girdle of Emperor Xian.[5]

Driven to fury by Xuande's recitation, Cao Cao ordered Xu Chu into the field. From behind Xuande, Zhao Zilong charged out with ready spear. The generals came to grips thirty times, but neither could prevail. Suddenly the ground trembled with battle cries as Lord Guan from the northeast and Zhang Fei from the southwest plunged into the action. Cao Cao's warriors, already fatigued from their long march, turned and fled. Xuande returned to base triumphant.

The next day Xuande sent Zhao Zilong to challenge the enemy, but Cao Cao's troops did not show themselves for ten days.[6] Zhang Fei was unable to provoke any response, either. While puzzling over Cao Cao's tactics, Xuande was informed that a grain shipment Gong Du was bringing in had been trapped. Xuande sent Zhang Fei to rescue it. No sooner had Zhang Fei set out than Xuande learned that Xiahou Dun was about to capture Runan from the back routes. "The enemy is in front and behind," Xuande cried, "where can I turn?" He sent Lord Guan to relieve Runan, but Runan fell that day. Liu Pi had fled, and Lord Guan was surrounded. Xuande became alarmed; then he heard that Zhang Fei, vainly trying to relieve Gong Du, had also been trapped. Xuande wanted to retreat but feared Cao Cao would attack from behind. Finally, a direct challenge came: Xu Chu stood before his camp to do battle.

Xuande held his ground until daybreak. He told his men to eat their fill and gave the order to break camp. The foot soldiers, followed by the cavalry, began moving out. False watches were announced to delay Cao Cao's attack. Xuande and his men had gone several *li* when, rounding a hill, they faced a row of torches. Above voices boomed, "Don't let Xuande escape! His Excellency has been waiting here especially for him!" Xuande despaired. Zhao Zilong said, "Do not fear, my lord. Follow me," and he plunged ahead, working his spear to cut a path as Xuande plied his twin swords. But then Xu Chu challenged them, followed by Li Dian and Yu Jin. Cao's commanders drove Xuande into the brush. Alone, he pushed deeper into the hills by unused trails. The sounds of battle receded. He had barely escaped.

Night dragged on. At dawn one thousand of his own defeated cavalry appeared, led by Liu Pi, who was escorting Xuande's family. Sun Qian, Jian Yong, and Mi Fang also rode up. "Xiahou Dun forced us from Runan," they said. "Lord Guan held off Cao Cao, and we got away." "Where is Lord Guan?" Xuande asked. "General, keep moving for now," Liu Pi replied. "We'll try to find him later."

After another few *li* a drum sounded and a body of troops surged in front of them. "Dismount and surrender!" cried the commander, Zhang He. Xuande tried to turn back. On a hill he saw enemy soldiers moving red flags in great sweeping circles. From a glen another company of men burst into view, commanded by Gao Lan. Xuande had no recourse. He cried to Heaven, "Why have you decreed this ordeal? Let me die!" He lifted his sword to his throat, but Liu Pi checked him. "I'll try to break through. Death does not daunt me!" he said. But Gao Lan cut him down at the moment of engagement. Xuande prepared himself to fight when a tumult arose in the rear of Gao Lan's force. A general tore into Gao Lan's back ranks and speared the commander. It was Zhao Zilong. Xuande was thankful to be saved.

Zhao Zilong, mounted, continued thrusting and stabbing as his horse reared and plunged. After putting Gao Lan's back ranks to flight, he reached the front and drove off Zhang He in a bitter struggle of thirty bouts. Zhao Zilong took a bloody toll until he found himself squeezed into a narrow valley blocked by Zhang He. He was rescued almost at once as Lord Guan, Guan Ping, and Zhou Cang arrived with three hundred men. Now squeezed himself, Zhang He was forced to withdraw. Zhao Zilong and Lord Guan came out of the defile and camped at a strongpoint in the hills. Xuande had Lord Guan look for Zhang Fei.

Zhang Fei had gone to relieve Gong Du, but Du was already in Xiahou Yuan's hands. Zhang Fei engaged Xiahou Yuan and forced him back. He pressed the attack but was himself surrounded by Yue Jin's men. Lord Guan, aided by stragglers, managed to track his way back to Zhang Fei, and together they drove off Yue Jin. The two brothers then returned to Xuande—only to hear that Cao Cao himself was coming in force. Xuande sent Sun Qian on with his family and began retreating with his comrades. In the end Xuande got far enough away, and Cao Cao called off the pursuit.

The harried remnants of Xuande's troops—now less than a thousand—pressed on. They reached a river known locally as the Han. Xuande pitched camp. People in the area brought lamb and wine especially to honor Xuande, and the gathering ate and drank at the river's edge. Then Xuande addressed his followers. "Good friends," he said sadly, "you are men with the talent to serve a king. Alas, following one whose fate is sealed has brought you only grief. For I possess nothing, not even the ground I stand on. I have led you far astray, I fear, and I urge you to seek out another more enlightened lord in whose service you may distinguish yourselves." His followers averted their faces and covered their eyes with their sleeves.

"Brother," Lord Guan said, "it is not so. At the beginning of the Han when the founding emperor suffered so many reverses in his struggle for mastery with Xiang Yu, his success in a single battle at Nine Mile Mountain enabled him to establish a four-hundred-year patrimony. Reverses are common in war and must not be allowed to affect morale." To this Sun Qian added, "There is a time for victory and for defeat. Do not lose heart. We are near Jingzhou, where Liu Biao controls the nine districts. He has a strong army and ample stores. And, like yourself, he is a Liu, a kinsman of the Han, who may protect us if we ask." "I doubt he'd grant us protection," Xuande replied. "Perhaps I can persuade him to receive you properly," Sun Qian suggested, and Xuande gave his approval.

Sun Qian presented himself before Liu Biao.[7] After the formalities Liu Biao said, "You serve Xuande. Why have you come here?" "My master," Sun Qian replied, "is one of the great heroes of the empire. At the moment his forces are at a low point, but he remains determined to sustain the sacred shrines of the Han. In Runan two utter strangers, Liu Pi and Gong Du, laid down their lives for him. Your Lordship and my master are both of the royal line. Recently Lord Liu suffered a setback and was thinking of taking refuge with Sun Quan in the Southland, but I took the liberty of saying to him, 'Why turn to a stranger? Nearby in General Liu Biao we have a kinsman, a leader who welcomes the worthy, who attracts men of talent, and who will welcome us all the more since both of you are Lius.' And so my master bid me offer his respects and learn your will."

Delightedly Liu Biao said, "I look upon Xuande as a younger brother; I have long wished to meet him but have never had the privilege. If he now so kindly seeks me out, it is fortunate indeed." However, Cai Mao objected: "That would be a serious mistake. Xuande first served Lü Bu, then Cao Cao, and after them, Yuan Shao. But he has served no one to the end. Doesn't that tell us enough about his character? If we welcome Xuande here, Cao Cao will turn on us. We will be involved in hostilities for no good reason. I would cut off this envoy's head and have it delivered to Cao Cao! That should raise your standing with the prime minister, my lord."

Sternly Sun Qian said, "I do not fear death. My master is loyal, heart and soul, to the Han. There is no comparison with a Cao Cao, a Yuan Shao, or a Lü Bu, whose service he entered only under duress. You, General Liu, are a descendant of the Han, a kinsman bonded in friendship, and that is why he seeks—despite all obstacles—to join you. How can Cai Mao purvey such slanders and show his jealousy of men of worth?" "I have made up my mind," Liu Biao said to Cai Mao in a tone of rebuke. "You need say no more." Shamed and resentful, Cai Mao left. Liu Biao had Sun Qian inform Xuande of his decision, and then he personally traveled thirty *li* outside the city to welcome his guest. At the reception Xuande showed great reverence for Liu Biao, who extended the most generous hospitality. Xuande introduced Lord Guan and Zhang Fei, who offered their respects, and all together they entered the city of Xiangyang. There the guests were assigned to suitable quarters.[8]

•   •   •   •   •

When Cao Cao discovered where Xuande had gone, he wanted to attack Jingzhou at once. Cheng Yu tried to dissuade him: "It is too risky with Yuan Shao threatening from the north. Return to the capital and build up your forces. After the spring thaw we can destroy Yuan Shao first and then take Xiangyang, sweeping north and then south in a single action." Cao Cao accepted this advice and took his army back to Xuchang.

In the first month of Jian An 7 (A.D. 202) Cao Cao reopened discussion of the campaign. He detailed Xiahou Dun and Man Chong to hold Runan and keep Liu Biao in check; he left Cao Ren and Xun Wenruo guarding Xuchang; and then he himself led the main army back to Guandu.

Yuan Shao, having recovered from the physical effects of last year's campaigns—catarrh and spitting of blood—was ready to plan another attack on the capital. Shen Pei argued against it: "In the battles at Guandu and Cangting last year our morale was badly hurt. We need to stay on the defensive and strengthen the army and the people." During this discussion, however, word came that Cao Cao had returned to Guandu and was preparing to attack Jizhou. "I don't think we can wait for the enemy to reach our walls and moats before we take the field," Yuan Shao said. "I will lead the main army myself." Then Yuan Shang, his youngest son, spoke up. "Father's condition does not yet permit a long campaign. Let me take command," he said. Yuan Shao consented and directed the other three provinces of his realm to gather their forces and defeat Cao Cao. Indeed:

> Hardly had the war drums died away at Runan
> When they began rolling again north of the river.

Could Cao Cao dominate both sides of the Yellow River?
READ ON.

32

Yuan Shang and His Brother Struggle for Jizhou;
Xu You Proposes Diverting the River Zhang

YUAN SHANG, WHO HAD KILLED Cao Cao's commander Shi Huan at Cangting, confidently marched his host of tens of thousands to Liyang without waiting for the armies of his brothers. At Liyang he engaged Cao Cao's vanguard. Zhang Liao rode out first, hot for combat. Spear braced, Yuan Shang answered the challenge but could not fend off Zhang Liao; he fled the field. Pressing his advantage, Zhang Liao drove the stunned Yuan Shang back to Jizhou. There Yuan Shao, in shock after his son's defeat, collapsed vomiting quantities of blood.

Lady Liu rushed Yuan Shao to a bedroom. His survival looked doubtful. She summoned Shen Pei and Pang Ji to his bedside to discuss the succession. Unable to speak, Yuan Shao answered by gestures. "Shall Shang succeed you?" Lady Liu asked. Yuan Shao nodded. Shen Pei wrote out his lord's testament. Yuan Shao rolled over, uttered a last cry, and passed away, blood spewing from his mouth.[1] A later poet wrote:

> From this noble and long-honored line
> Sprang a youth of unrestrained ambition,
> Who called three thousand champions up in vain
> And led his puissant armies to their ruin.
>
> No glory for this sheep in tiger's hide!
> No triumph for a chicken phoenix-plumed!
> The saddest part of this pathetic end:
> Both brothers of this fallen house were doomed.[2]

Shen Pei took charge of Yuan Shao's funeral. Lady Liu had all five of Yuan Shao's favored concubines put to death. Driven by jealousy, she had their heads shaved, their faces slashed, and their corpses mutilated, lest they try to rejoin their master in the netherworld. As a further precaution Yuan Shang killed the concubines' relatives. Next, Shen Pei and Pang Ji installed Yuan Shang as chief commanding officer and protector of the four provinces Ji, Qing, You, and Bing. After these measures were taken, they announced Yuan Shao's death.

Yuan Tan had already marched from Qingzhou to fight Cao Cao when he learned of his father's death. Guo Tu advised him, "My lord, hasten to Jizhou, or Shen Pei and Pang Ji will take advantage of your absence to put Shang in power." But Xin Ping cautioned, "Those two will be ready for us. Go now at your peril." "What should I do?" Yuan Tan asked. "Station troops outside the city and wait,"[3] Guo Tu said, "while I go in and survey the scene." Yuan Tan approved this plan; Guo Tu proceeded to Jizhou and presented himself to Yuan Shang.[4]

After the formalities Yuan Shang asked, "Where is my brother?" "With the army, convalescing. He couldn't come today," Guo Tu answered. "By my father's will," Yuan Shang said, "I am now lord. My brother is promoted to general of Chariots and Cavalry. Cao Cao threatens the southern border, and I want my brother to hold the front against him. I will bring reinforcement." Guo Tu replied, "We have no tacticians with the army. Could you let us have Shen Pei and Pang Ji?" Yuan Shang responded, "I depend on their counsel myself at all times. I cannot spare them." "Then," Guo Tu pressed, "would you send one of them?" Unable to refuse this request, Yuan Shang had the two men draw lots. Pang Ji was selected and went back with Guo Tu to deliver the seal and ribbon of command.

Finding Yuan Tan in perfect health, however, Pang Ji proffered the regalia with great anxiety. Yuan Tan would indeed have put Pang Ji to death, but Guo Tu dissuaded him: "With Cao Cao at the border, we'd better keep Pang Ji entertained to avoid provoking your brother. There'll be time enough to make our bid for Jizhou after Cao is defeated." Yuan Tan broke camp and advanced to Liyang. Deploying opposite Cao Cao, he sent Wang Zhao to challenge the enemy. Xu Huang rode forth to engage him. The duel had hardly begun when Xu Huang swept Wang Zhao to the ground with a stroke of his blade. Cao Cao's men pressed forward and fell upon the northerners. Yuan Tan retreated to Liyang and sought Yuan Shang's aid.

On Shen Pei's advice Yuan Shang sent a mere five thousand men. Cao Cao, learning of it, had Yue Jin and Li Dian intercept the relief force. The two generals surrounded the small unit before it arrived and wiped it out. When Yuan Tan learned that his brother had sent a small force and that Cao's commanders had swiftly eliminated it, he angrily summoned Pang Ji for an explanation. "Let me write to my lord and have him come himself," Pang Ji said. Yuan Tan agreed, and Pang Ji dispatched a letter.

Shen Pei advised Yuan Shang to turn down Pang Ji's request. "Guo Tu is full of tricks," Shen Pei argued. "Last time, Yuan Tan left without contesting Jizhou because Cao Cao was in our territory. But now, if he breaks Cao, he will try for Jizhou. Send your brother no aid. Let Cao's army take care of him." Yuan Shang did as Shen Pei advised. Enraged by his brother's treachery, Yuan Tan had Pang Ji executed immediately; then he discussed with his officers the possibility of surrendering to Cao Cao. Informed of his brother's intent, Yuan Shang said to Shen Pei, "If my brother surrenders to Cao Cao and they attack us jointly, we will be overcome." In the end Yuan Shang went to Liyang to relieve Yuan Tan.

Yuan Shang left Shen Pei and Commander Su You guarding the city and set out with a force of thirty thousand. The vanguard was led by two brothers who had volunteered, Lü Kuang and Lü Xiang. They reached Liyang, and Yuan Tan, pleased that his brother had come in person, dropped the idea of surrendering to Cao Cao. His troops, stationed inside the city, and Yuan Shang's, stationed outside, were positioned for mutual support. Before long, Yuan Xi and Gao Gan also arrived in force. Now the Yuans had three strongpoints. Every day they sent out troops to skirmish with Cao's. Again and again Yuan Shang was outfought by Cao Cao.

In the second month of Jian An 8 (A.D. 203) Cao Cao divided his army to attack the Yuans' positions and succeeded in his units' routing the Yuan brothers and Gao Gan, who abandoned Liyang. Cao Cao pressed on to Jizhou. Yuan Tan and Yuan Shang established a defense within the city; Yuan Xi and Gao Gan camped thirty *li* away and made a show of force.

Cao Cao's initial attacks on Jizhou failed to subdue the city. Guo Jia advised him, "Yuan Shao named the junior, not the elder, as his heir. The brothers are competing for power, and each has his faction. Threatened, they cooperate; otherwise, they quarrel. I think we should abandon this front and march south against Liu Biao in Jingzhou. When the Yuan brothers fall out again, Jizhou will be ours." Satisfied with this proposal, Cao Cao left Jia Xu governing Liyang and Cao Hong holding Guandu; then he started for Jingzhou.

· · · · ·

Yuan Tan and Yuan Shang congratulated each other on Cao Cao's withdrawal. Yuan Xi and Gao Gan went home to their respective provinces. Yuan Tan said to his advisers Guo Tu and Xin Ping, "Though the eldest, I have not been named heir. Shang is the son of a later wife, yet he has the title to my father's estate. I cannot put up with it!" "My lord," Guo Tu suggested, "hold your troops in readiness outside the city while you entertain your brother and Shen Pei. Have your men cut them down at the feast and settle this business!" Yuan Tan approved, but Assistant Inspector Wang Xiu, just arrived from Qingzhou, opposed it. He said to Yuan Tan, "Brothers are like two limbs. When locked in struggle with somebody, can you cut off your right arm and say, 'Now I'm sure to win'? Deny fraternal love and who will trust you, who will hold you dear? Give no heed, I beg you, to those who would set kinsmen at odds for passing advantage." But Yuan Tan rebuked Wang Xiu and issued the invitation.

Yuan Shang consulted Shen Pei. "Guo Tu's plotting," he said. "There is treachery in this. Now is the time to attack." Yuan Shang agreed. He donned his armor and rode out of the city at the head of fifty thousand men. Seeing that his brother had come with troops, Yuan Tan knew his plot had been exposed. He, too, armed himself and mounted. The two brothers faced off, hurling scorn at each other. "You poisoned Father," Yuan Tan cried, "and stole his estate. Now you come to kill your elder brother." The two engaged. Yuan Tan was defeated. Braving stones and arrows, Yuan Shang drove his opponent into the town of Pingyuan.[5]

On Guo Tu's advice Yuan Tan assigned General Cen Bi to renew the fight. Yuan Shang took the field again. Two opposed fronts formed, close enough for the troops on one side to see the banners and drummers on the other. Cen Bi and Lü Kuang clashed and Cen Bi fell. Defeated again, Yuan Tan retired once more to Pingyuan and would not come out. Yuan Shang besieged the city from three sides. "We are short on rations," Guo Tu told Yuan Tan. "The attackers are at full strength. Surrender to Cao Cao and try to get him to attack Jizhou. Yuan Shang will have to retreat to protect his city. Between Cao's army and ours, he will be taken. After Cao defeats him, we can seize his supplies and deny them to Cao. Too far from his base to feed his troops, he will have to withdraw, and Jizhou will be ours. Then we can plan further."

Yuan Tan asked, "Who will take Cao our message?" Guo Tu replied, "Xin Ping's younger brother Pi (styled Zuozhi), the prefect of Pingyuan and an eloquent scholar, may be trusted with this mission." Yuan Tan summoned the man, who came readily, provided him with a letter, and had him escorted past the border by three thousand men. Xin Pi took Yuan Tan's letter to Cao Cao at a time when Cao Cao was positioned at Xiping, preparing to attack Liu Biao. Liu Biao had sent Xuande to lead the vanguard against Cao Cao. Yuan Tan's envoy arrived before the battle.

Presenting himself to Cao Cao, Xin Pi explained Yuan Tan's proposal and delivered his letter. Cao Cao took it to his advisers. Cheng Yu said, "Yuan Tan is reeling from his brother's attack. Don't trust a man who comes under duress." Lü Qian and Man Chong also argued against turning the army around at the moment of battle, but Xun You favored the reversal. "You three gentlemen are mistaken," he said. "Liu Biao stays put between the Great River and the Han because, in my view, he lacks ambition. The Yuans, however, hold the four provinces north of the Yellow River and have hundreds of thousands under arms. If the two Yuan brothers get together to defend their land, the question of who rules the empire will remain unsettled. It is a rare occasion when one of the Yuans is desperate enough to come to us. Dispose of Yuan Shang, watch for the chance to destroy Yuan Tan, and you can control the empire. Do not let the opportunity pass."

Pleased with Xun You's advice, Cao Cao invited Yuan Tan's envoy to a banquet. "Is this surrender genuine?" Cao Cao asked Xin Pi. "Can Yuan Shang's army really be conquered?" "My lord," the envoy replied, "what need to ask? The situation speaks for itself. Year after year the Yuans have suffered defeat. Their armies are exhausted. Their advisers have been dismissed or executed. Slander and scheming have divided the brothers—and the realm. Add to that successive famines, natural disasters, and human crises—even a fool can see that the Yuans are on the verge of collapse. Heaven has doomed them. Now, my lord, you attack Ye, the administrative seat, and if Yuan Shang withdraws from Pingyuan to defend it, he loses his bastion. Yuan Tan will strike him from behind, and your mighty host will sweep away the wearied enemy as a storm does fallen leaves. Compare this to your present campaign against Liu Biao's Jingzhou, a prosperous territory, whose people and government enjoy a relationship far too harmonious for you to undermine. Besides, the north is your main problem. Once you have tamed it, your protectorship of the Emperor will be secure. Please consider this fully." Exuberantly, Cao Cao said, "How I regret coming to know you so late!" That same day Cao Cao supervised the shift of his armies to the north. Liu Xuande, well acquainted with Cao Cao's treacherous devices, pulled back to Jingzhou instead of pursuing him.

· · · · ·

Yuan Shang learned that Cao Cao had crossed the Yellow River. He called off the siege of Pingyuan and hastily led his troops back to Ye, with Lü Kuang and Lü Xiang bringing up the rear. Yuan Tan mobilized his troops at Pingyuan and gave chase for several dozen *li*. Suddenly a bombard sounded, and two units confronted him, Lü Kuang to the left, Lü Xiang to the right. Yuan Tan reined in and denounced them: "I always treated you well when my father was alive. How can you oppose me like this in my brother's service?" At Yuan Tan's words the two commanders offered to surrender. Yuan Tan said, "Surrender to the prime minister, not to me." They followed Tan back to his camp. When Cao Cao's army arrived, Yuan Tan conducted the brothers Lü into his presence. Cao Cao welcomed them with pleasure and promised Yuan Tan one of his daughters in marriage. Cao Cao had the Lü brothers arrange the match.

Yuan Tan appealed to Cao Cao to attack Jizhou. The prime minister replied, "We are still waiting for grain. Transport is a major problem. I'll have to recross the Yellow River and divert the Qi into the White Canal in order to open up a supply route. After that we can advance." Cao Cao quartered Yuan Tan in Pingyuan and then withdrew to Liyang. He granted the Lü brothers noble titles and placed them in his army with orders to hold themselves in readiness.

Guo Tu warned Yuan Tan, "This proposed wedding conceals Cao Cao's true intent. His generosity to the Lü brothers is meant to win over the northerners. It will end badly for us, though. My lord, have two seals of command carved and secretly delivered to the Lüs binding them to serve you. Then, after Cao defeats Yuan Shang, you can make your move." Yuan Tan adopted this plan, but the moment the Lü brothers received their seals, they turned them over to Cao Cao, who said with a laugh, "Tan has sent these so that you will help him after I defeat Shang. Very well. Accept the charge. I have my own way of handling it." Then and there Cao Cao decided to dispose of Yuan Tan.

In Ye, Yuan Shang said to Shen Pei, "Cao is moving grain through the White Canal. An attack must be coming. How shall we defend ourselves?" "First," Shen Pei replied, "have Yin Kai, our precinct master at Wuan, garrison Maocheng, where he can reach the Shangdang supply line. Next, have Ju Shou's son, Ju Gu, hold Handan to back up Yin Kai. You, my lord, will then send troops to Pingyuan and launch a lightning strike on Yuan Tan. Destroy Yuan Tan first, then Cao Cao." On this advice, Yuan Shang left Shen Pei and Chen Lin guarding Ye and sent generals Ma Yan and Zhang Yi to spearhead his attack on Pingyuan.

Yuan Tan informed Cao Cao that his brother Shang's troops were again approaching. The prime minister said, "This time I shall take Jizhou!" He was working out the tactics when Xu You arrived from the capital and said, "Your Excellency, what are you waiting for? For thunder to strike the Yuans?" "I have reached a decision," Cao responded with a smile. He dispatched Cao Hong to attack Ye while he moved against Yin Kai. In the action Xu Chu made short work of Yin Kai and scattered his ranks. Cao Cao welcomed all who surrendered, then guided his forces to Handan. There he found Ju Gu ready to do battle. Zhang Liao rode onto the field and fought with Ju Gu. The issue was quickly decided: Ju Gu fled in defeat. Zhang Liao raced after him and, as his mount narrowed the distance, brought him down with a single shot of his bow. Cao Cao dispersed Ju Gu's men and proceeded to Ye.

Cao Hong had already reached Ye. Cao Cao's troops ringed the wall around the city, piled up dirt mounds, and dug a tunnel out of the enemy's sight. Within the city Shen Pei issued stern orders on maintaining defenses and severely punished Feng Li, commander of the east gate, for drunkenness and negligence. The resentful Feng Li escaped through an underground passage and went over to Cao Cao. Cao Cao asked him how to reduce the city; Feng Li answered, "The earth is thick just behind the sally port.[6] Tunnel through there to get inside." Cao Cao then gave Feng Li three hundred men, and they began digging that night.

After Feng Li's defection Shen Pei mounted the wall himself to survey the scene. One night he noticed that there were no fires outside the wall by the sally port. "Feng Li must be digging his way in," Shen Pei whispered to himself. He ordered his best troops to crush the passage with heavy stones. It fell in, and Feng Li and his corps of three hundred perished underground.

Unable to penetrate the city, Cao Cao returned to the banks of the Huan to await Yuan Shang. Shang had heard of the defeat of Yin Kai and Ju Gu as well as the siege of Jizhou, so he broke off the battle at Pingyuan and started back to his city. A subcommander, Ma Yan, said to him, "Take the small road. Cao Cao will have an ambush on the main road. If we go by way of Xishan and come out at the head of the River Fu, we can raid his camp and break the siege." Yuan Shang approved the plan and left Ma Yan and Zhang Yi guarding the rear. Informed of Yuan Shang's movements, Cao Cao said, "If he takes the main road, we will avoid him. If he takes the small road out of Xishan, I can capture him in one battle. My guess is that he will signal with fire for reinforcement from the city: we will attack both him and the city." Cao Cao divided his troops in preparation for the action.

Yuan Shang passed the River Fu and went east to Yangping, where he established a position seventeen *li* from Ye, keeping near the water. During the night he made a bonfire to signal the city and sent his first secretary, Li Fu, to Ye disguised as one of Cao's inspectors. At the base of the wall, Li Fu shouted for entry. Shen Pei, recognizing the voice, admitted him. Li Fu said to Shen Pei, "Yuan Shang is at Yangping precinct waiting for reinforcement. When you send the men, light a fire as a signal." Shen Pei had the fires set to transmit the message. Li Fu continued, "The city is out of grain. Let the old and weak, the disabled and the women surrender to Cao. It'll put him off guard, and our troops, close behind them, can attack." Shen Pei approved this plan.

The next day a white flag went up on the wall proclaiming the surrender of the people of Jizhou. "They have no grain," Cao Cao said. "They'll push the old and weak out first, but the troops will be right behind." Cao Cao had Zhang Liao and Xu Huang conceal three thousand men on either side of his position; then, mounted, he spread the canopy of command and went to the city wall. He watched the people issuing from the gate, white flags in hand, supporting the elderly and pulling the children along. Soldiers rushed from the city in the wake of the exodus, but at a signal from Cao Cao's red flag Zhang Liao and Xu Huang emerged from hiding and drove the Jizhou troops back inside the city wall. Cao Cao raced to the side of the drawbridge, hoping to force an entry, but arrows rained down on him. One pierced his helmet and nearly killed him. His commanders pulled him back to the battle line for safety.

Cao Cao changed his armor and horse and led an attack on Yuan Shang's camp. Yuan Shang met him in the field, and the brigades of both sides swept into the fighting. Yuan Shang, severely beaten, withdrew to his camp at Xishan. Unknown to him, his outpost commanders, Ma Yan and Zhang Yi, had already accepted amnesty and enfeoffment as lords from Cao Cao.

Cao Cao attacked Xishan again the same day. At his order the Lü brothers, with Ma Yan and Zhang Yi, cut Yuan Shang's supply line.[7] Yuan Shang fled to Lankou in the night. But Cao Cao's men were waiting for him. Before he could pitch camp, Yuan Shang was encircled by torches and hidden troops. His soldiers, caught unprepared, were driven off fifty *li*. Desperate, Yuan Shang sent Yin Kui, imperial inspector of Yuzhou, to plead with Cao Cao to accept his surrender. Cao Cao pretended to heed the plea, even while sending Zhang Liao and Xu Huang to raid Yuan Shang's camp that night. Yuan Shang abandoned everything—regalia of office, tally of authority, and broadaxe of command, as well as armor and stores—as he fled north to Zhongshan district.

Once again Cao Cao turned his attention to Jizhou. Xu You advised him to divert the River Zhang and flood the enemy out. Cao Cao approved and had a moat forty *li* in circumference dug around the city. Shen Pei watched the digging from the wall. Observing that the trench was shallow, he thought smugly, "Cao will have to dig deep to flood this city," and took no measures for defense.

During the night, however, Cao Cao had the number of workers multiplied tenfold and by dawn the channel was nearly twenty spans wide and twenty deep. The Zhang was diverted into the trench, and the city was inundated. Soon rations ran out within the city and the defenders began to starve. Outside the wall Xin Pi held up to view Yuan Shang's seal, cord, and apparel, while offering amnesty to the resisters. In a rage Shen Pei executed eighty members of Xin Pi's family on the wall and threw down their heads. Xin Pi howled and groaned. Shen Pei's nephew Rong, a close friend of Xin Pi's, indignant at the slaughter of his friend's family, shot an arrow over the wall bearing an offer to surrender the city gate. The message was taken to Cao Cao.

Cao Cao issued an order: "When we enter the city, the old and young of the Yuan clan are to be spared; soldiers and civilians who surrender shall receive amnesty." The next morning Shen Rong opened the west gate to Cao Cao's army. Xin Pi leaped to the fore, and Cao Cao's commanders followed, slashing their way in. From the tower at the southeast gate Shen Pei saw the enemy inside the wall and tried to do battle. Xu Huang captured him and took him out of the city. On the way they met Xin Pi, who gnashed his teeth and whipped Shen Pei about the head, crying, "Thug! Cutthroat! Today you die!" "You're the traitor," Shen Pei retorted, "helping Cao Cao take our city. If only I had killed you."

Xu Huang brought Shen Pei to Cao Cao. "You know who yielded the city to us?" Cao Cao asked him. "No," Shen Pei said. "Your own nephew," Cao Cao said. "The vicious little brat!" Shen Pei responded angrily. "When I came to the wall," Cao Cao went on, "why were so many shots fired at me?" "Too few! Too few!" was Shen Pei's answer. "It was only natural," Cao Cao continued, "that you were loyal to the Yuans. Will you submit to me?" "Never! Never!" Shen Pei cried. Pleading from a prostrate position, Xin Pi wept. "This villain slaughtered eighty of my people," he cried. "Put him to death, Your Excellency, I pray you, to avenge my family." Shen Pei declared, "Alive, I served the Yuans. Dead I shall remain their loyal ghost. I'm not one of your fawning, wheedling villains. Get it over with!" Cao Cao ordered him executed. Facing death, Shen Pei shouted at the axeman, "My lord is to the north. I won't die facing south!" Turning north, Shen Pei kneeled and stretched his neck for the knife. Later a poet expressed his admiration for Shen Pei in these lines:[8]

> Above the northland's many famous men,
> Shen Pei truly rises all the more
> For laying down his life for feckless lord
> And standing fast as truest man of yore.
>
> Loyal and straight, to his lord a vassal frank,
> Pure and able, proof against temptation,
> He faced his lord as he faced his end:
> Let all defectors know their degradation.

Stirred by Shen Pei's spirit, Cao Cao had him interred north of the city wall. The commanders then invited the prime minister to enter Ye. Suddenly his guards hustled in a man whom Cao Cao recognized as Chen Lin. Cao Cao questioned him: "When you drew up the indictment of me for Yuan Shao, I understood that you had to denounce me. But why did you drag in my father and grandfather?" "The string sends the arrow," Chen Lin replied. Cao Cao thought it a pity to lose so talented a man. He rejected advice to execute him and made him an aide instead.[9]

•   •   •   •   •

Cao Cao's eldest son, Pi (Zihuan), was now eighteen. At his birth a cloud, purple in color and round like a canopy, hovered over the house all day. An observer of signs and auras told Cao Cao privately, "This is an imperial aura. Your son will know honors beyond naming." At the age of eight Cao Pi could write literary compositions that showed outstanding talent. He was knowledgeable about things ancient and modern, excelled in horsemanship and marksmanship, and was fond of sword fighting.[10]

In the conquered city of Ye, Cao Pi approached the residence of Yuan Shao with a few guards. A commander posted at the building warned him that the prime minister had banned entry, but Cao Pi brushed past and went into the private chambers wearing a sword. He found two women holding one another and sobbing. Cao Pi decided to kill them. Indeed:

Four generations of patricians and nobles, now a vanished dream;
Kith and kin of the Yuans faced disaster. [11]

What was their fate?
READ ON.

33

Cao Pi Exploits the Yuans' Troubles and Marries Lady Zhen;
Guo Jia Bequeaths a Plan to Secure Liaodong

As CAO PI BARED HIS SWORD before the sobbing women, a red light flashed before his eyes.[1] Putting up his weapon, he asked, "Who are you?" One of them replied, "I am Lady Liu, wife of the late General Yuan Shao." "And her?" Cao Pi said. "Lady Zhen," was the reply, "the wife of Yuan Xi, General Yuan Shao's second son. When the general sent Yuan Xi to administer Youzhou, Lady Zhen did not want to travel so far and stayed with us." Cao Pi drew Lady Zhen toward him, lifted her disheveled hair, and wiped her soiled face with his sleeve. With a face fair as jade, her skin flower-fresh, she was a beauty whose glance could topple kingdoms. Cao Pi said to her, "As the son of Prime Minister Cao Cao, I shall protect your family. Set your mind at ease." So saying, he posted himself inside the chamber, his hand on his sword.

Cao Cao arrived at Ye, the city he had conquered. Xu You approached him on horseback and, pointing to the gate with his whip, addressed the prime minister by his childhood name, Ah Man. "Without me," Xu You boasted loudly, "would you be entering in triumph today?" Cao Cao laughed, but his commanders were outraged.

Cao Cao rode first to the residence of Yuan Shao and asked the guard, "Has anyone entered?" "The young master is within," was the reply. Cao Cao scolded Cao Pi for violating his ban, but Lady Liu bowed and appealed to the prime minister, "If not for your son, our family would have perished. Allow me to offer Lady Zhen to serve in his household." Cao Cao summoned the woman, who prostrated herself. Cao Cao looked at her and said, "The perfect wife for my son!" and gave Cao Pi permission to take Lady Zhen as his wife.[2]

After taking control of Ye, Cao Cao made an offering at the grave of Yuan Shao. Making his kowtow, he wept bitterly. He then turned to his officials and said, "Years ago, when he and I were fighting Dong Zhuo, Yuan Shao asked me, 'If we cannot prevail now, which region would you choose to hold?' I asked his preference, and he replied, 'To my south, firm possession of the Yellow River; to my north, security against the rugged regions of Yan and Dai: if I had the desert peoples on my side, I could then turn my attention south of the river and make a bid for empire that might well succeed!' I replied to Shao, 'I prefer employing men of intelligence and energy and guiding them by my lights. That way I can accomplish whatever I set out to.' Our conversation seems as recent as yesterday. Now Yuan Shao is gone, and I can't help shedding a tear for him." The assembly was deeply moved. Cao Cao provided Yuan Shao's widow, Lady Liu, with gold, silk, and grain. He forgave all taxes for the current year in areas affected by the fighting. Then, after informing Emperor Xian, he assumed the protectorship of Jizhou himself.

One day Xu Chu was riding in through the east gate when he met up with Xu You, who hailed him and said, "Without me you could never have taken this city." Angered, Xu Chu said, "We all risked our lives in many a bloody battle for this place. What are you boasting about?" "You commonplace good-for-nothing!" Xu You taunted him. At those words Xu Chu lost his temper and killed Xu You; then he took the head to Cao Cao and described for him how Xu You had provoked him. "He and I were old friends," Cao Cao said, "so he felt free to tease us. Did you have to kill him?" He rebuked Xu Chu and buried Xu You lavishly.

Cao Cao ordered Jizhou scoured for men of worth and talent. People recommended Cavalry Commander Cui Yan (Jigui) from Dongwu in Qinghe. Cui Yan had retired on the pretext of illness after several futile attempts to counsel Yuan Shao on the defense of the northland. Cao Cao summoned Cui Yan, appointed him aide to the assistant inspector of Jizhou, and said to him, "The population registers I examined yesterday list three hundred thousand people. We have a considerable province here." Cui Yan responded, "The entire empire is going to pieces. The nine provinces of the realm[3] have been sundered from each other, and the plains of this one are covered with those who died in the battles between Yuan Shao's sons. What have the people to hope for unless Your Lordship will look into the moral and social conditions here and alleviate the crisis instead of calculating what the province may yield?" Cao Cao was abashed. He apologized and treated Cui Yan as an honored guest.

With Jizhou secured, Cao Cao sent for news of Yuan Tan. Yuan Tan had plundered Ganling, Anping, Bohai, Hejian, and other areas. He went on to attack Zhongshan after hearing that Yuan Shang had fled there. But Yuan Shang had no inclination to fight. He escaped to Youzhou to beg refuge of Yuan Xi. Yuan Tan accepted the surrender of all Yuan Shang's men and prepared to retake Jizhou. Cao Cao ordered Yuan Tan to present himself, but he would not come. Cao Cao angrily broke off the prospective marriage and marched against Pingyuan. In response Yuan Tan turned to Liu Biao for help.

Liu Biao consulted Liu Xuande, who said, "The conquest of Jizhou has strengthened Cao Cao enormously. He will capture the Yuan brothers shortly, and there's nothing you can do about it. Bear in mind that Cao Cao has had his eye on this city of yours for a long time. I'm afraid all we can do is continue training the soldiers and improving our defenses while avoiding reckless moves." "Then," Liu Biao asked, "how shall I explain to Yuan Tan our refusal to help him?" "We can do it in a roundabout way," Xuande suggested, "by urging both brothers to settle their differences." On this advice Liu Biao wrote first to Yuan Tan:

A man of honor will not turn to hostile lands to escape civil broils. Some time ago I was advised that you had bent the knee to Cao Cao, thus setting at naught your late father's unpaid blood debt and abandoning your fraternal responsibilities. Your actions have dishonored the alliance that once bound your father and me. Even if Yuan Shang failed you as a brother, you should have yielded to his demands all the same, waiting for the turmoil to subside before sorting out the rights and wrongs. Would that not have been the nobler course?

Liu Biao next wrote to Yuan Shang:

Yuan Tan is hasty-tempered by nature. He has become confused about right and wrong. The first thing is to get rid of Cao Cao and avenge your late father; after

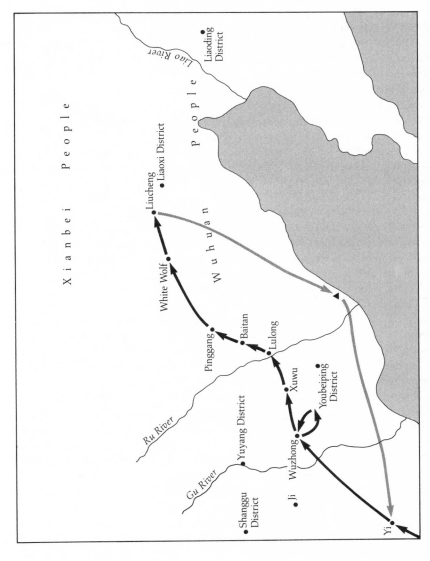

MAP 3. Youzhou province, showing Cao Cao's campaign against the Wuhuan people. Source: Liu Chunfan, *Sanguo shihua* (Beijing: Beijing chubanshe, 1981), p. 71.

that you can sort out your conflicting claims. Is this not the wiser course? Unless
you relent, you and your brother will end up like the hunting dog and the rabbit.
Both ran themselves to death, and a passing farmer picked them up.

Liu Biao's letter gave Yuan Tan no hope. He knew he could not withstand Cao Cao
alone and abandoned Pingyuan for Nanpi. Cao Cao pursued him. It was the harshest time
of winter. No supplies could be moved on the frozen river. Local laborers ordered by Cao
Cao to chop up the ice and pull his boats forward ran away. In a rage Cao Cao demanded
their arrest and execution, and the laborers gave themselves up. Cao Cao said to them, "If
I spare you, my orders will command no respect. But it would be sheer cruelty to kill
you. Go and hide yourselves in the hills so that my men don't find you." The people
wept for gratitude and departed.

Yuan Tan led his men forth to confront Cao Cao, and the two armies deployed. Cao
Cao rode out, and pointing his whip at Yuan Tan, said scornfully, "I treated you all too
well, and you betrayed me." "You invaded my territory," Yuan Tan retorted, "and seized
my cities—and you owe me a wife. Yet you say I betrayed *you!*?" Cao Cao sent Xu
Huang into the field. Peng An met him. The two horsemen clashed; Xu Huang downed
his opponent swiftly. The defeated Yuan Tan retreated to Nanpi, where Cao Cao hemmed
him in. In panic Yuan Tan sent Xin Ping to negotiate a surrender.

Cao Cao said to Yuan Tan's envoy, "This fellow Tan is one way one day, another way
the next. How can I trust him? You should stay with me. Your younger brother Xin Pi
has already been of great use to me." "Your Excellency," Xin Ping replied, "you mistake
me. As I understand it, 'the servant shares in his lord's glory—or his humiliation.' I have
served the Yuans a long, long time. Could I turn my back on them now?" Cao Cao realized Xin Ping was too resolute to be won over, and sent him back. Yuan Tan received
Xin Ping's report and said, "Isn't your brother already in Cao's service? What loyalty can
I expect from you?" Overwhelmed with indignation at this charge, Xin Ping collapsed
and died soon after. Yuan Tan regretted his words.

Guo Tu advised Yuan Tan, "We will have to drive the people out of the city and follow
with the army to stage a last-ditch battle." Yuan Tan approved. That night they rounded
up the inhabitants of Nanpi, armed them, and told them to stand by. The next morning,
with a mighty hue and cry, the crowd herded together and streamed through all four
gates toward Cao Cao's positions. Then, shielded by the populace, the army emerged and
a general melee ensued. The battle raged until noon with no clear outcome; the slain
covered the ground. Determined on a decisive victory, Cao Cao dismounted, climbed a
hill, and struck the drums himself. At the signal his men and officers resumed their advance. This time, giving their utmost, they routed Yuan Tan's army. Civilian losses were
enormous.

With a thrust of energy Cao Hong broke through a defending line and came face-
to-face with Yuan Tan. Slashing fiercely, Hong cut him down. In the confusion Guo Tu
dashed back to the city, but Yue Jin felled him with a perfect shot: man and mount toppled
into the moat. Cao Cao entered Nanpi and comforted the populace. Suddenly, another
contingent appeared, led by Jiao Chu and Zhang Nan, lieutenants to Yuan Xi. Cao Cao
maneuvered to engage them, but unexpectedly they threw down their arms in surrender.
Cao Cao granted them lordships. Zhang Yan, leader of the Black Hill bandits, also
surrendered with one hundred thousand. Cao Cao made him General Who Pacifies
the North.

Yuan Tan's head was set on display at the north gate. Despite Cao Cao's threat to
execute any mourners, a man in plain cap and hempen mourning coat was found weeping

below the severed head. Brought before Cao Cao, the offender identified himself as Wang Xiu, assistant to the imperial inspector of Qingzhou. Wang Xiu had been driven from his post for his forthright criticism[4] of Yuan Tan; nonetheless he came to pay his respects. Cao Cao demanded, "Did you know of my ordinance?" "I did," Wang Xiu replied. "And you have no fear of death?" Cao Cao asked. "I received office from Yuan Tan," Wang Xiu answered, "and not to mourn him would be disloyal. One cannot stand before the world holding life dearer than honor. If you would let me collect my lord's remains and inter them, I will accept the punishment of death without regret."

Cao Cao remarked, "Many indeed were the loyal servants of the north. And if the Yuans had made good use of them, I would never have set my sights on this territory." Cao Cao allowed Wang Xiu to bury Yuan Tan's body, treated him as an honored guest, and made him an officer in the Metals and Weaponry Division. Cao Cao then asked Wang Xiu, "Yuan Shang has taken refuge with Yuan Xi. How can I defeat him?" But Wang Xiu refused to reply, and Cao Cao remarked, "Truly a loyal servant to the Yuans."

Guo Jia advised Cao Cao, "Let the former Yuan generals, Jiao Chu and Zhang Nan, launch the attacks." Cao Cao approved the plan and strengthened the force with separate commands under Lü Kuang, Lü Xiang, Ma Yan, and Zhang Yi. They attacked Youzhou in three field armies. Cao Cao also dispatched Li Dian and Yue Jin to help Zhang Yan defeat Gao Gan, Yuan Shao's nephew, in Bingzhou.

Rather than face Cao Cao's army, Yuan Shang and Yuan Xi abandoned Youzhou and hurried to Liaoxi, taking refuge with the Wuhuan people.[5] At the same time the new imperial inspector of Youzhou, Chu of the Wuhuan, led the provincial officials in a joint vow to transfer their allegiance to Cao Cao: "We are surrendering to His Excellency Cao Cao, one of the great heroes of our age. Whoever violates this order dies." Each official stepped forward and validated his vow with a smear of sacrificial blood. Only Assistant Inspector Han Heng refused. He threw his sword to the ground and declared, "I have benefited from the kindness of the Yuans, the son as well as the father. Now in their hour of defeat I have neither the wit to save them nor the courage to die for them; I am lacking in loyalty. But to turn and serve Cao Cao is more than I can bring myself to do." The officials paled. Imperial Inspector Chu said, "Any great enterprise must rest upon the highest ethical principles. Our success depends on no one man. If such be Han Heng's bent, let him suit himself." Dismissing Han Heng from the assembly, the imperial inspector surrendered his army to Cao Cao, who with great satisfaction appointed Chu as General Who Quells the North.

Unexpectedly, Cao Cao was told that the assault on Bingzhou had failed: Yue Jin, Li Dian, and Zhang Yan could not break Gao Gan's defense at Wine Jar Pass. Cao Cao marched to the battleground. After learning of the commanders' difficulties, he called a general meeting. Xun You advised using the false surrender ploy, and Cao Cao approved. He summoned the recent defectors Lü Kuang and Lü Xiang to carry out the tactic.

The Lü brothers came to the pass with a few dozen men and called out, "We are former commanders of Yuan Shao's who have been forced to surrender against our will. Cao Cao is treacherous and unreliable and has used us ill. We want to work for our former lord again. Let us in at once." Gao Gan warily allowed only the two brothers up to the pass. They disarmed, left their horses, and went in to tell Gao Gan, "Cao Cao has only just arrived. Attack his camp tonight before they dig in. We will take the lead." Gao Gan accepted the proposal.

Following the Lü brothers with more than ten thousand men, Gao Gan approached Cao Cao's camps. Suddenly a roar went up behind him, and an ambush was sprung from all sides. Gao Gan dashed back to the pass but found it already in the hands of Cao Cao's commanders, Yue Jin and Li Dian. Gao Gan turned north and rode to seek refuge with the chief of the Xiongnu. Cao Cao took control of the pass and sent men after the fugitive.

Gao Gan entered the territory of the Xiongnu nation and came before their khan.[6] Dismounting and pressing himself to the ground, Gao Gan said, "Cao Cao has devoured my homeland. Now he has designs on yours. With your assistance we could protect the north." But the khan rebuffed him. "I have no quarrel with Cao Cao," he said. "Why should he invade my land? Are you trying to foment hostilities?" Thus rudely dismissed, Gao Gan began riding south to Liu Biao, his last hope. En route District Commander Wang Yan killed him and sent the head to Cao Cao, for which he received a lordship.

· · · · ·

With Bingzhou secured, Cao Cao began planning to attack the Wuhuan to the west. Cao Hong and others argued, "Yuan Xi and Yuan Shang have lost their men and officers. They are powerless, refugees in the remote desert. If we go after them now, the capital could fall: we could not reach it in time to meet an attack from Liu Biao and Liu Xuande. Rather than take that risk we should march home."

Guo Jia, however, said, "My colleagues are wrong. You are feared across the realm, my lord, while the desert tribes will be off guard, secure in their remoteness. A sudden strike is bound to succeed. Remember that Yuan Shao and the Wuhuan had close ties and that as long as the Yuan brothers survive, they will be a threat. Liu Biao, on the other hand, is an armchair strategist. He knows he can't dominate Liu Bei. If he gives Liu Bei a major task, he will lose control. If he gives Liu Bei a trivial task, he will refuse. The capital only appears to be vulnerable during this extended campaign. Actually, there is little risk." "Sound advice," Cao Cao decided and led the entirety of his forces, supported by thousands of supply wagons, to carry the war to the Wuhuan.

When Cao Cao came to the vast sea of yellow sand with its sudden windstorms and treacherous terrain, daunting to both man and beast, he wavered and consulted Guo Jia once again. Unfortunately, the adviser, unused to the punishing climate of the north, was lying ill in a wagon. Cao Cao wept and said, "Because of my wish to conquer the desert, you have been subjected to hardships that have broken your health. Now I will not know peace again." "I am grateful for Your Excellency's kindness," Guo Jia said. "My death could not requite one ten-thousandth of my debt." "The way is too dangerous," Cao Cao said. "I think we should turn back. What's your opinion?" "In war," Guo Jia answered, "speed is precious. On a march of this length the supply train requires too much time. You'd be better off with a small force that can reach the Wuhuan before they suspect anything. But you'll need someone who knows the routes." Cao Cao left Guo Jia recuperating in Yizhou.

Someone recommended Tian Chou, a former commander of Yuan Shao's, as a guide. Cao Cao called him for advice. "In summer and autumn," Tian Chou told him, "the routes are flooded, too deep for wagons and horses but too shallow for boats. I would turn back and go across Baitan through the defile at Lulong. You'll come out on open land. Advance to Liucheng and you should catch them unawares. Tadu can be overthrown in a single battle." Cao Cao accepted this advice, appointed Tian Chou Queller of the North, and assigned him to lead the way. Zhang Liao led the second contingent, Cao himself the rear.[7]

The small mounted force advanced double time to the White Wolf Hills, where they found Yuan Xi and Yuan Shang together with Tadu. There were tens of thousands of Wuhuan horsemen. Cao Cao guided his horse to a high point and surveyed the enemy.

The troops of Tadu were not organized into ranks and files. "Their lines are a mess," Cao Cao said. "We can attack." He gave the banner of command to Zhang Liao, who led Xu Chu, Yu Jin, and Xu Huang in a swift descent. The attackers routed Tadu, and Zhang Liao cut him down. The mass of horsemen surrendered. Yuan Xi and Yuan Shang fled east with a few thousand riders to Liaodong.

Cao Cao regrouped and entered Liucheng. He offered Tian Chou the lordship of Liu precinct to protect the township. But the guide, weeping bitterly, declined. "I am a faithless fugitive," he lamented. "Your kindness in sparing me is more than I deserve. How could I accept a reward for betraying Lulong? I prefer death to rank and office." Cao Cao acknowledged Tian Chou's sense of honor and made him a court counselor. Cao Cao comforted the Xiongnu. He had acquired ten thousand superb mounts as spoils of the campaign.

That very day Cao Cao started homeward. Through dry, bitter cold his army traveled two hundred *li*. There was no water and their grain was gone. They slaughtered horses for food and dug hundreds of spans into the earth for water.

On reaching Yizhou, Cao Cao rewarded first those who had opposed his expedition into the desert. "The campaign," he explained, "was too great a risk. Luck alone enabled us to succeed, and we can thank Heaven for it but never take it as an example to be followed. Your prudent objections deserve to be well rewarded. Please do not hesitate to speak out again." Guo Jia, the valued adviser, had died before Cao Cao reached Yizhou. His great outer coffin was placed in the main hall. Cao Cao offered sacrifice and wept sorely. "Heaven has taken you from me," he cried. Then, turning to his officers, he said, "Guo Jia was the youngest of our generation. I thought I would have his help in deciding on my heir, but his life has been cut short. It breaks my heart!" Guo Jia's attendants handed Cao Cao their master's last letter. "It is in his own hand," they said. "He told us that if Your Excellency followed his recommendations, the Liaodong problem could be settled." Cao Cao unsealed it. He sighed and nodded as he read it through, but he kept the contents to himself.

The next day Xiahou Dun and a group of leaders petitioned Cao Cao: "Gongsun Kang, governor of Liaodong, has not paid his respects in some time. Now that Yuan Shang and Yuan Xi have joined him, there could be trouble. Better to strike before they stir, and make Liaodong ours." "No need to put your mettle to the test this time," Cao Cao said with a smile. "A few days more and Gongsun Kang should be sending over the heads of the Yuan brothers." His bold statement left the commanders unconvinced.

Meanwhile, Yuan Xi and Yuan Shang had reached Liaodong, the district under Governor Gongsun Kang. Gongsun Kang came from Xiangping. He was the son of Gongsun Du, General of Martial Might under the Han. When the governor learned that Yuan Shao's sons were seeking his assistance, he consulted his officers. One of them, Gongsun Gong, said, "Yuan Shao was always trying to take us over. Now his sons have arrived like a pair of thieving cuckoos looking for a magpie's nest, utterly defeated, with nowhere to roost. Let them in and they'll plot against you. But if you lure them into the city and kill them, Cao Cao will be more than grateful for their heads!" "What worries me," the governor replied, "is that Cao Cao may try and conquer us. In that case we might be better off with the Yuan brothers' help." "Let's find out then," Gongsun Gong suggested. "If Cao Cao is coming, welcome the Yuans. If not, deliver the heads." And so Governor Gongsun Kang sent spies to discover Cao Cao's intentions.

Yuan Shang and Yuan Xi conferred before meeting the governor. Yuan Shang said, "Liaodong has tens of thousands of troops, more than enough to hold off Cao Cao. If they receive us, we can kill the governor, take his land, and rebuild our strength until we're ready to stand against the heartland region. That way we can recover the whole of the north." Thus agreed, the brothers presented themselves. But the governor, feigning illness, postponed their reception and kept them in a guesthouse.

Before long spies reported to the governor that Cao Cao was established in Yizhou and had no intention of marching to Liaodong. Delighted with the news, Gongsun Kang positioned armed men behind the wall hangings in the official hall and had the visitors shown in. The formalities concluded, the governor bade them be seated. It was bitter cold. Yuan Shang, seeing no cushions on the floor, asked, "May we have mats?" Glaring at them, the governor said, "Your heads are going on a long journey. What do you want mats for?" Yuan Shang was taken aback. Gongsun Kang shouted, "Guards! What are you waiting for?" The executioners rushed out and beheaded the brothers where they sat. The governor had their heads placed in a wooden box, which he dispatched to Yizhou.

At this time Xiahou Dun and Zhang Liao were impatiently petitioning Cao Cao: "If we aren't going to attack Liaodong, let's get back to the capital before Liu Biao becomes ambitious." "All I'm waiting for," Cao Cao said to them, "is the heads." The commanders snickered. But the arrival of the heads of the Yuan brothers caused general astonishment. Cao Cao read the accompanying letter from Governor Gongsun Kang and said, laughing, "Exactly as Guo Jia predicted." Cao Cao rewarded the messenger and made the governor lord of Xiangping and general of the Left. Finally, to satisfy his officers, Cao Cao produced Guo Jia's letter:

> I have learned that the Yuan brothers are seeking refuge in Liaodong. Your Lordship, do not use the army against it under any circumstances. The governor has always feared that Yuan Shao would annex his territory and will surely suspect his sons. If you attack, they will unite and resist; you may not succeed for some time. Give them no cause for alarm, and the brothers and the governor will intrigue against each other. That is what circumstances dictate.

The officers voiced their admiration; then Cao Cao led further ceremonies to honor the adviser's spirit. Guo Jia was thirty-eight when he died, had campaigned with Cao Cao for eleven years, and had many startling achievements to his credit. In the words of a later poet,

> Guo Jia, born with gifts divine,
> Excelled the heroes of Cao's court,
> His stomach filled with erudition,
> His mind deploying shield and sword.
>
> Like Fan Li of old, he worked his schemes.
> Like Chen Ping, he shaped and planned.
> Alas, he died before his time,
> A broken pillar of the land.[8]

Cao Cao sent Guo Jia's body on to the capital for solemn burial. Then he led his men back to Jizhou.[9]

Cheng Yu and others advised Cao Cao, "The north is now secure; it's time to plan the conquest of the south. We should start as soon as we return." "I've been thinking about it all along," Cao Cao responded with a smile. "Your proposal fits in perfectly with my own designs." That night in Jizhou, Cao Cao stood on the tower above the eastern corner of the wall. Leaning against the battlement, he stared into the sky. Xun You was beside him. Cao Cao pointed upward. "What dazzling signs of good fortune there to the south," he said. "But I am afraid we are not ready for that campaign." "Your Excellency," Xun You said, "who could withhold allegiance from your Heaven-sent prestige and power?" As they watched the heavens, a golden beam rose from the ground. "There is treasure there below," Xun You said. Cao Cao descended from the tower and ordered the light traced to its source and the spot dug up. Indeed:

> The stars pointed south,
> But an unexpected treasure appeared in the north.

What was to be unearthed?

READ ON.

34

Lady Cai Eavesdrops on a Private Talk;
Imperial Uncle Liu Vaults the River Tan on Horseback

AT THE SOURCE OF THE GOLDEN EMANATION Cao Cao unearthed a bronze bird. He asked Xun You what it portended. "In ancient times," the adviser replied, "Shun was born after his mother dreamed that a jade bird had entered her body. This discovery is auspicious."[1] Cao Cao was delighted with Xun You's interpretation and ordered a tower built to celebrate the omen. Workmen prepared the site, cut down trees, fired tiles, and polished bricks to construct the Bronze Bird Tower overlooking the River Zhang. A year was allotted for completion of the work.

One of Cao Cao's younger sons, Cao Zhi, proposed "A storied tower should comprise three structures: in the middle, the tallest: the Bronze Bird; another on the left: the Jade Dragon; and a third on the right: the Golden Phoenix. With two flying bridges traversing the space between, it will be a magnificent sight." Cao Cao responded, "A good idea, my son. And the completed towers may later serve to make my declining years more pleasurable."

Cao Cao had five sons. Among them Zhi alone was keen, quick-witted, and adept at composition. He was his father's favorite. Now Cao Cao left this son and his elder brother, Pi, in Ye to build the tower, and assigned Zhang Yan to defend the northern border; then with Yuan Shao's captured forces, which numbered some half a million, Cao Cao withdrew to the capital at Xuchang. Once established there, he ennobled those who had distinguished themselves; proposed that the Emperor honor Guo Jia with the posthumous title Faithful Lord; and arranged to have Guo Jia's son Guo Ye raised in his own household.

Once again Cao Cao assembled his council to discuss a southern campaign against Liu Biao. Xun You was opposed. "Our main force," he argued, "is not yet ready for mobilization after the northern campaigns. If we wait half a year to recover our strength and nourish our mettle, Liu Biao and Sun Quan too will fall at the first roll of our drums." Cao Cao accepted this advice and assigned the soldiers to settle and reclaim wasteland until the next call to arms.

· · · ·

Since Liu Xuande's arrival in Jingzhou, Liao Biao had treated him with kindness and generosity. One day as guests were gathering for a banquet, there was a report that the generals who had previously submitted, Zhang Wu and Chen Sun, were pillaging in Jiangxia and organizing an insurrection. Liu Biao said in alarm, "So, they have rebelled again. This may be serious." "Do not trouble yourself, elder brother," Xuande said. "Let me go and punish them." Delighted, Liu Biao gave Xuande a force of thirty thousand.[2]

A day later Xuande was in Jiangxia. The insurgents met him in the field. Xuande, Lord Guan, Zhang Fei, and Zhao Zilong rode to the front of their position. Ahead they could see Zhang Wu astride a magnificent horse. "An extraordinary animal!" Xuande exclaimed. At that moment Zhao Zilong braced his spear and rushed the enemy line. Zhang Wu raced to meet him. After three passages-at-arms the rebel, pierced through, dropped from his horse. In one motion Zhao Zilong seized the unguided animal's reins and pulled it back to his own line. The other rebel charged out to retake the horse. But Zhang Fei, shouting lustily, plunged into the fray and stabbed the pursuer. With both leaders slain, the rebel host broke and dispersed. Xuande pacified the remnants, restored order in the several counties of Jiangxia, and returned to the capital of Jingzhou. Liu Biao received him outside the walls and led him into the city.

At a banquet to celebrate the victory Liu Biao, warmed with wine, said to Xuande, "If this is an example of your valor and skill, our Jingzhou will be safe. But we still face constant raids by the Southern Viets, and Zhang Lu to the west and Sun Quan are an ever-present danger." "Elder brother," Xuande answered, "I have three commanders who are more than equal to such enemies. Let Zhang Fei cover the Southern Viet border, send Lord Guan to Guzi to restrain Zhang Lu, and have Zhao Zilong hold Three Rivers against Sun Quan. What will remain to worry about?"

Liu Biao was ready to adopt Xuande's recommendation, but there was opposition from Cai Mao, brother of Lady Cai, Liu Biao's wife. Cai Mao said to his sister, "If Xuande sends his three generals to those strategic points and remains in the capital himself, there's bound to be trouble." Accordingly, Lady Cai spoke to Liu Biao that night: "I've heard that a number of our people have entered into liaison with Xuande. You can't afford not to take precautions. It does us no good to let him stay in the capital. Why not send him elsewhere?" Liu Biao answered, "Xuande is a humane and benevolent man." "Others," Lady Cai responded, "may not be so well-meaning as you." Liu Biao pondered her words but did not reply.[3]

The next day outside the city wall Liu Biao noticed Xuande's magnificent horse. Someone told him it had been captured from the Jiangxia rebels. Liu Biao expressed such admiration that Xuande presented the animal to him. Liu Biao was delighted and rode back to the city. Kuai Yue found out the horse was a gift from Xuande and said to Liu Biao, "My late brother, Kuai Liang, an expert judge of horses, taught me something about them. Notice the little grooves or tear tracks under the eyes and the white spots on the side of his forehead. They call such horses 'marked';[4] they bring their masters bad luck. Zhang Wu fell in battle because of that horse, and you, my lord, must not ride it."

Impressed by this warning, Liu Biao told Xuande the following day, "I am deeply grateful for the horse you so generously gave me, but, worthy brother, you go off to war from time to time and will need it yourself. With all respect I return the gift." Xuande rose to thank him. Liu Biao went on, "Worthy brother, you have been here so long that your military skills are wasted. We have a prosperous county over in Xinye. What about establishing your command there?" Xuande agreed.[5]

The next day Xuande took formal leave of Liu Biao and led his force toward Xinye. As he was exiting the city gate, a man stepped before him, made a lengthy salutation, and said, "My lord, you should not ride that horse." It was Yi Ji (Jibo) of Shanyang, an adviser to Liu Biao. Xuande dismounted hurriedly. "Yesterday," Yi Ji explained, "I heard Kuai Yue say to my master, 'This horse has a marked head; it will bring its master ill

fortune.' That's the reason he returned it. Do not ride it any more.'' ''I am deeply grateful,'' Xuande replied, ''for your concern. But all men have their appointed time; that's
something no horse can change.'' To this wisdom Yi Ji deferred, and afterward he kept in
frequent touch with Xuande.

Liu Xuande's arrival at Xinye was a boon to soldier and civilian alike, for he completely reformed the political administration. In the spring of the twelfth year of Jian An
(A.D. 207) Xuande's wife, Lady Gan, bore him a son, Liu Shan. On the night of the birth
a white crane alighted on the *yamen*, sang some forty notes, and flew into the west. During parturition an unknown fragrance filled the room. Once Lady Gan had dreamed that
she swallowed the stars of the Northern Dipper and conceived as a result—hence the
child's milkname, Ah Dou, or Precious Dipper.

• • • •

Previously, when Cao Cao was campaigning in the north, Xuande had returned to the
capital of Jingzhou to persuade Liu Biao to take action.[6] ''All Cao's forces are engaged,''
Xuande argued. ''His capital stands vulnerable. With a surprise attack we can assume
control of the dynasty.'' But Liu Biao replied, ''I am content with the nine districts of
Jingzhou. What would I do with more?'' Xuande fell silent. Liu Biao invited him to his
private apartments for wine. Becoming mellow, Liu Biao sighed deeply, and Xuande asked
why. ''There is something on my mind,'' Liu Biao answered, ''that is difficult to speak
of. . . .'' Xuande had started to inquire further when Lady Cai emerged from behind a
screen. Liu Biao lowered his head and said no more. Shortly afterward they adjourned,
and Xuande rode back to Xinye.

• • • •

Winter came, and Cao Cao returned triumphant from his campaigns. Xuande despaired over Liu Biao's refusal to adopt his proposal. Unexpectedly, Liu Biao sent for him,
and Xuande went with the envoy. The ceremonies of greeting concluded, Liu Biao conducted Xuande to a banquet. ''We have had word,'' Liu Biao told him, ''that Cao Cao is
back in Xuchang with his forces, strengthening his position daily. Surely he covets this
land. Now I regret ignoring your excellent advice. We lost a perfect opportunity to attack.'' ''The empire,'' Xuande responded, ''is breaking apart. Armed clashes occur every
day. Do you think 'opportunity' no longer exists? If you can make the most of it in the
future, then 'regret' is premature.'' Liu Biao responded, ''What you say makes sense.''

They drank more and grew warmer. Suddenly Liu Biao began weeping profusely.
Xuande asked what was the matter. ''Something is on my mind,'' was the reply. ''I tried
to broach it that last time we were drinking but circumstances made it awkward.'' ''What
is the problem, elder brother?'' Xuande asked. ''If I can be of use, death itself could not
daunt me.'' ''I first married Lady Chen,'' Liu Biao began, ''who bore my first son, Qi—a
worthy enough lad, but too weak and timid to keep affairs of state on a steady course. My
second marriage was to Lady Cai. She bore my younger son, Zong, a bright and per-
ceptive boy. If I set aside the elder to make the younger my heir, I will be going against
tradition and law, but if I leave the elder as my heir, what do I do about the Cai clan? They
control the military and will stage a coup. This is my dilemma.''

Xuande responded, ''From most ancient times removing the elder and confirming the
younger has led to disaster. If you are worried about the extent of the Cai clan's power,
try paring it down a bit at a time. But on no account should you confirm the younger
because you dote on him.'' Liu Biao fell silent.

Lady Cai had been suspicious of Xuande from the start and eavesdropped on his con-
versations with Liu Biao whenever she could. On this occasion she was listening behind
a screen and bitterly resented what she heard. Xuande himself realized that he had said
more than he ought and rose to excuse himself. Doing so, he noticed the extra weight
around his middle. Suddenly he found tears welling in his eyes. When Xuande resumed
his place, Liu Biao asked what was distressing him. "I used to spend all my time in the
saddle," Xuande replied with a deep sigh. "Now it has been so long since I have been
riding that I am growing thick around the waist. Time is passing me by. My years come
on but my task languishes, and it grieves me."[7]

Liu Biao responded, "They say, worthy brother, that in the capital you and Cao Cao
once judged the heroes of the age over hot plum wine. Cao would acknowledge none of
the renowned men whom you proposed, saying, 'Of heroes, this world has but two—you
and me!' If Cao with all his power and influence did not rate himself above you, why are
you so concerned that your task is not being accomplished?" Under the effect of the wine
Xuande said more than he meant to when he replied, "If I had a real base, these tedious
types would no longer vex me." Liu Biao made no response. Xuande realized his mistake.
Alleging intoxication, he rose and went back to the guesthouse. Many years later a poet
wrote of Xuande:

> Lord Cao named the rivals that he owned:
> "Inspector, you're the second of the realm!"
> But Xuande felt his sinews going slack—
> How could he keep the world of Han intact?

Liu Biao made no reply, but Xuande's last comment had perturbed him deeply. He
retired to the company of Lady Cai, who said to him, "I overheard Xuande just now. How
contemptuous he is! It's easy enough to see he means to have our province. Unless he is
eliminated now, there will be great trouble." Liu Biao, however, simply shook his head
and kept silent. Lady Cai secretly summoned Commander Cai Mao, and they discussed
the matter. "I could go to Xuande's lodging and kill him," Cai Mao suggested. "We
would report it to His Lordship afterward." Lady Cai agreed, and Cai Mao called up soldiers for the purpose that night.

Meanwhile, Xuande was sitting in his quarters in the candlelight. He was about to
retire, a little after the third watch, when someone knocked on his door and came in. It
was Yi Ji, the man who had warned him about the marked horse. He had learned of the
plot to kill Xuande and had come to inform him. He described Cai Mao's scheme and
urged Xuande to get away immediately. "How can I leave before saying a proper farewell
to Liu Biao?" Xuande asked. "If you wait for that, Cai Mao will get you, I know."
Xuande therefore bade Yi Ji a grateful good-bye, summoned his followers, and rode off
before daybreak. By the time Cai Mao had reached the guesthouse with his soldiers,
Xuande was back in Xinye. Vexed that Xuande had eluded him, Cai Mao inscribed a poem
on the wall of Xuande's room and then reported to Liu Biao, "Xuande intends to rebel.
He wrote a seditious poem on his wall and then departed without bidding you good-bye."
Liu Biao, unwilling to believe this tale, went to Xuande's room, where he found the following:

> So many years in hard adversity,
> Staring back at the same old hills and streams—
> In a pond no dragon's meant to lie;
> He'll ride the thunder to the sky!

The verse enraged Liu Biao; he drew his sword and swore, "I'll kill the faithless in-grate!" But he reconsidered almost at once. "In all our time together," Liu Biao mused, "I have never known him to compose poetry. Some outsider may well be trying to estrange us." Liu Biao walked slowly back into Xuande's room and scratched out the poem with the point of his sword; then he threw down the weapon and mounted his horse. "My men are all in readiness," Cai Mao said. "We should go straight to Xinye and arrest Xuande." "Don't be so impetuous," Liu Biao replied. "It will take careful planning."

Unable to provoke his lord to act, Cai Mao planned privately with Lady Cai to hold a grand feast in Xiangyang for all the officials and to use the occasion to kill Xuande. The next day Cai Mao petitioned Liu Biao: "Let us have a gathering of officials at Xiangyang to show our satisfaction over the excellent harvests of recent years. Would Your Lordship be willing to make the trip?" "My breathing ailment has been acting up of late," Liu Biao replied. "My two sons may serve in my stead." "I am afraid," Cai Mao responded, "they are too young to do justice to the ceremony." "Then invite Xuande to officiate," Liu Biao suggested. Secretly delighted that his plan was working, Cai Mao sent a messenger to Xinye to request Xuande's presence in Xiangyang.

Xuande had fled back to Xinye well aware of the danger his careless comments had placed him in. He kept his own counsel, however, until the unexpected invitation arrived. "My lord," Sun Qian said to him, "you came home so distracted, I feared something had happened in Jingzhou. Now this invitation . . . We must consider it carefully." Xuande then confided to his companions the events of the preceding day. "Elder brother," Lord Guan said, "you are being overly suspicious if you think you misspoke. Liu Biao[8] is not holding it against you. Why should you believe a stranger like Yi Ji? But if you refuse to go to nearby Xiangyang, you will arouse Liu Biao's suspicions." "I agree," Xuande said, but Zhang Fei objected. "There's no such thing as a good banquet or a good con-ference," he asserted flatly. "Better not go!" Zhao Zilong said, "I will take three hundred men to escort you and prevent anything from happening." "That would be best," Xuande decided.

Cai Mao received Xuande and Zhao Zilong outside of Xiangyang and showed himself both modest and attentive. Following Cai Mao were Liu Qi and Liu Zong, Liu Biao's two sons, leading a delegation of officers and officials. They greeted Xuande, who felt some-what reassured by the presence of the sons. He was taken to the guesthouse, and Zhao Zilong set up the guard. Fully armed, he never left Xuande's side.

Liu Qi said to Xuande, "My father suffers from a breathing ailment. It is difficult for him to move. He especially wanted you, uncle, to receive the guests and give sympathetic encouragement to the officials who guard and govern our districts." "For myself," Xuande replied, "I would never dare undertake it. But since my elder brother commands it, I dare not decline." The next day it was reported that official personnel from the forty-two counties of Jingzhou had arrived for the celebration.

Before the ceremonies, Cai Mao conferred with Kuai Yue. "Xuande," he said, "is a hero of our age, and shrewd as an owl. If he remains with us, it means trouble. But today we have the chance to get him out of the way." "Don't you think," Kuai Yue replied, "that would risk our losing popular support?" "I already have Protector Liu's secret in-struction on this," Cai Mao replied.[9] "In that case," Kuai Yue answered, "let's get ready." Cai Mao said, "The east gate leads to Xian Hill. My brother Cai He is guarding that road. Cai Zhong is outside the south gate, and Cai Xun by the north gate. There's no point in covering the west: that direction is cut off by the rapids of the River Tan. Even if Xuande had tens of thousands of men with him, he still couldn't get through." "What about Zhao Zilong? He never leaves Xuande's side," Kuai Yue asked. "I have five hundred men hidden in the city," Cai Mao replied. "Have Wen Ping and Wang Wei host a dinner for the military commanders in one of the outer rooms," Kuai Yue proposed, "and get Zhao Zilong to attend. That's when we'll do it." Cai Mao approved the plan. That day oxen and horses were slaughtered for the feast.

Xuande, riding the marked horse, arrived at the Xiangyang *yamen*, where attendants hitched his mount in a rear courtyard. The officials assembled in the main hall. Xuande took the host's seat with Liu Biao's sons on either side, and the guests were placed according to rank. Zhao Zilong, armed with a sword, stood beside Xuande. As arranged, Wen Ping and Wang Wei invited Zilong to the commanders' feast. Zilong declined at first, but Xuande told him to go. Meanwhile, Cai Mao had sealed the place as tight as an iron barrel and sent Xuande's three hundred guards to their quarters. He was waiting only for the company to mellow with drink before giving the signal to strike.

During the third round of wine Yi Ji raised his cup and approached Xuande. With a meaningful look in his eye, Yi Ji murmured, "Excuse yourself!" Xuande took the hint and went at once to the privy. Yi Ji drained his cup and rushed to the back courtyard. Catching up with Xuande, he whispered, "Cai Mao plans to kill you. Outside the wall, all routes to the east, the south, and the north are patrolled. The only way out is west. Get away at once." In high alarm Xuande untied his horse, pulled it through the courtyard gate, and vaulted into the saddle. Without giving a second thought to his escort, he fled by the western gate of Xiangyang. To the challenge of the gatekeepers he made no reply. He laid on the whip and dashed off. The guards could not check him, but they reported his flight at once, and Cai Mao pursued with five hundred men.

Xuande had traveled only a *li* or two when a river loomed before him several rods broad, its waves whipping. It was the Tan, a spur of the Xiang; Xuande rode to the bank. Seeing he could not get across, he turned back only to see dust clouds in the distance, west of the city: his pursuers would soon arrive. Thinking his time had come, he turned again to the river. Cai Mao's troops were already close behind. At his wit's end, he charged into the racing current. After a few paces the horse lost its footing. As they began to sink, Xuande's surcoat became soaked. Belaboring the horse, he shouted, "A jinxed horse, indeed! Today you have brought me misfortune." But the horse reared and, making thirty spans with every thrust, gained the opposite shore. Xuande emerged from the wild water as if from cloud and mist. This ballad by Su Dongpo in the old style sings of Xuande crossing the Tan:

> Late one spring day official service took me by the Tan:
> The sun was low; the blossoms newly down.
> I stopped the carriage and paced the bank, gazing across;
> Shreds of catkin, stirred by the wind, caught the sun.
> I saw in them the dying fire of Double Suns, [10]
> That time dragon battled dragon and tiger, tiger.

> At Xiangyang the guests of honor reveled,
> While Xuande, marked for death, made his escape.
> Out the western gate he rode,
> Reaching the rushing mistbound Tan
> Moments ahead of an angry cavalry—
> The rider's shout urged the *dilu* in.

The pounding hooves break up the glassy waves,
Under a golden whip flailed like Heaven's wind.
Behind, to hear the clamor of a thousand cavalry!
Amid the waves, to see those dragons rear:
The noble hero who would rule the west,
Borne (by some design) upon the dragon-steed.

And eastward race the currents of the Tan;
The dragon-steed, its master—whither gone?
By river's edge, heartsore, to sigh, to sigh. . . .
The last rays touch the hills, deserted, void.
Was it more than dream—that age of kingdoms three?
More than idle traces in our memory?[11]

   Looking back across the Tan, Xuande saw Cai Mao on the far bank. "My lord," Cai Mao shouted over, "why have you fled our feast?" "We were never enemies," Xuande answered back, "why do you want to kill me?" "I never meant to," Cai Mao responded. "You give too much credence, my lord, to others." But Xuande had noticed Cai Mao reaching for his bow and arrow, so he headed his horse southwest and rode off. "Sheer providence!" Cai Mao said to his followers. At that moment he saw Zhao Zilong and his three hundred fighters racing toward him. Indeed:

The river-vaulting steed had saved its master.
Would the oncoming tiger take revenge on Cai Mao?

What was Cai Mao's fate?
READ ON.

35

Xuande Encounters a Recluse in Nanzhang;
Shan Fu Finds a Hero-Lord in Xinye

CAI MAO WAS TURNING BACK to the city of Xiangyang as Zhao Zilong hastened toward him with the three hundred guards. Earlier, during the banquet arranged for the military commanders, Zilong had noticed the movement of the host's cavalry and went to check on Xuande. Unable to find Xuande in the main hall, he went to the guesthouse. There he was told that Cai Mao and a party of troops had ridden west. Zhao Zilong, spear in hand, hastened after him. Now meeting up with Cai Mao he demanded, "Where is my lord?" "Lord Liu," Cai Mao replied, "left the banquet. We do not know where he is."

Circumspect by nature, Zhao Zilong did nothing rash. He rode on to the river and stared across its swift flow. Where could his lord have gone? He confronted Cai Mao again. "Lord Liu was your guest," he said. "Why were you chasing him?" "We have officials from the forty-two counties of Jingzhou's nine districts meeting here," Cai Mao answered. "As senior commander I am responsible for the security of them all." "Where have you driven my lord?" Zhao Zilong pressed him. "I was told," Cai Mao said evenly, "that Lord Liu had left unattended through the west gate. I went to look but could not find him." Alarmed but uncertain, Zhao Zilong returned to the edge of the river. He spotted a watery trail on the opposite shore and mused, "Could he have made it over on the horse?"

An extensive search turned up no trace of Xuande. Cai Mao returned to the city, and Zhao Zilong pressed the gate guards for information. They confirmed that Xuande had left by the west gate at a gallop. Zhao Zilong decided it was too dangerous to reenter the city and led his men back to Xinye.[1]

• • • • •

Having vaulted the Tan, Xuande was dazed with excitement. "I couldn't have spanned that broad a stretch," he thought, "except by Heaven's will." He rode on toward Nanzhang by a winding path. In the setting sun he saw an ox drawing closer. On its back a cowherd blew on a flute. "Oh, for such a life!" Xuande said with a sigh. He held his horse and watched the lad bring the beast to a halt. The cowherd stopped piping and scrutinized Xuande. "You must be General Liu Xuande," he said, "who destroyed the Yellow Scarves!" Startled, Xuande replied, "How does a lad from this out-of-the-way village come to know my name?"

The youth replied, "Not from my own knowledge, of course. But when guests come and I attend my master, I often hear talk of Liu Xuande—over six spans tall, arms reaching past his knees, eyes that can almost see behind him—one of the heroes of the age! The description fits, so I think you must be the man." "And who is your master?" Xuande asked. "He has a double surname, Sima," the youth replied. "His given name is Hui, his style Decao. He comes from Yingchuan and answers to the Taoist name of Still Water."[2] Xuande inquired about the master's companions, and the boy answered, "His closest friends are Pang Degong and Pang Tong, uncle and nephew, from Xiangyang. Pang Degong is styled Shanmin; he's ten years older than my master. Pang Tong is styled Shiyuan; he is five years younger than my master. One day Pang Tong came by while my master was picking mulberry leaves, and they spent the whole day talking without tiring. My master has the greatest affection for Pang Tong and regards him as a younger brother." "And where is your master now?" Xuande inquired. Gesturing toward the woods, the lad said, "The farm is over there." Xuande finally acknowledged his identity and asked to be taken to Master Still Water.

The cowherd guided Xuande some two *li* to a farmstead, where they dismounted. Entering through the central gate, they heard a lute being played. Xuande listened attentively to the exquisite sounds and asked the boy to wait before announcing him. The notes stopped, however, and the lute was struck no more. A man came out, smiling as he said, "The harmonies of the lute were somber yet distinct. Suddenly, through the melody a proud, assertive tone surged up. Some noble hero must have come to listen unobtrusively." "This is my master," the lad said to Xuande. Xuande remarked that he had the configuration of a pine tree, the bone structure of a crane. His physique and his aura were utterly extraordinary. Flustered, Xuande came forward to offer a greeting. His war coat was still soaking.

"My good lord," Still Water said, "today it was your blessing to be spared calamity." Xuande was struck speechless. Still Water invited him into his thatched cottage, where they sat as host and guest. Xuande saw written scrolls heaped on the shelves; pine and bamboo flourished outside the window. The lute lay on a stone frame. The atmosphere was pure and euphoric. "What brings you here, my lord?" Still Water asked. "I happened to be passing through," Xuande replied, "and thanks to the boy's assistance I now have the satisfaction of being able to pay homage to your venerable self."

Still Water smiled and said, "There is nothing to conceal or evade. You seek refuge, surely." This comment led Xuande to recount the details of his escape. "I knew. The look on your face bespoke the circumstances," the recluse said, and went on to ask, "I have long been acquainted with your great name, illustrious sir. But why has fortune frowned on you?" "The road ordained for me," Xuande conceded, "has not been smooth. That's why I am where I am." "There may be a different reason," Still Water continued. "It seems to me, General, that you have not found the right men to assist you." Xuande replied, "I know that I myself am not particularly capable. But among my civil officials I have Sun Qian, Mi Zhu, and Jian Yong; and among my military officers Lord Guan, Zhang Fei, and Zhao Zilong. The unstinting loyalty of these men sustains me, and I rely on their support." "Each of the warriors, it is true," Still Water responded, "is a match for ten thousand. The pity is that you have no one to make good use of them. As for your civil officials, they are no more than pasty-faced bookworms, not of a caliber to unravel the complexities of the age and see our poor generation through these troubled times."

"Actually," Xuande confessed, "I have been anxious to find a worthy man who has absented himself from the world of men. But, alas, I have yet to encounter him." Still

Water replied, "You can't have forgotten Confucius' words: 'Even in a hamlet of ten households one is sure to find loyalty and good faith.' Do not despair of finding the man you seek." "I am dull and unobservant," Xuande said, "and would be grateful for your guidance." Still Water asked him, "Have you heard the jingle going around the Xiangyang area?

> In nine years' time things start to waste;
> In thirteen years there isn't a trace.
> Heaven sends things where they're due;
> The mudbound dragon mounts the blue.

The song originates from the early years of Jian An. In the eighth year the death of Governor Liu Biao's first wife gave rise to domestic turmoil. 'Things start to waste' refers to this. As for 'there isn't a trace,' Liu Biao will shortly pass away himself, and his officials and officers will scatter to the four winds. 'Heaven sends things where they're due' and 'The mudbound dragon mounts the blue' find their echo in you, General.''

Xuande was alarmed. "How dare I?" he protested. "Now," Still Water replied, "the most extraordinary talents of the empire are gathered here. You should seek them out." "Where?" Xuande asked eagerly. "Where are these extraordinary talents? And who are they?" "Sleeping Dragon, Young Phoenix," Still Water answered. "With either of them you could settle our unsettled realm." "But who are they?" Xuande asked again. Rubbing his palms, Still Water laughed out loud. "Good! Good!" he said. "Good! Good! But it grows late. You should stay the night. We can discuss it further tomorrow." So saying, he ordered his young attendant to see to the needs of man and horse.

After his dinner, Xuande was taken to a room adjoining the thatched cottage. He lay down but could not sleep for thinking of Still Water's words. The night wore on. He heard a man knock and enter his host's room. "Yuanzhi!" Still Water said, "what brings you?" Xuande sat up in bed, attentive. He heard the visitor say, "I have long heard that Liu Biao treats both the virtuous and the wicked as they deserve, and so I made a point of presenting myself to him. But I found his reputation false. He favored the virtuous all right, but he couldn't use them in government. And though he recognized the wicked for what they were, he couldn't get rid of them. So I took my leave by letter and came here." Still Water replied, "You have the ability to be a king's right-hand man and should be more selective about whom you serve. What's the use of lowering yourself to go before Liu Biao—especially now when we have a heroic contender and enterprising champion right here with us? You have only failed to spot him!" "What you say makes sense," the visitor answered. Listening with elation, Xuande surmised that the visitor must be Sleeping Dragon or Young Phoenix. But much as he wanted to show himself, he was reluctant to appear undignified and so waited until daybreak before going to see Still Water.

"Who came last night?" Xuande asked Still Water. "A friend of mine," was the reply. Xuande expressed his desire to meet him. "He seeks," Still Water explained, "to commit himself to an enlightened ruler and has already gone elsewhere." Xuande asked his name, but Still Water only smiled, saying, "Good, good. Good, good." "Sleeping Dragon, Young Phoenix—who are these men?" Xuande pressed him. But Still Water kept smiling as he repeated, "Good, good. Good, good." Xuande then appealed to the recluse to leave the hills and join him in upholding the house of Han. But Still Water demurred. "Carefree recluses like me," he said, "are not fit to serve the world. There are men ten times my superior to aid you; you should take yourself to them."

While Xuande and Still Water were speaking, they heard noise and commotion out-side. A commander had ridden up with several hundred men. Xuande rushed out and was delighted to find Zhao Zilong. Dismounting, Zilong said, "Last night I went back to Xiangyang, but you were not there, so I tracked you here. My lord, you are needed at Xinye. Fighting could break out there anytime." Bidding Still Water good-bye, Xuande rode off with Zhao Zilong. En route they met Lord Guan and Zhang Fei. It was a joyful reunion. Xuande astonished everyone by describing how he had crossed the Tan.

Xuande reached Xinye county and took counsel with his advisers. Sun Qian said, "Be-fore anything else, Liu Biao must be informed of the recent events." Xuande thus sent Sun Qian with a letter to the governor. Liu Biao called Sun Qian before him and said, "I invited Xuande to preside over the provincial assembly in Xiangyang. What made him depart so unceremoniously?" Sun Qian handed him Xuande's letter detailing Cai Mao's attempt on his life and his escape over the Tan. The governor was outraged. He sum-moned Cai Mao, castigated him for threatening Xuande, and ordered him beheaded. Even Lady Cai's tearful pleas for mercy failed to temper the governor's wrath. But when Sun Qian argued, "If you kill Cai Mao, Imperial Uncle Liu will not be safe here," Liu Biao decided to release Cai Mao after further reproof. He also sent his older son, Liu Qi, back with Sun Qian to extend his personal apologies to Xuande.

At Xinye, Xuande received Liu Qi and prepared a banquet in his honor. As the wine mellowed them, Liu Qi began to weep. Xuande asked the reason. "Since she became my stepmother," the youth began, "Lady Cai has been intent on eliminating me—and I have no way to escape her. I would be most grateful for your advice, uncle." Xuande urged him to remain circumspect and scrupulously filial, and assured him no calamity would ensue. The next day Liu Qi bid Xuande a tearful farewell. Escorting the youth past the city wall, Xuande pointed to his own horse and said, "If not for him, I would have been a man of the netherworld."[3] "It was not the horse, uncle," Liu Qi responded, "rather your great good fortune." Thus they parted. Liu Qi was inconsolable.

Back in Xinye, Xuande rode through the market and saw a man in a linen scarf and plain cloth robe, black belt and black footgear, crooning as he approached Xuande:

> Heaven and earth are topsy and turvy, O!
> The "fire" is growing cold.
> A stately hall is coming down, O!
> It's hard for one beam to hold.
> But away in the valleys are worthy men, O!
> Who long for a lord to whom to repair.
> And though that lord is seeking the men, O!
> Of me he is all unaware!

Xuande heard the song and thought, "This must be one of the men Still Water spoke of—Sleeping Dragon or Young Phoenix." He got down and addressed the singer, inviting him into the county office. Xuande asked his name. "My surname is Shan, given name Fu; I am from Yingchuan," was the answer. "I have always thought Your Lordship hos-pitable to worthy men and have been hoping to enter your service. But rather than ap-proach you too directly, I decided to catch your attention by singing in the marketplace."

Delighted, Xuande treated Shan Fu as a guest of honor. "Could I have another look at your horse?" Shan Fu said. Xuande had it led unsaddled before the building. "Isn't he the *dilu*, the marked horse?" he inquired. "He may have phenomenal powers, but he will bring his master misfortune. Do not ride him." "But he has discharged his sign," Xuande said, and he related his crossing of the Tan. "Indeed," Shan Fu said, "that time the animal saved its master instead of ruining him. But in the end the horse will ruin *a* master—though I have a scheme for avoiding it." "I would like to hear it," Xuande said.

"If you have an enemy," Shan Fu continued, "give him the horse as a gift. Wait until its curse is spent upon that man, and then you can ride it without incident." Xuande turned color. "Sir!" he cried. "You come to me for the first time, and instead of advising me to be just and fair would have me harm another for my own gain. Excuse me if I decline to hear such advice." With a smile Shan Fu apologized. "Everyone," he explained, "holds Your Lordship to be humane and virtuous. But how could I simply accept the common view? I've used this idea to test you, that's all." Xuande's expression relaxed, and he too rose to apologize. "What humanity or virtue have I to benefit others?" he asked. "It is for you, good master, to show me." "When I arrived here," Shan Fu said, "I heard people in Xinye singing, 'Since Imperial Uncle Liu took Xinye in his care, / The people roundabout have enough and to spare!' This shows how Your Lordship's humane virtue has benefited the populace." After this, Xuande appointed Shan Fu director general and had him reorganize and train the army.

•   •   •   •   •

Cao Cao, since returning to the capital, had been determined to take Jingzhou, Liu Biao's province. For this purpose he assigned Cao Ren, Li Dian, and the recently surrendered generals Lü Kuang and Lü Xiang to assemble thirty thousand soldiers in the city of Fan. In Fan, Cao's generals, probing strengths and weaknesses, threatened the capital of Jingzhou, Xiangyang. The Lü brothers petitioned Cao Ren: "Xuande is now stationed at Xinye. He recruits troops and purchases horses, accumulates fodder and stores grain. His ambitions are not petty. You had better prepare your moves against him in good time. We two, since submitting to the prime minister, have achieved nothing. Grant us five thousand crack troops, and we will present Xuande's head to Your Excellency." Cao Ren agreed with pleasure, and the two generals marched their unit to Xinye to commence hostilities.

Spies rushed word to Xuande, who consulted Shan Fu. "They must not enter our territory," he advised. "Send Lord Guan with a company to meet their center from the left; Zhang Fei, to the right to meet their rear; and you, my lord, together with Zhao Zilong, will receive their vanguard. This way the enemy can be defeated." Xuande adopted Shan Fu's plan. He dispatched his two brothers to intercept Cao Ren's force; then, joined by Shan Fu and Zhao Zilong, he led two thousand men beyond his defense barrier to meet the attack.

Xuande had hardly advanced a few *li* when, lo, he saw dust rising behind the hills. Lü Kuang and Lü Xiang were drawing near. The two sides secured their flanks. Xuande emerged mounted from his bannered entrance and shouted out, "Who dares breach our boundary?" Lü Kuang rode forward to reply. "I am General Lü Kuang," he cried. "I bear the prime minister's mandate to seize you." With fierce determination Xuande ordered Zhao Zilong into battle. The two warriors closed in combat, and before many passages Zhao Zilong had unhorsed his man with a fatal spear thrust. Xuande motioned his forces to charge.

Unable to hold his ground, Lü Xiang drew back and fled; but Lord Guan's company attacked the retreating unit. After a short period of clash and slaughter, the bulk of Lü Xiang's unit was wiped out. He managed to flee, but he had hardly made ten *li* when another force blocked his path. The leader hoisted his lance and shouted, "Meet Zhang

Fei!" He took Lü Xiang at spearpoint, thrust him through, and overturned him under his horse. The rest of the enemy scattered. The units of the three brothers now combined and gave chase, capturing a great number. Afterward, Xuande withdrew to Xinye, where he feasted Shan Fu and rewarded the three contingents.

The report of the battle appalled Cao Ren. Li Dian said to him, "Our generals were killed because they took the enemy too lightly. All we can do now is hold our forces in place while we petition the prime minister for enough soldiers to wipe them out. That's the best strategy." "Not at all," Cao Ren countered. "In a single clash we have lost two commanders and a good number of men to boot. Reprisal must be swift. For a 'bowshot' of a place like Xinye, should we be troubling the prime minster?" Li Dian warned, "Xuande is a champion warrior. Do not underrate him." "Losing your nerve?" Cao Ren asked pointedly. "The rules of war," Li Dian retorted, "tell us that if you 'know the other side and know your own, then in a hundred battles, a hundred victories.' It's not that I'm losing my nerve but that victory is uncertain." "Perhaps it's your loyalty that's uncertain," Cao Ren shot back irritably. "I am going to take Xuande alive!" "If you go, " Li Dian said, "I will guard Fan." "If you refuse to go with me," Cao Ren said with finality, "your disloyalty is certain!" Li Dian had no alternative. Together they mustered twenty-five thousand, crossed the River Yu, and made for Xinye. Indeed:

> Lieutenants dishonored, corpses carted home;
> The general raises troops again to take revenge.[4]

Which side would prevail?

READ ON.

36

Xuande Surprises the Town of Fan;
Shan Fu Recommends Zhuge Liang

THAT NIGHT CAO REN STRUCK OUT across the River Yu in full force, determined to trample Xinye flat. Meanwhile, back in Xinye after the victory, Shan Fu warned Xuande, "Cao Ren is stationed at Fan. He knows the fate of his two commanders and is sure to attack in full force." Xuande asked him the best defense. "If Cao Ren comes," Shan Fu replied, "Fan will be vulnerable to capture." Asked for specific tactics, Shan Fu whispered certain things, to the delight of Xuande, who proceeded to make the suggested preparations.

Soon the outposts reported the attack Shan Fu had predicted. Xuande, following his adviser's counsel, put his forces into the field against Cao Ren. The opposed ranks were drawn up. Zhao Zilong issued the challenge to the enemy commanders. Cao Ren ordered Li Dian forth from the line to begin combat. Zhao Zilong and Li Dian crossed weapons several times. Li Dian saw he was no match for Zhao Zilong and wheeled back to his line. Zhao Zilong charged after him but was stopped by sustained volleys of arrows from both enemy wings. The two combatants returned to their camps.

Li Dian said to Cao Ren, "They have a crack company, one to be reckoned with. We would do better to return to Fan." "You!" Cao Ren hissed. "Even before the battle you were undermining morale. And we should have your head for that half-hearted performance in the field." Only the strenuous appeals of the asssembled commanders prevented Cao Ren from executing Li Dian. Cao Ren took over command of the vanguard and assigned Li Dian to the rear. The next day he advanced with the beating of drums, and deployed before Xinye. He sent a messenger to Xuande to ask if he recognized the formation he was using.

Shan Fu surveyed the enemy from an elevation and told Xuande: "They are using the formation called 'Eight Gates to Impregnable Positions.' The first gate is Desist; the second, Survive; the third, Injure; the fourth, Confound; the fifth, Exhibit; the sixth, Perish; the seventh, Surprise; and the eighth, Liberate. If you can enter through Survive, Exhibit, or Liberate, things will go in your favor. If you take Injure, Surprise, or Desist, you will suffer casualties. If you take Confound or Perish, you are doomed. These 'gates,' or points of articulation between units, are deployed perfectly, and yet the central mainstay or axis is missing. Surprise them at Survive from the southeast corner, move due west and out at Exhibit, and their ranks will be dislocated."

Xuande ordered his men to defend both ends of their advanced position and commanded Zhao Zilong to take five hundred men and do as Shan Fu had advised. Spear high, Zhao Zilong cut his way in, his horse leaping and thrusting, his men howling and yelling. Cao Ren retreated north. Instead of pursuing, Zhao Zilong burst through the west gate and swung round to the southeast again, throwing Cao Ren's forces into disarray. Xuande signaled his men to redouble their blows upon the foe, and Cao Ren fled the field in utter defeat. Shan Fu called off the action and recalled his contingents.

Cao Ren, who was beginning to see the merit of Li Dian's caution, said to him, "Someone very, very capable is in Xuande's army. My formations were completely destroyed." "While we are here," Li Dian responded, "I am worried about Fan." "Tonight then," Cao Ren said, "we'll raid their camp. If we succeed, we can take the next step. If not, we return to Fan." "It won't work," Li Dian said. "Xuande is sure to be ready for that." "How can we wage war without taking chances?" Cao Ren cried in exasperation. Ignoring Li Dian's advice, he took command of the vanguard, had Li Dian reinforce him, and marched to Xuande's camp that same night. It was the second watch.

Xuande and Shan Fu had been discussing the course of the battle when the seasonal northeast wind that visits the area began blowing up. "Cao Ren should strike tonight," Shan Fu predicted, "but we will be ready." Quietly he put his defense in place. By the second watch Cao Ren's men were nearing Xuande's camp. They found it surrounded by flames. The enclosing palisade had been set afire. "They were waiting for us!" Cao Ren thought. At once he ordered a retreat, but Zhao Zilong struck before the retreat could be effected. Cao Ren fled north to the river where he searched for boats; another contingent, led by Zhang Fei, confronted him. After hard fighting with Li Dian protecting him, Cao Ren managed to ferry himself across the river; most of his men drowned. He returned to Fan and called at the gate, but a barrage of drumming greeted him. A general came forward and shouted, "I took Fan long ago!" Cao Ren's brigade looked in awe at the general. It was Lord Guan. Cao Ren fled in fright, losing more men to Lord Guan's pursuing warriors, until he had made his way back to the capital, Xuchang. On the way, however, Cao Ren had discovered the identity of Xuande's new military adviser.

Xuande's victory was complete. Entering Fan, he was welcomed by Liu Mi of Changsha, the prefect of the county. Like Xuande, Liu Mi was an imperial kinsman. After the populace had been reassured, Liu Mi invited Xuande to his home and feasted with him. There Xuande noticed a pleasing youth with dignified deportment standing to the side. He asked the host who it was. "A nephew, Kou Feng," Liu Mi replied, "son of Kou, lord of Luo. He became our ward when his parents died." Xuande took a great liking to the lad and wished to adopt him. Liu Mi eagerly agreed. He had Kou Feng honor Xuande as his father and had the youth's name changed to Liu Feng. Xuande brought Liu Feng back from the feast and bid him honor Lord Guan and Zhang Fei as uncles. But Lord Guan said, "Elder brother, you already have a son of your own. What use do you have for another's? It will lead to trouble." "If I treat him as my son," Xuande insisted, "he will serve me as his father. What trouble can there be?" This answer left Lord Guan sulking.[1] Xuande turned to the problems of tactics. On Shan Fu's advice he returned to Xinye, ordering Zhao Zilong to guard Fan with a force of one thousand.

·   ·   ·   ·   ·

In the capital Cao Ren and Li Dian prostrated themselves tearfully before Prime Minister Cao Cao and confessed their failure. "A soldier must take the fortunes of war in his stride," Cao Cao said. "But I wonder who drafted the plans for Liu Bei." Cao Ren mentioned the name he had heard on the way home. "Shan Fu?" Cao Cao asked. "Who is he?"[2] Cheng Yu smiled and answered, "That's not his real name. In his youth he was an expert swordsman. Then, sometime toward the end of Emperor Ling's reign, he killed a man to avenge an injustice—and became a disguised fugitive. When he was finally apprehended, he refused to identify himself. The officers paraded him through the market area tied up on a cart. They beat the drums to collect a crowd, hoping someone would name him. But even those who did recognize the man would not speak up. Soon his comrades quietly freed him. He fled again, changed his name, and resolved to lead a scholar's life. He has paid his respects to all the well-known teachers and masters in our area and has studied with Sima Hui too. His real name is Xu Shu, and he's originally from Yingchuan. His style is Yuanzhi. Shan Fu is an assumed name."

Cao Cao asked Cheng Yu, "How does Shan Fu's ability compare with yours?" "Ten times greater," was the reply. "It is most unfortunate," Cao Cao said, "that Xuande is winning the loyalty of worthy and capable men. His wings are fully formed. What can we do?" "Although Shan Fu is with the other side," Cheng Yu said, "if Your Excellency is determined to have him serve you, there is an easy way to do it." "How can we win him over?" Cao Cao asked. "He is devoted to his mother," Cheng Yu replied, "his father having died when he was young. She is all he has. His brother Kang is also dead, so there is no one else to look after her. If you can entice his mother here and induce her to write Shan Fu to join her, he cannot refuse." Cao Cao was delighted with Cheng Yu's advice.

Shan Fu's mother, Madame Xu, was brought to the capital and treated royally. Cao Cao said to her, "They say your excellent son, Yuanzhi, is actually one of the extraordinary talents of the empire. Now he is in Xinye assisting the disobedient subject Liu Bei in his revolt against the court. For so precious a jewel to fall in the muck is truly regrettable. We would prevail upon you to write and call him back to the capital. I will guarantee him before the Emperor, who will reward him amply." Cao Cao ordered writing instruments brought.

"What manner of man is Liu Bei?" the matron asked. "A low-class sort, once based in Xiaopei," Cao Cao replied. "He makes preposterous claims to being an imperial uncle and is utterly without credibility or righteous commitment. He is a perfect example of 'a noble man on the outside, a base man within.'" Madame Xu reacted sharply to this indictment. "You!" she cried harshly. "What fraud and fabrication! I have long known Xuande to be a descendant of Prince Jing of Zhongshan, the great-great-grandson of Emperor Jing the Filial. Xuande is a man who humbles himself before men of ability and treats others with self-effacing respect. And he is renowned for his humanity. Why, callow youths and grey old men, herdsmen and wood-gatherers all know his name. He is one of the true heroes of our age. And if my son serves him, then he has found himself the right master. As for you, though you claim the name of prime minister to the Han, you are in reality a traitor who perversely takes Xuande to be the 'disobedient subject,' and would have my son forsake the light and elect the dark. Where is your shame?"

With that, Madame Xu struck Cao Cao with an inkstone. In a fury Cao Cao ordered armed guards to march the matron out and behead her. But Cheng Yu intervened. "The woman," he said, "antagonized you *in order* to die. If you kill her, you will earn yourself a vicious name even as you confirm her virtue; and once she is dead, Shan Fu[3] will commit himself to assisting Liu Bei avenge his mother. But if you detain her, the son's body will be in one place, his heart in another. That way, even if he remains with Liu Bei, he will not give his utmost. Furthermore, if we keep the woman alive, I think I can induce Shan Fu to come here and serve Your Excellency." Cao Cao concurred and spared the woman.

Madame Xu was held in custody and cared for. Cheng Yu visited her regularly and, pretending he had once sealed a pact of brotherhood with her son, attended her solicitously, as if she were his own mother. Cheng Yu honored her with gifts, always including

a personal note, and the matron would answer in her own hand. Having coaxed these
samples of her script out of her, Cheng Yu proceeded to imitate it. He then forged a letter
and had a henchman carry it to Xinye. A guard brought the messenger to Shan Fu, who,
knowing there was a letter from his mother, immediately received him. The messenger
said, "I am a house servant. Your mother sent me with this." The letter read:

> The recent death of your younger brother has left me with no other kin save you.
> In the midst of my sorrow and isolation, I never dreamed His Excellency Cao
> would lure me to the capital to denounce your betrayal and to put me in chains.
> My life has been spared only through Cheng Yu. If you surrender, I will be saved.
> When you read this, do not forget the hardships your mother endured to raise
> you. Come with all speed to fulfill your duty as a filial son. Afterward, we will
> bide our time until we can go home and tend our garden. That way we will avoid
> calamity. My life hangs by a thread. You are my sole hope of salvation. Need I
> implore further?

Tears flooded Shan Fu's eyes as he read the letter. He went to Xuande to acknowledge
his identity and explain his intentions. "At the beginning," Shan Fu said, "I went to
Governor Liu Biao, impressed by his reputation for welcoming men of learning. But in
advising him, I soon discovered how unfit he was. I took my leave by letter, went to the
farm of Still Water, and told him all that had happened. He took me to task for not recognizing my true lord, and then urged me to serve you.[4] I put on that mad show in the
market to attract Your Lordship's interest. I was favored by your gracious invitation
and given grave responsibilities. But what am I to do now that my mother has been
tricked and taken by Cao and threatened with harm? She has written herself summoning
me, and I cannot fail her. It is not that I am loath to toil for Your Lordship to repay your
confidence in me, but with my dear mother in his hands I would not be able to give
your cause my best. Permit me therefore to announce my departure. Surely we shall find
a way to meet again."

Xuande cried out at these words, but then he said, "Mother and son are nature's near-
est kin. You need not give further thought to me. I can wait until you have been reunited
with your mother for another opportunity to profit from your instruction." Shan Fu
prostrated himself in gratitude and begged permission to leave. Xuande prevailed upon
him not to leave at once but to remain the night for a final farewell dinner.[5]

Sun Qian took Xuande aside and said, "This extraordinary genius is thoroughly familiar by now with our military situation. If you let him go, they will use him at the
highest level, and we will suffer for it. Try your utmost, my lord, to get him to stay—
then Cao Cao will execute his mother, and to avenge her Shan Fu will fight all the more
fiercely against Cao Cao." But Xuande replied, "That I cannot do. It would be inhumane
to let them kill the mother so that we can use the son. It would be unjust and dishonorable to hold him against his will and keep mother and son apart. I would rather die
first." Xuande's firmness moved all who heard of it.

Xuande invited Shan Fu to drink. But Shan Fu said, "Knowing my mother is imprisoned, I could not swallow the most precious potion, the most exquisite liquor." "When
you said you were leaving," Xuande declared, "I felt as if I were losing my very hands.
The rarest delicacies will seem tasteless to me." The two men faced one another and wept,
then they sat down to await the dawn. Xuande's commanders had already arranged the
farewell banquet outside the walls of Xinye. Afterward, Xuande and Shan Fu rode out
of the city side by side. Reaching a pavilion, they dismounted and prepared to part.

Xuande, proposing a last toast, said, "My meagre lot, my paltry destiny keep us from remaining together. I hope you will serve your new master well and gain recognition for your merits."

Weeping freely, Shan Fu said, "Despite my insignificant talent and superficial knowledge, Your Lordship charged me with the gravest responsibilities. Now on my mother's account I have to leave, though our task remains incomplete. But no matter how Cao Cao pressures me, I will not propose a single strategy for him to my dying day." "Once you have gone, master," Xuande said, "I intend to withdraw to the mountain forest." "When I laid plans with Your Lordship for the royal cause," Shan Fu went on, "my meagre intelligence was all I had to count on. But now, because of my mother, I cannot think clearly. Even were I to remain, I would be of no use. My lord would do well to seek elsewhere some high-minded worthy to support and assist you in your great enterprise. You must not lose heart like this."

"Not one of the worthy men of our age," Xuande said, "surpasses you." "How can my useless, commonplace qualities deserve such high praise?" Shan Fu asked. Then, on the verge of parting, Shan Fu turned to the commanders and said, "It is my earnest wish that you all continue to serve our lord well. Leave behind a record of worthy deeds and shun my example of failing to finish what I have begun." The commanders grieved.

Xuande could not bring himself to say good-bye and saw him off one stage farther, then another stage. "You should not take the trouble to escort me so far," Shan Fu said. "Here I bid you farewell." Xuande took Shan Fu's hand. "Now we part," Xuande said, "to go to different worlds.[6] Who knows when we may meet again?" Xuande's tears fell like rain. Shan Fu, too, wept as he parted from his lord. Xuande poised his horse at the forest's edge, watching Shan Fu and his attendants race into the woods. "Gone!" Xuande cried. "What will become of me now?" Through blurry eyes he gazed into the distance, but a clump of trees blocked his line of vision. "I want those trees cut down," he shouted, "so I can see Shan Fu once again!"

At that very moment Shan Fu reappeared, whipping his horse to a gallop. "He's coming back! Can he have changed his mind?" Xuande cried and eagerly rode out to meet him. "Good sir," Xuande addressed him, "can it be that you are not leaving after all?" Shan Fu reined in and said, "My emotions were so conflicted, I forgot one thing. There is an extraordinary scholar in this area, in Longzhong, barely twenty *li* from Xiangyang. Your Lordship should seek him out." "Dare I trouble you to request that he come to see me?" Xuande inquired. "It would not be appropriate to send for him," Shan Fu replied. "Go to him in person, my lord. If you gain his services, it will be like the Zhou dynasty's winning Lü Wang, or the Han's winning Zhang Liang."[7]

Xuande asked Shan Fu, "Compared to yours, sir, what are his talents like?" "To compare him to someone like me," Shan Fu answered, "would be like comparing the fabled unicorn to a dray, a peafowl to a crow. He is in the habit of likening himself to Guan Zhong and Yue Yi—but he surpasses them in my view,[8] for he is perhaps the one man in the empire who can plot the interaction of the heavens and the earth." "I would hear his name," Xuande said. "He is from Yangdu in Langye," Shan Fu replied, "and bears the double surname Zhuge. His given name is Liang; his style, Kongming. He is a descendant of Zhuge Feng, former commander of the Capital Districts. His father, Zhuge Gui (styled Zigong), was a governor's deputy in Taishan district. Zhuge Gui died young, leaving Liang in the care of his younger brother Xuan. Zhuge Xuan, Liang's uncle, was a long-standing friend of Liu Biao, protector of Jingzhou. That is why they made their home in Xiangyang, under Liu Biao's protection. After Zhuge Xuan died, Liang and his younger brother Jun worked on the family's farm in Nanyang. Liang enjoyed chanting the Liangfu elegies.[9] Where they lived there was a stretch of hills known as Sleeping Dragon Ridge; he took the sobriquet Master Sleeping Dragon from that. His talents are indeed transcendent. Your Lordship, ignore his low estate and visit him—the sooner the better, for if he is willing to assist you, you need have no fear for the stability of the empire.''

Xuande said to Shan Fu, ''Master Still Water once said to me, 'If either Sleeping Dragon or Young Phoenix will help you, you can reestablish order in the realm.' Could the man you speak of be one of the two?'' ''Young Phoenix,'' Shan Fu replied, ''is Pang Tong of Xiangyang. Sleeping Dragon is none other than Zhuge Liang—Kongming.'' In his excitement Xuande leaped up and cried, ''Now I know what Still Water meant. These great men are before my very eyes. But for you, I should have remained blind to them.'' A later poet left these lines commemorating the moment Shan Fu recommended Zhuge Liang:[10]

> To part for aye made Xuande sore with grief.
> At road's fork they stopped; in each emotions deep.
> A word is dropped, like thunder's boom in spring,
> Rousing the dragon sleeping in Nanyang.

Having imparted Kongming's name, Shan Fu once again took leave. Xuande, now awakened to the meaning of Still Water's words, led his men back to Xinye to prepare gifts to take to Kongming in Nanyang.[11]

On the road, Shan Fu was moved by his lord's love and his unwillingness to say goodbye, but he began to wonder if Kongming would actually be willing to leave the hills and help guide Xuande's course. Before going to Cao Cao, therefore, Shan Fu rode straight to the young recluse in his thatched hut. Kongming asked his purpose in coming. ''My wish,'' Shan Fu said, ''was to serve Protector Liu,[12] but Cao Cao seized my mother, and she has written summoning me. What choice do I have? I'm on my way to her now. Just before leaving, I recommended you to Xuande; he should be coming to pay his respects. I hope you will not deny him, but will put at his disposal those great abilities you have always shown. It would be a blessing for us all.''

Kongming was annoyed. ''And you mean to make *me* the victim of this sacrifice?'' he said, and with a flick of his sleeves retired. Shan Fu retreated in embarrassment and resumed his journey. Indeed:

> Out of love for his lord, Shan Fu appealed to a friend;
> Out of love for his mother, he was homeward bound again.

What would the outcome be?

READ ON.

37

Still Water Recommends Another Noted Scholar;
Liu Xuande Pays Three Visits to Zhuge Liang

RIDING AT BREAKNECK SPEED, SHAN FU reached the capital. Informed of his arrival, Cao Cao had Xun Wenruo, Cheng Yu, and other advisers greet him at the city gate. From there Shan Fu went to the minsterial residence and paid his respects to Cao Cao. Cao Cao said to him, "How could so noble and enlightened a scholar as you, sir, lower himself to serve Liu Bei?" "In my youth," Shan Fu responded, "I fled my village and drifted through all sorts of places. Chance brought me to Xinye, where I formed a strong friendship with Xuande. But since my mother is here now in your care, I feel overcome with shame and gratitude." "Now that you are here," the prime minister said, "you will be able to tend and care for your honorable mother at dawn and at dusk as ritual prescribes. And I, too, perhaps may benefit from your superior learning." Shan Fu expressed his thanks and withdrew to his mother's chamber.

Shan Fu prostrated himself tearfully before his mother. "What brings *you* here?" she exclaimed in amazement. "I was in the service of Liu Xuande," he explained, "when your letter came. I rushed here at once." Mother Xu exploded in fury, swearing as she struck the table. "You disgraceful son," she shouted, "flitting hither and thither for so many years. I thought you were finally making progress with your studies. Now you've ended up worse than you started out![1] As a scholar, you should be aware that loyalty and filial devotion may conflict. How could you have failed to see Cao Cao for what he is—a traitor who has abused and ruined his sovereign—while Liu Xuande is widely known for humanity and righteousness? Moreover, he is a scion of the royal house. You had found yourself a proper master, but trusting a forged scrap of paper, which you never bothered to verify, you left the light for the dark and have earned yourself a name beneath contempt. Oh, you utter fool! With what kind of self-respect am I supposed to welcome you, now that you have shamed the spirit of your ancestors and uselessly wasted your own life?"

During his mother's tirade Shan Fu cowered on the ground, hands clasped over his head, not daring to look up. Suddenly, she turned and vanished behind a screen. Moments later a house servant appeared and called out, "The lady has hanged herself from the beams!" Beside himself, Shan Fu rushed to her, but her breath had ceased. Later someone wrote "In Praise of Mother Xu":[2]

> Mother's Xu's integrity
> Will savor for eternity.

She kept her honor free of stain,
A credit to her family's name.
A model lesson for her son,
No grief or hardship would she shun.
An aura like a sacred hill,
Allegiance sprung from depth of will.
For Xuande, words of approbation,
For Cao Cao, utter condemnation.
Boiling oil or scalding water,
Knife or axe could not deter her.
Then, lest Shan Fu shame his forebears,
She joined the ranks of martyred mothers.
In life, her proper designation;
In death, her proper destination.
Mother Xu's integrity
Will savor for eternity.

Seeing his mother dead, Shan Fu lay broken on the ground. Much time passed before he recovered. Cao Cao sent him ritual gifts of condolence and personally attended the sacrificial ceremonies. The coffin was interred in the high ground south of the capital. Shan Fu fulfilled the mourning and guarded the grave site. Everything that Cao Cao proffered he declined.

At this time Cao Cao was considering a southern expedition. But Xun Wenruo warned, "Winter is no time for that. After the spring thaw we can make an all-out attack." Cao Cao agreed. He then diverted water from the River Zhang to make a lake for naval training for the attack on the south. The lake was called the Pool of the Dark Tortoise.[3]

•   •   •   •   •

As Liu Xuande was preparing gifts for his visit to Kongming in Longzhong, the arrival was announced of an unusual-looking Taoist with a tall hat and broad sash. "Why, this must be Kongming himself!" Xuande said and attired himself formally to welcome him. It turned out, however, to be Still Water. Delighted, Xuande took him into his private quarters and led him to the seat of honor. Xuande said, "Since leaving your saintly presence, I have been beset by military concerns and thus failed to pay a courtesy call. Now I am honored by this visit, which gratifies my deeply felt longing and admiration." "I had heard," Still Water replied, "that Shan Fu was here and came especially to see him." "He went to the capital," Xuande explained, "in response to an appeal from his mother, whom Cao Cao had jailed."

"So he fell for the ruse!" Still Water said. "Mother Xu is known for her absolute integrity. Even if Cao imprisoned her, she would never agree to call for her son. The letter has got to be a forgery. By not going he could have saved her; his going dooms her." Agitated, Xuande asked for an explanation. "She lives according to the highest ethic," Still Water said, "and would be ashamed for her son." "As he was leaving," Xuande said, "he recommended Zhuge Kongming of Nanyang. What do you know about him?" "If Shan Fu had to leave, he had to leave," Still Water replied. "But why did he have to drag Kongming into this to sweat out his heart's blood?" "What do you mean by that, good master?" Xuande asked.

Still Water said, "Kongming befriended Shan Fu and three others: Cui Zhouping of Boling, Shi Guangyuan of Yingchuan, and Meng Gongwei of Runan. These four dedicated themselves to esoteric rituals of spiritual refinement. Kongming, however, was the only one who contemplated the doctrine in its entirety. Once while sitting embracing his knees and chanting in prolonged tones he remarked to his three friends: 'In official service any of you might advance to inspector or governor.' But when they asked what ambitions he had, he only smiled. He was wont to liken himself to Guan Zhong and Yue Yi. His ability is beyond measuring." "I wonder," Xuande commented, "why the Yingchuan area has produced so many great men." "Long ago," Still Water replied, "Yin Kui, a skilled observer of the constellations, remarked that with so many stars congregated in its part of the sky, the district was sure to have many worthy men."

Lord Guan, who had been listening to this conversation, interjected, "To my knowledge Guan Zhong and Yue Yi were outstanding figures of the Spring and Autumn and Warring States periods, men whose merit overarched the realm. Is it not presumptuous for Kongming to compare himself to them?"[4] "To my mind," Still Water replied smiling, "he might rather be compared to Jiang Ziya, who helped found the eight-hundred-year Zhou dynasty, or Zhang Liang, whose advice was responsible for the Han's four hundred years of glory." This praise left all hearers astonished. Still Water then took his leave, declining Xuande's invitation to stay. But on reaching the gate, he gazed upward and laughed aloud, "Sleeping Dragon has found his lord but not his time. A pity!" So saying, he was gone like a breeze. "Truly a recluse of great worth," Xuande said with a sigh.

The next day Xuande, Lord Guan, and Zhang Fei went to Longzhong. On the hills men were carrying mattocks to their acres, singing:

> The sky's a curving vault of blue,
> The level earth a chessboard,
> Where men their black and white divide,
> Disgrace or glory to decide.
>
> For the winners, peace and comfort,
> For the losers, tiring toil.
> In Nanyang someone lies secluded,
> Securely sleeping. Stay abed!

Xuande reined in and asked who had composed the song. "Why, Master Sleeping Dragon," was the reply. "Where does he live?" Xuande asked. A farmer answered, "A short way south runs a high ridge called Sleeping Dragon Ridge. In front is a thin wood where you'll find the little thatched lodge that he's made his refuge." Xuande thanked the man and rode on. Soon the ridge came into view. It was a soothing scene of extraordinary peace, as depicted in this old-style ballad:

> West of Xiangyang county twenty *li*,
> A rising ridge leans over a flowing stream.
> The twisting, turning ridge bears heavy clouds;
> The frothing, churning stream is liquid jade.
> Caught between the rocks, this dragon winds;
> Shadowed by the pines, this phoenix hides.
> A wattle gate half-screens a thatched retreat:
> Undisturbed, the recluse rests within.

The bamboo forms a veil of green outside,
Where year-round hedgerows exhale flowery scents.
Learned works are piled around his bed;
No common men have come before his seat.
Now and then a gibbon taps to offer fruit;
A crane, his gateguard, attends his nightly chants.
A brocade sack contains the precious lute;
The seven-star sword is hung upon the wall.
In this refined seclusion the master waits
And works his acres in his leisure hour,
Until spring thunder starts him from his dream
To calm the kingdom with one impassioned cry.

Xuande arrived at the farmstead and knocked at the brushwood gate. A lad answered the door and asked his name. "General of the Left under the Han," Xuande declared, "Lord of Yicheng Precinct, Protector of Yuzhou, Imperial Uncle Liu Bei comes to pay his respects to your master." "Too many names to remember," said the youth. "Just say Liu Bei is paying a call," Xuande urged him. "My master," the lad said, "went out for a bit earlier this morning." "Where to?" Xuande asked. "His movements are uncertain; I don't know where he has gone," was the reply. "When will he be back?" Xuande asked. "I don't know that, either," the lad said. "It could be three to five days or ten or more."

Xuande was greatly disappointed. Zhang Fei said, "Since we have failed to see him, let's go home and have done with it!" Xuande was for waiting a little longer, but Lord Guan also said, "We might as well be off. We can send someone later to inquire." Xuande finally agreed and told the lad, "When your master returns, will you say that Liu Bei came to call?"[5]

The brothers remounted and rode off. Several *li* later they reined in and looked back on the scenic figurations of Longzhong. Now the hills seemed more elegant than lofty, the streams more sparkling than deep, the land more smooth than spacious, the woods more lush than large, with gibbons and cranes joining in play, pine and bamboo blending their green. Xuande could not take his eyes away. Suddenly a man appeared, his countenance imposing, his bearing stately yet simple. A scarf was wound casually around his head; a plain black gown covered his frame. With a staff of goosefoot wood he trod down a hillside path.

"This must be Master Sleeping Dragon," Xuande said eagerly as he dismounted and made a gesture of respectful greeting. "Could you be Sleeping Dragon, master?" he asked. "Your name, General?" the man responded. "Liu Bei," he answered. "I am not Kongming," the man went on, "but a friend of his, Cui Zhouping of Boling." "Your name has been long known to me," Xuande said. "This is a meeting ordained by fortune. I would like to benefit from your instruction if you could find the time. . . . "

The two men sat on some rocks in the woods; Lord Guan and Zhang Fei stood to either side. Cui Zhouping began, "For what reason, General, do you wish to see Kongming?" "There is such disorder in the empire," Xuande replied. "The four quarters are as unsettled as the clouds. I would seek of Kongming the strategy to secure and stabilize the government and the country." "My lord," Cui Zhouping responded with a smile, "you are bent on bringing the disorder of our day to an end? However benevolent your intentions, since ancient times periods of discord and civic order have come and gone quite unpredictably. When the Supreme Ancestor of the dynasty slew the white serpent and embarked on the rising that destroyed the despotic Qin, that interval, which led to the founding of the Han, was a time of transition from discord to civil order. Two hundred years of peace and prosperity followed. Then, in the time of the Emperors Ai and Ping, Wang Mang usurped the throne and brought us again from order to disorder. But the first emperor of the Later Han, Guang Wu, revived the dynasty and, righting its foundations, brought us out of discord and back to civic order.

"Now after two another hundred years, during which the population has enjoyed peace and contentment, we find sword and shield around us. This only shows that we are moving again into a period of disorder, and one which cannot be quickly ended. For Kongming to try to reverse the course of events or mitigate what fortune has in store would be, I am afraid, a futile expense of mind and body. It is said, 'Adapt to Heaven and enjoy ease; oppose it and toil in vain.' It is also said, 'None can deduct from the reckoning, or force what is fated.'"

"There is great insight in your words," Xuande conceded. "But I, a Liu, scion of the Han, committed to maintain the dynasty's rule, may not leave the task to fate or reckoning." "A mountain rustic like myself," Cui Zhouping responded, "is hardly fit to discuss the affairs of empire. You honored me with your profound question, and I expressed myself rashly." "You have favored me with your insight and instruction," Xuande said, "but I would know where Kongming has gone." "I, too, was hoping to pay a call on him," Cui Zhouping replied, "so I could not tell you where he is." "Would you be interested, master," Xuande inquired, "in coming back with me to our humble county seat?" "My uncultured nature," Cui Zhouping replied, "has grown too fond of leisure's freedoms to give thought to success and fame. But there will be occasion for us to meet again." With that, the man left after making a deep bow. "We have failed to find Kongming," Zhang Fei said, "and bumped into that rotten pedant instead. Too much idle talk!" "That is how men in seclusion express themselves," Xuande admonished him.

A few days after returning to Xinye, Xuande made inquiries and was told that Kongming had come back from his rambles. Xuande ordered the horses readied for another visit. "Do you have to go yourself for that village bumpkin?" Zhang Fei demanded. "Have him summoned." "It looks," Xuande said sharply, "as if you do not know what the sage Mencius meant when he said, 'Trying to meet a worthy man in the wrong way is as bad as closing the door on an invited guest.' Kongming is one of the greatest men of our time, and yet you expect me to send out a summons?" And so a second time, attended by his brothers, Xuande went to Sleeping Dragon Ridge.

It was the dead of winter, severely cold. Dense, somber clouds covered the sky.[6] The brothers rode into a cutting northern wind. A heavy snow made the mountains gleam like arrowheads of white jade and gave the woods a silvery sheen. "The air is bitter," Zhang Fei said, "and the ground frozen solid. A bad time even for military operations, and yet you think we should be going this distance to meet someone of no use to us at all? Let's go back and get out of the storm." "I am determined," Xuande replied, "to show Kongming my earnest intentions. If you can't stand it, brother, go on back yourself." "If death doesn't frighten me," Zhang Fei retorted, "why should the cold? I just hate to see my elder brother waste his energy." "Then stop complaining," Xuande said, "and follow me." As they approached the thatched cottage, they were surprised to hear someone singing in a roadside wineshop:

No deeds, no fame achieved at manhood's prime:
Shall he ever find his lord or meet his time?

Remember when Jiang Ziya,[7]
The old sage of the Eastern Sea, quit his hazel wood
And followed Zhou's first king, Wen, as servant and as kinsman?
When, uncalled, eight hundred lords converged,
And a white fish flew into King Wu's boat[8]
As he forded at Meng
To battle the Shang at Grazing Field,
Where he shed a tide of blood
That bore off sword and shield,
As, fierce and majestic, an eagle on the wing,
He towered above King Wu's martial vassals?[9]
And when
The tippler from Gaoyang (as he liked to call himself),
Li Yiji, came and made a common bow[10]
To the "Big Nose Governor" in those dark hours
And spoke such startling truths of reign and rule
That the king-to-be dismissed his footwashers
And feasted Li Yiji, honoring his splendid spirit?
The surrender of the east soon followed:
Seventy-two cities and towns.
What man has followed in those footsteps?
Such were the deeds of Jiang Ziya and Li Yiji,
Heroes unsurpassed unto this very day.[11]

As soon as this song was finished, another man tapped the table and began to sing:

Han's first king took the realm by sword;
The house he founded lasted twenty score.
With Huan and Ling, Han's fire-virtue waned.
And evil men the chancelorship profaned.

They saw a serpent coiled beside the throne;
A rainbow in the consort-quarters shone.
Ant-like, outlaws gathered everywhere;
Villains rose like raptors in the air.[12]

We pound our hands and keen, but all in vain;
Our sorrows take us to the village inn.
Leading lives of simple decency,
Who needs a name that lasts eternally?

Their songs sung, the two men clapped and laughed aloud. Convinced that Sleeping Dragon was within, Xuande dismounted and entered the wineshop. The singers were leaning over a table drinking. One had a light complexion and a long beard, the other a fresh, ageless look. Xuande saluted them and asked, "Which of you is Master Sleeping Dragon?" "Who are you, sir?" the long-bearded one responded. "And what have you to do with him?" "I am Liu Bei," was the reply, "and I need the master's skill to aid my cause and succor our age." "I am not the man you seek," the long-bearded man replied, "nor is he. But we are friends of his. I am Shi Guangyuan of Yingchuan, and this is Meng Gongwei of Runan." "Noble names long known to me," Xuande exclaimed with delight. "I am favored by this fortunate encounter, and I have extra horses if you gentlemen would be willing to accompany me to Sleeping Dragon's farm." "Country idlers like us," Shi Guangyuan replied, "have no knowledge of the weighty matters that concern you. Do not waste time on the likes of us, sir, but resume your search yourself."

Xuande bade the drinkers good-bye and rode toward Sleeping Dragon Ridge. He dismounted at Kongming's farm and, finding the youth at the gate, asked, "Is your master in today?" "In the house reading," was the reply. Excitedly, Xuande followed the lad. Coming to the inner gate, they stopped before a couplet on the wall that read: "Only through austerity and quiescence can one's purpose shine forth; only through concentration and self-control can one's distant goal be reached."[13] As Xuande was studying the words, he heard someone singing inside. Standing attentively by the door of the thatched house, he peered in and saw a young man with his arms about his knees, chanting:

> The phoenix winging on the air
> Will choose no tree
> Except the *wu*.
>
> The scholar keeping to his lair
> Will have no lord
> Except the true.
>
> Oh, let me till these furrowed fields,
> By this sweet home
> That I call mine.
>
> In books and song I place my dreams
> And wait the time
> The fates assign.

When the singer stopped, Xuande entered and extended his courtesies. "I have long held you in admiration," Xuande began, "but wanted occasion to express it personally. The other day, thanks to Shan Fu's suggestion, I came to pay my respects at this retreat of yours. Unable to meet you, however, I went home disappointed. Now I come a second time, undaunted by the storm. This glimpse of your learned countenance is an untold blessing."

Flustered by this speech, the young man returned the greeting and then replied, "General, you must be Liu Yuzhou and, I believe, wish to see my elder brother."[14] "Master," Xuande said in astonishment, "then you are not Sleeping Dragon, either?" "No, I am his younger brother, Zhuge Jun. There are three of us brothers. The oldest, Zhuge Jin, is in the Southland advising Sun Quan. Kongming is the second brother." "Is the Sleeping Dragon at home?" Xuande inquired. "Yesterday," Zhuge Jun replied, "he was invited by Cui Zhouping to go on a jaunt." "Do you know where?" Xuande asked. "They might have gone rowing down some lake or river," Zhuge Jun answered. "Or to visit some Buddhist or Taoist on his hilltop retreat. Or to look for friends in the villages. Or they might have simply decided to entertain themselves with lutes and chess in some cavern den. My brother comes and goes quite unpredictably, and I have no idea where he might be."

"How meagre my lot!" Xuande exclaimed. "Twice now have I missed this excellent man!" "Sit awhile," Zhuge Jun suggested. "Let me offer you tea." But Zhang Fei broke in, "The master is not here. Let's get going!" "Why go back," Xuande answered him, "without having spoken to anyone?" With that, Xuande turned to Zhuge Jun and said, "Your esteemed brother is known for his mastery of military arts. They say he applies himself to the subject daily. Can you tell me more about this?" When Zhuge Jun said he knew nothing about it, Zhang Fei spoke again. "Look at that storm," he said. "Better be starting back." But Xuande told him sharply to be quiet. "Since my brother is not here," Zhuge Jun said, "I should not detain you officers. He will return your courteous call at a future time." "I would not want him to have to travel," Xuande replied. "I expect to be coming again in a few days. Could I trouble you, though, for a brush and paper? As an expression of the earnestness of my wish, I shall leave your elder brother a letter." The writing instruments were brought.

Xuande thawed the frozen hairs of the brush with his breath and unrolled the writing paper. His letter read:

> A longtime admirer of your honored name, I, Liu Bei, have come twice to present myself, only to leave again without having met you—a keen disappontment. I am humbly mindful that as a remote kinsman of the court, I have enjoyed prestige and rank far beyond my merits. When my thoughts turn to the rude displacement at court—our laws and customs crumbling and swept aside while countless contenders subvert the state and vicious factions abuse the sovereign—my heart breaks, my gall is rent. Whatever sincerity I may offer to the cause of delivering the Han perishes for want of strategy.
>
> I admire your humane compassion, your sense of loyalty and honor. If in your greatness of spirit you would unfold your mighty talents, talents comparable to those of Jiang Ziya, and apply your grand strategy in the manner of Zhang Liang, then the empire and the sacred shrines of the royal house would be doubly blessed. I am forwarding this to convey my intention, after further ceremonial purification, to pay homage yet again to your honored presence, respectfully offering my poor, simple sincerity and entreating your discerning consideration.

Xuande handed the letter to Zhuge Jun, bade him good-bye, and left. Zhuge Jun accompanied him past the gate, listening to his earnest reiterations. Finally they parted.

Xuande was starting homeward when he saw the lad beyond the fence waving and shouting, "The old master is coming!" Ahead, past a small bridge, a man in winter headdress and fox furs was riding a donkey through the descending snow. He was followed by a youth in simple black carrying a gourd of wine. Turning on to the bridge, the rider sang:

> Nightlong, north winds chill,
> Myriad-leagued, dusky clouds expand.
> Capering snow through an infinite sky
> Transforms the never-changing land.
>
> He looks into the ether's vastitude:
> Are jade dragons at war up there,
> Strewing their scales every which way,
> And filling up the hollow sphere?
>
> Alone,
> Sighing for the plum trees' battered blooms. [15]

Certain that Sleeping Dragon was coming, Xuande leaped from the saddle to extend his greetings. "It must be hard for you, master," he said, "to brave this bitter cold. I have long been awaiting you." The startled rider climbed off his beast and returned the salutation. Then Zhuge Jun came up and said, "This is not Sleeping Dragon; it is his father-in-law, Huang Chengyan."

"I happened to hear you chanting just now," Xuande said. "It sounded so elevated and poignant." "I was reading the 'Liangfu Elegies' in my son-in-law's home," the man replied. "I had that stanza in mind as I crossed the bridge; the plum blossoms near the fence moved me to sing. I never imagined an honored guest might hear me." "Have you seen your esteemed son-in-law?" Xuande asked. "Actually, I am coming to see him," was the reply. With that, Xuande took his leave, remounted, and headed home. The wind and snow grew fiercer. Giving a last look back over Sleeping Dragon Ridge, Xuande felt overwhelmed by sadness and uncertainty. As a poet of later times wrote,

> That stormy day he sought the sage in vain,
> And sore at heart, he started home again.
> The creek bridge, frozen; the land, sheer ice—
> His trembling horse has many *li* to cross.
>
> Pear-petal flakes descending from the skies,
> Antic willow puffs darting at his eyes,
> He turns and halts to view the scene behind:
> Banked with snow, the silvered ridges shine.

Back in Xinye time crept by until it was again spring. Xuande ordered the diviners to cast for a propitious time to visit Kongming. After three days' abstinence from meat and wine, Xuande bathed, smeared himself with ritual oils, changed his clothes, and went back to Sleeping Dragon Ridge. His two brothers expressed intense displeasure and protested.[16] Indeed:

> The worthiest has yet to bend the hero's will;
> Servility could shake his fighters' confidence.

What would Xuande say to them?

READ ON.

38

Kongming Determines the Realm's Division and Charts a Course;
Sun Quan Leads a Naval Attack and Exacts Revenge

DESPITE HIS TWO FRUITLESS VISITS, Liu Xuande resolved to pay another call on Kongming.
"Twice, brother," Lord Guan said, "you have respectfully presented yourself. Such courtesy is indulgence. It seems to me that Kongming has a false reputation and no real learning. That is why he avoids receiving you. Why are you so captivated by this man?" "You
fail to understand," Xuande replied. "Long ago Prince Huan of the state of Qi tried five
times before he succeeded in seeing the recluse of Dongguo, Guan Zhong. Getting to see
the wise and worthy Kongming may well demand even more of us."

"Dear brother," Zhang Fei declared, "I think you overrate this village bumpkin. What
makes him so wise and worthy? Spare yourself the trip. If he refuses to come, it will only
take a bit of rope to bring him here!" "I suppose," Xuande said with a scowl, "you've
never heard of King Wen, founder of the Zhou, presenting himself to Jiang Ziya. If King
Wen could show a wise man such respect, what excuses your utter discourtesy? This time
you may stay here. Lord Guan and I will go on together." "Since my elder brothers are
going," Zhang Fei replied, "I cannot stay behind." "Let us have nothing unsociable out
of you, then," Xuande warned. Zhang Fei agreed.

The brothers and their attendants rode toward Longzhong. Half a *li* from the hermitage they dismounted as a sign of respect. Approaching on foot, they met Zhuge Jun.
Xuande hastily extended a greeting and asked, "Is your honored brother at the farm?"
"He came home last night," was the reply, "and today, General, you may see him." With
that, Zhuge Jun sauntered away. "We're in luck this time," Xuande said. "We will see
the master." "What a rude fellow!" Zhang Fei exclaimed. "What would it have cost him
to walk us to the farm? Why did he make off just like that?" "He must have something
to attend to," Xuande remarked. "Don't be unreasonable."

The three went to the front gate and knocked. A youth received them. "May I trouble
you, young acolyte," Xuande said, "to report that Liu Bei has come especially to pay his
respects to the master?" "The master is at home today," the lad replied, "however, he is
napping in the cottage and has not yet awakened." "In that case, do not announce us for
now," Xuande said. He ordered his brothers to wait near the door, and slowly entered the
cottage himself. He saw the master lying on a couch and assumed a humble posture as he
stood below. A while passed; the master continued sleeping.

Growing impatient, Lord Guan and Zhang Fei came into the chamber and found
Xuande standing in attendance as before. Zhang Fei said angrily to Lord Guan, "The in-

solence! Our brother standing in attendance, while he pretends to sleep peacefully on! Let me go out and torch the rear. We'll see whether that gets him up or not!"[1] Lord Guan calmed his junior, and Xuande ordered both outside to resume their watch. When Xuande looked into the chamber again, the master was turning over and seemed about to wake, but then he rolled back toward the wall, sleeping soundly once again. The lad came in and tried to announce the visitor, but Xuande persuaded him not to disturb Kongming. After another hour or so Kongming finally rose and chanted a song:

> From this great dream who would waken first?
> All along I've known the part to play:
> To sleep in springtime, and to ask no more,
> Though outside, longer, longer grow the days.[2]

"Any callers from the outside world?" Kongming asked, turning to the lad. "Imperial Uncle Liu," he replied, "has been waiting here for some time." Kongming stood up. "You should have told me sooner! I need time to change my clothes," he said and hurried to his private quarters. It was another while before he reappeared, clothes and cap correct, and greeted his guest.

To Xuande, Kongming appeared singularly tall, with a face like gleaming jade and a plaited silken band around his head. Cloaked in crane down, he had the buoyant air of a spiritual transcendent. Xuande prostrated himself and said, "I, Liu Bei, a foolish fellow from Zhuo district, a distant scion of the house of Han, have long felt your mighty name thunder in my ears. Twice before I have presented myself and, failing to gain audience, finally set my worthless name to a letter. I have never learned whether it was brought to your discerning attention." "A simple rustic of Nanyang," Kongming replied, "negligent and indolent by nature, I am indebted to you, General, for the pains you have taken to travel our way. I have been remiss."[3] After further civilities they seated themselves as host and guest, and tea was served.

The conversation continued. "I could see in your letter," Kongming began, "a compassionate concern for the people and the dynasty. But I fear that you are mistaken in seeking the help of one so young and so limited in ability." "I don't think Sima Hui and Shan Fu would have praised you so highly without good reason," Xuande responded, adding, "I only hope that you will overlook my crudeness, my lack of status, and vouchsafe your edifying instruction." Kongming answered, "Sima Hui and Shan Fu are two of the noblest scholars of the age. I am but a common tiller of the soil. What right have I to speak of the empire? These gentlemen have made a preposterous recommendation. What good can it do, General, to pick the dull and useless stone but pass up the precious jewel?" "How can a man with the ability to shape the times waste himself among the groves and springs?" Xuande continued. "I beg you to consider the living souls of this land and for their sake enlighten me, free me of ignorance and folly." "I would like to know your aspirations, General," Kongming said with a smile.

Xuande dismissed everyone present, shifted his mat closer to Kongming's, and declared, "The house of Han teeters on ruin. Unscrupulous subjects have stolen the mandate of rule. Failing to recognize my limitations, I have tried to promote the great principle of true allegiance throughout the empire; but my superficial knowledge and inadequate methods have so far kept me from achieving anything. If you, master, would relieve my ignorance and keep our cause alive, the blessing would be truly ten-thousandfold."

"Since the time of Dong Zhuo's sedition," Kongming began, "powerful and aggressive figures have come into their own. Cao Cao could overcome Yuan Shao, though his strength was initially inferior, thanks to wise planning and favorable occasion. Now Cao has an army of one million and uses his hold on the Emperor to make the feudal barons do his bidding. There is no way you can cross spearpoints with him. As for Sun Quan, he has a firm grip on the Southland and represents the third generation of his family's power there. The territory is difficult of access, and the people are devoted to him. Hence, the south may serve as a supporting ally, but it is not a strategic objective.

"Now consider the central province, Jingzhou. To the north it commands the Han and Mian rivers; to the south it draws wealth from Nanhai;[4] eastward it communicates with the Southland districts; westward it offers access to the districts of the Riverlands—that is, Xichuan—Ba and Shu. Jingzhou—that's the place to fight for! Only a fitting ruler can hold it. And Jingzhou seems to be the very place that Heaven wants to give you, General, if you have the ambition for it.

"Yizhou in the west, strategically located, is an inaccessible frontier province whose fertile wildlands extend thousands of *li*—a kingdom rightly called Heaven's Cornucopia. The first emperor of the Han consummated his imperial enterprise by basing himself there. The present provincial protector, Liu Zhang, is benighted and feeble, and even though the people are well-off and the realm is thriving, he does not know how to care for either. Yizhou's men of insight and capability are yearning for enlightened rule.

"Now, General, you are known across the land as a trustworthy and righteous scion of the Han, one who keeps noble warriors in hand and thirsts for men of merit. If you sit astride these two provinces, Jing and Yi, guard well their strategic points, come to terms with the Rong tribes on the west, placate the Yi and the Viets to the south, form a diplomatic alliance with Sun Quan, and conduct a program of reform in your own territory—then you may wait for the right moment when one of your top generals will be able to drive north to Luoyang by way of Wancheng while you yourself mount an offensive from the Riverlands through the Qinchuan region.[5] And won't the good common folk 'basket food and jug wine' to welcome you, my general! Thus can your great endeavor be brought to fulfillment and the house of Han revived. This is how I would shape strategy for you, General. It remains for you to consider it."[6]

Kongming hung a map and continued: "These are the fifty-four counties of the west. To establish your hegemony, let Cao Cao in the north have the advantage of timely circumstance; let Sun Quan in the south have his geographical advantages; you, my general, will have the allegiance of men. First, take Jingzhou and make it your home base. Then move into the Riverlands and build your third of the triangle of power. Eventually, the northern heartland will become your objective."

Rising from his mat and joining his hands in respectful gratitude, Xuande said, "Master, you have opened the thicket that barred my view and have made me feel as if clouds and mists have parted and I have gained blue sky. The only thing is, Liu Biao of Jingzhou and Liu Zhang of the Riverlands are both, like myself, imperial kinsmen. How could I bear to seize what is theirs?" "Every night," Kongming replied, "I study the configurations of the heavens. Liu Biao will not be long among the living. And Liu Zhang has no ambition worthy of the name. In time he will transfer his allegiance to you." Xuande pressed his head to the ground to show his respect.

By this single interview Kongming, who had never left his thatched cottage, demonstrated his foreknowledge of the tripodal balance of power—truly an incomparable man in any generation! A poet of later times has recorded his admiration:

> Governor Liu, cast adrift, alone,
> By fortune found Nanyang's Sleeping Dragon.
> He sought to know the shape of things to be;
> Smiling, the master mapped his strategy.

Xuande humbly petitioned Kongming: "Though my name be inconsiderable, my virtue meagre, I beg you not to spurn me as a vulgar man of little worth. Come out from these hills to lend us your aid, and I will listen obediently to your enlightening instruction." Kongming replied, "Here I have long been content, with my plow and mattock, and hesitate to respond to the demands of the world. Forgive me if I am unable to accept such service." Xuande began to weep. "If you remain here," he said, "what of the living souls of this land?" Xuande's tears wet the sleeves of his war gown and soaked his lapel. Kongming, moved by the sincerity of his intent, said, "If you will have me, then, General, I shall serve you like a hound or horse."

Elated by Kongming's answer, Xuande called in Lord Guan and Zhang Fei. They offered the gifts Xuande had prepared, but Kongming adamantly declined until Xuande assured him, "Think of this not as a formal petition to a man of great worth, but simply as a humble expression of personal feeling." At last Kongming received the gifts. Xuande and his brothers stayed at the farm overnight. The next day Kongming told Zhuge Jun, who had come back, "I am accepting the kind generosity of Imperial Uncle Liu, who has favored me with three calls. I am obliged to go. Remain at your labors and do not let our acres go fallow. When my work is done, I shall return to resume my life of seclusion." A wistful poem, written in later times, goes:

> About to soar, he felt himself drawn back;
> His task complete, he'll think of this farewell.
> Only for the monarch, who pleaded and pleaded again:
> The "falling star," the "autumn winds"—the "last campaign."[7]

There is another ballad in the old style:[8]

> Han's founding king drew his snow-white sword
> And slew the silver serpent in the Mang-Dang Hills;
> He quelled Qin, smote Chu, and claimed Xianyang.
> Ten score passed; the line would have expired,
> But mighty Guang Wu revived its fortunes in Luoyang;
> The throne remained secure till Huan and Ling:
> Court rule broke down; Xiandi was moved to Xuchang.
> Bold spirits now arose at every turn:
> Cao Cao seized power; the times were in his favor;
> In the south, the Sun house founded its estate.
> Lost and sorely tried, Xuande roamed the realm;
> Off in Xinye, he took to heart the people's woes.
> Nanyang's Sleeping Dragon dreamed great dreams;
> In his mind deep strategies took form.
> If Shan Fu had not spoken Kongming's name,
> Could Xuande's triple quest have ever been?
> So Kongming at an age of three times nine
> Packed his books and lute and quit his fields.

"Take Jingzhou first and then take the west!"
Here was a plan to alter destiny.
Across the realm his words created storms.
Juggling stars that held men's fate, he smiled.
Dragons ramped, tigers stalked, sky and land stood calmed;
Time itself can never waste his name.

After bidding Zhuge Jun good-bye, Xuande returned to Xinye with his brothers and Kongming. Xuande treated Kongming as his mentor. They ate together and slept together and spent the days analyzing events in the empire. Kongming observed: "Cao Cao has built the Pool of the Dark Tortoise to train his fighters for naval warfare. That means he intends to invade the south. We ought to send agents south to find out what is happening." And it was done.[9]

•   •   •   •

After the death of Sun Ce,[10] Sun Quan had consolidated his hold on the Southland and extended the patrimony founded by his late father and brother. He brought into his government scholars of merit, and established a guesthouse in Kuaiji in Wuxian, commissioning Gu Yong and Zhang Hong to receive worthy guests from all regions. Over the years the following scholars came by mutual recommendation: Kan Ze (Derun) of Kuaiji; Yan Jun (Mancai) of Pengcheng; Xue Zong (Jingwen) of Pei county; Cheng Bing (Deshu) of Ruyang; Zhu Huan (Xiumu) and Lu Ji (Gongji) of Wujun; Zhang Wen (Huishu) of Wu; Luo Tong (Gongxu) of Wushang; Wu Can (Kongxiu) of Wucheng. These men received generous and courteous treatment in the Southland. A number of important military leaders came too: Lü Meng (Ziming) of Runan; Lu Xun (Boyan) of Wujun; Xu Sheng (Wenxiang) of Langye; Pan Zhang (Wengui) of Dongjun; Ding Feng (Chengyuan) of Lujiang. Sun Quan's civil and military officials worked in close cooperation, and the Southland gained a reputation as a land that fostered talent.

In the seventh year of Jian An, Cao Cao, having vanquished Yuan Shao, ordered his representative to the Southland to demand that Sun Quan send a son to the capital to serve the Emperor. Sun Quan could not decide whether or not to comply. His mother, Lady Wu, summoned Zhang Zhao and Zhou Yu. Zhang Zhao advised, "Cao Cao's attempt to get one of our lord's sons in his court is a traditional device for keeping the feudal barons under control. If we do not comply, he could raise an army and subjugate the Southland."

Zhou Yu, however, argued, "General Sun has inherited the task his father and brother began. He has brought together the population of the six districts.[11] His army is elite, his grain supplies ample. His officers and men are responsive to command. Why should we send hostages to anyone? Once we do, it will lead to an alliance with Cao Cao, and whenever he calls on us, we will have to go. Rather than become subject to his authority, I think it best to send no hostage but to observe how things develop and prepare a sound defense." "Zhou Yu is correct," Lady Wu decided. Sun Quan, in deference to his mother, cordially dismissed Cao Cao's representative and refused to send a son. After that Cao Cao was determined to subdue the Southland, but disturbances in the north gave him no respite for a southern campaign.[12]

In the eleventh month of the following year[13] Sun Quan attacked Huang Zu. They fought on the Great River, and Huang Zu's forces were demolished. But Sun Quan's commander, Ling Cao, racing ahead on a skiff into Xiakou, was shot down by Gan Ning,

Huang Zu's commander. The slain man's son, Ling Tong, a lad of fifteen, took a desperate chance and recovered his father's body. Seeing that the situation was unfavorable, Sun Quan brought his forces back to the Southland.

•   •   •   •   •

Sun Quan's younger brother, Sun Yi, governor of Danyang, was an inflexible, hard-drinking man whose excesses had been known to drive him to beat his men.[14] The district military inspector, Gui Lan, and the assistant governor, Dai Yuan, had long desired to murder Governor Sun Yi. Together with one of the governor's attendants, Bian Hong, the two officials decided to conspire against him.

Sun Yi had prepared a grand banquet on the occasion of a gathering of the generals and county prefects in the capital town of Danyang. On the day of the feast Sun Yi's wife, Lady Xu, a beautiful and intelligent woman, skilled at divination, cast a hexagram in the *Book of Changes* signifying dire misfortune. She urged her husband not to attend the reception, but he ignored her pleas and joined the festivities. Afterward, as the guests were dispersing, Bian Hong, armed with a knife, followed Sun Yi out the gate and cut him down.

The principal conspirators, Gui Lan and Dai Yuan, then charged their fellow plotter, Bian Hong, with the crime, and he was publicly beheaded. The murderers proceeded to plunder the governor's household, seizing his property and female attendants. Gui Lan found himself attracted to Sun Yi's wife and said to her, "I have avenged your husband's death, and you will have to live with me or die." "With my husband dead so recently," Lady Xu said, "I cannot bear to serve another yet. Would it be asking too much to wait until the last day of the month? Then, after I make the offerings and remove my mourning robes, we can solemnize the relationship." Gui Lan agreed.

Lady Xu summoned two confidants of the late governor's, Sun Gao and Fu Ying. Tearfully she appealed to them: "My husband often spoke of your loyalty and honor. Those two villains, Gui Lan and Dai Yuan, murdered my husband, then blamed Bian Hong and punished him for it, all the while helping themselves to our property and servants. Gui Lan even tried to possess me. I pretended consent to allay his suspicions. Now if you two could get word to Sun Quan and devise a plan to take care of the villains, my husband's death would be avenged and my honor redeemed; I would be eternally grateful." With that, Lady Xu flung herself to the ground.

Tears stood in the men's eyes. "We two," they said, "have ever been grateful for the late governor's generosity. We did not follow him in death only because we were trying to avenge him. What you command is ours to perform." And they sent secret messages to Sun Quan.

On the day appointed for the ceremony Lady Xu concealed her husband's two commanders behind the curtains in an inner chamber and commenced the sacrificial ritual in the main hall. That done, she removed her mourning attire, bathed and perfumed herself, and dressed seductively. She spoke to everyone with artful ease and gracious self-possession. Gui Lan was elated when informed of her behavior.

That night Lady Xu invited Gui Lan to her quarters, where she had prepared a feast. After he had drunk deeply, she led him to the inner chamber. Intoxicated as he was, the delighted guest went in. "Commanders, come forth!" Lady Xu cried out. Gui Lan had no time to defend himself. The two armed men leaped into view. Fu Ying felled Gui Lan with a single stroke of his blade, Sun Gao followed up with another cut, and Gui Lan lay dead. Lady Xu then sent Dai Yuan an invitation to the banquet; he too was killed when he arrived at the hall. All the followers and family members of the two slain murderers were executed. Lady Xu resumed her mourning attire and sacrificed the heads of her enemies before the altar of her dear lord, Sun Yi.

Before long Sun Quan himself arrived in Danyang with a party of soldiers. Since the two criminals had already been dispatched by Lady Xu, Sun Quan appointed Sun Gao and Fu Ying garrison commanders, put them in charge of Danyang, and took the widow, his sister-in-law, home with him that he might care for her for the rest of her life. The Southland celebrated Lady Xu's strength of character. A later poet wrote:

> So able and so chaste—in this world all too rare!—
> The widow lured two villains into her cunning snare.
> Vassals base chose treachery, vassals loyal chose death;
> To this Southland heroine does any man compare?[15]

Now all the rebels in the Southland had come under Sun Quan's control. And he had more than seven thousand war-boats on the Great River. At Sun Quan's behest Zhou Yu became supreme commander of the Southland's land and sea forces.

In winter, the tenth month of Jian An 12, Sun Quan's mother, Lady Wu, fell gravely ill. She called for Zhang Zhao and Zhou Yu and said to them, "Though originally a woman of Wu, I lost my parents when young and, following my younger brother, Wu Jing, settled among the Viets. Later I married Sun Jian and bore him four sons. At the birth of Ce, my eldest, I dreamed that the moon was coming into my body. When Quan, my second, was born, I dreamed that the sun had entered me. The diviners said, 'Such dreams portend great rank for your sons.' Alas, the eldest died too young, and now our patrimony passes to the second son. If I can count on you two gentlemen to concert your efforts to support him, I shall not die in vain."

Lady Wu then spoke her final charge to Sun Quan: "I want you to serve Zhang Zhao and Zhou Yu as if they were your teachers, without lapse or negligence. Remember, my younger sister was given in marriage with me to your father. She is your mother as well. Serve her as you would have served me. Care for your younger sister, too, and marry her well." With these words she passed away. Sun Quan wailed in grief. He duly fulfilled the ceremonies of mourning and interment.

In the spring of the following year, Sun Quan raised the question of attacking Huang Zu.[16] Zhang Zhao counseled caution: "We are still in the first year of the mourning period. It is not the time for military action." But Zhou Yu countered, "Avenging a humiliation brooks no waiting period." Sun Quan was brooding over the matter when District Commander Lü Meng was announced. "I was guarding Dragon's Gorge," he said, "when Gan Ning, one of Huang Zu's lieutenants, unexpectedly surrendered. Gan Ning's style is Xingba, and he comes from Linjiang in Bajun. On close questioning I found him to be a man of considerable learning, quite vigorous, and something of an 'honorable adventurer.' It seems he once led a gang of desperadoes who were active all over the region. Gan Ning always carried a brass bell at his waist. The sound of it put people to flight. He earned the nickname Bandit of the Colored Sails because he used Riverlands imported silk in his sails. Eventually he came to regret his earlier excesses, changed his ways, and entered the service of Liu Biao.

"Soon enough Gan Ning realized that Liu Biao would accomplish nothing, and he now desires to join us. At Xiakou, however, Huang Zu detained him. The last time we defeated Huang Zu he retook Xiakou only by the efforts of Gan Ning. Even then Huang Zu treated him most stingily. The chief of guards, Su Fei, tried several times to recommend

Gan Ning to Huang Zu, but Huang Zu always answered, 'Ning is a criminal who has preyed upon the people all along the river. I can't give him an important position.' So Gan Ning's resentment burned hotter and hotter.

"At this point Su Fei invited Gan Ning to dine at his home and said to him, ' Lord Liu Biao has refused you a fitting appointment despite my recommendations. The years are passing and life is short. It's time to plan ahead. I am going to set you up as a magistrate in Zhu county. You can look for a new lord from there.'[17]

"And that, my lord," Lü Meng concluded, "is how Gan Ning came to surrender to us. At first he was fearful that his having rescued Huang Zu and killed Ling Cao would be held against him, but I assured him that Your Lordship thirsted for worthy men and would never bear him a grudge, especially since he had acted out of loyalty. He has crossed the river with his men to present himself to you. I beg to know your will."

Sun Quan was jubilant. "This defection ensures Huang Zu's defeat," he said and had Gan Ning brought before him. After Gan Ning's formal salutations, Sun Quan told him, "Your coming wins our good will. There can be no thinking of old grudges. Be assured of that. We only hope you will show us the way to destroy Huang Zu." To this Gan Ning responded, "The sacred Han throne is in imminent danger. Cao Cao's ministry is bound to end in a usurpation, and Jingzhou is the place he will fight for. Its protector, Liu Biao, makes no provision for the future, and his two sons are clumsy mediocrities who could never keep what he has built up. My lord, make his territory yours—before Cao Cao makes it his. First, Huang Zu must be captured. He is old and apathetic, absorbed in profit and gain. He infringes upon the interests of his officials and exacts much from the populace. This has led to widespread disaffection. His military equipment is in disrepair; his army has no discipline. He will fall if you attack. And then—sound the drum and march west. Hold the Chu pass and aim for the Riverlands. Your hegemony can be achieved." "Precious advice," Sun Quan responded.

Sun Quan had made Zhou Yu supreme commander of all land and naval forces. He now made Lü Meng leader of the vanguard of the front unit and Dong Xi and Gan Ning, deputy commanders. Sun Quan himself took charge of the main army, which numbered one hundred thousand. Thus the expedition against Huang Zu began.

Huang Zu summoned his counselors as spies and scouts reported these developments back to Jiangxia.[18] He appointed Su Fei his chief general, assigned Chen Jiu and Deng Long to the vanguard, and mobilized the entire district. The two van leaders led a squad of war-boats and blocked the passage near Miankou.[19] Each boat held a thousand archers and crossbowmen. Heavy ropes linked the craft to steady them. When they sighted the Southlanders, the defenders rolled their drums and let fly volleys of arrows, driving the invaders back several *li*.

Gan Ning said to Dong Xi, "Having come this far, we can't turn back." They put five thousand crack troops on one hundred small craft; each carried twenty rowers and thirty men in armor. Steel swords in hand, braving the oncoming bolts, the sailors of the south drove toward the long junks. Drawing alongside, they severed the heavy ropes, causing the junks to drift away from each other. Gan Ning leaped onto the main ship and cut down Deng Long. Chen Jiu abandoned his ship.

Lü Meng sprang at once into a small boat, rowed directly into the enemy fleet, and set the junks afire. Chen Jiu struggled ashore, but Lü Meng, heedless of all risk, raced ahead of him and felled him with one stroke through the chest. By the time Su Fei arrived at the bank to assist, the Southlanders had already gained the shore in overpowering force. Huang Zu was routed. Su Fei took to his heels but was captured handily by Pan Zhang and brought to Sun Quan's ship. Sun Quan had him caged pending the capture of Huang Zu so that he could execute the two together. He then hastened on to Xiakou in full force. Indeed:

> Slighted by Liu Biao, the Bandit of the Colored Sails
> Blasted apart the war-junks of Huang Zu.

Huang Zu's fate hung in the balance.
READ ON.

39

Jingzhou's Heir Pleads Three Times for Advice;
The Director General Makes His Debut at Bowang

THE ATTACK SUN QUAN DELIVERED against Xiakou had wiped out Huang Zu's whole force.
Huang Zu abandoned Jiangxia and fled west toward Jingzhou.[1] Anticipating his line of
flight, Gan Ning had posted an ambush outside the eastern gate of Jiangxia. When the
defeated commander hurried through with a few dozen mounted followers, he found Gan
Ning's men massed across the way, shouting in unison. From horseback Huang Zu said
to Gan Ning, "I always did right by you in the old days. Why do you threaten me now?"
Scowling, Gan Ning replied, "All I ever got for my service was the title River Bandit. Do
you have anything else to say?" Denied mercy, Huang Zu wheeled about and galloped
off. Gan Ning pursued him.

A fresh commotion signaled the arrival of another Southland commander, Cheng Pu.
Gan Ning suspected Cheng Pu had come to take credit for the capture of Huang Zu, so
he drew his bow, felled Huang Zu, and severed his head. He subsequently rejoined Cheng
Pu, and the combined force rode back to Sun Quan. Gan Ning presented the enemy commander's head, and Sun Quan stored it in a wooden box until he could return to the
Southland and offer it at his father's altar.[2] The leader of the Southland rewarded his
army handsomely and elevated Gan Ning to district commander. Then he had to decide
whether to hold the city captured from Huang Zu.

"Jiangxia is too far from our bases to defend," Zhang Zhao argued. "Pull the men
back. Liu Biao will attack us the moment he hears of Huang Zu's fate. Let him come. His
overextended troops will soon yield to our well-rested soldiers, and then we can carry our
counterattack as far as Jingzhou's capital and capture it." Sun Quan approved Zhang
Zhao's advice and withdrew all units to the south.

Meanwhile, Su Fei was in the prisoner's cage. He appealed through someone for Gan
Ning's help. "Su Fei did not even have to mention it," Gan Ning told the emissary. "I
could never forget how he helped me." The Southland forces returned and Sun Quan
ordered Su Fei executed so that his head could be placed with Huang Zu's on Sun
Jian's altar.

Gan Ning came before Sun Quan to plead for his former patron: "Without Su Fei, I'd
be a pile of bones underground and never would have come to serve under you, General.
His offense, I grant, is capital. But in view of his past kindness to me, I beg to redeem him
with the office and rank you have so generously granted." "For your sake only," Sun
Quan said, "I pardon him—but what if he escapes?" "He would be too grateful to do

that," Gan Ning assured him. "But if he does, I will answer for it with my head." Thus Su Fei was spared, and Huang Zu's head alone was offered at the sacrificial altar.

After the ritual, a feast was held to congratulate the civil and military officials. As the wine was circulating one man rose, uttered a cry, and went for Gan Ning with drawn sword. Gan Ning used a chair to parry the attack. Sun Quan recognized the assailant as Ling Tong. Gan Ning had shot and killed his father, Ling Cao, while still in the service of Huang Zu at Jiangxia. Now Ling Tong wanted revenge.[3] Intervening, Sun Quan said, "When Gan Ning killed your father, he was bound to another lord. He was doing what he had to do. Now that we are all in the same family, old grudges must be forgotten—for my sake." "Blood debts must be paid!" Ling Tong shouted, pressing his forehead to the ground in front of Sun Quan, who, along with the officials present, tried to talk Ling Tong round. But the young warrior kept staring angrily at Gan Ning. Sun Quan made a quick decision to reassign Gan Ning to Xiakou with five thousand men and one hundred war-junks.[4] Gan Ning thanked him and left. At the same time Sun Quan appointed Ling Tong District Commander, Filial and Heroic, an offer the indignant son reluctantly accepted.[5]

The defense of the Southland was now begun in earnest, with a great boatbuilding campaign and the deployment of troops along the banks of the Great River. Sun Quan assigned his brother, Sun Jing, to guard Wujun while he positioned the main army at Chaisang.[6] Zhou Yu directed maneuvers on the Poyang Lakes daily, preparing his marines for the next invasion of Jingzhou.

·   ·   ·   ·   ·

The spies that Xuande had sent south now returned to Xinye with the following intelligence: "The southerners have struck. Huang Zu is dead. They're digging in at Chaisang." Xuande was discussing the new developments with Kongming when he was summoned by Liu Biao. Kongming said, "Since the Southland has routed Huang Zu, Liu Biao will want to see you to help plan his revenge. I'll go along to weigh the possibilities and advise you accordingly." Xuande agreed. He left Xinye in Lord Guan's hands and, joined by Kongming, went to the capital of the province. Zhang Fei and five hundred men escorted him.

As they rode, Xuande asked Kongming, "What should I say to Liu Biao?" "First of all," Kongming advised, "you must apologize for the incident at Xiangyang when you fled the banquet. Then, if he orders you to undertake a punitive expedition against the Southland, decline—no matter what he says. Tell him you need time to go back to Xinye and get your forces into condition."[7] Xuande approved. In Jingzhou the two men settled into a government guesthouse while Zhang Fei stood guard outside the city.

Liu Biao received Xuande and Kongming. The necessary formalities performed, Xuande expressed regret for his offense. "I am well aware, worthy brother," Liu Biao said, "of the mortal danger you were in. I was fully prepared to behead Cai Mao then and there to satisfy you but was induced by many appeals to forgive him. Will my worthy brother kindly not take offense?" "It was not really General Cai's doing," Xuande replied. "I assume the plot was hatched by his subordinates."

"Now that we have lost Jiangxia," the protector of Jingzhou continued, "and Huang Zu has met his death, I have called you here to take part in planning our retaliation." "Huang Zu was a violent sort," Xuande responded, "quite incapable of using men.[8] That's how he brought on this catastrophe. Now if we mobilize and march south, Cao Cao could strike from the north. What then?" "The years weigh on me," Liu Biao said. "My ailments multiply. I cannot cope with the affairs of this province. Worthy brother, if you come to assist me, you will become ruler of Jingzhou after I pass away." "Elder brother," Xuande cried out, "do not say that nor imagine that I would presume to undertake such a responsibility."

At this point Kongming eyed Xuande, who continued, "We must allow more time to devise a sound strategy." Xuande excused himself and returned to his lodgings. "My lord," Kongming said to him, "Liu Biao was ready to put the province in your hands. Why did you decline?" "The Protector," Xuande replied, "has treated me with consummate consideration and etiquette. To exploit his moment of peril by seizing his estate is the last thing I could bring myself to do." "What a kindhearted lord," Kongming said with a sigh.

While this discussion was going on, Liu Qi, the eldest son of Liu Biao, entered and tearfully importuned Xuande and Kongming. "My stepmother will suffer my existence no longer," he said. "I may be killed at any moment. Rescue me, uncle, for pity's sake." "This is a family matter, nephew," Xuande replied. "You cannot come to me with it." Xuande turned to Kongming, who was smiling faintly. "Yes," he said, "this is a family matter, with which I would not presume to acquaint myself." Afterward Xuande escorted the lad out and whispered to him, "Tomorrow I shall have Kongming return your call. Make sure to say thus and so . . . " Xuande proposed a ruse to obtain Kongming's advice, adding, "He should have some ingenious suggestions for you." Liu Qi thanked Xuande and left.

The next day Xuande put off all obligations, claiming a stomach ailment, and persuaded Kongming to repay Liu Qi's call alone. Liu Qi received Kongming in his private apartment. When they had finished tea, Liu Qi said, "My stepmother has no use for me. Master, favor me with a word to relieve my plight." "I am here as a guest," Kongming replied. "If people found out I had meddled for no good reason in a conflict among kinfolk, it could do us great harm." So saying, Kongming rose to leave. Liu Qi appealed to him: "You have honored me with your presence here. I must see you off with more ceremony than this." He led Kongming into another chamber and served him wine. "My stepmother," he reiterated, "has no use for me. I implore you to speak the word that can save me." "I may not give counsel in such matters," was the reply. Again Kongming asked to leave. "Master," Liu Qi went on, "if you will not speak, then there is nothing more to say. But must you leave so precipitately?"

Kongming returned to his place. "I have an ancient text," Liu Qi said, "that I would like you to examine." He guided his guest up to a small attic. "Where is the book?" Kongming asked. Bowing tearfully, Liu Qi said, "My stepmother has no use for me. My death is imminent. Do you mean to be so cruel as to deny me a single word of help?" Kongming rose angrily and tried to leave, only to find that the ladder they had ascended was gone. "I need a sound plan," Liu Qi appealed. "Your fear of discovery makes you reluctant to speak. Well, here we are, alone between Heaven and earth. Your voice can reach no ear but mine—therefore, bestow your wisdom." " 'Strangers never meddle among kin,' as the saying goes," Kongming replied. "I cannot give counsel." "If you are so resolved," Liu Qi said, "my life cannot be preserved. Let me end it before your eyes." With those words he drew his sword.

Kongming moved to restrain him, saying, "There is a way. You must remember the ancient story of the brothers Shensheng and Chong Er? The former stayed home and lost his life; the latter went into exile and saved himself.[9] Now, with Huang Zu's defeat, Jiangxia stands unguarded. Why not petition your father for a company of men to hold

Jiangxia? That might save you." Liu Qi thanked Kongming profusely and had the ladder replaced. Kongming returned to Xuande and informed him of the disposition of Liu Qi's problem. Xuande was delighted.

Liu Qi's petition for a defense force put Liu Biao in a dilemma. For advice he turned to Xuande. "Jiangxia is a crucial location," Xuande said. "You cannot have just anybody guarding it. Your son is the right man. And while your son takes care of the southeast, let me handle the northwest."[10] "I'm told," Liu Biao said, "that Cao Cao has built an artificial lake to train his forces for a southern expedition. We must be prepared." "We already know this," Xuande replied. "Do not be anxious, brother." Xuande returned to his base at Xinye, and Liu Biao assigned Liu Qi three thousand men to secure Jiangxia.[11]

•   •   •   •   •

It was at this time that Cao Cao terminated the duties of the three elder lords and attached their functions to his own office.[12] He made Mao Jie and Cui Yan his staff supervisers, and Sima Yi his chief of the Bureau of Documents. Sima Yi (Zhongda) came from Wen county in Henei district. He was the grandson of Sima Juan, governor of Yingchuan; the son of Sima Fang, governor of the western capital district Jingzhao; and younger brother of Sima Lang, chief of the advisory staff.[13] Having thus brought his civil staff up to full strength, Cao Cao held discussions with his generals on the southern campaign against Jingzhou. Xiahou Dun proposed: "We have been informed that Liu Bei has been steadily developing his fighting force in Xinye. We should plan to attack him before he becomes a serious problem." Cao Cao directed Xiahou Dun to take command of a hundred-thousand-man force, and Yu Jin, Li Dian, Xiahou Lan, and Han Hao to serve as his deputy generals. Their orders were to march to Bowang and keep Xinye under close watch.[14]

The adviser Xun Wenruo objected, however: "Xuande is one of the greatest heroes of our time and, with Kongming as his director general, is not to be recklessly confronted." "Xuande is a mouse that won't escape me," Xiahou Dun retorted. Then Shan Fu spoke: "General, do not underestimate Xuande. He is a tiger to whom Zhuge Liang gives wings." "Who is Zhuge Liang?" Cao Cao interjected. "His style is Kongming," Shan Fu replied, "his Taoist sobriquet, Master Sleeping Dragon. He is one of the rarest talents of the age. He can plot the motions of sky and land and design plans of divine perfection. On no account should you belittle him." "And how does he compare with you?" Cao Cao asked. "No comparison," Shan Fu said. "I am a firefly; he, the full-risen moon." "How absurd!" Xiahou Dun cried. "He's a straw reed to me. I fear him not. If in a single engagement I fail to capture Xuande and take this Kongming alive, the prime minister is welcome to my head." "Well then," Cao Cao replied, "send us an early report of victory and dispel our qualms." Filled with energetic determination, Xuahou Dun took his leave and commenced the operation.

•   •   •   •   •

Xuande's ritual acknowledgment of Kongming as his teacher caused his two brothers no little consternation. "Kongming is so young," they said to him, "what knowledge or ability could he have? Brother, you have obliged him beyond all reason—before even putting him to the test." But Xuande closed the matter by saying, "He is to me as water to the fish. Say no more, brothers." Rebuffed, Lord Guan and Zhang Fei silently withdrew.

One day someone presented Xuande with a yak's tail, and he wound it into a head-dress. When Kongming saw it, he said severely, "My illustrious lord must be forgetting his aspirations if this is all he has to devote himself to." Xuande tossed the yak's tail away and apologized. "I was only killing time, trying to forget my troubles," he said. "In your judgment," Kongming continued, "how do you and Cao Cao compare?" "I fall short," Xuande answered. "Your soldiers," Kongming went on, "number in the thousands. How would you deal with Cao's army if it appeared?" "That very question has been consuming me," Xuande admitted, "but I have not found a good answer." "You had better recruit a militia as quickly as possible," Kongming urged. "I will train them myself." On this advice Xuande called for volunteers. Three thousand men of Xinye joined the army, and Kongming instructed them intensively in field tactics.

Word of Cao Cao's approaching invasion force of one hundred thousand reached Xinye. Zhang Fei said to Lord Guan, "We'll have Kongming deal with it, and that will be that." When Xuande summoned his brothers to counsel, Zhang Fei said, "How about sending the one you call 'water'?" "For brains," Xuande retorted, "I have Kongming; for courage, you two. Don't bandy responsibilities!" The brothers left, and Xuande called Kongming to him. "My main concern," Kongming said, "is that Zhang Fei and Lord Guan obey my orders. If you wish to have me as your military executive, empower me with your sword and seal." Accordingly, Xuande turned these articles over to Kongming, who then assembled the commanders. "We might as well go along, too," Zhang Fei said to Lord Guan, "if only to see how he runs things."

Before the commanders Kongming issued his orders: "Left of Bowang are the Yu Hills; to the right, the forest of An—two good places for concealing men and horses. Lord Guan, you hide in the hills with a thousand fighters and let the enemy pass unopposed. Their equipment and food supplies will be in the rear. The moment you see fire on the southern side, unleash your men and burn the enemy's grain and fodder. Zhang Fei, you hide in the ravines behind the forest. When you see fire, head for the old supply depot at Bowang and burn it. I want Liu Feng and Guan Ping to take five hundred men with combustible materials and wait on either side of the area behind the slope of Bowang itself. At the first watch, when the enemy troops will be arriving, set fires." Kongming also ordered Zhao Zilong recalled from the town of Fan to lead the forward army, but with specific instructions to feign defeat. He concluded: "Our lord should lead one contingent as a rear support. All must act according to the plan without the slightest deviation."

Lord Guan's reaction was sharp. "So," he said, "we are all to go forth and engage the enemy. And when will we have the opportunity of reviewing your own role as director general?" "My role is simply to stay and guard our base," was Kongming's reply. Zhang Fei guffawed. "We all go to the slaughter," he cried, "while you sit home, perfectly content and comfortable!" "I have the sword and seal," Kongming said. "Whoever violates my orders will die." "Brothers," Xuande said, "have you forgotten? 'Plans evolved within the tent decide victories a thousand *li* away.' You must obey his orders." Smiling coldly, Zhang Fei left. "We shall see," Lord Guan said, "whether his ideas work. There will be time enough to confront him if they don't." With that, he followed Zhang Fei out. The commanders, uncertain about Kongming's strategy, remained doubtful but followed their orders.

Kongming said to Xuande, "My lord, station your troops at the foot of Bowang Hill. Tomorrow evening when the enemy arrives, abandon camp. At the fire signal, turn back upon them. I shall hold Xinye with Mi Zhu, Mi Fang, and five hundred guards."

Kongming then ordered Sun Qian and Jian Yong to prepare the victory feast and ready the honor rolls. Now complete, Kongming's orchestration had even Xuande perplexed.

· · · ·

Cao Cao's commanders, Xiahou Dun and Yu Jin, neared Bowang. They assigned half their troops to the front, half to guard the grain wagons. It was autumn. Strong winds began to blow. As the soldiers rushed ahead, their leaders noticed dust flying in the distance. Xiahou Dun drew up his forces and asked his guide to describe their position. "Ahead lie the slopes of Bowang," was the reply, "behind, the mouth of the River Luo."

Xiahou Dun had Yu Jin and Li Dian call a general halt while he rode in front of the line to scan the horizon. A force of cavalry was approaching them. Laughing loudly, Xiahou Dun said to his commanders, "Before the prime minister himself Shan Fu extolled Kongming as a divine strategist. Now look how he uses his troops! Sending such puny forces in the van is like sending sheep and dogs against tigers and panthers. I told His Excellency I would take Xuande and Kongming alive, and I shall make good my claim." So saying, he charged forward.

Zhao Zilong rode forth, and Xiahou Dun reviled him: "You and your men follow Xuande like lost souls chasing a ghost." Zilong gave his horse its head, and the two warriors closed. After several passages Zhao Zilong retreated, and Xiahou Dun chased him twenty *li*. Zilong turned and fought, then retreated again.

Cao's commander, Han Hao, raced up and warned Xiahou Dun that he was being drawn into an ambush, but he received a contemptuous answer: "Let them set a ten-sided ambush. I still have nothing to fear!" He pressed on to the slope. Thereupon, Xuande ordered his bombards to pound the enemy as he joined the battle. Engaging the new opponent, Xiahou Dun said derisively to Han Hao, "Is this the ambush you warned me about? I shall not halt again until we reach Xinye." And he moved forward, driving Xuande and Zhao Zilong in full retreat before him.

The sky was darkening. Thick clouds stretched across it. There was no moon. It had been gusty all day, and now the night winds were rising. Xiahou Dun was intent on the kill. His commanders, Yu Jin and Li Dian, reached a narrow point where dry reeds crowded the road on both sides. Li Dian said to Yu Jin, "'Despise your enemy and you will lose.' To the south the roads narrow, and the hills and river hem us in. The foliage is dense and tangled. What if they use fire?" "Of course!" Yu Jin exclaimed. "I'll go and warn the general-in-command. You go and halt the rear at once." But Li Dian could not arrest the forward momentum of the army. Yu Jin dashed ahead. "Stop the march!" he cried to Xiahou Dun. "They could use fire on these tight roads. The hills and the river have us hemmed in, and the undergrowth crowds us." How real the danger was now dawned on Xiahou Dun, but by the time he turned back to stop the advance, he caught the sound of fire hissing and rising in crescendo as arms of flame reached up through the dry reeds hugging the road. In moments the blaze, whipped by the wind, roared on all sides of them. Panic ensued. Cao Cao's soldiers trampled one another, adding to the incalculable losses. Zhao Zilong then returned to take a further toll on the enemy. Xiahou Dun, braving heat and smoke, broke through the walls of fire and fled.[15]

Li Dian, who had been watching this disastrous turn of events, raced for Bowang. But another contingent, illuminated in the fires, barred his way; at its head was Lord Guan. After a spell of confused and desperate fighting, Li Dian managed to escape; and Yu Jin too, seeing the wagons consumed in the flames, fled for his life. Xiahou Lan and Han Hao tried to save the grain and fodder; but Zhang Fei intercepted them, made short work of Xiahou Lan, and sent Han Hao into headlong flight. The slaughter went on until dawn. Corpses littered the land, and the blood ran in rivers. This poem commemorates the victory:

> With fire he broke the battle at Bowang,
> All smiles and small talk, giving each his cue.
> Striking fear deep into Cao Cao's soul,
> Thus Kongming scored a coup at his debut.

Xiahou Dun rounded up the survivors and returned to Xuchang.

Kongming recalled all units. Lord Guan and Zhang Fei said to one another, "He is a true hero, a champion!" The brothers had ridden only a short distance when they saw Mi Zhu and Mi Fang leading a party of soldiers. In their midst was a small carriage. A man, perfectly poised, sat inside. Lord Guan and Zhang Fei dismounted and bowed low before the carriage in acknowledgment of the director general's ability. Moments later Xuande, Zhao Zilong, Liu Feng, Guan Ping, and others arrived. The men regrouped into their companies, and the captured spoils were shared among officers and men. Afterward all marched back to Xinye. Along the road the townspeople prostrated themselves before the victors, exclaiming, "We are saved thanks to Lord Liu, who has won the service of an able man."

Back in the county seat, Kongming said to Xuande, "Xiahou Dun has beat a retreat, but Cao Cao himself will return in force." "What are we to do?" Xuande asked. "I think I know how to hold him off," Kongming replied. Indeed:

> After the victory neither man nor mount may rest:
> A perfect strategy is needed to avoid the next attack.

What was Kongming's plan?

READ ON.

40

Lady Cai Proposes Ceding Jingzhou to Cao Cao;
Zhuge Liang Burns Cao's Men in Xinye

XUANDE ASKED KONGMING HOW TO COUNTER CAO CAO, and Kongming said, "We cannot stay in a small town like Xinye. The latest news is that Liu Biao may be dying. The time has come to establish ourselves in Jingzhou and put ourselves in position to throw Cao Cao back." "It sounds sensible," Xuande said, "but I will not conspire against the man who has hosted us so kindly." "If you fail to take the province now," Kongming warned emphatically, "you will soon regret it." "I would rather die than do this dishonorable deed," Xuande responded. "This matter is going to come up again," Kongming said.

• • • • •

Xiahou Dun returned to Xuchang and presented himself in bonds before the prime minister. Touching his head to the ground, the defeated general offered to atone with his life for the losses at Bowang. But Cao Cao undid the ropes. "I fell afoul of Zhuge Liang's treacherous scheme," Xiahou Dun explained. Cao Cao said, "How could a man who has waged war all his life forget to guard against fire on those narrow pathways?" "Li Dian and Yu Jin tried to warn me," Xiahou Dun admitted, "but I did not heed them." Cao Cao rewarded the two commanders.[1]

"Xuande grows bolder," Xiahou Dun warned. "Action must be taken now." "Yes, Liu Bei and Sun Quan are our first concern," Cao Cao replied. "The others are not worth worrying about. The time has come to make the south submit." So saying, he ordered the mobilization of half a million soldiers into five equal contingents: the first, led by Cao Ren and Cao Hong; the second, by Zhang Liao and Zhang He; the third, by Xiahou Yuan and Xiahou Dun; the fourth, by Yu Jin and Li Dian; the fifth, by Cao Cao himself and his staff commanders. The expedition was scheduled to set out in the seventh month of Jian An 13.[2]

Imperial Mentor[3] Kong Rong opposed the expedition. "Liu Bei and Liu Biao," he argued, "are members of the imperial clan; imperial sanction is required before taking military action against them. Sun Quan has a powerful hold on the six districts of the Southland, and the Great River affords his territory a formidable natural defense. It is not an easy place to capture. Putting an army into the field without the justification such an enterprise must have will cost Your Excellency the confidence of the realm." Cao Cao responded angrily, "Liu Bei, Liu Biao, and Sun Quan have disobeyed imperial decrees.

Their chastisement is both necessary and proper." With that, he dismissed Kong Rong harshly and ordered any further protest punished by execution.

Kong Rong left Cao Cao's residence, lifted his eyes to Heaven, and sighed as he said, "How can the most inhumane of men succeed in war against the most humane of men? The former cannot win."[4] A household retainer of Imperial Censor Chi Lü overheard the remark and reported it to his master. The censor, whom Kong Rong held in disdain, deeply resented the scholar and gladly called the matter to Cao Cao's attention. "Day after day," Chi Lü added, "Kong Rong belittles you and slanders you. Moreover, he was friendly with Mi Heng. Mi Heng praised him as a second Confucius, and Kong Rong returned the compliment, calling Mi Heng another Yan Hui.[5] That time Mi Heng stripped himself at the drum concert and shamed you so—Kong Rong put him up to it." Shaking with fury, the prime minister ordered security officers to arrest the imperial mentor.

At the time Kong Rong's two young sons were at home playing chess. Their attendants said, "They've taken your father to be executed. Get away at once." "When the nest falls," the boys replied, "the eggs will break." Moments later the security officers swept in, seized all members of the household, including the two boys, and put them to death.[6]

Soon after, the imperial mentor's corpse was publicly displayed. Zhi Xi of Jingzhao kneeled over the body and wept. Cao Cao would have had him killed too, but Xun Wenruo dissuaded him, saying, "I have been told that Zhi Xi often warned Kong Rong that his obstinacy would ruin him. His mourning is no more than a token of his personal loyalty. I would spare him." Xun Wenruo's words carried weight, and Cao Cao took no action against Zhi Xi. Zhi Xi arranged a suitable burial for Kong Rong and his sons. A later verse sang the imperial mentor's praises:

> When Kong Rong Beihai district ruled,
> His mighty spirit spanned the sky.
> His house was always filled with guests;
> Their cups were always filled with wine.
>
> By rhetoric he held his age in awe;
> His wit put kings and dukes to shame.[7]
> Historians call him loyal and true
> In annals that preserve his rightful name.

After the execution of Kong Rong, Cao Cao ordered the five armies to commence their southern expedition. Xun Wenruo alone remained to protect the capital.

•   •   •   •   •

In Jingzhou, Liu Biao's illness had worsened. He called for Xuande, intending to entrust him with the care of his sons. Xuande, attended by his brothers, came before the protector. "My condition is incurable, worthy brother," Liu Biao began. "Before I die, I intend to place my sons in your charge. They are not fit to succeed me. After my death you should assume control of Jingzhou yourself." Xuande bowed and wept. "I shall give my utmost support to my nephews," he said. "I have no higher ambition." As the two kinsmen spoke, the approach of Cao Cao's armies was reported. Xuande took his leave and hastened back to Xinye. Liu Biao, severely shaken, decided that his rule should pass to his eldest son, Liu Qi, whom he placed in Xuande's protection. Lady Cai, infuriated at the decision, had the inner gates sealed and the outer gates guarded by her men, Cai Mao and Zhang Yun.

Liu Qi had already positioned himself at Jiangxia[8] when he learned that his father was near death. He hurried back to Jingzhou, only to find Cai Mao barring his entrance. "Young master," Cai Mao declared, "you were commissioned by your father to defend Jiangxia and have no authority to abandon your duties. What if the Southland soldiers strike? Your appearance here could only annoy the protector and aggravate his condition, which would be most unfilial. You should return at once." Liu Qi stood helplessly outside the gates; after a spell of lamentation he returned sadly to Jiangxia.

Liu Biao continued to fail. At last, despairing of his heir's arrival, he groaned loudly and passed away in the eighth month of Jian An 13 on the forty-fifth day of the chronological cycle. A poet of later times lamented the fate of Liu Biao:

> The Yuans held the Yellow River north,
> And Liu Biao the middle Yangzi.
> Till women's rule dragged their houses down,
> And without a trace they were gone.

With the provincial protector dead, Lady Cai, Cai Mao, and Zhang Yun forged a will appointing Liu Zong heir.[9] Then they commenced mourning and announced the funeral. Liu Zong, a shrewd lad though only fourteen, said to the assembled advisers: "My father has departed this world. My elder brother, Qi, is presently in Jiangxia. And my uncle, Liu Xuande, is in Xinye. You have chosen me to succeed my father, but they may well challenge my succession by force of arms. How are we to justify ourselves?"

Before anyone could reply, Li Gui, a military adviser, stepped forward and said, "Our young master speaks good sense. We must dispatch a letter to Jiangxia announcing the mourning and inviting the elder son to govern us. At the same time we should have Liu Xuande share the administrative duties. In that way we will be able to withstand Cao Cao to the north and repel Sun Quan to the south. This plan provides for all contingencies."

Cai Mao turned on the speaker. "Do you dare to subvert the late protector's will?" he demanded sharply. But Li Gui stood firm and denounced Cai Mao: "After conspiring with your cohorts, you published a false will and then instated the junior son and deposed the senior. We will soon see the nine districts of our province fall into enemy hands. If our late lord's ghost be present, let him punish this crime." Cai Mao angrily ordered the officer removed and beheaded. Li Gui's curses ended only with his life.

Cai Mao set up Liu Zong as ruler of Jingzhou, and key members of the Cai clan assumed control of the province's military. He ordered Deng Yi, secretary to the protector, and Liu Xian, assistant protector, to guard the capital. Lady Cai and her son, Liu Zong, stationed themselves at Xiangyang to check any move by Liu Qi or Liu Xuande. Then, without informing Liu Qi or Xuande, Cai Mao had Liu Biao interred in the hills south of the River Han, east of Xiangyang.

Lady Cai and Liu Zong had hardly settled into Xiangyang when they discovered they were directly in the line of Cao Cao's march. Panicked, Liu Zong called Kuai Yue and Cai Mao for counsel. One of their staff supervisers, Fu Xuan, said to Liu Zong, "Cao Cao is not the only danger. Neither your elder brother in Jiangxia nor Xuande in Xinye has been informed of the funeral. If they move against us, Jingzhou could be lost. I have a plan, however, that will make our people as secure as Mount Tai and save your own rank and office as well." "What do you have in mind?" Liu Zong asked. "I advise you to offer the province to Cao Cao," Fu Xuan said. "He will surely treat you generously, my lord."

"What!" Liu Zong exclaimed. "Do you expect me simply to surrender the patrimony I have only now made mine?" Kuai Yue broke in: "Fu Xuan is right. The choice between rebellion and submission has to be made in broad perspective. The disparity between the strong and the weak cannot be overcome. Cao Cao has undertaken his expeditions north and south in the name of the imperial court. By resisting him, my lord, you win no name for obedience. Moreover, you are newly instated. Your hold on the territory is not firm. Problems abroad give us no peace, and problems at home are beginning to brew. Our people quail at the news of Cao's advance before a single battle has been fought. How can we make a stand with frightened men?" "My lord," Liu Zong conceded, "there is merit in your arguments, and I would be ruled by them, but to turn my late father's estate over to a stranger is bound to make me the mockery of the realm."

At this point someone strode boldly into the chamber and declared: "Fu Xuan and Kuai Yue have advised you well. You must act accordingly." All eyes turned to Wang Can (Zhongxuan), a man from Gaoping in Shanyang. Wang Can had a frail appearance and was short of stature. In his youth he had been received by the famed imperial courtier, Cai Yong. On that occasion, Cai Yong did Wang Can the honor of rising eagerly to greet him, even though he had many distinguished guests to meet. This gesture caused Cai Yong's startled retainers to ask him, "Why does the master single out this lad for such honor?" "Wang Can has extraordinary gifts," Cai Yong replied, "far beyond any I may have." Wang Can was widely informed and had a prodigious memory. He once recited the entire text of a roadside inscription after a single viewing. Another time he reconstructed perfectly a complex chess game after it had been played. He was also skilled in arithmetic, and he surpassed his contemporaries in rhetoric and poetry. At the age of seventeen he was advanced by the Emperor to attendant in the Inner Bureau, but he did not assume the post. Some time after that, to avoid the civil wars in the northeast, he came to Jingzhou, where Liu Biao had received him as an honored guest.

Now Wang Can asked Liu Zong, "How do you compare with Cao Cao, my lord?" "There is no comparison," he replied. "Cao Cao," Wang Can continued, "has a powerful army, brave commanders, and a staff of able tacticians. He captured Lü Bu at Xiapi; put Yuan Shao to flight at Guandu; chased Liu Xuande to Longyou; defeated the Wuhuan in the White Wolf Hills; and no man can count the others he has beheaded, eliminated, and swept aside, or the cities he has taken. If he comes in force, we cannot hold him off. Follow the proposal of Fu Xuan and Kuai Yue or suffer the consequences." "Excellent advice," Liu Zong answered, "but I shall have to inform my mother." At these words Lady Cai appeared from behind a screen and said, "That will not be necessary, since these three have agreed that you should tender the province to Cao Cao."

Having chosen his course, Liu Zong secretly sent his letter of surrender. The bearer, Song Zhong, was received in the city of Wancheng and richly rewarded by the prime minister. Cao Cao instructed Song Zhong to have Liu Zong welcome him in front of the city gate of Jingzhou; in return he would confirm Liu Zong's rule for all time.

Song Zhong was on his way back to Jingzhou with Cao Cao's answer when, nearing a river, he spied a party of soldiers under Lord Guan's command. Song Zhong tried to slip away but was called to a halt. Initially he evaded Lord Guan's questions, but persistent interrogation eventually forced him to disclose the nature of his mission. Astonished, Lord Guan took his prisoner back to Xuande, who wept at the story Song Zhong told.

"Under the circumstances," Zhang Fei said, "we have to behead the courier, take Xiangyang, do away with the Cai clan and Liu Zong, and go to war with Cao Cao." "Enough," Xuande retorted, "I will keep my own counsel on this." He then turned to

Song Zhong and demanded, "If you knew of these moves, why didn't you inform me at once? I could have your life, but what good would it do? Get out!" Reiterating humble thanks for this reprieve, Song Zhong scurried off.

At this moment of deep dilemma for Xuande, Liu Qi's envoy, Yi Ji, arrived. Xuande was grateful to Yi Ji for having saved his life, so he descended the steps, welcomed him personally, and thanked him profusely.[10] "My master, Liu Qi," the envoy began, "was in Jiangxia when he learned of his father's death. Lady Cai and Cai Mao did not announce the funeral and colluded to establish Liu Zong. My master has verified this. Thinking Your Lordship might not have heard, my master sent me to convey his expression of grief and to request that Your Lordship march to Xiangyang with your finest troops and make the Cais answer for their crime."

Xuande read Liu Qi's letter. "Your information about Liu Zong's usurpation is correct," he said to Yi Ji, "but do you know that they have offered the province to Cao Cao?" "Who told you that, my lord?" Yi Ji asked aghast. Xuande then described the capture of Liu Zong's messenger. "In that case," Yi Ji said, "hasten to Xiangyang on the pretext of attending mourning ceremonies for Liu Biao. Lure Liu Zong out to receive you, seize him, and wipe out his clique, and Jingzhou will be yours, my lord." "Good advice," Kongming remarked. But Xuande began to sob. "In his last hours," he said, "my elder brother entrusted his son to me. How could I face him in the netherworld if I laid hands on the other son and his estate?" "If you won't do it," Kongming said, "how do you propose to fight off Cao Cao when his troops are even now at Wancheng?" "We shall retreat to Fan," Xuande answered.[11]

The advance of Cao Cao's army to Bowang was announced. Xuande sent Liu Qi's envoy back to Jiangxia with instructions to prepare for battle. He then sat down with Kongming to discuss tactics. "Put your mind at ease," Kongming said. "Last time we burned out half of Xiahou Dun's army at Bowang. This time we'll make another trap for him. But Xinye is no place for us now. We must hasten to Fan." Proclamations of the impending move were posted at the four gates of Xinye. The text read:

> Without regard to age or sex, let all those willing to follow us proceed directly to Fan for temporary refuge. Do not endanger yourselves by remaining.

Sun Qian arranged to move the populace across the river, and Mi Zhu escorted the families of the officials to Fan. At the same time Kongming assembled the body of commanders. His first instruction was to Lord Guan: "Hide a thousand men at the upper end of the White River and provide each one with bags of sand to dam the waters. Tomorrow, after the third watch, the moment you hear men and horses downstream, pull the bags out of the river and flood the enemy. Then hurry down to reinforce us."

Next, Kongming instructed Zhang Fei: "Hide a thousand men at the Boling crossing, where the river runs slow. If Cao's men are in danger of drowning, that's where they'll try to escape. I want you to join the battle at that point of vantage."

He then gave orders to Zhao Zilong: "Divide three thousand men into four contingents. Take one yourself and hide outside the eastern gate to Xinye. Have the other three contingents cover the remaining gates. Before you leave the city, place plenty of sulphur and saltpeter on the house roofs. When Cao enters, his soldiers will want to rest in the people's homes. Tomorrow evening the wind should be strong. The moment it starts blowing, have the men covering the three other gates shoot flaming arrows into the town. As the fire peaks, let those three contingents raise a great commotion—but leave the east gate open for the enemy to exit through. When they come through, attack from behind. Then catch up with Lord Guan and Zhang Fei and bring your three thousand, along with their men, over to Fan."

Finally, Kongming instructed Mi Fang and Liu Feng: "Station two thousand on Magpie Tail Hill, thirty *li* from Xinye: one thousand under blue flags, one thousand under red. When Cao's army comes up, have the red group flee left, the blue group right. This will confuse their leaders and prevent pursuit. Next, deploy an ambush and fall on the foe as soon as you see flames over Xinye. After you're finished, come to the upper end of the river and help us out." All parts of their plan now in place, Kongming and Xuande climbed to an observation point to await reports of victory.

· · · · ·

In the lead of Cao Cao's army was the hundred-thousand-man force commanded jointly by Cao Ren and Cao Hong. Its three-thousand-man shock force fit out in iron armor and under the command of Xu Chu was sweeping toward Xinye. Around midday Xu Chu reached the slopes of Magpie Tail and saw soldiers massed under blue and red flags. As he advanced, Liu Feng and Mi Fang began their prearranged maneuvers. Xu Chu called a brief halt. "There must be an ambush ahead," he said. "We'll hold here." He then hastened back to inform Cao Ren, who was leading the main force. "It's only a decoy," Cao Ren said to him. "There's no ambush there. Press on. We will follow."

Xu Chu returned to his forward position and resumed the advance. The contingent reached a small wood and stopped. The place looked deserted. The sun had set. As Xu Chu prepared to move forward again, the hilltops seemed to speak with the blaring of horns and the beating of drums. Xu Chu looked up into a field of flags and banners surrounding two umbrellas, one over Xuande, the other over Kongming. They were seated face-to-face enjoying something to drink. Maddened, Xu Chu sought a way up, but his ascent was prevented by the stone and wooden missiles that came pelting down. As thunderous shouts from behind the hill rang in the air, Xu Chu struggled to get his forces into action, but the light of day had already left the sky.

When Cao Ren's main force arrived, he ordered Xinye occupied in order to shelter and rest the horses. He reached the walls, had all four gates flung wide, and entered the evacuated city unchallenged. "As you see," Cao Hong remarked, "having neither strength nor strategy to oppose us, they have scurried off, followed by the entire population." Spent and famished, the invaders settled into whatever lodgings were at hand and began preparing their meals. Cao Ren and Cao Hong entered the *yamen*, there to enjoy the respite from war.

After the first watch strong winds blew up. Guards at the gates reported minor fires, but Cao Ren dismissed the danger, saying, "Take it easy. They must have been caused by our army's cooks." But more reports kept coming in, followed by the news that three of the city's gates were on fire. Frantically, Cao Ren ordered his commanders to mount, but the whole city was already ablaze. Flames covered the ground and reached into the sky— a conflagration that dwarfed the one that had foiled Xiahou Dun at Bowang. As a later poet wrote,

> The evil genius of the northern plain
> Marched his legions to the River Han.
> Within Xinye's walls he felt the wind god's wrath,
> And down from blazing Heaven the fire god ran.

Cao Ren led his men through the smoke and fire, dashing for any avenue of escape. Someone called out that the east gate was not burning, and everyone bolted for it in a mad rush that left many trampled to death. Cao Ren had barely made it out of the burning city when he heard voices roaring behind him. Zhao Zilong was charging up. In the melee the beaten invaders—too demoralized to fight—fled for their lives. Then Mi Fang hit them hard, inflicting more casualties. Cao Ren continued his flight. Again he was attacked, this time by Liu Feng. By the fourth watch the bulk of his force had been crushed. The remnant reached the edge of the White River, thankful that the water was low enough to cross. Men and horses waded in and drank their fill amid great clamor and neighing.

Upstream Lord Guan had dammed the current. At dusk he had seen the flames over Xinye. Now at the fourth watch he heard the men and horses downstream and ordered his troops to pull the sandbags from the river. The pent-up water burst forth, drowning men and mounts in its powerful surge. In order to cross, Cao Ren led the survivors to Boling, where the current was slower, only to be confronted by another party of soldiers. Suddenly their shouts filled the night, and before him stood Zhang Fei. "Cao, you bastard, I'll have your life!" he cried to the astonished enemy. Indeed:

> In the city Cao Ren witnessed the belching flames;
> At the river a new menace confronted him.

Would Cao Ren survive?[12]

READ ON.

41

Liu Xuande Leads His Flock over the River;
Zhao Zilong Rescues Master Liu Single-handedly

As LORD GUAN RELEASED THE TORRENTS of the White River upstream, Zhang Fei joined the battle downstream, intercepting Cao Ren with a powerful offensive. Zhang Fei and Xu Chu suddenly came face-to-face, but Xu Chu had lost his taste for combat; he fled. Zhang Fei caught up with Xuande and Kongming, and all together they marched upriver to the boats that Liu Feng and Mi Fang had waiting to take them to Fan. After the crossing Kongming ordered the ships and rafts burned.

· · · ·

Cao Ren collected the battered remnants of his troops and stationed them in Xinye, sending Cao Hong to Cao Cao with a full report. "Zhuge, the bumpkin! How dare he!" Cao Cao raged. He then mobilized his entire force and blanketed the region around Xinye. He ordered the hills scoured, the White River blocked, and his host divided into eight field armies. His objective was to take Fan in a concerted attack.

"My lord," Liu Ye said, "you have barely arrived in Xiangyang and must win the affections of the people before all else. Liu Bei has moved the entire population of Xinye over to Fan; a direct attack would wreak havoc on both counties. I suggest sending an envoy to offer Liu Bei the opportunity to submit. If he refuses, we will have made plain our wish to spare the people. If he accepts, Jingzhou will be ours without a fight." Cao Cao approved and asked whom to send. "Shan Fu is close to Liu Bei. Why not send him?" Liu Ye suggested. "What if he does not return?" Cao Cao countered. "And make himself a laughingstock?" Liu Ye responded. "Have no fear of it, my lord."

On this advice Cao Cao summoned Shan Fu and said, "My original thought was to crush Fan. But I hesitate to put the common people through such suffering. If you can convince Liu Bei to surrender, I shall forgive his offenses and grant him rank. If he clings to his delusions, soldier and civilian alike will perish, and not a stone will be left unscathed. I know you for a loyal and honorable man. That is why I delegate you. I trust you will not fail me." Shan Fu set out.[1]

Liu Xuande and Kongming received Shan Fu at Fan, and the three shared memories of former times. Then Shan Fu said, "Cao Cao sent me to call for your surrender, my lord. But it is only a pretext for winning popular approval. He has formed eight armies and filled in the bed of the river for his advance. I fear this city cannot be defended. You must find a way to leave as soon as possible." Xuande wanted Shan Fu to stay, but the former adviser said, "I would be universally scorned. Be assured, my mother's death burns fresh in my heart. Though I stay with Cao in body, I am sworn never to devise a stratagem for him. With Sleeping Dragon's help you need not despair. I must go back. Please forgive me." Xuande did not press the matter. Shan Fu reported that Xuande had no intention of submitting, and Cao Cao, began the southern campaign in a great show of anger that very day.

Xuande turned to Kongming, who said, "We have to leave at once. We can take Xiangyang and rest there temporarily." "These common folk have stayed by us so long," Xuande said, "are we to abandon them now?" "Send round word," Kongming said, "that those who wish to may follow you." He sent Lord Guan to the river to prepare the boats, and ordered Sun Qian and Jian Yong to issue the following proclamation: "Cao Cao's army is approaching. Our city cannot hold out. Those who wish to will have to follow us across the river." The people of Fan as well as those of Xinye shouted out in unison, "We will go with Lord Liu—even if we must die."

That same day, amid cries and tears, the exodus began. Bracing up elders, taking the young in hand, leading sons and daughters, the human tide traversed the water like great waves rolling on and on. Unabating cries rang out from the shores. On his boat surveying the scene, Xuande was profoundly shaken. "If I have made these good people suffer this for my sake, what will be left to live for?" He attempted to throw himself into the river but was restrained by those around him. His words pierced all who heard him with sorrow. After reaching the south shore, Xuande looked back to those still waiting anxiously and tearfully to cross. He had Lord Guan urge the boatmen to greater efforts. Then at last he mounted.

Xuande led the mass march to the east gate of Xiangyang. He found the top of the wall crowded with banners, the moat below thick with sharp staves and barbed branches. Xuande reined in and shouted, "Liu Zong, worthy nephew, I seek but the succor of these people. Open the gates for us—and quickly!" But Liu Zong was afraid to show himself. Cai Mao and Zhang Yun raced to the tower and urged the archers to unleash their volleys on the human throng outside the wall. Staring upward, the people voiced their appeal. One commander inside the town raced to the tower with several hundred guards and bellowed, "Cai Mao! Zhang Yun! Traitors to the Han! How dare you reject Governor Liu, a man of humane character who comes seeking refuge for the people in his care!"

Who was this man, eight spans tall, with a face swarthy as dark dates? It was Wei Yan (Wenchang) of Yiyang. Then and there Wei Yan cut down the gate guards with broad sweeps of his sword, threw open the gates and let down the drawbridge. "Imperial Uncle Liu," he shouted, "lead your men into the city and let us slay these tyrants together." Without hesitation Zhang Fei started forward, but Xuande checked him. "Don't create panic," he warned.

Wei Yan was doing his utmost to induce Xuande to enter the city, when another soldier rode forth and denounced him: "Wei Yan, common footslogger! Will you incite sedition? It's I, General Wen Ping!" Outraged, Wei Yan raised his spear and rode forth to engage his challenger. The men of both sides then fell upon one another at the base of the city wall in a wild mutual slaughter that made the ground shake. "I have brought the people the harm I meant to spare them," Xuande said. "We shall not enter Xiangyang!" "Jiangling is another strategically located town," Kongming said. "Let's take it and settle in." "My idea, exactly," Xuande responded. And with that he turned the throng away from Xiangyang and on toward Jiangling. In the commotion many people from Xiangyang slipped out and joined Liu Xuande.

Meanwhile, the fight between Wei Yan and Wen Ping continued. By afternoon Wei Yan's force had been decimated. He finally rode from the field, hoping to locate Xuande but ended up taking refuge with Han Xuan, governor of Changsha.

More than one hundred thousand soldiers and commoners, thousands of carts and carriages, and innumerable carriers and bearers came together in the procession. When they came upon Liu Biao's grave, Xuande led his commanders in ritual worship. In a trembling voice he declared, "Elder brother, I, wanting in virtue and lacking in talent, have failed to fulfill the heavy charge you laid on me. This shameful offense is mine alone and does not touch these good people. Brother, let your splendid spirit descend and save the people of Jingzhou."[2] Xuande's voice conveyed such sad intensity that neither soldier nor civilian could contain his emotions.

A scout reported: "Cao Cao's main force is camped at Fan. They're gathering boats and rafts to cross over here today." "We can defend ourselves from Jiangling," the commanders assured Xuande, "but with such a multitude on our hands we're barely covering ten *li* a day. Who knows when we will make Jiangling? And how could we engage Cao's army if it found us now? Wouldn't it be expedient to leave the people behind for now and go on ahead ourselves?" Xuande replied with deep feeling, "The human factor is the key to any undertaking. How can we abandon those who have committed themselves to us?" These words became known, and all were deeply moved. Much later a poet left these lines commemorating the desperate flight across the waters:

> In mortal straits, good of heart, he kept his flock from harm;
> Riverborne, the tearful leader won his army's love.
> And still today men mark the site with solemn piety;
> And older folks keep Lord Liu in cherished memory.

Xuande advanced slowly in the midst of his multitude. "They will overtake us soon," Kongming warned. "Dispatch Lord Guan to Jiangxia. Have him ask young Liu Qi for boats to meet us at Jiangling." Accordingly, Xuande put this request in a letter, which Lord Guan and Sun Qian, guarded by five hundred riders, carried to Liu Qi. Xuande had Zhang Fei watch the rear, Zhao Zilong protect the members of his family, and the remaining leaders take care of the commoners. On they marched. In the course of one day they covered little more than ten *li*.

·   ·   ·   ·

From Fan, Cao Cao sent a messenger across the river to summon Liu Zong. Liu Zong was afraid to appear before the prime minister, and so Cai Mao and Zhang Yun asked permission to go in his stead. Wang Wei secretly urged Liu Zong, "You, General, have surrendered, and Xuande is gone. Cao Cao's guard will be down. Why not organize your men, place them strategically, and surprise Cao Cao? Once he is captured, you will command the empire's respect and a general call to arms in your name would bring peace to the whole of the northern heartland. Such an opportunity rarely arises. Don't miss it!" Liu Zong took this proposal to Cai Mao, who berated Wang Wei and said, "How absurd! What do you know of the Mandate of Heaven?" To this, Wang Wei retorted, "Traitor! What I wouldn't give to devour you alive!" At this point Kuai Yue intervened to prevent Cai Mao from killing Wang Wei.

Cai Mao and Zhang Yun traveled to Fan and presented themselves in a most ingratiating manner before Cao Cao. "Tell me," the prime minister asked, "what are Jingzhou's resources in men, horses, cash, and grain?" "Fifty thousand horse soldiers," Cai

Mao replied, "one hundred and fifty thousand foot soldiers, eighty thousand marines. Most of the coin and grain is in Jiangling; the rest is stored in various places—a year's supply." "How about the war-boats?" Cao Cao continued. "And who are the naval commanders?" "All told," Cai Mao answered, "seven thousand boats. Myself and Zhang Yun here are in command."

Then and there Cao Cao conferred on Cai Mao the title of Lord Who Controls the South and named him superintendent of the Naval Forces, and he made Zhang Yun Lord Who Upholds Obedience and lieutenant superintendent of the Naval Forces. Delighted with their new positions, the two men expressed respectful gratitude. The prime minister said, "I shall report to the Emperor Liu Biao's death and his son's submission, so that the proper heir may rule Jingzhou permanently." The two commanders withdrew, highly pleased with the outcome of their interview.

Xun You said to Cao Cao, "Why did you grant such exalted titles to those craven toadies? And why make them naval superintendents into the bargain?" "Do you think I don't know them for what they are?" Cao Cao replied. "Don't forget, we have an army of northerners unused to naval warfare. Those two can be of help at the moment. When we have accomplished what we want, they will be dealt with as they deserve!"

Cai Mao and Zhang Yun returned to Jingzhou and appeared before Liu Zong. "Cao Cao," they said, "has assured us that he will recommend your permanent control of Jingzhou to the Emperor." Liu Zong was delighted. The next day he and his mother, Lady Cai, prepared the seal of office and the tally of command and crossed the river to welcome Cao Cao and do him the honor of presenting the instruments of government personally.

Cao Cao offered words of comfort to the young prince. Then, to prepare his entrance, he directed the generals of the expeditionary army to station troops by the walls of Xiangyang. Cai Mao and Zhang Yun ordered the residents to welcome the prime minister with burning incense. Again, Cao Cao spoke kind and reassuring words to one and all. He entered the city and seated himself in the governmental hall. First, he summoned Kuai Yue and said to him, "Acquiring your services means more to me than the whole province." He made Kuai Yue governor of Jiangling and lord of Fan. Next, he made Fu Xuan and Wang Can honorary lords, and Liu Zong imperial inspector of Qingzhou, with orders to report to his post forthwith. Startled, Liu Zong declined, saying, "I have no wish to become governor of another province, only to remain on my parents' native soil." Cao Cao replied, "Qingzhou is close to the capital. I am making you an official attached to the court lest you come to harm here." Cao Cao overcame Liu Zong's objections, and the youth set off for Qingzhou, as required, with Lady Cai. They were accompanied only by the former general Wang Wei. The other members of Liu Zong's court returned after seeing him to the river.

Cao Cao called Yu Jin aside and said, "Take a few riders; overtake Liu Zong and his mother, and do away with them. That should prevent further trouble." Yu Jin soon overtook the little party. "I bear the prime minister's command," he declared. "Prepare to die!" Lady Cai cradled the boy and cried bitterly as Yu Jin's men set to work. Wang Wei put up a fierce struggle but was finally slain. Lady Cai and Liu Zong were subsequently killed swiftly. Yu Jin reported the success of his mission to Cao Cao, who rewarded him richly.[3] Cao Cao also searched for Kongming's family in Longzhong, but on Kongming's instructions they had long since moved to Three Rivers—to Cao Cao's great frustration.

After Cao Cao had Xiangyang under his control, Xun You counseled him, "Jiangling, with its ample supplies of money and grain, is one of the keys to the province. Xuande will be well positioned if he gets hold of that town." "The thought has never left my mind," Cao Cao said and ordered that one of his generals in Xiangyang be selected to spearhead a move to Jiangling.

The planning session, however, was not attended by Wen Ping, and Cao Cao demanded to know the reason. When Wen Ping finally appeared, Cao Cao asked him, "Why are you late?" "A loyal subject who has failed to protect his master's lands cannot show his face," Wen Ping said and began to sob and weep. "A loyal follower and true," Cao Cao said. He promoted Wen Ping to governor of Jiangxia, granted him the title of honorary lord, and ordered him to lead the expedition to Jiangling.

At this moment spies reported: "Liu Bei is accompanied by a multitude of common folk. They're only three hundred *li* from here and moving at barely ten *li* a day." Cao Cao ordered five thousand crack horsemen to overtake Liu Bei within one day. The force set out that night, followed closely by Cao Cao's main army.

•   •   •   •

Xuande was now at the head of more than a hundred thousand common folk and three thousand cavalry, all struggling to reach Jiangling. Zhao Zilong had charge of Xuande's two wives and young son. Zhang Fei was defending the rear. "We have heard nothing of Lord Guan," Kongming said, "since we sent him to Jiangxia. I wonder what came of his mission." "Perhaps we could trouble you to go there yourself," Xuande responded. "Liu Qi will never forget the good advice you once gave him, and if he sees you in person, we should get what we want." Kongming agreed and, joined by Liu Feng and five hundred men, set out for Jiangxia in quest of aid.

Liu Xuande pressed on. With him were Jian Yong, Mi Zhu, and Mi Fang. Suddenly a violent gale scooped up the dust in front of the horses and sent it skyward, blotting out the sun. "What does this signify?" Xuande asked in alarm. Jian Yong, who had some insight into the laws of *yin* and *yang* that govern all, took augury and said uneasily, "Great ill fortune should strike tonight, my lord. Abandon these people with all speed and be gone." "They have followed from as far as Xinye," Xuande replied. "I cannot abandon them." "If you continue like this, disaster is imminent." "What lies ahead?" Xuande asked. "Dangyang county," his attendants answered, "site of Scenic Mountain." Xuande ordered camp pitched at the mountain.

Autumn was passing into winter. Chill winds pierced the marchers' bones. As the day darkened, wailing voices filled the wilderness. By the fourth watch, the dead of night, the encamped multitude began to hear them—out of the northwest—the shouts of men that shook the ground as they came. Xuande leaped to his horse and led two thousand of his own crack troops to meet them. But Cao Cao's force had the advantage of numbers. Opposition was impossible. Xuande was fighting for his life. At just this juncture of mortal extremity Zhang Fei arrived with a body of men and cut a route for Xuande, enabling him to escape eastward. Wen Ping challenged Xuande, but Xuande denounced him: "Faithless traitor! To dare to stand before men!" Wen Ping, his face suffused with shame, turned away and headed northeast.

Zhang Fei stayed beside Xuande. They fought as they fled. By dawn the hue and cry of war had receded. For the first time Xuande rested his horse. Only a hundred riders remained with him. He had become hopelessly separated from the mass of his followers, from Mi Zhu, Mi Fang, Jian Yong, and Zhao Zilong, and also from his family. "One hundred thousand living souls," he lamented, "have borne these woes for remaining with us. Of the fate of our commanders and of my family we know nothing. Even a man of clay or wood would have to grieve."

In this moment of despair Xuande saw Mi Fang, his face pierced through with arrows, stumble toward him, crying, "Zhao Zilong has defected to Cao!" "So old a friend would not betray me," Xuande said heatedly. "He sees our position is hopeless," Zhang Fei said, "our strength spent, and probably expects wealth and rank from Cao Cao." "He has stayed with us through our worst tribulations," Xuande answered. "He has a will of iron; wealth and rank would not move him." "I saw him heading northwest," Mi Fang said. "I will find him," Zhang Fei said. "And when I do, this spear will do the rest." "Mistrust him not!" Xuande cautioned. "You should remember how our second brother, whom you likewise suspected, made short work of Cao's generals Yan Liang and Wen Chou. Zhao Zilong must have good reason for his absence. I cannot believe he has abandoned us."

Zhang Fei would not be reasoned with. He took twenty horsemen to Steepslope Bridge. A wood to the east gave him an idea: "If I cut some branches, tie them to the horses' tails, and trot the beasts back and forth in the wood, the dust they raise will suggest numbers that should deter the enemy's approach." Having thus instructed his men, Zhang Fei, spear ready, mount poised, rode onto the bridge and scoured the west for any sign of Zhao Zilong.

During Cao Cao's raid Zhao Zilong had attacked the enemy at the fourth watch and continued battling until daybreak. But he had become separated from Xuande's family and was unable to find them again. He thought: "Lord Liu placed his two wives, Lady Gan and Lady Mi, in my care, along with his child, Master Ah Dou. Having lost them in the fighting, I cannot show myself before my lord again. The least I can do is die in battle trying to locate his loved ones." With only thirty or forty riders behind him, Zhao Zilong charged into the tangle of fighters.

The common people of two counties, Xinye and Fan, shook Heaven and earth with their wails as they fled the scene of battle. Beyond all numbering, pierced by arrows, lanced by spears, they abandoned their young. Zhao Zilong, in search of his charges, came upon Jian Yong lying in the brush. "Have you seen our mistresses?" Zilong asked. "They abandoned their carriages," Jian Yong answered, "and fled on foot with Ah Dou. I was rounding a hill, racing after them, when one of Cao's captains stabbed me. I fell, and he took my horse. I could not move, much less fight." Zilong gave him the mount of one of his followers. He also detailed two men to help Jian Yong get to Xuande and report that he meant to seek high and low for Xuande's wives and son, or die on the field.

Zhao Zilong was galloping toward Steepslope Bridge when a soldier hailed him. "Where to, General Zhao?" "Who are you?" Zhao Zilong countered, reining up. "I was escorting our lord's wives," the man replied, "when an arrow knocked me down." Zilong asked for details. "Just now," the soldier said, "I saw Lady Gan, disheveled and barefoot, fleeing south with a group of women, commoners." At once Zhao Zilong turned away and raced south. He passed hundreds of civilians, men and women, helping each other make their way. "Is Lady Gan among you?" Zilong cried. To the rear of the crowd Lady Gan spotted Zilong and called out. Zilong dismounted and planted his spear in the ground. "Letting you slip from my sight was a dreadful crime," he said tearfully. "Where are Lady Mi and the young master?" "When Cao's troops chased us," Lady Gan said, "we quit the escort and fell in with these refugees. Another troop attacked us. We scattered, and I was separated from them. Somehow I escaped alive."

At that instant a fresh outcry announced another troop charging the crowd. Zhao Zilong flourished his spear and remounted to observe. In front of him was Mi Zhu, a prisoner in bonds. Just behind him, at the head of a thousand men, was Chunyu Dao, Cao Ren's corps commander, waving his sword. He had captured Mi Zhu and was going to claim his reward. With a short, sharp cry Zilong, spear leveled, went straight for Chunyu Dao. Chunyu Dao, unable to counter, was lanced and thrust under his horse. Zhao Zilong then rescued Mi Zhu and made off with two horses. He sat Lady Gan on one and, cutting a bloody swath, brought her to Steepslope Bridge.

Zhang Fei, poised on the bridge with leveled sword, confronted him. "Zhao Zilong!" he called at the top of his voice, "explain why you betrayed our brother!" "I couldn't find our mistresses or the young master," Zilong answered, "so I dropped back. What do you mean by 'betrayed'?" "If Jian Yong had not already vouched for you, you would not pass!" Zhang Fei said. "Where is our lord?" Zilong asked. "Ahead, not far," Zhang Fei replied. Zhao Zilong turned to Mi Zhu and said, "Go on with Lady Gan. I'm going back to look for Lady Mi and the young master." He took a few riders and left.

Along the way Zilong saw a captain with an iron spear in his hand and a sword strapped to his back. Behind him a dozen horsemen advanced at a gallop. Without wasting words, Zilong challenged the leader and dropped him in a single engagement. The dozen riders fled. The slain man was Xiahou En, Cao Cao's personal attendant and sword bearer.

Now, Cao Cao had two swords of exceptional value. One was called Heaven's Prop, the other Black Pommel. Cao wore the first himself, Xiahou En the second. Its blade could slice through iron as if it were mud, and its point was dagger sharp. Before he crossed Zhao Zilong, Xiahou En had let himself become separated from Cao Cao, for he never doubted his skill. Intent only on what he and his men could plunder, Xiahou En had little expected to lose his life, let alone the treasured weapon. Zhao Zilong, examining the sword, saw the words "Black Pommel" engraved in gold on the handle and realized the value of the weapon. He thrust it into his belt, raised his spear, and resumed his assault on the enemy ranks. Looking back, he could no longer see his riders behind him.

Undaunted, Zilong continued searching for Lady Mi, questioning any civilian he passed. Finally, someone pointed ahead, saying, "The mistress has the child. Her left leg is wounded, and she can't walk. She's sitting there in a crevice in the wall." Zhao Zilong hastened to the spot and found a dwelling with an earthen wall that had been damaged by fire. Lady Mi was sitting at the base, near a dry well, weeping. Zilong dismounted and pressed his palms and head to the ground.

"With you here, General," Lady Mi said, "I know Ah Dou will live. I pray you, pity the father who, after half a lifetime of being tossed hither and roaming thither, has nothing in this world but this scrap of blood and bone. Guard him well, General, that he may see his father once again—and that I may die without regret." "My negligence is responsible for the ordeals you have suffered," Zhao Zilong said. "Say no more, but take this horse. I intend to fight on, on foot and bring you safely through the enemy's lines." "I will not have it that way," Lady Mi responded. "You must keep the horse. You are the child's only protection. My wounds are heavy, and my death is of no moment. I pray, General, take the child on ahead, and quickly. Do not delay for my sake." "I hear pursuers," Zhao Zilong said. "Mount the horse." "No," she said. "Do not lose two lives." She held Ah Dou out to Zhao Zilong and added, "His life is in your hands." Steadfastly, she refused his offers. The enemy was closing in. Their shouts were everywhere. Zilong's tone grew more anxious. "My lady, what will you do when they come?" Without answering again, Lady Mi set Ah Dou on the ground, turned, and threw herself into the well. A poet of later times honored her sacrifice in these lines:[4]

> The embattled captain had to have his steed;
> On foot he could not save the little prince.
> Her death preserved the Liu dynastic line:
> For bold decision mark this heroine.

To prevent the enemy from taking his mistress's corpse, Zhao Zilong pushed over the earthen wall, burying the well. He then loosened his armor straps, lowered his breast-plate, and placed Ah Dou against his bosom. Hefting his spear, Zilong remounted.

By this time one of Cao Hong's corps commanders, Yan Ming, had brought up a body of foot soldiers. Wielding a two-edged sword with three prongs, he set on Zhao Zilong. After a brief clash Zilong ran him through. He dispersed Yan Ming's squad, killing several, and broke open a path. But another unit—commanded by a general—arrived and blocked Zilong. Their standard bore the words, large and clear, "Zhang He of Hejian." Without a word, Zilong raised his spear and joined battle. After more than ten passes Zilong had to break off the contest. He fled, and Zhang He gave chase.

Zhao Zilong applied the whip, but unfortunately his horse went crashing into a ditch, and Zhang He approached for the kill. Suddenly, a beam of reddish light formed an arc from the ditch, and the horse, as if treading on thin air, leaped out of the hole. The rescue of the prince is described in this verse of later times:

> The cornered dragon bathed in red took wing
> And cleaved the enemy lines by Steepslope Bridge.
> In two score years and two the babe will reign;
> Zhao's superhuman might thus earned his fame.

Zhang He fell back at the miraculous sight.

Zhao Zilong was in full flight when he heard two voices behind him: "Halt, Zhao Zilong!" Two more commanders before him, displaying weapons, blocked his way. Bringing up the rear were Ma Yan and Zhang Yi; blocking the way in front were Jiao Chu and Zhang Nan: all four had served Yuan Shao before surrendering to Cao Cao. Zhao Zilong fought them mightily. Cao Cao's men came trooping up. Zilong drew the sword Black Pommel and began slashing wildly. Wherever he struck, the blade cut through the armor, drawing blood. In this manner he slowly drove back the swarm of commanders and got through the encirclement.

From his vantage on Scenic Mountain, Cao Cao observed the general whom none could best and asked his attendants who it was. Cao Hong sped down the hill to find out, shouting: "Let the fighter speak his name!" "Zhao Zilong of Changshan!" was the instant reply. Cao Hong relayed the news to Cao Cao, who said, "There's a tiger-warrior for you! Try and get him here alive." He sent swift riders to inform various stations: "If Zhao Zilong comes your way, deliver him to the prime minister alive. No potshots!" And so, Zhao Zilong was able to get away. Was this too not the result of Ah Dou's good fortune?

After cutting through the encircling troops, the baby prince still on his breast, Zhao Zilong downed two standards and captured three spears. The sum total of noted captains speared or slashed by Zilong amounted to more than fifty. His exploits are remembered in these lines written long after the events:

In bloodsoaked battle gown and armor bloody red,
He faced down every foe at Dangyang town.
Of all who ever fought to keep a king from harm,
Who excels Zhao Zilong, hero of Changshan?

Zhao Zilong, his surcoat drenched in blood, had brought Ah Dou safely away from the main battleground when two armed companies intercepted him by the foot of the slope. They were led by two brothers, Zhong Jin and Zhong Shen, corps commanders under Xiahou Dun. Zhong Jin was wielding a giant axe; Zhong Shen, a figured halberd. "Dismount and submit, Zhao Zilong!" they shouted. Here was an instance, indeed,

Of facing the waves in the dragon's pool
Moments after escaping from the tiger's lair.

Would Zhao Zilong manage to get free?
READ ON.

42

Zhang Fei Makes an Uproar at Steepslope Bridge;
Xuande, Defeated, Flees to the Han River Ford

ZHAO ZILONG WORKED HIS SPEAR against the two attackers. Zhong Jin came on first, swinging a giant battle-axe. The riders tangled. Zilong downed his man neatly and rode on. Zhong Shen gave chase, halberd in hand, drawing close enough for his horse to touch the tail of Zilong's mount. The reflection of his halberd flashed in the back of Zilong's armor. Suddenly Zilong pulled up short and lurched around, confronting his pursuer: to the left, Zilong's spear checked the halberd; to the right, he swung Black Pommel, cutting through Zhong Shen's helmet and cleaving his skull in two. Shen's escort quickly vanished.

Riding unhindered, Zilong headed for Steepslope Bridge. Suddenly he felt the ground trembling behind him. Wen Ping was leading a company in pursuit. Man and mount spent, Zilong reached the bridge and saw Zhang Fei upon it, lance raised, horse steady. Zilong hailed him: "I need help, Yide!" "Hurry across!" Zhang Fei said. "Leave the pursuers to me!" Zilong guided his horse over the bridge and rode another twenty *li*. Finally he found Xuande resting under a tree, surrounded by a group of men. Zilong dismounted and placed his head and hands to the ground. Lord and vassal wept.

Still breathing hard, Zilong said, "Ten thousand deaths could not redeem my offense. Lady Mi was wounded so badly that she refused my horse and threw herself down a well. I could do nothing but knock over an earthen wall to cover her body. Then, holding the young master on my chest, I broke through the enemy's lines, and by the favor Heaven bestows on you, my lord, I survived. A moment ago the young master was crying. But he's stopped moving now, and I fear . . . " Zilong untied his armor and looked inside. The infant was asleep. "Safe and sound," he announced happily. "Fortune smiles." He handed Ah Dou carefully to Xuande, who flung him to the ground the instant he received him. "For the sake of a suckling like you," Xuande cried, "I risked losing a great commander!"[1] Zilong swept the child off the ground and prostrated himself, saying through his tears, "If I cut my heart out here, I could not repay your kindness to me." A poet of later times described the scene:

> The tigers sprang from Cao Cao's fighting line;
> Safe on Zhao Yun's breast the little dragon curled.
> How did the liege requite his liege man's love?
> Down before the horse, Xuande his own son hurled!

• • • • •

Wen Ping, meanwhile, had tracked Zilong to the bridge. There he found Zhang Fei, tiger-whiskers upcurled, eyes two rings of fury, snake-lance in hand. Mounted and poised, Zhang Fei looked out from the bridge. Wen Ping spotted dust rising out of the adjacent copse to the east. Suspecting an ambush, he reined in. Soon Cao Cao's leading generals joined him—Cao Ren, Li Dian, Xiahou Dun, Xiahou Yuan, Yue Jin, Zhang Liao, Zhang He, Xu Chu, and others. Cao's commanders contemplated Zhang Fei's menacing glare and leveled lance. And, too, they remembered Kongming's clever traps. They dug in west of the bridge, therefore, and posted a man back to Cao Cao. News of the standoff decided Cao Cao to hurry to the scene.

Zhang Fei's probing eye made out Cao Cao's blue silk umbrella in the distance, his feathered battle-axe and fringed banner. "So he came to see for himself," Zhang Fei thought. He called out: "I am Zhang Fei of Yan! Have you a man who'll fight it out to the death?" The power of Zhang Fei's voice unnerved Cao Cao's men. Cao Cao ordered the command umbrella removed. Turning to his attendants, he said, "Once Lord Guan told me that Zhang Fei had taken the head of a chief general before the eyes of his own legions as easily as removing an object from a sack. Today we have crossed his path and must take care." As Cao Cao spoke, Zhang Fei widened his eyes and shouted again: "Here he stands! Zhang Fei of Yan, who'll fight to the death any man that dares!" But Cao Cao, daunted by the warrior's indomitable spirit, was content to draw back.[2]

Zhang Fei watched the rear lines of Cao Cao's army shuffling about. He lifted his spear and bellowed: "What's it to be? Don't want to fight? Don't want to leave?" The mighty voice still commanded the air when Xiahou Jie, right beside Cao Cao, collapsed and fell from his saddle, panic-stricken. Cao Cao turned and rode back, followed by his commanders. Indeed, what suckling babe can bear the peal of thunder; what injured woodsman can stand the roar of tigers and leopards? At that moment Cao Cao's soldiers threw down their spears and helmets and trampled one other as they fled—a tide of men, an avalanche of horses. Later a poet expressed his awe:

> Zhang Fei's war blood rose at Steepslope Bridge:
> Spear leveled, horse poised, eyes round-fixed.
> With a single thunderous cry that shook the ground,
> Alone he turned Cao's mighty host around.

Zhang Fei's awesome presence had terrified Cao Cao. Dashing west, he let his cap and hairpin drop, and his hair streamed out behind him. Zhang Liao and Xu Chu overtook him and seized his horse's bridle. Cao Cao had lost control. "Do not panic, Your Excellency," Zhang Liao said. "Is one Zhang Fei so fearsome? Turn the army round again and fight. Liu Bei can be taken!" At these words Cao Cao got hold of himself and sent Zhang Liao and Xu Chu back to the bridge to find out what they could.

Zhang Fei dared not pursue Cao Cao's withdrawing army. He summoned his original retinue of twenty riders, had them remove the branches from their horses' tails, and ordered them to pull down the bridge. He then reported back to Xuande. Xuande said, "Your bravery, brother, is beyond question, but not your tactics." Zhang Fei began to protest. "Cao Cao is a man of many schemes," Xuande continued. "You should have let the bridge stand. Now he's sure to be back." "If a single shout sent him reeling several *li*," Zhang Fei argued, "he won't be back for more." "Had you let it stand," Xuande explained, "fear of ambush would have continued to deter him from attacking. Now that it's down, he'll know we were afraid, having no troops around. His million-man host could ford the Han and the Great River simply by filling them in! How could razing one

bridge stop him?'' With that, Xuande set out at once on the side roads, moving diago-
nally toward Mianyang by way of Hanjin.

Zhang Liao and Xu Chu examined the bridge and reported back to Cao Cao: ''Zhang
Fei destroyed it and left.'' ''So he was afraid,'' Cao Cao said and decided to cross the river
that same night. He ordered ten thousand men to set up three floating spans. ''This could
be one of Zhuge Liang's tricks,'' Li Dian warned. ''Do not be reckless.'' ''Zhang Fei's a
foolhardy warrior. He knows no tricks,'' Cao Cao retorted and commanded his men to
advance swiftly.

Approaching Hanjin, Xuande saw dust rising in the air behind him. Drumbeats filled
the air, and war cries shook the ground. ''The Great River lies ahead,'' he said, ''the enemy behind. What can we do?'' He ordered Zhao Zilong to prepare a defense.

Cao Cao instructed his men: ''Liu Bei's a fish in our pot, a tiger in our trap. If we don't
take him, here and now, we'll be letting the fish back into the sea, setting the tiger free
in the hills. Press forward and spare no effort.'' With renewed vigor Cao's men started off
one by one to get their man. But suddenly they heard a burst of drumming as a body of
men and riders dashed forth from behind a hill. ''We've been waiting for you a long
time,'' the leader called out. It was Lord Guan, sitting astride Red Hare and gripping his
Green Dragon. He had borrowed ten thousand men from Liu Qi in Jiangxia. Hearing of
the great battles at Dangyang and Steepslope Bridge, he had come to intercept Cao Cao's
band of pursuers. The moment Cao Cao sighted Lord Guan, he cried in despair, ''Another
of Zhuge Liang's traps!'' and called a swift retreat.

Lord Guan chased Cao Cao's army for many *li* before he rode back to see Xuande
safely to Hanjin, where boats had been readied. Lord Guan bade Xuande and Lady Gan
seat themselves in one of them and had Ah Dou placed securely inside. He asked, ''Why
don't I see my other sister-in-law?'' Xuande told him of Lady Mi's death in Dangyang.
''Had you let me kill Cao Cao on the hunting field at Xuchang,'' Lord Guan said with
emphasis, ''you might have spared yourself these woes.'' ''I had to consider how such an
act could injure us,'' Xuande replied.[3]

War drums from the southern shore intruded on their conversation. Boats were
swarming across, sails to the wind. On the lead craft Xuande saw a man in white battle
gown and silvery armor standing on the prow. ''Uncle,'' he called out, ''have you been
well since we parted? I fear I have failed to serve you as a nephew should.'' It was Liu Qi.
He boarded Xuande's boat and, tearfully prostrating himself, said, ''I heard Cao Cao was
closing in, uncle, so I have come to relieve you.'' Xuande was overjoyed. He merged the
forces and continued his journey by water.

Xuande was describing the recent events for Liu Qi when a line of war-boats, stretching across the water from the southwest, came smartly up, borne by a full wind. ''All my
Jiangxia forces are here,'' Liu Qi said anxiously. ''These must be Southland ships coming
to cut us off—if they're not Cao Cao's! What are we to do?'' Xuande surveyed the approaching craft. Seated in the front was Kongming, robed like a Taoist hermit with a band
round his head. Behind him stood Sun Qian. Xuande excitedly hailed Kongming and
asked how he had managed to turn up here. ''As soon as I reached Jiangxia,'' Kongming
explained, ''I sent Lord Guan by land to meet you at Hanjin. I expected that Cao Cao
would chase you, and that you, my lord, would cut over to take Hanjin rather than go on
to Jiangling. That's why I had Master Qi here reinforce you. Then I went to collect the
soldiers at Xiakou and lead them here.''

Xuande could not have been more delighted. With all his forces reunited, he started
planning to defeat Cao Cao. Kongming said, ''Xiakou enjoys natural defenses and has

ample cash and grain. It can be held indefinitely. I advise you, my lord, to station your-self there. Let Master Qi return to Jiangxia, work his navy into fighting condition, and prepare his weapons. We can hold Cao Cao off by thus placing our forces in pincer for-mation. For us to return to Jiangxia together would leave us isolated." "Wise counsel," Liu Qi said. "However, uncle, I thought I would invite you to stop at Jiangxia first and put your forces in shape. After that there'll be time enough for you to proceed to Xia-kou." "My worthy nephew has a point," Xuande said and, after dispatching Lord Guan to Xiakou with five thousand men, he headed for Jiangxia with Kongming and Liu Qi.

· · · · ·

Lord Guan's intervening land force had deterred Cao Cao from pursuing Xuande. Fearing an ambush, Cao Cao marched directly to Jiangling lest Xuande, traveling by water, take it before him.

In Jiangling the provincial secretary Deng Yi and the assistant inspector Liu Xian had already learned that Liu Zong had surrendered Xiangyang to Cao Cao. Unable to offer any defense against Cao Cao, the two officials led their armed forces out past the walls of the capital and submitted to the prime minister. Cao Cao entered the city and, after calm-ing the populace, freed Han Song and put him in charge of protocols.[4] Other officials were given fiefs and handsome gifts.

Cao Cao said to his generals, "Xuande has fled to Jiangxia. If he forms an alliance with Sun Quan, our problems will multiply. What is the best way to defeat him?" "Now that we are in the field on a grand scale," Xun You advised, "send a messenger to the Southland summoning Sun Quan to join you in Jiangxia for a hunting party—with Xuande as the quarry! Offer Sun Quan half of Jingzhou to seal your amity. He will be too frightened, too confused not to submit. Our cause will thrive." Cao Cao approved this advice and sent an envoy south. At the same time he called up a force of eight hundred and thirty thousand—infantry, cavalry, and marines—which he rumored numbered a full million. Cao Cao's host advanced by land and sea. The cavalry rode along the Great River parallel to the long line of war-boats stretching westward back as far as Jiangling and the gorges, and eastward as far as Qichun and Huangzhou. The encampments ex-tended for three hundred *li*.

· · · · ·

In the Southland Sun Quan, stationed at Chaisang, heard that Cao Cao had accepted Liu Zong's submission and was marching on Jiangling double time. He therefore assem-bled his counselors to discuss the defense of the Southland. Lu Su said, "Jingzhou adjoins our territory. Rivers and mountains protect it. Its people are prosperous. If we can seize and hold the province, we will acquire the resources to establish our rule over the empire. I propose that you send me to Jiangxia to offer your official condolences on the occasion of Liu Biao's death. I believe I can persuade the newly defeated Liu Bei to encourage Liu Biao's commanders to make common cause with us against Cao Cao. Liu Bei's coopera-tion would provide a firm basis for our grand strategy." Sun Quan adopted the proposal and dispatched Lu Su to Jiangxia with mourning gifts.

· · · · ·

At Jiangxia, Xuande, Kongming, and Liu Qi were conferring. "Cao Cao is too pow-erful. We cannot oppose him," Kongming said. "The best we can do is turn to Sun Quan for support. If the south keeps Cao Cao at bay to the north, we can pluck advantage from between them—and why not?" "The Southland is well endowed with worthy men," Xuande said. "They are bound to have their own long-range plans and have little need of us." With a smile Kongming responded, "Cao leads a million-man host. He's perched like a tiger on the Great River and the Han. You can be sure the south will be sending someone to find out about his strengths and weaknesses. And when he comes, I'll take a little sail south down the river. Trust my three inches of limber tongue to induce the south and the north to devour each other. If the southern armies are prevailing, we'll join them, settle Cao, and retake Jingzhou. If the northern armies are prevailing, we will have the possibility of taking the Southland itself!" "A profound estimation of the situation," Xuande said. "But how do we get a Southlander to come here?"

That very moment Lu Su was announced. He had arrived by boat bearing Sun Quan's condolences for the death of Liu Biao. "Our plans will carry," Kongming said with a smile. Turning to Liu Qi, he asked, "When Sun Ce died, was anyone sent to the services?" "There was deep enmity between our houses," Liu Qi replied, "for we had slain his father, Sun Jian. Exchanging ceremonial embassies would have been unthinkable." "Then," Kongming said, "Lu Su comes for no obsequies, but to sound out the military situation." Turning to Xuande he went on, "My lord, if Lu Su questions you concerning Cao's movements, simply plead ignorance. If he persists, send him to me." His analysis completed, Kongming had Lu Su escorted into the city.

After accepting the ritual gifts for the bereaved, Liu Qi bade Lu Su present himself to Xuande. After the formal introduction Xuande invited the envoy to a private chamber, where wine was served. "Long has the imperial uncle's great name been known to me," Lu Su began, "though I have never had occasion to pay the man himself due homage. Our fortunate meeting today now satisfies that wish. They say you have joined battle with Cao Cao. I presume, therefore, that you know something about his strengths and vulnerabilities, and I venture to ask the approximate number of his forces." "Our own numbers," Xuande replied, "are insignificant, our generals few. No sooner do we hear of his approach than we make off. So, actually, I am unable to answer your question." "But I'm told," Lu Su pressed, "Zhuge Kongming twice succeeded in burning out Cao Cao and that Cao Cao twice lost his nerve. Your answer is difficult to accept." "If you must know the details," Xuande replied, "you will have to put your questions to Kongming himself." "Where would I find him?" Lu Su asked. "A meeting is what I desire." Xuande bade Kongming come forth and meet Lu Su.

The introduction concluded, Lu Su spoke: "Your talents and your virtue have ever been the objects of my esteem. But I have not had the honor of being presented to you. Now that fortune has made it possible, I would learn your view of the present state of affairs." Kongming replied, "I am well informed of Cao Cao's cunning devices. But, alas, our strength falls far short of his, and we have been avoiding engagement."[5] "Will the imperial uncle be remaining here, then?" Lu Su asked. "Lord Liu," Kongming answered, "has an old friend, Wu Ju, governor of Changwu, south of Jingzhou, in northern Jiaozhou. He will entrust himself to his care." "Wu Ju hasn't enough grain or men to protect himself, let alone someone else," Lu Su said. "It will do for now, until we can make other plans," was Kongming's reply.

"General Sun Quan," Lu Su said earnestly, "holds the six districts of the Southland firmly in his hands. His soldiers are keen, his grain abundant. And because he shows the utmost courtesy to men of worth, heroes from all along the Great River have joined his cause. What could better serve your interest than to send a man you trust to the south for the purpose of forging an alliance with us to plan the conquest of the realm?" "Lord

Liu and General Sun," Kongming said, "had no ties in the past. Your lord would turn a deaf ear to us, I fear. And we have no one to send." "Your own elder brother," Lu Su responded, "presently serving the Southland as an adviser, looks forward daily to seeing you. I myself have nothing to contribute. But I beg to go with you, sir, to see General Sun, so that we can confer on the future of the empire."

Finally, Xuande intervened. "Kongming is my mentor," he said. "I cannot spare him, even for a brief time. He may not go." Xuande feigned resistance to Lu Su's repeated appeals until Kongming said, "Matters are urgent. If you will authorize it, there's no harm in seeing what might come of a visit down there." At these words Xuande granted permission. Lu Su bade Xuande and Liu Qi good-bye and, together with Kongming, boarded his boat for the sail to Chaisang. Indeed:

> Because Kongming traveled south,
> Cao Cao's armies would taste sudden defeat.

The following chapter tells what Kongming meant to do.[6]

READ ON.

43

Kongming Debates the Southern Officials;
Lu Su Rejects the Consensus

LU SU AND KONGMING BADE XUANDE AND LIU QI good-bye and sailed for Chaisang. On board they reviewed the situation. "When you see General Sun, sir," Lu Su emphasized, "be sure to avoid mentioning how large and well-commanded Cao Cao's army is." "There is no need, Su, to keep reminding me of this," responded Kongming. "I will make my own replies to him." When their boat docked, Lu Su invited Kongming to rest at the guesthouse while he went ahead to see Sun Quan.

Sun Quan was already in council with his officers and officials. Informed of Lu Su's return, Quan summoned him and asked, "What did you learn in Jiangxia about the state of Cao Cao's forces?" "I have a general idea," replied Su, "but I will need time to report in full, sire." Quan showed him Cao Cao's summons and said, "Cao Cao had this delivered yesterday. I have sent the envoy back while we debate our response." Cao's note said:

> Under a recent imperial mandate, I have authority to act against state criminals. Our banners tilted southward; Liu Zong bound his hands in submission. The populace of Jingzhou, sensing the direction of events, has transferred its allegiance to us. We have one million hardy warriors and a thousand able generals. We propose that you join us, General, in a hunting expedition to Jiangxia in order to strike the decisive blow against Liu. Then, sharing the territory between us, we may seal an everlasting amity. Please do not hesitate but favor us with a speedy reply.

After he had read the document, Lu Su said to Sun Quan, "What is your most honored view, my lord?" "A decision has yet to be reached," he responded. The adviser Zhang Zhao joined the discussion, saying, "Commanding a host of one million, cloaked in the Emperor's authority, Cao Cao has campaigned the length and breadth of the land. To resist is to rebel. Moreover, your major advantage was the Great River—until Cao Cao took Jingzhou. Now we share the river's strategic benefits with him. Really, there is no opposing him, and in my poor estimation we would do better with the total security which submission will afford." "Zhang Zhao's views," the counselors declared in unison, "conform to the wishes of Heaven itself." But Sun Quan pondered in silence. "Have no doubts, my lord," Zhang Zhao continued. "If we submit to Cao, the people of the region will be protected and the six districts of the Southland preserved."[1] Sun Quan lowered his head and said nothing.

A moment later Sun Quan rose to go to the privy. Lu Su followed. Aware that Su did not share the views of Zhang Zhao, Quan turned to him and asked, "But what is your mind on this?" "The majority's view, General, will be your ruin," Su replied. "They can submit to Cao, but you cannot" "What are you saying?" Quan asked. "For someone like me," Su went on, "submission means being sent home to my clan, my village. Eventually I'll regain high office. But what have you to go home to? A minor estate? A single carriage? A single mount? A handful of followers? And what of your claim to royalty? Your advisers all consider only themselves. You must not heed them. It is time to make a master plan for yourself."

At these words Sun Quan sighed. "Their counsel fails my hopes," he said. "But the point you make—the master plan— accords well with my thinking. You come to me by Heaven's favor.[2] Cao Cao, however, has Yuan Shao's legions as well as the troops of Jingzhou. He seems impossible to resist." "I have brought back with me," Su went on, "Zhuge Jin's younger brother, Liang. Put your questions to him, my lord, and he will explain how things stand." "Master Sleeping Dragon is here?" exclaimed Quan. "Resting in the guesthouse," answered Lu Su. "It's too late to see him today," Quan said. "Tomorrow I shall gather my civil and military officers so he can get acquainted with the eminent men of the south before we proceed to formal discussion." Lu Su went to arrange things accordingly.

The following day Lu Su came for Kongming. Again he warned the guest not to mention the size of Cao Cao's army. "Let me respond as I see fit," Kongming said with a smile. "Nothing shall go amiss, I assure you." Lu Su conducted Kongming to the headquarters of General Sun, where he was introduced to Zhang Zhao, Gu Yong, and some twenty other officials and officers of the first rank. As they sat erect in full dress, with their high formal caps and broad belts, Kongming was presented to each in turn. The formalities concluded, Kongming was shown to the guest's seat.

From Kongming's air of self-assurance and dignified, confident carriage, Zhang Zhao and the others understood that he had come to exert his powers of persuasion. Zhao initiated the discussion with a provocative comment: "I, the least of the Southland's scholars, have been hearing for some time how you, ensconced in Longzhong, have compared yourself to the great ministers of antiquity, Guan Zhong and Yue Yi. Have you actually made such claims?" "There could be some slight basis for the comparison," was Kongming's reply. "I have also heard that Liu Xuande,[3] protector of Yuzhou, solicited you three times at that thatched hut and, considering himself fortunate to get you—'a fish finding water' was how he put it—expected to roll up Jingzhou in the palm of his hand. Now that the province belongs to Cao Cao, we await your explanation."

Aware that Zhang Zhao was Sun Quan's foremost adviser—the man he had to confound or else lose all hope of convincing Quan himself—Kongming replied, "In my view that province on the River Han could have been taken as easily as one turns one's palm. But my master, Lord Liu, precisely because he conducts himself humanely and honorably, could never bear to steal a kinsman's estate and refused to do so. The adolescent Liu Zong, the victim of insidious counsel, secretly surrendered himself, giving Cao Cao a free hand in the region.[4] My master, however, with forces stationed at Jiangxia, has promising prospects of his own, not to be lightly dismissed."

"Then your words and deeds do not agree," said Zhang Zhao. "For the men with whom you are wont to compare yourself helped their lords win fame and power. The patriarch Huan dominated the feudal lords and kept the realm together during Guan Zhong's tenure as minister; and Yue Yi helped the feeble state of Yan subdue the seventy cities of mighty Qi. Those two had the talent to set the empire to rights. But you, sir, have dwelled in a thatched hut, delighting yourself with the breeze and moon, profoundly absorbed in meditation. After you entered Lord Liu's service, we expected you to promote the welfare of the living souls of the realm and to root out and destroy treason and sedition.[5]

"Before Lord Liu obtained your services, he was already a force to be reckoned with wherever he went, seizing this or that walled town. Now that he has you, people are saying that the ferocious tiger has grown wings and that we will witness the restoration of the Han and the elimination of the Caos. Old servants of the court and recluses of the mountains and forests have begun rubbing their eyes in expectation, imagining that the sky will clear, that the sun and moon will shine again. They hope to see the salvation of the people and the deliverance of the empire in their time.

"One can only wonder why, then, after you had committed yourself to him, Lord Liu scurried for safety the moment Cao Cao stepped into the field, abandoning his obligations to Liu Biao for the security of the people of Jingzhou, and failing to sustain Liu Zong in the defense of his land. And what followed? Lord Liu quit Xinye, fled Fan, lost Dangyang, and bolted to Xiakou for refuge. But no one will have him! The fact is that Lord Liu was better off before you came. How does that measure up to what Guan Zhong and Yue Yi did for their lords? Kindly forgive my simple frankness."

Kongming broke into laughter. "The great roc ranges thousands of miles," he said. "Can the common fowl appreciate its ambition? When a man is gravely ill, he must be fed weak gruel and medicated with mild tonics until his internal state is readjusted and balanced and his condition gradually stabilizes. Only then can meat be added to his diet and powerful drugs be used to cure him. Thus is the root of the disease eradicated and the man's health restored. If you do not wait until breath and pulse are calm and steady but precipitately use powerful drugs and rich food, the attempt to cure the patient is sure to fail.

"When Lord Liu suffered defeat at Runan, he threw himself on Liu Biao's mercy. He had less than a thousand men and no generals at all, except for Lord Guan, Zhang Fei, and Zhao Zilong. He was like a man wasted by disease. Xinye, a small town off in the hills, with few people and scant grain, was no more than a temporary refuge, hardly a place to hold permanently. And yet, despite our poor weapons, weak city walls, untrained forces, and day-to-day shortages of grain, we burned Cao out at Bowang, flooded him out at the White River, and put his leading generals, Xiahou Dun and Cao Ren, in a state of panic and dismay. I am not sure that Guan Zhong and Yue Yi surpassed us in warfare.

"As for Liu Zong's surrender to Cao Cao, the truth is that Lord Liu knew nothing about it. Nor could he bear to exploit the treason of the Cais to steal a kinsman's estate—such is his great humanity and devotion to honor. In the case of the Dangyang defeat, Lord Liu had several hundred thousand subjects, including the elderly and many young people, who were determined to follow him. Could he leave them to their fate? He was moving a mere ten li each day but never thought of racing ahead to capture Jiangling. He was content to suffer defeat with his people if he had to—another instance of his profound humanity and sense of honor.

"The few cannot oppose the many, and a warrior learns to endure his reverses. The founder of the Han, Gao Zu, was defeated over and over by Xiang Yu, but the final victory at Gaixia was the result of Han Xin's good counsel, was it not? The same Han Xin who, in his long history of service to Gao Zu, had compiled no impressive record of victories! For the grand strategy of the dynasty, the security of our sacred altars, truly there is a master planner, one utterly different from the boasting rhetoricians whose empty reputations overawe people, who have no peer in armchair debate and standing discussions, of whom not even one in a hundred has any idea how to confront a crisis or cope with its rapid development. What a farce to amuse the world!"

To this oration Zhang Zhao had no reply, but another rose to the challenge. "Cao Cao has in place one million men and a roster of a thousand commanding officers. He can prance like a dragon while they glare down on us like tigers who could swallow Jiangxia with ease. What then?" Kongming eyed the speaker narrowly. It was Yu Fan. "Cao Cao did indeed bring into his fold the swarming hosts of Yuan Shao," Kongming replied. "And he stole the ill-organized soldiers of Liu Biao. But even his million are not that much to worry about!" With an icy smile Yu Fan countered: "Your forces were ruined at Dangyang. Your plans came to naught at Xiakou. You're desperate for any scrap of support and yet would boastfully deceive us by saying, 'Don't worry.'"

"And how," Kongming responded, "was Lord Liu to hold off a million murderous men with a few thousand troops dedicated to humanity and honor? We retired to Xiakou to bide our time. In the Southland the men are well trained and grain is plentiful. The Great River is your natural defense. And yet, giving no thought to the disgrace or to the mockery it would incur, you would have your lord crook his knee and submit to a traitor! By your standards it's not Lord Liu who fears the villain Cao!"

To this speech Yu Fan made no reply. But Bu Zhi rose to challenge Kongming, saying, "Are you not playing the part of those seductive diplomats of ancient times, Zhang Yi and Su Qin, striving to prevail upon our country to serve your ends?" Kongming turned his gaze to the speaker; then he responded: "You take those two for mere rhetoricians, forgetting their distinguished achievements. Su Qin held the highest office in six different kingdoms, while Zhang Yi twice served as chief minister to the state of Qin. Both men gave counsel that enlightened and strengthened their ruler, and are hardly to be put in a category with those who cringe before the mighty, victimize the weak, and cower before the sword. You gentlemen, hearing Cao Cao's empty threats, urged surrender with craven dispatch. Are you the ones to mock Zhang Yi and Su Qin?" Bu Zhi fell silent.

"What is your view of Cao Cao the man?" another asked. Kongming eyed the questioner, Xue Zong. "A traitor to the Han," he replied. "Is there any doubt?" "You are in error, sir," Xue Zong went on. "The mandate of the Han has devolved from sovereign to sovereign down to this day; now the dynasty's Heaven-ordained period draws to its close. Already Cao Cao possesses two-thirds of the empire, and all men tender him allegiance. Lord Liu, however, refuses to recognize the season of history, and in forcing the issue will fail as surely as an egg dashed against a rock."

Kongming answered harshly: "So, then, you mean to deny both king and father? In man's short life between Heaven and earth, loyalty and filial devotion are the foundation of personal integrity. Since, sir, you are a subject of the Han, when you see a man who disavows his duty as a subject, you are pledged to help destroy him—for such is a true subject's obligation. Cao Cao, far from honoring his debt to the Han for sustaining his forebears in office, bears within him a seditious usurper's heart, to the indignation of all. In tendering him allegiance on grounds of 'Heaven-ordained numbers,'[6] you deny both king and father and render yourself unfit to speak in the company of men." Xue Zong was too humiliated to reply.

Another from the council picked up the argument. "Though Cao Cao enjoins the nobles through coercion of the Emperor, yet he is himself a descendant of the Supreme Ancestor's prime minister, Cao Shen. Lord Liu claims descent from Prince Jing of Zhongshan, but that has never actually been verified. As far as anyone can tell, he is a mere mat-weaver, a sandal merchant, hardly a worthy contender with Cao Cao." Kongming regarded this speaker, Lu Ji. A smile crossing his face, he asked, "Didn't you once steal an orange at one of Yuan Shu's banquets? I'd like you to sit still while I tell you something. If Cao Cao is the descendant of the great minister Cao Shen, then the Caos have been the subjects of the Han from that day to this. For him to monopolize power and recklessly wield it, deceiving and abusing the sovereign, is more than negation of the emperor, it is nullification of his own sacred ancestor. This makes Cao Cao more than a seditious subject; it makes him a traitorous son. Lord Liu has the dignity of an imperial scion. He is a man to whom the present Emperor has granted recognized status in accordance with the official genealogy. How can you say there is no verification? Consider further that the Supreme Ancestor, who began his career as a precinct magistrate, in the end took possession of the empire. And what is there to be ashamed of in mat-weaving or selling sandals? Your puerile point of view makes you an unworthy participant in the discussions of distinguished scholars." Lu Ji was confounded.

Suddenly, another man rose and spoke: "Kongming's rhetoric is bereft of reason. His distorted judgments are not worth consideration. I beg to inquire, what classics have you mastered?" Kongming turned to the speaker, Yan Jun, and said, "How can the textbound pedant revive our nation or further our cause? And what of the ancient sages—Yi Yin, who tilled the soil in Shen, or Jiang Ziya, who fished the River Wei? What of men like Zhang Liang and Chen Ping, Zheng Yu and Geng Yan? These worthies sustained their kings in time of peril. What canons did they master? Do you really think they simply spent their days confined between the pen and the inkstone like schoolmen arguing over texts, flourishing words, wielding brushes?" Deflated by Kongming's denunciation, Yan Jun lowered his head and made no reply.

Yet another protested loudly: "You, sir, are certainly given to exaggeration. I am not so sure that there is any real learning in you, that you won't end up as the butt of scholars' ridicule." The speaker was Cheng Deshu of Runan. Kongming answered the man so: "There are scholars of noble character and scholars with petty interests. The former are loyal to their sovereign and devoted to his government; they preserve their integrity and detest renegades—for they are intent on making their influence felt in their time and making their names known to later ages. But the latter bend their efforts to polishing rhymes, knowing no skill but that of trivial composition. Authors of grandiose odes in their youth, by old age they've digested the classics. In one sitting a thousand words may flow from their pens, but inside of them not a single useful idea is to be found. Take the scholar Yang Xiong who made a great reputation in his time only to disgrace himself by serving Wang Mang—for which he jumped to his death from the upper story of a building. He is an example of the petty scholar.[7] Let him produce a ten-thousand-word rhapsody every day. What value does it have?" Cheng Deshu, like the others, was too confounded to reply. The assembly was unnerved at Kongming's exhibition of mastery in debate.

Two others, Zhang Wen and Luo Tong, were about to raise their objections when someone entered the chambers and cried, "Kongming is one of the rarest talents of our age. Belaboring these issues is hardly the way to show due respect to our guest. With Cao Cao, backed by a huge army, looking hungrily across our borders, what's the point of sterile polemics? We should be considering instead how to drive the enemy back." The assembly turned to see Huang Gai (Gongfu), a man from Lingling, presently serving as a commissariat officer in Dongwu.

"With your permission," Huang Gai said to Kongming. "Sometimes one carries the day by holding one's peace. Save your invaluable opinions for our lord rather than continuing this debate." "These gentlemen," said Kongming, "are unaware of the exigencies of our age, and their objections had to be answered." With that, Huang Gai and Lu Su took Kongming to see Sun Quan. At the entrance to the government hall they encountered Zhuge Jin, Kongming's elder brother, and saluted him. "Worthy brother," said Jin, "since you are in the Southland, why haven't you come to see me?" "For one in the service of Lord Liu," Kongming replied, "it is only fitting that public concerns take precedence over private ones. As long as these require my attention, I must beg your forgiveness." "Worthy brother," said Zhuge Jin, "come over and catch up on things after you have seen the lord of the Southland."

After Jin had departed, Lu Su said, "What I cautioned you about before—let there be no slip." Kongming nodded. As they reached the official chambers, Sun Quan himself appeared and descended the stair to welcome them, offering his highest regards. After the exchange of salutations he showed Kongming to a seat. Quan's officials stood in attendance, civil officials in one row, military in another. Lu Su watched as Kongming conveyed Liu Xuande's good wishes. Kongming stole a glance at Sun Quan. Jade green eyes and a purplish beard—an imposing presence. "His appearance is extraordinary," Kongming mused. "A man to be incited, not won over by argument. But I must wait for him to question me."

After the presentation of tea Sun Quan spoke: "Lu Su has told me of your great abilities. Now that we have the good fortune to meet you, I make bold to seek the benefit of your teaching." "One unfit and unlearned as I," Kongming responded, "could never do justice to your enlightened questions." "Recently," Sun Quan went on, "you assisted Lord Liu on strategic decisions in the war with Cao Cao. This must have given you profound knowledge of the enemy's military position."

"Lord Liu," answered Kongming, "is hardly in a position to resist Cao Cao. His forces are paltry, his generals all too few; on top of this, Xinye is a small town without grain supplies." "But how large a force does Cao have?" Sun Quan asked. "Mounted, foot, and naval, all told, over one million troops," replied Kongming. "This has to be a trick!" exclaimed Sun Quan. "No trick," Kongming went on. "He had the Qingzhou army of two hundred thousand when he took charge of Yanzhou. When he vanquished Yuan Shao, he added another five or six hundred thousand to that. Recently he recruited another three or four hundred thousand from the north-central plains. And now he has gained two or three hundred thousand more from the conquest of Jingzhou. It adds up to no less than one and a half million. I said 'one million' for fear of scaring off your warriors."

Stunned, Lu Su paled and tried to catch Kongming's eye. But Kongming pretended not to notice. "And how many military commanders?" Sun Quan asked. "He has competent, inventive advisers and hardened, seasoned leaders—over a thousand or two, easily," Kongming stated. "Now that he has conquered Jingzhou," Quan pressed, "has he greater ambitions?" "At the moment," replied Kongming, "he is making his way down the Great River, leaving a trail of camps in preparation for naval action. What other territory could his ambition lead him to, if not the Southland?" "If he means to swallow and assimilate us," said Quan, posing his question, "must we fight or not? I crave your judgment on this." "I do have an opinion," Kongming conceded, "but I am afraid you would be reluctant to accept it." "I would know your esteemed view," was Quan's reply.

At this invitation Kongming began to speak: "When the realm was in turmoil, you formed a state in the south and Lord Liu rallied his hosts below the River Han in order to contest the empire with Cao Cao. Now Cao has freed himself of his greatest difficulties and has stabilized his position to a certain degree. This fresh triumph in Jingzhou has made him feared throughout the land, and whatever heroes would oppose him lack the base for waging war. That is why Lord Liu made good his removal to this region. I would urge you to weigh your strength and address the problem. If you can lead the forces of the south in contention with the north for mastery of the area, then break with Cao Cao at once. Otherwise, why, follow your advisers' judgment, lay down your arms, face north, and submit to his rule."

Before Sun Quan could respond, Kongming continued: "General, you have let it be known that you incline toward submission, but I know how torn you are. The situation is precarious. Act before disaster strikes." "If all you say is true," Sun Quan said, "why hasn't Lord Liu submitted?" "Tian Heng," answered Kongming, "the stalwart loyalist of Qi, held fast to his honor and refused to disgrace himself. A scion of the royal house, renowned in his time, looked up to by men of learning everywhere, how could Lord Liu do less? His failures are ordained and not of his own making. He will not be humiliated."[8]

His composure breaking, Sun Quan swept his robes about him and retired to his private apartments. The assembly dispersed, snickering. Lu Su berated Kongming: "What was the point of saying such things? My sovereign's temper is too liberal, fortunately, to censure you directly. But what you said has demeaned him." Kongming tilted his head and laughed. "Why is he so excitable?" he said. "I have my own plan for destroying Cao Cao. But he did not ask, so I did not mention it." "If you actually have a sound strategy," said Lu Su, "I will ask my lord to seek your instruction." "To me," Kongming rejoined, "Cao's host is like a million ants waiting to be pulverized with one swipe of the hand!" At these words Lu Su went to the rear chamber to talk to Sun Quan.

Quan's anger had not subsided, and he said pointedly to Lu Su, "His insolence is insufferable!" "I rebuked him for it," Lu Su responded, "but he only said that you were too 'excitable,' and that he was reluctant— on his own initiative—to broach the subject of Cao Cao's destruction. Why not solicit his plan, my lord?" Sun Quan's consternation passed, and his tone softened. "So he had a strategy all along. That's why he incited me. I was not thinking clearly at the moment and nearly spoiled everything." So saying, Sun Quan reappeared in the hall together with Lu Su and invited Kongming to resume discussions. Quan received Kongming with an apology: "Just now I recklessly sullied your high name. Kindly overlook the offense." Kongming conveyed his regrets too: "It was I who spoke offensively, and I beg your forgiveness for it." Sun Quan bade Kongming join him in his private apartments, where he had wine set out.

After several rounds Sun Quan began: "Cao Cao's lifelong enemies were Lü Bu, Liu Biao, Yuan Shao, Yuan Shu, Lord Liu, and myself. The first four heroes are no more. Lord Liu and I remain. I cannot give the Southland into another's control, not even to preserve it. That is certain. And none save Lord Liu can oppose Cao Cao. But after his recent defeats how can he continue to hold firm in adversity?" "Lord Liu's defeats notwithstanding," Kongming began, "Lord Guan commands ten thousand elite troops, and Liu Qi's fighters from Jiangxia number no less. Cao Cao's host is exhausted, having come so far. In their recent pursuit of Lord Liu, their light cavalry was covering three hundred *li* a day—clearly a case of 'a spent arrow unable to pierce fine silk.' Consider too that the northerners are unused to naval warfare and that the officers and men from Jingzhou follow Cao by coercion, not by choice. General, if you can unite hand and heart with Lord Liu, the destruction of Cao's army and his return to the north can be guaranteed. Then with the strengthening of the Southland and Jingzhou, a tripodal balance of power will come into being in the empire. The means to shape the outcome are in your hands today. It is for you to use them."

Sun Quan was exhilarated. "Hearing you, master, is like breaking out of a thicket and into a clearing. My mind is made up. I have no further doubts. Discussion of joint action to wipe out Cao Cao shall begin this very day." With these words Sun Quan commanded Lu Su to inform all officials of his intentions and escort Kongming to the guesthouse.

When Zhang Zhao heard the news, he said to the counselors, "We have fallen into Kongming's trap." He rushed to Sun Quan and said: "We have heard, my lord, that you mean to meet Cao Cao on the battlefield. How do you think you compare to Yuan Shao, whom Cao conquered with a roll of the drums when his own forces were still relatively weak? Do you think you can oppose him today when he has one million in his command? Listen to Kongming and undertake this ridiculous mobilization, and you will be carrying kindling to put out the fire."

Sun Quan lowered his head and said nothing. Another adviser, Gu Yong, added his arguments: "Because he suffered defeat at Cao Cao's hands, Liu Bei wants to use our forces to drive him back. Why should we serve his ends? I pray you will heed Zhang Zhao's advice." Sun Quan pondered and lapsed into indecision. Zhang Zhao and his party left, and Lu Su reentered to plead further: "Zhang Zhao and his faction oppose the mobilization and favor submission because they fear for the safety of themselves and their families. I beg my lord to ignore such self-interested calculations." Sun Quan continued to ponder his dilemma. "If you delay, my lord," Lu Su said, "you will be ruined by them." "Retire for now, my good vassal," Quan said, "and let me reflect." Lu Su withdrew. The military officers were divided, but the civil officials all advocated submission. All sorts of conflicting opinions were expressed.

Sun Quan retired, his mind deeply divided. He was unable to eat or sleep. His mother, Lady Wu,[9] offered a sympathetic ear. "Cao Cao is camped on the river," he said to her, "intent on subduing our land. I have put the question to our civil and military advisers. Some would capitulate, some would wage war. If we risk battle, I fear our fewer numbers will not be able to stand against their greater. If we risk submission, I fear Cao Cao will not accommodate us. I waver, therefore, unable to act resolutely." "Have you forgotten my elder sister's dying words?" his mother asked. This question woke Sun Quan from his quandary. Indeed:

Because Sun Quan remembered his mother's last words,
Zhou Yu would do great deeds of war.

What had she said?
READ ON.

44

Kongming Cunningly Moves Zhou Yu to Anger;
Sun Quan Decides on a Plan to Defeat Cao Cao

To solve her nephew's dilemma Lady Wu said, "My late sister passed on to us your brother's dying words: 'Consult Zhang Zhao on domestic difficulties, Zhou Yu on external ones.' Isn't Zhou Yu's counsel wanted now?" Pleased with Lady Wu's suggestion, Sun Quan sent a messenger to the Poyang Lakes where Zhou Yu was directing naval exercises, inviting him to join in the discussions. But even before the messenger left, Cao Cao's arrival at the River Han had compelled Zhou Yu to go to Chaisang for a military conference. There Lu Su was the first to meet Zhou Yu and brief his close friend. "No need to worry," Zhou Yu reassured Lu Su, "I think I know what we have to do. But you must get Kongming here for a meeting right away." Lu Su rode off to find him.

As Zhou Yu settled into his lodgings, a delegation of four was announced: Zhang Zhao, Gu Yong, Zhang Hong, and Bu Zhi. Zhou Yu showed them in, and the five men seated themselves. The amenities concluded, Zhang Zhao began: "Commander, do you know the trouble the Southland is in?" "I have not been informed," was his reply. "Cao Cao has one million men on the River Han. Yesterday he summoned our lord to join his 'hunting party' at Jiangxia. Though he means to swallow us up, he has made no overt move. We are advocating submission to spare the Southland a debacle; we never expected that Lu Su would bring back Liu Bei's military director, Zhuge Liang. Liang has his own scores to settle and will make sure to stir our lord with his all-too-convincing points, while Lu Su clings stubbornly to his illusions, refusing to recognize reality. We turn to you, Commander, to make the final decision." "Do you have a consensus, gentlemen?" asked Zhou Yu. "We have conferred and we concur," Gu Yong responded. "Such has been my own wish for some time," Zhou Yu said. "I beg you all to return to your quarters. Early tomorrow I am to present myself before our lord, when the debate will be settled accordingly." Zhang Zhao and his delegation excused themselves and left.

Soon Cheng Pu, Huang Gai, and Han Dang, representing the military faction, came to see Zhou Yu. After he had received them and greetings had been exchanged, Cheng Pu began: "Have you heard, Commander, that soon the Southland must lose its independence and be annexed to another power?" "I have not been so informed," was the reply. "We have followed General Sun," Cheng Pu went on, "in the founding of this domain through hundreds of battles, great and small. Thus we have come into possession of the towns and cities of our six districts. What shame we would suffer, what regret, if our lord should heed the advocates of surrender. But we who choose death before disgrace count on you to convince him to muster the troops—a cause to which we dedicate our all." "Is there consensus among you, Generals?" asked Zhou Yu. Huang Gai rose and, striking his palm to his forehead, said hotly, "This shall roll before I submit." The group echoed his oath. "To decide the issue by combat," said Zhou Yu, "is precisely what I desire. How could I acquiesce in surrender? I beg you, Generals, return. After I meet with our lord, the debate will be settled accordingly." Cheng Pu and his party took their leave.

Soon afterward a party of civil officials led by Zhuge Jin and Lü Fan was welcomed in. Greetings exchanged, Zhuge Jin began: "My younger brother Liang has come downriver to tell us that Lord Liu seeks our cooperation in operations against Cao Cao. Our civil and military officials remain locked in debate. Since my own brother is Lord Liu's representative, I have stood aside, biding my time until you would arrive to settle the question." "What is your own assessment?" Zhou Yu asked him. "Surrender means cheap security," replied Jin. "War puts all at risk." "I have some ideas of my own," Zhou Yu responded with a smile. "Join us tomorrow in the council hall, where we shall settle things."

As Zhuge Jin and his party withdrew, another group, this led by Lü Meng and Gan Ning, was announced. Zhou Yu invited them in and they expressed their views. Some insisted on surrender, some were determined to fight. They argued back and forth until Zhou Yu said, "This is enough discussion for now. Join us tomorrow in the council hall, where we shall settle things." Long after the group had departed, a cynical smile remained on Zhou Yu's face.

That evening Lu Su brought Kongming to pay his respects. Zhou Yu came from the central gate to escort them inside. After the formalities they seated themselves as host and guest. Lu Su began with a question to Zhou Yu: "Cao Cao has launched an offensive against the Southland, and between the two courses, war or peace, our lord cannot decide. In this matter he is yours entirely. I would inquire what your own view is." "Cao Cao acts in the name of the Son of Heaven, the Emperor himself," said Zhou Yu. "His host cannot be driven back. His power has grown to the point where it would be futile to risk engagement. If we fight, defeat is certain. If we surrender, security is cheaply bought. I have made my decision. Tomorrow before our lord I shall advocate sending a representative to convey our submission."

Lu Su was appalled. "But this is most misguided!" he responded. "The estate we have founded now spans three generations. How can we abandon it to strangers on the spur of the moment? The last words of Lord Sun's brother, Sun Ce, charged us to entrust external matters to you. What will befall us if you follow the counsel of cowards now, at the very moment we must rely on you—as if you were the great Mount Tai itself—to preserve the house of Sun?" To this appeal Zhou Yu replied: "The living souls in the six districts of the Southland are more than can be numbered. If we bring upon them the disasters of war, they will lay their grievance to us. That is why I have decided to sue for peace." "How wrong that would be!" cried Lu Su. "With a general of your mettle and the sure defensibility of the land, Cao is far from assured of fulfilling his ambitions." The two men argued round and round while Kongming looked on, detached, smiling with sangfroid.

"What makes you smile so disdainfully?" Zhou Yu asked him. "Your antagonist Lu Su, of course, who refuses to recognize the exigencies of the occasion," said Kongming. Lu Su snapped back, "Now you're mocking me for 'refusing to recognize the exigencies of the occasion'?" Kongming replied, "Zhou Yu advocates submission. It seems perfectly reasonable." "Any scholar who recognizes realities—and Kongming is surely one—must be of the same mind," said Zhou Yu. "You too argue this way?" Lu Su asked Kongming. "Cao Cao is a master of warfare," Kongming explained, "whom none in the empire dares engage. Those who did—Lü Bu, Yuan Shao, Yuan Shu, and Liu Biao—have been annihilated. And no such men remain in the empire—save Lord Liu, who has refused to 'recognize the exigencies of the occasion' and struggles with Cao for mastery. But Lord Liu stands alone in Jiangxia, his very survival in question. The general's plan to submit to Cao ensures his family's safety and protects his wealth and status. What if the sacred throne of the house of Sun is transferred to another house? Why, ascribe it to the Mandate of Heaven. What do we need these things for?" Lu Su was moved to wrath. "You would see our sovereign crook his knee and endure disgrace before a treasonous rogue?" he exclaimed. [1]

Kongming went on: "I have thought of another possibility that might well save the ritual gifts of sheep and wine as we transfer our lands and render up the seals of state. You would not even need to cross the river yourself, but merely to send a solitary representative to escort two persons to the river. If Cao Cao can get hold of these two, his million-man host will discard their armor, furl their banners, and retire from the field." Zhou Yu spoke: "And with what two persons do you propose to effect this reversal?" "The Southland's parting with these two," Kongming continued, "may be likened to an oak shedding a leaf, a granary diminished by a grain of millet. Yet if he gets them, Cao Cao will depart content." Again Zhou Yu asked, "Well, what two persons?"

"When I was in residence at Longzhong," Kongming continued, "I heard that Cao was building a new tower on the banks of the Zhang. It is called the Bronze Bird Tower—an absolutely magnificent edifice, and elegant. He has searched far and wide for beautiful women to fill its chambers. Cao Cao, who is basically inclined to wantonness, has known for some time that the Southland patriarch Qiao has two daughters, beauties whose faces would make fish forget to swim or birds to fly, abash the very blossoms and outshine the moon. He has vowed: 'First, I'll sweep the realm and calm it and build an empire; next, I'll possess the Southland's two daughters Qiao and install them in the Bronze Bird Tower so that I may have pleasure in my later years and die without regret.' Cao Cao may lead his million-fold host to menace the Southland, but in reality he comes for the sake of these two women. General, why not seek out the patriarch Qiao, procure his girls with a thousand pieces of gold, and dispatch someone to deliver them to Cao? Once he has them, he will be content and return to the capital. Long ago Fan Li of Yue succeeded with a similar plan when he presented the beauty Xi Shi to the king of Wu. Why not act at once?" [2]

"Can you verify Cao's desire to possess these two women?" asked Zhou Yu. "He once commissioned his son, Zhi (styled Zijian), a writer of great genius, to compose a rhapsody. The result was the 'Bronze Bird Tower Rhapsody.' Its theme is the fitness of his house for sovereignty and his vow to wive the daughters Qiao." [3] "Can you recall it?" Zhou Yu asked. "Infatuated with its gorgeous language, I committed it to memory," Kongming replied. "May I request a recitation?" said Zhou Yu. Then and there Kongming recited:

> A pleasant promenade beside His Majesty:
> They mount the tiered tower, delight their spirits,
> And view the teeming richness of the realm,
> The sphere his sagely virtue rules.
> These gates he built pierce the mid-sky;

The double pylons float to the crystalline.
Splendid viewing rooms sit suspended there,
Linked chambers seem to hang above the western wall.
They peer down on the ever-flowing Zhang,
Whose gardens give promise of teeming glory.[4]

Aloft on either side, twin towers—
Left, Jade Dragon; right, Golden Phoenix—
To hold his brides, the Southland daughters Qiao,[5]
With whom he will take his pleasure, morning, evening.
Look down on the royal city's spacious elegance;
Behold the shimmering tints of distant clouds.
Rejoice in the confluence of many talents;
Auspicious dreams of aid will be fulfilled.[6]

Look up! The gentle solemnity of spring;
And hear! the lovelorn cries of every bird.
May these proud towers stand till Heaven's end.
Our house has gained a twin fulfillment.
Our benevolent influence spreads across the realm,
Winning universal homage for our capital.[7]
Even the splendor of Huan and Wu, ancient hegemons,
Pales beside his sagely grace and wisdom.
Most blessed! Most marvelous!
His generous favor, extending far and wide.
Lend the sovereign house your aid
That unto the four corners peace may reign.
Our king is on a scale with Heaven and earth,
Radiant as the light of sun or moon,
Ever honored as the ultimate principle,
Immortal as the sky's sovereign star.[8]

Driving the dragon banners round the royal circuit,
Guiding the phoenix chariot round the realm:
His clement influence bathes the kingdom's corners;
Prize offerings to him heap high—the people prosper.
May these towers stand firm for all time,
For pleasure never failing and without end.

When Kongming's performance was done, Zhou Yu started violently from his seat and pointed north.[9] "Old traitor! Rogue!" he cried. "You abuse us past endurance." Kongming rose too, swift to check him. "Remember when the khan, chief of the Xiongnu, encroached on our border," he said, "and the Emperor of Han granted him a princess to forge amity through kinship? Can we not now spare two female commoners?" "There is something you are not aware of," Zhou Yu replied. "The elder daughter of the patriarch Qiao was the first wife of the late general Sun Ce. The younger is my own wife." "Truly, I did not know," said Kongming, feigning astonishment. "I have said something unforgivable and offended you most gravely. A thousand pardons!" "Cao, old traitor," Zhou Yu went on, "you and I cannot share footing on this earth. So I swear." "The situation calls for careful consideration," Kongming cautioned, "lest our actions entail regret." But Zhou Yu continued, "I had our late lord Sun Ce's solemn trust and could never crook the knee to Cao. I only meant to test you. When I left the Poyang Lakes I resolved to take up arms against the north. The executioner's axe upon my neck could not alter my resolve. I hope for your stout aid, Kongming, that together we may smite the traitor Cao." "If you would accept my humble efforts, I would toil unsparingly, like a dog or a horse, entirely at your service." "Tomorrow," Zhou Yu responded, "I will present myself to our lord to debate the mustering of the troops." With that, Kongming and Lu Su bid Zhou Yu good-bye and left.

On the morning of the next day Sun Quan ascended the assembly hall: to his left, some thirty civil officials led by Zhang Zhao and Gu Yong; to his right, thirty or more military officials led by Cheng Pu and Huang Gai. The caps and robes of the officials rustled against each other, and the swords and pendants of the officers jostled and clanked. All stood at attention in their respective lines. Moments later Zhou Yu appeared.

After formal salutations and a few kind words from Sun Quan, Zhou Yu said, "I have been told that Cao Cao has marched south, stationed his forces along the River Han, and sent us a letter. I wonder, my lord, what your own honorable wishes might be?" Sun Quan passed the letter to Zhou Yu, who read it and smiled. "The old traitor," he said, "must imagine we have no men worthy of the name in the Southland, to approach us so insolently!" "What is your own view?" Quan asked. "Have you discussed the matter thoroughly with your officers and officials, my lord?" responded Zhou Yu. "For days on end," replied Quan. "Some advocate submission, some war. Because I have not yet reached a final decision, I appeal to you to resolve it once and for all." "Who are those urging submission?" asked Zhou Yu. "Zhang Zhao and his party," said Sun Quan. Turning to Zhang Zhao, Zhou Yu said, "I beg to hear your reasons."

"Cao Cao controls the Emperor," Zhao began, "and his campaigns across the land enjoy the sanction of the court. His recent victory in Jingzhou makes his power all the more formidable. The Great River was the Southland's only hope of blocking him. But now he has thousands of light attack craft and war-boats; a combined advance by land and sea could never be stopped. It is better to submit for now and live to plan another day."

"The twisted reasoning of a pedant!" cried Zhou Yu. "Now, in the third generation since the founding of the Southland, how could we bear to throw it all away overnight?" "So then," Quan said to Zhou Yu, "what is your grand strategy to be based on?"

Zhou Yu replied: "Posing as prime minister of the Han, Cao Cao is in reality a traitor to the dynasty. But you, General, true heir to your father and your brother, have possession of this territory. Your martial skill is godlike, your troops are keen, and your grain stores are ample. Now is the time to make your might felt the length and breadth of the empire and eliminate a cruel and violent enemy for the sake of the ruling house. How can we submit! Furthermore, by coming here, Cao has broken the most sacred rules of military science. While the north is still untamed and while Ma Teng and Han Sui threaten his rear, he is losing time on this campaign. That's the first rule broken. With troops unused to naval warfare, Cao has put away his saddles and steeds and taken to boats to contest for this land of mariners. That's the second rule broken. Now the height of winter is upon us, and his horses want for hay. That's the third rule broken. He has driven his northerners far afield to unfamiliar rivers and lakes, into a strange clime where disease is rife. That is the fourth rule broken. However numerous his men, they will be defeated. This is the moment to make Cao Cao your captive. I appeal to you: grant me between fifty and a hundred thousand crack troops to place at Xiakou,[10] and I will destroy the invaders for you."

Eyes flashing, Sun Quan stood up. "Long, too long," he cried, "has the traitor sought to remove the Han and establish his own house. Four of those he had to fear—Yuan Shao, Yuan Shu, Lü Bu, and Liu Biao—are gone. I alone remain. One of us—the old traitor or I—must fall. That is my oath. Good vassal, your voice for war meets my own thoughts. You must have come to me by Heaven's grace." "I am resolved upon the bloody course and shrink from no extremity. Yet I fear, General, that you remain undecided," Zhou Yu responded. Sun Quan drew his sword and sheared off a corner of the table at which he received the petitions of his ministers. "Any officer or official who advocates submission will be dealt with so!" he declared and, handing the sword to Zhou Yu, honored him as first field marshal. Cheng Pu was made second field marshal, and Lu Su consulting commander.

In giving his sword, Sun Quan had empowered Zhou Yu to execute any officer or official who disobeyed. Zhou Yu accepted the weapon and addressed the assembly: "I am authorized to lead you in battle to destroy Cao Cao. Tomorrow all commanders and subordinate officers are to assemble at my headquarters on the riverbank to receive further orders. Anyone who delays or interferes with our mission will be punished in accordance with the Seven Prohibitions and the Fifty-four Capital Offenses."[11] With these words, Zhou Yu took leave of Sun Quan and left the building. The officials adjourned without further comment.

Back at his quarters Zhou Yu summoned Kongming. "Now that the debate is settled," Zhou Yu began, "what would you consider a sound plan for defeating Cao Cao?" "General Sun's resolve is weak. We cannot make any decision," Kongming answered. "What do you mean, 'his resolve is weak'?" responded Zhou Yu. "The sheer size of Cao Cao's army still intimidates him," Kongming went on. "He wonders if the few can withstand the many. Before our cause can succeed, General, you will have to reassure him by making an analysis of the enemy's numerical strength." "Your judgment, master, is correct," said Zhou Yu, and he went back to see Sun Quan.

"Only a matter of some importance," said Sun Quan, "would bring you back so late at night." "My lord," replied Zhou Yu, "are you still in doubt about beginning the expedition tomorrow?" "My only concern," said Sun Quan "is the numerical imbalance between our forces." With a smile Zhou Yu reassured him: "I have come to set your mind at ease on precisely this point, my lord. Your fears and uncertainties arise from mention in Cao's letter of his million-man land and sea force. And you have taken his claim at face value. Let us lay out the facts: Cao Cao is leading no more than one hundred and fifty or sixty thousand northern troops, who are almost entirely exhausted. The soldiers he took over from Yuan Shao number some seventy or eighty thousand, the greater part of whom have little trust in their new leader and consequently little commitment. You have little to fear from one long-wearied army and another with no fixed purpose, whatever their numbers. Fifty thousand men are all I need to break them. Let Your Lordship worry no further." Sun Quan placed his hand gently on Zhou Yu's shoulder and said, "You have allayed my fears. Zhang Zhao has no sense[12] and has deeply disappointed me. Only you and Lu Su share my view. You two and Cheng Pu should pick your forces at once and advance. I will reinforce you with more soldiers and plenty of supplies. If your vanguard runs into difficulties, come back to me at once, and I will meet the traitor Cao in combat personally. My doubts are dispelled."

Zhou Yu expressed his gratitude and left, observing inwardly, "Kongming divined my lord's state of mind before I did! In strategy, too, he excels me. In the long run such brilliance bodes danger to our land; we would be well rid of him now." That night Zhou Yu sent for Lu Su and confided his thoughts to him. Lu Su responded, "Never! To kill a valuable ally before Cao Cao falls would be self-defeating." "The man is an asset to Liu Xuande, not to us," retorted Zhou Yu. "He will cause the Southland trouble." "Zhuge Jin is his elder brother," said Lu Su. "Wouldn't it be wonderful if Jin could induce Kongming to come over to the Southland?" Zhou Yu approved the suggestion.

As dawn broke the following morning, Zhou Yu entered his riverside headquarters and ascended the commander's seat in the main tent of the central army. Left and right stood swordsmen and axemen. Officials and officers crowded below to hear his instructions. But Cheng Pu, the second marshal, was resentful at having to serve under Zhou Yu, who was his junior in age and now his superior in rank. Cheng Pu excused himself on grounds of illness and sent his eldest son, Cheng Zi, in his place.

Zhou Yu issued his commands to the assembly: "The king's law favors no man: let each of you good men perform his duty. Cao Cao's tyranny exceeds even Dong Zhuo's: he holds the Emperor prisoner in Xuchang; and now his ruthless army stands poised at our borders. Today by our sovereign's authority I mean to bring him to justice. I call on you to give your all to this action. Wherever you march, the population is not to be disturbed. Rewards and punishments will follow the strictest standards."

Having delivered the charge, Zhou Yu dispatched the vanguard, Han Dang and Huang Gai, to take command of the naval force and proceed to Three Rivers,[13] there to establish camp and await further orders. The second brigade was led by Jiang Qin and Zhou Tai; the third, by Ling Tong and Pan Zhang; the fourth, by Taishi Ci and Lü Meng; and the fifth, by Lu Xun and Dong Xi. The first marshal further assigned Lü Fan and Zhu Zhi to facilitate and supervise land and sea operations of all units and assure their strict coordination. When these assignments had been made, the various commanders put their boats and armaments in order and set out.

Cheng Zi reported to his father that Zhou Yu's measures were the model of military procedure. Cheng Pu, greatly impressed, said, "I mistook Zhou Yu for a coward, a man unworthy to lead. But if he can do this, he is a true general, and I must not show disrespect." He then presented himself at Zhou Yu's headquarters and apologized for his conduct. Zhou Yu accepted his apology graciously.

The next day Zhou Yu said to Zhuge Jin, "Your brother has the talent to be a king's minister. It is beneath him to serve Liu Xuande. His fortunate arrival in the Southland offers the occasion for persuading him to stay, if I might trouble you to undertake the mission. Our lord would then have a valued adviser and you would be reunited with your brother. What could be more desirable? Be so kind as to pay him a little visit." "I have accomplished nothing, I regret to say, since coming to the Southland, but I shall do all that I can to carry out the field marshal's command." So saying, Jin rode directly to see Kongming. Receiving him at the guesthouse, Zhuge Liang prostrated himself tearfully, and the two brothers gave vent to their deep love for one another.

"Dear brother," Zhuge Jin began, sobbing, "surely you remember the tale of Bo Yi and Shu Qi?"[14] "Hmm," thought Kongming, "Zhou Yu must have sent him to win me over." He answered, "You mean the worthy sages of antiquity?" "Though they died of hunger at the foot of Mount Shouyang, the two brothers stayed together," Zhuge Jin continued. "You and I came from the same womb, suckled at one breast. But now we serve different lords and lead divergent lives. Reflecting on the character of Bo Yi and Shu Qi, can you help feeling a pang of shame?" "What you speak of, brother," Kongming replied, "pertains to the realm of sentiment. What I must preserve is in the realm of honor. You and I are men of the Han. Imperial Uncle Liu is a scion of the royal house. If you could leave the Southland and join me in serving the imperial uncle, then you would have no 'pang of shame' as a true subject of the Han, and we, as brothers, would be reunited. In this way, neither the principle of sentiment nor of honor would be impaired. I venture to inquire how you view this proposal." "I came to ply him," thought Zhuge Jin, "and end up being plied." He had no answer to make, so he rose and took his leave.[15]

Zhuge Jin returned to Zhou Yu and related all that Kongming had said. "How do you feel about it?" asked Zhou Yu. "I have received General Sun Quan's grace and generosity. I could never leave him." "Good sir," responded Zhou Yu, "if you will serve our lord with loyal heart, there is no need to say more. I think I know the way to make Kongming give in." Indeed:

> When wits are matched, it's best if they agree;
> But when talents clash, it's hard for them to yield.

Would Zhou Yu outwit his rival yet?
READ ON.

45

Cao Cao Suffers Casualties at Three Rivers;
Jiang Gan Springs a Trap at the Congregation of Heroes

ZHUGE JIN RECOUNTED HIS CONVERSATION with Kongming. As Zhou Yu listened, his hostility deepened, and he made up his mind that he would have to dispose of Kongming.

The following day, after reviewing his commanders, Zhou Yu went to take leave of Sun Quan. "You proceed," said Quan, "I will bring up the rear with another force." Zhou Yu withdrew and, together with Cheng Pu and Lu Su, commenced the expedition. He also invited Kongming, who accepted eagerly. With the four on board, the ship hoisted sail and began tacking toward Xiakou. Some fifty *li* from Three Rivers the convoy halted. Zhou Yu, commanding the center, established his headquarters and ordered a ring of camps built along the shore around the Western Hills. Kongming betook himself to a little boat of his own.

His arrangements completed, Zhou Yu called Kongming to his tent. After the formalities, Zhou Yu said, "In an earlier campaign Cao had far fewer troops than Yuan Shao; but he won all the same by following Xu You's advice and cutting off Shao's food supply at Wuchao. Now Cao has eight hundred and thirty thousand men to our fifty or sixty thousand. How can we resist? Only by cutting off his supplies. According to information I have already gathered, everything is stored at Iron Pile Mountain. Since you have lived on the River Han and are familiar with the terrain, I wonder if I could prevail upon you, together with Lord Guan, Zhang Fei, and Zhao Zilong—as well as the thousand men that I will give you—to go at once to the mountain and sever their supply line. This would be in the interest of both our lords. I hope you will accept." Kongming mused: "He is scheming to murder me because I will not agree to leave Lord Liu. Rather than look foolish, I'll go along and figure out later what to do." And so, to Zhou Yu's satisfaction, Kongming accepted the assignment enthusiastically.

After Kongming had left, Lu Su said privately to Zhou Yu, "What's behind this sending Kongming to steal their grain?" "Killing Kongming would only invite ridicule," Zhou Yu explained. "Let Cao Cao be the one to save us future trouble." Lu Su then went to Kongming to find out what he knew. But Kongming, betraying no anxiety, was gathering his forces for roll call, preparing to set out. The kindhearted Lu Su said pointedly, "What chance does this mission have, good sir?" With a smile Kongming replied, "I have mastered the fine points of every form of warfare, naval, foot, horse, and chariot. I fear no failure—unlike Southland leaders like you, sir, or Zhou Yu, who have only one specialty.'' ''What do you mean?'' answered Lu Su. Kongming replied: ''Isn't there a children's rhyme going around the south, 'To ambush a trail or hold a pass, Lu Su's the man to trust; / For marine war, Commander Zhou Yu's a must'? So it seems that you're not good for more than a roadside ambush or guarding a pass and that Zhou Yu can fight on water but not on land.''

Lu Su reported this conversation to Zhou Yu, who exclaimed angrily, ''So he thinks I can't fight on land! Fine. Let him stay here. I'll raid Cao's supplies myself with ten thousand men.'' Lu Su carried this new development back to Kongming, who smiled as he said, ''All Zhou Yu really wanted was for Cao Cao to kill me. So I teased him with that remark. He is touchy, though. This is a critical moment. My only wish is for Lord Sun and Lord Liu to work together, for then we may succeed. Plotting against one another will undo our cause. The traitor Cao has plenty of tricks. In his career as a general he's made a specialty of severing enemy supply lines; his own storage is sure to be well prepared for raids: if Zhou Yu goes they'll only capture him. What is called for now is a decisive engagement on the river to blunt the enemy's mettle while we try to work out a plan for their defeat. It's up to you to explain this to Zhou Yu in a reasonable way.''

As Lu Su recounted Kongming's words that night, Zhou Yu shook his head and stamped his feet, crying, ''He is ten times my better. If we don't destroy him now, he will destroy this land of ours.'' ''At this critical time,'' Lu Su argued, ''I hope you will consider the Southland above all. There will be time enough for such schemes after Cao Cao is defeated.'' Zhou Yu had to agree.

·   ·   ·   ·   ·

Liu Xuande charged Liu Qi with the defense of Jiangxia, while he and his commanders moved ahead to Xiakou. In the distance they saw flags and banners shadowing the river's southern shore, and row upon row of spears. Surmising that the Southland had already mobilized, Xuande shifted all the Jiangxia troops across the Great River and east to Fankou. He then addressed his followers: ''We have had no word from Kongming since he went south, and no one knows how things stand. Who will find out for us and report back?'' Mi Zhu volunteered, and Xuande, having provided him with sheep, wine, and other gifts, instructed him to go to the Southland and learn what he could while pretending to feast the southern troops.

Mi Zhu piloted a small boat downriver and arrived in front of Zhou Yu's camp. After being received, Mi Zhu prostrated himself, conveyed Xuande's respects, and presented the articles he had brought. Zhou Yu accepted the gifts and called a banquet to welcome Mi Zhu. ''Kongming has been here too long,'' Mi Zhu declared. ''I would like to bring him back with me.'' ''But he is consulting with us on the campaign against Cao Cao,'' said Zhou Yu, ''he can't simply leave. I, for my part, desire to see Lord Liu in order to confer with him. But, alas, I am personally directing the army and cannot leave the scene. How gratifying it would be, though, if Lord Liu would consider traveling here to visit me.'' Mi Zhu assented and returned to Xuande.

Lu Su said to Zhou Yu, ''Why do you want to see Xuande?'' ''He's the craftiest owl on earth,'' responded Zhou Yu. ''I must be rid of him. This is my chance to lure him here and kill him, and save our house future grief.'' Lu Su argued over and over against such measures—to no avail. Zhou Yu issued a secret order: ''If Xuande comes, I want fifty armed men hidden behind the wall curtains. I'll throw a cup to the ground as the signal to strike.''

Mi Zhu returned to Xuande and relayed Zhou Yu's invitation. Xuande called for a swift boat and set out. Lord Guan objected: "Zhou Yu is a schemer; moreover, we have no letter from Kongming. I see treachery in this. Let's think it over some more." "But they are our allies in the struggle against Cao Cao," said Xuande. "Not to go when they call violates the spirit of the alliance. Constant mutual suspicion will ruin our cause." "If you insist on going, brother," said Lord Guan, "I shall join you." "And I too," added Zhang Fei. "No. Let Lord Guan accompany me," Xuande replied. "You and Zhao Zilong can guard the camp, and Jian Yong can guard Exian. I will return soon."

Xuande and Lord Guan boarded a light craft and, with a small guard of some twenty men, sped downriver to the Southland. Xuande viewed the cutters and war-boats of his ally, their flags and armored men, their orderly array, with mounting excitement. His arrival was swiftly reported to Zhou Yu, who asked, "With how many boats?" "Just one," he was informed, "and about twenty men." "His life is mine," said Zhou Yu, smiling. He deployed his men and went forth to greet his guest. Xuande, with Lord Guan and his guards, followed his host to the main tent. Salutations exchanged, Zhou Yu saw Xuande to the seat of honor. "General," Xuande protested, "you are renowned throughout the empire. I am a man of no talent. Do not trouble so much over ceremony." They partook of a banquet as host and guest.

At the riverside Kongming discovered that Xuande and Zhou Yu were having a meeting. Anxiously entering the main tent to see what was afoot, he noted a murderous look in Zhou Yu's eye and the armed guards behind the wall curtains. "What am I to do about this?" he said to himself in alarm. He turned and observed Xuande chatting and laughing, completely at ease, while Lord Guan stood behind him, hand on his sword. "He is safe," Kongming thought and left to return to the river.

Host and guest had savored several rounds of wine when Zhou Yu stood up, cup in hand. Observing Lord Guan, hand on sword, Yu inquired who he was. "My younger brother, Guan Yunchang," replied Xuande. "Not the one who cut down generals Yan Liang and Wen Chou?" Zhou Yu asked nervously. "The same," Xuande answered. Zhou Yu, alarmed, broke into a sweat. He poured a cup for Lord Guan and drank with him. Moments later Lu Su came in. "Where's Kongming?" Xuande asked him. "Could you bring him here?" "There'll be time enough for meeting when Cao Cao is defeated," said Zhou Yu, closing the subject. Lord Guan eyed Xuande, who sensed his brother's intent and rose. "I shall bid you farewell for now," Xuande told Zhou Yu, "but I will return expressly to celebrate with you the defeat of Cao Cao." Zhou Yu made no effort to detain his guest and escorted him out the main gate.

Xuande and Lord Guan reached the edge of the river, where they found Kongming in his boat. Xuande was elated. "My lord," said Kongming, "you were in more danger than you knew!" Aghast, Xuande said, "No!" "He would have killed you, but for Lord Guan," Kongming remarked. Xuande, only then realizing the actual situation in the Southland, begged Kongming to return with him to Fankou. But Kongming said, "Here in the tiger's mouth I am as secure as Mount Tai. What you have to do is prepare your forces for action. On the twentieth day, first of the cycle, of the eleventh month, send Zhao Zilong in a small boat to wait for me at the south shore. There must be no slip-up." Xuande asked what he was planning, but Kongming simply replied, "Look for a southeast wind. That's when I'll come back." Xuande wanted to know more, but Kongming hurried him aboard and returned to his own boat.

Xuande, Lord Guan, and their followers had sailed but a few *li* when they saw fifty or sixty boats speeding downriver toward them; in the lead was General Zhang Fei, spear at

the ready. Fearing some mishap to Xuande, he had come to back up Lord Guan. And so
the three brothers returned to their camp together.

·   ·   ·   ·

Zhou Yu, having seen Xuande off, returned to camp. Lu Su asked, "You lured Xuande
here. Why didn't you strike?" "Lord Guan is the fiercest of generals. He never leaves
Xuande's side. If I had acted, he would have slain me," Zhou Yu explained. Lu Su was
astounded at the awe Lord Guan had inspired.

At that moment an emissary from Cao Cao arrived, bearing an envelope with the
words "The prime minister of the Han authorizes Field Marshal Zhou to open this."
Zhou Yu angrily tore the envelope, unopened, into pieces and threw them to the ground.
He then ordered the bearer put to death. "Two kingdoms at war don't kill each other's
envoys," Lu Su urged. "I do so to show my confidence in our strength," answered Zhou
Yu. The envoy was executed, and his head was given to his attendants to carry back to
Cao Cao. Zhou Yu then commanded Gan Ning to lead the van, Han Dang to lead the left
wing, and Jiang Qin to lead the right, reserving for himself the task of relief and reinforcement. The next day they breakfasted at the fourth watch and sailed out at the fifth,
drums and battle cries heralding their advance.

·   ·   ·   ·

The news that Zhou Yu had destroyed his letter and beheaded his messenger infuriated
Cao Cao. At once he organized a vanguard led by Cai Mao, Zhang Yun, and other Jingzhou commanders who had submitted to him. Cao Cao himself took command of the rear
and supervised the transfer of the fleet to Three Rivers. Soon he saw the approaching
war-boats of the southerners spread across the length and breadth of the river. Their lead
general, seated in the prow of one boat, shouted out, "Gan Ning comes! Who dares oppose?" Cai Mao sent his younger brother, Xun, to meet him. The two boats drew near.
Gan Ning steadied his bow and toppled Xun with one shot. Gan Ning pressed ahead, his
archers massing their bolts; Cao Cao's forces reeled before the assault. Following up,
Jiang Qin sailed from the right and Han Dang from the left, straight into the center of the
northerners' position. Most of Cao's soldiers, coming from the provinces of Qing and Xu,
were unused to naval warfare and lost their balance on the rolling ships. This gave the
southerners—now augmented by Zhou Yu's force—control of the waterway. Thousands
of Cao Cao's men fell by bombard or arrow in a battle that lasted from midmorning to
early afternoon. But despite his advantage, Zhou Yu, still wary of Cao Cao's greater
numbers, beat the gong recalling his boats.

After his defeated troops had returned, Cao Cao appeared in his land headquarters and
directed the reordering of his forces. He rebuked Cai Mao and Zhang Yun: "The troops
of the Southland, though few, have defeated us—because you lack commitment." Cai
Mao protested, "We were defeated because the Jingzhou sailors have been off their training and because the Qingzhou and Xuzhou troops have no experience in naval warfare.
The thing to do now is to establish a naval camp, placing the Qingzhou and Xuzhou
troops inside, the Jingzhou troops outside, and train them every day until they are fit for
combat." To this Cao replied, "You are already the chief naval commander and can perform your duties at your discretion. There's no need to petition me."

Cai Mao and Zhang Yun undertook the training of a navy. Along the river they set up
a row of twenty-four water lanes for communication; the larger boats formed the outer
rim, enclosing the smaller like a city wall. At night the torches lit up the sky and river,

while on land the camps, which stretched for three hundred *li*, sent up smoke and fire day and night.

•   •   •   •   •

The triumphant Zhou Yu had returned to camp, rewarded his troops, and sent news of the victory to Sun Quan. After nightfall Zhou Yu surveyed the scene from a height: the glow in the west reached the horizon. "The fires and torches of the northern army," his aides said. Shocked, Zhou Yu decided to investigate Cao's naval encampment himself the following day. He ordered a two-tiered boat outfitted with drums and other instruments. Accompanied by his ablest commanders, all armed with longbows or crossbows, he boarded and set out.

The craft threaded its way upriver. When it reached the edge of Cao Cao's camp, Zhou Yu dropped anchor. The instruments began playing, and Zhou Yu observed how the camp responded. "They have mastered the finest points of naval warfare," he exclaimed. "Who's in general command?" "Cai Mao and Zhang Yun," his assistants reported. "Longtime residents of the Southland, they're skilled in naval tactics," Zhou Yu mused. "I'll have to put them out of the way before I can defeat Cao." At that moment Cao Cao was informed of the spy ship's presence and ordered it captured. Zhou Yu saw Cao Cao's signal flags in motion and had the anchor raised; the oarsmen had pulled the two-tiered vessel more than ten *li* into open water by the time Cao Cao's boats came forth. Finding the Southland vessel out of range, the captains returned and reported to Cao Cao.

Cao Cao conferred with his commanders. "Yesterday," he said, "we lost a battle and our momentum. Now they've sailed in again, close enough to spy on our camp. How can we defeat them?" As he spoke, one man stepped forward and said, "Zhou Yu and I have been close since childhood when we were students together. Let me try my powers of persuasion on him and see if I can get him to surrender."[1] Cao Cao turned a grateful eye on the man. It was Jiang Gan (Ziyi) of Jiujiang, a member of his council. "You are on good terms with Zhou Yu?" Cao Cao asked. "Your troubles are over, Your Excellency," said Jiang Gan. "When I go south, I shall not fail." "What will you need?" asked Cao. "A page to accompany me, two servants to row me across." Cao Cao, immensely pleased, regaled Jiang Gan with wine and saw him off. The envoy, dressed in hempen scarf and plain weave robe, sped downriver, straight to Zhou Yu's camp. His arrival was announced—"An old friend comes to pay a call"—just when Zhou Yu was in conference. Delighted by the news, he turned to his commanders and said, "The 'persuader' has come." Then he told each of them what to do, and they left to perform their duties.

Zhou Yu adjusted his cap and garb and, surrounded by several hundred in brocade clothes and decorated hats, came forth. Jiang Gan approached boldly and alone, save for his one young attendant who was dressed in plain black. Zhou Yu received him with low bows. "You have been well since we parted, I trust," said the visitor. "My friend, you have taken great trouble, coming so far to serve as Cao Cao's spokesman," Zhou Yu responded.[2] Taken aback, Jiang Gan said, "We have been apart so long, I came especially to reminisce. How could you suspect me of such a thing?" With a smile Zhou Yu answered, "My ear may not be so fine as the great musician Shi Kuang's, but I can discern good music and good intentions too."[3] "Dear friend," Jiang Gan replied, "if this is how you treat an old friend, I must beg my leave." Still smiling, Zhou Yu took Jiang Gan by the arm and said, "I was afraid, brother, that you were working for Cao, that's all. If you have no such purpose, there is no need to rush. Please stay." And so the two of them went into the tent. After the ritual greetings they seated themselves, and Zhou Yu summoned the notables of the south to meet his friend.

Chief officials and generals in formal dress and subordinate officers and commanders clad in silvered armor entered shortly in two columns. Zhou Yu had each dignitary introduced to Jiang Gan and seated in one of two rows to the side. A great feast was spread and victory music performed. Wine came too, round after round. Zhou Yu addressed the assembly: "Here is one of my schoolmates, a close friend. Although he has come from north of the river, he is not serving as a spokesman of Cao Cao's cause. Set your minds at ease on that score." He then removed the sword at his side and handed it to Taishi Ci, saying, "Wear the sword and supervise the banquet. We will speak of friendship today and nothing else. If anyone so much as mentions the hostilities between Cao Cao and the lord of the Southland, take off his head!" Taishi Ci acknowledged the order and sat at the feast, his hand resting on the sword. Terror-stricken, Jiang Gan said little.

"Since taking command of the army," Zhou Yu declared, "I have drunk no wine. But today, in the company of an old friend, with no lack of trust, let us have our fill and then some." With that, he laughed loudly and drank deeply. The toasts came thick and fast. When they had grown flushed and mellow, Zhou Yu took Jiang Gan by the hand, and the two friends strolled outside the tent. To the left and right of them stood soldiers in complete outfit, armed with dagger and halberd. "Formidable, are they not?" Zhou Yu asked. "Ferocious as bears, fierce as tigers," Jiang Gan agreed. Then Zhou Yu led his guest around behind the headquarters where hills of grain and fodder were stored. "Enough for any eventuality, don't you think?" Zhou Yu asked his guest. " 'Crack troops and full bins.' Your high reputation is not for nothing," Jiang Gan agreed again.

Feigning intoxication, Zhou Yu laughed heartily. "To think we were once students together!" he said. "Who would have foreseen a day like today?" "Brother," said Jiang Gan, "with your supreme abilities, such accomplishment is only too fitting." Gripping Jiang Gan's hand, Zhou Yu said, "As a man of honor all my life and one having the good fortune to serve a lord who appreciates me, I am as obligated to that honored bond between liege and liege man as I am by my kinsmen's love. What I say, he does. What I propose, he approves. His misfortunes and his blessings are mine as much as his. Were the great rhetoricians of old—Su Qin, Zhang Yi, Lu Jia, Li Yiji[4]—were they to walk the earth again, delivering speeches like cascading streams and wielding their tongues like sharp swords, they could not move me!" Having spoken, Zhou Yu burst into laughter. Jiang Gan's face was ashen. Zhou Yu led his guest back into the tent, and the general carousing resumed. Zhou Yu pointed to his commanders and said, "These are the flower of the Southland. And this gathering today shall be known as the Congregation of the Heroes." The company kept on drinking until it was time to light the lamps. Then Zhou Yu rose and performed a sword dance, singing:

> In this life a man must make his name:
> A good name is a comfort all life long.
> A lifelong comfort: Oh, let me feel the wine,
> And flushed with wine, I'll sing my wildest song.

When he finished, the whole table laughed gaily. As the night advanced, Jiang Gan prepared to take his leave. "The wine was too much for me," he said. Zhou Yu dismissed the guests, and the commanders departed. "We have not shared a couch for many a year, my friend," Zhou Yu said. "Tonight we share a bed foot-to-foot." Again feigning intoxication, he led Jiang Gan arm in arm into his bedchamber and there collapsed, sprawling into bed fully dressed and vomiting copiously. How could Jiang Gan sleep? He lay on his pillow, listening. The drum sounded the second watch. Lifting his head, he saw the wasted candle still giving light. Zhou Yu was snoring heavily. On the table Jiang Gan noticed a sheaf of documents. He rose and stealthily looked through them: among the correspondence was a letter from Cao Cao's two naval commanders, Cai Mao and Zhang Yun. He peeked at the contents:

> We surrendered to Cao by dint of circumstance, not for wealth or rank. We have tricked the northern army by enclosing it inside the large ships. The moment we have the chance, we will deliver the traitor Cao's head to you. Someone will come with further information. Have no doubts. Herein our respectful reply.

Jiang Gan said to himself, "So Cai Mao and Zhang Yun are in league with the Southland!" and stowed the letter in his clothes. He was going to look at some of the other papers, but Zhou Yu turned over in bed. Jiang Gan extinguished the lamp and lay down. Zhou Yu began to mumble, "My friend, wait a few days and you'll see the head of that traitor Cao!" Jiang Gan managed a reply. Again Zhou Yu said, "Do stay a while . . . you'll see Cao Cao's head . . ." Jiang Gan tried to question him, but saw that he had fallen fast asleep.

Jiang Gan lay on the bed. The fourth watch was near. He heard someone come into the tent and call out, "Is the marshal awake yet?" Zhou Yu, giving the appearance of a man startled from his dreams, asked the man, "Who is this sleeping on my bed?" "Marshal," was the reply, "you invited Jiang Gan to share your bed. Can you have forgotten?" In a repentant tone, Zhou Yu said, "I never allow myself to get drunk. I was not myself yesterday. I don't remember if I said anything." "Someone came from the north," said the man. "Lower your voice!" said Zhou Yu urgently. He then called Jiang Gan, but Gan feigned sleep. Zhou Yu slipped out of the tent. Gan listened intently. Outside someone was saying, "Zhang Yun and Cai Mao said, 'We are not able to take quick action . . .'" The remainder was spoken too low for Jiang Gan to make out.

Moments later Zhou Yu reentered the tent and called his friend again. Jiang Gan continued the pretense by pulling the blanket over his head and making no response. Zhou Yu took off his clothes and lay down. Jiang Gan thought, "Zhou Yu is a shrewd man. He is sure to kill me in the morning when he discovers the letter is gone." Jiang Gan rested until the fifth watch, then rose and called Zhou Yu. No answer. He put on his hood and slipped out of the tent, called his young companion and headed for the main gate. "Where to, sir?" the guard asked. "I'm afraid I have been keeping the field marshal from his work, so I am saying good-bye for now." The guard made no attempt to stop them.[5]

Jiang Gan boarded his boat and sped back to see Cao Cao. "How did it go?" the prime minister asked. Jiang Gan said, "Zhou Yu is too high-minded to be swayed by speeches." Angrily Cao replied, "The mission failed. And we end up looking like fools!" "Though I could not persuade him to join us, I did manage to find out something of interest for Your Excellency. Would you ask the attendants to go out?" So saying, Jiang Gan produced the stolen letter and related point by point all that had happened in the bedchamber. "That's how the villains repay my kindness!" roared Cao Cao and summoned Cai Mao and Zhang Yun to his quarters at once. "I want you two to begin the attack," Cao Cao said to them. "The training is still unfinished. It would be risky," they replied. "And when the training is completed, will my head be delivered to Zhou Yu?" said Cao. Cai Mao and Zhang Yun could make no sense of this and were too confused to respond. Cao Cao called for his armed guards to put them to death. But the moment the two heads were brought in, Cao Cao realized he had been tricked.[6] A poet of later times left these lines:

> Cao Cao, a master of intrigue,
> Fell for Zhou Yu's cunning ruse.
> Cai and Zhang betrayed their lord
> And fell to Cao Cao's bloody sword.[7]

Cao Cao's commanders wanted to know the reason for the executions. But Cao Cao was unable to admit his mistake. "They flouted military rules; therefore, I had them killed," he said. The stunned commanders groaned and sighed. Cao Cao chose Mao Jie and Yu Jin to serve as the new chief naval commanders.

Meanwhile, spies reported the executions to Zhou Yu. "I feared those two the most," he said with satisfaction. "With them out of the way, I have no problems." "Commander," said Lu Su, "if you can wage war this well, we will have nothing to worry about. Cao will be beaten." "My guess is that none of our commanders knows what happened," said Zhou Yu, "except for Kongming, who knows more than I do. I doubt if even this plan fooled him. Try to sound him out for me. Find out if he knew. And tell me right away." Indeed:

> His success in dividing his rivals would not be complete
> Until he knew what the stony-eyed observer on the side was thinking.

Once again Lu Su went to see Kongming for Zhou Yu. Could he keep the alliance from breaking up?[8]

READ ON.

46

Kongming Borrows Cao Cao's Arrows Through a Ruse;
Huang Gai Is Flogged Following a Secret Plan

ZHOU YU SENT LU SU to find out if Kongming had detected the subterfuge. Kongming welcomed Lu Su aboard his little boat, and the two men sat face-to-face. "Every day I am taken up with military concerns and miss your advice," Lu Su began. "Rather, I am the tardy one, having yet to convey my felicitations to the chief commander," answered Kongming. "What felicitations?" asked Lu Su. "Why," replied Kongming, "for that very matter about which he sent you here to see if I knew." The color left Lu Su's face. "But how did you know, master?" he asked. Kongming went on: "The trick was good enough to take in Jiang Gan. Cao Cao, though hoodwinked for the present will realize what happened quickly enough—he just won't admit the mistake. But with those naval commanders dead, the Southland has no major worry, so congratulations are certainly in order. I hear that Cao Cao has replaced them with Mao Jie and Yu Jin. One way or another, those two will do in their navy!"

Lu Su, unable to respond sensibly, temporized as best he could before he rose to leave. "I trust you will say nothing about this in front of Zhou Yu," Kongming urged Lu Su, "lest he again be moved to do me harm." Lu Su agreed but finally divulged the truth when he saw the field marshal. Astounded, Zhou Yu said, "The man must die. I am determined." "If you kill him," Lu Su argued, "Cao Cao will have the last laugh." "I will have justification," answered Zhou Yu. "And he will not feel wronged." "How will you do it?" asked Lu Su. "No more questions now. You'll see soon enough," Zhou Yu replied.

The next day Zhou Yu gathered his generals together and summoned Kongming, who came eagerly. At the assembly Zhou Yu asked him, "When we engage Cao Cao in battle on the river routes, what should be the weapon of choice?" "On the Great River, bow and arrow," Kongming replied. "My view precisely, sir," Zhou Yu said. "But we happen to be short of arrows. Dare I trouble you, sir, to undertake the production of one hundred thousand arrows to use against the enemy? Please favor us with your cooperation in this official matter." "Whatever task the chief commander assigns, I shall strive to complete," replied Kongming. "But may I ask by what time you will require them?" "Can you finish in ten days?" asked Zhou Yu. "Cao's army is due at any moment," said Kongming. "If we must wait ten days, it will spoil everything." "How many days do you estimate you need, sir?" said Zhou Yu. "With all respect, I will deliver the arrows in three days," Kongming answered. "There is no room for levity in the army," Zhou Yu snapped. "Dare

I trifle with the chief commander?" countered Kongming. "I beg to submit my pledge under martial law: if I fail to finish in three days' time, I will gladly suffer the maximum punishment."

Elated, Zhou Yu had his administrative officer publicly accept the document. He then offered Kongming wine, saying, "You will be well rewarded when your mission is accomplished."[1] "It's too late to begin today," said Kongming. "Production begins tomorrow. On the third day send five hundred men to the river for the arrows." After a few more cups, he left. Lu Su said to Zhou Yu, "This man has to be deceiving us." "He is delivering himself into our hands!" replied Zhou Yu. "We did not force him. Now that he has publicly undertaken this task in writing, he couldn't escape if he sprouted wings. Just have the artisans delay delivery of whatever he needs. He will miss the appointed time; and when we fix his punishment, what defense will he be able to make? Now go to him again and bring me back news."

Lu Su went to see Kongming. "Didn't I tell you not to say anything?" Kongming began. "He is determined to kill me. I never dreamed you would expose me. And now today he actually pulled this trick on me! How am I supposed to produce one hundred thousand arrows in three days? You have to save me!" "You brought this on yourself," said Lu Su. "How can I save you?" "You must lend me twenty vessels," Kongming went on, "with a crew of thirty on each. Lined up on either side of each vessel I want a thousand bundles of straw wrapped in black cloth. I have good use for them. I'm sure we can have the arrows on the third day. But if you tell Zhou Yu this time, my plan will fail." Lu Su agreed, though he had no idea what Kongming was up to, and reported back to Zhou Yu without mentioning the boats: "Kongming doesn't seem to need bamboo, feathers, glue, or other materials. He seems to have something else in mind." Puzzled, Zhou Yu said, "Let's see what he has to say after three days have gone by."

Lu Su quietly placed at Kongming's disposal all he had requested. But neither on the first day nor on the second did Kongming make any move. On the third day at the fourth watch he secretly sent for Lu Su. "Why have you called me here?" Su asked. "Why else? To go with me to fetch the arrows," Kongming replied. "From where?" inquired Lu Su. "Ask no questions," said Kongming. "Let's go; you'll see." He ordered the boats linked by long ropes and set out for the north shore.

That night tremendous fogs spread across the heavens, and the river mists were so thick that even face-to-face people could not see each other. Kongming urged his boats on into the deep fog. The rhapsody "Heavy Mists Mantling the Yangzi" describes it well:

Vast the river! Wide and farflung! West, it laps the mountains Mang and E. South, it grips the southern shires. North, it girdles the nine rivers, gathers their waters, and carries them into the sea, its surging waves rolling through eternity.

Its depths hold monsters and strange forms: the Lord of the Dragons, the Sea Thing, the river goddesses, the Ocean Mother, ten-thousand-span whales, and the nine-headed centipede. This redoubt of gods and spirits, heroes fight to hold.

At times the forces of *yin* and *yang* that govern nature fail, and day and darkness seem as one, turning the vast space into a fearful monochrome. Everywhere the fog, stock-still. Not even a cartload can be spotted. But the sound of gong or drum carries far.

At first, a visible gloom, time for the wise leopard of the southern hills to seclude itself. Gradually darkness fills the expanse. Does it want the North Sea

leviathan itself to lose its way? At last it reaches the very sky and mantles the
all-upbearing earth. Grey gloomy vastness. A shoreless ocean. Whales hurtle on
the waves. Dragons plunge and spew mist.

It is like the end of early rains, when the cold of latent spring takes hold: everywhere, vague, watery desert and darkness that flows and spreads. East, it blan-
kets the shore of Chaisang. South, it blocks the hills of Xiakou. A thousand war-
junks, swallowed between the river's rocky steeps, while a single fishing boat
boldly bobs on the swells.

In so deep a fog, the deep-domed heavens have gone dark. The countenance of
dawn is dull: the day becomes a murky twilight; the reddish hills, aquamarine jade.
Great Yu, who first controlled the floods, could not with all his wisdom sound its
depths. Even clear-eyed Li Lou could not use his measures, despite his keen vision.

Let the water god calm these waves. Let the god of elements put away his art.
Let the sea creatures and those of land and air be gone. For now the magic isle of
Penglai is cut off, and the gates of the polar stars are shrouded.

The roiling, restless fog is like the chaos before a storm, swirling streaks resembling wintry clouds. Serpents lurking there can spread its pestilence, and evil
spirits can havoc wreak, sending pain and woe to the world of men, and the storms
of wind and sand that plague the border wastes. Common souls meeting it fall
dead. Great men observe it and despair. Are we returning to the primal state that
preceded form itself—to undivided Heaven and earth?

By the fifth watch Kongming's little convoy was nearing Cao Cao's river base. The
vessels advanced in single file, their prows pointed west. The crews began to roar and
pound their drums. Lu Su was alarmed. "What if they make a sally?" he asked. Kongming smiled and replied, "I'd be very surprised if Cao Cao plunged into this fog. Let's
pour the wine and enjoy ourselves. We'll go back when the fog lifts."

As the clamor reached Cao Cao's camp, the new naval advisers Mao Jie and Yu Jin sent
reports at once. Cao Cao issued an order: "The fog has made the river invisible. This
sudden arrival of enemy forces must mean an ambush. I want absolutely no reckless
movements. Let the archers and crossbowmen, however, fire upon the enemy at ran-
dom." He also sent a man to his land headquarters calling for Zhang Liao and Xu Huang
to rush an extra three thousand crossbowmen to the shore. By the time Cao's order
reached Mao Jie and Yu Jin, their men had already begun shooting for fear the southerners would penetrate their camp. Soon, once the marksmen from the land camp had
joined the battle, ten thousand men were concentrating their shots toward the river. The
shafts came down like rain.

Kongming ordered the boats to reverse direction and press closer to shore to receive
the arrows while the crews continued drumming and shouting. When the sun climbed,
dispersing the fog, Kongming ordered the boats to hurry homeward. The straw bundles
bristled with arrow shafts, for which Kongming had each crew shout in unison: "Thanks
to the prime minister for the arrows!" By the time this was reported to Cao Cao, the light
craft, borne on swift currents, were twenty *li* downriver, beyond overtaking. Cao Cao
was left with the agony of having played the fool.

Kongming said to Lu Su, "Each boat has some five or six thousand arrows. So without
costing the Southland the slightest effort, we have gained over one hundred thousand
arrows, which tomorrow we can return to Cao's troops—a decided convenience to us!"
"Master, you are indeed supernatural," Lu Su said. "How did you know there would be

such a fog today?" "A military commander is a mediocrity," Kongming explained, "unless he is versed in the patterns of the heavens, recognizes the advantages of the terrain,
knows the interaction of prognostic signs, understands the changes in weather, examines
the maps of deployment, and is clear about the balance of forces. Three days ago I calculated today's fog. That's why I took a chance on the three-day limit. Zhou Yu gave me
ten days to finish the job, but neither materials nor workmen. He plainly meant to kill me
for laxity. But my fate is linked to Heaven. How could Zhou Yu have succeeded?" Respectfully, Lu Su acknowledged Kongming's superior powers.

When the boats reached shore, five hundred men sent by Zhou Yu had already arrived
to transport the arrows. Kongming directed them to take the arrows—upward of one
hundred thousand of them—from the boats and to deliver them to the chief commander's
tent. Meanwhile, Lu Su explained in detail to Zhou Yu how Kongming had acquired
them. Zhou Yu was astounded. Then, with a long sigh of mingled admiration and despair,
he said, "Kongming's godlike machinations and magical powers of reckoning are utterly
beyond me!"[2] A poet of later times left these lines in admiration:

> That day thick fog covering the river
> Dissolved all distance in a watery blur.
> Like driving rain or locusts Cao's arrows came:
> Kongming had humbled the Southland's commander.

Kongming entered the camp. Zhou Yu came out of his tent and greeted him with cor-
dial praise: "Master, we must defer to your superhuman powers of reckoning." "A petty
subterfuge of common cunning," Kongming replied, "not worth your compliments."
Zhou Yu invited Kongming into his tent to drink. "Yesterday," Zhou Yu said, " Lord Sun
urged us to advance. But I still lack that unexpected stroke that wins the battle. I appeal
to you for instruction." "I am a run-of-the-mill mediocrity," replied Kongming. "What
kind of unique stratagem could I offer you?" "Yesterday I surveyed Cao's naval stations," Zhou Yu continued. "They are the epitome of strict order, all according to the
book, invulnerable to any routine attack. I have one idea, but it may not be workable.
Master, could you help me to decide?"[3]

"Refrain from speaking for a moment, Chief Commander," Kongming said. "We'll
write on our palms to see whether we agree or not." Zhou Yu was delighted to oblige. He
called for brush and ink, and, after writing on his own masked hand, passed the brush to
Kongming, who wrote on his own. Then the two men shifted closer to one another,
opened their hands, and laughed. The same word was on each: fire. "Since our views
coincide," said Zhou Yu, "my doubts are resolved. Protect our secret." "This is our common cause," answered Kongming. "Disclosure is unthinkable. My guess is that even
though Cao Cao has twice fallen victim to my fires, he will not be prepared for this.[4] It
may be your ultimate weapon, Chief Commander." After drinking they parted. None of
the commanders knew of their plan.

•   •   •   •

Cao Cao had lost a hundred and fifty or sixty thousand arrows with nothing to show
for it, and a surly temper ruled his mind. Xun You put forward a plan: "With Zhou Yu
and Zhuge Liang framing strategy for the Southland, there is little hope of defeating
them in a quick strike. Rather, send a man to the Southland claiming to surrender, one
who can serve as our spy in their camp. Then we will have a chance." "I was thinking
much the same thing," said Cao. "Whom would you choose for the mission?" "We've

executed Cai Mao. His clansmen are all in the army: Cai Zhong and Cai He are now lieutenant commanders. Bind those two to you, Your Excellency, with suitable favors and then send them to declare their submission to the Southland. They will not be suspected." Cao Cao agreed.

That night the prime minister secretly called the two into his tent and gave them their instructions: "I want you to take a few soldiers south and pretend to surrender. Send covert reports of all you observe. When your mission is done, you will be enfeoffed and amply rewarded. Do not waver in your loyalties." "Our families are in Jingzhou," they replied. "How could our loyalties be divided? Rest assured, Your Excellency. We will secure the heads of Zhou Yu and Zhuge Liang and place them before you." Cao Cao paid them handsomely. The next day Cai Zhong and Cai He sailed south in several boats, accompanied by five hundred men and headed for the southern shore on a favorable wind.

Zhou Yu was working on preparations for his attack when it was reported that the ships approaching from the north shore were bringing two defectors, kinsmen of Cai Mao's, Cai He and Cai Zhong. Zhou Yu summoned them into his presence, and the two men prostrated themselves, weeping as they spoke: "Cao Cao has murdered our elder brother, an innocent man. We want to avenge him. So we have come to surrender in the hope that you will grant us a place. We want to serve in the front line." Delighted, Zhou Yu rewarded them handsomely and ordered them to join Gan Ning in the vanguard. The two men gave their respectful thanks, believing their plan had worked.

Zhou Yu, however, secretly instructed Gan Ning: "This is a false surrender. They have not brought their families. Cao Cao has sent them here to spy. I want to give him a taste of his own medicine by giving them certain information to send back. Be as solicitous of them as possible, but on your guard. The day we march, we will sacrifice them to our banners. Take the strictest precautions against any slip-up." Gan Ning left with his orders.

Lu Su said to the chief commander, "The surrender of Cai Zhong and Cai He is undoubtedly a pretense. We should not accept it." Zhou Yu rebuked him: "They have come to avenge their brother whom Cao Cao murdered. What 'pretense' are you talking about? If you are so full of suspicions, how are we going to open our arms to the talents of the realm?" Silently, Lu Su withdrew and went to inform Kongming, who smiled but said nothing. "What are you smiling at?" Lu Su demanded. "At your failure to detect Zhou Yu's plan. Spies cannot cross the river so easily. Cao Cao sent them to defect so that he could probe our situation. Zhou Yu is fighting fire with fire and wants them to transmit certain information. 'There is no end of deception in warfare'—Zhou Yu's plan exemplifies the adage." And so Lu Su left enlightened.

•   •   •   •

One night Zhou Yu was sitting in his tent, when Huang Gai stole in. "You must have a fine plan to show me, coming in the night like this." said Zhou Yu. "The enemy is too numerous," said Huang Gai, "for us to maintain this standoff long. Why don't we attack with fire?" "Who told you to offer this plan?" Zhou Yu asked. "No one," he replied. "It's my own idea." "Well, it's exactly what I mean to do," said Zhou Yu. "That's why I'm keeping those two false defectors: to convey false information to Cao's camp. But I need a man to play the same game for us." "I am willing to do it," Huang Gai answered. "What credibility will you have," said Zhou Yu, "if you show no sign of having suffered?" "To requite the favor and generosity that the house of Sun has bestowed on me," Huang Gai answered, "I would freely and willingly strew my innards on the ground."

Bowing low, Zhou Yu thanked him, saying, "If you are willing to carry out this trick of being flogged to win the enemy's confidence, it will be a manifold blessing to the Southland." "Even if I die, I will die content," was Huang Gai's reply. He took leave of Zhou Yu and departed.

The next day Zhou Yu sounded the drums, convening a general assembly of his commanders outside his tent. Kongming too was in attendance. Zhou Yu began: "Cao Cao's million-strong horde, deployed along a three-hundred-*li* stretch of land and shore, will not be defeated in a single day. I am ordering the commanders to take three months' rations and prepare to defend our line." Huang Gai came forward, interrupting him. "Never mind three months'—thirty months' rations won't do the job," he said. "If we can beat them this month, then let's do it. If not, what choice have we but to go along with Zhang Zhao's advice, throw down our weapons, face north, and sue for peace?"[5]

Zhou Yu exploded in fury. "I bear our lord's mandate," he cried, "to lead our troops to destroy Cao Cao. The next man to advocate surrender dies! Now at the very moment of confrontation between the two armies, how dare you weaken our morale? If I spare you, how will I hold my men?" Roughly, he barked orders to his guards to remove Huang Gai, execute him, and report back when done. Huang Gai turned to denounce him: "My service to Lord Sun's father, General Sun Jian, has taken me the length and breadth of the Southland through three successive reigns. Where do the likes of you come from?" Zhou Yu ordered immediate execution.

Gan Ning rushed forward and made an appeal: "Huang Gai is one of the Southland's elder leaders. I beg you to be lenient." "What are you trying to do, destroy the rules of the army?" Zhou Yu shouted back and barked orders to his guards to drive Gan Ning from the assembly with their clubs. At this point the entire assembly got on their knees, attempting to intercede: "No doubt Huang Gai deserves to die for his offense, but that would not be in the interests of the army. Let the chief commander be lenient and simply make note of his act for the present time. There will be time enough to dispose of him after we have beaten Cao Cao." Zhou Yu would not relent, but in the face of the strenuous protests of his commanders, he said, "If not for my consideration for your views, he would lose his head. But I shall spare him for now." Then, turning to his attendants, he added, "Throw him to the ground. One hundred strokes across the back should teach him a proper lesson." The commanders renewed their appeals for Huang Gai, but Zhou Yu overturned his table, silenced them with a gesture, and ordered the whipping carried out.

Huang Gai was stripped and forced facedown to the ground. After fifty blows of the rod the officers once again appealed for mercy. Zhou Yu jumped to his feet and, pointing at Huang Gai, said, "You have dared to show your disrespect! The other fifty will be held in reserve. Any further insults will be doubly punished." Still muttering angrily, he reentered his tent. The officers helped Huang Gai to his feet. His skin was broken everywhere and his oozing flesh was crossed with welts. Returning to his camp, he fainted several times. All who came to express their sympathy wept freely. Among the callers was Lu Su.

Afterward Lu Su went to Kongming's boat. "Zhou Yu made Huang Gai pay for it today," Lu Su said. "As his subordinates, we couldn't plead too hard and incur Zhou Yu's displeasure. But you, sir, are a guest. Why did you stand by so apparently unconcerned?" Kongming smiled and answered, "Don't mock me, Lu Su." "Since crossing the river together," Lu Su protested, "when have I mocked you? Do not say such things!" "Don't tell me, my friend," Kongming went on, "you didn't know today's beating was all a trick. What would be the point of having me oppose it?" These words awakened Lu Su to the meaning of what had happened. "Without the 'battered-body trick,'" Kongming re-marked, "how could Cao Cao be taken in? Zhou Yu will be sending Huang Gai over to 'defect,' so he wants Cai Zhong and Cai He to report today's events to Cao Cao. But it is imperative that Zhou Yu not know that I know. Tell him simply that I too resented the beating."

After leaving Kongming, Lu Su went to Zhou Yu, and the two men conferred pri-vately. "Why did you condemn Huang Gai so bitterly today?" Lu Su asked. "Did the commanders resent it?" responded Zhou Yu. "Most of them were disturbed," answered Lu Su. "And Kongming?" Zhou Yu asked. "He too expressed unhappiness at your ex-treme intolerance," replied Lu Su. "This time around I have deceived him," said Zhou Yu. "What?" Lu Su asked. "The beating was a ruse," Zhou Yu explained. "I wanted Huang Gai to feign defection, and his body had to be badly bruised to make it convincing. While Huang Gai is in their camp, we will attack with fire; victory will be ours." Lu Su marveled to himself at Kongming's insight but dared not breathe a word.[6]

•   •   •   •   •

Huang Gai lay in his tent. All the commanders came to sympathize. Gai moaned but did not speak. When the military counselor Kan Ze arrived to pay his respects, Huang Gai dismissed his attendants. "I can't believe you have made an enemy of the chief com-mander," Kan Ze said. "I haven't," Huang Gai replied. "Then your punishment must be a trick to win the enemy's confidence," Kan Ze said. "How did you know?" asked Huang Gai. "I was watching Zhou Yu's every move," Kan Ze responded, "and guessed the truth pretty much." "The house of Sun has been my benefactor under three masters," said Huang Gai. "I proposed this plan for destroying Cao because of my appreciation, and I submitted to this beating willingly. But there is no one in the army I could trust to help me, except for you, who have a loyal and honorable mind and the courage to serve our lord without question." "Do you mean," Kan Ze said, "that you want me to deliver the letter of surrender?" "That is my wish. Are you willing?" Huang Gai asked. Eagerly, Kan Ze accepted. Indeed:

> A brave general requites his lord without a thought for his own safety;
> A counselor serves his land with the selfsame devotion.

What would Kan Ze say next?
READ ON.

47

Kan Ze's Secret Letter Offering a Sham Surrender;
Pang Tong's Shrewd Plan for Connecting the Boats

KAN ZE (DERUN) CAME FROM SHANYIN COUNTY in Kuaiji district. His family was poor, but he was a devoted student and performed menial chores in exchange for the loan of books. Kan Ze could grasp a text in one reading and was eloquent in argument. Even as a youth he had the courage of his convictions. When Sun Quan summoned Kan Ze to serve as a consultant, Huang Gai, impressed by his ability as well as his mettle, befriended him; and this is how Huang Gai came to choose Kan Ze to present his sham appeal to Cao Cao.

Kan Ze responded eagerly to Huang Gai's proposition: "The man of honor will decay and vanish like a plant unless he can make his mark in this world. Since your life is pledged to requite your lord, can I begrudge my own worthless self?" Huang Gai rolled down from his bed and prostrated himself in gratitude. "This matter brooks no delay," Kan Ze said. "Let's start at once." "The letter is written," Huang Gai said and handed it over.

Disguised as a fisherman, Kan Ze guided a small craft to the north shore that very night under a winter sky filled with stars.[1] At the third watch he reached Cao's camp. The river patrol who captured him reported to Cao Cao. "A spy for sure," he said. "Only a fisherman," said the guard, "but he claims to be Kan Ze, consultant to Sun Quan, with something confidential to present to you." Cao Cao had Kan Ze brought before him. In Cao's tent, lit by flaming candles, Kan Ze could see Cao Cao sitting rigidly at his desk. "If you are an adviser to Sun Quan," Cao said, "what brings you here?"

"People say," Kan Ze began, "that Your Excellency yearns for men of ability. But your question belies your reputation. Oh, Huang Gai, you have miscalculated once again!" "I am about to go to war with Sun Quan," Cao Cao said. "and you come stealing over here! How can I not ask?" "On Zhou Yu's orders," Kan Ze went on, "Huang Gai, who has served three rulers of the house of Sun, was brutally and gratuitously beaten today in front of all the generals. Outraged and vengeful, he wants to defect and has placed his case in my hands, for he and I are as close as flesh and blood. I have come directly to present his secret letter. I wish to know if Your Excellency is willing to take him in." "Where is the letter?" Cao asked. Kan Ze passed it up to the prime minister. Cao slit the envelope and read the letter beneath the burning candles. It said in essence:

As a beneficiary of the Suns' generous favor, I should never waver in my loyalty. But it is evident to all that the soldiers of the six southern districts have no chance whatsoever of stopping the north's million-fold host. All the southern generals and officials, even the most obtuse, recognize the impossibility of it—except for that rascal Zhou Yu, who, out of shallow willfulness and an exaggerated sense of his own ability, seems determined to "smash a rock with an egg." He has, moreover, assigned rewards and punishments without reason so that the blameless suffer and the deserving are ignored. And I, humiliated without cause after long years of service to the house of Sun, feel heartfelt hatred. Believing that Your Excellency handles all situations with true sincerity and welcomes men of ability with true humility, I have decided to lead my men in surrender to you, both to establish my merit and to erase my shame. Provisions and equipment will be offered in accompanying ships.[2] Weeping bitter blood, I speak bent to the ground. Never doubt me![3]

Seated there, Cao Cao read the letter over and over. Suddenly he struck the table and, eyes widening in anger, cried, "It's the old trick of being flogged to win the enemy's confidence! Huang Gai had you carry a letter of sham surrender, fishing for advantage in the confusion. You dare trifle with me, do you?" He ordered Kan Ze removed and executed. But Kan Ze's expression did not alter as the guards hustled him off. He simply looked to the sky and laughed. Cao Cao had him dragged back and said viciously, "I have seen through your scheme. What are you laughing at?" "Not at you," replied Kan Ze, "but at Huang Gai for thinking he knows men." "Meaning?" asked Cao. "Kill me and be done with it," said Ze. "Why bother with questions?" "From my youngest days," said Cao, "I have studied manuals of warfare and am well acquainted with the ways and means of deception. This trick of yours might have fooled someone else, but not me." "Where do you find trickery in this letter?" Kan Ze responded. "I'll tell you so that you may die content," Cao said. "If this surrender were genuine, the letter would specify a time. Can you talk your way out of that?" Kan Ze laughed out loud again. "What a shame! And all that bragging about your knowledge of manuals. You'd better take your forces home as soon as you can, for if you fight, Zhou Yu will capture you. Know-nothing! More's the pity that I should die at your hands." "Why 'know-nothing'?" Cao demanded. "Because you know nothing of strategy or principles," answered Kan Ze. "All right, then," said Cao, "point out my errors." "You mistreat the worthy—why should I say it?" said Ze. "Let me die and be done." "If you talk sense," said Cao, "of course I will show you due respect."[4] Kan Ze continued, "You must know the adage, 'There's no set time for betraying one's lord.' Were Huang Gai to set a time and then at the crucial moment find himself unable to act while the other side was already making its move, why, the whole thing would be exposed. One can only wait for the convenient moment. How can such a thing be arranged ahead of time? If you don't understand even this basic principle and are determined to kill a well-meaning friend, that is indeed the height of ignorance."[5]

On hearing this speech, Cao Cao relaxed his expression, came down from his seat, and apologized to Kan Ze, saying, "To be sure, I have been blind, and I have offended your dignity, too. But do not hold it against me." "Huang Gai and I," said Ze, "are coming over to your side with full hearts, like infants turning to their parents. There is no deception in this." Delighted, Cao Cao said, "If the two of you can achieve real merit, you will be rewarded far above all others." "It is not for rank or emolument that we come," answered Ze. "We are doing what Heaven ordains and men approve." Cao poured wine to entertain him.

In a little while someone entered the tent and whispered to Cao, who said, "Bring me the letter." The man presented a secret missive, which seemed to give Cao great satisfaction. Kan Ze said to himself, "This must be Cai Zhong and Cai He's report on the beating of Huang Gai. Cao looks pleased because this verifies that my surrender is genuine." "I will trouble you, sir," Cao Cao said to Kan Ze, "to return south to complete the arrangements with Huang Gai. Let me know when he will be coming, and my men will help him." "I cannot go south now that I have left," Kan Ze said. "I beg Your Excellency to send another trusted man." "If I do," Cao said, "our plans will be discovered." Kan Ze held back until at long last he said, "Then I must return here swiftly."

Refusing Cao Cao's parting offer of gold and silk, Kan Ze sailed back to the Southland, where he saw Huang Gai and related the details of his mission. "If not for your clever replies," Huang Gai said, "I would have suffered for naught." "I am going to Gan Ning's camp to find out what Cai Zhong and Cai He have been up to," Kan Ze said. "A good idea," replied Huang Gai.

Kan Ze was received at Gan Ning's camp. "Yesterday, General," Ze said, "you were humiliated by Zhou Yu for trying to save Huang Gai. I am outraged at the injustice done you."[6] Ning smiled and made no reply. At that moment Cai Zhong and Cai He entered. Ze eyed Ning, who caught his meaning and said, "Zhou Yu is all too confident of his own abilities and takes us for granted. I have been humiliated, disgraced before the notables of the south." So saying, he clenched his teeth, slammed the table, and shouted. Kan Ze then spoke softly into Gan Ning's ear. Ning lowered his head but only uttered a few sighs. Cai He and Cai Zhong, sensing their discontent, asked pointedly, "General, what vexes you? And you, good sir, what injustice have you suffered?" "How could you know the bitterness in our hearts?" Kan Ze said. "Could it be that you wish to turn from Sun Quan to Cao Cao?" asked Cai He. Kan Ze paled. Gan Ning drew his sword and stood up. "We are discovered!" he cried. "We must kill them lest they betray us." The two Cais said urgently, "Fear us not, gentlemen. We have something to confess."

"Out with it," said Gan Ning. "Cao Cao sent us as false defectors," said Cai He. "If you gentlemen are minded to give allegiance to the rightful ruler, we can arrange it." "Is what you say true?" asked Gan Ning. In unison the two Cais replied, "How could we falsify something like this?" Feigning pleasure, Gan Ning said, "Then Heaven sends this opportunity." "The disgrace that you and Huang Gai suffered has already been reported to the prime minister," the two Cais assured them. Kan Ze said, "I have already delivered to His Excellency a letter of surrender from Huang Gai. I have come to Gan Ning today to ask him to join us." "When a man of action meets a wise lord," said Gan Ning, "he should put himself wholeheartedly at his disposal." After these words the four men drank together and spoke in tones of deepest confidentiality. The two Cais informed Cao Cao at once of these developments, adding in their letter, "Gan Ning will be working with us from within." Kan Ze penned a separate letter, to be sent by secret courier, informing Cao Cao that "Huang Gai desires to come and awaits the opportunity. Look for a boat with a blue-green jack at the prow. That will be him."[7]

•   •   •   •   •

Meanwhile, Cao Cao, having received the two letters, had yet to reach a decision. He summoned his advisers. "Gan Ning of the Southland," Cao began, "disgraced by Zhou Yu, has decided to collaborate with us. Huang Gai, condemned by Zhou Yu, has sent Kan Ze to negotiate his surrender. I remain dubious about both. Can anyone here get into

Zhou Yu's camp and find out what's going on?'' Jiang Gan proposed, ''I still feel a sting of shame for the failure of my last visit to Sun Quan. I'd like to try again now, whatever the risk, in order to bring some solid information back to Your Excellency.'' Delighted, Cao Cao had Jiang Gan provided with a boat. Jiang Gan reached the camp on the river's southern shore and sent someone to announce him. Zhou Yu was overjoyed. ''This man will bring me success again,'' he said. Zhou Yu also told Lu Su: ''Now I want to see Pang Tong . . .''

Pang Tong (Shiyuan), originally from Xiangyang, had earlier come south to escape the disorders in the north,[8] and Lu Su had recommended him to Zhou Yu. Though Pang Tong had not yet presented himself, Zhou Yu, through Lu Su, had solicited Pang Tong's advice on how to defeat Cao Cao. ''You must use fire,'' Pang Tong had privately told Lu Su. ''But on the river if one boat burns, the others will scatter unless someone can convince Cao to connect up his ships—you know, the 'boat-connecting scheme.' That's the only way it will work.'' Impressed with this advice, Zhou Yu had told Lu Su, ''Only Pang Tong can get that done for us.'' ''Cao Cao is too cunning,'' said Lu Su. ''He won't succeed.''

So things stood, with Zhou Yu brooding over the possibilities, when the announcement of Jiang Gan's arrival roused the chief commander to action. He ordered Pang Tong to carry out his plan. Remaining in his tent, Zhou Yu had his men receive the guest. Jiang Gan, uneasy because Zhou Yu had not met him personally, ordered his boat tied up at an out-of-the-way spot before appearing.

''Why have you deceived me so dreadfully?'' Zhou Yu, looking wrathful, said to Jiang Gan. Jiang Gan smiled. ''I was just thinking,'' he said. ''You and I are brothers from way back. I have come to reveal something of particular import. Why do you speak of deception?'' ''You want to talk me into surrendering,'' said Zhou Yu, ''or else the ocean has dried up and the mountains have melted. Last time, mindful of our long-standing friendship, I invited you to drink with me and share my couch. But you stole a personal letter, left without saying good-bye, and betrayed me. Cao put Cai Mao and Zhang Yun to death and thereby ruined my plans.[9] Now you come again, but what for? You certainly don't mean me well. Were it not for our old friendship, I'd have you cut in two! I was going to send you back, but we expect to attack the traitor Cao in a day or two. And I can't keep you here, either, or my plans will get out.'' Zhou Yu ordered his aides: ''Escort Jiang Gan to the Western Hills retreat to rest,'' adding, ''After Cao's defeat we'll send you home.''

Jiang Gan tried to speak, but Zhou Yu had already walked away. The aides provided Jiang Gan with a horse to ride to the retreat, where two soldiers attended him. Inside, Gan found himself too depressed to sleep or eat. Stars filled the sky; dew covered the ground. Alone he stepped outside and behind the dwelling. Somewhere someone was reading aloud. He walked on and saw by the cliffside several thatched huts, lit from within. Jiang Gan went over and peeked into one: a man sat alone, sword hanging in front of the lamp, intoning the military classics of Sunzi and Wu Qi.[10] ''He must be someone extraordinary,'' thought Jiang Gan. And he knocked on the door, seeking an interview.

An unusual-looking man came out and met Jiang Gan. Gan asked his name, and he replied, ''Pang Tong.'' ''Not Master Young Phoenix!'' exclaimed Jiang Gan. ''The same,'' he said. ''Your great name has long been known to me,'' Jiang Gan went on. ''But what has brought you to this remote spot?'' ''Zhou Yu has the greatest confidence in his own ability,'' replied Pang Tong, ''but he is too intolerant, so I have hidden myself here. Who are you, sir?'' ''Jiang Gan,'' he replied. Pang Tong invited him into his dwelling, where they sat and spoke freely. ''A man of your talents,'' Jiang Gan said, ''could prosper wherever he went. If you would consider serving Cao Cao, I could arrange it." "I have wanted to leave the Southland for a long, long time," Pang Tong said. "If you are willing to arrange the introduction, I will make the trip now. If I delay, Zhou Yu will hear of it and I will be killed."

And so Pang Tong left the hill that same night with Jiang Gan. They reached the shore and found the boat that had brought Jiang Gan south. Swift rowers brought them to the north shore. At Cao's camp Jiang Gan came before Cao first and related the events of the past days. Cao Cao, hearing of Master Young Phoenix's arrival, came out of his tent to escort him in personally. When they had seated themselves as host and guest, Cao Cao said, "Zhou Yu is immature. Overconfident of his abilities, he oppresses his followers and rejects sound strategy. Your great name has long been familiar to me, and we welcome your gracious regard. May I hope that you will not deny us advice and instruction?"

Pang Tong replied, "People have always said that Your Excellency's use of military forces sets the standard. But I would like to look over the features of your deployment for myself." Cao called for horses and invited his guest to review his land bases. From an elevation they viewed the scene below. Pang Tong said, "Backed up against woody hills, easy signaling from front to rear, exits and entries, labyrinthine passages—if the ancient masters of the art of war, Sunzi, Wu Qi, Sima Rangju, were reborn they could not surpass it."[11] "You should not overpraise me, master," said Cao, "I still look to you for improvement."

Next, they reviewed the naval stations. There were twenty-four openings facing south, and in each the attack boats and warships[12] were laid out like a city wall, within which clustered the smaller craft. For passage there were channels, and everything proceeded in good order. Smiling delightedly, Pang Tong said to Cao Cao, "Excellency, if your use of forces is like this, your reputation has not preceded you for naught!" So saying, Pang Tong pointed across the river and cried, "Zhou Yu, Zhou Yu, the day of your doom is fixed!"

Immensely pleased, Cao returned to camp and invited Pang Tong into his tent to share his wine and talk of military machinations. Pang Tong spoke with profundity and eloquence. Cao Cao felt his admiration and respect deepen, and treated his guest with solicitous hospitality. Feigning intoxication, Pang Tong said, "You have good medical services for the troops, no doubt?" "Of what use would that be?" Cao asked. "There is much illness among the sailors," responded Pang Tong, "and good physicians are needed to cure them."

The truth was that at this time Cao's men, unable to adjust to the southern clime, had been seized with nausea and vomiting, and many had died. Cao Cao was preoccupied with the problem and was naturally receptive to Pang Tong's remark. "Your Excellency," Pang Tong went on, "your methods for training a navy are superb—only, unfortunately, something is missing." Cao Cao importuned him until Pang Tong replied, "There is a way to free the sailors of their ailments, to make them steady and capable of success." Cao Cao was delighted and eager to learn.

"On the Great River the tide swells and recedes," Pang Tong continued, "and the wind and the waves never subside. These northern troops, unaccustomed to shipboard, suffer from the pitching and rolling. This is the cause of their ailment. Reorganize your small and large vessels: marshal them in groups of thirty or fifty and make them fast with iron hoops, stem to stem and stern to stern. Then, if wide planks are laid so that horses as well as men can cross from ship to ship, however rough the waves or steep the swells, what will you have to fear?"

Cao Cao quit his seat to express his deep gratitude: "But for your sound advice, master, I could never destroy Sun Quan." "My uninformed views," responded Pang Tong, "are for Your Excellency to use as he sees fit." Cao Cao issued an immediate order for all blacksmiths in the army to manufacture hoops and large nails to bind the boats. The news cheered the men. In the words of a later poet,

> In Red Cliffs' bitter trial, they fought with fire:
> Fire's the perfect weapon, all agreed.
> But it was Pang Tong's boat-connecting scheme
> That let Zhou Yu accomplish his great deed.

Pang Tong turned to Cao Cao and added, "In my view, most of the great families of the south have deep grievances against Zhou Yu. Let me use my limber little tongue to persuade them on Your Excellency's behalf to join our side. If Zhou Yu can be isolated, he will be yours. And once Zhou Yu is defeated, Liu Bei will have nowhere to turn." "Master," replied Cao Cao, "if you can indeed accomplish so much, I will personally petition the Emperor to honor you as one of the three elder lords." "I do not care for wealth and status," Pang Tong answered. "My one concern is the common people. When you cross the river, Your Excellency, spare them, I pray you." "I act for Heaven," said Cao, "to promote the rightful way of government. How could I bear to do anything cruel?"

Pang Tong next requested a letter to ensure the safety of his own clan. "Where are the members of your family, now?" Cao asked. "They're all near the river," Tong answered. "Your letter will ensure their safety." Cao Cao ordered an official document for which Pang Tong thanked him saying, "After I go, advance quickly. Waste no time, lest Zhou Yu realize what is up." Cao Cao agreed.

Pang Tong departed. He had reached the riverbank and was about to embark, when he spied someone on shore wearing a Taoist priest's gown and a hat of bamboo. With one hand the Taoist grabbed Pang Tong and said, "Your audacity is remarkable! Huang Gai works the 'battered-body scheme,' Kan Ze delivers the letter announcing Huang Gai's sham defection, and now you submit the plan for linking the boats—your only concern being that the flames might not consume everything! Such insidious mischief may be enough to take in Cao Cao, but it won't work on me." This accusation terrified Pang Tong, who felt as if his heart and soul would flee his body. Indeed:

> Can the southeast ever prevail in victory
> When the northwest holds men of genius, too?

Who challenged Pang Tong?
READ ON.

48

Feasting on the Great River, Cao Cao Sings an Ode;
Linking Its Boats, the North Prepares for War

ASTOUNDED BY THE STRANGER'S WHISPERED WORDS, Pang Tong turned and found himself looking at his old friend Xu Shu.[1] Tong became calm at once and, sure of their
privacy, said, "If you reveal my plan, the inhabitants of the Southland's eighty-one
departments will suffer disaster." "And what of the lives and fate of the eighty-three
legions over here?" Xu Shu asked with a grin. "You don't mean to give me away?"
Pang Tong pleaded. "I will always be grateful for Imperial Uncle Liu's kindness, and I
intend to repay it. Cao Cao sent my mother to her death; I promised then I would
never frame strategy for him. Of course I am not going to expose your very effective
plan. The problem is, I am here with Cao Cao's army, and when they are destroyed,
the jewel won't be distinguished from the rock. How do I avoid disaster? Suggest some
device to save me, and I will sew up my lips and remove myself." Smiling, Pang Tong
said, "Someone as shrewd and far-seeing as you should have no difficulty." "I crave
your guidance," Xu Shu insisted, and so Pang Tong whispered a few vital words into his
ear and received his heartfelt thanks. Thus Pang Tong left his friend and sailed back to
the Southland.

That night Xu Shu secretly had a close companion spread rumors through Cao's
camps. The following day the rumors were on everyone's lips. Soon informants reported
to Cao Cao: "The whole army is talking about Han Sui and Ma Teng, saying they have
rebelled and are on their way from Xiliang to seize the capital." Alarmed, Cao Cao summoned his advisers. "My greatest concern when I undertook this expedition," he said,
"was the danger from the west, Han Sui and Ma Teng. Whether the current rumors are
true or not, we must take measures."

Xu Shu came forward with a proposal: "I have the honor of being in Your Excellency's
employ, but to my dismay have not in any way justified your confidence. I wish to request three thousand soldiers to take at once to San Pass to seal this key point of access
against invasion from the west. In the event of an emergency, I will report immediately."
Delighted, Cao said, "With you at the pass, I need not worry. Take command of the
troops already there. I will give you three thousand more, mounted men and foot soldiers, and Zang Ba to lead the vanguard. Leave without delay." Xu Shu bid Cao Cao
good-bye and set out with Zang Ba.[2] Thus Pang Tong saved Xu Shu's life. A poet of later
times wrote:

Cao's southern march—every day a trial,
As rumors spread of fresh calamity.
Pang Tong counseled Xu Shu what to do:
Once let off the hook, the fish swims free.

After dispatching Xu Shu to the north, Cao Cao's mind was easier. He rode to the riverbank to review the army camps and the naval stations. Boarding one of the larger ships, he planted in its center a banner marked "Supreme Commander." To his left and right the naval stations stretched along the river; aboard the ship a thousand crossbowmen lay in wait. Cao Cao stood on the deck. It was the thirteenth year of Jian An, the fifteenth day of the eleventh month (December 10, A.D. 208). The weather was clear and bright, the wind calm, the waves still. Cao Cao ordered a feast and entertainment for the commanders that evening. The complexion of the heavens reflected the advancing night as the moon climbed over the eastern mountains and beamed down, turning night to day. The Great River lay slack, like a bolt of white silk unrolled.

Aboard ship, Cao Cao was surrounded by several hundred attendants in damask coats and embroidered jackets. They all shouldered lances and each man held a halberd. The officers and officials were seated in order. Cao Cao took in the picturesque Southern Screen Hills. To the east he could see the boundary marked by Chaisang. To the west he contemplated the course of the Great River before it reached Xiakou. To the south he looked out on Mount Fan; and to the north he peered into the Black Forest of Wulin. Wherever he turned, the view stretched into infinity, gladdening his heart. He spoke to the assembly: "We have raised this loyalist force to purge evil and dispel threats to the ruling family, for I have sworn to scour the realm, to calm the empire by my sure sword. The Southland alone remains outside our sphere. Today I possess a million heroic fighters. And with you to apply our commands, need we fear for our success? When we have received the submission of the Southland and the empire is at peace, we shall share with you the enjoyments of wealth and station to celebrate the Great Millennium."[3] The audience rose as one to give their leader thanks: "May the song of victory soon be on your lips! May we live by Your Excellency's favor all of our days."

Cao Cao was gratified and ordered the wine sent round. The night of drinking wore on, and Cao Cao was well in his cups when he pointed south and said, "Zhou Yu! Lu Su! How little you know the appointments of Heaven. These defectors to our cause will be your ruin. You see, Heaven itself lends us aid." "Say no more, Your Excellency," Xun You warned, "lest the wrong people hear." Cao laughed and said, "Every man here— whether attendants or companions of our table—is in our deepest trust. Let us be free with one another." He turned toward Xiakou and, pointing again, said, "Liu Bei! Zhuge Liang! You have failed to measure your antlike strength in attempting to shake Mount Tai. What folly!" To his generals he said, "Now I am fifty-four. If we take the Southland, I shall have my humble wish. Long ago I befriended the patriarch Qiao, knowing that his two daughters were the beauties of the empire. To think that Sun Ce and Zhou Yu would take them to wife before me! Recently I built the Bronze Bird Tower on the River Zhang. If I win the Southland, I will take these women to wife and install them in the tower to pleasure me in my advanced years. And all my wishes will be satisfied!" With that he burst into laughter. The Tang dynasty poet Du Mu wrote these lines:

Half-rusted, broken in the sand, this halberd,
Scraped and cleaned, calls up an era past.[4]

> Had that east wind not done Zhou Yu a turn,
> Two Qiaos in spring would have gone to the tower.

Cao Cao was still laughing and talking when they all heard a raven cawing as it flew southward. "Why does the raven cry in the night?" Cao asked. Those around him replied, "It supposes the brilliance of the moon to be the dawn. That is why it has left its tree and cries." Cao laughed again. Already drunk, he set his spear in the prow of the boat and offered wine to the river. Then he quaffed three full goblets and, leveling his spear, said to his commanders, "Here is the weapon that broke the Yellow Scarves, took Lü Bu, eliminated Yuan Shu, subdued Yuan Shao, penetrated beyond the northern frontier, and conquered the east as far as Liaodong. In the length and breadth of this land no man has withstood me. My ambitions have always been those of a man of action, a leader among men. And now the scene before us fills my soul with profound passion. I shall perform a song, and you must join me." Cao Cao recited:

> Here before us, wine and song!
> For man does not live long.
> Like daybreak dew,
> His days are swiftly gone.
>
> Sanguine-souled we have to be!
> Though painful memory haunts us yet.
> Thoughts and sorrows naught allays,
> Save the cup Du Kang first set.[5]
>
> "Deep the hue of the scholar's robe;
> Deeper, the longing of my heart."[6]
> For all of you, my dearest lords,
> I voice again this ancient part.
>
> Nibbling on the duckweed,
> "Loo! Loo!" the lowing deer.[7]
> At our feast sit honored guests
> For string and reed to cheer.
>
> The moon on high beckons bright,
> But no man's ever stayed it.
> Heart's care rises from within,
> And nothing can deny it.
>
> Take our thanks for all your pains;
> Your presence does us honor.
> Reunited on this feasting day,
> We well old loves remember.
>
> The moon is bright, the stars are few,
> The magpie black as raven.
> It southbound circles thrice a tree
> That offers him no haven.
>
> The mountaintop no height eschews;
> The sea eschews no deep.
> And the Duke of Zhou spat out his meal[8]
> An empire's trust to keep.[9]

As Cao Cao finished, the assembly took up the singing amid general enjoyment, until someone stepped forward and said, "Great armies stand opposed. Our officers and men are ready for action. Why does Your Excellency utter ominous words at such a time?"

Cao Cao turned to the speaker, imperial inspector of Yangzhou, Liu Fu (Yuanying) from Xiang in the fief of Pei, Cao Cao's home district. Liu Fu had started his career at Hefei where he established the provincial seat of government. He collected those who had fled or scattered, established schools, expanded the "soldier-tiller" acreage, and revived orderly administration. During his long service to Cao Cao he had many accomplishments to his credit.

On this occasion Cao Cao leveled his spear and asked, "And what do you find 'ominous' about my words?" Liu Fu replied, "You sang,

The moon is bright, the stars are few,
The magpie black as raven.
It southbound circles thrice a tree
That offers him no haven.

These are ominous words." "You dare to wreck our delight and enthusiasm!" Cao cried angrily. With a single heave of his spear Cao Cao pierced Liu Fu through, killing him. The assembly was aghast. The banquet was dismissed. The following day, sobered and wracked with remorse, Cao Cao wept as he told Liu Xi, the son who had come to claim the body, "Yesterday while drunk I did your father a terrible injustice, for which I can never atone. He shall be interred with the highest honors, those reserved for the three elder lords." Cao Cao sent soldiers to escort the coffin for burial in Liu Fu's native district.

•   •   •   •   •

The next day the new naval commanders, Mao Jie and Yu Jin, informed Cao Cao: "The large and small boats have been joined together. All flags and weapons are in order. Everything is at Your Excellency's disposal. We await your command to launch the attack." Cao Cao took up his position on a large ship in the center of the fleet and called his commanders together for their instructions. Naval and land forces were divided into units under flags of five colors: yellow for the naval center, commanded by Mao Jie and Yu Jin; red for the forward, under Zhang He; black for the rear, under Lü Qian; green for the left, under Wen Ping; white for the right, under Lü Tong. The forward cavalry and infantry unit, under Xu Huang, flew a red flag; the rear, under Li Dian, a black flag; the left, under Yue Jin, a green flag; the right, under Xiahou Yuan, a white flag. Serving as reinforcement for naval and land forces were Xiahou Dun and Cao Hong. Protecting communications and overseeing the battle were Xu Chu and Zhang Liao. The remainder of Cao Cao's brave commanders returned to their respective squads.

When these arrangements were complete, three rounds of drumbeats thundered through the naval camp; Cao Cao's navy steered through the station gates and onto the river. The wind gusted sharply out of the northwest. The ships let out their sails, beating upon wave and billow yet steady as if on flat ground. On board the northerners, bounding and vaulting to display their courage, thrust their spears and plied their swords. The various units maintained ranks under the discipline of signal flags. Some fifty small craft patrolled the great floating war camp, monitoring its progress. Cao Cao stood in the command tower and surveyed the exercise, immensely pleased, thinking he had found the secret of certain victory. He ordered sails dropped, and all ships returned to the camps in good order.

Cao Cao proceeded to his tent and said to his advisers, "Divine decree has come to our aid in the form of Young Phoenix's ingenious plan. With iron bonds linking the ships, we can actually cross the river as if we were walking on land." To this Cheng Yu replied, "Though the linked ships are level and stable, if the enemy attacks with fire it will be hard to escape. This we must be prepared for." Cao Cao laughed loudly. "Despite your provident view," he said, "there are still things you do not know." "Cheng Yu's point is well taken," Xun You added. "Why is Your Excellency making fun of him?" "Any attack with fire," Cao explained, "must rely on the force of the wind. Now at winter's depth, there are only north winds and west winds—how could there be a south wind or an east wind? Our position is northwest; their troops are all on the southern shore. If they use fire, they will only burn out their own troops. What have we to fear? If it were the season for a late autumn warm spell, I would have taken precautions long ago." The commanders bowed respectfully. "Your Excellency's insight," they said, "is more than we can match." Cao turned to his commanders and added, "The men from Qing, Xu, Yan, and Dai lack naval experience. If not for this expedient, how could they negotiate the treacherous Great River?" Just then two commanders rose and said, "Though we are from the north, we have some skill at sailing. To prove it, we volunteer to take twenty patrol craft direct to Xiakou, seize their flags and drums, and return."

Cao Cao eyed the two: Jiao Chu and Zhang Nan, formerly under Yuan Shao's command. "You men," said Cao, "born and raised in the north, may find shipboard hard to take. The southern soldiers, accustomed to moving by water, have honed their sailing skills. If I were you, I would not trifle with my life." "If we fail," the two replied, "we are content to accept what martial law decrees." "The larger boats have already been made fast," said Cao. "There are only small ones free. They hold twenty men each. Too few, perhaps, to engage the enemy." Jiao Chu said, "If we were to use the large ships, we would not impress the enemy. Let us have twenty small ones: ten for me and ten for Zhang Nan. Before the day is out, we will hit their camp and return with their standard and a general's head." Cao Cao said, "Then I shall give you twenty boats and five hundred crack troops, experts with long spears and crossbows. Tomorrow morning the flotilla will make a show of force from the main camp, and Wen Ping will escort you back with thirty patrol boats." Gratified and eager for battle, Jiao Chu and Zhang Nan withdrew.

Early the next day at the fourth watch the men were fed; by the end of the fifth they were ready, and drums and gongs sounded in the naval camp. The main fleet emerged and fanned out on the water, their blue and red flags forming a pattern above the Great River. Jiao Chu and Zhang Nan led their twenty scouting craft through the camp and onto the river. Then they raced south.

During the night the beating of drums and the din of battle preparation had reached the southern shore, where the defenders watched Cao Cao's navy maneuvering in the distance. The Southland's intelligence brought word to Zhou Yu. He went to a hilltop to observe, but the force had already pulled back. The next day the same sounds from the north rent the sky. The southern warriors climbed quickly to a viewing place, from where they saw the twenty small boats moving south, breasting the waves. The news was sped to Zhou Yu, who called for volunteers. Han Dang and Zhou Tai stepped forward. Well pleased by their offer, Zhou Yu ordered a strict vigil at all camps as Han Dang and Zhou Tai led their five-boat squadrons from the left and the right out onto the river.

Now Cao's volunteers, Jiao Chu and Zhang Nan, were relying on little more than raw nerve. As their swift-oared boats approached the southern craft, Han Dang, wearing a breastplate, stood on the prow of his boat, a long spear in hand. Jiao Chu arrived first and ordered his archers to shoot, but Han Dang defended himself with his shield. Next, Jiao Chu crossed spears with Han Dang, but Dang slew him with a single thrust. Then Zhang Nan came forth, shouting, and Zhou Tai darted out from the side. Zhang Nan stood at the prow, his spear leveled. Arrows flew in volleys and counter-volleys. Plying his shield with one arm, his sword with the other hand, Zhou Tai leaped onto Zhang Nan's approaching boat and handily cut him down. Zhang Nan's body sank in the river, as Zhou Tai slashed wildly at his crew. The other attackers rowed swiftly back to the north shore. Han Dang and Zhou Tai gave chase but were checked in the middle of the river by Wen Ping. The boats of both sides took battle formation and set about the slaughter.

Zhou Yu and his commanders stood on the hilltop surveying the fighting craft and warships deployed along the river's northern shore. The flags and emblems were in perfect order. The southerners watched as Cao's commander Wen Ping met the furious attack of Han Dang and Zhou Tai, then fell back, reversed course, and fled. The two southern commanders gave swift chase, but Zhou Yu feared they might sail too far into the enemy's strength; and so he raised the white flag summoning them to return while the gongs were struck.[10]

Han Dang and Zhou Tai swung their boats around and rowed south. From his hilltop Zhou Yu watched Cao's warships across the river crowding into the camp. Turning to his commanders, Zhou Yu said, "Their ships are as dense as reeds. And Cao Cao is a man of many schemes. What plan do we have for defeating them?" Before anyone could answer, they saw the tall pole in the center of the enemy camp snap in the wind and its yellow flag drift into the river. With a hearty laugh Zhou Yu said, "Not a good sign for them!" Then erratic winds blew up and whipped the waves against the shore. Caught by a gust, a corner of Zhou Yu's own flag brushed his face. Suddenly a dreadful thought came to Zhou Yu. With a loud cry he fell over backwards, blood foaming up in his mouth. The commanders rushed to his assistance, but their leader had lost consciousness. Indeed:

> One moment laughter, the next a cry of pain;
> What hope did the south have in its battle with the north?

What happened to Zhou Yu? Would he survive?[11]

READ ON.

49

On Seven Star Altar Kongming Supplicates the Wind;
At Three Rivers Zhou Yu Unleashes the Fire

AFTER ZHOU YU HAD BEEN CARRIED to his tent, the southern commanders came inquiring about his condition. Agitatedly they said to one another, "A million-strong host, set to pounce and devour us, holds the north shore. With our chief commander stricken, how can we cope with Cao Cao's army?" They sent a report to Sun Quan and called for a physician to treat Zhou Yu.

The turn of events caused Lu Su great anxiety. He went to Kongming, who asked, "What is your view?" "A blessing for Cao, a catastrophe for us," was Lu Su's reply. Kongming smiled and said, "Such an illness even I could cure!"[1] "What a boon that would be!" Lu Su responded, and the two men went to see Zhou Yu. Lu Su, entering the tent first, found the chief commander on his back, bedclothes pulled over his head. "Commander, how is your condition?" Su inquired. "My insides feel unsettled and tender, and the fits return from time to time," he answered. "What medicines have you been taking?" Lu Su wanted to know. "I reject everything, can't keep the medicine down," was his reply. "I have just seen Kongming," Lu Su said. "He says he can cure you, Commander. He's outside now. Should we trouble him to try his remedy?" Zhou Yu ordered Kongming admitted and had himself propped up to a sitting position on the bed.

"It is many days since we last met, my lord," Kongming began. "But I never imagined that your precious health was failing." "A man may have good luck when the day begins, bad luck when it ends. Who can tell beforehand?" Zhou Yu replied. "And the winds and the clouds above come when least expected," Kongming said, smiling. "You never can tell." At these words Zhou Yu lost his color and moaned. "Commander," Kongming continued, "do you seem to feel vexation gathering inside you?" Zhou Yu nodded. "You must take a cooling tonic to dispel it," Kongming advised. "I have," was Zhou Yu's reply, "to no effect." "You must first regulate the vital ethers," Kongming explained. "When the vital ethers are flowing smoothly and in the proper direction, then in a matter of moments your good health will naturally be restored." Zhou Yu, sensing that Kongming must know his unspoken thought, tested him by saying, "What medicine would you recommend to get the vital ethers flowing in the proper direction?" "I have a prescription to facilitate this," said Kongming, smiling still. "I shall benefit from your advice," said Zhou Yu. Kongming called for writing brush and paper and, waving away the attendants, wrote sixteen words for Zhou Yu's eyes alone:

> To break Cao's back
> With fire we attack.
> Everything is set, save
> The east wind we lack!

Kongming handed the note to Zhou Yu, saying, "This is the source of the chief commander's illness." Zhou Yu was astounded and thought, "Truly beyond all belief. He realized my problem at once. I'll simply have to tell him the truth." And so with a chuckle he said, "Master, since you already know the cause of my suffering, what medicine shall we use to cure it? The situation is moving swiftly to a crisis, and I look for your timely advice." To this appeal Kongming answered, "Though I myself have no talent, I once came upon an extraordinary man who handed on to me occult texts for reading the numerology of the heavens. Their method can be used to call forth the winds and rains.[2] If the chief commander wants a southeast wind, erect a platform on the Southern Screen Hills, call it the Altar of the Seven Stars.[3] It should be nine spans high, three-tiered, surrounded by one hundred and twenty flag bearers. On the platform I will work certain charms to borrow three days and three nights of southeast wind to assist you in your operations. What do you say?" "Never mind three days and three nights," Zhou Yu cried, "with one night's gales our endeavor can be consummated! But time is of the essence. Let there be no delay." "On the twentieth day of the eleventh month, the first day of the cycle, we will supplicate the wind," Kongming said. "By the twenty-second day, third of the cycle, the winds will have died away." Elated, Zhou Yu sprang to his feet. He ordered five hundred hardy soldiers to begin work on the altar, and he dispatched one hundred and twenty guards to hold the flags and await further instructions. Kongming then took his leave.[4]

Accompanied by Lu Su, Kongming rode to the Southern Screen Hills to take the lay of the land. He commanded the soldiers to build the altar of the ruddy earth of the southeast. It was a structure of some two hundred and forty spans all around, with three three-span tiers. On the lowest tier were twenty-eight flags representing the twenty-eight zodiacal mansions. Along the eastern face were seven blue-green flags for the eastern mansions—Horn, Neck, Root, Room, Heart, Tail, Basket—arrayed in the shape of the Sky-blue Dragon. Along the northern face were seven black flags for the northern mansions—Southern Dipper, Ox, Girl, Void, Rooftop, Dwelling, Wall—laid out in the form of the Dark Tortoise. On the western side flew seven white flags for the western mansions—Straddling Legs, Bonds, Stomach, Bridge, Net, Turtle, Triaster—in the menacing crouch of the White Tiger. On the southern side flew seven red flags for the southern mansions—Well, Ghost, Willow, Star, Drawn Bow, Wings, Axle—making the outline of the Vermillion Bird.[5]

The second tier was encompassed by sixty-four yellow flags, one for each set of oracular lines in the *Book of Changes*, divided into in eight groups of eight. On the top tier stood four men, hair tightly bound and heads capped, wearing black robes of thin silk, wide sashes emblematic of the phoenix, vermillion shoes, and squared kilts. At front left, one man held up a long pole fledged at the tip with chicken feathers to catch any sign of the wind. At front right, another held up a long pole with the banner of the Seven Stars fastened to the top to show the direction of the wind. At the left rear, a man stood respectfully holding a prized sword; at the right rear, a man held a cresset. On the outside, the platform was surrounded by twenty-four men holding, severally, emblemed flags, ceremonial canopies, large halberds, long dagger-axes, ritual gold battle-axes, white yak-tail banners, vermillion pennants, and black standards.

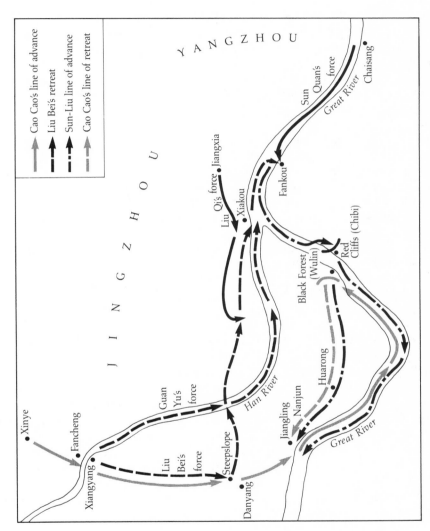

MAP 4. The battle at Red Cliffs. Source: Liu Chunfan, *Sanguo shihua* (Beijing: Beijing chubanshe, 1981), p. 101.

On the twentieth of the eleventh month, an auspicious day, Kongming performed the required ablutions, fasted, and assumed the sacred vestments of a priest of the Tao. Barefoot, hair flowing behind, he came to the front of the altar and instructed Lu Su: "Return now and help Zhou Yu with the deployment. Blame me not if my prayer draws no response." After Lu Su's departure Kongming instructed the guards: "No one here is to leave his position without authorization. The men are forbidden to engage in conversation or to make any irregular remarks or react as if anything were out of the ordinary. Whoever disobeys will be executed."[6] The men acknowledged the order. Having surveyed all stations, Kongming ascended with deliberate steps, lit incense, and poured water into a vessel. Staring into the heavens he uttered a silent incantation, after which he descended and entered his tent for a brief respite, allowing the soldiers to eat in shifts. That day Kongming ascended and descended three times, but of a southwest wind no sign was seen.

•   •   •   •

Cheng Pu, Lu Su, and other military leaders joined Zhou Yu in his tent, where they waited to start the offensive the moment a southeast wind arose. Zhou Yu also reported developments to Sun Quan, who was to direct the reinforcement. Huang Gai had already prepared twenty fireboats, whose prows were studded with nails. Each boat was packed with reeds and kindling soaked in fish oil and covered with an inflammable compound of sulfur and saltpeter. The materials were wrapped with black oilcloth. At the boats' prows, notched banners of the Green Dragon of the East;[7] to the stern, light craft.[8] Before the chief commander's tent Huang Gai and his men awaited the order to move. Gan Ning and Kan Ze kept Cai He and Cai Zhong snug and secure in their water camp and plied them with wine day after day, never permitting a single northern soldier on shore. The Southland guards made sure that not an iota of information got through to them. Everyone was watching for the command tent's signal.

Zhou Yu was with his advisers when a liaison man reported: "Lord Sun Quan's boats are moored eighty-five *li* away, ready for the chief commander's word." Zhou Yu sent Lu Su to inform all commanders, officers, and men under him: "Keep your craft, weapons, and rigging in readiness. Once the order comes down, the slightest delay will be punished with the severity of martial law." The troops prepared themselves, rubbing their hands in anticipation of battle. That day everyone watched the sky intently as evening drew on, but the heavens held clear and no wind stirred. Zhou Yu turned to Lu Su and said, "How absurd are Kongming's claims! There can be no east wind in the dead of winter." "I can't believe Kongming would make absurd claims," replied Lu Su. Toward the third watch they heard, as if from nowhere, the sound of wind. The banners and pennons began to loll to and fro, and when Zhou Yu came out to look, the fringes of the flags were actually fluttering to the northwest. Within moments a stiff gale was coming up out of the southeast.

In consternation Zhou Yu said, "This man has snatched some method from the creative force of Heaven and earth, some unfathomable technic from the world of departed spirits. Why allow him to remain among us and cause trouble, when his elimination would save such great grief?" Zhou Yu immediately called two military commanders, Ding Feng and Xu Sheng, into his presence and told them: "Take a hundred men each— Xu Sheng on the river, Ding Feng on the shore—and go to the Altar of the Seven Stars in the Southern Screen Hills. Take Kongming's head—no questions asked—and bring it to me for your reward." The two commanders left to carry out their assignment. Xu Sheng embarked with one hundred swordsmen working the oars; Ding Feng rode to his destination with one hundred archers astride battle mounts. Both companies moved against the rising southeast wind. In the words of a poet of later times,

> Sleeping Dragon stood on Seven Star Altar,
> As all night eastern winds roiled the Jiang.
> Had Kongming not devised his artifice,
> Could Zhou Yu have played the strategist?

Ding Feng's land force arrived first. He saw the flag bearers on the altar, standing into the wind. Ding Feng dismounted, drew his sword and climbed the platform. Kongming was not there. Distressed, he asked a guard, who said, "He stepped down just moments ago." As Ding Feng descended the platform, Xu Sheng was arriving by water, and the two men met at the shore. A soldier reported to them: "Last night a light craft stopped at that shallow stretch ahead of us. I saw Kongming, his hair all unbound, get into it a short while ago. Then the boat sailed upriver."

Ding Feng and Xu Sheng gave chase by land and sea. Xu Sheng ordered his sails raised in an attempt to catch the wind. The boat was not too far ahead. Xu Sheng stood in the bow and hailed Kongming across the water: "Do not depart, Director. The chief commander sends his invitation." And there was Kongming, standing in the stern of his boat, laughing. "Tell the commander for me," he shouted, "to use his forces well. I am returning to Xiakou for now, but the time will come for us to meet again." "Stay a moment," Xu Sheng pleaded, "I have something urgent to say." Kongming replied, "I realized long ago that the chief commander could never abide me. I've been expecting him to try to kill me and arranged some time ago for Zhao Zilong to meet me here. You had best turn back."

Xu Sheng saw that Kongming's boat had no sail, so he pressed ahead despite the risk. As he pulled nearer, Zhao Zilong drew his bow and rose from the stern. "I am Zhao Zilong of Changshan," he cried, "sent to receive the director general. How dare you pursue us? A single arrow would serve to cut you down and signal the end to our two houses' amity. Instead, let me give you a demonstration of marksmanship." Zilong fitted an arrow and shot away Xu Sheng's sail cord, causing the sheet to drop into the water and the boat to veer sideways. Zilong then ordered his own sail raised and rode the strong wind west. His boat, hardly touching the water, could not be overtaken. From the shore Ding Feng called Xu Sheng back: "Kongming is a wizard of matchless ingenuity, and Zilong a warrior of peerless courage. Remember his performance at Steepslope in Dangyang? There's nothing we can do but return and make our report." And so the two men presented themselves to Zhou Yu and described how Kongming had escaped. The astonished Zhou Yu cried in despair, "How weary I am of his endless schemes!"[9] "Why not wait until after Cao Cao has been defeated before taking further measures against him?" Lu Su suggested.

This met with Zhou Yu's approval. He called together his commanders to receive their orders. First he told Gan Ning: "Take Cai Zhong and the surrendered soldiers along the southern shore. Fly only the flag of the northern troops. Capture the area around the Black Forest, directly opposite Cao Cao's grain depot. Penetrate his camp, then signal with fire. Leave Cai He here, outside my tent. I have a particular use for him." Next, he called Taishi Ci and instructed him: "Take three thousand men to the Huangzhou boundary to intercept Cao's reinforcement from Hefei. Attack immediately and signal us by fire. Look for the red flag: it will mean that Lord Sun Quan is coming to your aid." Gan Ning and Taishi Ci had to travel farthest, and so they went off first.

The third to receive orders was Lü Meng, who was told to take three thousand men to the Black Forest to back up Gan Ning and to burn down Cao's fortifications. Ling Tong, fourth, was ordered to cut off all traffic from Yiling and then shift to the Black Forest area with his three thousand men when he saw flames shooting skyward. Zhou Yu gave Dong Xi, fifth, three thousand troops for a direct assault on Hanyang; he was also told to attack Cao's camp from the River Han on seeing white flags. Zhou Yu told Pan Zhang, sixth, to take three thousand men under white flags to Hanyang and there to support Dong Xi. The six marine squads departed to perform their separate missions.

Following these assignments, Zhou Yu ordered Huang Gai to ready the fireboats and speed word to Cao that he would surrender that very night. At the same time he directed four squads of warships to cover Huang Gai from the rear: the first under Han Dang; the second, Zhou Tai; the third, Jiang Qin; the fourth, Chen Wu. Each unit included three hundred warships and was preceded by twenty fireboats.

Zhou Yu and Cheng Pu oversaw the preparations from the deck of a large attack boat while Xu Sheng and Ding Feng stood guard on either side. Lu Su, Kan Ze, and a few advisers were the only ones left to hold the camp. Cheng Pu was deeply impressed by the order and logic of Zhou Yu's disposition of forces. At this point an envoy from Sun Quan appeared with military credentials, saying that Lord Sun had sent Lu Xun with the vanguard to attack the area around Jichun and Huangzhou with Sun Quan himself in support. In addition, Zhou Yu sent men to the Western Hills to release fire rockets and to the Southern Screen Hills to raise signal flags. All preparations now in order, they waited for dusk.

·   ·   ·   ·   ·

In Xiakou, Liu Xuande eagerly awaited Kongming's return. He spotted a squad of boats arriving, but it turned out to be Liu Qi coming for news.[10] Xuande invited him to the observation tower and said, "The southeast wind has been blowing for some time. Zilong went to meet Kongming, but so far no sign. I'm very worried." A petty officer pointed toward the harbor at Fankou and said, "There's a single sail coming in on the wind. It has to be the director general." Xuande and Liu Qi climbed down to meet the boat, and moments later Kongming and Zilong came ashore. Xuande was elated.

After formal greetings Kongming said, "Let us put all else aside for now. Are the land and sea forces we called up before I left now ready?" "Ready long ago," Xuande said, "and awaiting your deployment." Kongming, Xuande, and Liu Qi seated themselves in the main tent, and Kongming began assigning battle stations. First he said to Zilong, "Take three thousand men across the river and seize the trails and bypaths in the Black Forest. Where the trees and reeds are thickest, place your men in ambush. Tonight after the fourth watch Cao Cao is sure to flee that way. When they pass, use your torches. You may not get them all, but you'll get half." "The Black Forest has two roads," said Zilong, "one to Jiangling, the other to Xiangyang. Which one will he use?" "Jiangling is unsafe," replied Kongming. "He'll head for Xiangyang and then repair to Xuchang with his main force." Zilong departed with his assignment.

Next Kongming summoned Zhang Fei: "Yide," he said, "you take three thousand across the river, cut off the road to Yiling, and set your ambush at Gourd Valley. Cao Cao wouldn't dare flee by South Yiling, only by North Yiling. After tomorrow's rain passes, they will set their pots in the earth to prepare a meal. The moment you see smoke, start fires on the hillside. I doubt that you will capture Cao Cao, but your accomplishment should be considerable." Zhang Fei left with his assignment. Then Kongming instructed Mi Zhu, Mi Fang, and Liu Feng[11] to cover the river by boat and capture the defeated troops and their weapons. They too left to carry out their orders.

Kongming rose and said to Liu Qi, "The area in sight of Wuchang is absolutely vital. Please go back there with your own men and deploy them at all points up and down the shore. Some fugitives from Cao's defeat are bound to come, and you should be there to seize them—but do not risk leaving the city walls without good reason." So instructed, Liu Qi took leave of Xuande and Kongming. Then the director general turned to Xuande. "My lord," he said, "station your men at Fankou, find yourself a high vantage point, then sit back and watch Zhou Yu do great deeds tonight!"

All the while, Lord Guan had been waiting at the side, but Kongming spared him not even a glance. Unable to endure it further, Lord Guan cried out, "I, Guan, have followed in elder brother's wake through long years of war, and have never been left behind. Today we close with a great enemy, but the director has given me no assignment. What does this mean?" Kongming smiled. "Do not take offense, Yunchang," he said. "My intention was to trouble you to hold an absolutely crucial pass, but—forgive me—something held me back, and I was reluctant to ask." "What 'held you back'?" Lord Guan replied. "I want an explanation here and now."

"Once," Kongming went on, "Cao Cao treated you most generously, and you are bound somehow to repay him.[12] When his host is defeated, Cao will take the road to Huarong. If we ordered you there, I was certain, you would let him pass. That is what held me back." "How mistrustful of you!" Lord Guan responded. "True, Cao Cao treated me well. But did I not repay him when I beheaded Yuan Shao's general, Yan Liang, and put to death General Wen Chou? And again when I broke the siege at Baima? Do you think I'd let him go today?" "But if you should, then what?" Kongming said, pressing the point. "Let military law be applied to my misdeed!" said Lord Guan. "Well and good," Kongming answered. "Now put it in writing." Lord Guan executed the document, saying, "And if Cao Cao does not take that route?" "I give you a formal commitment that he will!" Kongming answered, to Lord Guan's complete satisfaction, and then added, "But why don't you pile up dry brambles around the trails and hills by Huarong? At the right time, set them afire. The smoke should draw Cao Cao that way."

"Smoke would make Cao Cao think there's an ambush," Lord Guan protested. "It would keep him away." "Have you forgotten," Kongming responded, "the tactic of 'letting weak points look weak and strong points look strong'? Cao may be an able strategist, but this should fool him. The smoke will make him think we are trying to create an impression of strength where we are weak and thus draw him to this route. But I must remind you again, General, to refrain from showing him any mercy." Lord Guan accepted this assignment and taking his son Ping, Zhou Cang, and five hundred practiced swordsmen, headed for Huarong Pass to set up the ambush.

When Lord Guan had left, Xuande said to Kongming, "His sense of honor is very strong. If Cao Cao actually takes that route, I am afraid my brother will let him pass in the end." "Last night I surveyed the constellations," Kongming replied. "The traitor's doom is not written there. And to leave a good turn for Lord Guan to do is a rather nice touch, after all." "Master," Xuande said, "your superhuman calculations are more than any man could match." Kongming and Xuande then set out for Fankou to observe Zhou Yu's assault, leaving Sun Qian and Jian Yong to guard Xiakou.

•   •   •   •   •

Cao Cao and his advisers were in the main tent awaiting news of Huang Gai's defection. That day the southeast wind blew strong. Cheng Yu went in and said, "We should be taking measures against this wind." But Cao Cao smiled and replied, "The winter's *yin* phase is spent; the *yang* now begins its cycle. A southeast wind is quite normal. There is nothing to be alarmed about." At that moment soldiers reported the arrival of a small craft from the south bringing a secret letter from Huang Gai. Cao Cao immediately had the bearer shown into his presence. The letter said in part:

> Zhou Yu has held me under tight surveillance, and so I have had no means to get away. Now we have a new grain shipment from the Poyang Lakes. Zhou Yu has put me on patrol, and opportunity presents itself. I will find a way to cut down one of our eminent commanders and present his head with my submission. Tonight at the second watch, look for a boat with the Green Dragon jack—that will be the shipment.

Delighted, Cao Cao and his generals went to the great ship to watch for Huang Gai.

It was almost night. In the Southland Zhou Yu ordered Cai He brought before him, bound, and thrown to the ground. "I have committed no crime," Cai He cried. "Who do you think you are," said Zhou Yu, "pretending to come over to our side? Today we lack the ritual articles suitable for sacrifice to the flags. Your head will have to serve instead." Cai He, unable to deny the charge, shouted, "Your own Kan Ze and Gan Ning were in on it!" "As arranged," answered Zhou Yu. To what avail were Cai He's regrets now? Zhou Yu ordered him brought to the riverbank beneath the black standard, where they offered libations and burned paper. Cai He was beheaded, and his blood was poured in sacrifice to the flag. After that, the ships set sail.

Huang Gai was in the third fire vessel, wearing a breastplate and holding a sharp sword; on his banner, four large characters: "Vanguard Huang Gai." Riding the favoring wind, he set his sights for the Red Cliffs. By now the gale was in full motion. Waves and whitecaps surged tumultuously. Cao Cao scanned the river and watched the rising moon. Its reflections flickered over the waters, turning the river into myriad golden serpents rolling and sporting in the waves. Cao faced the wind and smiled, thinking he would achieve his ambition. Suddenly a soldier pointed out: "The river is serried with sails from the south bank riding in on the wind!" As Cao strained his eyes from the height, the report came: "They fly the Green Dragon jack; among them, a giant banner, 'Vanguard Huang Gai.'" Cao Cao smiled. "Huang Gai's defection is Heaven-sent." But Cheng Yu studied the approaching boats and warned, "It's a ruse. Don't let them near our camp." "How do you know?" asked Cao. "If they held grain," Cheng Yu answered, "they would be low and steady in the water. But the boats coming on are so light, they are practically skimming the surface. Besides—with the force of this southeast wind, could you evade a trap?"

Then the truth dawned on Cao Cao, and he called for a volunteer to stop the oncoming boats. "I have experience as a mariner," said Wen Ping. "Let me go." He leaped into a small craft and went forth, followed, at a signal from his hand, by a dozen patrol boats. Standing in the prow of his ship, Wen Ping shouted: "By the prime minister's authority, the ships from the south are to approach no farther but to anchor in midriver!" Wen Ping's warriors cried out in unison: "Lower your sails!" These words were hanging in the air when an arrow sang, and Wen Ping, struck in the left arm, toppled over in his boat. There was commotion on board, and the squad raced back to the naval station.

The ships from the south were now only two *li* from Cao's fleet. At the signal from Huang Gai's sword, the first line of onrushing ships was torched. The fire was sped by the might of the wind, and the boats homed in like arrows in flight. Soon smoke and flame screened off the sky. Twenty fiery boats rammed into the naval station. All at once Cao's ships caught fire and, locked in place by their chains, could not escape. Catapults sounded from across the river as the burning ships converged. The face of the water where the three rivers joined could scarcely be seen as the flames chased the wind in piercing currents of red that seemed to rise to the heavens and pass through the earth.

Cao Cao looked back to his shoreside camps; several fires had already broken out. Huang Gai sprang into a small boat and, followed by a few men, braved smoke and fire to find Cao Cao. Desperate, Cao Cao was about to jump back on shore, but Zhang Liao steered a small cutter toward Cao and helped him down from the large ship, already on fire. Zhang, with some dozen men protecting Cao Cao, raced for a landing point. Huang Gai had spotted someone in a scarlet battle gown lowering himself into a boat and, surmising it was Cao Cao, made for him. "Go no farther, traitor!" he cried, sword in hand. "Huang Gai has come!" A series of angry cries broke from Cao Cao's throat. Zhang Liao hefted his bow and fitted an arrow, squinting as Huang Gai drew nearer. Then he let fly. The wind was roaring. Huang Gai, in the center of the firestorm, could not hear the twang of the bowstring. The arrow struck him in the armpit, and he fell into the water. Indeed:

> When fatal fire reached its height, he met his fate in water;
> When wounds from wooden clubs had healed, he fell to a metal arrow.

Would Huang Gai survive the victory he had made possible?[13]

READ ON.

50

Kongming Foresees the Outcome at Huarong;
Lord Guan Releases, and Obligates, Cao Cao

AFTER HIS SHOT HAD KNOCKED HUANG GAI into the water, Zhang Liao brought Cao Cao safely ashore, where they found horses and fled. Cao's army was in utter disorder.

The southern commander Han Dang, steering through smoke and fire, attacked the naval station. Suddenly a soldier reported: "Someone hanging onto the rudder is calling you." Han Dang, straining, heard his name: "Dang, save me!" Recognizing Huang Gai's voice, Han Dang had him pulled aboard. He saw the wound and yanked the shaft out with his teeth, but the arrowhead remained in Huang Gai's flesh. He then removed Gai's soaked garments, dug the metal head out with his sword, and bound Gai's arm with a strip of his flag. Wrapping his own battle gown around Huang Gai, Han Dang sent him back to the main camp for treatment. Huang Gai was used to the water, so he managed to survive the experience even though it was midwinter and he wore armor.

That day fires rolled across the river like waves, and the cries of men shook the earth. On the left, boat squads led by Han Dang and Jiang Qin attacked from the west of the Red Cliffs; to the right, Zhou Tai and Chen Wu guided in their craft from the east; in the center, Zhou Yu, Cheng Pu, Xu Sheng, and Ding Feng arrived in force. Their fighters spared not what the fires had spared, and the fires lent the fighters added strength. Such indeed was the naval battle at Three Rivers and the bloody trial of war at Red Cliffs. On Cao Cao's side, those who fell to spear or arrow, or burned to death or drowned were beyond numbering. A poet later wrote:

> Wei and Wu waged war to rule the roost;
> The northland's towered ships—to smoke reduced.
> Spreading flames illumined cloud and sea:
> Cao Cao went down; 'twas Zhou Yu's victory.

Another verse reads:

> High hills, a tiny moon, waters vague and vast—
> Look back and grieve: what haste to carve the land!
> The Southland had no wish for Cao's imperium;
> And the wind had a mind to save its high command.

• • • •

While the sea war raged, on land Gan Ning ordered Cai Zhong to bring him deep into Cao's camp. Then he struck Zhong a single blow, and he fell dead from his horse. Gan Ning began setting fires at once. Southland commander Lü Meng, seeing flames above Cao Cao's central camp, set his fires in response. Pan Zhang and Dong Xi did the same, and their troops made a great uproar, pounding their drums on all sides.

Cao Cao and Zhang Liao had little more than one hundred horsemen. Fleeing through the burning wood, they could see no place free of fire. When Mao Jie rescued Wen Ping, another dozen riders caught up with them. Cao Cao demanded that they find an escape route. Pointing to the Black Forest, Zhang Liao said, "That's the only area that seems free and clear," so Cao Cao dashed straight for the Black Forest. A troop of soldiers overtook him as their leader shouted, "Cao Cao! Stand, traitor!" Lü Meng's ensign appeared in the fiery glare.

Letting Zhang Liao deal with Lü Meng, Cao pushed on, only to be confronted by a fresh company charging out of a valley, bearing torches. A shout: "Ling Tong is here!" Cao Cao felt his nerve fail, his courage crack. Suddenly a band of soldiers veered toward him. Again, a shout: "Your Excellency, fear not, it's Xu Huang!" A rough skirmish followed. Cao Cao managed to flee some distance north before he encountered another company stationed on a slope ahead. Xu Huang rode over and found Ma Yan and Zhang Kai, two of Cao's commanders, formerly under Yuan Shao, with their force of three thousand northerners arrayed on the hill. They had seen the night sky full of flames and had hesitated to move. Now they were perfectly positioned to receive Cao Cao. He sent the two commanders ahead with one thousand men to clear a path and reserved two thousand as his personal guard.

Fortified by this fresh body of men, Cao's mind was easier. Ma Yan and Zhang Kai rode swiftly on, but within ten *li* voices rent the air, and another band of soldiers materialized. Their commander cried, "Know me for Gan Ning of the Southland!" Ma Yan tried to engage him, but Ning cut him down with one stroke. Zhang Kai raised his spear and offered combat. Whooping, Ning struck again with his sword, and Zhang Kai fell dead. Soldiers in the rear raced to inform Cao Cao.

Cao had been counting on support from troops in Hefei, unaware that Sun Quan already controlled all routes to the east. Assured of victory by the conflagration on the river, Sun Quan had Lu Xun signal Taishi Ci with fire. The moment he saw it, Taishi Ci joined Lu Xun and raced toward Cao, forcing him to flee toward Yiling; on the way Cao met up with Zhang He, whom he ordered to guard the rear.

Cao Cao whipped his horse into a dead run. At the fifth watch he looked back: the great fire had receded into the distance, and he felt steadier. "Where are we?" he asked. "West of the Black Forest," his attendants said, "and north of Yidu." Cao looked at the tangled woods and steep hills. He raised his head and laughed without stopping. "What does Your Excellency laugh so hard at?" the commanders asked. "At nothing. Nothing but the folly of Zhou Yu and the shallowness of Kongming. If I had been in their place, I would have laid an ambush right here. I, Cao Cao, would've been done for." Even as he spoke, drums thundered from both sides and flames shot upward. Cao nearly fell from his horse. A band of soldiers appeared. Then, a shout: "Zhao Zilong, here! On orders from the director general! And waiting a long time too!" Cao had Xu Huang and Zhang He engage Zilong together, while he turned into the smoke and flame and fled. Zilong made no attempt to pursue, intent only on capturing the flags. Again, Cao Cao made good his escape.

The night sky was beginning to grey. Dark clouds spread out above. The southeast wind had not let up. Suddenly torrential rains came down, soaking everyone. Cao Cao braved the downpour and pressed on. His men were wan with hunger. Cao ordered food seized from nearby villages and some embers gathered for cooking fires. Before they could start, a company of men arrived at the rear. Cao Cao despaired, but it was only Li Dian and Xu Chu guarding the prime minister's advisers. Delighted, Cao Cao ordered his men to continue advancing. "What's the area just ahead?" he asked. "On one side is the South Yiling road; on the other, the North Yiling road," he was told. "Which one runs to Nanjun's seat, Jiangling?" "The easiest way," the soldiers said, "is to take the southern road through Gourd Crossing." Cao ordered them to take it and soon they reached the crossing.

Cao's men, famished, could barely march on. The horses, too, were fatigued, and most of them had fallen. Cao called a brief halt. Some horses carried cauldrons; others, grain seized in the villages. Near a hillside they found a dry spot, set their pots in the earth, and began cooking. They fed on horseflesh; then they stripped and hung their clothes in the breeze to dry. The mounts were unsaddled, left to roam free and graze. Cao Cao sat in a sparse wood, threw back his head, and laughed loudly. His officials said, "The last time Your Excellency laughed at Zhou Yu and Kongming, it brought Zhao Zilong down on us, and we lost plenty of men and mounts. What are you laughing at now?" "At Kongming and Zhou Yu, whose knowledge and planning is in the end rather deficient," he replied. "Had I been in command, I would have set an ambush right here to meet our exhausted troops with their well-rested ones. Even if we had escaped with our lives, we'd have been mauled. But they did not see that far. And that's why I am laughing." At that moment shouts rang out, ahead and behind.

Terrified, Cao Cao flung aside his armor and mounted. But most of his soldiers, with smoke and fire closing in, had no time to get to their horses. Before them an enemy troop had control of the pass through the hills. Their commander, Zhang Fei of Yan, spear leveled, poised on his mount, bellowed at Cao, "Where goes the traitor?" Officers and men quaked at the sight of Zhang Fei, but Xu Chu mounted bareback and made ready to fight, and Zhang Liao and Xu Huang converged on Zhang Fei. Then the horsemen on both sides jammed together in close action. Cao broke free first. Others followed. Zhang Fei pursued hotly. Cao fled in a meandering pattern, slowly leaving the enemy behind.

Cao Cao observed that most of his commanders bore wounds. One soldier respectfully asked, "There are two roads ahead; which one does Your Excellency think we should take?" "Which is shorter?" Cao asked in response. "The main road is fairly flat, but more than fifty *li* longer. The trail toward Huarong is fifty *li* shorter, but narrow and treacherous and hard-going." Cao Cao ordered some men to climb a hill and survey the roads. "Smoke is rising from several places along the trail," one reported back. "But there seems to be no activity on the main road." Cao Cao ordered the front ranks on to the Huarong Trail. "Those smoke signals mean soldiers," the commanders protested. "Why go down there?" "Don't you know what the military texts say?" Cao said. "'A show of force is best where you are weak; where strong, feign weakness.' Kongming is a man of tricks. He purposely sent his men to some nooks in the hills to set fires to deter us from going that way, while placing his ambush on the main road. That's my judgment. I won't fall into this trap!" "Your ingenious calculations are beyond compare," the commanders agreed and directed their troops toward the Huarong Trail.

By now the men were staggering from hunger. The horses could barely move. Some men had burns; others bore wounds from spear or arrow. On they plodded with walking sticks, dragging themselves painfully along, their clothing and armor drenched. No one had escaped unscathed, and weapons and standards were carried in no semblance of good order. Few mounts had had gear since the rout north of Yiling, when saddles and bridles had been cast aside. It was midwinter, and the cold was severe. Who can fairly describe their sufferings?

Cao Cao saw the front line come to a halt and asked why. The report came back: "The hills ahead are rarely crossed; the paths are too narrow, and the horses have bogged down in the ditches after the morning's rains." In an exasperated tone Cao Cao said, "Are you telling me that an army that forges through mountains and bridges rivers can't get through a little mud?" Then he sent down the command: "Let the old, the weak, and the wounded follow as best they can; the able-bodied are to carry earth, wood, grass, and reeds to fill in the road. The march must resume, and whoever disobeys dies." As ordered, the soldiers dismounted and cut trees and bamboo by the roadside to rebuild the road. Cao Cao, fearing pursuit, had Zhang Liao, Xu Chu, and Xu Huang lead a hundred riders with swords bared to cut down slackers.

At Cao Cao's order the troops, starved and exhausted, trudged ahead, trampling over the bodies of the many who had fallen. The dead were beyond numbering, and the sound of howls and cries on the trail did not cease. Angrily, Cao said, "Fate rules life and death. What are all these cries for? I'll behead the next to cry." One third of the men fell behind; another third lay in the ditches; one third stayed with Cao Cao. They passed a treacherous slope. The road began to flatten out. Looking behind, Cao saw that he was left with a mere three hundred mounted followers, not a one with clothing and armor intact. Cao urged them forward. The commanders said, "The horses are spent; they need a short rest." "Push on. There'll be time for that in Jiangling," Cao answered.

They rode another *li* or two. Cao Cao raised his whip and laughed again. "Why is Your Excellency laughing?" the commanders asked. "Everyone thinks Zhou Yu and Kongming are such shrewd tacticians," he replied. "But as I see it, neither is especially capable. If they had set an ambush here we could only have surrendered quietly." That moment a bombard echoed. Five hundred expert swordsmen flanked the road. At their head, raising his blade Green Dragon, sitting astride Red Hare, the great general Lord Guan Yunchang checked Cao's advance. Cao's men felt their souls desert them, their courage die. They looked at one another helplessly.

"It is the last battle, then," said Cao, "and we must fight it." But the commanders replied, "Even if the men will fight, their horses lack the strength. We cannot fight again." "Lord Guan," said Cheng Yu, "is known to disdain the high and mighty but to bear with the humble. He gives the strong short shrift but never persecutes the weak. He knows clearly the difference between obligation and enmity, and he has ever demonstrated good faith and honor. In times past, Your Excellency showed him great kindness; now, on your personal appeal to him, we might be spared."

Cao Cao approved and guided his horse forward. Bowing, he addressed Lord Guan: "You have been well, I trust, General, since we parted?" Lord Guan bowed in return and said, "I bear orders from the director general and have been awaiting Your Excellency for some time." "My army is defeated and my situation critical," Cao Cao said. "At this point I have no way out. But I trust, General, you will give due weight to our old friendship." "Though I benefited from your ample kindness," Lord Guan replied, "I fulfilled the debt when I destroyed two enemy generals and relieved the siege at Baima. In the present situation I cannot set aside public duty for personal considerations."

"You still recall, do you not," Cao went on, "how you slew my commanders at five passes when you left my service? A man worthy of the name gives the greatest weight to good faith and honor. With your profound understanding of the *Spring and Autumn Annals*, you must be familiar with the story of the apprentice Yugongzhisi who pursued his archery instructor, Zizhuoruzi, only to release him, unwilling to use the man's own teachings to destory him."[1] And Lord Guan, whose sense of honor was solid as a mountain, could not put Cao Cao's many obliging kindnesses or the thought of the slain commanders from his mind. Moved, despite himself, at the sight of Cao's men distracted and on the verge of tears, Lord Guan softened. He swung away his mount and said to his soldiers, "Spread out on all sides," clearly signaling his intent to make way. When Cao Cao saw Lord Guan turn aside, he and his commanders bolted past, and when Lord Guan came back, they were gone.

Lord Guan gave a powerful shout. Cao's soldiers dismouted, prostrated themselves, and wept. Lord Guan's sense of pity seemed to grow on him, and he hesitated. Then Zhang Liao came racing up, and Lord Guan was reminded of their old friendship.[2] With a long sigh, he let all the remaining troops pass.[3] A poet of later times has written:

> Cao Cao fled along the Huarong Trail,
> But Lord Guan barred his passage hardily.
> Then, weighing obligation once incurred,
> He slipped the lock and let the dragon free.

Cao Cao rode on to the mouth of the gorge. Looking back, he saw all of twenty-seven riders behind him.

It was dark when he neared Jiangling. Masses of torches lit up the area, and a cluster of troops blocked his path. "This is the end," Cao Cao cried in fear. But he was relieved to find a patrol under Cao Ren, who greeted him saying, "I knew of the defeat but chose to keep to my post so that I could meet you on your return." "I might never have seen you again," Cao Cao said and gathered everyone into Jiangling for the night.

Soon Zhang Liao rode up and told Cao Cao of Lord Guan's kindness. Cao Cao checked his commanders and lieutenants. Many were wounded. Cao ordered them all to rest. Cao Ren set forth wine to dispel Cao Cao's sorrow, and his advisers joined him. Suddenly Cao Cao lifted his head and cried out in grief. His advisers said, "Your Excellency, when you escaped the tiger's den you showed neither fear nor anxiety. Yet now that we are safe inside these walls, the men fed, the horses provisioned, the time come to reorganize ourselves for counterattack, you cry out in grief. Why?" "I mourn for Guo Jia. He could have prevented this dreadful defeat," Cao said. He beat his breast and howled: "I grieve for you, Guo Jia. Oh, what a loss, what a loss!" His advisers remained quiet, shamed.

The next day Cao Cao told Cao Ren, "I am going back to the capital briefly to replenish my forces for the counterattack. Keep guard here over Jiangling. I have a plan to leave with you, but you must keep it sealed—except in emergency. Should you have to use it, the Southland will never succeed with its designs on Jiangling." "Who will guard Hefei and Xiangyang?" asked Cao Ren. "Jingzhou is in your hands," Cao replied. "And I've tapped Xiahou Dun to hold Xiangyang. The most critical point is Hefei. Zhang Liao will be in charge there, assisted by Yue Jin and Li Dian. The moment something arises, inform me." His arrangements completed, Cao Cao rode back to Xuchang, the capital, taking with him the remainder of his army as well as those originally under Liu Biao's ad-

ministration who had subsequently submitted to him. Cao Ren sent Cao Hong to defend
Yiling and Jiangling against Zhou Yu.

∙   ∙   ∙   ∙   ∙

Before Lord Guan brought his men home, the other commanders assigned by Kongming had already returned to Xiakou with their booty of horses, grain, money, and
equipment. Only Lord Guan came back empty-handed, having taken neither man nor
mount. Kongming was in the midst of congratulating Xuande when Lord Guan's return
was reported. Kongming rushed forth from his place, bearing the cup of congratulation,
to greet him. "It is time to rejoice, General," he said, "in your epoch-making achievement—ridding the empire of a monstrous evil. I really should have made the effort
to receive you on the road." Lord Guan was silent. "General," Kongming continued,
"can it be that you are displeased because we did not come far enough to meet you?"
He turned to his attendants and added, "Why did you not report his approach before
he arrived?"

"I come only to request capital punishment," Lord Guan said. "You do not mean to
tell me that Cao Cao did not take the Huarong Trail?" Kongming asked. "He did, in fact,
come that way," Lord Guan answered. "But I was so inept, he got away from me."
"What commanders and soldiers have you captured, then?" Kongming went on.
"None," came the reply. "That means," said Kongming, "that you purposely released
him, mindful of his past generosity. Nonetheless, since you made a formal commitment,
we have no choice but to enforce it under martial law." Kongming shouted for the guards
to execute him. Indeed:

> Lord Guan risked his life to thank a benefactor;
> And men forever after held his name in honor.

Cao Cao had escaped his doom; would Lord Guan?
READ ON.

51

Cao Ren Battles the Southland Troops;
Kongming Spoils Zhou Yu's Victory

KONGMING WAS ABOUT TO EXECUTE LORD GUAN, but Xuande intervened, saying, "When my brothers and I pledged mutual faith, we swore to live—and die—as one. Now Yunchang has broken the law, but I haven't the heart to go against our former convenant. I hope you will suspend the rule this time and simply record his fault, allowing him to redeem his offense by future merit." With that, Kongming pardoned Lord Guan.

• • • •

Zhou Yu recalled his forces, reviewed his commanders' accomplishments, and reported them to Sun Quan. He also sent all surrendered northerners back across the river. After feasting and rewarding his southern troops, Zhou Yu mounted an attack on Nanjun.

His first echelon camped at the edge of the river, in five sites from van to rear. Zhou Yu occupied the central site. He was in the midst of conferring on the tactics of the campaign when a report came in: "Liu Xuande has sent Sun Qian to congratulate the chief commander." Invited into Zhou Yu's presence, Sun Qian performed the ritual salute and said, "My lord, Liu Xuande, has commanded me to convey his respectful gratitude for your magnanimity, and to tender these poor courtesies." "Where is Xuande?" Zhou Yu asked. "As far as I know," Sun Qian replied, "he has moved his troops into position at the mouth of the You River."[1] Startled, Zhou Yu asked, "Is Kongming there too?" "He is with Lord Liu," Sun Qian answered. "Then please return; I shall go there myself, later, to express my gratitude."

Zhou Yu accepted the gifts and sent Sun Qian back ahead of him. Lu Su asked Zhou Yu, "Whatever made you lose your composure just now, Commander?" "If Xuande is at the River You," Zhou Yu answered, "it means he plans to take Nanjun! We are the ones who expended so many men and horses, who consumed so much coin and grain—and now Nanjun is ours for the plucking. But if they harbor such ruthless ambition as to snatch our prize, they'll have to reckon with the fact that I am still around." "What strategy could force them back?" Lu Su wanted to know. "I'm going to talk with Xuande myself. If all goes well, fine. If not, I'll not wait for him to take Nanjun; I'll finish him off first!" "I should go with you," said Lu Su. With three thousand light cavalry the two men headed for Xuande's camp on the You River.

When Sun Qian told Xuande that the Southland commander was on his way, Xuande asked Kongming, "What is he coming for?" Kongming smiled. "Hardly for trivial courtesies," he said. "He is coming for Nanjun." "If he comes with troops, what do we do?" Xuande asked. Kongming suggested certain replies for Xuande to make to Zhou Yu, and then ordered the warships arrayed on the river and the land forces along the shore.

The arrival of Zhou Yu and Lu Su and their battalion was announced. Kongming had Zhao Zilong take a few riders and greet them. Zhou Yu observed uneasily the strength and vigor of Xuande's military position. Soon he was taken to the main tent where he was well received by Xuande and Kongming. When the formalities were done with, a banquet was spread. Xuande raised his wine cup to thank Zhou Yu for his part in the difficult campaign. After several rounds, Zhou Yu began, "Lord Liu, are we to understand that in moving your forces here, you intend to take Nanjun?" "I had heard, Commander," Xuande replied, "that you wished to take it, and so I have come to lend my assistance. If you do not take it, of course, I shall." Zhou Yu smiled. "We in the Southland have long wished to assimilate the area around the Great River and the Han," he said. "Now Nanjun is within our grasp. How could we not take it?"

"The outcome of any engagement is hard to foretell," Xuande said. "Before returning north, Cao Cao assigned Cao Ren to defend Nanjun and other neighboring points. He is sure to have left some surprises for us, not to speak of Cao Ren's unchallengeable bravery. My only concern is whether you will be able to capture the city, Commander." "In the event that we fail," Zhou Yu answered, "you are welcome to try." To this, Xuande replied, "Lu Su and Kongming are here as witnesses. Do not go back on your word, Commander." Lu Su hemmed and hawed without answering, but Zhou Yu said, "When a man worthy of the name gives his word, there is no going back." "Your position, Commander, is certainly fair-minded," Kongming commented.[2] "Let Lord Sun Quan go to take Nanjun first. If he does not subdue it, my Lord Liu will try. What objection can there be to that?"

After Lu Su and Zhou Yu had departed, Xuande asked Kongming, "All the same, those replies you had me make seem unjustified now that I think it over. I am isolated and destitute, without a place to set my feet. I sought Nanjun as an expedient refuge. If Zhou Yu takes the city for the Southland, where am I supposed to go?" Kongming laughed heartily. "Remember, my lord," he said, "when I tried to get you to take Jingzhou? How you ignored me? But today you yearn for it!" "Then it was Liu Biao's land," Xuande replied. "I could not bear to take it. Now that it is Cao Cao's, I'd be justified." "Never mind fretting and worrying, my lord," said Kongming. "Let Zhou Yu do a bit of the fighting now, and I will have you sitting in power within Nanjun's walls soon enough." "And how will you manage that?" asked Xuande. Kongming whispered a few phrases that dispelled Xuande's anxiety. He consequently held his troops in tight check at the mouth of the River You.

•　　•　　•　　•

Zhou Yu and Lu Su returned from their mission to Xuande. "Commander," Lu Su asked, "how could you consent to Xuande's capture of Nanjun?"[3] "I can take it with a snap of the fingers," said Zhou Yu. "I have simply granted them a favor that will cost us nothing." Then he called for a volunteer to lead the attack. His call was answered by Jiang Qin. "You will have the vanguard," said Zhou Yu. "Xu Sheng and Ding Feng will be your lieutenants. Select five thousand of our finest soldiers and cross the river. I will bring up the rear."

In Nanjun, Cao Ren had sent Cao Hong west to guard Yiling and create a pincer defense. When the crossing of the river by southern troops was reported, Cao Ren said,

"Defend stoutly but do not give battle." Valiant Commander Niu Jin protested energet-
ically: "To refuse to fight an enemy at our walls is cowardice. More than ever we need
to put new heart in our men after our recent defeats. I volunteer to take five hundred and
destroy them or die trying." Cao Ren approved and granted Niu Jin the fighters. Ding
Feng raced forward to meet him. After four or five bouts Feng feigned defeat, and Niu Jin
chased him beyond his own line. At a signal from Feng, Niu Jin was surrounded. He
charged the encircling enemy right and left but to no avail.

From the city wall Cao Ren could see Niu Jin trapped in the enemy camp. He donned
his armor, mounted, and rode out, followed by several hundred horsemen. Cao Ren tore
into the enemy line, his blade wheeling. Xu Sheng went forth but broke before the assault. Cao Ren fought his way to the center of the camp and rescued Niu Jin. A few dozen
riders were still trapped, so he turned again and did bloody slaughter until he had brought
them out of the encirclement—only to find Jiang Qin barring his way. Cao Ren and Niu
Jin fought with might and main to break up the enemy lines. Cao Ren's brother, Chun,
came to their aid, and a melee ensued. The southern troops fell back and Cao Ren returned victorious. Jiang Qin, standing before an angry Zhou Yu, escaped punishment of
death only through the commanders' intercession.

Zhou Yu tallied his forces for the struggle with Cao Ren himself. But Gan Ning said,
"Let the chief commander not be so impetuous. Cao Ren has put Cao Hong in charge of
Yiling as one point of a pincer. I would like to have three thousand men to seize Yiling;
then you can seize Nanjun." Zhou Yu was persuaded, and Gan Ning set out. Cao Ren was
quickly informed of these moves and conferred with Chen Jiao. "If anything goes wrong
at Yiling," Jiao warned Ren, "we won't be able to hold Nanjun. Reinforce it immediately." Cao Ren therefore sent Cao Chun and Niu Jin quietly over to Yiling to support
Cao Hong.

Cao Chun had sent a man ahead to inform Hong and have him leave the city as an
enticement to the enemy. When Gan Ning came before the walls in force, Cao Hong
went forth to engage him. After twenty bouts, Cao Hong fled in defeat, and Ning took
possession of Yiling. Then, at dusk, Cao Chun and Niu Jin arrived and swiftly laid siege
to Yiling.

The reports that Gan Ning was trapped in Yiling stunned Zhou Yu. Cheng Pu said to
him, "We must send more men there at once." "Our own position is at the center of
things. We can't spare troops. What if Cao Ren attacks us here?" Zhou Yu countered.
"Gan Ning is one of our top generals. We can't leave him there," said Lü Meng. "I would
go myself," said Zhou Yu, "but who would take my place?" "Let Ling Tong stand in for
you here," said Lü Meng. "I will take the van. You cover the rear, Commander. And
inside of ten days, we will be celebrating a victory." "We have yet to hear if Ling Tong
is willing," Zhou Yu said. "For ten days, yes," Ling Tong responded. "But longer than
that—the responsibility would be too much." Delighted, Zhou Yu left Ling Tong with
about ten thousand troops and struck out for Yiling that same day.

On the way Lü Meng said to Zhou Yu, "At the southern edge of Yiling is a little road,
the easiest way to Nanjun. Send five hundred men there to fell trees and block it off. The
northerners will have to take that road if they are defeated; and when they find they have
to flee on foot, they'll leave us their horses." Zhou Yu approved and sent the soldiers to
carry out the scheme.

When the main body of southern troops approached Yiling, Zhou Yu called for someone to break through the siege and rescue Gan Ning. Zhou Tai volunteered. Bracing his

sword and giving his horse free rein, he hewed a bloody track through Cao Hong's ranks until he reached the city wall. Gan Ning emerged to greet him. "The chief commander himself is coming," said Zhou Tai. Gan Ning sent out an order for his men to dress for battle and eat their fill, that they might be ready to coordinate with the rescuers.

Cao Hong, Cao Chun, and Niu Jin soon learned of the approach of Zhou Yu's force and sent a messenger to Nanjun to inform Cao Ren. At the same time they assigned a portion of their army to hold off the attackers. The southerners arrived, and Cao's troops met them in battle. At that moment Gan Ning and Zhou Tai came out of the city and joined in the fighting. Cao's army disintegrated, and the southerners bore down on the foe from every side. As predicted, the three leaders, Cao Hong, Cao Chun, and Niu Jin, fled Yiling by the small road. Blocked by heaps of timber, they fled on foot, abandoning to the southerners some five hundred mounts. Zhou Yu pressed hotly on to Nanjun—only to encounter Cao Ren's rescue force. The armies fell upon each other and fought wildly until dark. Then they returned to their respective positions.

Cao Ren went back into Nanjun and conferred with his commanders and counselors. "We have lost Yiling," Cao Hong said, "and we are in great peril. We should have a look at the secret plan the prime minister left before he went to Xuchang." "My thought exactly," replied Cao Ren. Reading the secret instructions, Cao Ren's anxiety lifted. He ordered mess to be served at the fifth watch and all units to abandon the city at dawn. Around the wall he left his colors waving as a false show of force. Then his army vacated the city through its three gates.

Having rescued Gan Ning, Zhou Yu ranged his troops before the walls of Nanjun. He observed the evacuation from his general's platform. He saw the flags sticking up from the unguarded battlement; and he noted the sacks tied to the waists of the retreating soldiers. Surmising that Cao Ren must have prepared this move well ahead of time, Zhou Yu descended from his observation post and split his army into two wings. He commanded the forward unit, if successful, to press on no matter what, retreating only when the gong sounded. Then he commanded Cheng Pu to supervise the rear army, while he himself prepared to take possession of the city.

To the powerful beating of drums Cao Hong rode out to challenge the southerners. Zhou Yu directed Han Dang to meet him in combat. After thirty clashes Hong retreated. Cao Ren himself joined the battle, and Zhou Tai went forth to engage him. After ten clashes, Cao Ren retired. As Cao's line was breaking apart, Zhou Yu summoned his two wings into action. It was fast becoming a rout. Zhou Yu led his riders to the wall of Nanjun. Cao Ren, instead of entering the city, turned northwest and fled. Han Dang and Zhou Tai swept mightily after him. Seeing the main gate open and the walls deserted, Zhou Yu ordered his men to seize the city. A few dozen horsemen went in first, with Zhou Yu behind, racing forward, right into the space between the outer and inner walls.

In the archer's tower Chen Jiao watched Zhou Yu entering and muttered to himself, "The prime minister's brilliant schemes are almost miraculous." At the signal of a watchman's rattle, his crossbowmen let fly from both sides. Bolts pelted the field like heavy rain. Those who managed to struggle into the city fell head over heels into ditches and pits. Zhou Yu tried desperately to turn back, but a quarrel from a crossbow struck him squarely in the left side, knocking him from his horse. Niu Jin then came out slashing, bent on capturing Zhou Yu. Xu Sheng and Ding Feng sped to his rescue, throwing caution to the wind.

Cao's army now thrust forward from the city, pushing back the southern soldiers. As they trampled each other, many fell into the moat. Cheng Pu desperately called for retreat. But Cao Ren and Cao Hong turned the columns they had led out of the city back into the fray. The southerners, though badly mauled, were not routed only because Ling Tong, charging in from an angle, managed to hold off the northerners. Cao Ren led his victorious solders back into Nanjun, and Cheng Pu took his defeated troops back to their camp. Ding Feng and Xu Sheng carried Zhou Yu to his tent and called for an army surgeon to extract the arrow with forceps. He applied medication for wounds caused by metal, but the pain was unbearable. Zhou Yu could take neither food nor drink. The medical officer said, "The tip was poisoned. There can be no swift recovery. Fits of choler will only reopen the wound."[4]

Cheng Pu ordered the southern army to make no move and permitted no one to give battle. Three days later, Niu Jin came to denounce the southern foe, but Cheng Pu would not respond. Niu Jin hurled taunts until sunset and resumed them the following day, but Cheng Pu did not inform Zhou Yu lest his condition worsen. The third day, Niu Jin rode directly to the camp gate to rail upon the southerners, declaring in every word his intention to capture Zhou Yu. Cheng Pu decided on a temporary retreat until Sun Quan could be consulted.

Despite his physical suffering, Zhou Yu was aware of what was going on: that Cao's army had come before the camp to denounce him and that his commanders were holding something back. One day Cao Ren came as usual, his army beating drums, truculently demanding to fight. Cheng Pu held fast and would not go forth. Zhou Yu called his commanders into his tent and asked them, "Where is the drumming and shouting coming from?" "We're training the troops," was the reply. "Don't try to fool me!" Zhou Yu declared angrily. "I know full well Cao's men are in front of the camp abusing us. Cheng Pu shares military authority with me. Why has he done nothing?" He called for Cheng Pu and asked him the same question.

"Seeing that you were ill from the wound and that the doctor said you were not to be angered," replied Cheng Pu, "I didn't report the enemy's provocations." "What is your purpose in refusing to fight?" Zhou Yu asked. "The commanders," Cheng Pu answered, "want to take the army back to the south and wait for your recovery before undertaking further action." At these words Zhou Yu started from his couch. "A man worthy of the name, who takes his sustenance in the service of his lord, considers it a boon to die on the battlefield, to be sent home wrapped in horsehide. You can't bring our cause to naught on my account." So saying, he put on his battle dress and mounted, leaving his commanders in a state of shock.

Zhou Yu led several hundred fighters to the front of the camp. Cao's troops were already positioned for combat. Cao Ren sat poised on his horse under the commanding general's banner. He raised his whip and shouted, "Zhou Yu, you baby! I thought you'd die in your cradle and never again dare to look upon my men." Cao Ren was still shouting when Zhou Yu shot forward from the soldiers massed around him, crying, "Cao Ren, you scum, can you see me?" Cao Ren's men looked in fear. Ren turned to his commanders and said, "Curse him!" And the army raised its voice in a thunderous outcry.

Roused to fury, Zhou Yu sent Pan Zhang to give battle. But before the warriors had engaged, the Southland's chief commander cried out sharply and toppled from his horse, blood rushing from his mouth. Cao's men advanced swiftly. The southern commanders held them back, and, after brief but violent fighting, brought Zhou Yu back to his tent. Cheng Pu asked him, "Commander, what ails you?" "It's a ruse," Zhou Yu whispered.

"How will it work?" Cheng Pu asked. Zhou Yu continued: "There's nothing wrong. I want them to think I'm dying so that they will drop their guard. Have some of our trusted men pretend to surrender; tell them I have died. Cao Ren is sure to raid our camp this night—but we will have soldiers on all sides ready for them. Cao Ren will be ours in a single roll of the drums!" "A brilliant plan!" Cheng Pu exclaimed and, leaving the tent, raised the cry of mourning. Fear swept the southerners as word spread that the chief commander had died from his reopened wound. Everyone in camp wore the white of mourning.

Cao Ren was conferring with his counselors, discussing Zhou Yu's fall from his horse and his expected death from the reopened wound, when the announcement came: "Over ten southern soldiers have come to submit, two of them our own, previously captured by the south." Cao Ren hurriedly summoned them for questioning. The soldiers said, "Zhou Yu's wound burst when he was at the front today, and he died back at camp. The commanders are dressed in white and have raised the cry of mourning. All of us, here, have come to surrender and report the news because Cheng Pu mistreated us." Cao Ren was overjoyed, and began planning a night raid to carry off Zhou Yu's corpse so that he could send the chief commander's head to the capital.

Chen Jiao said, "This calls for speed. Let us not delay." Cao Ren put Niu Jin in the van, himself in the center, and Cao Hong and Cao Chun in the rear. Chen Jiao was left guarding the city with a handful of men. All the rest joined the attack force. They left the city after the first watch and made straight for Zhou Yu's camp. On reaching the gate, they saw not a single soul, only a few pennoned spears idly stuck in the ground. Sensing a trap, they strove to pull back, but the Southland's bombards were already homing in.

From the east came Han Dang and Jiang Qin; from the west, Zhou Tai and Pan Zhang; from the south, Xu Sheng and Ding Feng; from the north, Chen Wu and Lü Meng. They closed in for the kill, knocking Cao Ren's entire army to pieces; van and rear could not aid each other. Ren and a dozen riders broke the encirclement and met up with Cao Hong; the two fled with what remained of their forces. The slaughter continued into the fifth watch. The fleeing commanders were close to Nanjun when, to the pounding of drums, Ling Tong checked their passage. A sharp clash ensued. Cao Ren and his men fled off at an angle, only to meet Gan Ning, who took another heavy toll. Afraid to return to Nanjun, Cao Ren headed down the main route to Xiangyang. The southerners pursued briefly, then returned.

Zhou Yu and Cheng Pu regathered their troops and set out for Nanjun. Reaching the walls of the city, they saw a host of flags and banners, and a general calling to them from the wall tower: "My apologies, Chief Commander. On orders from our director general, I have taken possession of the city. I am Zhao Zilong of Changshan." In a fury, Zhou Yu ordered his men to attack. Arrows rained down from the wall. Zhou Yu withdrew and, after conferring with his commanders, decided to send Gan Ning with several thousand troops to take Gong'an, and Ling Tong to take Xiangyang, before renewing the assault on Nanjun.

As Zhou Yu was making these assignments, scouts raced in to report: "After Zhuge Liang seized Nanjun, he used captured military credentials to deceive the guard at Jingzhou into coming to help. Then he had Zhang Fei seize the city." This was followed by another report: "Xiahou Dun was holding Xiangyang when Zhuge Liang sent someone with credentials claiming that Cao Ren needed his help. Dun was lured out of the city, and Lord Guan captured it. The two cities have come into Liu Xuande's possession without the least effort on his part." "How did Zhuge Liang get hold of the military tallies?" asked

Zhou Yu. "When Chen Jiao was captured, he had all the tallies on him," was the explanation. Zhou Yu cried out, and his wound reopened. Indeed:

> The walls and moats of several districts—not a one for me?
> Campaigns and bitter fighting—for whose sake all that toil?

The conflict between Sun Quan and Liu Xuande had taken a new turn.[5]
  READ ON.

52

Zhuge Liang Temporizes with Lu Su;
Zhao Zilong Captures Guiyang

AFTER KONGMING CAPTURED NANJUN AND XIANGYANG, Zhou Yu passed out from exasperation, rupturing his wound. When he came to himself, his commanders tried to soothe him, but Zhou Yu said, "Nothing less than the life of Zhuge Bumpkin will quell my discontent. Cheng Pu can help me retake Nanjun for the Southland." At this point Lu Su entered, and Zhou Yu said, "I am going to assemble an army to recover our cities and have it out with Xuande and Kongming. Will you help me?" "Nothing doing," replied Lu Su. "With our struggle against Cao Cao undecided and with Lord Sun's advance on Hefei stalled, we become easy prey for Cao Cao if we turn on one other. Our whole position will crumble. What's more, Liu Xuande was once Cao Cao's good friend. If we push him into tendering his cities to Cao Cao and the two of them unite against us—then what?"[1] "It is insufferable," cried Zhou Yu. "Our strategy, our casualties, our costs in coin and grain—and for what? A ready victory for them!" "Bear with it, my friend," Lu Su urged. "I shall go and reason with Xuande myself. If I fail to make him see things our way, there will be time enough for hostilities." Zhou Yu's commanders welcomed this idea.

Lightly attended, Lu Su headed for Nanjun. He came to the city gate and shouted up to be admitted. When Zhao Zilong came out, Lu Su said, "I have something to say to Liu Xuande." Zilong replied, "Lord Liu and the director general are over in Gong'an." Lu Su turned and headed there. At Gong'an he found the flags and banners in brilliant array and the appearance of the army magnificent. To himself he admitted boundless admiration for Kongming. The visitor's arrival was reported. Kongming ordered the city gate opened wide and ushered Lu Su into the *yamen*. Formal greetings completed, they seated themselves as host and guest.

After tea had been served, Lu Su began: "Lord Sun Quan and his chief commander, Zhou Yu, have sent me to communicate their emphatic view to the imperial uncle. When we first undertook this campaign, Cao Cao had command of a million men and threatened to descend on the Southland. His real objective, however, was the imperial uncle, whom by fortune's grace the Southland saved in a massive campaign that drove back the northerners. Jingzhou's nine imperial districts should now properly become part of the Southland. But the imperial uncle has used a subterfuge to seize and hold the area, handily reaping a benefit for which the Southland has vainly expended its coin, grain, and men. I doubt that this is consonant with accepted principles."

"My friend," Kongming said, "on what grounds does a high-minded and enlightened scholar like yourself make such statements? It is commonly agreed that 'things belong to their owners.' Jingzhou's nine districts are not the Southland's territory, but rather the estate of Liu Biao,[2] and Lord Liu, as everyone knows, is his younger brother. Though Liu Biao himself is dead, his son is still alive. For an uncle to support a nephew in taking Jingzhou—what can there be to object to?"[3] "If in fact the patriarchal son were holding the territory," Lu Su conceded, " I might understand. But he is in Jiangxia; he is obviously not here."

"Would you care to see him?" asked Kongming. He motioned to his attendants, and before Lu Su's very eyes, steadied by two supporters, Liu Qi came out from behind a screen and spoke to Lu Su: "My ill health prevents me from performing the proper courtesies; please forgive my offense." Lu Su swallowed his amazement and kept silent for some time. Then he said, "And if the patriarch's son were to die . . . " "He lives from day to day," Kongming replied. "Should he die, there will be something to negotiate." "When he dies," said Lu Su, "the territory reverts to the Southland." "I think your position is correct," Kongming said finally. A banquet was then prepared to fete Lu Su.

Lu Su bore the news to his own camp that night. Zhou Yu said, "Liu Qi is in the prime of youth and unlikely to die. When will we ever get Jingzhou back?" "Chief Commander," Lu Su replied, "rest assured that the responsibility is mine alone. I will see to it that Jingzhou is restored to the Southland." "You have something up your sleeve?" Zhou Yu asked. Lu Su replied: "Anyone could see how dissipated in vice and luxury Liu Qi is. Disease has penetrated his vitals. His face looks feeble and wasted. His breathing is troubled, and he spits blood. The man cannot live beyond six months. At that time I shall go to claim Jingzhou, and Liu Bei should have no excuses whatsoever to put me off."

Lu Su's assurances gave Zhou Yu little comfort. But an unexpected messenger from Sun Quan resolved the matter. "Lord Sun," he announced, "has surrounded Hefei. Unable to subdue it after many battles, he now orders the chief commander to shift his forces over there." Zhou Yu had no choice. He withdrew to Chaisang to allow his wound time to heal and sent Cheng Pu in command of a naval force to serve Sun Quan.

•   •   •   •   •

Liu Xuande, overjoyed with the acquisition of the key cities of Gong'an, Nanjun, and Xiangyang, began considering how they could be held permanently. Suddenly, a man entered his reception chamber to offer counsel. It was Yi Ji.[4] In recognition of his earlier help in saving his life, Xuande showed him great courtesy and invited him to be seated. Then Yi Ji spoke: "If you seek a plan to keep Jingzhou for good, why not solicit the advice of the worthy scholars of the region?" "Where are they?" Xuande asked. "There is the Ma family of Jingzhou," Yi Ji replied. "The five brothers are noted for their talent: the youngest is Ma Su (styled Youchang); the most able, Ma Liang (styled Jichang), famous for the white hairs between his eyebrows. As a popular saying has it: 'Of the Mas' five Changs, the best is white-browed Liang.' This is the man to consult."

Accordingly, Ma Liang was invited. Xuande treated him with high courtesy and asked him how to maintain his hold on Jingzhou. Ma Liang responded: "The province, exposed to attack from four directions, cannot hold out long. Keep young master Liu Qi here nursing his illness, summon former leaders to guard the place, then petition the Emperor to make Liu Qi imperial inspector of Jingzhou. This will relieve the anxieties of the population. Once that is done, you can march south on the four districts Wuling, Changsha, Guiyang, and Lingling to gather coin and grain and build a base area. This is how to make the province yours for good."[5] Delighted with this advice, Xuande asked, "Which of the four should we capture first?" "Lingling," he replied, "west of the River Xiang, is closest. It should be first, followed by Wuling. Then, east of the river, take Guiyang, and finally Changsha."[6]

After this conference Xuande appointed Ma Liang an assistant to the imperial inspector and Yi Ji, his deputy. Xuande called on Kongming to arrange Liu Qi's return to Xiangyang and to bring Lord Guan back to Gong'an. Next, he directed his troops to capture Lingling. He sent Zhang Fei in the van and Zilong in the rear, while he and Kongming made up the center. In all they had fifteen thousand men. Lord Guan was left to guard Gong'an; Mi Zhu and Liu Feng defended Jiangling.[7]

The governor of the district of Lingling was Liu Du. Informed of the approach of Xuande's army, he took counsel with his son, Liu Xian. "There is no need to worry, Father," Liu Xian said. "Although Xuande has brave warriors like Zhang Fei and Zhao Zilong, we have in Xing Daorong a top general who can withstand legions. He will be able to hold them off." The governor then ordered Liu Xian and Xing Daorong to lead ten thousand men some thirty *li* out of the city, there to camp hard by a stream, their back to the hills.

Scouts brought word that Kongming was approaching with a company of men, and Daorong went forth to battle. The opposing lines moved into position. Daorong charged out, wheeling a great mountain-cleaving axe. "Renegade! Traitor!" he shrieked. "You dare violate our territory?" Suddenly a group of yellow flags came into view, and where they parted a four-wheeled carriage emerged. On it sat a single figure wearing a garment of crane feathers, a plaited band wrapped around his head in the Taoist fashion. He held a feathered fan, with which he motioned to Xing Daorong. "I am Zhuge Kongming of Nanyang," he said. "With a few little tricks I wrecked Cao Cao's million-man host. You are no match! I come today to offer you amnesty. The sooner you surrender, the better for you."

In response Daorong laughed out loud. "Zhou Yu's genius," he shouted, "won the day at Red Cliffs. You had no hand in it. Begone with your absurd claims." Wheeling his great battle-axe, he charged. Kongming withdrew into the open center of his line, which closed behind him. Daorong hurtled forward. The line quickly split into two as either half peeled away from the field. In the distance Daorong saw the cluster of yellow flags and, thinking to find Kongming there, charged again.

Sweeping past the foot of the hills, Daorong found the yellow flags, but from their midst a mounted warrior bounded forth, spear raised, and went for Daorong with a shout. It was Zhang Fei. Daorong held high his axe and advanced; but after several clashes he felt his powers fail, so he fled. Zhang Fei came pounding after him, and his troops came forth from hiding. The air rang with warcries. Daorong plunged on for his life. Another warrior blocked his passage. "Ever hear of Zhao Zilong of Changshan?" he cried. Unable to resist or flee, Daorong dismounted and submitted. Zilong took him, bound, to Xuande and Kongming.

Xuande ordered the prisoner beheaded, but Kongming quickly stopped him. He said to Daorong, "Capture Liu Xian for us, and we will accept your surrender." Daorong assented eagerly. "How will you do it?" Kongming asked him. "If the director general will release me," he replied, "I have an idea. This evening have your men raid the camp. I will work from within, capture Liu Xian alive, and deliver him to you. After that Governor Liu Du's surrender will be a matter of course." Xuande mistrusted the man, but Kongming released him, saying, "The commander is not fooling."

After being sent home, Daorong informed Liu Xian truthfully of all that had passed. "What are we to do?" asked Xian. "Fight fire with fire," was Daorong's reply. "Place our men outside of the camp in ambush. Leave our flags in the camp as a decoy. When Kongming attacks, we can seize him then and there." Liu Xian agreed.

At the second watch a band of men appeared at the camp. Each had a clump of dry straw, which he set afire. Liu Xian and Daorong struck, drove the torch-bearing soldiers back, and pursued them. But after a chase of some ten *li* they could find no one. Frightened, Liu Xian and Daorong hurried back to their camp, only to find the firebrands blazing there. A warrior dashed out from the camp: Zhang Fei. Liu Xian said to Daorong, "We cannot enter. Let us raid Kongming's camp instead." They retraced their steps; but before they had gone ten *li*, Zhao Zilong led a company out from the side. With one thrust he stabbed Daorong dead. Liu Xian wheeled and tried to flee, but Zhang Fei overtook him from behind, swept him onto his own saddle, and presented him, bound, to Kongming.

Liu Xian pleaded: "Xing Daorong made me do this. It was never my idea." Kongming ordered him freed. He gave him fresh clothes, some wine to calm him, and had him escorted back to the city to persuade his father to submit or face the loss of the city and the extermination of his family. Liu Xian returned to Lingling to see his father, Liu Du. He recounted in detail the kindness of Kongming and urged submission. Liu Du agreed. He raised the flag of surrender on the city wall, opened wide the gate, and, bearing the seal and cord of authority, left his city to present himself at Xuande's camp. Kongming arranged for Liu Du to remain as governor and for his son, Xian, to go to Gong'an and serve in the army. The population of the district of Lingling was universally content with the outcome.

After Xuande had assured the city of its safety and rewarded his army, he took counsel with his commanders. "Lingling is ours," he said. "Who will capture Guiyang?" Zhao Zilong volunteered, but Zhang Fei thrust himself forward and demanded to go. As the two heroes argued, Kongming said, "After all, Zilong volunteered first. Let him be the one." Zhang Fei still would not agree, so Kongming had them draw lots. Zilong was the winner. Angrily, Zhang Fei said, "I need no one to help me. All I want is three thousand men and I will guarantee the capture." Zilong then retorted, "All I want is three thousand; and if I fail, let me suffer the penalty dictated by military law." Elated, Kongming had the document drawn up and sent Zilong off with three thousand picked troops. Xuande gruffly ordered the indignantly protesting Zhang Fei to retire.

Zhao Zilong's advance toward Guiyang was soon reported to the governor, Zhao Fan, who called an urgent meeting of his advisers. Chen Ying and Bao Long, his military commanders, offered to meet the invaders in battle. These two officers came from families of hunters in the Guiyang Hills. Chen Ying was a master in hurling forked weapons, and Bao Long had once killed a pair of tigers with bow and arrow. Both had great confidence in their martial skills. To Zhao Fan they said, "If Xuande comes, we want to be in the front lines." Zhao Fan replied, "They say that Liu Xuande is an imperial uncle of the Emperor of Han, that his chief adviser, Kongming, is a superb strategist, and that Lord Guan and Zhang Fei are the bravest of warriors. The man who leads this invasion is Zhao Zilong, who had no trouble with a million-man enemy at Steepslope in Dangyang. How many can our little Guiyang put in the field? Let us surrender." "Let me go forth," Chen Ying said. "If I fail to capture Zilong, there will be time enough for Your Lordship to submit." Zhao Fan was persuaded to let him try.

Chen Ying, at the head of three thousand, soon saw Zhao Zilong approaching. Drawing his line into formation, Chen Ying raced forward with his flying pike. Zilong appeared, spear braced, and denounced Chen Ying: "The lord I serve is Liu Xuande, younger brother to Liu Biao. We uphold the patriarchal son, Liu Qi, in joint rule of Jingzhou province and we have come to allay the people's fears. How dare you offer battle!" Chen Ying swore back: "We bow to the rule of Prime Minister Cao Cao, not to Liu Bei."

Roused to fury, Zilong hoisted his spear and charged. Ying gripped his weapon. The horsemen locked and fought four or five bouts. Overpowered, Chen Ying wheeled and fled. Zilong gave chase. Chen Ying looked back at his pursuer and hurled his flying pike, but Zilong caught it and flung it back. As Ying dodged, Zilong drew alongside, plucked him from the saddle, and threw him to the ground. Then he had his men bind him and take him back to camp.

The defeated soldiers scattered. Zilong returned to camp and confronted Chen Ying: "Did you think you could stand up to me?" he said harshly. "I spare you only so you can talk Zhao Fan into surrendering, and the sooner the better." Grateful for his life, Chen Ying hastened to Guiyang and told Zhao Fan how he had been taken. "It was my idea to submit," Zhao Fan said. "You insisted on fighting. Now you see the result." He sent Chen Ying from his presence and, bearing the governor's seal and cord, led a dozen riders to Zilong's camp to surrender.

Zhao Zilong came forth from the camp and received Zhao Fan with full courtesy. They then shared the ritual wine, and Zhao Zilong accepted the seal and cord. After several rounds Zhao Fan said, "General, you have the surname Zhao, as I do. Five hundred years ago we were one family.[8] You are from Zhending; that is my hometown, too. If it is agreeable to you, I would like to tie the fraternal bond. It would be a great boon." Zhao Zilong was overjoyed, and both men related the precise time of their births. Since Zilong was four months older, Zhao Fan recognized him as his elder brother. The two men rejoiced in the discovery that they shared the same hometown, year of birth, and surname.

They parted late that evening and Zhao Fan returned to his city. The next day Fan called Zilong into the city to reassure the people. Zilong did not mobilize his men, but took only some fifty cavalry. The people welcomed him on the road, some holding incense, some prostrating themselves. Zhao Zilong promised them their safety. Zhao Fan invited him to a banquet in the government headquarters. After they had drunk amply, Zhao Fan invited Zilong to his private chambers to drink further. Zilong was beginning to feel intoxicated.

Suddenly Zhao Fan summoned a woman to serve the wine. Zilong observed that the woman, dressed in white mourning silk, was an extraordinary beauty, the kind that overturns nations and cities. Zilong asked his host who she was. "My sister-in-law from the Fan family," was the reply. Softening his expression, Zilong extended his courtesies to her, and after she had presented his cup, the host ordered her to be seated. But Zilong expressed uneasiness at her joining them, and Lady Fan retired. "Worthy brother," Zilong asked, "why trouble your sister-in-law to present the wine?"

"I have a reason," Zhao Fan replied, all smiles. "I beg you, elder brother, bear with me. Her husband, my elder brother, departed some three years ago. I don't think she should pass the rest of her life a lonely widow; and though I have often urged her to remarry, she says, 'I will marry only the man who fulfills these three criteria: he must be renowned for accomplishment in both letters and martial skills; of noble mien and stature; and of the same surname as my late husband.' Tell me where in the world I might find such a combination of qualities! But now, you, honored elder brother, fulfill the three conditions my sister has set. If you will deign to accept a woman of such common looks, I am willing to provide her dowry so that she may serve you, General, as a wife, and thus bind us in future generations. What do you say?"

Zilong rose angrily, answering in harsh tones, "If you and I have bound ourselves as brothers, then your sister-in-law is as good as my own. How can we violate the laws of morality with this incest?" Zhao Fan, covered with shame and humiliation, said, "I only meant you well. There is no need for such rudeness," and glanced meaningfully toward his guard, intending to have Zilong murdered. But Zilong sensed the danger and struck Zhao Fan down with a blow of his fist. He then strode out of Zhao Fan's quarters, mounted his horse, and rode out of the city.

Zhao Fan called for Chen Ying and Bao Long at once. After a brief discussion, Ying said, "He left so outraged, we can only fight." "I don't know if we can beat him," responded Zhao Fan. "Let us two pretend to surrender," proposed Bao Long. "Then, Your Lordship, lead the troops out to challenge them, and we will seize him in the battle line." "We'll need to take some troops," Chen Ying added. "Five hundred cavalry should do," Bao Long said. That night the two men and their company surrendered to Zhao Zilong.

Zilong, knowing full well what Chen Ying and Bao Long were up to, allowed them into his camp. The two commanders entered his tent and said, "Zhao Fan was using a woman to deceive you, General. He meant to wait until you were drunk, kill you in his chambers, and send your head to Cao Cao. That's how ruthless he is. When you departed so angrily, we decided to surrender rather than suffer the consequences of our part in the crime." Zilong feigned great pleasure and drank heartily with the two men.

As soon as they were good and drunk, Zilong tied them up and squeezed the truth out of one of their subordinates. He called together their guard of five hundred, gave each man wine and food, and issued a command: "It was Chen Ying and Bao Long who sought my life. None of you is involved. And if you will carry out a plan for me, you will be well rewarded." The soldiers expressed their gratitude.

Zilong had the two leaders beheaded on the spot. Then he had the five hundred lead the way back to Guiyang that same night while he followed with a thousand warriors. At the gates the soldiers said that Chen Ying and Bao Long were returning after having killed Zhao Zilong and that they wanted to confer with the governor. Seeing his own men in the glare of the torches, Zhao Fan hurried out and was seized immediately. Zilong entered the city for the second time, assured the people of their safety, and sped the news back to Xuande.[9]

When Xuande and Kongming came to Guiyang, Zilong welcomed them into the city. He shoved Zhao Fan to the ground before the steps leading up to the main hall of the *yamen*. In answer to Kongming's questions, Fan related the details of the marriage offer he had made Zilong. "Why, this is an excellent thing," Kongming said to Zilong. "Why are you acting this way?" "In the first place," Zilong answered, "marrying my brother's sister-in-law would provoke contempt. Secondly, it is her second marriage; I would be causing her to forsake the life of chastity proper to a widow. And thirdly, it's not easy to read the intentions of someone who has just surrendered. Lord Liu has just taken control of the area around the Jiang and Han rivers, and he is preoccupied with a difficult situation. How could I put aside my lord's great cause for the sake of a woman?" "Today, our cause is secure," Xuande said. "I can arrange for you to marry this woman. What do you say?" "The world is full of women," said Zilong. "I seek fame, not a wife." "Zilong," said Xuande, "you are indeed manly." He freed Zhao Fan and restored him as governor of Guiyang. Zhao Zilong was richly rewarded.

Now Zhang Fei thundered in dismay: "Let Zilong have all the credit! And let me remain a useless man! Oh, give me but three thousand to take Wuling, and I'll bring that
governor Jin Xuan back alive!" Kongming was delighted with Zhang Fei's zeal. "There is
no reason you should not go, Yide," he said, "but you must promise one thing." Indeed:

> Kongming's endless tricks won the day;
> And the warriors vied for martial fame.

What did Kongming want to say?

READ ON.

53

Lord Guan Spares Huang Zhong;
Sun Quan Battles Zhang Liao

KONGMING TURNED TO ZHANG FEI. "Before Zilong marched to Guiyang district," he said, "he gave us written oath. Now, Yide, you want to capture Wuling; we will have to ask for the same oath before assigning men to you." Zhang Fei gave his pledge, eagerly took command of his three thousand soldiers, and set out at once for Wuling.

As soon as Governor Jin Xuan learned of Zhang Fei's approach, he gathered his commanders and lieutenants, requisitioned his finest troops and weapons, and went forth from the city to meet the invaders. A staff officer, Gong Zhi, warned him: "Surrender is the best course. Do not go to war with Liu Xuande, imperial uncle of the Han and renowned through the empire for his humanity and honor, nor with Zhang Fei, warrior of peerless courage." "Are you planning to collaborate with these criminals?" Jin Xuan demanded and thereupon ordered Gong Zhi executed. But the assembly interceded. "To kill one of our own," they appealed, "bodes ill for the army." The governor therefore dismissed Gong Zhi gruffly and took personal command of the army.

Jin Xuan met Zhang Fei some twenty *li* from the city. Spear and horse poised for action, Zhang Fei challenged Jin Xuan. The governor's commanders declined to step forward, so he sallied forth himself, flourishing his sword. Zhang Fei roared, and his voice had the power of a thunderclap; Jin Xuan fled in terror. Zhang Fei pursued, his men close behind. As the governor reached the wall around Wuling, arrows hailed down at him and he spied Gong Zhi on the top. "You have brought disaster on yourself," he shouted down, "flouting the course of Heaven. The people of Wuling and I have decided to submit to Liu Xuande." As Gong Zhi spoke, an arrow flew, striking Jin Xuan square in the forehead. He toppled from his horse, and an officer cut off his head to present to Zhang Fei. Gong Zhi then came out and surrendered, and Zhang Fei told him to deliver the seal and cord of authority to Xuande in Guiyang. Delighted with the outcome of the campaign, Xuande directed Gong Zhi to assume the governorship.

Liu Xuande then came to Wuling to reassure the people of their safety. He informed Lord Guan by special messenger that Zilong and Zhang Fei had each taken a district. Lord Guan's reply read: "I hear that Changsha is yet to be taken. If elder brother does not despise my lack of ability, I would be happy to undertake this task." Gratified by Lord Guan's offer, Xuande sent Zhang Fei to relieve Lord Guan in Gong'an.

Lord Guan presented himself to Xuande and Kongming. "Zilong has taken Guiyang," Kongming said, "and Zhang Fei has taken Wuling. Each had three thousand fighters. The governor of Changsha, Han Xuan, poses no problem. But he has a general, Huang Zhong (styled Hansheng), from Nanyang. Before entering Han Xuan's service, as corps commander under Liu Biao, he was responsible for the defense of Changsha together with Biao's nephew, Pan. Though nearly sixty, Huang Zhong is invincibly courageous. Do not take him lightly. You will need extra troops." Lord Guan retorted, "Why is the director general playing up another's mettle and dampening our own spirits? That old warrior doesn't worry me. Not only do I not need three thousand men, with my own company of five hundred expert swordsmen, I guarantee that the heads of Huang Zhong and Han Xuan will be laid beneath your command flag yet." Xuande objected strenuously, but Lord Guan would not yield and went off with his five hundred followers. Kongming said to Xuande, "Lord Guan is underestimating Huang Zhong. Something is likely to go wrong. You should go, my lord, and support him." On this advice, Xuande set out for Changsha with his own troops.

Han Xuan, governor of Changsha, was widely hated for his unstable temper and an unfortunate tendency to kill whoever displeased him. On hearing of the approach of Lord Guan, he called his veteran general Huang Zhong to counsel. "There is no cause for worry," Huang Zhong said. "With this sword and this bow, if a thousand come, a thousand die!" Huang Zhong was a man who could pull a bow of over two hundred and fifty pounds yet never miss a shot. At that moment someone stepped forward below the governor's platform and said, "Why should the great general have to fight? I have a plan to capture that fellow Guan alive." Governor Han Xuan looked at the speaker. It was his commandant, Yang Ling. Deeply gratified, Han Xuan assigned Ling a thousand men, and Ling swiftly rode into the field.

Yang Ling had traveled some fifty *li* when he saw Lord Guan's company charging through the dust. Yang Ling raised his spear and rode to the front of his line to rail at Lord Guan. In silent rage, Lord Guan waved his sword and came for Yang Ling. Ling leveled his aim and closed with his attacker. The clash was brief. A hand rose, a blade fell, and Yang Ling went down. Lord Guan's company drove on to the city wall, slaughtering Ling's retreating troops.

Astonished at the news, Han Xuan sent Huang Zhong into the field and himself climbed the city wall to observe. Huang Zhong, sword in hand, raced over the lowered drawbridge, followed by his five hundred. Lord Guan recognized the old general. He ranged his five hundred swordsmen in a single line. Then, sword leveled across his saddle, he asked, "Can it be General Huang Zhong?" "If you know my name, what have you to do in my territory?" replied the general. "I come for your head," Lord Guan retorted. The riders grappled. They had struggled through one hundred passes without a victor when Han Xuan, fearing for Huang Zhong, rang the gong calling Zhong and his men back into the town. Lord Guan withdrew ten *li* and camped. He mused, "That old general—he deserves his reputation. In a hundred passes he wasn't nicked once. Tomorrow I'll have to use the 'trailing sword trick' and get him while he gives chase."

The next morning after the early meal Lord Guan appeared to taunt the defenders. Han Xuan, sitting on the wall, sent Huang Zhong out. Once again the old general took his men across the drawbridge and battled Lord Guan to a draw after fifty or sixty bouts carried out to the cheers of the soldiers of both sides. When the drumbeat accelerated, Lord Guan wheeled and fled. Huang Zhong followed close. Lord Guan was preparing to sweep round and strike, when he heard a clatter to the rear. Glancing back, he saw that Huang Zhong had been thrown to the ground. Lord Guan rode back, lifted his sword with both hands, and cried fiercely, "I spare you. Get another horse and let's finish this!'' Huang Zhong brought his horse to its feet, remounted, and sped back to Wuling.

To the astonished Han Xuan, Huang Zhong said, "The horse has been out of combat too long. That explains his mishap." "You're a crack archer," said the governor. "Why don't you shoot?" "In tomorrow's battle," replied Zhong, "I'll feign defeat, lure him to the bridge, and shoot him." The governor provided a black horse from his own stable, and Zhong retired, expressing profound thanks. But another thought came to him: "Where would one find a man so honorable as Lord Guan? Can I bear to shoot down the man who forbore to kill me? Can I disobey an order?" He spent the night in indecision.

The following dawn Lord Guan's arrival was announced, and Huang Zhong led his troops out. Having failed twice to overcome the old general, Lord Guan was chafing with frustration and came to grips with Huang Zhong, making a great show of his confident spirit. After thirty passages-at-arms Zhong feigned defeat and fled. Lord Guan pursued. Huang Zhong, unable to put Lord Guan's act of mercy from his mind, could not shoot. Putting up his sword, he plucked his bowstring. Lord Guan ducked at its strong note but saw no arrow and resumed the chase. Huang Zhong repeated the motion, and Lord Guan bent low, but again, no arrow. "A poor shot," thought Lord Guan, and he rode on securely to the drawbridge. Huang Zhong was already there. He watched Lord Guan get closer. Then he put an arrow on the string and let fly. It lodged at the base of the knob atop Lord Guan's helmet. The defending soldiers roared. Overcome with alarm, Lord Guan rode back to camp, the arrow firmly in place. Finally, aware that Huang Zhong had used his superlative marksmanship to repay the earlier act of mercy, Lord Guan ordered a general retreat.

When Huang Zhong reentered Changsha, Governor Han Xuan ordered him arrested. "I have committed no crime," Zhong shouted; but Han Xuan said angrily, "I have been watching for three days. Do you think you can fool me? Two days ago you didn't put up a real fight. Was it because you had interests of your own? Yesterday your horse slipped and the foe spared you. Was there some understanding between you? Today you snapped an empty bowstring twice, and the third time hit only his helmet. What can explain this except some liaison? If I let you live now, I will only pay the price later on." The governor ordered armed guards to execute Huang Zhong in front of the city gate, and forestalled all pleas by saying, "Whoever appeals for mercy will be taken as his sympathizer."

The executioner had pushed Huang Zhong out of the gate and was about to deal the death blow when from nowhere a commander swooped down, slaughtered the executioners, and carried off Huang Zhong. "This man is the shield of Changsha," he shouted. "To kill Huang Zhong is to kill the people of Changsha. Governor Han is ruthless and violent; he slights the worthy and insults men of learning. He should be put to death by common, concerted action. Those who will, follow me!" Everyone turned to the man. His face was ruddy as a date, his eyes as clear as stars. It was Wei Yan of Yiyang.

Wei Yan had come from Xiangyang in search of Xuande but, unable to find him, sought service with Han Xuan. The governor, however, offended by his easygoing manner and his inattention to ceremonial affairs, chose to let Wei Yan remain idle in the neighborhood rather than give him the position his talents warranted.

That day, after rescuing Huang Zhong and rousing the people against Han Xuan, Wei Yan bared his arm and mobilized hundreds with a single shout. Huang Zhong was powerless to stop them. Wei Yan fought his way to the top of the city wall and cut Han Xuan in half with a single blow. He took the governor's head, led the people out of the city, and offered himself to Lord Guan. Delighted by Wei Yan's surrender, Lord Guan entered Changsha and calmed the populace. He invited Huang Zhong to audience, but Zhong pleaded illness. Then Lord Guan sent for Xuande and Kongming.

Xuande had begun organizing a support detachment the day Lord Guan left for Changsha. It was already on the way when its blue-green standard fell over and rolled up. At the same time a south-flying crow passed them, croaking three times. "What do these signs mean?" Xuande asked. Kongming took an augury on horseback and replied, "Changsha district is ours! And we have won over important generals. We will learn more this afternoon." Soon a petty officer reported, "General Guan has taken Changsha and received the surrender of generals Huang Zhong and Wei Yan. He awaits the arrival of Lord Liu." Xuande rejoiced and entered the city. Lord Guan welcomed him into the main hall of the government compound and described his encounter with Huang Zhong. Xuande then went to Huang Zhong's home to extend the invitation to submit. Huang Zhong submitted, requesting only permission to have Han Xuan buried east of the city. A poet of later times has memorialized General Huang Zhong:

> His martial powers set him high as Heaven,
> Yet in the end this greybeard went in bonds.
> Resigned to death, he held no man to blame;
> Surrender made him hang his head in shame.
> His dazzling sword bespoke demonic daring;
> His barded mount, wind-breathing, inspired his combat-lust.
> This hero's noble name defies oblivion,
> Trailing the orphan moon above the Xiang and Tan.

Xuande was generous to Huang Zhong; but when Lord Guan led in Wei Yan, Kongming ordered him executed. "The man has merits and is without fault. Why must he die?" Xuande said anxiously. "To kill the lord that fed you is disloyal; to deliver your homeland is dishonorable. I see treachery in Wei Yan. Eventually, he will turn against us. Kill him now and you will prevent it."[1] Thus Kongming replied. "Why then," said Xuande, "everyone who surrenders will fear for his life. I pray you, relent." Kongming pointed to Wei Yan and said, "I spare you, then. Repay your new lord with all your loyalty and never think to deceive him—or in the end I will have your head." With that, Wei Yan retired, anxiously nodding in agreement.

Huang Zhong recommended to Xuande the nephew of Liu Biao, Pan, presently residing in You county without office. Xuande appointed him governor of Changsha. With four districts now under his control, Xuande marched back to Jingzhou city, also known as Youkou, which he now renamed Gong'an.[2] From this time forward, Xuande had ample supplies of grain and coin, and many worthy men tendered him their service. He dispatched cavalry commanders to defend all strategic points and passes.

· · · · ·

Chief Commander Zhou Yu, nursing his wound in Chaisang, sent Gan Ning to Baling[3] and Ling Tong to Hanyang to defend these two districts with war-junks pending further orders. After that, Cheng Pu took the rest of the commanders and officers to Hefei, where Sun Quan had been battling Cao Cao's forces since the fighting at Red Cliffs. Not daring to pitch camp near the city after a dozen indecisive engagements, Sun Quan camped fifty *li* away.

The news of Cheng Pu's arrival buoyed Sun Quan's spirits, and he personally went out from his encampment to reward the troops. Lu Su was the first to be received. Sun Quan dismounted to welcome him, and Lu Su flung himself to the ground in ritual prostration. All the commanders were amazed by Sun Quan's extraordinary deference. Sun Quan invited Lu Su to remount and the two rode side by side. Sun Quan asked him softly, "Was greeting you on foot recognition enough?" "No, my lord," Lu Su replied. "What wish remains unfulfilled?" "To see my illustrious lord's awesome virtue prevail through-out the land, to see every province under your sway, to see your imperial enterprise con-summated and my name written down in the histories—then and only then will I be satisfied with my 'recognition.'" Sun Quan rubbed his palms together and laughed heartily. The two walked to the command tent for a grand banquet, at which the men and officers of the Red Cliffs campaign were feasted and rewarded. Then Sun Quan and Lu Su took up the question of how to subdue Hefei.

As they spoke, a defiant letter from Zhang Liao was brought in. Sun Quan read it and said angrily, "Now, Zhang Liao, you go too far! You taunt me to combat knowing Cheng Pu has arrived. But I'll send no fresh troops against you. I'll be in the field tomorrow and will give you the fight you're looking for." Sun Quan issued an order for all armies to leave for Hefei at the fifth watch. The march was in progress when Cao's forces inter-cepted it in midmorning. The opposing sides arrayed their warriors. Sun Quan rode forth in golden helmet and armor: to his left, Song Qian; to his right, Jia Hua. Both com-manders bore halberds with twin side blades. The triple drumroll ended. In the center of Cao's army the gate flags parted, and three commanders in full battle gear stood before their line: in the center, Zhang Liao; to the left, Li Dian; to the right, Yue Jin. Zhang Liao charged to the front and called Sun Quan to combat.

Sun Quan set his spear and prepared himself. But from his own line another com-mander bolted ahead to take the challenger. It was Taishi Ci. Zhang Liao whipped his sword around, and the warriors clashed seventy or eighty times with no decision. Li Dian called out to Yue Jin: "That one, in the golden helmet, is Sun Quan. If we catch him, we'll avenge the eight hundred and thirty thousand lost at Red Cliffs."

At these words Yue Jin angled into the field, a lone rider with a single sword, streaking toward Sun Quan like a bolt of lightning. His hand rose, his sword fell, but the two hal-berdiers, Song Qian and Jia Hua, blocked his blow. Jin's sword struck off both men's hal-berd blades; and they reached for their opponent's horse with the bare staves. While Yue Jin swung his horse around, Song Qian seized a spear from a soldier and raced for Yue Jin; but Li Dian put an arrow to his string and shot Song Qian in the breast. The rider went down as the string hummed. Taishi Ci saw the man fall, abandoned Zhang Liao, and headed back to his line. Zhang Liao, seeing the battle turn in his favor, came on strong. The southern forces broke and scattered. Zhang Liao headed for Sun Quan at top speed. Another company, under Cheng Pu, spotted Zhang Liao, and plunged into the fray, in-tercepting the attack and thus saving Sun Quan. Zhang Liao collected his fighters and went back to Hefei.

Guarded by Cheng Pu, Sun Quan returned to the main camp, his defeated troops to their encampments. The sight of Song Qian's fall caused Sun Quan to give voice to his grief. One of his chief lieutenants, Zhang Hong, said, "My lord, confidence in your own vigor led you to underestimate the enemy and led our men to be disappointed by Your Lordship's rashness. Suppose you had killed a commander and seized a flag, and in so doing had dominated the battleground; it would still have been no more than the service expected of a lower-ranking commander, not of the lord of the land. Let my lord suppress his desire to display the raw valor of a Meng Ben or a Xia Yu[4] and embrace the strategies of a king or a hegemon. Your disdain for the foe has cost Song Qian his life. Hereafter it will be essential that your person be kept safe." In response Sun Quan acknowledged his fault and promised to correct it.

Soon Taishi Ci entered the command tent and said to Sun Quan, "I have in my company one Ge Ding, the brother, as it happens, of a groom in Zhang Liao's service. This servant harbors a deep resentment from having suffered continual rebuke. Tonight he has sent word that he will kill Zhang Liao to avenge Song Qian and will signal us with fire when he has completed the deed. I am requesting troops to support him from without." "And where is Ge Ding?" asked Sun Quan. "He has already entered Hefei undetected. I beg you for five thousand men." At this point Zhuge Jin intervened. "Zhang Liao," he argued, "is full of schemes. They may have been forewarned. Do not act rashly." But Taishi Ci was insistent, and Sun Quan, eager for revenge on Song Qian's killers, met Taishi Ci's request for troops.

Ge Ding was a fellow townsman of Taishi Ci. Disguised as a soldier, he had entered Hefei and found his brother. "I have already sent word to General Taishi Ci," Ding told him. "They will coordinate with us tonight. How are you going to work it?" The groom replied, "We are too far from the central camp to get in before nightfall. Let's simply stack some hay here and set it afire. You cry rebellion in front of the city to create a panic among the troops. In the midst of it all I'll stab Zhang Liao, and the rest of the army will disperse." "A perfect plan!" responded Ge Ding.

That night Zhang Liao returned victorious. He rewarded his troops handsomely but forbade them to disarm or sleep through the night. His lieutenants protested, "Today our victory was complete; we drove the enemy far off. Why don't you unhook your armor, General, and rest?" "That would be a mistake," Zhang Liao responded. "In war one must never rejoice in victory nor grieve in defeat. If the enemy thinks we are unguarded and attacks, how will we defend ourselves? Tonight we should be even more alert than usual." As Zhang Liao spoke, fires shot up from behind the camp, and a shrill voice calling for revolt was answered by a battery of others.

Zhang Liao left his tent and mounted his horse, summoning his closest commanders and lieutenants. A dozen of them stood in the roadway. "The voices sound urgent," they said. "We'd better go and look." "How could the whole city rise in revolt?" cried Zhang Liao. "This is the work of troublemakers trying to frighten our men, that's all. Anyone joining the disorder is to be executed." Moments later Li Dian captured Ge Ding and his brother, the groom; and Zhang Liao, as soon as he discovered the truth, had them executed on the spot. Directly, a great clamor of gongs and drums rose outside the city. "That must be the southerners working with the rebels. We'll turn the tables on them." He ordered his men to start a fire inside the main gate and raise the cry of revolt as they opened it and lowered the bridge.

Taishi Ci saw the doors part and, thinking the rebellion had succeeded, raced inside with spear raised. From the wall a bombard crashed and archers raked the ground with arrows. Taishi Ci tried to pull back but was wounded several times. From behind, Li Dian and Yue Jin came out for the kill. More than half of the Southland troops were killed as Cao Cao's commanders pursued them to the edge of their camp. Then Lu Xun and Dong Xi came out fighting and rescued Taishi Ci, and Cao's men went back to Hefei.

Sun Quan grieved at the sight of Taishi Ci's wounds. On Zhang Zhao's appeal he halted the campaign and ordered his warriors to their boats. The expedition returned to Nanxu and Runzhou. By the time the southern army had redeployed, Taishi Ci was near death. Sun Quan sent Zhang Zhao to see him. Taishi Ci exclaimed: "A fighting man, born into an age of trouble, must carry a three-span sword to immortalize his name.

Alas, my hopes are defeated. Let death come." With these words he died; his age was forty-one. A poet of later times has praised Taishi Ci:

> Loyal and true, this dedicated son—
> Taishi Ci of Donglai earns our praise.
> His name lent glory to the far frontiers;
> His bow and horse confounded mighty foes.
> For Kong Rong, his mother's comforter,
> Heartily he fought, requiting courtesy.
> His final stand bespoke a sturdy will.
> In every age he draws men's sympathy.

Sun Quan mourned Taishi Ci and ordered him richly interred at the foot of Beigu Hill in Nanxu; then he took Ci's son, Taishi Heng, into his own home.

· · · ·

In Gong'an city Liu Xuande had reorganized his fighting force. Learning of Sun Quan's defeat at Hefei and his retreat to Nanxu, he called Kongming to counsel. "Last night I was watching the heavens," Kongming said. "A star fell to earth in the northwest: a member of the imperial house must have died." That very moment they received a report that Liu Qi had passed away. Xuande wept sorely at the news. "Life and death are predetermined," Kongming said consolingly. "Such grief could injure you, my honored lord. Look at things in perspective for now. We must send someone to guard the city and see to the funeral." "Whom can we send?" Xuande asked. "Guan is the man," replied Kongming. And so Lord Guan was sent to defend Xiangyang. "Now that Liu Qi is dead," Xuande said, "the southerners will claim Jingzhou. How should we respond?" "If anyone comes," Kongming reassured him, "I know what to say." Two weeks later Lu Su arrived to convey his lord's condolences. Indeed:

> Once the plan is set,
> The claimant can be met.

What would Kongming say to the envoy from the Southland?
READ ON.

54

State Mother Wu Meets the Bridegroom in a Temple;
Imperial Uncle Liu Takes His Bride to the Wedding Chamber

XUANDE AND KONGMING GREETED LU SU outside the city walls and ushered him into the government buildings. After the reception Lu Su said, "My lord Sun Quan, learning of your honored nephew's passing, offers these trifling gifts and sends me to participate in the obsequies. Chief Commander Zhou Yu, moreover, conveys his sincerest respects to Imperial Uncle Liu and Master Zhuge Liang." Xuande and Kongming, rising, expressed thanks for the Southland's gracious sentiments and accepted the gifts. They then set wine before their guest, who continued, "On my previous visit Imperial Uncle Liu said that the province of Jingzhou would be restored to the Southland in the event of Liu Qi's death. Now that the young master has died, we expect its return as a matter of course. Would you inform us when the province can be transferred?" "Enjoy your wine, and we will discuss it," replied Xuande.

Lu Su steeled himself, and after swallowing several cups of wine, he again attempted to broach the subject. Before Xuande could reply, Kongming interrupted. "You're being quite unreasonable," he said with a stern expression, "if I have to speak plainly.[1] The Supreme Ancestor slew the white serpent and rebelled against the Qin to found this great dynasty, which has enjoyed unbroken sovereignty to this very day. Now in these evil times treacherous contenders arise everywhere. Each one seizes a corner of the realm for himself, while the world waits for the rule of Heaven to be restored—under the rightful sovereign. Lord Liu Xuande is descended from Prince Jing of Zhongshan, of the progeny of Emperor Jing the Filial. And he is an uncle of the reigning Emperor. Is he not eligible to be enfeoffed as a feudal lord? All the more so when he is the younger brother of the late Liu Biao! Where do you find impropriety in a younger brother succeeding to an elder's estate? Your lord, son of a minor officer from Qiantang, has rendered no meritorious service to the Han court. At the present time, depending on sheer military power, he has possession of the six districts and eighty-one townships of the Southland. Yet his greed is not satisfied. He wants to devour more Han territory. In a realm ruled by the Liu family, my lord, a Liu himself, has no rightful share, while yours, a Sun, actually means to wrest this land from him. Don't forget that in the battle at Red Cliffs my lord bore the brunt of the fighting, and his commanders risked their lives in the field. Do you mean to tell us that the victory was due to the strength of the south alone? If I hadn't been able to borrow the force of the southeast winds, what strategy would Zhou Yu have used? Had the south fallen, not only would the ladies Qiao have been moved to the Bronze Bird

Tower, even the safety of your own family could not have been guaranteed. The reason Lord Liu did not answer you just now is that he regards you as a high-minded gentleman who may be expected to understand such things on his own. How could you be so undiscerning?"

During this tirade Lu Su sat silent. At long last he commented, "There is some truth, I'm afraid, in what you say. The thing is, it puts me in a most difficult position."[2] "How is that?" Kongming asked. "When the imperial uncle was in straits in Dangyang," Lu Su answered, "it was I who took Kongming to meet my lord. Later when Zhou Yu wanted to march on Jingzhou, I was the one who stopped him. When you told me you would return Jingzhou after Liu Qi died, once again I committed myself and guaranteed your word. If you do not honor your promise today, what kind of answer would you have me take to my lord, who, as much as Zhou Yu, can well be expected to resent the injury?[3] If I must die for the failure of my mission, so be it. My only fear is that if the southerners are incited to arms, the imperial uncle will not be able to enjoy possession of Jingzhou and—all for naught—will end up the object of ridicule."

To this Kongming replied, "Cao Cao commands a million-man host and acts in the name of the Emperor, yet he causes us no concern. Do you expect us to fear a little boy like Zhou Yu? If it's a bit of face you're afraid of losing, I can have Lord Liu give it to you in writing that we are borrowing the province as our temporary base, and that once Lord Liu has completed his arrangements for taking another, he will return Jingzhou to the Southland. What do you think of that?" "What place do you expect to take over?" Lu Su wanted to know. "The north," Kongming replied, "is too unsettled for us to have hopes there. But the western province of the Riverlands, Yizhou, has in Liu Zhang a governor both foolish and weak. That's where Lord Liu is setting his sights. If we succeed, we will return Jingzhou."

Lu Su had to accept this arrangement. Xuande personally wrote out the document and affixed his seal. And Zhuge Kongming affixed his own, saying, "Since I am in the service of the imperial uncle, it hardly suffices for me to act as guarantor. May we trouble you, sir, to sign as well? I think it will look better when you see Lord Sun again." "I doubt," replied Lu Su, "that a man of humanity and honor like the imperial uncle would betray his commitment." With that, he added his seal and gathered up the document.

The banquet ended, Lu Su bade his hosts good-bye. Xuande and Kongming escorted him to the water's edge. Kongming left him with this parting admonition: "When you see Lord Sun, speak well of us—and do not get any strange ideas. If our document is not accepted, we'll show a different face and your eighty-one townships will be lost. Both sides need good relations or the traitor Cao will make fools of us all." Lu Su made his good-byes and climbed into his boat.

He traveled first to Chaisang to see Zhou Yu. "Well, how did you make out with our claim to Jingzhou?" Zhou Yu asked. "I have the document right here," Lu Su replied, handing it to Zhou Yu. Zhou Yu stamped his foot and cried, "So he's fooled you again! In name he borrows the province; in reality he's reneged. They say they'll give it back when they take the Riverlands. And when will that be? In ten years? Does that mean they'll keep Jingzhou for ten years? A document like this—what use is it? And you actually countersigned it! You will be implicated if they don't return it. Should our lord take offense, then what?" Zhou Yu's words left Lu Su numb. After a time he said, "I don't think Xuande will sell me out." "Oh, what a sincere soul you are," Zhou Yu exclaimed. "Liu Bei is a crafty old owl, and Zhuge Liang a sly and wily sort. They don't think the way you do." "Then what shall we do?" asked Lu Su. "You are my benefactor,"

Zhou Yu answered, "and I shall always remember your kindness in sharing your grain with us. How could I let you suffer? Just relax and sit tight for a few days, until our spies bring word from the north. I have something else in mind." But Lu Su's agitation did not subside.

Several days later spies reported that Jingzhou city—that is, Gong'an—was all decked out with ceremonial flags, that a new burial site was being constructed outside the wall, and that the whole army was in mourning. Surprised by the news, Zhou Yu asked, "Who has died?" "Liu Xuande's wife, Lady Gan," was the reply. "They are arranging the funeral and the interment now." Turning to Lu Su, Zhou Yu said, "I have a plan that will deliver Liu Bei and Jingzhou into our hands with no effort at all." "What is that?" asked Lu Su. "If Liu Bei's wife is dead, he'll need another. Our lord has a younger sister, a tough, brave woman with a retinue of several hundred females who normally carry swords and who have chambers filled full of weapons. She is a woman to outman any man. I am going to propose to our lord that he send a go-between to Jingzhou and convince Liu Bei to marry into the family. When he bites the bait and comes to Nanxu, he'll find himself held prisoner instead of getting married. Then we'll demand Jingzhou in exchange for his release. After they hand over the territory, I'll have further plans. You need not be involved in any way." Lu Su expressed his gratitude.

Zhou Yu drafted his proposal and put Lu Su on a fast boat for Nanxu. There Su told Sun Quan the result of his mission to Jingzhou and showed him the agreement with Xuande and Kongming. "What a fool you were!" exclaimed Sun Quan. "What good is an agreement like this?" "Chief Commander Zhou sends this proposal," responded Lu Su, handing him the letter, "with which he says we can recover Jingzhou." Sun Quan read it through and nodded, secretly pleased, and began asking himself whom to send as the go-between. The name that sprang to mind was Lü Fan.

Sun Quan summoned Lü Fan and said to him, "Recently we have had news of the passing of Liu Xuande's wife. I desire to invite him to marry into my family by taking my younger sister to wife. Bound thus in lasting kinship, we can join wholeheartedly in the struggle to defeat Cao Cao and uphold the house of Han. You are my choice for go-between. I count on you to present our case in Jingzhou." Lü Fan accepted the assignment, readied a boat, and, lightly attended, set out.

·   ·   ·   ·   ·

Liu Xuande was sorely distressed by the loss of Lady Gan. One day while speaking with Kongming, he was informed of the arrival of Lü Fan from the Southland. Kongming smiled. "Zhou Yu's up to something; he's still after Jingzhou," he said. "I'll just step behind this screen and listen in. Go along with anything he says, my lord, and when he is resting up in the guesthouse, we can talk further."

Xuande invited Lü Fan to enter. Formalities completed, they took their places. After tea had been served, Xuande asked, "Well, what have you come to tell us?" "Imperial Uncle, I heard recently," Lü Fan began, "that Lady Gan's demise has left you a widower. Now, I have the perfect match for you, and even at the risk of arousing your mistrust have come to arrange it. May I ask your own wishes in this matter?" "To lose a wife in one's middle age is a great misfortune," replied Xuande. "I could not bear to talk about marriage, with my late wife still warm in her grave." "A man without a spouse," said Lü Fan, "is a house without a beam. One cannot abandon this fundamental relationship in mid-life. My lord has a younger sister, a woman both beautiful and worthy, who can 'serve you with dustpan and broom.' If the two houses of Sun and Liu ally through matrimony as the ancient states of Qin and Jin once did, the traitor Cao will never again dream of confronting the south. Such a union would benefit both families and both states. Please do not mistrust us, Imperial Uncle. The only thing is, the queen mother, Lady Wu, dotes on her youngest and is loath to send her away. We must request that the imperial uncle come to the Southland instead."

To this proposal Xuande replied, "Has Lord Sun been informed of this?" "Would I dare speak to you on my own without first presenting the idea to Lord Sun?" Lü Fan replied. "I am already fifty," said Xuande. "My temples are streaked with white. Lord Sun's sister is but a young woman, barely nubile. I wonder if she's the right mate for me." "Although still a girl," Lü Fan answered, "Lord Sun's sister has more strength of will than a man. She has often said, 'I will marry only a true hero.' Imperial Uncle, you are known in the four corners of the realm. This is the ideal match of 'the comely lass and the goodly man.'[4] Why raise questions because of disparity in age?" "Remain with us a while," Xuande said, "and I will sleep on it."

That day a banquet was laid out, and Lü Fan was received in the guesthouse. In the evening Xuande consulted Kongming, who said, "I already know what he's here for, and I have divined great good fortune and prosperity from the *Book of Changes*. So, my lord, you may give your assent. But first have Sun Qian return with Lü Fan to confirm the agreement with Lord Sun face-to-face. Then we can select an auspicious day for the marriage." "Zhou Yu plans to murder me," responded Xuande. "How can I walk lightly into this trap?" Kongming gave a hearty laugh and said, "I doubt if he can outwit me. I have a little 'plan' of my own to make sure Zhou Yu gets nowhere while you make Sun Quan's sister your wife without the slightest risk to Jingzhou." Kongming's boast left Xuande bewildered.

At Kongming's behest Sun Qian accompanied Lü Fan south and presented himself before Sun Quan for the purpose of sealing the marriage alliance. "It is my desire," Sun Quan began, "to welcome Xuande here as my sister's groom. In this we are utterly sincere." Sun Qian bowed down and expressed thanks. He then returned to Jingzhou and declared to Xuande, "The lord of the Southland expectantly awaits Your Lordship's arrival that you may join his family through marriage." Xuande remained hesitant to go. Kongming said to him, "I have settled upon three stratagems, but only Zilong can carry them out." He called Zhao Zilong and whispered a few confidential words: "I leave our lord in your care when you enter the Southland. Take these three brocade sacks. Each contains a useful scheme. Use them in the correct order." Zhao Zilong secreted the sacks on his person. Kongming had already sent an envoy ahead with gifts; everything was ready.

It was the fourteenth year of Jian An (A.D. 209), winter, the tenth month. Xuande, together with Zhao Zilong and Sun Qian, selected ten swift vessels and five hundred followers to accompany them to Nanxu. All affairs in Jingzhou were left in Kongming's hands.

Xuande was unable to compose himself. As they reached Nanxu and his boat came along shore, Zilong said, "It is time to read the first of the director general's stratagems." He opened the first brocade sack and read the enclosed instructions, then gave certain orders to the five hundred warriors, who left to carry out their assignments. After that, Zilong suggested Xuande pay his respects to State Elder Qiao, the father of the two eminent ladies Qiao, who resided in Nanxu.[5] Xuande got ready sheep and wine, went to the home of the respected elder, and explained the nature of his visit. His guard of five hundred, gaily clad in red, covered Nanxu, purchasing various articles and spreading the news that there would be a new son-in-law in the house of Sun. Soon everyone in the city knew of the affair. Learning of Xuande's arrival, Sun Quan had Lü Fan entertain him and provide for his comfort in the guesthouse.

State Elder Qiao, after receiving Xuande, went at once to offer his congratulations to the state mother, Lady Wu. "And what would be the occasion?" she asked. "Your beloved daughter has been promised to Liu Xuande. He has already arrived," he said. "Are you trying to fool me?" the state mother said in surprise. "No one told me!" She called for Sun Quan so that she could question him. At this time a man she had sent into town to learn what he could reported back: "The rumor is true. The prospective son-in-law is presently resting in the guesthouse, and five hundred of his soldiers are all over town buying up pigs and sheep and fruit in preparation for the marriage feast.[6] The go-between on our side is Lü Fan, on theirs Sun Qian. Both of them are being entertained in the guesthouse." The news astonished Lady Wu.

When Sun Quan came to see his mother in her private quarters, she was beating her breast and weeping. "What is the matter, Mother?" Quan asked. "So this is how you regard me," she sobbed, "as a thing of no consequence. Have you forgotten my elder sister's last injunction?" Startled by this outburst, Sun Quan responded, "Speak plainly, Mother. Why are you so distressed?" She replied, "When a man is grown, he must take a wife; and a woman, when grown, must be married. This is how things have been done since most ancient times. I am your mother. For such an event my approval should have been sought first. How could you invite Liu Xuande to join our family behind my back? She is my daughter!" Sun Quan, taken aback, demanded, "What are you saying?" "'If you don't want it known, don't let it happen!' The whole city knows, and you're still trying to fool me!" Lady Wu exclaimed. Then State Elder Qiao spoke: "I myself learned of it many days ago. I came here to congratulate the state mother." "You've got it all wrong!" cried Sun Quan in despair. "It was a scheme of Zhou Yu's to retake Jingzhou. We used the pretext of a marriage to trick Xuande into coming here so that we could detain him and then trade him back for Jingzhou, or kill him if they refused. That was the plan. There was no actual marriage intended."[7]

The state mother, angrier than ever, directed her wrath toward Zhou Yu. "You, chief commander of our six districts and eighty-one townships," she cried, "have no better strategy for recovering Jingzhou than to use my daughter in a 'seduction scheme' that would leave her a widow before she ever was a bride? Who will seek her hand after this? Her life will be ruined. You are all preposterous!" "Even if the scheme succeeded," the state elder Qiao added, "we would be the butt of general ridicule. Such a plot could never work." Sun Quan sat glum and silent.

The state mother continued her denunciation of Zhou Yu, but State Elder Qiao said, "Since things have progressed as far as they have, let us not forget that Imperial Uncle Liu is after all related to the imperial house. I would advise making the invitation to marry your sister genuine before we make utter fools of ourselves." "But they are so far apart in age," Sun Quan objected. "Imperial Uncle Liu is one of the eminent men of our day," replied Elder Qiao. "To have him marry your sister is no disgrace to her." "I have yet to see the imperial uncle," the state mother interjected. "Arrange for us to meet in the Temple of Sweet Dew[8] tomorrow. If he fails to suit me, you are free to do as you like. If he does suit me, I will personally give your sister to him."

Sun Quan, a man of the deepest filial devotion, quickly assented to his mother's demand. On leaving her presence, he instructed Lü Fan to arrange a banquet in the reception hall of the Temple of Sweet Dew so that the state mother could receive Liu Bei. "We could have Jia Hua hide three hundred men in the flanking corridors," suggested Lü Fan. "At the first sign of Her Grace's displeasure, you would have only to say the word and the soldiers would take Liu Bei and his attendants." On this advice Sun Quan summoned Jia Hua and ordered him to await the state mother's view.

State Elder Qiao, returning home after his visit with Lady Wu, sent word to Xuande: "Tomorrow Lord Sun and the state mother will receive you personally. Do be careful!" Xuande took counsel with Sun Qian and Zhao Zilong. "This meeting tomorrow," Zilong said, "is more ominous than auspicious. I will take our five hundred guards along."

On the following day State Mother Wu and State Elder Qiao arrived first at Sweet Dew Temple and took their seats in the abbot's chamber. Sun Quan arrived next, leading a retinue of counselors, and sent Lü Fan to the guesthouse to escort Xuande. Xuande, dressed in light metal armor under a brocade surcoat, was attended closely by his personal guard, swords slung over their shoulders. The party rode with Lü Fan to the temple. Zhao Zilong was in full battle dress at the head of the five hundred guards. They reached the temple and dismounted. Sun Quan received them first and, noting Xuande's extraordinary bearing and appearance, felt a queasy sensation come over him. The two leaders concluded the formalities and entered the abbot's quarters to present themselves before the state mother.

State Mother Wu was delighted at the sight of Xuande. Turning to State Elder Qiao, she said, "This is the son-in-law for me!" "He has the earmarks of an emperor," he replied.[9] "A man, moreover, to combine anew humanity and virtue and manifest them throughout the world. You are truly to be congratulated on acquiring so excellent a son-in-law." Xuande prostrated himself and voiced his thanks. The feast began; Zilong came in presently, armed with a sword, and stood by Xuande. "Who is this?" the state mother asked. "Zhao Zilong of Changshan," replied Xuande. "Not the man who rescued your son, Ah Dou, at Steepslope in Dangyang?" the state mother went on. "Yes it is," Xuande answered. "A good and worthy general," she said, ordering wine for him.

At this point Zilong said quietly to Xuande, "I was just looking around the hallways and saw armed men hidden in the rooms. They mean us no good. You'd better inform the state mother." Xuande kneeled in front of Lady Wu and tearfully appealed to her: "If you would have me killed, then let it be here." "What are you saying?" she exclaimed. "Armed men are hidden in the corridors," he said, "what other purpose could they have?" The state mother turned wrathfully on Sun Quan and berated him: "Today Xuande has become my son-in-law; that is to say, he is my child. Why have you placed men in ambush in the corridors?" Feigning ignorance, Sun Quan demanded an explanation of Lü Fan, who put the blame on Jia Hua. The state mother summoned Jia Hua, who bore her denunciation in silence. The state mother would have ordered him executed, but Xuande intervened. "To kill a general," he said, "bodes no good to bonds of kinship. I would not be able to serve you as a filial son for long." State Elder Qiao added his own pleas, and Lady Wu relented, dismissing Jia Hua with a sharp rebuke. His armed followers beat a shamefaced retreat.

Xuande walked outside to wash his hands. There, in front of the temple hall he saw a large rock. Borrowing a sword from an attendant, he raised his eyes to Heaven and pledged, "If I am to return to Jingzhou and complete my hegemon's mission, let this sword cleave this stone. If I am to die here, let the stone not split." So saying, he struck a blow, and the stone broke apart in a shower of sparks. Sun Quan, who had been observing from behind, asked, "Lord Xuande, what grudge do you bear this stone?" "Though nearly fifty," Xuande replied, "I have failed to purge the dynasty of traitors, a matter of acute distress. Now—honored by the state mother as son-in-law—now is the most fortunate moment of my life. So I put a question to Heaven: if we are to destroy Cao and revive the Han, let the stone crack—and it happened!" Sun Quan mused, "Can Liu Bei be trying to put something over on me?" Gripping his own sword, he said, "I too shall put a question to Heaven!" But to himself he swore, "If I am to regain Jingzhou and if the Southland is to thrive, let the rock split in two." He brought the sword down upon the giant stone, and it broke again. To this day there remains a Rock of Rue bearing this oath. In later times a poet visiting the site composed these lines in admiration:

> The treasured sword, the rock that split in two,
> Engendering sparks where two sharp blades struck true:
> Two houses' fortune Heaven here ordained;
> From this moment, threefold power reigned.

The two men left their weapons and hand in hand reentered the hall. After several more rounds Sun Qian looked meaningfully at Xuande, who announced apologetically, "The wine is too much for me. I beg to retire." Sun Quan escorted Xuande to the front of the temple, where the two men stood side by side contemplating the scenery. "There is no sight to equal it!" Xuande exclaimed. To this day a stele by the temple bears these words, "There is no sight to equal it." A later poet has left these lines of appreciation:

> Rain clearing o'er the scape; winecup firm in hand.
> Our realm is free of care; content prevails.
> Where long ago two heroes fixed their gaze
> Stony cliffs still beat back wind-blown waves.

The two leaders looked on as the wind swept the river. Great waves rolled and foamed, and white breakers snatched at the heavens. Among the breakers a slip of a boat was moving as if on flat land. Sighing, Xuande said, " 'Southerners steer boats; northerners ride horses.' How true." Sun Quan thought, "He's trying to make fun of my riding," and had his aides bring over a horse. He leaped on and charged down the slope; then laying on the whip, he raced up again. Smiling, he remarked to Xuande, "Southerners can't ride, you say?" At this, Xuande threw off his cloak and sprang to horseback. He flew down and swept back in a swift career. The two men stayed their mounts on the rise and laughed as they swung their whips. Today the spot is known as Halting Hill. A later poet wrote:

> What spirit in their charging dragon-steeds!
> Mounted side by side, they viewed the hills and vales:
> For Wu and Shu—east, west—two hegemons.
> And the Halting Hill remains, untouched by eons.

The two men returned riding side by side, and the people of Nanxu voiced their approval to a man.

Xuande went back to the guesthouse. Sun Qian said to him, "My lord, plead with State Elder Qiao to conclude this marriage as soon as possible before something else goes wrong." The next day Xuande was received into the home of Elder Qiao. After the formalities and tea, Xuande stated his desire: "Too many people in your land seek to do me injury. I'm afraid I cannot stay." "Rest easy," replied the elder. "I will speak to the state mother in your behalf and have her see to your safety." Xuande bowed low, thanked him, and returned to the guesthouse.

State Elder Qiao went to see the state mother and told her of Xuande's fears and his anxiousness to return home. The state mother replied angrily, "Who would dare to harm my son-in-law?" and had him moved into her private study until the wedding day. Xuande informed the state mother that it was not convenient to have his lieutenant Zhao Zilong outside and his soldiers removed from his authority. And so she moved all the visitors from Jingzhou out of the guesthouse and into her residence for their safety. Xuande was delighted.

A few days later a great banquet was held and the young Lady Sun was married to Liu Xuande. It was late at night before the guests dispersed. Xuande went to his chambers flanked by two rows of red candles, in whose light he took note of the many weapons stored within and of the sword-bearing serving maids standing to either side. Xuande was so frightened, he felt his very soul divide from his body. Indeed:

> Amazed to find armed maids in the bridal suite,
> Liu Bei suspected another Southland trap.

What were they doing there?

READ ON.

55

Xuande Incites Lady Sun to Flee the South;
Kongming Riles Zhou Yu for the Second Time

XUANDE TURNED PALE GLANCING around Lady Sun's chamber; it was well stocked with spears and swords, and armed maidservants lined its walls. The keeper of the princess's quarters said to him, "Fear not, worthy sir. Our mistress is fond of martial arts, and her maids perform combat for her amusement. That explains what you see." "Hardly the proper thing for a lady to be watching," Xuande replied. "It gives me the chills. Send them out for a while." The keeper made a suggestion to Lady Sun: "This array of weapons unnerves our son-in-law. Have them removed for now." Lady Sun laughed. "A man half a lifetime on the battlefield," she said, "and afraid of these?" But she had the weapons taken away and her maids put by their swords before waiting on her and her husband.

That night man and wife consummated their marriage in mutual bliss. Xuande distributed gold and silk to Lady Sun's attendants to win their goodwill. He also sent Sun Qian back to Jingzhou to tell Kongming the glad tidings. Meanwhile, day after day he indulged in wine. The state mother showed him deep love and due respect.

Sun Quan sent a messenger to Zhou Yu in Chaisang with the news: "My sister and Liu Bei are married—at my mother's insistence! It never occurred to me that our ruse would turn into a reality. What are we to do?" Zhou Yu was shocked; he racked his brains until an idea struck him. He then drafted a secret letter to Sun Quan, which he gave the messenger to take back. In essence it said:

> It is hard to believe that my plan has turned against us! Given the outcome, however, we must think up another. Liu Bei, the very model of the crafty owl, has three great generals, Lord Guan, Zhang Fei, and Zhao Zilong, and Zhuge for his chief adviser. He won't stay long under anyone's authority. I suggest keeping him with us in congenial confinement. Give him sumptuous quarters to sap his will to fight. Send him plenty of alluring women and amusements to beguile his senses. Try to alienate him from Guan and Zhang and keep him as far as possible from Zhuge Liang. Then we can defeat him militarily and achieve our objective. But once we free him and he reaches the clouds, he will never again be content in a pond. I pray, most wise lord, you will consider this plan carefully.

Sun Quan, having read the letter, showed it to Zhang Zhao, who said, "I am in full agreement with Zhou Yu. Liu Bei is a man of obscure origins, and in all his scuttling around the empire he has yet to have a taste of wealth and dignity. Let him enjoy a

luxurious mansion with servants and riches, and divisions are bound to develop. Kongming, Guan, and Zhang will begin to resent him. And then we can plan to retake Jingzhou. Act quickly on Zhou Yu's advice, my lord."

Sun Quan was delighted. He ordered renovation of the eastern palace and its garden
richly planted for his young sister and Xuande. He had the rooms opulently furnished
and had scores of female musicians as well as gifts of gold, jade, ornamental silk, and
other things sent to the palace for their pleasure. The state mother, who took it to be a
gesture of goodwill from Sun Quan, was overjoyed. Xuande himself began to lose his
sense of purpose among these enchantments of song and dance and gradually put returning to Jingzhou from his mind.

•   •   •   •   •

Posted at Xuande's new quarters, Zhao Zilong and his five hundred soldiers whiled
away their time shooting and racing outside the city wall. Almost unnoticed, the year had
come to an end. Zilong thought, "Kongming put three brocade bags in my hands and told
me to open the first in Nanxu, the second when the year ended, and the third in a moment of desperation. The third contains some uncanny trick to guarantee the safe return
of our lord. Now the year has drawn to a close. I never see my lord anymore, for he
indulges his lusts continually: time to open the second bag for a plan of action." Zilong
did so and found a marvelous plan.

As directed, Zhao Zilong went immediately to the mansion at the eastern palace and
demanded to see Xuande. A serving maid announced him: "Zhao Zilong is here on urgent business." Xuande summoned him and asked his purpose in coming. Putting on an
appearance of surprise and apprehension, Zilong said, "My lord, dwelling in such splendid chambers, do you still remember Jingzhou?" "What is the cause of your concern?"
Xuande responded. "This morning," said Zilong, "Kongming sent word that Cao Cao
means to avenge his defeat at Red Cliffs and is heading for Jingzhou with half a million
crack troops. He bids Your Lordship return at once to deal with the emergency." "I must
discuss this with my wife," was the reply. But Zilong said, "If you do, she won't let you
go. Better to say nothing and set out tonight. Delay and all is lost." "You may leave
now," Xuande said. "I know what I am doing." Zilong stressed the urgency of the situation several times before going out.

Xuande went to Lady Sun. Silently, he shed tears. "What troubles you, my lord?" she
inquired. Xuande replied, "The fate that has driven me to the ends of the realm and to
strange climes has kept me from fulfilling my duties to my parents and from sacrificing
to my ancestors. I have failed as a filial son. The coming of another year fills me with
boundless sadness." "You needn't bother trying to fool me," Lady Sun responded. "I
know full well what Zhao Zilong just reported—that Jingzhou may fall into enemy
hands. They want you to return and you are giving me an excuse." Kneeling before her,
Xuande pleaded, "Since you know already, my lady, I shall speak openly. If I stay and
let the province fall to Cao, the world will have its laugh. But I cannot bear to lose
you. This is the dilemma that torments me." "I have married you," she replied, "and
shall follow wherever Your Lordship goes." "Though you may feel this way," said
Xuande, "I doubt that the state mother and Lord Sun Quan will allow you to leave.
If you have any compassion for me, we shall have to part for a while." He finished speaking and wept profusely.

"Stop fretting," Lady Sun urged him. "I'll plead with my mother with all my heart;
she will let me go with you." "She may agree," Xuande said. "But Sun Quan will surely

stop us." Lady Sun remained silent for a long time; then she said, "When we offer our New Year's respects, I shall tell them we are going to sacrifice to your ancestors at the river. We can leave without announcing it. What do you think?" Xuande kneeled again and expressed his thanks: "If you do this for me, I will never forget it, not in this world nor in the next. But secrecy must be absolute." Thus their plan was made.

Xuande secretly called Zhao Zilong and instructed him: "On New Year's Day lead your men out of the city very early and wait for me on the main road. I will tell them that I am making an ancestral sacrifice and will leave with Lady Sun." Zilong nodded. On the first day of the new year, Jian An 15,[1] Lord Sun Quan held a great congregation in the state hall. Xuande and Lady Sun entered and prostrated themselves to honor the state mother. Lady Sun said, "The resting place of my husband's parents and ancestors, to the north in Zhuo county, has been much in his thoughts, causing him to grieve day and night. Today he wants to go to the river and send his gaze northward to pay homage to that far-off holy site. We take this opportunity to inform you." The state mother replied, "This is filial piety. How could we oppose it? Though you have never met your husband's parents, you should go with him and take part in the ceremony, as befits a daughter-in-law." Husband and wife touched their heads to the ground in gratitude and departed.

Sun Quan was left in the dark. Lady Sun in her carriage, having taken only the barest necessities, and Xuande riding behind, attended by several horsemen, left Nanxu city. They met up with Zhao Zilong, whose five hundred warriors served as the van and brought up the rear; the procession proceeded at a doubled pace.

That day Sun Quan had gotten drunk and had had to be helped back to his private rooms. His counselors and commanders had all returned to their own homes, so it was already evening by the time the disappearance of Xuande and Lady Sun was discovered. Sun Quan slept on till the fifth watch and could not be informed. When he learned of their flight the following day, he summoned his court. Zhang Zhao said, "The departure of Xuande will mean trouble before long. Pursue him immediately." Sun Quan ordered Chen Wu and Pan Zhang to take five hundred crack soldiers and bring back the fugitives as soon as possible. The two commanders departed to perform their duties.

Sun Quan expressed his hatred for Xuande by smashing the jade inkstone on his desk into a thousand fragments. Cheng Pu said, "My lord, your anger is in vain. And I know your two commanders will never capture that fellow." "They would disobey me?" said Sun Quan. "Lady Sun," Zhang Zhao replied, "has fancied the martial arts all her life. She is severe, resolute, firm, and forthright. All the commanders fear her. Since she means to do as Liu Bei bids her, she must have left with him. How could the pursuers carry out your orders once they see her?" Sun Quan gripped his sword and summoned Jiang Qin and Zhou Tai. "Take this sword," he ordered them sharply, "and bring me the heads of my young sister and Liu Bei—or lose your own!" The two commanders, with one thousand men between them, joined the chase.

Xuande laid on the whip and gave his mount free rein. The horses ran well. At night the fugitives stopped to rest in the carriage for two watches. Then they rushed on. But even as they neared the border at Chaisang, telltale dustclouds were rising not far behind them. "We are being pursued," someone reported. "What shall we do?" Xuande asked Zilong in desperation. "You go on, my lord," he replied. "I will take up the rear."

They rounded the foot of a hill to find a body of horsemen blocking their advance. Two commanders shouted stridently, "Dismount, Liu Bei, and submit to arrest! I bear orders from Chief Commander Zhou Yu. We have long been awaiting you."

Earlier, Zhou Yu, anticipating Xuande's escape, had sent Xu Sheng and Ding Feng ahead with three thousand men, and they had camped at this strategic point. Scouts had been sent to watch from a height, because Zhou Yu knew that Xuande had to come this way if he came by land. Xu Sheng and Ding Feng had sighted Xuande's party in the distance and were brandishing their weapons to block his escape.

Xuande nervously swung his horse around and addressed Zilong: "Soldiers are blocking the road. More are coming from behind. There is no way out. What do we do?" "Steady, my lord," replied Zilong. "The director general placed three stratagems in those brocade bags. The first two proved most effective. I have the third one here. His instructions were to open it as a last resort. I think it is time now to look at it." He opened the little sack and presented the note to Xuande, who, after reading it, rushed to the front of Lady Sun's carriage and appealed tearfully to her, "I have something to tell you." Lady Sun replied, "Do so; hold nothing back." "When Sun Quan and Zhou Yu conspired to call me to the Southland to marry you," Xuande said, "they did not do so for your sake. All they wanted was to confine me so that they could retake Jingzhou, and after that to kill me. Truly, you were but the bait on the hook. But the threat did not deter me; I came, knowing you had a brave and manly heart and would have sympathy for me. Yesterday I heard that Lord Sun Quan intended to murder me, and I pretended there was urgent business in Jingzhou simply as a means to get home. It was my blessing that you chose to stay by me. Now Lord Sun Quan and Zhou Yu's troops are behind and before us, and no one but you can save me. If you are not willing, I prefer to die here before your eyes to requite your kindness."

Lady Sun replied angrily, "If my brother does not know how to treat his own flesh and blood, I have no wish to see him again! This crisis I'll resolve myself." So saying, she sharply ordered her carriage brought forward. Rolling up the front curtain, she shouted to Xu Sheng and Ding Feng: "Are you two in revolt?" The two commanders hurriedly dismounted and threw down their weapons, voicing respectful greetings as they approached. "Would we dare? Chief Commander Zhou Yu posted us here to wait for Liu Bei." "Zhou Yu! That renegade, that traitor!" she cried. "What injury has the Sun family ever done you? Xuande is an imperial uncle of the great Han dynasty. And he is my husband. Both my mother and my brother were informed that I would return to Jingzhou. Does this blockade mean you're going to plunder our goods?"

Xu Sheng and Ding Feng protested their loyalty, saying submissively, "Would we dare? Spare us your wrath, my lady, for this is none of our doing. We act on orders from the chief commander." Lady Sun rebuked them: "So you fear the chief commander more than you fear me! He has the power of life and death over you. But do I not have the power of life and death over him?" She denounced Zhou Yu roundly and then ordered her carriage moved forward. Xu Sheng and Ding Feng reflected: "Who are we underlings to dispute the princess?" And, taking careful note of the fury in Zhao Zilong's face, they finally chose to let the princess's party pass.

The carriage had hardly advanced five or six *li* when the second pair of commanders, Chen Wu and Pan Zhang, arrived. Xu Sheng and Ding Feng gave them a full explanation. "It was a mistake to let them go," Chen and Pan said. "We were authorized by Lord Sun Quan himself to hunt them down and bring them back." The four thereupon formed a single company and raced furiously after Lady Sun and Xuande.

Xuande soon heard the clamor of pursuit. Once more he turned to Lady Sun. "We are being pursued again. What can we do?" "Husband," she replied, "you proceed. Zilong and I will hold the rear." Xuande took three hundred men and headed for the river.

Zilong wheeled round and drew up beside the carriage. His men fanned out to await the Southland generals.

When the four generals saw Lady Sun they dismounted, clasped their hands, and stood at attention. "Chen Wu! Pan Zhang!" she cried, "your purpose in coming?" "We bear orders from our lord to request that you and Xuande return." Lady Sun regarded them sternly and spoke reproachfully: "It is all your fault, you and the likes of you; you have come between my brother and me. I am married to Xuande. This is not an elopement. My mother has sanctioned our trip back to Jingzhou. Even my brother has to conform to what ritual enjoins. Do these weapons mean you want to murder me?" The four commanders stared at one another helplessly, one thought running through their minds: "Lady Sun and Sun Quan will always be brother and sister. And she has the sanction of the state mother. A man of profound filial piety like Lord Sun could never violate his mother's wishes. Tomorrow he'll change his mind and we'll end up in the wrong! It would be better to show them a kindness." The four generals had one other thing to consider. Though Xuande was nowhere to be seen, Zhao Zilong was right before them, ready for bloody combat, eyes angry and wide-staring. At last the four generals, bowing repeatedly, withdrew; and Lady Sun ordered the servants to push on.[2]

Xu Sheng said, "I think the four of us should go together to the chief commander to make our report." They were debating this suggestion when Jiang Qin and Zhou Tai rode up like a whirlwind. "Have you seen Liu Bei?" they asked. "He passed this morning, a good while ago," the four replied. "Why didn't you hold him?" Jiang Qin demanded. The four related what Lady Sun had said. "That is what Lord Sun was afraid of," said Jiang Qin, "and so he pressed his seal to this sword in confirmation of his order to kill first his sister and then Liu Bei. Disobedience is to be punished by death." "They are already far off," said the four. "What can be done?" "Most of them are on foot," said Jiang Qin, "and can't travel too fast. Generals Xu Sheng and Ding Feng, you report back to the chief commander at once and have some fast boats sent after them. We four will pursue them along the shore. Whoever overtakes them first must kill them before they can speak." At that, Xu Sheng and Ding Feng raced back to Zhou Yu. Jiang Qin, Zhou Tai, Chen Wu, and Pan Zhang led their troops along the edge of the river.

In the meantime, Xuande's column of riders had put some distance between themselves and Chaisang.[3] Only on reaching Liulangpu did Xuande begin to feel easier. He searched the shore for a crossing point, but the river loomed wide and no boat was to be found. Xuande lowered his head and mused. "My lord," Zilong said, "has escaped the tiger's mouth, and we are close now to our own territory. I am sure the director general will have arranged something. There is nothing to worry about now." But Xuande's thoughts turned to his life of luxury in the south, and tears of sadness came into his eyes. A poet of later times has left these lines on the marriage:

> Upon these shores the South and West were wed:
> Pearl-screened paths and golden rooms were shared.
> None thought the girl would spurn her status royal,
> Of those who meant Liu's kingly mind to guile.

Xuande was told of the pursuit after he had sent Zilong scouting ahead for a boat. Xuande climbed to a rise and viewed the plain: it was swarming with riders. Sighing, he said to himself, "Fleeing for days on end, my men and horses are exhausted. Again we are chased. If they catch us, who will give my corpse a resting place?" The noise from the plain grew louder. At this desperate moment Xuande spied a string of some twenty boats, sails down, hugging the shore. "A godsend," said Zilong. "Let's take them across quickly and then plan our next step." Xuande and Lady Sun climbed aboard. Zilong followed with his five hundred. At that moment they spotted someone in the cabin dressed in plain Taoist garb, a band wound round his head. It was Zhuge Liang, laughing loudly as he emerged and said, "What a pleasure, my lord. I have been waiting here for some time." On board were Jingzhou sailors disguised as passengers. Reunited with his men at last, Xuande was overjoyed.

Presently, the four Southland generals reached the river. Pointing at them, Kongming grinned and shouted, "I arranged this long ago. All of you, return and take Zhou Yu this message: no more seduction schemes!" Arrows from the shore began flying at them, but the boats were already out of range. The surprise rescue left Jiang Qin and the others gasping.

As Xuande and Kongming proceeded homeward, a mighty roar echoing over the water announced the approach of a vast fleet behind them. Zhou Yu had brought the Southland's most seasoned navy under his command banner; Huang Gai and Han Dang flanked him left and right. The southern war-boats moved with the speed of a horse in full gallop, a star coursing through the sky. As they drew near, Kongming had his oarsmen row straight for the north shore, where everyone fled on horseback or in carriages. Zhou Yu made shore moments later and pressed the chase on land. All his sailors were on foot; only the captains had horses. Zhou Yu took the lead, followed closely by Huang Gai, Han Dang, Xu Sheng, and Ding Feng.

"Where are we?" Zhou Yu asked. "The Huangzhou border is up ahead," a soldier replied. Seeing that Xuande's party had not gone far, Zhou Yu resumed pursuit. But that moment he heard drums pounding as a troop of swordsmen came charging out of a mountain covert; their commander, Lord Guan. Confounded, Zhou Yu swung round and fled. Lord Guan pursued. Zhou Yu gave his mount its head as he raced for his life. Then two more generals struck—from the left Huang Zhong, from the right Wei Yan—and the southerners were routed. Zhou Yu retreated frantically to his boats as Kongming's soldiers jeered from shore: "Young Master Zhou's brilliant plan of conquest has cost you the lady, and officers and men to boot." Exasperated by the taunts, Zhou Yu shouted to his men, "Let's make one last try!" But Huang Gai and Han Dang firmly refused.

Zhou Yu reflected, "My plan has failed. How am I to face Lord Sun?" A howl broke from his lips, and his wound reopened as he collapsed on the deck. Men rushed to aid him, but he had lost consciousness. Indeed:

> Trapped a second time in his own tricks,
> Zhou Yu tasted humiliation added to rage.[4]

What was Zhou Yu's fate?

READ ON.

56

Cao Cao Feasts at Bronze Bird Tower;
Kongming Riles Zhou Yu for the Third Time

UNDER KONGMING'S DIRECTION THE THREE COMPANIES—Lord Guan's, Huang Zhong's, and Wei Yan's—had ambushed and defeated Zhou Yu's southern troops. Huang Gai and Han Dang had brought Zhou Yu safely aboard their boat, but countless sailors were lost in the operation. Later, the defeated southern leaders watched Xuande, Lady Sun, and their party of attendants relaxing on a knoll safely beyond reach. Rage welled up in Zhou Yu; his wound burst, and he fainted. His commanders struggled to revive him as they steered downriver toward safety. Ordering no pursuit, Kongming returned to Jingzhou with Xuande to celebrate and to reward the imperial uncle's commanders.

Zhou Yu went back to Chaisang; the others marched on to Nanxu and reported to Sun Quan. Quan's first angry impulse was to send Cheng Pu as chief commander to capture Jingzhou. Zhou Yu, hoping to redeem his disgrace, also proposed new action. But Zhang Zhao argued: "Day and night Cao Cao ponders revenge for Red Cliffs. Fear alone restrains him—fear of the alliance that Liu Xuande and Lord Sun maintain against him. My lord, annexing Xuande's Jingzhou for a moment's satisfaction would expose the Southland to extreme danger of an attack by Cao Cao."

Gu Yong added his views: "Do you think Xuchang[1] has no spies here? At the first sign of conflict, Cao Cao will try to work something out with Liu Bei. And if Bei turns to Cao for protection, will the Southland know another single day of peace? Would not the wiser course be to send a petition to the throne recommending Liu Bei's appointment as protector of Jingzhou? That should deter Cao Cao from moving in this direction and alleviate any grievance on Liu Bei's part. It will also put us in a position to pit our enemies Cao and Liu against each other and to our advantage."

"There is wisdom in Gu Yong's words," said Sun Quan. "But whom shall we send to court?" "There is someone here," Gu Yong replied, "someone whom Cao Cao admires and respects." Sun Quan asked his name, and the adviser went on, "What would you say to Hua Xin for this mission?" Pleased by this suggestion, Sun Quan dispatched Hua Xin to the capital to present his memorial to the throne.[2] But the envoy reached Xuchang only to find that Cao Cao had gone to Ye to celebrate the completion of his Bronze Bird Tower. And so Hua Xin continued his journey to Ye in hopes of being received.

Cao Cao was indeed determined to avenge his great defeat at Red Cliffs, but the united strength of the Sun and the Liu houses deterred him. In the spring of the fifteenth year of Jian An (A.D. 210) the Bronze Bird Tower that Cao Cao had ordered built was completed. To honor the event Cao Cao held a grand banquet in Ye at which he entertained both court officials and army officers. The structure overlooked the River Zhang: the central tower was the Bronze Bird; to the left stood the Jade Dragon Tower, and to the right the Golden Phoenix. Each side tower rose some hundred spans high and was linked by an overhead walkway to the central tower. There were innumerable entrances and doorways, and the interplay of gold and jasper was striking to the eye. On this day Cao Cao donned a golden cap inlaid with jade and wore a fine gown of green damask; he had a belt of jade tesserae and pearl-sewn shoes. Below the height where he sat his civil and military officials stood in rank.

Cao Cao wished to observe his military officers compete in marksmanship. He had an attendant drape a Riverlands red brocade battle gown on the branch of a poplar, beneath which a mound with a target had been raised. The marksmen—officers divided into two groups—were to shoot from one hundred paces. All members of the Cao clan wore red. Other officers wore green. Each carried a carved bow and long arrows as, mounted, they held their horses in until the signal to begin. The rules were: "Whoever strikes the red center on the target wins the damask battle gown. Whoever misses must drink a penalty cup." The first order was given, and a young commander from the Cao clan charged into the lists. All eyes turned to Cao Xiu as he made three flying passes up and down the field. Then, fitting arrow to string, he drew, shot, and hit the target! Gongs and drums sounded in unison, and shouts of acclaim filled the air.

A delighted Cao Cao watched from the terrace. "Our champion colt!" he said admiringly and was about to have the prize fetched for Cao Xiu when a horseman raced out from the green ranks, crying, "His Excellency's precious battle gown should go to an outsider. You should not allow your own clansman to preempt it." Cao Cao regarded the man closely. It was Wen Ping. The commanders said, "We might as well see what Wen Ping can do."

Wen Ping hefted his bow and in swift career hit the red bull's eye. The commanders hailed the shot, and the gongs and drums sounded wildly. Wen Ping shouted, "Bring the gown at once!" But from the red ranks of the Cao clan another commander dashed into the lists, demanding stridently, "Cao Xiu made the first shot. How dare you try to take it from him? Watch as my arrow takes its place between your two." The speaker bent his bow to the full, and his arrow too struck home. The spectators cheered again.

Who was the marksman? Cao Hong. Now Hong, the famed commander, went to take the battle gown. But another commander from the green ranks came forth, holding his bow high. "There's nothing exceptional in the marksmanship of you three," he cried. "Watch this!" The audience turned to Zhang He as he rode like the wind into the arena, twisted himself round, and shot with his back to the target. Another bull's eye! Four shafts in a row were now stuck in the center of the target. "A great shot!" the crowd declared. "The prize belongs to me!" Zhang He cried.

His claim was still ringing in the air when a commander from the red party raced out to make his challenge. "I see nothing to marvel at in your parting shot," he cried. "Watch me top you all." The spectators turned to view Xiahou Yuan. Yuan charged to the very end of the lists, turned around, and let fly. His arrow landed in the center of the other four. The gongs and drums burst out afresh. Xiahou Yuan reined in, braced his bow and said, "That shot must win the prize!" But in response yet another contender from the green side appeared.

"Leave the gown for Xu Huang," he cried. "What skill can you display," cried Xiahou Yuan, "to take this prize from me?" "Your last shot was nothing special," answered Xu

Huang. "Watch me take down the damask gown." His long-range shot snapped the slender branch that held the gown; it dropped to earth. Xu Huang raced forward and seized the garment. He draped it over himself, then charged up to the dais and chanted ritually, "My thanks to Your Excellency for this battle gown."

Cao Cao and his retinue voiced their approval. But as Xu Huang started back to his place, a green-coated commander sprang out from beside the dais, shouting, "Where are you going with that battle gown? Leave it here right now." The assembly turned to Xu Chu. "The gown is mine," Xu Huang said. "What right have you to demand it?" Making no reply, Xu Chu rode out to snatch the prize. As the two horses closed, Xu Huang lifted his bow to strike Chu, but Chu held it fast with one hand, nearly wrenching Huang out of the saddle. Huang quickly dropped his bow and slid to the ground. Chu also dismounted, and the two men wrestled wildly. Cao Cao had someone pull them apart. But the battle gown was torn to shreds.

Cao Cao ordered the two men to the dais. Xu Huang's eyes were wide with wrath. Xu Chu gnashed his teeth. They both lusted for combat. Laughing, Cao said, "Courage is all I admire. That gown means nothing." And he had each commander ascend the dais to receive a roll of Shu silk.[3] After the commanders had given their thanks, Cao Cao had them seated in order of rank, and music rose harmoniously as delicacies from land and sea were served. Officials and officers exchanged toasts and congratulations.

Cao Cao turned to his civil officials and said, "The military leaders have enjoyed themselves with feats on horseback and marksmanship in a gratifying display of strength and daring. Now perhaps you learned scholars who share the dais would present us with some excellent stanzas to commemorate this splendid occasion?" The officials bowed low and said, "It is our desire to comply with your puissant command."

At this time the civil staff included Wang Lang, Zhong You, Wang Can, and Chen Lin. Each of them submitted verses lauding Cao Cao for his towering achievements and magnificent virtue and asserting his fitness to receive the Mandate of Heaven and rule as emperor himself. Cao Cao read each in turn and smiled. "Gentlemen," he said, "your praise goes beyond the measure. I am but a crude and simple man who began his official career by being cited for filial devotion and integrity. Later on, because of the disorder in the realm, I built a retreat fifty *li* east of the fief at Qiao, where I wished to devote myself to reading in spring and summer and hunting in autumn and winter until tranquility returned to the world and I could enter public life. Beyond all my expectations the court assigned me to serve as commandant for Military Standards, and so I forsook my life as a recluse and dedicated myself to achieving distinction by punishing the rebels in the Emperor's behalf. If after I die my tombstone reads 'Here Lies the Late Lord Cao, Han General Who Conquers the West,' my lifelong ambition will have been fulfilled.

"Let it be remembered that since bringing Dong Zhuo to justice and rooting out the Yellow Scarves, we have eliminated Yuan Shu, defeated Lü Bu, wiped out Yuan Shao, and won over Liu Biao. Thus peace has been restored in the realm. I have become the Emperor's highest servant, the chief steward of his realm. What greater ambition could I have? If not for me, who knows how many would have declared themselves emperor, or prince of a region?

"There are those who have drawn unwarranted conclusions concerning my power, suspecting me of imperial ambitions. This is preposterous. I remain constantly mindful of Confucius' admiration for King Wen's 'ultimate virtue.' His words burn bright in my heart.[4] I long only to relinquish my armies and return to my fief as lord of Wuping. But practically speaking I cannot; for once I relinquish power, I might be murdered—and that would imperil the house of Han. I cannot expose myself to real dangers for the sake of reputation. So it seems, gentlemen, that not one of you understands my thinking."[5] The officials rose as one and made obeisance. "Not even the great prime ministers of old, Yi Yin and the Duke of Zhou," they said, "approach Your Excellency." A poet of later times wrote:

> Once Zhougong feared the slander of the world;
> Once Wang Mang treated scholars with respect.
> What if they had perished then, misjudged,
> Their chronicles forever incorrect?

The wine had inspired Cao Cao. He called for writing brush and inkstone, intending to celebrate the Bronze Bird Tower in verse[6] and was about to set pen to paper when someone announced: "Lord Sun Quan has sent Hua Xin with a petition recommending Liu Bei as protector of Jingzhou. Sun Quan's sister is now Liu Bei's wife, and most of the nine districts along the River Han already belong to Liu Bei." This report shattered Cao Cao's composure, and he threw the brush to the ground.

Cheng Yu said, "Your Excellency has led tens of thousands of men, faced slings and arrows in the heat of battle, and never once lost his nerve. Why does Liu Bei's capture of Jingzhou trouble you so?" "Liu Bei," Cao Cao replied, "is a veritable dragon among men, but he has never found his element. Now the dragon is confined no more; he has reached the open sea. Of course I am troubled." "Do you know what Hua Xin really wants?" Cheng Yu asked. "No," Cao replied. "Liu Bei worries Sun Quan," Cheng Yu explained. "Quan wants to attack him but fears that Your Excellency might attack the Southland while he is occupied with Liu Bei. That is why he has sent Hua Xin to recommend the appointment: to reassure Liu Bei and thus deter any move by Your Excellency against the south." "True enough," said Cao Cao, nodding.

Cheng Yu continued: "I have a plan, however, for turning Sun and Liu against each other. It would allow Your Excellency to maneuver both enemies into ruining each other—two vanquished at one stroke!" Cao was delighted and asked for details. "The pillar of the south," Cheng Yu went on, "is Zhou Yu, the chief commander. Your Excellency should petition the throne to appoint Zhou Yu governor of Nanjun and Cheng Pu governor of Jiangxia;[7] and Hua Xin should be kept here at court and given an important position. Zhou Yu will then consider Liu Bei his mortal enemy, and we will profit from their conflict. Does this not seem apt?"[8]

"My thought exactly," Cao Cao responded. He called Hua Xin to the dais and bestowed rich gifts on him. After the banquet Cao Cao led his officials and officers back to Xuchang, where he submitted the appointments for Zhou Yu and Cheng Pu to the Emperor. Hua Xin was made junior minister of justice and kept in the capital. The documents confirming the appointments were then sent to the south, and Zhou Yu and Cheng Pu accepted their new offices.

·　·　·　·　·

Now governor of Nanjun, Zhou Yu pondered his revenge against Xuande even more intently. His first step was to petition Lord Sun Quan to have Lu Su try again to reclaim Jingzhou. Accordingly, Sun Quan commanded Lu Su: "You served as guarantor when we loaned Jingzhou to Liu Bei. But he's dragging things out. How long must we wait to get it back?" "The document," Lu Su said, "provides for its return only after they acquire the Riverlands." This answer provoked Sun Quan to say, "That's all I hear, but so far they haven't sent one soldier west. I don't intend to wait for it until I've grown old." "Let me go and speak to them," responded Lu Su. And so he sailed to Jingzhou once more.

In Jingzhou, Xuande and Kongming had gathered ample supplies of grain and fodder, upgraded their armed forces, and attracted talented men from far and wide. When Xuande asked the meaning of Lu Su's visit, Kongming replied, "Recently Sun Quan proposed you, my lord, as protector of Jingzhou out of fear of Cao Cao. Cao Cao countered by appointing Zhou Yu governor of Nanjun, intending to set our two houses at odds and to pluck his advantage from between. Coming after Zhou Yu's appointment, Lu Su is here to demand Jingzhou." "How do we handle him?" Xuande asked. "If he refers to the question of Jingzhou," Kongming answered, "just bellow and wail, and at the height of the scene I will step forth and make certain representations." Thus the plan was made.

Lu Su entered Xuande's headquarters. After the formalities, he was offered a seat. "Now that the imperial uncle is a son-in-law of the Southland," he began, "he is my master too. How dare I sit in his presence?" "You are my old friend," Xuande said, smiling. "Such modesty is unnecessary." With that Lu Su seated himself. Tea was served. "I bear today the important mandate of Lord Sun Quan," Lu Su began. "My mission concerns Jingzhou. Imperial Uncle, you have occupied it too long and its return is overdue. Now that Sun and Liu are kinsmen, the territory should be returned as soon as possible in the interests of family harmony." At these words Xuande covered his face and burst into tears.

Startled, Lu Su asked, "What is this?" Xuande continued crying as Kongming stepped out from behind a screen and said, "I have been listening for some time. Do you know why my master cries?" "Indeed I do not," was the reply. "Is it not apparent?" Kongming said. "When my lord first borrowed the province, he promised to return it after taking the Riverlands. I have given this matter careful thought. Yizhou province is ruled by Liu Zhang, my master's younger cousin, who, like himself, belongs to the imperial family. Were Xuande to march on Liu Zhang's capital, the world would lose all respect for him. But if he returns Jingzhou to you, where will he live? And if he doesn't, he offends his brother-in-law. Torn by this dilemma, Lord Liu cries from heartfelt pain."

Kongming's words seemed to strike Xuande deeply, for he smote his breast and stamped his feet, wailing as bitterly as before. Lu Su tried to assuage him. "Imperial Uncle," he said, "do not fret and grieve like this. Perhaps Kongming has some plan." "I would trouble you," Kongming said, "to return to Sun Quan and, sparing no details, sincerely describe to him this most distressing scene that you are witnessing and beg him to allow us a little more time." "And if he will not?" Lu Su asked. "Lord Sun has given his own sister to the imperial uncle. How can he refuse? We are counting on you to place the matter before him in the right way." Lu Su, the soul of generosity and benevolence, was moved to act on Xuande's complaint. Xuande and Kongming offered their respectful thanks. The banquet ended, they escorted their guest to his boat.

Lu Su sailed straight to Chaisang and delivered the message. Zhou Yu stamped his foot and said, "He's trapped you once again. Back when Liu Biao ruled Jingzhou, Liu Bei was already dreaming of taking over. Why should he have any scruples about Liu Zhang's land? This last bit of foolery may land you in trouble, old friend. I have a plan, however, that should confound even Zhuge Liang—but it will mean another trip." "Let me hear your esteemed strategy," Lu Su replied. "You will not go to Lord Sun," said Zhou Yu. "Rather, you will go back to Jingzhou and tell Liu Bei this: 'The Suns and the Lius are now one family. If you cannot bear to take the Riverlands, the Southland will raise an army and do so. We will then turn it over to you as a dowry, and you can return Jingzhou to us.'''

To this proposition Lu Su responded: "The Riverlands is too far to be easily conquered. I wonder if your plan is feasible, Chief Commander." "You are too virtuous," said Zhou Yu. "Do you think I really mean to take the Riverlands and give it to them? It is only a pretext. I mean to catch them unprepared and capture Jingzhou. As our army moves west via Jingzhou, we will ask them for coin and grain; and when Liu Bei comes out of the city to receive our men, we will kill him and take control. That will redeem my name and get you out of trouble."

This plan won Lu Su's immediate approval, and he returned to Jingzhou. Xuande took counsel with Kongming. "Lu Su can't have seen Sun Quan in so short a time," Kongming said. "He probably went to Chaisang, and he and Zhou Yu have cooked something up. Whatever he says, watch me. If I nod, give consent." Xuande agreed to act accordingly.

Lu Su entered; the formalities were concluded. "Lord Sun Quan," Su began, "sends his praise of the bounteous virtue of the imperial uncle. Having taken counsel with his command, he has decided to raise an army to capture the Riverlands for the imperial uncle—as a kind of dowry. Once this is done, you may give us Jingzhou. When our army passes through, however, we will expect a little cash and grain from you." At these words Kongming hastened to nod. "Such kindness from Lord Sun!" he said. Xuande, folding his hands in a gesture of respect and gratitude, added, "We owe this entirely to your persuasiveness." "When your heroic legions come," Kongming assured him, "we shall go out of our way to see that they are amply provided for." Inwardly pleased with his reception, Lu Su took his leave after the banquet had ended.

"What are they up to?" Xuande asked Kongming. "Zhou Yu does not have long to live," Kongming said with a loud laugh. "He's making plans that wouldn't fool a child, using the ancient ruse of 'passing through on the pretext of conquering Guo.'[9] Their real objective is Jingzhou, not the Riverlands. They want you to come out of the city so they can nab you, 'attacking the unprepared, doing the unanticipated.'" "But what can we do?" asked Xuande. "It's nothing to despair over," Kongming said reassuringly. "Just keep in mind that 'it takes a hidden bow to catch a fierce tiger, and delicate bait to hook a giant tortoise.' When we get through with him, Zhou Yu will be more dead than alive." Next, Kongming communicated certain instructions to Zhao Zilong. Xuande was delighted with Kongming's scheme. According to the verse of later times,

> Zhou Yu framed a plan to take Jingzhou
> Whose opening move Liang knew from history.
> Yu thinks his bait secure below the tide;
> The hook that's meant for him he does not see!

Lu Su reported back to Zhou Yu his hosts' enthusiasm for the plan and their willingness to come out of the city and provide for the Southland army. Zhou Yu laughed aloud and said, "This time I will have them!" He told Lu Su to inform Sun Quan and to have him send Cheng Pu with reinforcements. Zhou Yu's arrow wound had gradually healed and his condition was good. He placed Gan Ning in the van, while he himself and Xu Sheng and Ding Feng formed the second contingent; Ling Tong and Lü Meng made up the rear. Counting land and naval forces, they had fifty thousand men marching toward Jingzhou.

On his boat Zhou Yu chuckled to himself, confident that Kongming was trapped. When his advance guard reached Xiakou, Zhou Yu asked, "Has Jingzhou sent anyone to greet us?" "Imperial Uncle Liu," he was told, "has sent Mi Zhu to receive the chief commander." Zhou Yu summoned the man and demanded to know how his forces would be provisioned. "Lord Liu," Mi Zhu replied, "has made all the preparations and arrangements." "And where is the imperial uncle?" Zhou Yu asked. "He is outside the gates of Jingzhou awaiting the moment to offer you a toast," Mi Zhu responded.

Zhou Yu said, "For the sake of your house, we have undertaken a long expedition. The provisioning of our forces is not to be taken lightly." Mi Zhu took Zhou Yu's admonition back to the city. The Southland's war-boats advanced in order up the river. Soon they made Gong'an, but not a single soul nor war-boat was there to meet them. Zhou Yu urged his fleet on. Barely ten *li* from Jingzhou, he saw that the river was calm and quiet. Scouts reported back to him: "The city wall flies two white flags,[10] but the city seems deserted."

Perplexed, Zhou Yu went ashore and rode on horseback to the city; Gan Ning, Xu Sheng, and Ding Feng, leading three thousand picked troops, followed him. They reached the foot of the wall but there was no sign of life. Zhou Yu reined in and had his men shout to open the gate. Someone above asked who had come. A Southland soldier answered, "The Southland's chief commander, Zhou Yu himself." At that moment they heard the rap of a stick as a row of soldiers armed with spears and swords appeared on the wall. From the guard tower Zhao Zilong emerged and said, "Chief Commander, what is your purpose in coming here?" "I have come to capture the Riverlands for your master," he answered. "Don't tell me you know nothing of it!" But Zilong answered back: "Director General Kongming knows full well that the chief commander means to 'borrow passage to destroy Guo.' That's why he left me here. As for my lord, he said that because Governor Liu Zhang of the Riverlands is, like himself, an imperial kinsman, it would be dishonorable to seize his province. If you Southlanders actually mean to seize the Riverlands, he said, he will have to unbind his hair and go off into the hills rather than lose the trust of men forever."

At these words Zhou Yu swung away; just then he saw a man holding the command banner and standing before his horse. "Four field corps," he reported, "are converging on us: Guan from Jiangling, Zhang Fei from Zigui, Huang Zhong from Gong'an, Wei Yan from Chanling. We don't know how many they have in all, but the hills are ringing for a hundred *li* with shouts that they want to capture Zhou Yu!" The chief commander gave a shout and fell from his horse. Again his wound opened. Indeed:

> A subtle move is hard to counteract;
> Every shift he tried came to naught.

Would the marriage-sealed alliance break apart?[11]

READ ON.

57

Sleeping Dragon Mourns Zhou Yu at Chaisang;
Young Phoenix Takes Office at Leiyang

ZHOU YU, HIS CHEST POUNDING, toppled from the saddle; aides carried him aboard ship. When he recovered, they informed him that Xuande and Kongming had been sighted on a hilltop, drinking and enjoying themselves. Zhou Yu said grimly, "They think I can't take the Riverlands, but I swear I will." At that moment Sun Yu, Sun Quan's younger brother, arrived. Zhou received him and described the battle. "My brother sends me with orders to help you, Chief Commander," Sun Yu said; and so Zhou Yu directed him to advance on Jingzhou. Soon, however, Zhou Yu learned that Sun Yu's troops had been stopped at Baqiu by Xuande's commanders Liu Feng and Guan Ping, who already controlled the upper course of the Great River.[1] The news deepened Zhou Yu's distress. Soon after, a messenger brought him a letter from Kongming:

> Director General for the Han, Imperial Corps Commander Zhuge Liang, addresses the eminent Chief Commander of the Southland, Master Zhou Yu: Since we parted at Chaisang, you have been much in my thoughts. When I heard that you were planning to take the Riverlands, I felt it could not be done. The people are sturdy, the terrain is rough, and Protector Liu Zhang, admittedly a bit foolish and feeble, can still manage to defend it.
>
> Now your army has commenced a long campaign and will face many trials and uncertainties before victory is secure. Even the great strategists of old, Wu Qi and Sun Wu, could not guarantee their calculations nor ensure an outcome. I must remind you that revenge for the defeat at Red Cliffs is not absent from Cao's thoughts for a single moment! If he strikes while your army is far off, the Southland will fall. To prevent such an unbearable loss I have written this note which I hope you will favor with your attention.

Zhou Yu sighed, called for brush and paper, and wrote a statement for Sun Quan. Next, he summoned his commanders and said, "Far be it from me to withhold the service I owe to our land, but my time on earth ends here. No one can help that. I want you all to serve Lord Sun to the best of your ability and bring his great cause to fruition." With those words Zhou Yu lost consciousness, then seemed to revive momentarily. Looking Heavenward, he cried, "After making me, Zhou Yu, did you have to make Zhuge Liang?" He groaned several times and passed away; his age was thirty-six. A later poet wrote of Zhou Yu:

Glory had crowned this hero since Red Cliffs,
From earliest years hailed a champion.
In lute-set song he showed his sense of grace;
With cup in hand he bade his friend farewell.[2]
Three thousand bushels from Lu Su he once begged;
Ten legions took the field at his command.
Baqiu, now Zhou Yu's final resting place,
Still draws men who mourn in heartfelt grief.

While Zhou Yu lay in state in Baqiu, his testament was taken to Sun Quan, who grieved uncontrollably for his chief commander. Quan then read the document, which recommended Lu Su as his replacement:[3]

Despite my commonplace abilities, I was favored with exceptional recognition as confidential adviser and supreme military commander. Could I do otherwise than strain every fiber of my being attempting to render due service? Alas, the day of death is never known beforehand; life's duration is destined. That my flesh should succumb before my humble purpose has more to show overwhelms me with remorse.

At present, with Cao Cao to the north, our borders are uneasy. With Liu Bei living in our land, we are rearing a tiger. The leadership of the realm remains in doubt, and it is imperative that all vassals of our court remain ever vigilant and that the sovereign exercise careful judgment.

Lu Su, distinguished for his loyalty and dedication, serious and scrupulous in all affairs, may replace me as chief commander. A man's dying words are his best, they say. If this letter receives your consideration, I have not died in vain.

Sun Quan finished reading and said tearfully, "Zhou Yu, with the talent of a king's right-hand man, is dead, suddenly and prematurely. Whom else have I to depend on? How can I ignore his recommendation?" That day he appointed Lu Su chief commander and ordered Zhou Yu's coffin sent home for burial.

•   •   •   •   •

In Jingzhou, Kongming pondered the constellations. Observing a falling "general" star, he smiled and said, "Zhou Yu has died." The next morning he told Xuande, whose spies soon confirmed it. "What shall we do now?" Xuande asked Kongming. "Lu Su is bound to be the new chief commander," was the reply. "I have been watching the 'general' stars clustered in the east. I think I should take a trip to the Southland, ostensibly to offer condolences, and see if any of their worthy men would be willing to serve you, my lord." "What if they harm you, master?" Xuande asked. "I was not afraid while Zhou Yu lived; what have I to fear now?" was his reply.

And so with Zhao Zilong and five hundred warriors and an assortment of funerary gifts, Kongming sailed to Baqiu. En route he learned that Sun Quan had already made Lu Su chief commander and that Zhou Yu's coffin had been returned to Chaisang, so Kongming headed for Chaisang, where Lu Su received him according to protocol. Zhou Yu's commanders wanted to kill Kongming, but Zilong's armed presence deterred them. Kongming had his funerary gifts placed before the coffin. Then he personally offered a libation, kneeled on the ground, and read his eulogy:

Alas, Gongjin! Woefully fallen in your prime! Heaven numbers our days and leaves man to grieve. Heartbroken, I spill this flask of wine. May your spirit savor my libation.

I pay homage to your youth, remembering your deep friendship with Sun Ce. You stood for honor and disdained wealth, and you offered him your home. I pay homage to your early manhood when you flexed your wings like the storm-embracing roc[4] and constituted a new state in the south. I pay homage to your mature years when in the fullness of your powers you made Baqiu an outpost of the Southland: pressure for Liu Biao, relief for Sun Quan. I pay homage to your style and the dignity you wore when you took the junior Lady Qiao to wife. Son-in-law to a Han minister, you were a man who graced the court. I pay homage to your bold spirit, when you argued against sending Cao Cao tribute. You held your ground and ended up the stronger. I pay homage to your conduct at Poyang, when you resisted Jiang Gan's blandishments, showing self-possession, superb character, lofty ideals. I pay homage to your scope of talents, your capable administration, and worthy strategies,[5] which broke the foe with fire, subduing a stronger enemy.

I think back to that time, your dashing mien and brilliance. I weep for your untimely demise, head bowed, heartsore. Loyal and honorable of mind, noble in spirit! Three twelve-year spans of life, a name for a hundred ages. I mourn, distraught, my insides knotted with grief. While a heart beats here, this sorrow cannot end. Heaven darkens over. The whole army blanches with despair. Your lord mourns; your friends pour out their hearts.

I have no talent, yet you sought my counsel. We aided the Southland against Cao Cao, supported the Han, and comforted the Liu. Our mutual defense was perfectly coordinated, and we did not fear for our survival. Alas, Gongjin, the living and the dead can never meet. You preserved your integrity with simple devotion, and it will survive the mists of death and time. Perhaps the dead can discern our thoughts, but what man alive truly knows me now? Alas, alas. Partake of this offering.

Kongming finished his eulogy and prostrated himself on the ground. Tears of grief gushed forth. The southern commanders remarked, "Everyone said they were enemies; but after watching him at the ceremony, we don't believe it." Lu Su, also deeply moved, thought, "Kongming is a man of such depth! Zhou Yu was narrow. He brought on his own death." A poet of later times wrote:

> Before Nanyang's Sleeping Dragon woke,
> Another star was born in Shucheng town.
> When fair blue sky brought Gongjin into being,
> Did sullied earth have to make Kongming?

Lu Su feasted Kongming. Then Kongming took his leave. He was about to descend into his boat, when a man in a Taoist robe and bamboo-leaf hat, a black sash of plaited silk and plain sandals accosted him. "You drove Master Zhou to his death," he said, laughing, "and yet have the nerve to come and pay your victim homage—as if to mock the Southland for having no one of stature!" Kongming turned and faced the man. It was Master Young Phoenix, Pang Tong.[6] Kongming laughed in turn, and the two men entered the boat hand in hand, recounting all that had passed during their long separation. Then

Kongming handed his old friend a letter and said, "My guess is that Sun Quan won't have much use for you. If so, come to us in Jingzhou and work for Xuande. Here is a note to him. I think you'll find my lord tolerant and humane, a man of ample virtue who will put your vast learning to good use." Pang Tong nodded and left. Kongming returned to Jingzhou.

. . . . .

Lu Su escorted Zhou Yu's coffin to Wuhu, where Sun Quan received it. Weeping freely, he made ritual offerings and ordered a lavish burial for the late chief commander in his native village. Sun Quan provided handsomely for Zhou Yu's sons, Xun, the elder, and Yin, as well as for Zhou Yu's daughter.

These matters settled, Lu Su said to Sun Quan, "A man of middling abilities like myself should never have received Zhou Yu's strong recommendation for an office I am unworthy to fill. Would Your Lordship permit me to suggest someone to assist you? The man is thoroughly versed in astronomy and geography; his plans rival those of Guan Zhong and Yue Yi. And his stratagems rank with those of Sun Wu and Wu Qi. Zhou Yu often used his ideas, and Kongming himself respects his knowledge. He is presently in the Southland. I think you should offer him a high position."

Delighted, Sun Quan asked the man's name, and Lu Su replied, "He comes from Xiangyang; his surname is Pang, his given name Tong; his style is Shiyuan. He also has a Taoist name, Master Young Phoenix."[7] "A name long known to me, too," Sun Quan said. "Since he is here, have him present himself." Accordingly, Lu Su invited Pang Tong to come before Sun Quan. But after the introduction Lord Sun Quan found himself disturbed by Tong's strange appearance, his bushy brows and tilted nose, his dark complexion and short beard. At last Quan asked, "What have you spent your time studying principally?" "I stick to no particular subject," Pang Tong answered, "coping as occasions arise." "How do your ability and knowledge compare to the late Zhou Yu's?" Sun Quan inquired. "My studies differ greatly from Gongjin's," Pang Tong replied, smiling. Sun Quan, offended even more by Tong's tone of disdain for the man he had so admired, simply said, "You may withdraw for now. We will call on you when we need you." Pang Tong gave a long sigh and left Sun Quan's presence.

To Lu Su's question, "My lord, why have you made Pang Tong no offer?" Sun Quan answered, "He's unorthodox, not a well-balanced scholar. What would I gain?" "Before the battle at Red Cliffs," Lu Su protested, "he was the one who persuaded Cao Cao to tie his ships together. He achieved the highest merit. My lord must have recognized that." "That time," Sun Quan responded, "Cao Cao wanted the boats linked. It may well have had nothing to do with the chap. He shall not serve me."

Lu Su left Sun Quan's presence and said to Pang Tong, "My strong recommendation notwithstanding, Lord Sun is not inclined to use you. Please have patience." Pang Tong lowered his head, sighed again, and said nothing. "You must have lost interest in remaining here?" Lu Su asked. Pang Tong did not answer. Lu Su pressed him: "You have the talent to see a king through times of trouble, and wherever you go you will succeed. You must answer me truthfully: where do you mean to go?" "To Cao Cao," Pang Tong finally said. "What value has a shining pearl in darkness!" Lu Su cried. "Go to Imperial Uncle Liu in Jingzhou. He will undoubtedly employ you according to your ability." "I would really prefer that. My first answer was not serious," Pang Tong admitted. "Let me give you a letter of introduction," said Lu Su. "In guiding Xuande, remember that above all the houses of Sun and Liu must remain friendly and united against Cao Cao." "That has been my lifelong commitment," Tong replied. He asked for the letter and headed for Jingzhou.

Kongming was still away inspecting the four southern districts of Jingzhou that Liu Bei had asked him to administer, when the gate guards reported to Xuande: "The noted Southland scholar Pang Tong has come to offer his services." Xuande was familiar with the visitor's reputation and issued him an invitation to audience. Tong appeared but, instead of prostrating himself, merely gave a low bow. Xuande was dismayed by the man's ugly face, just as Sun Quan had been. He remarked, "Such a long trip must have been difficult for you." Without showing Xuande his letters from Kongming and Lu Su, Pang Tong answered simply, "The imperial uncle's reputation for receiving scholars induced me to offer my services." "The region has hardly settled down," Xuande responded, "and unfortunately we have no unoccupied offices. However, one hundred and thirty li to the northeast, in Leiyang county, they have no prefect—if such an assignment would be no imposition? When a more important post opens, I shall transfer you."

Pang Tong thought, "He's not taking me seriously," and started to urge his case more earnestly, but noting Kongming's absence, he grudgingly took his leave and went to Leiyang. After assuming his post, Pang Tong ignored county affairs and spent his time drinking and amusing himself, leaving all fiscal and legal matters unattended. His negligent performance was made known to Xuande, who said angrily, "How dare this pedant make a mess of my administration?" and ordered Zhang Fei to investigate the affairs of the southern Jingzhou counties. "If you see anything unfair or unlawful," Xuande instructed him, "gather all the facts and pass judgment on the spot. Take Sun Qian with you just in case."

As assigned, Zhang Fei went with Sun Qian to Leiyang county. They were met before the walls by the local civil and military officials. Pang Tong, however, was not to be seen. "Where is the prefect?" Zhang Fei asked. His staff officers replied, "Prefect Pang, from the moment he took office nearly one hundred days ago, has totally neglected county affairs. Every day he drinks wine, dallying in the land of the intoxicated from morning to night. Right now he is still sleeping off last night's binge." Zhang Fei was outraged and wanted to arrest him. But Sun Qian said, "Pang Tong is a high-minded man. Before we condemn him, let's go to his office and ask some questions. There will be time enough to take measures if he can't justify himself."

Zhang Fei entered the county offices, seated himself in the main hall, and summoned the prefect, who came tottering in, dress and cap in disarray. "My elder brother," Zhang Fei said angrily, "trusted you when he put this county in your hands. How dare you fail in your duties?" Pang Tong smiled and replied, "What duties do you find have been neglected, General?" "You've spent the last one hundred days here in a drunken stupor," Zhang Fei shot back. "How could you manage the county in such a state?" "I reckoned," responded Pang Tong, "that in a county this small, the few petty public matters we had shouldn't take much deciding. Wait here a bit while I dispose of them." Pang Tong called for the cases that had accumulated during the hundred days. His officers flocked into the hall carrying the papers. Petitioners and defendants formed a circle below Pang Tong's seat. The prefect wrote out judgments and delivered oral decisions as he heard the litigation, establishing right and wrong in each case with uncanny precision. The people knocked their heads to the ground and prostrated themselves to show reverence for his wisdom. Within half a day judgment had been passed in all the hundred days' cases. Pang Tong tossed his writing brush to the ground and said to Zhang Fei, "Well, show me the 'neglected business' now. Cao Cao? Sun Quan? They're an open book to me—so this scrap of a county is no bother at all!" Amazed, Zhang Fei rose from his sitting mat and apologized: "My unworthy self has failed to recognize great talent, master. I will recommend you strongly to my brother when I return."

Only then did Pang Tong produce the letter of recommendation given him by Lu Su. "Master," Zhang Fei exclaimed, "why didn't you show this to begin with?" "Because," Tong replied, "I didn't want to rely solely on the letter." Zhang Fei turned to Sun Qian and said, "We would have lost a most worthy man had you not stopped me!" Zhang Fei bade Pang Tong good-bye and returned to Jingzhou, where he gave Xuande a full account of Pang Tong's abilities. The astounded Xuande commented: "This mistreatment of a highly capable man is entirely my fault." Zhang Fei handed his lord the letter from Lu Su, which read:

> Pang Tong has too great a talent for a petty administration. He should be assigned to government documents or made assistant to a governor; then he will display his powers. If you judge him by his appearance, you run the risk of ignoring his learning; and he will end up in another's service—which would be a great pity.

Xuande read the letter and sighed deeply. At that moment Kongming returned and, after the formalities, began by asking, "Has Director General Pang Tong[8] been in good health and spirits of late?" "I put him in charge of Leiyang," responded Xuande, "but his love of drink led him to neglect his office." Kongming smiled and said, "He is no minor talent. He has ten times more in his head than I do. Did he show you the letter of introduction I left with him?" "Today," Xuande replied, "I saw one from Lu Su, but none from you." "A great talent," Kongming said, "given minor office often loses himself in wine and neglects his tasks." "If not for Zhang Fei, I'd have lost him," Xuande admitted, and he sent Zhang Fei back to Leiyang with a new offer.

When Pang Tong arrived back in Jingzhou, Xuande descended the hall steps and acknowledged his error. Pang Tong handed him Kongming's letter of introduction recommending him for a major post without delay. Xuande was immensely pleased and said, "Sima Decao told me I could pacify the world with the help of either Sleeping Dragon or Young Phoenix.[9] Now that I have both, the house of Han will rise again." Xuande made Pang Tong deputy-director general and Imperial Corps commander, in which capacities he joined Kongming in all strategy sessions and took over responsibility for training the army for the northern expedition.[10]

. . . .

Reports soon reached Cao Cao in Xuchang that Liu Bei, guided by Zhuge Liang and Pang Tong, was recruiting troops, gathering grain and fodder, and maintaining the Southland alliance in preparation for a northern campaign. In response, Cao Cao proposed another southern campaign to his advisers. At the meeting Xun Wenruo said, "Now that Zhou Yu is dead, you should first take Sun Quan and next attack Liu Bei." "If we undertake a distant campaign," Cao said, "Ma Teng could surprise the capital. During the Red Cliffs battle our camps hummed with rumors that Teng's Xiliang army would sack the capital. We must take every precaution." "Why not make Ma Teng General Who Conquers the South on the pretext of sending him to punish Sun Quan?" Xun Wenruo proposed. "Once we lure him into the capital and do away with him, we can advance south unhindered."[11] Cao Cao welcomed this advice and sent a decree summoning Ma Teng from Xiliang.[12]

Ma Teng (Shoucheng) was a descendant of the famous general Ma Yuan, Tamer of the Deep.[13] Teng's father, Su (Zishuo), had been a justice of the peace in Tianshui's Langan county during the reign of Emperor Huan. Removed from office, Ma Su was stranded in Longxi and had settled among the Qiang people. He married a Qiang,[14] and she gave birth to Teng. Ma Teng, though some eight spans tall, with a heroic physique and striking features, was of a gentle nature and widely respected. He recruited militia and aided the Han pacifications of the Qiang rebellions that plagued the end of Emperor Ling's reign. During the reign era Chu Ping, "Beginning Stability" (A.D. 190–94), Ma Teng was elevated to General Who Conquers the West in recognition of his successful campaigns. He had sworn brotherhood with Han Sui, General Who Garrisons the West.[15]

On receiving the imperial summons, Teng said to his eldest son, Ma Chao: "Since Dong Cheng gave me Emperor Xian's secret mandate,[16] Liu Xuande has been my sworn ally in the loyalist campaigns. Alas, Dong Cheng is dead, and Liu Xuande has suffered numerous defeats while I, off in this remote western corner, have been able to do little for him. The news of Xuande's conquest of Jingzhou has rekindled my longstanding ambition to help the Han—but now a summons comes from Cao Cao. What am I to do?" Ma Chao replied, "Cao Cao acts with the Emperor's sanction. If you refuse to go, he will charge us with sedition. Take advantage of his summons and go to the capital. Make use of the occasion to fulfill your 'longstanding ambition.'"

But Ma Teng's nephew, Ma Dai, said, "Who can fathom Cao Cao's purposes? You could be going to your doom, uncle." Ma Chao then volunteered, "What's to stop me from following you to the capital with the whole Xiliang army and ridding the empire of this evil?" To this suggestion Ma Teng replied, "You remain here guarding Xiliang with your Qiang troops. My other sons, Xiu and Tie, and my nephew Ma Dai can follow me. When Cao Cao sees that you have stayed in Xiliang, assisted by Han Sui, he won't dare harm me." "Father," Ma Chao answered, "if you must go, do not enter the capital without precautions. Size up the situation and act according to the circumstances." "Don't worry," Ma Teng said, "I know what I'm doing." And so Ma Teng took five thousand Xiliang fighters with him, putting Ma Xiu and Ma Tie in the vanguard and Ma Dai in the rear. Following a tortuous route, they advanced to within twenty *li* of Xuchang before pitching camp.

Informed of these developments, Cao Cao summoned the imperial officer Huang Kui[17] and instructed him: "Ma Teng is on a southern expedition. I am ordering you there to represent me as adjutant general. Go to Ma Teng's camp and greet his army; tell him I say that Xiliang is too far away for easy movement of supplies and that he is to take only a small force because I will be providing an army to support him. Have him enter the capital tomorrow and present himself before the Emperor; I will see to his grain and fodder at that time."

As ordered, Huang Kui went to see Ma Teng, who received him cordially and served him wine. After several rounds Kui said, "My father Huang Wan died in the coup of Li Jue and Guo Si,[18] something I have always bitterly resented. I never thought I would meet up with another traitor!" "Who is a 'traitor'?" Ma Teng demanded. "Cao, the traitor who victimizes the Emperor. Do you have to ask?" Fearing Kui had been sent by Cao Cao to test him, Ma Teng stopped him at once, saying, "Eyes and ears are everywhere. Do not speak nonsense!" But Kui replied indignantly, "Have you really forgotten the imperial decree sewn into the clothing?" Ma Teng now knew that the envoy spoke sincerely, and quietly disclosed the real nature of his mission.

"Cao Cao wants to present you to the Emperor," Huang Kui said. "His intentions are anything but good; precautions must be taken. Station your men at the wall. When Cao Cao comes out to review them, kill him on the spot, and our work will be done." Their conference concluded, Huang Kui returned home, angrier than ever. His wife tried to find out what was bothering him, but he would say nothing. Unbeknownst to Kui, however, his concubine, Li Chunxiang, was having an affair with his brother-in-law, Miao Ze. Miao Ze had always wanted Chunxiang for himself but had no way to get her. Chunxiang, noting her master's indignation, said to Miao Ze, "Imperial Officer Huang seemed so perturbed after his military conference. I wonder why?" "Why don't you see if you can get something out of him?" Miao Ze suggested. "Ask him why everyone calls Liu Xuande humane and virtuous and Cao Cao a treacherous villain, then see how he responds."

That night Huang Kui went to Li Chunxiang's room, and the concubine coaxed the drunken man into saying, "Even a woman like you can tell the true from the twisted. Do you think I cannot? My deepest longing is to kill Cao Cao." "How could you do that?" she wanted to know. "I've arranged it with General Ma Teng," Huang Kui answered. "Tomorrow he'll be killed while reviewing the troops." Chunxiang reported her master's words to Miao Ze, who informed Cao Cao. Cao Cao alerted Cao Hong and Xu Chu, as well as Xiahou Yuan and Xu Huang, and gave each his instructions. Meanwhile, he had Huang Kui's entire family taken into custody.

The next day Ma Teng led his Xiliang army close to the wall of the capital. In front of him he saw a cluster of red flags flying the prime minister's insignia. Ma Teng, assuming that Cao Cao had come to inspect his force, raced forward. Suddenly a bombard sounded and the flags parted. Archers and crossbowmen fired simultaneously. Cao Hong had the lead command. As Ma Teng urgently turned, another round of bombards sounded. On the left Xu Chu came forth for the kill; on the right came Xiahou Yuan. To the rear Xu Huang cut off the Xiliang army, leaving Ma Teng and his two sons surrounded. Realizing he was trapped, Teng fought furiously. His son Tie was quickly brought down in a barrage of arrows; his other son, Xiu, stayed close to Teng, thrusting left and lunging right, but could not break free. Father and son were badly wounded. Their horses had already fallen and both were captured. Cao Cao ordered Ma Teng, Ma Xiu, and Huang Kui bound and brought before him.

"I am innocent," Huang Kui cried, but Miao Ze contradicted him. Ma Teng denounced Huang Kui: "Low-down bookworm! You have ruined our cause. But my failure today is Heaven's work." Cao Cao ordered him dragged out as the curses poured from his lips. Thus, Ma Teng and his son Xiu met their doom. A later poet left these lines of admiration:

> Equal glory for the father and the sons!
> Loyal and pure, they dignified their house.
> They gave their lives to keep the royal house safe;
> Their plighted faith requites their liege lord's love.
> The sacred oath, blood-written, still remains;
> The pact to punish treachery still stands.
> This scion of Xiliang
> Was worthy of the Sea Tamer Ma Yuan.

Miao Ze said to Cao Cao, "I desire no reward, only Chunxiang for my wife." But Cao Cao said with a laugh, "For the sake of a woman you ruined your brother-in-law's entire family. A man so faithless does not deserve to live." With that, Cao Cao had Miao Ze, Chunxiang, and Huang Kui and his entire family executed in the public square. The spectators heaved sighs of despair. A poet of later times left these lines:

> For lust Miao Ze condemned the loyalist:
> He gained no bride, and Cao Cao sealed his doom.
> Not even a vicious tyrant could condone
> The base and futile plan Miao Ze had spun.

After the executions Cao Cao offered amnesty to the Xiliang troops, exonerating them of Ma Teng's plot. At the same time he ordered the passes sealed until Ma Dai was apprehended. Ma Dai, who had one thousand men in the rear, learned of the disaster from Ma Teng's escaping soldiers. Dai abandoned his men and fled, disguised as a traveling merchant.

After the execution of Ma Teng and the others, Cao Cao resolved to begin the southern campaign. Suddenly he received a report that Liu Bei was training troops and gathering weapons for an attempt on the Riverlands. Cao Cao was shocked. "If Liu Bei takes the western river region, he will have flown full-fledged beyond our reach." At these words someone stepped forward saying, "I know how to foil the Liu Bei–Sun Quan alliance so that both the Southland and the Riverlands will end up in Your Excellency's hands." Indeed:

> Even as calamity befell the bold spirits of the west,
> It threatened the southern heroes, too.

Who had a stratagem to offer?
READ ON.

58

Ma Chao Avenges His Father in the Field;
Cao Ah Man Throws Down His Coat and Cuts Off His Beard

THE MAN WHO STEPPED FORWARD to advise Cao Cao was Chen Qun (Zhangwen), an imperial censor in charge of petitions. "Do you have a sound plan, Zhangwen?" Cao Cao asked. He replied, "Liu Bei and Sun Quan depend on each other like lips and teeth. But Liu Bei's desire to seize the Riverlands offers Your Excellency a splendid opportunity: order your chief generals to join the armies now at Hefei for a direct strike on the south. Sun Quan will seek Liu Bei's help; but a Liu Bei bent on taking the west will care little about helping his eastern ally. And Sun Quan, without Bei's help, should offer little resistance, Your Excellency. Once you have the Southland, Jingzhou will fall with a roll of the drums. From there we can conquer the west at our leisure—and make the realm our own at last!" "Chen Qun speaks my thoughts!" Cao Cao exclaimed. He called up three hundred thousand troops for the campaign and ordered Zhang Liao at Hefei to prepare the necessary supplies.

Swift spies informed Sun Quan, who called his commanders together. His senior adviser Zhang Zhao said, "Have Lu Su write at once to Xuande, asking his help against Cao Cao. Xuande should agree, as he owes Lu Su a great deal. Moreover, Xuande is our son-in-law, honor-bound not to refuse. His help will keep our land safe." Sun Quan accepted the proposal, and Lu Su accordingly sent a letter.

After quartering the messenger at a guesthouse, Xuande sent to Nanjun for Kongming. Kongming returned to Jingzhou to advise Xuande on the Southland's request; he said, "There's no need for them or for us to mobilize. I'll see to it that Cao Cao never turns his eyes southward again." He then wrote Lu Su: "You may sleep in peace. If the northerners make the slightest move, the imperial uncle has the perfect plan for driving them back." With this reply Kongming sent the envoy home.

Xuande asked Kongming, "Master, what plan do you have for keeping three hundred thousand troops, plus the army at Hefei, from advancing en masse?" "Cao constantly worries about the Xiliang troops," Kongming replied. "He has killed Ma Teng; Teng's son, Chao, now commands that army and burns for revenge on the traitor. My lord, write a letter opening relations with Ma Chao. If he will march on the north, what freedom will Cao have left for a southern campaign?" Highly satisfied with this advice, Xuande sent a trusted courier off to Xiliang.[1]

· · · · ·

In Xiliang, Ma Chao dreamed that tigers had attacked him when he fell in the snow. Waking in panic, he gathered his commanders and advisers to consider the meaning of the omen. "An evil sign!" a follower said. Everyone turned to Pang De (Lingming), one of the Ma's trusted commandants. "Speak your thoughts," Ma Chao said. "To meet tigers in the snow," Pang De responded, "is a dire dream portent. Can it be that the old general, Ma Teng, has met with some mishap in the capital?" Even as he spoke, a warrior scrambled in and flung himself to the ground, weeping. "Uncle and both cousins are dead," he cried. It was Ma Dai. "Uncle Teng," Ma Dai continued, "planned with Imperial Officer Huang Kui to kill Cao; but, alas, the scheme got out and all were executed publicly. Your brothers Tie and Xiu also met their doom. Only I, disguised as a merchant, managed to escape." At this news Ma Chao collapsed in tears and had to be helped to his feet. Ma Chao ground his teeth in hatred for Cao. At that moment Liu Xuande's envoy arrived with the letter from Jingzhou. Ma Chao read it:

> My thoughts dwell on the misfortune that has befallen the house of Han. Because the traitor Cao has usurped power and wronged the sovereign, the common people are in misery. In the past your honored father and I received a secret decree on which we swore to punish the traitor. Now your honored father has been murdered by Cao; it is a crime that must be avenged. If you will lead your forces against Cao from the west, I shall check him to the south with my Jingzhou army. Then the renegade can be apprehended, the rebel party eliminated, your father avenged, and the house of Han restored. This letter tells but a fraction of my thoughts. I await your response anxiously.[2]

Brushing aside his tears, Ma Chao wrote a response to Xuande's letter and sent it back to Jingzhou with the envoy; he then mustered his army. Chao was about to march east when Han Sui, governor of Xiliang, called for him. Ma Chao went to Han Sui's residence and was shown a letter from Cao Cao that said, "If you will deliver Ma Chao to the capital, I will have you enfeoffed at once as lord of Xiliang." Ma Chao flung himself to the ground and said, "Uncle, I beg you, deliver me and my cousin, Dai, to Xuchang and spare yourself the ordeals of war." Han Sui raised Ma Chao to his feet. "Your father and I were sworn brothers," he said. "Could I harm his son? Take the field and I shall give you every support." Ma Chao thanked Han Sui profoundly. Han Sui had Cao Cao's messenger put to death. He then detailed eight companies to march east under his personal command. The eight commanders—Hou Xuan, Cheng Yin, Li Kan, Zhang Heng, Liang Xing, Cheng Yi, Ma Wan, and Yang Qiu—joined Pang De and Ma Dai, who were under Ma Chao's command. All told, two hundred thousand western troops marched on Chang'an.[3]

The governor of Chang'an, Zhong Yao, sped the news to Cao Cao, then drew his forces up to repel the enemy, deploying them on open ground.[4] The vanguard of the Xiliang troops under Ma Dai, numbering fifteen thousand, moved across the land like a flood tide, covering the hills and filling the valleys. When Governor Zhong Yao rode forth to answer the invaders, Ma Dai brought his fine sword into play. But moments later the governor fled in defeat as Dai raised his sword and pursued him. Ma Chao and Han Sui arrived with the main armies and surrounded Chang'an. Zhong Yao ascended the wall, from there to direct the city's defense.

Once the site of the capital of the Western Han, Chang'an had formidable walls and moats, which saved it from succumbing at once to Ma Chao's assault. After the city had withstood a continuous siege for ten days, Pang De advised: "Inside, the soil is hard and the water too saline for drinking. They have no firewood, either. The siege has reduced army and inhabitants to hunger. Let us pull back for a time to see what happens. I think Chang'an will fall into our hands." "An ingenious plan!" exclaimed Ma Chao and sent his command banner around to each field army ordering a retreat, while he personally guarded the rear. The various commands gradually withdrew.

The next day Governor Zhong Yao mounted the wall and viewed the evacuated field skeptically. Only when his scouts reported that the invaders were indeed far off did he relax enough to allow the inhabitants and soldiers out of the city to find fuel and water, and to open the main gates to traffic. On the fifth day the return of Ma Chao's forces was reported, and everyone flocked back into the walls, which Zhong Yao sealed and guarded once again.

Now, Zhong Yao's younger brother Jin was defending the west gate, and it was somewhere near there during the third watch that fire broke out.[5] When Zhong Jin rushed to the scene, a man rode hard toward him from the wall, sword bared, shouting, "Pang De is here!" Before Zhong Jin could defend himself, Pang De had cut him down, dispersed his guard, and broken open the entrance. Ma Chao and Han Sui entered with their forces, and the governor abandoned the city by the east gate. Ma Chao and Han Sui took possession of Chang'an and rewarded their armies. Governor Zhong Yao retreated to Tong Pass and informed Cao Cao of what had occurred.[6]

The loss of Chang'an put an end to all discussion of a southern campaign. Cao Cao summoned generals Cao Hong and Xu Huang and instructed them: "Take a force of ten thousand and help Zhong Yao hold Tong Pass. If in the next ten days the pass is lost, both of you will be executed. After ten days your responsibility ends. I will bring up the main army." The two generals sped to the pass with their orders. Cao Ren, however, raised an objection: "Cao Hong is unstable. He could ruin everything." Cao Cao said, "You deliver the supplies, then, and reinforce the front."

Cao Hong and Xu Huang reached the pass and helped Zhong Yao guard the cross-points but did not show themselves to the enemy. Ma Chao led his troops below the pass and loudly defamed Cao Cao, his father, and his grandfather. Outraged, Cao Hong wanted to descend and fight, but Xu Huang said, "He only wants to provoke you. Do not engage him. When His Excellency arrives with the main army, he will have a master plan." Ma Chao's troops hurled up their taunts day and night, but Xu Huang managed to restrain Cao Hong. On the ninth day they saw from the height that the western soldiers had freed their horses and were lounging on the grass. Most were sleeping on the ground, exhausted. Cao Hong called for horses and detailed three thousand to go down from the pass and slaughter the enemy. The western soldiers fled, abandoning weapons and horses, and Cao Hong tracked them.

Xu Huang, who had been tending the grain supplies at the pass, was shocked to hear that Cao Hong had gone down to fight. He lit out after him to call him back. But shouts to the rear brought him up short. Ma Dai accosted him for battle. Cao Hong and Xu Huang tried desperately to escape. But at the signal of pounding sticks two more armies cut them off: to the left, Ma Chao; to the right, Pang De. A frenzied clash ensued. Cao Hong could not hold his ground. Half his men were lost before he broke through the enemy lines and bolted for the pass. The Xiliang troops gave chase, and Hong fled, abandoning the pass. Pang De plunged on through and saw that Cao Ren had rescued Cao Hong. At that moment Ma Chao arrived and took the pass with Pang De.

Cao Hong rushed back to Cao Cao. "You had a limit of ten days," Cao said, "and yet you lost the pass on the ninth." "The western soldiers abused us so foully that when their discipline looked lax, I seized the chance, little expecting a trap," Hong explained.

"You are young and unstable," Cao Cao responded. "But, Xu Huang, you should have known better." "I did all I could to stop him," Xu Huang said. "That day I was above the pass inspecting the grain wagons. Before I knew what was happening, our young commander here had gone down to fight. I was afraid something would go wrong and raced after him—but too late." Cao Cao, in great anger, called for Cao Hong's execution. On his commanders' appeal, however, the order was suspended. Cao Hong acknowledged his offense and withdrew.

Cao Cao marched straight to Tong Pass. Cao Ren said, "Camp before you attack." Cao Cao ordered barricades built with felled trees and sited three camps: on the left, Cao Ren's; on the right, Xiahou Yuan's; in the center, his own. The next day Cao Cao led the men and officers of the three camps en masse in a charge on the crosspoints. When they confronted the Xiliang army, each side assumed formation. Cao Cao rode out below his banners to observe the enemy: all of them brave and hardy warriors, veritable heroes. He also noted Ma Chao: a visage as light as if coated with powder; lips as red as if daubed with vermillion; narrow-waisted, broad-shouldered, with a powerful voice and vigorous physique; clad in white battle gown and helmet.[7]

Gripping a long spear, Ma Chao, flanked by Pang De and Ma Dai, sat poised on his horse in front of his line. Cao Cao pondered the scene with admiration, then he rode toward Ma Chao and said, "You are descended from a renowned general of the Han. Why do you rebel?" Grimacing, Ma Chao replied, "Thief! Traitor who wrongs our Emperor! Execution would be too light. Murderer of my father and my brothers! We two are 'enemies who cannot share one sky.' If I catch you alive, I'll chew your flesh!" So saying, he held his spear high and charged.

From behind Cao Cao, Yu Jin emerged and engaged Ma Chao but retired defeated after eight or nine clashes. Zhang He suffered the same fate after some twenty clashes. Li Tong came out. Ma Chao, flaunting his powers, took him on and, in only a few bouts, dropped him with a thrust of his spear. Then the Xiliang troops, beckoned by a wave of Ma Chao's spear, came up in full career and did bloody work with Cao Cao's troops, whose commanders broke before the fierce onslaught of the western army. Ma Chao, Pang De, and Ma Dai plunged into the center camp to capture Cao Cao. In the confusion Cao Cao heard the westerners cry, "Cao's in the red battle gown!" No sooner had Cao Cao stripped off the garment[8] than he heard another cry, "Cao Cao—with a long beard!" In panic Cao Cao cut his beard with his knife. Someone informed Ma Chao, who spread the word that Cao Cao now had short whiskers. Hearing this, Cao Cao tore off a corner of his banner and wound it round his neck. A poet of later times wrote of the rout at Tong Pass:[9]

> For Cao Cao, dire defeat and frantic flight:
> He shed his gorgeous surcoat for disguise
> And hacked his beard, driven by his fright,
> While Ma Chao's fame was mounting to the skies.

Fleeing, Cao Cao turned to confront the rider closing in—Ma Chao! Cao panicked. His commanders bolted, leaving Cao Cao to fend for himself. Ma Chao cried harshly, "Stand your ground!" The whip fell from Cao's trembling hand. Moments later Ma Chao, overtaking him, thrust with his spear. Cao Cao ducked behind a tree. The point stuck fast in the trunk. As Ma Chao struggled with it, Cao moved off. Ma Chao raced for him but, rounding a hill, found a warrior who shouted to him, "Stand back from my lord! Cao Hong here!" His sword whirling, Hong confronted Ma Chao, enabling Cao Cao to get away. Hong and Chao fought forty or fifty bouts until gradually Hong's swordplay became confused and his energy flagged. When Xiahou Yuan arrived with several dozen horsemen, Ma Chao turned and rode back, fearing foul play. Xiahou Yuan did not give chase.

On returning to camp Cao Cao found few losses, thanks to Cao Ren's determined defense. Cao Cao entered his command tent and said, "Had I not spared Cao Hong, I would have died at Ma Chao's hands." He summoned Cao Hong and rewarded him handsomely. He then collected the defeated troops, mounted vigilant defense over the camps, and adopted a strictly defensive posture.[10]

Every day Ma Chao came before the camps to revile Cao Cao and hurl battle taunts. Cao banned all response and ordered any unauthorized move punished by death. The commanders said, "All the westerners wield long spears. We should hit back with our archers and crossbowmen!" "To fight or not to fight," Cao Cao replied, "rests with me, not with the rebels. Can those long spears reach us here? Keep to the walls, gentlemen, and watch; they will retire of their own accord." But the commanders grumbled among themselves, "His Excellency has always taken the van. Maybe Ma Chao's victory has shaken his confidence."

Several days later a spy reported, "Ma Chao has added twenty thousand fresh troops, men from the Qiang tribes." The news delighted Cao Cao. His commanders said, "What does this mean? Ma Chao is reinforced, and Your Excellency is delighted?" "I'll explain it to you when I have defeated them," Cao Cao retorted. Three days later Cao Cao learned that the pass had been reinforced a second time. Cao again expressed satisfaction and held a congratulatory banquet in his tent. His commanders snickered. Cao Cao challenged them: "Do you think I have no plan for destroying Ma Chao? What do you propose?" Xu Huang came forward and said, "Your Excellency has ample troops here. The rebels, too, are concentrated at the pass, leaving the western side of the river vulnerable. We could make things pretty difficult for them if we sent one company secretly across Cattail Shoal and cut off their retreat while Your Excellency struck the rebel troops from the north before they could be aided." "Exactly my thought," Cao Cao said.

Cao Cao sent Xu Huang and Zhu Ling with four thousand picked troops to cross to the western side of the Yellow River[11] and set ambushes in the terrain. Cao told them to wait until he too had crossed the Yellow River for a joint attack. As assigned, Xu Huang and Zhu Ling crossed with four thousand, while Cao Hong readied rafts at Cattail Shoal. Cao Ren guarded the camps. Cao Cao prepared to lead his men north across the Wei River.

Spies informed Ma Chao, who said, "Instead of attacking Tong Pass, Cao Cao is making rafts to cross the river. He means to interdict us. I shall take a company upstream along the west bank and block his crossing. Within twenty days his supplies on the east side will give out. When his men begin protesting, I'll drop back south along the river and take him." Han Sui said, "Is that really necessary? Don't you know the rule of military science, 'Strike while they're halfway across'? Wait for Cao Cao's men to get halfway over, then strike from the southern shore. They'll all perish in the river." "Good advice indeed, uncle," said Ma Chao and sent spies to discover the time of Cao Cao's crossing.

Cao Cao completed his deployment into three armies and advanced to the river. His men reached the juncture of the rivers at sunrise.[12] First, Cao sent a select team over to the northern shore to break ground for camps. Then, with one hundred personal guards, Cao sat on the south shore, hand on sword, watching the troops embark. Suddenly a report came: "A general in white behind us!" It had to be Ma Chao. The men made for the boats, shouting furiously as they clambered aboard. But Cao Cao, hand firmly on his sword, did not budge, intent on calming the uproar.

The battle cries of the enemy and the wild whinnying of their horses preceded the onslaught. A commander leaped ashore and shouted, "It's the rebels! Get in this boat, Your Excellency." Cao Cao turned to Xu Chu; the words "Who cares?" were still in his mouth when he spotted Ma Chao barely one hundred paces away. Xu Chu dragged Cao Cao toward the boat, but it had moved some ten spans from shore. Xu Chu put Cao on his back and vaulted in. Cao's guards jumped into the water and clutched the gunwales, causing the little craft to tip. Xu Chu hacked wildly at their hands, slicing many off into the water. The boat then shot downriver, Xu Chu in the stern working a pole to punt it. Cao Cao crouched at his feet.

Ma Chao came to the river's edge and watched Cao's boat pulling away. He hefted his bow and fitted an arrow to the string, shouting to his mounted commanders who outraced the boat and raked it with bolts. Xu Chu held up his saddle to shield Cao Cao, but Ma Chao's shots took their toll: one after another the oarsmen toppled into the water. On board dozens lay wounded. The boat began to swerve and spin in the swift stream. In a burst of energy Xu Chu wrapped his legs around the tiller and guided the boat, poling with one arm and using the other to protect Cao Cao with his saddle. Meanwhile, from a hill to the south, Ding Fei, prefect of Weinan county, had been watching Ma Chao gaining on Cao Cao. Ding Fei urgently ordered all oxen and horses in his care driven into the open country, causing the Xiliang troops to lose all heart for pursuing Cao as they chased the herds, hoping to catch a prize for themselves. Thus Cao Cao finally escaped.

When Cao reached the north shore, he sank his rafts. His commanders who had heard of his escape were already on shore to assist as he landed. The leather cuirass of Xu Chu's heavy armor was studded with arrows. The commanders escorted Cao Cao to a bivouac, where they prostrated themselves and expressed concern for Cao. But he only laughed and said, "That little rebel nearly got me today!" "Somebody lured the rebels away with animals," Xu Chu added, "or they would have done their utmost to get across." Cao Cao asked who the man was, and someone replied, "Ding Fei, prefect of Weinan."

Shortly afterward, Ding Fei appeared before the prime minister. Cao Cao thanked him and said, "They would have caught me except for your excellent trick." Cao then appointed him a commandant for military standards.[13] Ding Fei said, "They may be gone for now, but they'll return tomorrow. We'll need a good defense." "I am ready for them," Cao Cao said. He called on his commanders to split up and picket the corridor along the river to make a temporary barrier. Behind the pickets, battle banners served as decoys while troops were deployed outside in case of attack. Cao's men also dug trenches along the bank and covered them with reeds and brush, hoping to entice the rebels to land there.

Meanwhile, Ma Chao had met with Han Sui, to whom he said, "We almost caught Cao Cao! But some commander in a display of courage bore him back to the boat. I wonder who it was." "They say," Han Sui responded, "that Cao Cao has placed around him a select guard of superb warriors known as the Tiger Guard, led by the Valiant Cavalier generals Dian Wei and Xu Chu. Since Dian Wei is dead, it must have been Xu Chu who rescued him. He has extraordinary strength and courage and has been dubbed the Mad Tiger. Not a man to risk opposing." "A name long known to me, too," replied Ma Chao. "Cao Cao has crossed the river," Han Sui went on, "and means to surprise us from behind. We must attack before he can fortify, or we'll never clear him out." "My own preference, uncle," Ma Chao said, "would be to deploy on the north shore of the Wei and keep them from crossing it." "Worthy nephew," Han Sui answered, "you guard the camp while I advance along the riverbank to fight Cao Cao. What do you say?" "Let Pang De take the van for you," was the reply. And so Han Sui and Pang De took fifty thousand to Weinan. Cao Cao told his commanders to lure them on from both sides of the picketed shore road. Pang De struck first with one thousand armored cavalry. They crashed down into the covered pits before their hoots and cries had faded from the air.

Pang De, however, with a mighty lunge succeeded in getting back to flat ground where he smote Cao's men as he marched forward to break the encirclement. He turned back to save Han Sui but was blocked by Cao Ren's field captain, Cao Yong. Pang De felled him with a sword stroke and seized his horse. Mounted, Pang De pulled Han Sui from danger, cutting a bloody swath, and fled to the southeast. Behind him, Cao Cao's troops were catching up, but Ma Chao came to his aid and sent them reeling back, so that the better part of the western army was saved. The battle lasted until dark. Surveying the toll, Ma Chao found that he had lost commanders Cheng Yin and Zhang Heng, as well as more than two hundred men in the pits.

Ma Chao and Han Sui took counsel. "Delay," Ma Chao said, "will enable Cao Cao to establish permanent fortifications north of the river. We have to raid their camps with a small cavalry force tonight." "We'd better divide our forces so we can assist each other," Han Sui replied. Ma Chao accordingly took the forward army and put Pang De and Ma Dai in command of the rear, preparing to march that night.

Cao Cao gathered his troops and positioned himself north of the River Wei. He told his commanders, "The rebels will attack our bivouacs as we have not yet built forts. Hide troops all around but leave the core area vacant. A bombard will signal the moment to come out; we will capture them on the first onslaught." The command was carried out.

That night Ma Chao did not come himself, however. He sent Commander Cheng Yi ahead with thirty mounted scouts. Seeing no one, Cheng Yi went straight to the center of the camps. Cao Cao's men saw the western riders and sprang their ambush, only to find a mere thirty horsemen in their trap. Cheng Yi fell to Xiahou Yuan. But Ma Chao then came on from behind, together with the armies of Pang De and Ma Dai, and stormed the scene in a murderous assault. Indeed:

> Though Cao had laid an ambush for the foe,
> Their able leaders were striving to excel.

How would this crucial engagement turn out?[14]

READ ON.

59

Xu Chu Strips Down and Duels with Ma Chao;
Cao Cao's Doctored Letter Turns Ma Chao Against Han Sui

BOTH ARMIES FOUGHT FIERCELY, their formations deteriorating, until recalled at dawn. By then Ma Chao had the mouth of the Wei and was dispatching troops steadily to harass Cao Cao front and rear.

Cao Cao linked his boats and rafts, making three bridges to the southern shore; Cao Ren built camps on both sides of the river and made a barrier out of his freight wagons. Ma Chao, intent on stopping Cao Cao from establishing a fortified position, provided his men with sheaves of hay and other kindling. Then Chao and Han Sui carried the fight to the enemy camps where they set bonfires with the piles of straw, forcing the northerners to flee as the wagon train and floating bridges went up in flames. The triumphant westerners now held the River Wei. Cao Cao, unable to fortify his positions, was apprehensive. Xun You advised using soil, so Cao Cao assigned thirty thousand men to carry mud from the river to make a defensive wall. But Ma Chao had Pang De and Ma Dai harass the workers with small cohorts of five hundred. On top of that, the mud did not solidify and the walls kept collapsing. Cao Cao was at his wits' end.

It was the end of the ninth month (A.D. 211) and bitterly cold. Dense clouds covered the sky day after day. Cao Cao brooded in his tent, wondering what to do. An attendant reported: "An old man is here to see Your Excellency to speak of tactics." The visitor admitted to Cao Cao's presence was a man of great age, thin and angular like a crane, craggy and austere like a pine tree. He turned out to be Lou Zibo from Jingzhao, a recluse, who dwelt in the Zhongnan Mountains and had the Taoist name Hermit Who Dreams of Plum Blossoms. Cao Cao treated him as an honored guest.

"Your Excellency," Zibo said, "has long been trying to fortify both sides of the River Wei. Is this not the ideal moment?" "The earth is too sandy," Cao Cao replied. "What I build doesn't hold up. Perhaps a retired man of learning like yourself would have some useful advice?" "What surprises me," responded the visitor, "is that a master of military operations like yourself is not taking the climate into account. It's been overcast for days on end. With the first gales from the north, everything will freeze. After that happens, have your men move the earth and wet it down. By dawn the walls can be completed." Cao Cao saw his point. Lou Zibo then left, declining Cao's offer of a rich reward.

That night the north wind blew. Cao Cao ordered every soldier to bring up mud and wet it. Having no pots or jars, they carried water in watertight silk pouches, pouring it on the wall as they built. By dawn the water and sand had frozen and the walls had firmed.

Spies informed Ma Chao, who came and gazed at the finished structure, which he thought could be nothing less than the result of divine action. The next day he gathered his army and advanced to the rolling of his drums. Cao Cao rode out of the camp, attended only by Xu Chu. Flourishing his whip, he shouted, "Cao Cao comes, alone. Let Ma Chao come forth and answer for himself." Spear held high, Ma Chao rode out. Cao Cao said, "You were too confident that we couldn't build this wall. I have built it in a single night. Why have you not surrendered yet?" Angered, Ma Chao started for Cao, but suspecting the guard behind him was Xu Chu—monstrous, wide-staring eyes, blade in hand, set to charge—he flourished his whip again and cried, "Where is that Tiger Lord of yours?" Xu Chu raised his sword and shouted, "Xu Chu of Qiao." His eyes emitted a supernatural light. His fighting spirit was palpable. Ma Chao froze, then turned his horse and retired. Cao Cao, too, led Xu Chu back to camp. Both armies watched, dumbfounded.

Cao Cao said to his commanders, "Even the rebel can see that Xu Chu is a Tiger Lord." From then on the name stuck to Xu Chu. "Tomorrow," Xu Chu vowed, "I will capture him." "He's a splendid warrior," Cao Cao warned. "Don't take chances." "I shall fight to the death," Xu Chu declared and had a letter sent in the name of the Tiger Lord challenging Ma Chao to single combat. The letter angered Ma Chao, who said, "He dares express such contempt for me?" He swore to kill the "Mad Tiger" the next day.

On the morrow the opposing armies deployed. Ma Chao placed Pang De on his left, Ma Dai on his right; Han Sui held down the center. Ma Chao, spear high, rode swiftly to the front of his line and cried, "Let's have the Mad Tiger!" Cao Cao, beneath his banners, turned to his commanders and was saying, "Ma Chao is another Lü Bu!" when Xu Chu rode out to battle, his blade dancing. The warriors closed and fought a hundred bouts, but neither could prevail. Each got a fresh horse and returned to the combat. Another hundred clashes produced no victor. Xu Chu's blood was up. He dashed back to his lines and stripped off helmet and armor, revealing muscles that stood out all over his body. Sword in hand, he remounted and came for Ma Chao once again. The armies watched, breathless.

After another thirty passages, Xu Chu swung a mighty blow in a burst of energy; but Ma Chao ducked, then charged, leveling his spear at Xu Chu's heart. Xu Chu threw down his sword to clasp the oncoming spear under his arm. The two riders struggled for the spear. Xu Chu, the more powerful, roared and snapped the shaft in two, leaving them each with a fragment with which they belabored one another. Cao Cao, fearing for Xu Chu, ordered Xiahou Yuan and Cao Hong into the battle. Pang De and Ma Dai on Ma Chao's side signaled mailclad horsemen from either wing to join the fray. In the murderous melee that followed, Cao Cao's troops became disorganized. Xu Chu took two arrows in his arm, and Cao's panicked commanders withdrew into camp. Ma Chao fought his way to the riverside. Half his troops fallen, Cao Cao ordered the camp sealed. No one could go out.

Ma Chao returned to the mouth of the Wei and said to Han Sui, "I've never seen such a vicious fighter. Mad Tiger, indeed!" Cao Cao, however, judged Ma Chao vulnerable to trickery and secretly ordered Xu Huang and Zhu Ling to cross the Yellow River slightly above its angle and fortify the west bank for a two-fronted attack. Several days later Cao Cao observed Ma Chao from the wall approach his front outworks with a few hundred riders and there race back and forth. After watching him for a long time, Cao Cao threw his headgear to the ground and cried, "This Ma must die! Or I shall have no burying place!" Xihou Yuan answered hotly, "I will crush the Ma rebels or die here in the attempt." So saying, he led his thousand men into the field, and Cao Cao, unable to stop him yet fearing for his life, hastily mounted to support him.

Ma Chao, seeing the enemy in the field again, switched his van and rear squadrons and deployed in a single file. As Xiahou Yuan arrived, Ma Chao engaged his force directly. Ma Chao, surrounded by the turmoil of battle, spotted Cao Cao in the distance and went at him, shaking off Xiahou Yuan. Frightened, Cao Cao wheeled and fled. His order of battle began falling apart. Ma Chao gave hot pursuit but pulled back to camp on the stunning news that Cao Cao's men had fortified the west bank. Ma Chao consulted with Han Sui. "They saw their opening and crossed to the west bank," Chao said. "They have us, van and rear. What to do?" Lieutenant Commander Li Kan said, "Offer them a piece of our land, and let each side withdraw. Let us get through the winter, and we'll think of something else when spring comes." "Good advice," Han Sui said. "Take it."

Ma Chao hesitated. But the other commanders, Yang Qiu and Hou Xuan, urged him to seek peace. And so Han Sui sent Yang Qiu to Cao Cao with an offer of territory. Cao Cao said to the envoy, "You may return to your camp. I will send my answer tomorrow." Yang Qiu departed. Jia Xu entered Cao Cao's tent and said, "What is Your Excellency's decision?" "What's your view?" Cao Cao replied. "In warfare," Jia Xu said, "there can never be too much trickery. Agree to it now and later we can find a way to turn them against each other. If Han Sui and Ma Chao become suspicious of each other, we won't have much trouble destroying them." Cao Cao clapped his hands with satisfaction and said, "Great thinkers think alike! Your plans accord perfectly with my own thinking."

Cao Cao returned the following answer: "Give us time to pull back and we will return the west bank." Accordingly, Cao Cao had his pontoon bridges set up as an indication of his intention to recross the river and withdraw. On receiving this note, Ma Chao said to Han Sui, "Although Cao Cao has agreed to a peace, he is too treacherous to read clearly. Unless we are prepared, we could fall into his hands. Let's rotate our forces. Today you take Cao Cao, uncle, and I'll take Xu Huang; tomorrow we'll switch. Our separate defense should foil any tricks they try." Ma Chao and Han Sui proceeded accordingly.

A courier soon apprised Cao Cao of these tactics. "Now we will succeed," Cao said privately to Jia Xu. Then he asked the runner, "Whom will I be facing tomorrow?" "Han Sui," was the reply. The next day Cao Cao rode out of camp, a lone rider conspicuous in the midst of his accompanying lieutenants. Han Sui's soldiers, few of whom had ever seen Cao Cao, stared at him. Cao Cao cried: "You'd like a look at Lord Cao? I'm only human; I haven't got four eyes or two mouths—I'm just full of ideas, a bit smarter, that's all!" Han Sui's men blanched. Cao sent a message: "His Excellency earnestly requests a meeting with General Han."

Han Sui appeared and, seeing Cao Cao completely unarmed, put off his own gear and rode forth alone. As the horses touched heads, their masters reined in and began talking. "General," Cao Cao said, "your father and I were cited as filial and honest in the same year, and he was ever like an uncle to me. You and I, moreover, have both served the Emperor. The years have slipped by. How old are you now, General?" "Forty," was his reply. "Those days in the capital," Cao Cao went on, "that was our springtide, our youth. Who would have expected the middle years to come so soon! If only the world were at peace, if we could have the pleasure of one another's company . . ." And Cao Cao continued making small talk about the past, never alluding to the military situation. After two hours they parted, Cao laughing heartily, and returned to their respective camps.

As soon as the incident was reported to Ma Chao, he hurried to Han Sui and demanded, "What was Cao Cao talking about today?" "Nothing—the old days in the capi-

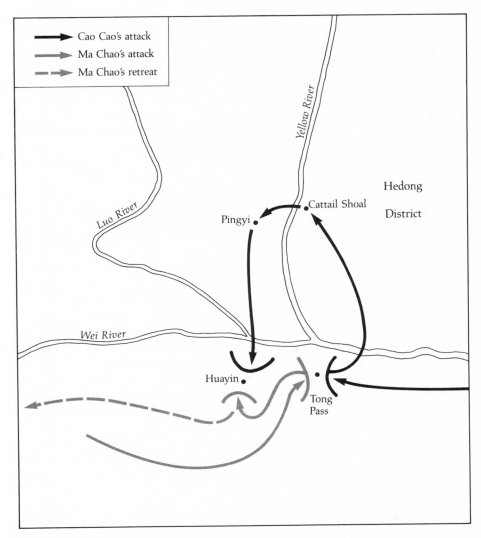

MAP 5. The battle at the Wei River. Source: Liu Chunfan, *Sanguo shihua* (Beijing: Beijing chubanshe, 1981), p. 114.

tal," was Han Sui's reply. "Why did you say nothing about the fighting?" Ma Chao demanded. "He didn't mention it," answered Han Sui, "how could I?" But suspicion had been planted. Ma Chao withdrew without another word.

In camp Cao Cao asked his adviser Jia Xu, "Did you know the purpose of my conversation with Han Sui?" "It was an ingenious one," Jia Xu responded, "but not enough to divide your enemies. I know a way, however, to engender hatred between them." "Yes?" Cao Cao inquired. "A brawny brute like Ma Chao," Jia Xu went on, "knows nothing of intrigue. Your Excellency, write Han Sui in your own hand, something vague in content, smearing or scratching out words and writing over others in the important parts. Send it to Han Sui, sealed, but make sure Ma Chao knows so that he'll be certain to ask to see the letter. The alterations will make him suspect that Han Sui has doctored it to keep him from discovering some secret activity. This will confirm his suspicions about the conversation on horseback—suspicions that will breed confusion between them. Furthermore, if we can quietly create friction between him and Han Sui's commanders, Ma Chao will be as good as dead." "An excellent plan!" Cao Cao said and wrote Han Sui as Jia Xu had advised, conspicuously sending a number of his followers to bear the envelope.[1]

As expected, Ma Chao soon learned of the letter and went directly to Han Sui, demanding to see it. When Han Sui handed him the letter, Ma Chao, noting the deletions and changes, asked, "Why are these passages all blotted out?" "That's how it came," Han Sui replied. "I don't know why." "Why would he send a rough draft?" Ma Chao continued. "Uncle, you must have changed something so that I wouldn't find out certain details." "He must have sealed the draft by mistake," Han Sui countered. "I'm not convinced," Ma Chao said. "Cao Cao is far too meticulous for that. You and I, uncle, have joined to fight that traitor. Why are you double-crossing me?" "If you do not trust me," replied Han Sui, "then let me lure Cao Cao into conversation again tomorrow; you can race out and kill him with a spear stroke." "That would show your sincerity, uncle," was Ma Chao's reply. So it was agreed.

Next day Han Sui led five commanders—Hou Xuan, Li Kan, Liang Xing, Ma Wan, and Yang Qiu—onto the field. Ma Chao was concealed in the shadows of the opening of the formation. Han Sui sent a man to Cao Cao's camp. "General Han Sui," he called out, "requests that the prime minister come forth and continue the talk." Cao Cao had Cao Hong lead a few score horsemen out to answer Han Sui. Cao Hong rode to within a few feet of Han Sui, bent forward over his horse, and said, "His Excellency was most gratified by your words last night. Let there be no slipup." He then rode back to his line. Ma Chao overheard and flew into a rage. Raising his spear, he forged ahead and struck at Han Sui. The five commanders intervened and tried to get Ma Chao back to camp. "Worthy nephew," Han Sui cried, "you must not doubt me. I bear you no malice." But Ma Chao, having lost all confidence in Han Sui, left in a vengeful mood.

Taking counsel with his five commanders, Han Sui asked, "How can this be made right?" Yang Qiu said, "With his martial skill, Ma Chao thinks too highly of himself; he has always tended to bully you. Even if Cao Cao is defeated, Chao will continue in his arrogance. In my humble opinion we should secretly enter Lord Cao's service; later you will have a lordship for sure." "Ma Teng and I were sworn brothers," Han Sui said. "I cannot bear to betray that trust." "There is no choice, at this point,"[2] responded Yang Qiu. "Then who will take the message?" Han Sui asked. "I'll do it," Yang Qiu answered. And so Han Sui sent Yang Qiu to Cao Cao's camp with a secret offer of surrender.

Cao Cao received this letter with great delight. He had Han Sui enfeoffed as lord of Xiliang and Yang Qiu as governor. The other commanders received official appointments all. They agreed on signal fires to coordinate their moves against Ma Chao. After taking leave, Yang Qiu reported to Han Sui in full, adding, "Tonight at the signal, those inside and those outside will work together." Well pleased, Han Sui ordered his men to accumulate kindling behind the tents of the central army. The five commanders waited with their weapons near to hand. Han Sui had also proposed holding a banquet in order to murder Ma Chao, but this plan had not yet been put into action.

Little did Han Sui know that Ma Chao had already discovered the details of the plot against him. Taking a few trusted followers, Ma Chao went directly to Han Sui, sword in hand. Pang De and Ma Dai followed close behind. Ma Chao silently entered Han Sui's tent. There were the five commanders whispering with Han Sui; and there was Yang Qiu actually saying, "This cannot be delayed. It must be done now." Roused to fury, Ma Chao confronted them, swinging his sword as he bellowed, "You pack of thieves would murder me?" Everyone was astounded. Ma Chao sliced at Han Sui's face. Sui tried to ward off the blow; the blade swiftly severed his left hand. All five commanders then rushed Chao waving their swords. Ma Chao strode outside but was quickly surrounded by the five, who flailed wildly at him. Wielding his fine sword, Ma Chao took them on. Wherever his blade flashed, fresh blood shot forth: he cut down Ma Wan and hacked Liang Xing to death; the other three fled. Ma Chao went back into the tent to finish off Han Sui, but Sui's attendants had already pulled him to safety.[3]

Behind the tent a torch flared, and the troops in every camp began stirring. Ma Chao mounted swiftly. Pang De and Ma Dai too joined in the furious combat. By the time Ma Chao had forced his way free, Cao Cao's units were on all sides: Xu Chu in front, Xu Huang behind; Xiahou Yuan to the left, Cao Hong to the right. The Xiliang troops began fighting among themselves. Ma Chao, having lost sight of Pang De and Ma Dai, took up a position on Wei Bridge with a hundred riders. Day was starting to break. Li Kan, one of Han Sui's five commanders, appeared with a small force. Ma Chao put him to flight but broke off the chase when Yu Jin, Cao's commander, arrived. Yu Jin, coming from behind, shot at Ma Chao. Detecting the hum of the string, Ma Chao leaned away, and the arrow struck down Li Kan instead. Then Chao turned on Yu Jin; but Jin galloped away, and Chao subsequently resumed his place on the bridge.

Cao Cao's main force reached the scene, his famed Tiger Guard in the fore. Arrows rained on Ma Chao from two sides, but he managed to deflect many with his spear as his guard made short, murderous charges. Alas, Cao Cao's mass of troops was too solid to break through. From the bridge Ma Chao gave a deafening yell, then dashed away to the north of the stream. His guard was completely cut off. All alone now, Chao tried to force his way out, but the bolt from a sniper's crossbow knocked his mount from under him. Cao Cao's men closed in.

At this moment of dire peril, a body of men flashed into view on the northwest, led by Pang De and Ma Dai. They brought Ma Chao to safety and gave him a horse. Then they pushed forward, leaving a bloody trail, and escaped to the northwest. Hearing of Ma Chao's getaway, Cao Cao ordered his commanders: "Ride day and night till you ride him down. A thousand pieces of gold and a fief of ten thousand households to the man who takes his head. And the man who takes him alive will be supreme general." His commanders set out one after the other in quest of the prize fugitive. Ma Chao, meanwhile, heedless of his own fatigue or his mount's, dashed on, gradually leaving his followers behind. Those on foot were mostly taken captive. Attended by only thirty riders, Ma Chao, Pang De, and Ma Dai headed for Lintao in Longxi.

•   •   •   •   •

Cao Cao personally pursued Ma Chao as far as Anding before returning to Chang'an, where he received all his returning commanders. Han Sui, crippled by loss of his left hand, was permitted to remain in Chang'an and was made lord of Xiliang. Yang Qiu and Hou Xuan were enfeoffed as lords of the first rank and ordered to defend Weikou. Cao Cao gave the order for all to withdraw east to Xuchang. At that moment a Liangzhou military adviser, Yang Fu (Yishan), presented himself before Cao Cao and said: "Ma Chao has the prowess of a Lü Bu, and the Qiang hold him dear. If Your Excellency does not remove him before he regains his strength, the dynasty will never again control the western districts. I pray Your Excellency not to go back to the capital."

"Initially," Cao Cao replied, "I had intended to leave a force to conquer him. But, alas, the northern heartland has troubles enough of its own, and the south, too, has yet to be controlled. I cannot remain here. You shall have to undertake it for me." Yang Fu assented and requested the appointment of Wei Kang as imperial inspector of Liangzhou to help him defend Jicheng against Ma Chao. Fu also asked Cao Cao to leave well-armed troops in Chang'an for support. "I have arranged it," Cao Cao replied. "Don't worry." Yang Fu took his leave.

Cao Cao's commanders put a question to him: "When the rebels first took Tong Pass, the way north was wide open. Why did Your Excellency contest the pass so long before crossing to the north and attacking Pingyi from the east bank of the Yellow River?" Cao Cao replied, "When they had the pass, if we had gone for the east bank right away, the rebels would have fortified the crossing points and kept us from getting over to the west bank. Instead, by concentrating my troops at the pass I forced the rebels to throw everything into defending themselves on the south side of the river, leaving the west bank to their north undefended. That way, Xu Huang and Zhu Ling were able to cross first; then I followed, linking up the carriages and posts to make a sheltered road, and building walls of iced mud—all in order to make the rebels so confident of our weakness that they would fail to prepare their own defenses. Next, I used trickery to divide our enemies while conserving our soldiers' strength so that we could break them with a surprise attack—an example of what is meant by 'There's no time to cover the ears after thunder peals.' The possibilities in warfare are manifold."

The commanders asked: "Your Excellency, every time an increase in the rebels' troop strength was announced, you seemed pleased. Why?" "Guanzhong is a remote region," Cao Cao responded. "If the rebels had kept to their strongpoints, it would have taken us a year or two to restore order. But when they gathered in one place, despite their numbers, their lack of unity made it easy to cause dissension and annihilate them in a single action. That's what pleased me." The commanders expressed their profound respect, saying, "Your Excellency's marvelous tactics far surpass anything we would have devised." "I could not do without the efforts of my officers and officials," Cao Cao replied and distributed rewards to the various corps. He left Xiahou Yuan in Chang'an to redeploy the surrendered soldiers into several commands. Xiahou Yuan recommended to Cao Cao that Zhang Ji (Derong) from Gaoling in Pingyi serve as governor of Jingzhao district, defending Chang'an jointly with himself.

After these arrangements Cao Cao brought the army home to Xuchang. Emperor Xian personally welcomed him before the walls. By imperial proclamation, Cao Cao was excused from using his given name before the Emperor; he was also permitted to enter the court without hurrying forward with his body bowed, and to enter the principal hall shod and armed with a sword—all after precedents set for the first prime minister of the Han, Xiao He. From this time forward Cao Cao's reputation flourished and spread at home and abroad.

•   •   •   •   •

Details of these events made their way to Hanzhong, alarming Zhang Lu, the governor of Hanning. Zhang Lu was originally from Feng in the fief at Pei. His grandfather, Zhang Ling, the Taoist of the Swan Call Hills in the Riverlands, led people astray with faked miracles that won him a great name. After Zhang Ling's death, his son Heng followed in his footsteps. Those among the people intending to study the Tao had to contribute five pecks of rice; thus, Zhang Heng earned the popular sobriquet Rice Rebel. Zhang Heng died, and Zhang Lu carried on his work in Hanzhong. He styled himself lord-preceptor, and his disciples were known as the Ghost Squad. Captains were known as libationers; and those commanding large numbers were called head libationers.

The principal concern of this sect was sincerity; neither lying nor deception was condoned. Anyone who became ill was placed in a quiet room in a sanctuary so that he could reflect on his past mistakes and make a clean breast of them. Then all prayed for the patient. A control-libationer directed the prayer session. The method was as follows. The sick man's full name was written out, his penance explained, and three copies of his "petition to the three realms" were made: one to place on a hilltop in appeal to Heaven, one to bury in the ground in appeal to earth, and one to drop in the water in appeal to the masters of the netherworld. After this was done, and once the illness had passed, the patient donated five pecks of rice as an expression of gratitude.

This Taoist sect also had public bins filled with rice, fuel, and meat. Anyone who came was allowed whatever he could consume, though he would be punished by Heaven for taking more than an honest share. Within the dominion of the sect, offenders were forgiven three times. Only those who refused to mend their ways suffered punishment. There were no court officials; all were attached to the libationer. Thus had Hanzhong been ruled for thirty years. The court regarded it too far away to be worth an expedition, and so simply commissioned Zhang Lu as Imperial Corps Commander Who Garrisons the South and governor of Hanning; his only responsibility was to forward local tribute.

When Zhang Lu heard that Cao Cao had defeated the western army and was making his might felt in the region, he called his advisers to counsel. "Ma Teng of Xiliang," he said, "has met his doom, and Ma Chao has taken a beating. That means Cao Cao will attack us. I am going to declare myself prince of Hanning and take charge of the resistance. What are your views?" Yan Pu said, "The people of the Han River region, numbering over one hundred thousand households, have great wealth and ample grain as well as natural fortification on all four sides. Ma Chao's defeat has sent tens of thousands of Xiliang soldiers through the Zi-Wu valley and into Hanzhong. In my humble view, Liu Zhang, the protector of Yizhou, the Riverlands, is too muddled to govern with any effect. Let us first seize the forty-one departments of the Riverlands as our base before we take the step of declaring an independent kingdom." Zhang Lu accepted this advice with pleasure and consulted with his brother Zhang Wei on the mustering of the troops.[4]

News of these developments soon reached the Riverlands. The province's protector, Liu Zhang (Jiyu), was the son of Liu Yan and a descendant of Prince Gong of Lu.[5] During

Emperor Zhang's reign of Primal Harmony (Yuan He, A.D. 84–86), Prince Gong's kingdom was shifted to Jingling, and so the clan's sons settled there. Later Liu Yan's position was shifted to that of protector of Yizhou; he died of an ulcer during the first year of Prosperous Tranquility (Xing Ping, A.D. 194). The main officials of the province, Zhao Wei and others, supported Liu Zhang as his replacement.

Liu Zhang and Zhang Lu were enemies, for the protector had killed Lu's mother and younger brother. Accordingly, Liu Zhang had set up Pang Xi as governor of Baxi to serve as a buffer against Zhang Lu. Informed by the governor that Zhang Lu meant to march on the Riverlands, the protector, a timid sort, became unnerved and confused. But at an emergency meeting of Liu Zhang's advisers, someone stepped boldly forth and said, "Set your mind at ease, my lord. I don't have much ability, but this tough little tongue of mine can forestall Zhang Lu's plan to take our territory." Indeed:

> Because a man of Shu stepped forward with a plan,
> The Jingzhou champions were drawn into the game.

Who was that man of Shu?
READ ON.

60

Zhang Song Confounds Yang Xiu;
Pang Tong Proposes the Conquest of Shu

THE PLAN WAS PROPOSED BY ZHANG SONG (Yongnian), the lieutenant inspector of Yizhou. Zhang Song was a most unusual looking man. He had an angular brow and a tapered skull; his nose was flat, his teeth protruding; he was under five feet tall; and his voice was plangent as a bronze bell. To Inspector Liu Zhang's question, "Lieutenant, what can be done about the threat Zhang Lu poses from Hanzhong?" Zhang Song responded, "Cao Cao, based in Xuchang, has swept the northeast of seditious elements, wiping out Lü Bu, Yuan Shao, and Yuan Shu.[1] Today, after defeating Ma Chao, he has emerged unrivaled. My lord, prepare gifts for me to take to the capital. If I can persuade Cao Cao to march on Hanzhong, Zhang Lu will have little time to concern himself with our territory of Shu." Delighted with this counsel, Liu Zhang collected gold and pearls and rich textiles for his lieutenant to take to the capital. Meanwhile, after quietly providing himself with maps of the Riverlands, Zhang Song set out attended by a few horsemen. His movements were soon reported in Jingzhou, and Kongming sent men to the capital to bring back information on Zhang Song's mission.[2]

Having arrived in Xuchang, Zhang Song sought audience daily at Cao Cao's ministerial quarters. Now Cao Cao, swelled with pride after his victory over Ma Chao, held banquets regularly and kept to his residence, from which he conducted government business. It took Zhang Song three days to get his name announced. Finally, after bribing Cao's attendants, he gained admittance. Zhang Song presented himself to Cao Cao, who was seated in the main hall, and prostrated himself. Cao Cao asked, "Your master, Liu Zhang, has submitted no tribute for years. Why?" "The routes are virtually impassable," Zhang Song replied. "With so many highwaymen, we have been unable to send tribute." Cao Cao said derisively, "I have cleaned up the north; where are there any thieves?" "To the south there is Sun Quan," Zhang Song answered, "to the north, Zhang Lu; and to the west, Liu Bei—the least of whom has a hundred thousand under arms. How can you call this an era of general peace?"

Cao Cao, already unfavorably impressed by Zhang Song's wretched appearance, reacted to these provocative remarks. He stood up, flicked his sleeves, and retired to his private chambers, leaving his aides to rebuke the visitor. "An emissary," they admonished, "should display some understanding of proper ceremony instead of blindly crossing his host. Luckily the prime minister, in view of your long journey, did not take offense. Now go back as quickly as you can." "You won't find any craven toadies among us Riverlanders," Zhang Song replied smugly.

This fresh jibe was suddenly answered by someone at the base of the stair leading to the main hall. "You Riverlanders have no skill in flattery, do you?" he shouted. "Do you think we northerners do?" Zhang Song regarded the man. He had thin eyebrows and narrow eyes, a light face and fine features. He was the son of the former grand commandant Yang Biao, Yang Xiu (Dezu), presently first secretary to the prime minister, in charge of the treasury. Yang Xiu had broad learning and a competence in argument that few could surpass; and his skill in debate was well known. Zhang Song had a mind to put him in his place. Yang Xiu had supreme confidence in his talent and disdained other scholars of the realm. After Zhang Song's sarcastic response, Yang Xiu invited him to join him in the library.

The two scholars seated themselves as host and guest. Yang Xiu said, "The road from Shu is rough indeed. Such a long journey must have tired you." "At my lord's command," Zhang Song replied, "I would walk through fire or boiling water." "Tell me something of the way of life in Shu," Yang Xiu requested. "Shu comprises the districts of the west," Zhang Song began, "under the ancient name Yizhou. Access by water is by the difficult Jin River; by land, through the formidable Saber Gateway Road. It would take two hundred and eighty stages to make the round trip from Shu, and its area exceeds thirty thousand *li*. Cocks crow and dogs bark everywhere, for the common folk are ceaselessly active. The fields are fertile and the soil productive, and neither flood nor drought plagues us. Thus, the state is wealthy and its people prosper, enjoying in due season the delights of music and song. No place under Heaven can produce such mountains of goods."

"And what men of note have you produced?" Yang Xiu asked. "In the civil arts we have had men as gifted as the great rhapsodist Sima Xiangru; in the military, leaders as capable as Ma Yuan; in medicine, physicians as able as Zhang Ji;[3] in divination, seers as profound as Yan Zun. Furthermore, in the various schools of philosophy and religion we have produced more exemplary men of talent and learning than I could begin to name." So Zhang Song replied.

"And," Yang Xiu went on, "could you also tell me something about the men now in Liu Zhang's service? Are there more like yourself?" "In both civil and military departments," Zhang Song said, "we have a full complement of talented men—wise, brave, loyal, honorable, and noble-minded—numbering in the hundreds. As for those like me, men of the most limited capacity, we come by the cartload, the bushelful, too many to be counted." To this Yang Xiu responded, "And what position do you presently occupy?" "I am filling in as a lieutenant inspector, but I am unqualified for the position. And what office do you hold at court, sir? May I inquire?" "Presently," Yang Xiu replied, "I am first secretary to the prime minister." "It is said you come from successive generations of officeholders," Song said. "Why are you not an assistant to the Emperor instead of an insignificant staff officer in the prime minister's service?"

At these words Yang Xiu flushed crimson. Controlling his expression he answered with effort, "Although I am a minor aide, His Excellency has entrusted me with the administration of money and provisions for the army, a weighty responsibility that has taught me much, under His Excellency's constant guidance. That is why I took the position." Zhang Song smiled. "I have heard," he said, "that His Excellency knows nothing of the way of the ancient sages Confucius and Mencius and that he falls short of Sunzi and Wu Qi in military strategy. He is said to be a man whose high office serves wholly to enhance his power. What could you possibly learn under such 'guidance'?"

"Living in a backwater as you do," Yang Xiu responded, "you may be excused for not appreciating His Excellency's talent. Perhaps you should be given an opportunity to see something of it." With that Yang Xiu summoned his aides, who brought a cased scroll to Zhang Song. Glancing at the title, *New Writings of Mengde*, Zhang Song read it from beginning to end, all thirteen chapters containing Cao Cao's major teachings on military science, and remarked, "What book is this?" "It was written by the prime minister; it is drawn from history and the current situation and is modeled on the thirteen chapters left by Master Sun. You ridicule His Excellency for having no talent. Here's something worthy of being handed on to future generations, I should say." Zhang Song laughed as he replied, "What? The children in our land of Shu know this sort of stuff by heart! Why call it new? It was written in the Warring States era by an unknown hand and has now been plagiarized by Prime Minister Cao. He seems to have put one over on you, at any rate."

"Although it has grown into a volume, the prime minister's work is kept in private, never made public," Yang Xiu explained. "As for the children of Shu being able to recite it, that's all bluff." "If you don't believe it," countered Zhang Song, "let me recite for you." With that, he recited the contents of the volume in a clear, loud voice, every word in place. Yang Xiu was astonished. "You memorized it at a glance," said Yang Xiu. "Truly a man of rare talent." A poet of later times left this description of Zhang Song:

> A cranky man, peculiar to describe:
> Pure and upright, but coarse in countenance,
> Whose words poured forth like rapids through the gorge,
> Who mastered pages in a single glance.
> His courage topped them all in western Shu.
> To every learned sphere he stretched his pen.
> In philosophy and literature he was read,
> So widely that no point escaped his ken.

Zhang Song began to take his leave, but Yang Xiu said, "Don't go quite yet. Let me plead your case one more time. Perhaps His Excellency will see you." Zhang Song expressed his thanks and withdrew.

Yang Xiu approached Cao Cao. "Why did you rebuff Zhang Song just now, Your Excellency?" he asked. "He was rude," Cao Cao replied. "You showed tolerance for Mi Heng once," Yang Xiu argued. "Couldn't you receive Zhang Song now?" "Mi Heng was a noted writer," Cao Cao said, "so I spared him. What talent does Zhang Song have?" "Superb rhetorical powers," was the reply. "He is an unbeatable debater and has a broad knowledge and accurate memory all too rarely found. I have just shown him Your Excellency's *New Writings*, and he recited them verbatim after merely glancing over them. He said the book was an anonymous work of the Warring States era and that even the children of Shu are familiar with its contents." "Could it by chance be in accord with writings of the ancients?" Cao Cao said; he ordered his book burned.

"I think you should see this man and show him the magnificence of the imperial court," Yang Xiu continued. "Tomorrow I'll be reviewing troops in the west field," Cao Cao replied. "Bring him over before it starts. I want him to witness the abundance of our power and let the westerners know that the day after we conquer the south, we will be coming for the Riverlands." The following day Yang Xiu brought Zhang Song to the parade ground. Fifty thousand marched before Cao Cao. His Tiger Guard and elite fighting units were spread in formation. Helmets and armor gleamed over brilliant surcoats; gong and drum resounded to the heavens; halberd and spear glinted in the sun; echelons of warriors stretched in the eight directions; bunting and banner spangled and streamed; men on horses pranced and vaulted against the horizon. Zhang Song glanced sidelong at the pageant. After a while Cao Cao summoned Song and, gesturing outward, said, "Does your Riverlands have such splendid, gallant heroes?" "In the land of Shu," Song answered, "I have never seen such a display of military force. We govern ourselves only by humanity and justice."

Cao Cao's countenance altered as he regarded Song, but Song looked unconcerned as Yang Xiu tried in vain to catch his eye. Cao responded, "Those 'river-rats'[4] of Shu are nothing but dirt. Where our army goes, it conquers. What it attacks, it takes. Those who obey us live. Those who resist die. Do you know that?" "That Your Excellency conquers and captures wherever he directs his forces," Zhang Song replied, "I am only too well aware—when you met Lü Bu at Puyang and Zhang Xiu at Wancheng, for example, or Zhou Yu at Red Cliffs and Lord Guan at Huarong Pass; when you cut off your beard and dropped your battle gown at Tong Pass; when you fled under a hail of arrows on the River Wei. Certainly, it all goes to show that you have no equal in the empire."

Cao Cao was inflamed. "What petty pedant dares hold up my failures before my face?" he cried and ordered Zhang Song executed. Yang Xiu protested: "Though he deserves to die, he does bear tribute from the remote Riverlands, and if we kill him we risk losing the confidence of men from afar."[5] Finally, Xun Wenruo convinced the outraged prime minister to spare the envoy, and Zhang Song was driven from the ministerial quarters with a sound thrashing.

At his lodgings Zhang Song was preparing to return directly to the Riverlands when something occurred to him: "I was only trying to offer the territory to Cao Cao. I never expected to find him so insolent. I gave Inspector Liu Zhang some pretty big assurances; and to go home now disappointed and with nothing to show, as it were, must earn me the mockery of my countrymen. They say Liu Xuande of Jingzhou has a great reputation for humanity and justice. I could make a side trip there before returning, just to see what he is like. I shall keep my own counsel about this."

Thus Zhang Song led his small suite toward the province border. Soon he saw a squadron of some five hundred cavalry. Their leader, a ranking commander, lightly equipped and without armor, guided his horse forward and asked, "Could our visitor be Lieutenant Inspector Zhang Song?" "The same," Song replied. The commander dismounted hastily and announced himself after due salutation: "Zhao Yun, here. I have been expecting you." Zhang Song dismounted and returned the greeting: "Not Zhao Zilong of Changshan?" "The same," Zilong replied. "My lord, Liu Xuande, has assigned me to host Your Honor and relieve the fatigue so long a journey must entail."[6] With that, Zilong's attendants, kneeling humbly, carried over refreshments, which Zilong respectfully proffered.

Zhang Song began to think Liu Xuande's reputation for magnanimity and hospitality well deserved. He joined Zhao Zilong in a few cups; then they remounted and proceeded together, reaching Jingzhou by nightfall. At the inn there, Zhang Song was greeted by one hundred men standing in lines leading to the door; beating drums welcomed him. A commander came before Zhang Song's horse to extend his courtesies. "My elder brother put me under orders to clean up this station for you to rest yourself in after the rigors of the road," said Lord Guan introducing himself. Zhang Song dismounted and was brought into the guesthouse. After the amenities, a banquet was spread and the two hosts urged their guest to enjoy himself. They drank until late into the night and then retired.

The next day after breakfast Zhao and Zhang rode a little way and then encountered Xuande himself, accompanied by Sleeping Dragon and Young Phoenix.[7] As Zhang Song approached, the three dismounted and waited. Song also dismounted hurriedly. "Your resounding reputation has long been known to me," Xuande began. "How we rue the distance that clouds and mountains impose, preventing us from profiting by your advice. Hearing you are homebound, we have come here especially to greet you. If you will only accept the hospitality of our poor province to break your journey and gratify our hopes, truly, it would be a blessing ten thousand times over." Delighted, Zhang Song rode into the city with his hosts.

In the main hall of the government buildings ritual greetings were exchanged and a banquet was laid. Throughout the repast Xuande confined himself to commonplace conversation, studiously avoiding any reference to the western Riverlands.[8] Zhang Song probed: "I wonder how many districts the imperial uncle holds in Jingzhou?" "Jingzhou is only on loan to us from the Southland," Kongming replied with a smile, "and they are always sending somebody to reclaim it. However, Lord Liu, as a brother-in-law of Sun Quan, has been granted temporary tenure." "Does that mean," Zhang Song continued, "that the Southlanders are not satisfied, despite their six districts and eighty-one regions, the strength of their people and the wealth of their state?" "Lord Liu," Pang Tong said, "though an imperial uncle of the dynasty, has never taken a piece of the realm, unlike those grubbing traitors to the Han who depend on forced seizures. But men of true understanding decry this injustice."

"Refrain from such statements, gentlemen," Xuande said. "What virtue have I to justify ambition?" "Not so," Zhang Song said.[9] "My enlightened lord, you are a royal kinsman whose humanity and sense of honor reach far and wide. Far more than 'a piece of the realm'—it is not beyond expectation that you might one day occupy the imperial throne as a successor in the legitimate line." Xuande joined his hands and made a gesture of disavowal. "Good sir," he said, "you far overestimate whatever I may deserve."

And there the matter lay during three days of feasting. Then, at a parting banquet at the first way station, Xuande toasted Zhang Song: "We are deeply grateful to you for sharing these three days with us. But now the time to take leave of one another has come, and I wonder when I may again have the benefit of your advice." Having spoken, Xuande shed tears freely, while Zhang Song wondered inwardly, "He is magnanimous and humane, a lover of learned men. Can I pass over him? Better to persuade him to take the Riverlands." Song said aloud, "I have long wished to be of service to you but despaired of finding the occasion. From Jingzhou, I see Sun Quan on the east, like a tiger ready to strike, and to the north Cao Cao with a whale's appetite. This place can hardly have enduring appeal for you."

Xuande replied, "I know it all too well. But there is not a place I can put my foot down safely." "The province of Yi, the Riverlands," Zhang Song said, "is protected by formidable barriers. Its fertile territory extends thousands of *li*. The people are thriving and the state prospers. Our wise and capable officials have long held the imperial uncle's virtue in high regard. If you will mobilize your forces to make the long trek west, your hegemony can be established and the house of Han restored." "How could I undertake such a thing?" Xuande said. "The provincial protector, Liu Zhang, is a royal kinsman like myself, and he has long dispensed favor throughout the land of Shu. What third party could upset things?"

"I am not one to sell my sovereign for high position," Zhang Song answered. "But having met with Your Lordship, I must bare my innermost thoughts. Liu Zhang, though in possession of Yizhou, is endowed with so ignorant and irresolute a nature that he has kept worthy and competent men from office. Now with the threat from Zhang Lu in the north, confidence is shaken, and people's thoughts turn to acquiring an enlightened lord. This excursion of mine was for the sole purpose of making an offer to Cao Cao; but in him, to my surprise, I found a perverse traitor who uses deceit for statecraft, who disdains the worthy, who insults those willing to serve. For these reasons I have made a point of coming to see you. My lord, take the Riverlands and make it your base, plan an attack on the Hanzhong buffer, then go on to incorporate the northern heartland and set the dynasty to rights. Your fame will pass into history and you will outshine all rivals. Should you be inclined to adopt this suggestion, I would be willing to do whatever is necessary to coordinate matters from within. Let me know your esteemed decision."

"Your concern touches me deeply," Xuande responded. "Alas, Liu Zhang and I share the same ancestor. If I attacked him, I would be reviled and repudiated by all." "A man of noble ambition," Zhang Song said, "spares no effort to establish his worth and his estate. Apply the whip and assume the lead! For if you do not take Yizhou, others will— and then it will be too late for regrets." "They say the roads are so hilly and rough," Xuande remarked, "that neither carriage nor horse can ride abreast. Even if I wanted to take it, what strategy would work?"

Producing a map from his sleeve, Zhang Song said, "I am moved by my lord's ample virtue to present this. A single glance will apprise you of the road system of the River-lands." Casually, Xuande unrolled the map and examined it. The geographic details of the region were fully spelled out: topography and marching stages, dimension and distance of roads, strategic intersections, repositories of coin and grain. "Strike now, my lord," Zhang Song urged. "My two close and trusted friends there, Fa Zheng and Meng Da, can be counted on. Should they come to Jingzhou, you may consult them in complete confidence." Xuande raised his clasped hands in an expression of gratitude. "You will be well rewarded when the plan is realized," he said, "as sure as the hills stay green and the rivers ever run." "I look for no reward," Zhang Song asserted. "Having met a lord who is wise and enlightened, I could do nothing but make known to him all the facts of the case." With that, they parted. Kongming ordered Lord Guan and the others to escort the guest several dozen *li*.

• • • • •

Back in Yizhou, Zhang Song went first to see his close friend Fa Zheng (Xiaozhi), a man from Mei in West Fufeng, son of the worthy officer Fa Zhen. Zhang Song gave Fa Zheng a complete account of his interview.[10] "Cao Cao," he began, "has utter contempt for learned, honorable men. He turns to them in trouble, and from them in success. I have promised our province to Imperial Uncle Liu, and I want to discuss it with you, brother." "In my judgment," replied Fa Zheng, "Liu Zhang is an incapable leader. I have had my eye on Liu Xuande for some time. Since I share your view, you need have no doubts."

A while later Meng Da (Ziqing) arrived. He was a fellow townsman of Fa Zheng's. Seeing the two talking together, Meng Da said, "It looks like you are ready to surrender the province." "Such is our wish," answered Zhang Song. "What is yours, elder brother? Who is the best choice?" "Xuande! Who else?" responded Meng Da. Each of the three clasped his hands and laughed. Then Fa Zheng said to Zhang Song: "And what will you say to Liu Zhang tomorrow, brother?" "I am going to recommend that he send both of you to Jingzhou as his envoys," Zhang Song replied. The others agreed.

The next day Liu Zhang received Zhang Song and asked, "How did you fare?" "Cao is a traitor to the Han!" Zhang Song exclaimed. "His lust for power is unspeakable. He is after our land." "Then what are we to do?" asked Liu Zhang. "I have a plan for keeping both Cao Cao and Zhang Lu from invading us," Zhang Song answered. "Yes?" said Liu Zhang. "Imperial Uncle Liu Xuande of Jingzhou," Zhang Song began, "is a member of the royal house, my lord, as you yourself are. Benevolent, kind, magnanimous, liberal, he has the aura of a man who is honest and self-respecting. Since the battle at Red Cliffs, the mere mention of his name throws Cao Cao into panic, not to speak of Zhang Lu! I think, my lord, that you would do well with such friendship and support from the outside in your struggle against Cao Cao and Zhang Lu."

"I have been thinking along these lines for some time," the imperial inspector said. "Whom could we send as envoys to Jingzhou?" "Fa Zheng and Meng Da," Zhang Song replied, "no one else will do." Liu Zhang summoned the two men. He gave Fa Zheng a letter to establish good relations with Xuande, and Meng Da five thousand men to escort Xuande and his supporting force into the province. But while this discussion was under way, a man burst into the room, his face covered with perspiration. "My lord, listen to Zhang Song," he cried, "and your forty-one departments will pass into the hands of another."

Zhang Song stared at him in astonishment. It was Huang Quan (Gongheng) from Xi-langzhong in Ba, presently serving Imperial Inspector Liu Zhang as first secretary. "Xuande and I are royal kinsmen," Liu Zhang said. "That is why I enlist his support. How can you make such a statement?" "I am quite familiar with Xuande's magnanim-ity," was the reply, "how his gentle approach has overcome the hardest resistance the empire's heroes have put up so far. He has won the allegiance of men from afar, and gratified the hopes of those he has ruled. On top of that, he has two wise counselors in Zhuge Liang and Pang Tong; and he has the support of such valiant warriors as Guan, Zhang, Zhao Zilong, Huang Zhong, and Wei Yan. If you call him into Shu and treat him as a subordinate, how long do you think he will be willing to remain compliant? On the other hand, if you accord him the reception of an honored guest—well, one kingdom can't hold two kings. Heed my words and our rule can be secure as Mount Tai. Heed them not and your own position will become as precarious as a pile of eggs. Zhang Song must have arranged something with Xuande when he passed through Jingzhou. Execute Zhang Song, break off with Liu Bei, and the Riverlands will enjoy unlimited good fortune."

"And how am I going to stop Cao Cao and Zhang Lu?" Inspector Liu Zhang asked. "Seal the borders and close the passes," Huang Quan replied. "Improve defenses and wait for the threat to blow over." "With the enemy at our borders, we cannot waste time," Liu Zhang said; he rejected Huang Quan's strategy in favor of Fa Zheng's mission. But another man cried out in opposition. It was Wang Lei, an aide in Liu Zhang's personal service. Touching his head to the ground, Wang Lei said, "My lord, Zhang Song's advice spells disaster." "No!" Liu Zhang shot back. "Alliance with Xuande will block Zhang Lu." "Zhang Lu," Wang Lei continued, "is a superficial problem. Liu Bei represents a threat to our vitals, for he is the most treacherous of villains. Once he served Cao Cao; then he plotted his destruction. Next, he joined Sun Quan and ended up stealing Jing-zhou. Can you coexist with such duplicity? If you summon him, it means the end of the Riverlands!"

Liu Zhang dismissed the speaker sharply: "Stop this nonsense! Would a kinsman steal my estate?" The inspector had attendants escort the protesters from the hall and sent Fa Zheng to Jingzhou.

Fa Zheng went straight to Jingzhou and was granted audience. After presenting him-self, Fa Zheng handed Liu Xuande a written proposal.[11] It read:

Your cousin, Liu Zhang, respectfully commends the following to the attention of General Xuande as an elder of the clan. Long have I esteemed your lofty name, but the difficult roads of Shu have prevented me from sending tribute. For this I feel deepest shame. They say, "Share trouble, bear trouble." This goes for friends, not to speak of kinsmen. Now Zhang Lu's army on our northern borders gives me no peace, and so I send this earnest petition for your weighty consideration. If you decide to take cognizance of our common ancestry and preserve honor among brothers, you will raise an army at once to rid us of these violent marauders. In that way we will remain mutual adherents, "lips and teeth," and you will be richly rewarded. No letter can say all that I wish. I expectantly await your arrival.[12]

Xuande exulted on reading the letter. He ordered a banquet for Fa Zheng. As the wine was circulating, he dismissed his attendants and said confidentially, "I have long admired your splendid name, and Zhang Song has spoken much of your ample virtue. This op-portunity to benefit by your counsel answers hopes long held."

Disclaiming the compliment, Fa Zheng replied, "A minor official from the Riverlands is hardly worth notice. But they say horses whinnied when they met the master trainer Bo Luo: a man will sacrifice all for one who appreciates him. General, have you thought further on Lieutenant Inspector Zhang Song's proposal?" "My life as an exile," Xuande replied, "has never been free of woe and discontent. I often think of the little wren that keeps a cozy spot for itself and the cunning hare that maintains three holes in case of escape. Men should do the same. Don't think I would not have your overabundant land—but I cannot bring myself to conspire against my clansman." "The Riverlands is a natural storehouse," Fa Zheng responded. "A sovereign who cannot keep control cannot last. Liu Zhang has proved unable to assign good men to office, and his patrimony is doomed to pass to someone else. It would be unwise, General, not to take what he offers you so freely. As the saying goes, 'He who gets to the rabbit first, wins the chase.' I stand pre-pared to give you my full support." Xuande folded his hands in a gesture of appreciation and said, "Much yet remains to be discussed."

After the banquet Kongming personally escorted Fa Zheng to the guesthouse. Xuande was alone, pondering, when Pang Tong approached him and said, "It is a foolish man who fails to resolve a matter that demands resolving. You are high-minded and understanding, my lord. Why hesitate?" "What do you think we should do?" Xuande asked. Pang Tong replied, "Jingzhou's present situation—Cao Cao to the north and Sun Quan to the east—confounds our ambitions. But the Riverlands, in population, territory, and wealth, offers the wherewithal for our great endeavor. If Zhang Song and Fa Zheng are going to help us from within, that is a godsend. Do not hesitate!"

"The man who is my antithesis," Xuande responded, "who struggles against me as fire against water, is Cao Cao. Where his means are hasty, mine are temperate; where his are violent, mine are humane; where his are cunning, mine are truehearted. By main-taining my opposition to Cao Cao, my cause may succeed. I can't throw away the world's trust and allegiance for personal gain." Smiling, Pang Tong said, "My lord, that accords well enough with sacred universal principles. But in a time of division and subversion, when men strive for power by waging war, there is no high road to follow. If you cling to accustomed principle, you will not be able to proceed at all. Rather, you should be flexible. You know, 'to incorporate the feeble and attack the incompetent,' to 'take power untowardly but hold it virtuously,' was the way of the great conquerors, kings Tang and Wu.[13] When things are settled, and if you reward Liu Zhang honorably with a big fief, what trust will you have betrayed? Remember that if you do not take power, another will.[14] Give it careful consideration, my lord.''

Inspired by these words, Xuande answered, ''Your memorable advice shall be inscribed on my heart.'' Soon after he consulted with Kongming about raising a force to move west. ''Jingzhou is too important to leave undefended,'' Kongming said. ''Then,'' Xuande replied, ''I shall go ahead with Pang Tong, Huang Zhong, and Wei Yan. You remain behind with Lord Guan, Zhang Fei, and Zhao Zilong.'' Kongming agreed and assumed overall responsibility for Jingzhou province, assigning Lord Guan to defend the route into Xiangyang from the pass at Qingni; Zhang Fei to take charge of the four districts along the river; and Zhao Zilong to hold Jiangling and protect Gong'an, the seat of Xuande's administration.

Xuande, with Huang Zhong as forward commander and Wei Yan as rear guard, took command of the center, with Liu Feng and Guan Ping assisting. Pang Tong was made director general. All told, their forces numbered fifty thousand. At this time Liao Hua offered his services, and Xuande assigned him to assist Lord Guan in guarding against Cao Cao.

In the winter Xuande marched west. Meng Da greeted him, explaining that inspector Liu Zhang had provided five thousand troops for the reception. Earlier, Xuande had notified Liu Zhang of his route, and the imperial inspector had instructed the localities along the way to supply the arriving soldiers with grain and cash. Liu Zhang himself meant to greet Xuande at Fucheng and had therefore ordered splendid carriages, tents, flags, and armor for the occasion. But First Secretary Huang Quan again protested: ''My lord, if you go, Xuande will kill you. I have served you for many years, and it pains me to see you walking into a trap. Please reconsider.'' Zhang Song countered: ''Huang Quan is trying to divide kinsmen while aiding our enemies. His advice is worthless.'' Liu Zhang cried: ''I have made up my mind. Cross me no more!'' Thus rebuked, Huang Quan struck his head to the ground until blood ran; he bit down on the hem of Liu Zhang's clothing to stop him. Enraged, Liu Zhang arose, yanking his garment free of Huang Quan's clenched mouth, breaking his front teeth. Zhang shouted to have Huang Quan removed. Lamenting bitterly, Quan returned home.

As Liu Zhang prepared for the journey to meet Xuande, someone bowed at the stair and warned, ''My lord, rejecting Huang Quan's loyal advice will only speed your doom.'' Liu Zhang looked on Li Hui from Yuyuan in Jianning. Striking his head to the floor, he cried, '''A lord will profit from his minister's warning, and a father from his son's.' Huang Quan's loyal and honorable words cannot be ignored. In Liu Bei you're welcoming a tiger at the front gate.'' ''Xuande is a senior member of our clan,'' Liu Zhang retorted. ''He would never murder me. The next protester dies.'' And he had Li Hui thrust from his presence.

''The officials of the Riverlands,'' Zhang Song said, ''care only for their wives and children and will never give their all for Your Lordship; the military leaders are arrogant, content with their accomplishments, eager for external contacts. Without Imperial Uncle Liu, you will be attacked and destroyed by enemies both inside and out.'' ''Your planning,'' Liu Zhang said, ''serves my interest profoundly.''

The next day Liu Zhang rode to Elm Bridge Gate. There he was told that his aide Wang Lei had strung himself upside down above the city portals, a written protest in one hand, a sword in the other, and was threatening to cut the rope and dash himself to death if his warnings were not heeded. Liu Zhang called for the protest note, which said in essence:

> Your aide Wang Lei weeps blood, appealing in all sincerity. "Effective medicine is bitter to the mouth but remedies disease. Loyal words offend the ear but benefit one's conduct." In ancient times King Huai of Chu ignored the advice of Qu Yuan and covenanted at Wuguan, falling prey to Qin. Now Your Lordship lightly leaves his home district to welcome Liu Bei at Fucheng. Will you return the way you came? If only you would put Zhang Song publicly to death and break off with Liu Bei, the entire population of Shu as well as your own house would benefit.

Angered by what he had read, Liu Zhang said, "I go to meet a humane and benevolent man, a kindred spirit of noble intent. How often do you mean to affront us this way?" Wang Lei uttered a single cry, severed the rope, and crashed to his death. A poet of later times left this tribute:

> Suspended from the city gate, the protest note in hand,
> So he chose to die in the service of Liu Zhang.
> Huang Quan, with his broken teeth, gave in at the end;
> Wang Lei alone exemplifies fidelity unstained.

Liu Zhang set off for Fucheng with thirty thousand soldiers. Behind him rolled a thousand carts loaded with grain, money, and silk.

· · · · ·

Xuande had advanced as far as the River Dian. Because the westerners had provisioned his army and because his soldiers had been warned on pain of death not to touch anything belonging to the people, Xuande's forces maintained discipline wherever they passed. Young and old thronged the thoroughfares to catch a glimpse of the arriving army, burning incense to pay their respects. Xuande spoke kindly and reassuringly to the people.

Meanwhile, Fa Zheng confided to Pang Tong: "I have a secret letter from Zhang Song. He wants us to move against Liu Zhang at the meeting in Fucheng, not to delay." "Say nothing for now," replied Pang Tong. "Wait until they are face-to-face. If this gets out, things could go awry." Fa Zheng kept his counsel. Fucheng was three hundred and sixty *li* from Chengdu, the capital of Yizhou. On arriving, Liu Zhang sent a man to welcome Xuande. The two armies settled in above the River Fu. Then Xuande entered the city to meet Liu Zhang, and the two men expressed their fraternal feelings. The overtures concluded, they wept freely, speaking their affection. After feasting, each returned to his camp to rest.

Liu Zhang told his assembled officials: "Those absurd suspicions of Huang Quan and Wang Lei! Little did they understand my clan-brother's good heart. Now I see how humane and honorable a man he really is. With his support, we have nothing to fear from Cao Cao or from Zhang Lu. And we have Zhang Song to thank for it!" So saying, he removed the green robe he was wearing and sent it with five hundred taels of gold to Zhang Song in the capital. His subordinates, however, Liu Gui, Ling Bao, Zhang Ren, Deng Xian, and other officers and officials said, "Restrain your enthusiasm a little, my lord. Liu Bei has an iron hand under that soft touch, and his motives are not easy to fathom. We had best take precautions." "You are overanxious," Liu Zhang replied. "There is no duplicity in my kinsman." His officials sighed in frustration and withdrew.

•   •   •   •

Meanwhile, Xuande had returned to his base, where Pang Tong came to him. "Your Lordship," he said, "what was your sense of Liu Zhang at the banquet?" "A sincere and honest man," Xuande replied. "He is a good man," Pang Tong agreed, "but his men, Liu Gui and Zhang Ren, seemed most aggrieved. With them our fortune is uncertain. My advice is to invite Liu Zhang to a banquet tomorrow. Have a hundred men placed behind the wall hangings beforehand. During the banquet you can signal them by throwing a cup down and have him put to death. We can then enter Chengdu en masse and conquer it without lifting our swords from their scabbards or fitting an arrow to a string." "Liu Zhang is my kinsman," Xuande responded. "He has treated me with all sincerity. Moreover, we are newcomers in the west. Our favor and trust have yet to be established. Heaven would not condone, nor the people forgive, a thing like that. Not even the power-hungry hegemons of old would have done what you propose."

"It is not what I propose," Pang Tong explained, "but a suggestion from Zhang Song conveyed in a confidential letter to Fa Zheng calling for swift action. The time must come sooner or later." As Pang Tong was speaking, Fa Zheng himself entered. "We are not acting for ourselves," he said, "but in conformity with the Mandate of Heaven." "Liu Zhang is my kinsman. I cannot do it," was Xuande's answer. "You are mistaken, my enlightened lord," Fa Zheng continued. "If you do not do it, Zhang Lu, who holds our state responsible for his mother's death, will attack and seize it. Your Lordship has come all this way across hills and streams; your men and horses have suffered hardship. To go forward is to your advantage; to withdraw is profitless. If you persist in these doubts and scruples and let the time pass, our cause will fail. And if our plans are discovered, they will do us in. Seize this moment when Heaven and man concur, when Liu Zhang suspects nothing: establish your estate. That is our best move." Pang Tong added his own exhortations. Indeed:

> The ruler holds an honorable course
> While clever ministers urge on him their schemes,

for Liu Xuande must have a place to rule! What kind of decision would Liu Xuande reach?

READ ON.

61

Zhao Zilong Recovers Ah Dou at the River;
Sun Quan's Letter Causes Cao Cao to Retreat

PANG TONG AND FA ZHENG tried to convince Xuande that the Riverlands could be handily won by murdering Liu Zhang at the banquet. But Xuande stood firm against their counsel, saying, "Having just entered the realm, we have neither good will nor credibility. It would never work."

The next day Xuande feasted with Liu Zhang in the city.[1] The two men expressed their deep feeling for one another in tones of earnest friendship. When the company was well into its wine, Pang Tong suggested to Fa Zheng, "At this point there's nothing my master can do to stop us," and told Wei Yan to ascend into the banquet hall and assassinate Liu Zhang while giving a sword dance. Wei Yan bared his weapon and presented himself, saying, "Our gathering lacks entertainment. Let me perform the sword dance for your amusement." As Wei Yan spoke, Pang Tong had armed guards line up below the hall in anticipation of the deed.

Some of Liu Zhang's commanders were alarmed at the unfolding scene. An aide to Imperial Inspector Liu, Zhang Ren, gripped his sword and stepped forth. "This is a dance to perform in pairs," he said. "I shall accompany General Wei Yan." The two men moved gracefully before the company. At a glance from Wei Yan, Liu Feng also drew his blade and joined the dance, followed quickly by Liu Gui, Ling Bao, and Deng Xian, who said, "To add to the merriment." At this point Xuande, thoroughly alarmed, took hold of a follower's sword and stood up; he addressed the gathering: "I meet Liu Zhang at this feast today as a brother. Mistrust has no place here. This is no Hongmen![2] The sword dance is uncalled for. Let each throw down his blade or die." Liu Zhang added his own rebuke, "This reunion requires no weapons," and ordered his followers to disarm. Everyone rushed from the banquet hall.

Xuande summoned Liu Zhang's captains to the feast and rewarded them with wine as he said, "We two are kinsmen, blood and bone, conferring on matters of import. Duplicity has no place. You should all be clear about that." At these words Liu Zhang's captains prostrated themselves in gratitude. Deeply moved, Liu Zhang took Xuande's hand and said, "Your good will, brother, will never be forgotten." The two men continued carousing until late hours. Back at his camp, Xuande reproved Pang Tong: "Were you and the others trying to dishonor me? Don't let such a thing ever happen again." Sighing profoundly, Pang Tong withdrew.

When Liu Zhang returned to his camp, Liu Gui said, "My lord, you saw that scene at the banquet today? Let us go home while we are still alive." "My brother Liu Xuande is unlike other men," replied Liu Zhang. But his officers retorted, "Xuande himself may harbor no ill will, but those around him aim to take over the Riverlands in pursuit of their own interests." "Do not come between two brothers," Liu Zhang answered, and he remained deaf to all persuasion during his days spent with Xuande.

Suddenly it was reported that Zhang Lu had brought a well-organized force before Jiameng Pass. Liu Zhang requested Xuande to defend the pass, and Xuande, generously agreeing, went there at once with his troops. Liu Zhang's commanders urged Zhang to have his main force seal off all points of access in case of a mutiny by Xuande's army. After much urging, Liu Zhang finally agreed to have two leading military officers of Baishui, Yang Huai and Gao Pei, guard the pass at the River Fu. Liu Zhang then returned to Chengdu. Xuande kept his soldiers on tight discipline in the Jiameng Pass area, winning the favor of the inhabitants by his many acts of largess.[3]

·   ·   ·   ·

Spies had already reported these events to the Southland command. Lord Sun Quan was consulting with his civil and military officials when Gu Yong proposed: "Now that Liu Bei has taken a part of his forces so far to the west, I think we should send a company to cut off the mouth of the river and prevent his return. Then a general military action will bring us an easy victory in Jingzhou. This is not an opportunity to let slip." "An excellent plan!" responded Sun Quan. But during the session someone stepped forward from behind a screen, shouting, "The author of this plan should be killed for trying to murder my daughter." The assembly was startled at the sight of State Mother Wu. Angrily, she said, "I have only one daughter, and she is married to Liu Bei. If you attack him, what of my daughter?" Then she turned on Sun Quan: "You hold your father's and your brother's estate in your hands. Is comfortable possession of the eighty-one regions of the south not enough for you? Must you risk your own flesh and blood for some trifling gain?" Sun Quan voiced his respectful submission over and over again. "Whatever my revered mother requires will be performed," he answered and dismissed the assembly. The state mother left indignantly.

Standing by the porch railing, Sun Quan mused, "If I miss this chance, Jingzhou could be lost forever." Zhang Zhao entered and asked, "My lord, what troubles you?" "I'm still thinking of what Gu Yong said," responded Sun Quan. "Nothing could be simpler," Zhang Zhao went on. "Slip a trusted commander and five hundred men into Jingzhou with a letter for Lady Sun saying that the state mother is critically ill and wants to see her daughter. That should bring her back as soon as possible. See that she brings Xuande's only son with her—Xuande will be only too glad to exchange Jingzhou for his son. And if he refuses, you are free to use force." "An excellent plan!" cried Sun Quan. "I have a man, Zhou Shan, so trusted by my brother that since his youth he used to enter his private chambers. He's the man to send." "This must be kept absolutely secret," said Zhang Zhao. "Give him his orders to start out here and now."

Zhou Shan took five hundred men disguised as merchants and five boats. He was provided with false papers in case anyone questioned him on the way. Weapons were concealed on board. As commanded, Zhou Shan sailed for Jingzhou. Reaching the capital area, he docked and had the gate guards report his arrival to Lady Sun.

Lady Sun summoned Zhou Shan to audience, and he presented her the secret letter. Reading of her mother's condition, Lady Sun tearfully expressed her deep concern. Prostrating himself, Zhou Shan said plaintively, "Throughout her terrible illness the state mother has had you alone in her thoughts. If you delay, you might never see her again. She bids you take Ah Dou with you to see her." "The imperial uncle," replied Lady Sun, "is on a remote campaign. I will have to inform Director General Kongming before returning south." "And what," Zhou Shan answered, "if he has to have the imperial uncle's approval?" "If I depart without taking leave," said Lady Sun, "we will be blocked." "Boats are now waiting in the river," said Zhou Shan. "I beg Your Ladyship, mount your carriage at once and leave the city."

The news of her mother's condition made Lady Sun's head spin. She hurried the seven-year-old Ah Dou into her carriage and, followed by some thirty armed guards, left the city of Gong'an for the river's edge. She had already embarked at Sandy Head before her attendants could report it.

Zhou Shan was about to set sail when he heard a shout from the shore: "Hold on! Let me see my lady off!" It was Zhao Zilong. Returning from patrol, Zhao Zilong was shocked to discover Lady Sun had departed. Riding like the wind, he had reached the shore with but five horsemen. Gripping a long spear, Zhou Shan cried out, "Who dares thwart the lady?" and ordered the boat launched as armed soldiers lined the decks. The wind favored them and the current sped the five boats on.

Zhao Zilong rode along the shoreline, shouting, "Lady Sun is free to leave. But I must make one appeal to her." Zhou Shan took no notice and urged the little fleet forward. Zilong followed another ten *li*. Suddenly he sighted a fishing vessel moored at the bank. Dismounting, he seized his spear and jumped aboard. Zilong and one follower steered urgently after the boat carrying Lady Sun. Zhou Shan ordered his men to shoot. But Zilong knocked the arrows harmlessly aside with his spear. As he drew to within ten feet of the main craft, the soldiers stabbed wildly at him. Zilong set aside his spear and took hold of the black-hilted sword at his waist. Finding a break in the menacing spears, he scrambled aboard the southern boat.

The sailors fell back, astonished. Zilong entered the cabin and saw Lady Sun cradling Ah Dou at her bosom. "How dare you!" she cried. Zilong put away his sword and paid his respects, saying, "Where is my lady bound? Why have you not informed the director general?" "My mother is at death's door," she replied. "There was no time to inform anyone." "Does a visit to the state mother require taking the young master?" asked Zilong. "Ah Dou is my child now," was the reply. "There was no one to leave him with in Jingzhou." "Not so, my lady," responded Zilong. "This bit of blood and bone, my master's only progeny, was saved by your humble commander from a battlefield of a million by Steepslope Bridge in Dangyang. Why does my lady wish to carry him off?"

Angrily Lady Sun said, "What has the likes of you, a ruffian in service, to do with my family affairs?" "You are free to leave," Zilong replied. "But our young lord must stay." Lady Sun shouted, "You jump onto my boat midway—it means revolt!" "If you don't leave the child, I will face ten thousand mortal perils before I'll let Your Ladyship go," said Zilong. Lady Sun called her female attendants to seize the intruder, but Zilong thrust them aside, snatched Ah Dou, and carried him safely onto the deck. He wanted to get close to shore, but there was no one to help; neither had he cause for violent action. There was no way out.

Lady Sun called her women to recover Ah Dou. Zilong held the boy in one arm and fended off the attendants with the other; no one dared approach him. To the rear Zhou

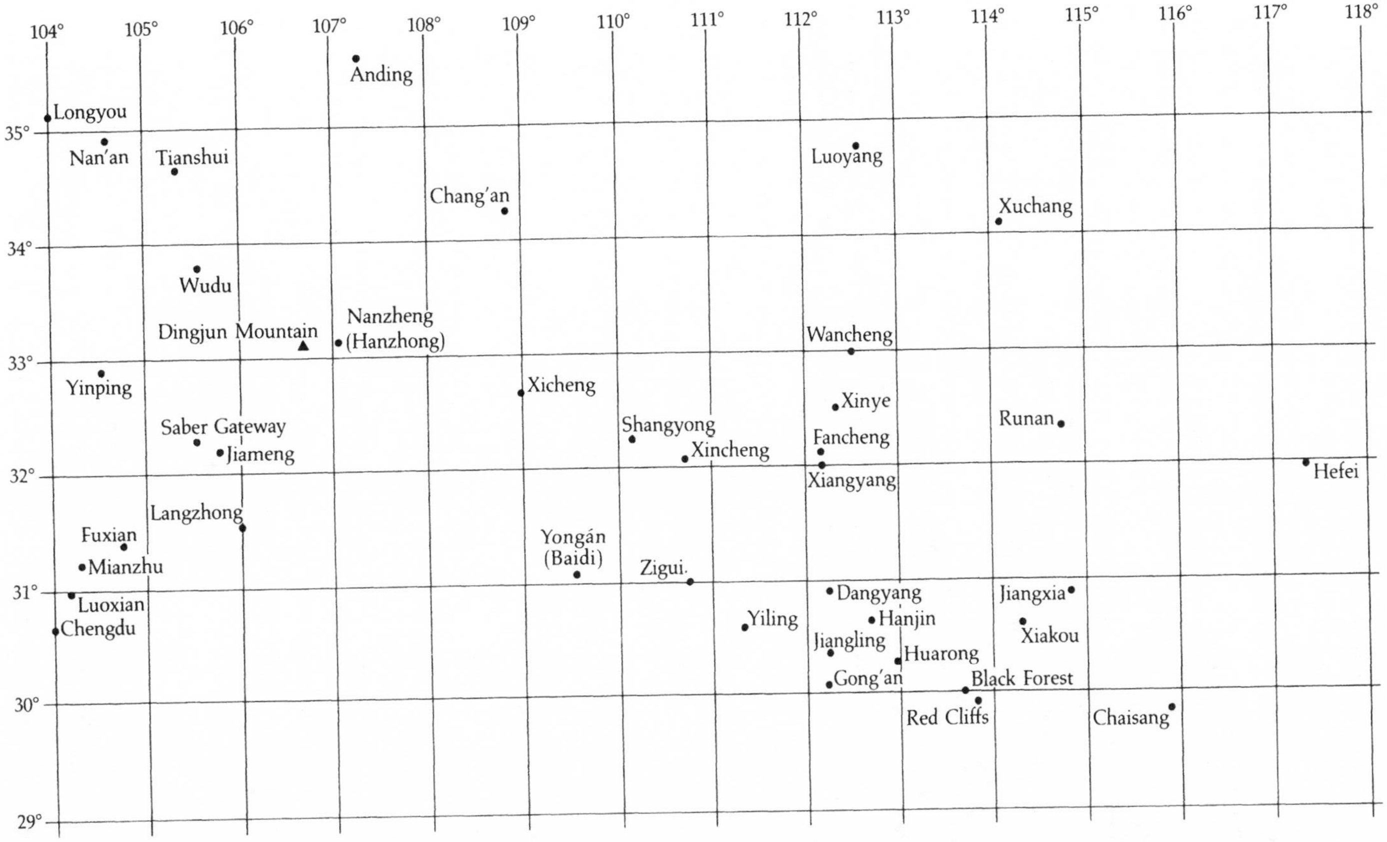
104°
105°
106°
107°
108°
109°
110°
111°
112°
113°
114°
115°
116°
117°
118°
35°
34°
33°
32°
31°
30°
29°
Anding
Longyou
Nan'an
Tianshui
Luoyang
Chang'an
Xuchang
Wudu
Dingjun Mountain
Nanzheng
(Hanzhong)
Wancheng
Yinping
Xicheng
Xinye
Saber Gateway
Jiameng
Shangyong
Xincheng
Fancheng
Runan
Xiangyang
Hefei
Langzhong
Fuxian
Mianzhu
Yongán
(Baidi)
Zigui
Dangyang
Jiangxia
Luoxian
Chengdu
Yiling
Hanjin
Jiangling
Xiakou
Huarong
Gong'an
Black Forest
Red Cliffs
Chaisang

MAP 6. Approximate latitude and longitude of key centers and strongpoints east and west of the 112th meridian. Source: Tan Qixiang, chief ed., *Zhongguo lishi dituji* (Shanghai: Cartographic Publishing House, 1982), II:42–58.

Shan held the rudder steady, bent on his downstream course. Sped by wind and current, the boat moved toward midstream. Zilong was helpless. With Ah Dou in his arms, how could he shift the boat toward shore?

At this critical moment, from an inlet downstream, a row of ten boats emerged, flags waving, drums rolling. Zilong thought, "This time the Southland has me!" Then he saw a commander on the boat ahead. A long spear was in his hand. "Sister-in-law!" he bellowed. "Leave my nephew!" It was Zhang Fei; he had learned of Lady Sun's departure while on his rounds and had rushed to the mouth of the River You. Encountering the southern ships, he hastened to bar their advance. In moments Zhang Fei had boarded the main craft, sword at the ready. Zhou Shan sprang to meet him, but Zhang Fei cut him swiftly down and flung his severed head at Lady Sun's feet. "How could you commit such an outrage, brother-in-law?" Lady Sun cried in alarm. "The outrage, sister," Zhang Fei went on, "is that you are quietly taking yourself home without giving a thought to my elder brother." "My mother is dying," she replied. "If I waited for your elder brother's approval, it would be too late. Let me go home or I will throw myself into the water."

Zhang Fei observed to Zilong, "To drive her to her death is no way for loyal men to act. Let's take Ah Dou and leave it at that." So Zhang Fei said to Lady Sun, "My brother, imperial uncle of the great Han, has always treated Your Ladyship as befits your dignity. Now you are leaving us. But if my brother's kind affection for you be in your thoughts, you will come back soon." So saying, Zhang Fei took Ah Dou in his arms and returned with Zilong to his boat. Lady Sun was permitted to pass. A later verse pays tribute to Zilong:

> In Dangyang once he saved the little heir;
> Now he hurls himself upon the Jiang.
> The southern sailors feel their spirits die
> Before the prowess of this paragon.

Another verse praises Zhang Fei:

> Once by Steepslope Bridge at fury's pitch
> The tiger growled and Cao's men gave ground.
> Today he stands beside his menaced prince
> And makes a name for evermore renowned.

The two men sailed homeward well pleased with themselves. Before they had covered many *li*, Kongming met them with a large naval force. He was delighted to have Ah Dou safely back. The three men continued their journey on horseback. Kongming sent a letter to the Jiameng Pass to inform Xuande of what had happened.

•   •   •   •

Lady Sun told her brother, Sun Quan, that Zhang Fei and Zhao Zilong had intercepted her boat, killed Zhou Shan, and wrested Ah Dou from her. Angrily Sun Quan said, "My sister has returned to us. Xuande is my relative no more. The death of Zhou Shan must be avenged." He met with his advisers to consider the conquest of Jingzhou. But during their discussion of the assignment of units, Sun Quan learned that Cao Cao was coming with an army of four hundred thousand to avenge his defeat at Red Cliffs. Astounded, Sun Quan set aside the question of Jingzhou and turned to the threat from Cao Cao.

At this moment a messenger announced the death of the senior adviser Zhang Hong, who had earlier pleaded illness and returned home. His last words had been put down in a letter urging Sun Quan to shift his capital to Moling, a site, he claimed, that had an imperial aura in its hills and streams and would sustain an enduring estate. After perusing the letter, Sun Quan wept and addressed his followers: "Zhang Hong urges me to remove to Moling. How can I ignore his counsel?" He ordered the seat of government shifted to Jianye,[4] where he built the City of Stones.

Lü Meng offered his counsel: "Since Cao's troops are coming, we should build a rampart near the mouth of the Ruxu River to hold them back." The commanders all said, "There's no need for a wall. We can attack from shore, or wade barefoot into our boats." To this Lü Meng responded, "The fortunes of war are never constant; victory is never sure. In an abrupt confrontation, with infantry and cavalry jostling together, our men may not have time to reach the water much less board the boats." Sun Quan commented, "Improvidence invites danger. Lü Meng wisely looks ahead." So saying, he sent tens of thousands of soldiers to build a rampart at the Ruxu, and by dint of unremitting toil the project was completed according to plan.

•　　•　　•　　•

Cao Cao was in Xuchang, the capital. Day by day his power and fortune grew. Senior Adviser Dong Zhao proposed: "Since antiquity no servant of the throne has achieved what His Excellency has achieved. Neither the Duke of Zhou nor Lü Wang approaches him. These thirty years he has faced the utmost rigors in his campaigns to clear our realm of rebels, relieve the people's plagues, and revive the house of Han. How could he be ranked with other servants of the imperial house? He merits the position of lord patriarch of Wei and the award of the Nine Dignities to glorify his virtue and his achievements." What are the Nine Dignities?

1. Chariot and Horse: one great wain of state or golden chariot, one military chariot, two quadriga of dark stallions, eight cream-colored mounts;
2. Royal Raiment: Dragon-figured robe and squared headdress matched with vermillion shoes;
3. Suspended Chimes: music suited to audience with a king;
4. Vermillion Doors: a gateway of fortune for his residence;
5. Inner Staircase: protected, for him to ascend;
6. Imperial Tiger Escort: three hundred guards to secure his palace gates;
7. Imperial Axes: ceremonial axes and battle-axes;
8. Bows and Arrows: one red-striped bow and one hundred red-striped arrows, ten black bows and a thousand black arrows;
9. Implements for the Ritual Offering of Black Millet Wine, Herb-Scented: jade tablet and libation cup, one bowl of millet and wine each (the tablet and cup matching, the millet black); seasoned wine to sprinkle on the ground to attract the gods below; tablet and libation cup, ritual instruments of the ancestral temple for sacrificing to the former kings.[5]

Privy Counselor Xun Wenruo said, "This may not be! His Excellency has raised a loyalist army in support of the house of Han and must follow humble and retiring ways to maintain his loyalty and integrity. The noble man shows his love of fellow man through his virtue—not like this." Cao Cao was indignant at Xun Wenruo's stand. Dong

Zhao said, "Can one man thwart the general wish?" and submitted a memorial to the throne calling for Cao Cao to be honored as lord patriarch of Wei and awarded the Nine Dignities. Xun Wenruo sighed and said, "Little did I expect to witness such a thing!" Cao Cao, deeply angered by Wenruo's objections, no longer regarded him as a dependable friend.

In the winter of Jian An 17 (A.D. 212), the tenth month, Cao Cao mobilized his army to crush the Southland. He ordered Xun Wenruo to accompany him; but Wenruo had anticipated Cao's intent and, pleading illness, remained in Shouchun. Cao sent the adviser a container for food sealed with his handwritten inscription, but Wenruo found the box empty when he looked inside. There was no mistaking Cao Cao's point. The counselor took poison and died. He was fifty years old. A poet of later times left this appreciation of Xun Wenruo:

> A splendid talent, admired of all men!
> His folly lay in serving Cao Cao's power.
> Liken him not to Zhang Liang, Lord of Liu:[6]
> Wenruo was 'shamed to face Han's Emperor!

Xun Wenruo's son, Xun Yun, informed Cao Cao of his father's passing. The prime minister deeply regretted his action and had Wenruo buried richly and honorably with the posthumous title lord of Jing.

Cao Cao's main force reached the Ruxu. He sent Cao Hong ahead with thirty thousand armored cavalry to scout the shoreline. The report came back: "Banners along the river far as the eye can see. But troop concentrations not visible." His confidence shaken, Cao Cao went to the Ruxu himself and deployed his force. He took one hundred men to a height and observed squadrons of southern warships in orderly array, flying flags of all colors, weapons gleaming smartly. On a large craft positioned in the center, beneath an umbrella of blue-green silk sat Sun Quan, flanked by attendants, counselors, and advisers.

Pointing with his whip, Cao Cao said, "Oh, for sons like Sun Quan! Liu Biao's were pigs and pups." As he spoke, a noise rang out. Swift boats were attacking from the south. From behind the Ruxu barrier an armed force emerged and attacked. Cao Cao's troops turned and fled, heedless of commands to stop. Suddenly hundreds of pursuers raced to the hillside; at the lead, a man with jade-green eyes and a purplish beard. Everyone recognized Sun Quan himself, leading a squad of cavalry. Cao Cao panicked and turned as Sun Quan's generals—Han Dang and Zhou Tai—joined the fray. Xu Chu dashed up to cover Cao Cao and, working his sword, checked the two southern generals' advance. Thus, Cao Cao got away and back to camp. Xu Chu fought thirty bouts with the two before retiring.

Back at camp Cao Cao rewarded Xu Chu well. He then scolded the rest of his commanders: "To retire in the face of the enemy blunts morale. Those who break ranks again will face execution." That night during the second watch an earthshaking clamor arose outside Cao's camp. Cao took to his horse in time to see fires spring up on all sides as the southern troops forced their way into the site. The killing went on until dawn. Cao's men retreated fifty li and camped. Sick at heart, Cao Cao browsed among his military manuals. Cheng Yu said to him, "Your Excellency knows the art of warfare well. Can you have forgotten the dictum that nothing is more precious than 'superhuman speed'? Your operations took too long and Sun Quan had ample time to prepare. He walled the Ruxu River on both sides, making it difficult to attack. I think we should retreat to the capital and reformulate our plans." Cao refused this advice.

Cheng Yu left, and Cao Cao rested his head on a low table. A noise like the surge of the tide or the stampede of ten thousand horses filled his ears. Cao went to look outside and saw in the midst of the river a great rolling sun whose blaze dazzled his eyes, and up in the sky a pair of suns. Suddenly the sun in the river rose from the water and dropped to earth in the hills before his camp, making a terrific peal. With a start Cao Cao awoke from his dream. They were announcing the noon hour.

Cao Cao had his horse readied and rode with fifty men to where he had seen the sun fall. There by the hillside he saw a body of soldiers. The leader wore gilded armor and helmet. It was Sun Quan. Cao's arrival seemed to make no impression on Sun Quan. Betraying no uneasiness, he reined in his horse and, pointing at Cao with his whip, said, "The prime minister has full control of the northern heartland and has attained the height of his fortunes. What greed prompts him to invade the south?"

To this Cao Cao responded, "You are a vassal who shows no respect to the royal house. The Son of Heaven has mandated me to bring you to justice." With a laugh Sun Quan replied, "What an outrage! Who in the world does not know that you coerce the Son of Heaven to compel the obedience of the feudal lords? Far from not respecting the Han court, I am going to bring you to justice so that the dynasty may be set to rights." Enraged, Cao Cao shouted to his commanders to take the hill and capture Sun Quan. Suddenly there was a tremendous drumming as two companies came from behind the hill: on the right, Han Dang and Zhou Tai; on the left, Chen Wu and Pan Zhang. The four commanders had three thousand archers unleash a storm of arrows on Cao's position. Cao beat a swift retreat, but the four southern commanders gave chase. Midway, Xu Chu managed to block the pursuers with Cao's personal guard and pull Cao to safety. The southern troops burst into a victory song and returned to the Ruxu naval base.

Returning to his own camp, Cao Cao thought, "Sun Quan is no ordinary man. The sign of the red sun means he will eventually reign." Yet though he saw the wisdom of pulling back, he feared the ridicule of the southerners. And so the two sides remained at a standoff for over a month, each scoring small victories. By the first lunar month of the following year, continuous rains had flooded the roadways, and Cao Cao was anxious over the suffering of his troops in the mud. Some counseled retreat; others argued that the spring thaw would assist the campaign. Cao Cao remained undecided. At this point a messenger from the south brought a letter to Cao Cao. The text read:

> Your Excellency and myself act equally in the service of the court. Yet Your Excellency, giving no thought to his debt to the dynasty or the welfare of the people, resorts unreasonably to arms, causing dreadful suffering to the common people. Is this the conduct of a humane man? Now that the spring floods have erupted, you should depart quickly, lest you suffer another Red Cliffs. Kindly give this your consideration.

On the back of the document was another sentence: "I shall have no peace while you live."

Cao Cao laughed at what he read. "Sun Quan speaks no lie," he said. After rewarding Sun's envoy, Cao ordered a general retreat to the capital. He instructed the governor of Lujiang, Zhu Guang, to garrison Huancheng and took the army back to Xuchang himself. Sun Quan, too, retired to Moling. There he set a proposal before his advisers: "Cao Cao has gone back, and Liu Bei remains away at Jiameng Pass. Why not use the soldiers who were fighting Cao Cao to capture Jingzhou?" Zhang Zhao, however, opposed this plan, saying, "It's still not time to use the army. I have a plan that will prevent Liu Bei's return to Jingzhou." Indeed:

> The moment Cao Mengde's power moved back north,
> Sun Quan's ambitions for the south revived.

Would Zhang Zhao's proposal return Jingzhou to Sun Quan's hands at last?
READ ON.

62

Yang and Gao Lose Their Heads in the Conquest of Fu;
Huang and Wei Vie for Credit in the Attack on Luo

"Refrain from military action," Zhang Zhao advised. "The moment you mobilize, Cao Cao will return. Instead, write two letters: the first, telling Liu Zhang that Liu Bei is allied with us in an effort to capture the Riverlands—that will turn Liu Zhang against Liu Bei; the second, urging Zhang Lu to attack Jingzhou and cut off Liu Bei's link to his base area. That should assure the success of our campaign for Jingzhou." Following this suggestion, Sun Quan dispatched two envoys.

· · · · ·

Xuande, after many months at Jiameng Pass, had won popular support in the locality. Receiving Kongming's letter informing him that Lady Sun had returned south and hearing of Cao Cao's attack on the Ruxu, Xuande turned to Pang Tong: "Cao has attacked Sun Quan. Whoever wins will take Jingzhou. What are we to do?" "There is nothing to fear," Pang Tong replied. "With Kongming there, I doubt the south will invade Jingzhou. Speed a letter to Liu Zhang, though, as follows: 'Sun Quan seeks aid from Jingzhou against Cao Cao. Quan and I stand or fall as one; I must help him. Zhang Lu is digging in now and won't dare attack the Riverlands. I would like to join forces with Sun Quan, but, alas, I don't have enough grain or men. I wonder if I could presume on our relationship as kinsmen to request thirty or forty thousand crack troops and a hundred thousand bushels of grain for the march? Please fail me not.' If Liu Zhang grants our request, we can plan the next step."

On Pang Tong's advice Xuande sent a man to Chengdu. He was received at the pass at the River Fu by Yang Huai and Gao Pei. Leaving Gao Pei to guard the pass, Yang Huai accompanied Xuande's envoy into Chengdu, where Liu Zhang accepted the petition. After reading it, Zhang asked Yang Huai why he had escorted the envoy. "Solely on account of this appeal," Yang Huai replied. "Since entering our region, Liu Bei has exhibited benevolence and virtue and has won the people's love thereby. He therefore means us harm. His present request for men, money, and grain must not be honored. To do so would be to add kindling to the fire."

"Xuande and I are like brothers," Liu Zhang replied. "How can I fail him?" Someone stepped forward and said, "Liu Bei's a crafty owl. To keep him in Shu is like letting a tiger into your house. And now to grant him what he requests is to add wings to that tiger." The speaker was Liu Ba (Zichu) from Zhengyang in Lingling. His argument gave Liu

Zhang pause. Then Huang Quan, too, urged his opposition. Liu Zhang consequently decided to lend Liu Bei four thousand inferior troops and only ten thousand bushels of grain. He sent his answer to Xuande and told Yang Huai and Gao Pei to guard the gateway to Chengdu.

Liu Zhang's envoy presented the letter to Xuande at Jiameng Pass. "I hold off your enemies," the outraged Xuande cried, "wearing myself out in mind and body, while you amass wealth and stint rewards. Is that the way to get the troops to give their utmost?" So saying, he destroyed the letter and stood up, denouncing Liu Zhang. The envoy ran back to Chengdu. Pang Tong said, "My lord, you give too much importance to humanity and honor. Today your display of anger has ended your friendship with Liu Zhang." "If so, what can be done?" asked Xuande. "I have three strategies," Pang Tong replied. "I pray Your Lordship, choose one and make use of it."

"Well?" said Xuande. "All you have to do," Pang Tong replied, "is to select your best men and make a lightning raid on Chengdu. That's the best plan. Yang Huai and Gao Pei are two famous generals of Shu. They have tough troops guarding the entrance to Chengdu. If you pretend to be seeking passage back to Jingzhou, they will come to see you off. Put them to death then and there, take the pass, and capture Fu; then take Chengdu. That's the second-best plan. Retire to Baidi and then go back to Jingzhou by rapid marches and make further plans there. That's the least preferable. If you stay here brooding, you are in for more trouble than you can get out of." Xuande replied, "Director General, plan one is too impetuous, plan three too slow. The second seems best. Let's try it."

Xuande wrote to Liu Zhang to say that Cao Cao had ordered Commander Yue Jin to Qingni township with more men than could be held off, that he had to help defend Qingni[1] himself, and that he was writing to bid farewell because there was no time to take leave in person. When the letter reached Chengdu, Zhang Song assumed that Xuande really was returning to Jingzhou, so he drafted a letter to Xuande himself. While he was looking for a courier, his brother Zhang Su, governor of Guanghan, arrived. Zhang Song hid the letter in his sleeve and began chatting idly. Zhang Su became suspicious at his brother's aimlessness. Song poured wine for Su and in offering the cup dropped the letter on the ground. One of Su's men recovered it. After the party ended, he showed it to Su. It read:

> Recently I made my views known to the imperial uncle. Everything I wrote was sound and sensible. Why have you yet to act? "Rough in conquest, smooth in rule" is what the ancients prized. Everything lies in your hands. I cannot grasp why you are leaving for Jingzhou now. When you get this, march on Chengdu at once. I will coordinate from within. You must not let yourself down.

Astounded by what he had read, Zhang Su thought, "My brother conspires to treason. I shall have to turn him in." He took the letter directly to Liu Zhang and denounced Zhang Song for plotting to deliver the Riverlands to Liu Bei. Liu Zhang cried in outrage, "All along I have treated him generously. How could he plot against me?" He ordered Zhang Song's family executed in the center of the city. A later poet expressed his regret:

> Though gifted with a memory most rare,
> Zhang Song let the crucial secret fall.
> Before Xuande's kingly cause was crowned,
> He fell to bloody swords before his town.

Liu Zhang proceeded to gather his advisers. "Liu Bei means to steal my estate," he told them. "What is to be done?" In reply Huang Quan said, "The situation brooks no delay. Tighten control at the passes and let no man from Jingzhou through." Liu Zhang approved and had all points notified.[2]

·   ·   ·   ·   ·

Xuande brought his forces back to Fu. He notified the pass guards and asked Yang Huai and Gao Pei to come out for the formal parting. Yang Huai asked, "What is Xuande up to this time?" Gao Pei replied, "Xuande comes to get killed. Let's carry daggers and do it at the parting. That will put an end to our lord's problems." "An excellent plan!" Yang Huai agreed. The two commanders took but two hundred men down to see Xuande through the pass and on his way. The rest of the guard stayed above.

Xuande's entire force had advanced to the edge of the River Fu. Pang Tong said to Xuande, "If Yang Huai and Gao Pei come eagerly, be on your guard. If they don't come, capture the pass directly." As they were speaking, a sharp gust of wind blew down the command flag before Xuande's horse. "What does this signify?" Xuande asked Pang Tong. "It's a warning," was the reply. "Those two mean to kill you. Be prepared." Xuande accordingly donned thick armor and belted on his fine sword. The approach of the two commanders was announced. Xuande ordered his men to halt. Pang Tong instructed Wei Yan and Huang Zhong: "As many as they are, not one is to go back, cavalry or foot." Wei Yan and Huang Zhong went to carry out their orders.

Meanwhile, Yang Huai and Gao Pei, carrying concealed weapons and attended by two hundred men, had brought sheep and wine to Xuande's soldiers. Seeing no particular precautions, they secretly rejoiced at the prospects for their scheme. They entered the command tent, saw Xuande and Pang Tong seated inside, saluted, and said, "We heard the imperial uncle was taking the long trip homeward and have come to send him off with a few trifles." So saying, they offered Xuande wine. "Your responsibilities at the pass are not light," responded Xuande. "You should drink first." The visitors drank as Xuande went on: "I have something to discuss with you two in secret. Everyone else should retire." He dismissed the two hundred followers, then ordered his men to arrest the two commanders. From behind the curtains Liu Feng and Guan Ping responded instantly. Yang and Gao began to struggle, but Liu and Guan took them prisoner. Xuande shouted at them: "Your lord and I are brothers of the same clan. How dare you conspire to divide us?" Pang Tong ordered them searched, and the knives were brought forth. Tong ordered them beheaded, but Xuande hesitated. "They meant to kill Your Lordship," Tong said. "For their crime death is too generous." And so Xuande ordered Yang Huai and Gao Pei put to death in front of the tent.

Huang Zhong and Wei Yan had already taken prisoner all two hundred followers of Yang Huai and Gao Pei. Xuande summoned them before him and offered them wine to calm their fears. "Yang Huai and Gao Pei," Xuande said, "meant to turn Liu Zhang and myself against each other. They were carrying weapons to commit an assassination, and for that reason we have had them executed. None of you is involved, and none needs fear for his safety." The soldiers prostrated themselves gratefully.

Pang Tong said, "Help us get to the pass so that we can capture it, and you will be well rewarded." The soldiers assented. That night the two hundred, with Xuande's main army close behind, reached the pass. "Our commanders return on urgent business," they shouted up. "Let us in. Hurry!" Those above, hearing familiar voices, opened the barrier at the pass. Xuande's men poured in and took Fu Pass without staining their swords. The

Shu troops surrendered to a man. Xuande rewarded them well and set up his own defenses.

The next day he feasted the troops in the great hall. Warmed with wine, Xuande turned to Pang Tong and said, "Today's gathering is cause for celebration!" Pang Tong said, "To take up arms against another's state and then celebrate it is not the way a humane man wages war." "I have heard," Xuande replied, "that in ancient days King Wu celebrated his victory over Zhou. Was King Wu not a humane warrior? Why are you so unreasonable? I advise you to withdraw." Pang Tong rose and laughed aloud. The attendants conducted Xuande into his private quarters. After several hours' sleep, he awoke from his stupor and, on being told that he had dismissed Pang Tong, was overcome with remorse. Early next morning he appeared in the main hall and apologized. "I was intoxicated yesterday and gave offense. Please do not remember it and hold it against me." Pang Tong spoke and laughed as if nothing had happened. "Truly I was in the wrong," Xuande insisted. "Lord and vassal both," replied Pang Tong. "Not Your Lordship alone." Xuande too laughed, and good will was restored.

•   •   •   •   •

Liu Zhang was dismayed to learn that Xuande had killed Yang Huai and Gao Pei and taken the pass at the River Fu. "Who would have thought this day would come?" he cried and assembled his advisers to discuss strategy for forcing Xuande's army back. Huang Quan said, "Reinforce Luoxian at once. That will give you control of the key road. The finest troops, the fiercest commanders will not get through." Accordingly, Liu Zhang commanded Liu Gui, Ling Bao, Zhang Ren, and Deng Xian to guard Luoxian with fifty thousand men.

On the first stage of the march Liu Gui said, "In the Damask Screen Hills dwells a remarkable man whose Taoist name is High Priest of the Azure Realm. He can foretell life and death, and things to come as well. When we march by those hills today, let's ask him how we'll fare." But Zhang Ren objected: "Warriors of mettle on their way to meet a foe don't seek answers from hermits." "I disagree," Liu Gui retorted. "The sage has said, 'Those who sincerely follow the way have foreknowledge.' A wise and lofty man may show us whether good or ill lies ahead." And so the four took fifty or sixty riders to the foot of the hills where they asked a woodcutter how to reach the sage's dwelling. Following his directions, the four ascended to a little hermitage on top of the hill.

A Taoist acolyte met them, took their names, and led them inside where the High Priest was seated on a rush mat. The four visitors bowed and expressed their wish to know of things to come. The High Priest replied, "We poor followers of the way are castaways in the wilderness; what do we know of the blessings or woes fate has in store?" Only after Liu Gui had repeated his request several times did the master call for writing brush and paper. He wrote eight lines, which he gave to Liu Gui. They read: "A dragon left, a phoenix right, he flies into the Riverlands. Young Phoenix drops to earth; Sleeping Dragon soars on high. One gain, one loss, as Heaven's lots dictate. Act as opportunity beckons and avoid perishing below in the Nether Springs."

"And our own individual fates?" Liu Gui continued. "What is ordained," the master answered, "is inevitable. No more questions." Liu Gui persisted, but the High Priest lowered his brows, closed his eyes, and made no further reply. The four climbed down the hill. "One must have faith in what these immortals say," Liu Gui commented. But Zhang Ren said, "He's a mad old fool whose words are worthless." The four remounted and proceeded to Luoxian, where they dispatched their men to guard the several strongpoints.

"Luoxian is vital to the defense of Chengdu: lose Luoxian, lose Chengdu," Liu Gui said. "The right thing would be for two of us to guard the city while the other two pitch their camps in front of the town at strategic points near the hills—to keep the enemy from approaching." Ling Bao and Deng Xian said, "We will prepare the camps." Gratified, Liu Gui assigned them twenty thousand men. They pitched camp sixty *li* from Luoxian, and Liu Gui and Zhang Ren guarded the city itself.

Having taken the pass at the River Fu, Xuande was deliberating with Pang Tong on how to capture Luoxian. When Liu Zhang's countermeasures—the advance of the four commanders and their men—were reported to them, Xuande convened his own commanders. "Who will win merit first," he demanded, "by seizing their forward encampments?" Veteran Huang Zhong responded promptly: "Here's a ready old soldier!" "Take your own men," said Xuande, "and proceed to Luoxian. You will be richly rewarded for taking the forts of Ling Bao and Deng Xian."

Huang Zhong, delighted, was about to set out when someone stepped forward and said, "The veteran general is too old to go. Though this junior commander has no talent, he begs to be sent." Xuande eyed the speaker—Wei Yan. "I have my orders," Huang Zhong protested. "How dare you interfere?" "The value of the elders does not lie in their sinews," was Wei Yan's reply. "Ling Bao and Deng Xian are famed generals of Shu, in the prime of their powers. I fear you are no match for them and could well ruin our lord's cause. That is why I beg to replace you. I mean no harm." Angrily Huang Zhong said, "If you think I'm too old, perhaps you will match martial skills with me." "Here before Our Lordship," answered Wei Yan. "The winner goes—agreed?"

Huang Zhong hastened from the hall and called for his sword. Xuande checked him swiftly. "No!" he shouted. "Today's campaign against the Riverlands depends entirely on the efforts of both of you. If two tigers fight, one will be wounded—and my cause will surely suffer. I appeal to you, do not continue this dispute." Then Pang Tong added, "What's the point of your arguing? Ling Bao and Deng Xian have two camps. Each of you attack one. The first to succeed gets top honors." Thus it was decided that Huang Zhong would attack Ling Bao's camp, and Wei Yan, Deng Xian's. After the two had set out, Pang Tong said, "They are likely to fight on the way. Your Lordship, follow with reinforcements." Xuande left Pang Tong guarding the town while he, Liu Feng, and Guan Ping went after Huang Zhong and Wei Yan with five thousand men.

Back at camp, Huang Zhong ordered mess ready at the fourth watch and finished by the fifth so that they could set out at dawn and approach through a ravine to the left. Meanwhile, through a spy he had planted among Huang Zhong's men, Wei Yan learned of the veteran's plans. Keeping his satisfaction to himself, Wei Yan instructed his army to prepare mess at the second watch and to march at the third so that he could reach Deng Xian's camp by dawn. The soldiers ate their fill; bells were stripped from the horses, the men gagged, flags furled, and armor bound—all to ensure silence before storming the camp.

During the third watch Wei Yan's force left camp. Halfway there, Wei Yan reflected, "Simply to attack Deng Xian's camp is no display of my prowess. I'll attack Ling Bao's camp and then Deng Xian's, so I'll have two victories to my credit." Abruptly, he ordered his troops to take the left road round the hill. By dawn they were nearing Ling Bao's position. Wei Yan's soldiers enjoyed a respite while the gongs, drums, and flags, as well as spears, swords, and other devices were arrayed for use.

Ling Bao, however, was well prepared, thanks to a sentinel's timely report. At the first shock of the bombards his men mounted and came out fighting. Wei Yan, sword upraised, raced to meet Ling Bao. The two generals tangled and fought some thirty bouts. The Riverlands troops formed themselves into two companies and surprised the Han army under Wei Yan's command. Finally, men and horses too weary to fight on after the night's march, the Han army retreated and fled. Hearing the disorganized march of his men, Wei Yan broke off his combat with Ling Bao and raced for safety. The Riverlands troops came on in hot pursuit. The Han forces sustained a grave defeat.

Before they had fled five *li*, the rumble of drums behind a hill announced a body of troops—led by Deng Xian himself—coming out of the ravine to bar their way. "Wei Yan! Dismount and surrender!" the call rang out. Laying on the whip, Wei Yan rode for his life, but the horse stumbled, fell forward, and flung Wei Yan to the ground. Deng Xian raced up and had raised his lance to dispatch Wei Yan when a bowstring hummed, and Deng Xian collapsed on his horse. Ling Bao was about to come and rescue Deng Xian, but a commander sprang into view crying fiercely, "The veteran Huang Zhong stands here!" and took on Ling Bao point-blank. Unable to withstand the charge, Bao turned and fled. Huang Zhong, pressing his advantage, routed the Riverlanders.

Huang Zhong's men rescued Wei Yan, put Deng Xian to death, and charged on to the campsite. Ling Bao now turned to engage Huang Zhong. They had clashed less than ten times when a mass of cavalry surged up from behind. Ling Bao abandoned his eastern camp and brought his defeated troops to the western camp, only to find the flags there completely changed. Astonished, he held his horse steady; before him was an imposing general in gilded armor and brocade war gown—it was Liu Xuande, flanked by Liu Feng and Guan Ping. "The camp is ours!" he cried. "Where are you going?" Xuande, who had originally set out to support Huang Zhong and Wei Yan, had later seized the opportunity to capture Deng Xian's camp. Ling Bao had no exit before or behind, so he took to mountain trails, heading for Luoxian. But before he had traveled ten *li*, he sprung an ambush on the narrow road, and men armed with hooked poles took Ling Bao alive. Wei Yan had realized his earlier mistake and established an ambush here with the help of some Riverlands troops. Thus, they were ready for the enemy. Ling Bao was bound and delivered to Xuande.

Xuande raised the flag of amnesty, ensuring that those who laid down their arms would be spared and that anyone harming a prisoner would forfeit his life. He then informed the body of surrendered Riverlands troops: "You are natives of the Riverlands; you have parents and families here. Those willing to come over to us shall be integrated into the army. Those unwilling are free to return to their homes." The cheering of the soldiers rocked the earth.

Huang Zhong established the foundation for his camp and then went to see Xuande, before whom he reported Wei Yan's violation of military regulations and demanded capital punishment. Xuande summoned Wei Yan, who brought in his prize captive, Ling Bao. "Such an achievement redeems your fault," Xuande said. He commanded Wei Yan to acknowledge his debt to Huang Zhong for saving his life and forbade further contention between them. A contrite Wei Yan pressed his head to the ground. Xuande rewarded Huang Zhong handsomely. Next, he had the prisoner Ling Bao brought before him. Xuande removed the bonds and offered him wine to reassure him. "Do you consent to surrender?" Xuande asked. "For sparing my life, I stand in your debt. Of course I consent. Liu Gui and Zhang Ren are my dearest comrades. If you let me go back, I shall invite them to surrender and tender Luoxian to you." Xuande was delighted; he arrayed Ling Bao and provided him a mount and sent him back to Luoxian. "Don't let him go,"

Wei Yan urged. "Once he's free, he'll never return." But Xuande responded, "I treat men with humanity and honor, and they never betray me."

Back in Luoxian, Ling Bao presented himself to Liu Gui and Zhang Ren. Without alluding to his capture and release, he simply said, "I killed a dozen men, snatched a horse, and got away." Liu Gui sent for help to Chengdu, where Liu Zhang, alarmed at the loss of Deng Xian, called an emergency conference. He eldest son, Liu Xun, requested a command to defend Luoxian. "Who will support him?" Liu Zhang asked. A man stepped forth to volunteer. It was his wife's brother, Wu Yi. "This offer gratifies us," said Liu Zhang. "Who will serve as deputy commander?" he asked. Wu Yi recommended Wu Lan and Lei Tong and detailed twenty thousand to proceed to Luoxian.

Liu Gui and Zhang Ren received them at the strongpoint and provided a complete account of the recent events. "The enemy is upon us," Wu Yi observed. "The defense will not be easy. What is your view?" Ling Bao said, "This region is flanked by the swift-flowing Fu River. Their fortifications stand before us at the foot of the hills, where the land is low. Give me five thousand men with spades and hoes to divert the river, and we can drown Xuande's army." Wu Yi followed the suggestion and ordered Ling Bao to cut a gap for the water. With Wu Lan and Lei Tong furnishing support troops, Ling Bao prepared the equipment.

Xuande left the two captured camps in charge of Huang Zhong and Wei Yan and returned to Fu, where he conferred with Pang Tong. Spies reported to them, "Sun Quan of the Southland is trying to conclude an agreement with Zhang Lu of Dongchuan³ concerning an attack on Jiameng Pass." Startled, Xuande said, "If we lose the pass, we'll be cut off from behind, unable to advance or retreat. What would we do?" Pang Tong turned to Meng Da and said, "This is your homeland, and you know the terrain well. Suppose you go and help guard the pass; are you willing?" "If I could recommend someone to go there with me, I will guarantee its security," was Meng Da's reply. "He was an Imperial Corps commander under Liu Biao when Biao governed Jingzhou. His name is Huo Jun (styled Zhongmiao). He hails from Zhijiang in Nanjun." Delighted, Xuande sent Meng Da and Huo Jun to defend Jiameng Pass.

When Pang Tong returned to his quarters, the gatekeeper told him a special visitor had come. Pang Tong went forth to receive a man of majestic appearance, well over six spans tall. His cut hair, disheveled, hung about his nape. His clothes were slovenly. "Who are you, sir?" asked Pang Tong. Without answering, the stranger stepped up into Pang Tong's quarters and lay down on the bed. Puzzled, Pang Tong repeated his question until the man replied, "A moment please, and then I will speak to you of the fate of the empire." Bewildered, Pang Tong ordered wine and food for the man. He rose from the bed and ate his fill unabashedly. Then he went to sleep.

Pang Tong did not know what to do. Fearful that the stranger was a spy, he summoned Fa Zheng to observe him. Fa Zheng listened to Pang Tong explain the circumstances of the stranger's visit. "Could it be Peng Yungyan?" Fa Zhang said, and ascended the stairs to look. The stranger leaped up and said, "Fa Zheng, I trust you have been well since we parted?" It came to pass, indeed:

> That the Riverlander found an old friend,
> And the River Fu was not turned from its course.

Who was the stranger?⁴

READ ON.

63

Zhuge Liang Weeps for Pang Tong;
Zhang Fei Obliges Yan Yan

FA ZHENG AND THE STRANGER looked at one another; then each clapped his hands and laughed. "This is Peng Yang (styled Yungyan) from Guanghan, a Riverlander of high repute," Fa Zheng explained to Pang Tong. "His frankness rubbed Liu Zhang the wrong way, so he was put to slave labor, his hair cut and his neck closed in a metal ring. That's why his hair is short." Pang Tong welcomed him as a guest and asked why he had come. "I have come to save the lives of tens of thousands of your men," was his answer, "as I will explain to General Liu when I see him." Fa Zheng swiftly informed Xuande, who came to interview the visitor personally.

"How many men in your forward camp, General?" the visitor asked. Xuande told him the number and identified the two commanders, Wei Yan and Huang Zhong, by name. "Shouldn't a general be better informed about topography?" asked Peng Yang. "Your fortifications are too close to the River Fu. If the enemy breaches its banks and bottles you up—van and rear, no one will escape." Xuande saw at once the danger of his position. "The handle of the Dipper is turned west," Peng Yang went on, "Venus lowers overhead: something ill-starred is on the horizon. Exercise utmost caution." Xuande appointed Peng Yang to his council of advisers and secretly alerted Wei Yan and Huang Zhong to patrol the river vigilantly. The two generals agreed to alternate the watch daily and inform each other of any enemy movements.

That night as a great storm blew up, Ling Bao took his five thousand men along the river in order to cut a channel. Suddenly he heard a jumble of voices behind him and, seeing that the enemy was on guard, beat a quick retreat. But Wei Yan overtook Ling Bao, and the Riverlands troops panicked. Ling Bao stumbled into Wei Yan, who captured him after a brief struggle. Then Ling Bao's support force, led by Wu Lan and Lei Tong, arrived, only to be cut to pieces by Huang Zhong. Wei Yan delivered his prisoner to Fu Pass, where Xuande denounced him: "I treated you humanely and honorably when I let you go. How could you betray me? How can I forgive you?" So saying, he had Ling Bao executed and Wei Yan rewarded richly.

Xuande was hosting a banquet for Peng Yang when Ma Liang, carrying a message from Director General Zhuge Liang, was announced. Xuande summoned Ma Liang, who, after performing the ritual courtesies, told him, "All is well; nothing in Jingzhou need concern Your Lordship." He delivered Kongming's letter:

I have been marking the Guardian star of the Polar Palace. This year Jupiter advances to the midpoint of the cycle. The handle of the Dipper points west. Observing other celestial phenomena, I see Venus lowering over Luoxian: that means our commanders are likely to incur misfortune. The utmost caution is essential.

Xuande read the letter and told Ma Liang to return. "I, too, shall return to Jingzhou to discuss this matter," he said. But Pang Tong thought: "Kongming, resentful of our conquest of the Riverlands and my own achievements, has written to deflect us." Pang Tong then said to Xuande, "I, too, have been marking the Guardian star and the westward turn of the handle of the Dipper. These signs correspond to Your Lordship's acquisition of the Riverlands and bode no ill. I, too, have read the stars and marked Venus looming above Luoxian—an evil omen signifying that we have already killed the Shu general Ling Bao, and nothing more. Your Lordship, do not waver. Now we must press our attack."

Urged on by Pang Tong, Xuande advanced. Huang Zhong and Wei Yan took him into camp, while Pang Tong asked Fa Zheng about the routes to Luoxian. Fa Zheng sketched them in the dirt, and Xuande checked them against the maps Zhang Song had left with him; they matched perfectly. Fa Zheng said, "North of the hills runs a major road by which Luoxian's east gate can be taken. South of the hills is a trail to the west gate. Both can be used by troops." Pang Tong said to Xuande, "I have ordered Wei Yan to the van: he will advance by the southern route. Your Lordship should order Huang Zhong to proceed by the northern. They can join forces in Luoxian."

"Horse and bow are second nature to me," Xuande said. "And I have much experience on narrow roads. Director General, you take the east gate from the main route, and I will take the west gate." "There will be enemy troops to intercept us on the main road; they will be better dealt with by you. I will take the narrow road," Pang Tong replied. "Better not," responded Xuande. "Last night I dreamed a divine being struck my right arm with an iron bar, and the arm hurt after I awoke. Our sortie may be ill-fated." "A brave soldier," Pang Tong said, "expects wounds, if not death. Can a dream make you waver?" "It is rather Kongming's letter," Xuande continued, "that gives me pause. Why don't you maintain guard at Fu Pass?" Laughing loudly, Pang Tong said, "Kongming is deceiving you, my lord. He has no wish for me to achieve great merit on my own, and he wrote that letter to make you doubt. Your doubts gave rise to dreams. What ill fortune is in this? I would gladly die the cruelest death fulfilling my heartfelt purpose. Please say no more, my lord, but make ready for an early start tomorrow."

Xuande had the morning meal scheduled at the fifth watch; they departed at dawn. Huang Zhong and Wei Yan took the lead. Xuande and Pang Tong, together again, were firmly in their saddles when Pang Tong's horse balked and stumbled, throwing its rider to the ground. Xuande leaped down and collared the horse. "Director General, why do you ride such a nag?" he asked. "I've had him a long time. He's never done this before," Pang Tong replied. "To balk on going into battle endangers the rider's life. My white is docile. Please take him. He will never fail you. Let me ride that wretch," Xuande said and exchanged horses with Pang Tong, who replied, "Not even my life could repay your kind generosity." Each remounted and rode on, but watching Pang Tong leave, Xuande could not suppress a sense of foreboding.

•   •   •   •   •

At Luoxian, Wu Yi and Liu Gui were considering the loss of Ling Bao. Zhang Ren said, "Off to the southeast there's a small but crucial road. I'll take a company and guard it. You gentlemen defend Luoxian. Let there be no slips." Suddenly they learned that Han forces were closing in on the city by both roads. Zhang Ren hurried off with three thousand men. He placed them in ambush along the narrow route, lying low as Wei Yan's troops passed. Pang Tong's forces were following from behind. Zhang Ren's soldiers pointed to the chief general in the distance, saying, "That must be Liu Bei—on the white horse." Excited, Zhang Ren issued his orders.

Pang Tong advanced along the twisting route. He noticed how the hills pressed close and the vegetation grew thick. It was summer's end, when the leaves grow thickest. "Where are we?" he asked, warily coming to a halt. He had freshly surrendered troops among his own, who said, "This is Fallen Phoenix Slope." Astonished, Pang Tong said, "My Taoist name is Young Phoenix. That name bodes no good." He ordered an immediate retreat, but the bombard had sounded, and bolts converged like locusts on the white horse. Helpless, Pang Tong perished in the barrage; his age was thirty-six. A later poet left these lines of lamentation:

> Afar, old Xian Hill in a hazy pile;
> In one snug nook, the home Pang Tong once knew.
> There lads could tell the turtledove's homing call,
> And news of his great deeds was known by all.[1]
>
> Pang Tong foretold a kingdom cut in thirds:
> Far he sought but never found his place.
> Alas, that savage Sky Dog charging down
> Never let him have his proud return.[2]

Prior to Pang Tong's death a children's ditty circulated in the northeast:

> Phoenix and Dragon joined as two,
> Minister and general came to Shu.
> Hardly halfway down the Luoxian trail,
> On the eastern slope the Phoenix fell.
>
> Winds bring rains;
> Rains chase winds.
> When Han rises next, the road to Shu'll be free.
> But when it's free, a dragon's all there'll be.[3]

Zhang Ren had shot Pang Tong down, and the Han army—caught in a vise, unable to advance or retreat—lost half its men. The bad news was rushed to Wei Yan, who immediately tried to swing his troops around. But the narrow mountain trail cramped their movement and Zhang Ren's archers and crossbowmen, shooting from a knoll, cut off their retreat. Wei Yan was at a loss. On the advice of one of the Shu soldiers who had surrendered, Wei Yan fought his way through to the main road and went on toward Luoxian. Amid rising dust ahead, a company of the defenders appeared, commanded by Wu Lan and Lei Tong. To the rear, Zhang Ren was catching up. Ringed by Riverlands soldiers, Wei Yan could not break free. Suddenly, he saw the troops of Wu Lan and Lei Tong becoming disorganized at the rear; the two commanders raced off. Seeing his chance, Wei Yan charged ahead—toward a commander who was swinging his sword and slapping his horse. "Wei Yan, I've come to save you," he cried. It was Huang Zhong!

Wei Yan and Huang Zhong turned the tables on Wu Lan and Lei Tong. Attacking van and rear, Xuande's generals crushed their enemies and forged ahead to Luoxian. Liu Gui came forth to do battle, but Xuande had now arrived with support troops, and Huang Zhong and Wei Yan hurried back to safety. By the time Xuande raced back to camp, however, Zhang Ren had cut the narrow road, and Liu Gui, Wu Lan, and Lei Tong were moving in. Xuande could not defend his two camps. He fought, fled, and fought again until he neared Fu Pass, hotly pressed by the victorious soldiers of Shu.

Xuande and his mount were spent. Bent only on flight, he had no taste for combat. As he neared Fu Pass, Zhang Ren's pursuers pressed closer. Xuande was saved only when Liu Feng and Guan Ping seized the road with thirty thousand fresh troops and forced Zhang Ren back in heavy fighting. Xuande's two commanders pursued Zhang Ren for twenty *li*, recovering many war-horses. After Xuande's force had reentered Fu Pass, Xuande asked for news of Pang Tong. Men who had escaped the massacre reported that he had fallen in the heat of battle under volleys of arrows. Xuande faced west and wept uncontrollably. A ceremony for recalling the soul was held, though they were away from the site of the incident. The commanders wept too.

"With Director General Pang Tong dead," Huang Zhong commented, "Zhang Ren will attack Fu Pass. What should we do? I think we should send to Jingzhou for Director General Zhuge to come and advise us how to take over the Riverlands." Even as he spoke, they learned that Zhang Ren was at the walls issuing battle taunts. Both Huang Zhong and Wei Yan wanted to take the field, but Xuande said, "Your mettle is blunted now. We'll dig in until the director general gets here." The two commanders did as ordered. Xuande wrote out a letter and instructed Guan Ping, "Go to Jingzhou for me; request the director general to come." Guan Ping hastened to Jingzhou, while Xuande himself defended the walls, refusing all challenges to battle.

• • • •

Meanwhile, in Jingzhou, on the festive evening of the seventh day of the seventh month, Kongming had assembled a grand congregation of officials to feast and discuss the conquest of the Riverlands. Due west in the night sky he witnessed a falling star, its head the size of a bowl, plunge to earth, spewing plumes in every direction. Kongming lost his composure and flung down his wine cup. "Alas! Grieve, then!" he cried, covering his face. The officials asked him why. "Earlier," Kongming answered, "I'd calculated that the handle of the Dipper's pointing west this year boded the director general no good. With Sky Dog[4] in the same degree as our army, and Venus above Luoxian, I have already respectfully advised Lord Liu to take every possible precaution. But I never expected that falling star this evening. Pang Tong must have died." So saying, he wept again before continuing, "My lord has lost a limb." The officials were astounded, yet doubtful. "In a few days," he added, "we will hear." The company adjourned, leaving the feast unfinished.

Several days later Kongming and Lord Guan were conferring when Guan Ping was announced. Before the astonished officials Lord Guan's foster son delivered Xuande's letter to Kongming. It read: "On the seventh day of the seventh month Director General Pang was slain on Fallen Pheonix Slope by Zhang Ren's archers." Kongming wept freely, and the officials did so, too. He then said, "I shall have to go. Lord Liu is in trouble at Fu Pass." "If you leave, Director General, who will guard this base so vital to our fortunes?" Lord Guan asked. "Although this letter does not say so specifically," Kongming replied, "I think I know our lord's mind."

Showing Xuande's letter to the officials, Kongming said, "Our lord has has placed the responsibility for Jingzhou upon me, with instructions to appoint whomsoever I deem fit. Nonetheless, today Guan Ping is here with a letter whose intent is that Lord Guan assume this heavy task. Yunchang, be ever mindful of the honor-binding oath in the peach garden and do your utmost to defend this province. So weighty a task will require the utmost diligence."

Lord Guan, without pausing to make the ritual refusal, readily accepted. At a magnificent feast Kongming proffered the seal and cord of authority, which Lord Guan extended both hands to receive. "Everything now depends on you," Kongming said, holding forth the seal. "An honorable man," Lord Guan responded, "perseveres until death." At the mention of death Kongming became uneasy, and he would have put off the transfer of authority had he not already committed himself.

"And if Cao Cao attacks?" Kongming asked him. "I will repel him vigorously," was the reply. "And if Cao Cao and Sun Quan attack?" Kongming pressed. "I will divide my army and repel both," was Lord Guan's response. "That would jeopardize Jingzhou," said Kongming. "Let me give you eight words of advice; if you commit them to memory, General Guan, they will keep Jingzhou safe." "What eight words?" Lord Guan asked. "North—repel Cao Cao. East—conciliate Sun Quan," was Kongming's answer. "The director general's words are engraved in my heart," Lord Guan said. Kongming tendered the seal and cord of office and commanded the civil officials—Ma Liang, Yi Ji, Xiang Lang, and Mi Zhu—as well as the military officers—Mi Fang, Liao Hua, Guan Ping, and Zhou Cang—to support Lord Guan in the defense of Jingzhou.[5]

Kongming took personal command of a force to enter the Riverlands. He placed ten thousand picked troops under Zhang Fei, ordering him to cut through west of Bazhou and Luoxian, and offering top prizes for those who arrived first. Then he dispatched another body of men, with Zhao Zilong in the van, to follow up the Great River and meet the first group at Luoxian. Kongming himself was to follow with Jian Yong and, in the capacity of secretary, Jiang Wan (Gongyan), a noted scholar of the Jingzhou capital, originally from Xiangxiang in Lingling.

Kongming himself had fifteen thousand men. He set out the same day as Zhang Fei. Before departure Kongming said to Fei, "The Riverlands has many mighty warriors to be reckoned with. Along the way your men must observe strict discipline; looting will alienate the common people. We must show compassion everywhere; and toward our own men we must not indulge in brutality—no whipping or flogging them. I trust you will reach Luoxian quickly, General. Do not fail us."

Zhang Fei eagerly accepted his command and set out. He met no opposition; no one surrendering to him was harmed. But when he reached Bazhou by the Hanzhong-Riverlands route, a spy reported that the governor of Bajun, Yan Yan, was refusing to surrender. Yan Yan, one of the Riverlands' most famous generals, had all his powers despite his advanced years. He could draw a heavy bow, wield a big sword; and he had the courage to confront ten thousand. Zhang Fei ordered camp pitched ten *li* from the city. He then sent a man into Bazhou to "tell the old fool to hurry up and surrender and spare his people, or I'll flatten the city and kill all within."

It happended that Yan Yan had been strongly opposed to inviting Xuande into the Riverlands. When told that Liu Zhang had authorized Fa Zheng to extend the invitation, he beat his breast and sighed, "A case of calling a tiger to guard someone alone in the hills." Later, told that Xuande had seized Fu Pass, he restrained his wish to attack the pass only for fear of a counterattack on his city. Now he was determined to stand against Zhang Fei with five or six thousand warriors.

Someone offered Yan a piece of advice: "At Steepslope Bridge in Dangyang, Zhang Fei drove back Cao Cao's mighty host of one million with a single shout. Cao Cao himself sensed Fei's strength and backed off. Do not rush to engage him. For now, it is best to dig in and defend tenaciously. They have no grain and will have to retreat within a month. Then, too, Zhang Fei has an explosive temper and makes a point of flogging his men. If we refuse battle, he will be piqued and will be sure to maltreat his soldiers in some fit of temper. When his soldiers revolt, we can strike and capture Zhang Fei." Yan Yan accepted this advice and ordered his entire force to defend the walls. At this point Zhang Fei's emissary arrived and was admitted. The soldier identified himself and delivered his message bluntly. Enraged, Yan Yan swore at him: "Lout! Barbarian! Will General Yan ever submit to traitors? Tell him that!" He had the man's ears and nose cut off and sent him back.

Zhang Fei listened to his envoy's bitter recitation of Yan Yan's insults. Gnashing his teeth and opening his eyes wide, Zhang Fei donned full armor and led several hundred riders to the walls of Bazhou to provoke the defenders to battle. But they threw every manner of epithet back down at him. Temper flaring, Zhang Fei fought to the drawbridge several times and would have crossed the moat, but volleys of arrows drove him back. By nightfall, however, not a man had emerged, and Zhang Fei returned to camp swallowing his rage.

At dawn Zhang Fei returned. From the observation tower Yan Yan shot a bolt through Fei's helmet. Fei pointed up and cried wrathfully, "If I catch you, old fool, I'll feed on your flesh!" Evening fell, and Zhang Fei went back to camp again without having fought. The third day, followed by his company, Zhang Fei circled the wall, reviling Yan Yan. It so happened that Bazhou, a hill town, was itself surrounded by groups of hills. Zhang Fei looked down from one of them into the city and saw the soldiers all readied in their armor and arrayed in ranks but keeping hidden behind the walls, determined to stay in their hold. He also watched the common folk moving back and forth transporting bricks and stones for the city's defense. Fei ordered his horse soldiers to dismount and his foot soldiers to sit down, hoping to draw the defenders out—but to no avail. After a futile day of full-throated curses, Zhang Fei went back to camp as he had before.

Zhang Fei mused: "I bellow at their wall all day long, but no one comes out. What can I do?" A solution struck him: keep the main body of troops standing by fully armed in camp and send only a few dozen warriors to the wall to draw out Yan Yan's men. But three days of such sallies by these common soldiers failed to draw forth a single fighter, and so Zhang Fei revised his strategy: he had his men fan out to chop firewood and explore the roads around the city without challenging the enemy to battle.

Wondering what Zhang Fei was up to, Yan Yan had a dozen men, disguised as Zhang Fei's woodcutters, slip out of the city to mingle with the enemy troops and find out what was going on in the hills. Back at his camp Zhang Fei sat amid his men stamping his feet. "That damned old fool will drive me mad!" he cried. A few men by the entrance to his tent were then heard saying to him, "General, why distress yourself? We have discovered a path that will take us past Bazhou unobserved." Zhang Fei deliberately shouted loudly enough to be heard, "Why did you wait till now to tell me this?" "We just found out," they replied together. "We must act at once," Zhang Fei declared. "Mess today at the second watch; break camp at the third when the moon is bright. Gag the men and strip the horses of bells for the march. I will go ahead and clear the way. You all follow in order." Zhang Fei's command was circulated throughout the camp.

Once these plans were known to Yan Yan's spies, they returned to Bazhou. The news pleased Yan Yan, who said, "I figured you couldn't control yourself, you damned fool. Sneaking over that road with your grain and supplies in the rear! When I intercept you from behind, how will you feed your men? Brainless idiot! I'll have you now!" Yan Yan ordered the army to prepare for battle: "Mess for us, too, at the second watch. At the third we leave the walls and hide where the trees grow thickest. Wait for Zhang Fei to come through the neck of this little road. When their wagons pass, hit them hard at the roll of the drum."

Night fell soon after the order was issued. Yan Yan's army, fed and well appointed, left Bazhou silently and spread out into an ambush, awaiting the signal to strike. Yan Yan himself entered a nearby thicket with a dozen lieutenants. Some time after the third watch he spotted Zhang Fei marching on, spear leveled for action, his warriors behind him, silent; three or four *li* further behind came the wagon guard—in plain view of Yan Yan. From all sides the ambushers emerged and were about to fall upon the wagon guard, when a gong rang out and a body of warriors overwhelmed the ambushers. "Stay where you are, you old scab!" a voice boomed. "This is a timely meeting." Turning swiftly, Yan Yan saw a powerful general—a pantherine head and wide-staring eyes, swallow-like jaw and a tiger's whiskers—wielding a ten-span spear and riding a deep black horse. It was Zhang Fei!

Gongs shattered the air as Zhang Fei's men came in for the kill. Seeing Zhang Fei, Yan Yan felt his skill depart him. After a few bouts on horseback Zhang Fei feigned a fall and allowed his foe an opening. Yan Yan swung hard. Fei ducked, then charged, grabbed Yan Yan's armor straps, pulled him over, and flung him to the ground; Fei's men bound him tightly. Actually, the first man on the path had been made to look like Zhang Fei. The real Zhang Fei had gongs rung ahead of the anticipated drums. That signaled his own onslaught, which caused the bulk of the Riverlands troops to throw down their arms and surrender.

Zhang Fei reached the wall of Bazhou in heavy fighting after his support troops had already entered the city. He ordered an amnesty and guaranteed the population's safety. His warriors pushed Yan Yan forward into the main hall where Zhang Fei sat, but Yan Yan refused to kneel. Through clenched teeth Fei shouted, "Why did you refuse to surrender to this general? How dare you continue to resist?" Without a trace of fear on his face, Yan Yan shouted back, "No man of honor in this bunch! Invading our province— you can have a headless general, but never a surrendering one." Zhang Fei angrily called for his executioners. "Villain and fool!" cried Yan Yan. "Take the head! Why waste anger?"

Yan Yan's strong, dignified voice and unflinching expression caused Zhang Fei to alter his mien. Coming down from his seat and waving off his attendants, he removed Yan Yan's bonds, gave him suitable clothes, and guided him to the central seat of honor. Then, inclining his head, he bowed, saying, "Just now I spoke harshly. Please take no offense. I have always known you for a noble warrior." Grateful for this demonstration of high-minded generosity, Yan Yan fell to his knees. A poet of later times wrote of the general:

> This grand, grey man of Riverlands,
> Whose spotless name the whole realm knows,
> Proved constant as the bright and lofty moon;

> Within the Jiang his mighty spirit rolls.
> He'd part with his head but would not give
> His knee in base subjection curled.
> Age-honored general of Bazhou,
> Who can find his equal in this world?

Another poem, praising Zhang Fei, reads:

> Bravest of all for taking Yan Yan alive,
> Valiant Zhang Fei won the hearts of all.
> Today in western shrines his image we revere,
> Where services keep springtime round the year.[6]

Zhang Fei asked Yan Yan the best way to enter the Riverlands. "A defeated general," Yan Yan replied, "indebted for such generosity, will toil like a beast of burden to requite his benefactor. The capital at Chengdu can be reached without resort to bow and arrow." Indeed:

> Because this general gave himself to Zhang Fei heart and soul,
> A string of cities would pass into Xuande's hands.

What plan had Yan Yan to offer Zhang Fei?

READ ON.

64

Kongming Sets a Scheme to Capture Zhang Ren;
Yang Fu Borrows Troops to Vanquish Ma Chao

IN ANSWER TO ZHANG FEI, Yan Yan said, "From here to Luoxian my men hold all the strongpoints, and they will do what I tell them. Allow me to lead the march to repay your kindness. The pass guards will surrender at my call." Zhang Fei thanked him from the bottom of his heart. Yan Yan went forth, followed by Zhang Fei, and the defenders indeed delivered each strongpoint to him. To win over those who hesitated, he said, "If I have surrendered, why not you?" In this way he advanced unopposed.

· · · · ·

Kongming had already informed Xuande of his intended departure date, designating Luoxian as the meeting place. In council with his advisers, Xuande said, "Kongming and Zhang Fei are taking separate routes into the Riverlands. We are to join them at Luoxian and proceed to Chengdu together. Their chariots and boats set out on the twentieth of the seventh month and should be arriving shortly. We can begin to march."

"We have steadily refused Zhang Ren's challenges," Huang Zhong said. "Their troops are getting lax, lowering their guard. If we send a company out to sack their camp tonight, it will be even better than a daylight rout." Xuande approved the plan and sent Huang Zhong to the left, Wei Yan to the right; he himself took the center. At the second watch the three forces set out together. In fact, Zhang Ren was utterly unprepared. The Han troops surged into the main fortification, setting fires that quickly mounted high. That night the Riverlands troops fled back to Luoxian where they found refuge. Xuande withdrew and camped on the road. The following day he advanced, encircled the city, and attacked it. Zhang Ren kept to his walls. On the fourth day Xuande personally led an attack on the west gate while Huang Zhong and Wei Yan went against the east; they left the north and south gates open to traffic. Xuande did not bother to guard the south gate, which led into mountainous roads, nor the north, which gave onto the River Fu.

In the distance Zhang Ren watched Xuande at the west gate to the city, riding back and forth, directing the assault through the morning hours. Observing that Xuande's forces were tiring, Zhang Ren ordered Wu Lan and Lei Tong to lead their men out of the north gate and swing over to the east, there to confront Huang Zhong and Wei Yan. Zhang Ren himself came out of the south gate and swung west to take on Xuande alone. Within the city soldiers and dwellers mounted the walls to beat drums and shout encouragement.

488

As the sun reddened in the western sky, Xuande ordered his rear contingent to pull back first. His troops were trying to turn when a great shout rose from the wall: Zhang Ren had charged out of the south gate and was heading straight for Xuande. Xuande's forces were becoming disorganized, and Wu Lan and Lei Tong had checked Xuande's two generals, Huang Zhong and Wei Yan. Cut off from their help, Xuande fell back and fled along a narrow mountain trail; Zhang Ren was close behind. Alone, Xuande raced ahead, Zhang Ren and a few horsemen giving chase. Riding straight ahead, Xuande laid on the whip. Suddenly a body of soldiers burst into view. "An ambush!" Xuande cried bitterly. "I'm trapped. Heaven has doomed me." Then he realized that the leader of the force ahead was Zhang Fei.[1]

Zhang Fei and Yan Yan had been coming along that very road when they spotted dust in the distance, a sure sign of a battle in progress. Zhang Fei hurried forward and clashed with Zhang Ren. After ten bouts Yan Yan arrived in force, and Zhang Ren fled. Zhang Fei chased him to the city wall, but Zhang Ren passed through the gate to the city and hauled up the drawbridge.

Zhang Fei rode back to Xuande. "The director general is still making his way upriver," he reported. "It looks like I won the race." "The roads are so treacherous," Xuande responded, "and you must have met opposition. How could you come so far so fast?" "There were forty-five strongpoints, but Yan Yan, the veteran commander, gets the credit for taking us through without difficulty," Zhang Fei said and explained how he had won Yan Yan's allegiance by freeing him. He then introduced Yan Yan. "But for you, General, my brother could not have made it," Xuande said gratefully as he removed his gilded armor and gave it to Yan Yan. Yan Yan prostrated himself before Xuande. As they were arranging a banquet, a scout rode back and reported: "Huang Zhong and Wei Yan are locked in combat with two Riverlands commanders, Wu Lan and Lei Tong. When Wu Yi and Liu Gui came out to aid the enemy, our forces could not fight off the combined attack. Huang Zhong and Wei Yan have fled east in defeat."

On hearing this, Zhang Fei requested that Xuande divide his field army into two forces to relieve Huang Zhong and Wei Yan. Fei led one force and Xuande the other as they charged to the rescue. Wu Yi and Liu Gui, hearing the tumult to their rear, retreated into the city in confusion; Xuande and Zhang Fei then intercepted Wu Lan and Lei Tong, who were closing in on Huang Zhong and Wei Yan. The latter two turned on their pursuers, catching them in the middle. Wu Lan and Lei Tong offered their surrender, which Xuande accepted. He then camped near the city.

Zhang Ren was sorely distressed by the loss of the two commanders. "The military situation is extreme," said Wu Yi and Liu Gui. "Without a fight to the death, we'll never repel them. We should report the emergency to Lord Liu Zhang in Chengdu while we think of a way to hold them in check." Zhang Ren advanced a proposal: "Tomorrow I shall challenge them to battle, feign defeat, and lead them around north of the city. At the right moment, rush out with a company and intersect their army. Victory can be won!" Wu Yi responded, "Let Liu Gui support our lord's young Master Liu Xun in the defense of the city. I shall conduct the attack at the north wall." And so it was decided.

The next day Zhang Ren led several thousand out of the city. Waving their pennants and shouting raucously, they taunted the army of Xuande. Zhang Fei rode out to confront them and without sparing a word engaged Zhang Ren. After ten clashes Ren feigned defeat and fled along the city wall. As Zhang Fei came after Ren at top speed, Wu Yi struck at the appointed moment and Zhang Ren turned his company rearward, thus trapping Zhang Fei between them. In despair, Zhang Fei spotted a company fighting its way up from the edge of the River Fu, a general at its head. Spear high, horse in full career, the general crossed points with Wu Yi. Within moments he had taken Wu Yi alive, thrown back the enemy troops, and plucked Zhang Fei from their midst. The warrior was Zhao Zilong. "Where is the director general?" asked Fei. "He has already arrived," Zilong answered. "He must be with Lord Liu by now." The two brought Wu Yi back to camp, and Zhang Ren retreated into the east gate.

On their return Zhang Fei and Zhao Zilong found that Kongming, Jian Yong, and Jiang Wan were already gathered in Xuande's tent. Fei dismounted and came to see the director general. "How did you get here before me?" asked Kongming in astonishment. Xuande related how Yan Yan had been released under obligation and had aided the march. "General Zhang certainly knows his strategy," commented Kongming as he congratulated Fei. "This is a boundless blessing for Your Lordship." Next, Zilong delivered Wu Yi to Xuande. "Will you submit?" Xuande asked. "How can I refuse? I've been taken alive," Wu Yi replied. Delighted, Xuande personally undid the prisoner's bonds.

Kongming asked Wu Yi, "How many men are inside guarding the city?" "There is Liu Xun, son of Inspector Liu Zhang, and two supporting commanders, Liu Gui and Zhang Ren. The former is no problem, but Zhang Ren is from Shu district and has great courage. Do not risk confrontation with him lightly." "We'll have to capture Zhang Ren before we can take Luoxian," Kongming said. "What bridge stands east of the city?" "Gold Goose Bridge," Wu Yi answered. Kongming rode directly to the spot to survey the river. On returning, he summoned Huang Zhong and Wei Yan and commanded them, "Along the river, five or six *li* south of Gold Goose Bridge, both banks are thick with reeds and rushes—a perfect place for an ambush. I want Wei Yan to hide a thousand spearmen on the left—they will stab at the commanders on horseback—and Huang Zhong to hide a thousand swordsmen on the right—they will cut down their mounts. Once their force is dispersed, Zhang Ren will have to come out by the small road east of the hills. That's where I want Zhang Fei with a thousand men in hiding—they will take him alive." Last, he ordered Zhao Zilong to wait at the north end of the bridge: "Destroy it as soon as I get Ren to cross. Then deploy your men north of the bridge to prevent his flight to the north. When he moves south, I'll have him!" His directions given, the director general went himself to draw the enemy out.

•   •   •   •   •

Meanwhile, Riverlands Inspector Liu Zhang had sent two commanders, Zhuo Ying and Zhang Yi, to reinforce Luoxian. Zhang Ren left Zhang Yi and Liu Gui to defend the city while he and Zhuo Ying went forth, Ren in the van and Ying at the rear, to drive the enemy off. Kongming led a rather disorderly troop over the bridge and arrayed them against Zhang Ren. Kongming himself appeared in a four-wheeled carriage, holding a feather fan, surrounded by his hundred cavalry. Pointing at Zhang Ren, he cried, "Cao Cao had a million men, but he fled at the mention of my name. Who are you to refuse surrender?" Zhang Ren, noting the careless look of Kongming's lines, smiled coldly from horseback. "It seems there is little reality in Zhuge Liang's reputation as a marvel among strategists," Zhang Ren said and with his spear motioned his force into action.

Kongming abandoned his carriage and retreated across the bridge on horseback, Zhang Ren in hot pursuit. When Ren crossed the bridge, he saw Xuande to the left and Yan Yan to the right, both charging toward him. He strove to pull out of the trap, but the bridge behind him was already down. He started north, but saw Zhao Zilong's men arrayed on the opposite shore and decided to flee south around the river. Riding some five or seven *li*, he reached the thicket of reeds and rushes. Wei Yan's men sprang out, stabbing furiously with their long spears while Huang Zhong's men slashed at the horses' legs with their long swords. The entire cavalry force was downed, the horsemen captured and bound. How could the infantry follow?

Zhang Ren fled to the hills with a few dozen riders, but Zhang Fei blocked his way. Ren tried to retreat, but a shout from Fei brought his whole force to the fore, and Zhang Ren was taken alive.[2] His rear guard commander, Zhuo Ying, had seen the trap closing and had surrendered to Zhao Zilong, who brought him back to the main camp. Xuande rewarded Zhuo Ying.

Zhang Fei brought Zhang Ren in when Kongming was seated in the command tent. Xuande said to Zhang Ren, "The other generals of Shu have submitted. Why not you? The sooner you do, the better." Eyes glaring, Zhang Ren shouted back, "No loyal vassal serves a second lord!" "You fail to recognize how times have changed," Xuande went on. "Submit and save your life." "I might for today," Ren replied. "But not for long! Kill me quickly!" Xuande could not bear to give the order, but Zhang Ren continued to denounce him. Finally Kongming had him executed to preserve his reputation for loyalty. A poet of later times wrote of Zhang Ren:

> No constant man consents to serve two lords;
> Loyal and brave, he died a deathless death.
> Now he shines like the heavens' circling moon,
> Lighting up the city Luo beneath.

Xuande was inconsolable. He had the body interred beside the Gold Goose Bridge to honor Zhang Ren's devotion to his master.

The next day Yan Yan, Wu Yi, and a group of surrendered commanders in the van marched to Luoxian and shouted out, "Open the gates and submit. Spare the people of the city." From the wall Liu Gui shouted back defiance. As Yan Yan put an arrow to his bow, a commander on the wall suddenly drew his sword and cut down Liu Gui. The gate was opened and the city delivered to Xuande. Liu Xun exited from the west gate and headed for Chengdu.

Xuande comforted the population. The man who had killed Liu Gui was Zhang Yi of Wuyang. With Luoxian firmly in hand, Xuande rewarded his commanders richly. "Luoxian has fallen," Kongming said, "and Chengdu will soon be ours. But I am concerned about the outer districts. It would be advisable to have Zhang Yi and Wu Yi lead Zhao Zilong in a campaign to pacify Jiangyang and Jianwei and the regions they administer along the Great River, while Yan Yan and Zhuo Ying lead Zhang Fei in a campaign to pacify Deyang and its subdistricts in Baxi.[3] After they have appointed officials there, they can return and move on Chengdu." Zhao Zilong and Zhang Fei set off at once to fulfill their missions.

Kongming next asked about the strongpoints on the road to Chengdu. The former Riverlands commanders replied, "Only Mianzhu is well defended. Once that falls, the capital is easily taken." Kongming called a conference on commencing the attack. Fa Zheng said, "With Luoxian in our hands, the district of Shu cannot stand. If, my lord, you mean to win over the people here by means of humanity and justice, defer taking action while I write to Liu Zhang setting forth the perils of his situation. That should induce him to surrender." "This advice is most pertinent," Kongming added. And so a letter was sent to Chengdu.

Liu Xun, meanwhile, after his escape from Luoxian, had returned to Chengdu to inform his father of its fall. Inspector Liu Zhang hurriedly gathered his advisers. An assistant, Zheng Du, proposed: "Despite his victories, Liu Bei still lacks troops and the adherence of the officials and the population. He feeds his men with wild grains, and he has no supply train. I suggest that we drive the people of Zitong in Baxi west across the River Fu and burn all their stored foodstuffs and all grain in the field. Then we can dig in quietly and wait them out, refusing to engage when they come to fight. Without supplies, they will have to leave inside of one hundred days. That will give us the opportunity to strike and capture Liu Bei." "I doubt it," responded Liu Zhang. "They say one drives off an enemy to secure the people. But who has ever heard of dislodging the people to prepare for the enemy? This is no way to ensure our safety."

During this discussion Fa Zheng's letter arrived. It read:

Only recently I was charged with binding Liu Bei to us in friendship. Little did I expect the opposition of those around Your Lordship would bring us to this pass. Yet Bei remains mindful of our longstanding amity and shared ties of kinship. If Your Lordship would reverse course and tender your allegiance, I am sure you would be treated most generously. We pray you will reflect and make your wishes known.

Infuriated, Liu Zhang ripped the letter to shreds. "Fa Zheng is a traitor! A mercenary, glory-seeking, faithless ingrate!" he cried and drove the messenger from the city. He ordered his wife's younger brother, Fei Guan, to reinforce the defense at Mianzhu. Fei Guan recommended Li Yan (Zhengfang) of Nanyang as his co-commander. They took thirty thousand troops to Mianzhu.[4] The governor of Yizhou, Dong He (Youzai) from Zhijiang in Nanjun, submitted a proposal to seek help from Hanzhong. Inspector Liu Zhang, however, rejected it. "Zhang Lu is my mortal enemy," he said, "and would never rescue me." Dong He responded, "Nonetheless, with Liu Bei in Luoxian, the situation is critical. And you still serve Lu as a buffer. It would to be his advantage to oblige." And so a messenger was sent to Hanzhong.

•   •   •   •   •

It was now more than two years since Ma Chao had suffered defeat and gone to live among the Qiang; he formed an alliance with them and seized the district of Longxi.[5] Every city there had surrendered to him; only Jicheng remained unconquered. Imperial Inspector Wei Kang had sent a number of messengers to Chang'an asking Xiahou Yuan for aid, but the latter would not act without Cao Cao's approval. Despairing of assistance, Wei Kang was inclined to surrender to Ma Chao. But his military adviser, Yang Fu, protested bitterly, "How can you submit to a rebel against the Emperor's authority?" "What else can we do?" said Wei Kang, and he ordered the gates opened to the conqueror, despite Yang Fu's strong objection.

Ma Chao said angrily, "You submitted out of desperation, not sincerity," and he executed Wei Kang and all forty members of his clan. Someone urged him to execute Yang Fu for urging Wei Kang not to submit; but Ma Chao said, "He kept his honor. We will not kill him." And so Yang Fu became a military adviser to Ma Chao. Fu in turn recommended Liang Kuan and Zhao Qu, who subsequently joined Ma Chao as officers. Yang Fu appealed to Ma Chao for two months' leave to bury his wife, who had died at Lintao. Ma Chao assented.

On the way, in Licheng, Yang Fu visited his cousin Jiang Xu, General Who Protects Remote Peoples.[6] (Xu's mother, aged eighty-two, was Yang Fu's paternal aunt.) On entering Jiang Xu's home, Yang Fu paid his respects to his aunt and then said to her tear-fully, "I have failed to defend the city placed in my care. I have failed to follow my lord in death. How can I face you again? Ma Chao is a rebel who has wantonly murdered district officials. He is hated throughout the province. My cousin sits tight here in Licheng and has no interest in bringing the traitor to justice. Is that how a servant of the Emperor should act?" So saying, he wept sorely.

Jiang Xu's mother summoned her son and berated him: "Imperial Inspector Wei Kang's death is on your shoulders." She turned to Yang Fu and said, "You have submitted and accepted office; why would you turn around and think of attacking him?" To this reproach Yang Fu responded, "I have followed the traitor and preserved my worthless life only to avenge my lord." "Ma Chao is a fighter of great courage," said Jiang Xu, "not an easy adversary." "Brave but incapable," answered Yang Fu, "no great problem. I've already secretly arranged for the cooperation of Liang Kuan and Zhao Qu should you be willing to take the field." To this Jiang Xu's mother added, "Act now. There will be no better time. All men must die, but to die for loyalty, for honor, is to die nobly. My life matters little; and if you do not heed your cousin's advice, I'll end it and end your worries too."

Jiang Xu took counsel with his commanders, Yin Feng and Zhao Ang. It so happened that Ang's son, Zhao Yue, was a subordinate commander under Ma Chao. The day Ang accepted Jiang Xu's assignment, he returned to his wife, Lady Wang, and said, "Today Jiang Xu, Yang Fu, Yin Feng, and I discussed avenging the murder of Inspector Wei Kang. But I am afraid that once we take the field, our son will be killed immediately by Ma Chao. What can we do?" His wife replied loudly and indignantly, "To cleanse the shame of king or father one should gladly sacrifice even one's own life. If you fail to act simply in order to save his life, I will take my own." Zhao Ang was resolved. The next day he joined the march against Ma Chao. Jiang Xu and Yang Fu stationed their forces in Licheng; Yin Feng and Zhao Ang, in Qishan. Lady Wang personally donated her jewelry and silks to the Qishan army to reward the troops and raise their morale.

When Ma Chao learned that Jiang Xu, Yang Fu, Yin Feng, and Zhao Ang were joining forces against him, he executed Ang's son, Yue. He then ordered Pang De and Ma Dai to attack Licheng in full force. Jiang Xu and Yang Fu went forth to meet them. Both sides assumed battle formation as Yang Fu and Jiang Xu appeared in white battle gowns. "Rebel! Dishonored traitor!" they shouted. Ma Chao plunged toward them, and the two armies fought. Overwhelmed, Jiang Xu and Yang Fu fled in defeat. Ma Chao took after them; but to his rear loud cries announced a fresh attack by Yin Feng and Zhao Ang. Ma Chao tried to reverse course, but pressed front and back, his army became divided.

At the height of the battle a new force came into play. Xiahou Yuan, having received Cao Cao's command, had come to destroy Ma Chao. Ma Chao's army was demolished by the combined strength of the three forces, and the remnant fled. Chao rode through the night, arriving at daybreak at the gates of Jicheng; demanding entrance, he was met with a storm of arrows and curses from Liang Kuan and Zhao Qu standing on the wall. They brought out his wife, Lady Yang, cut her down, and flung her corpse from the wall. Next, three of Ma Chao's infant sons and a dozen close kin were butchered one by one and pieces of their bodies were thrown to the ground. His bosom bursting, Ma Chao nearly toppled from his mount. To his rear Xiahou Yuan was catching up. The danger was too great. Ma Chao lost all taste for battle. With Pang De and Ma Dai, he fought his way free. Jiang Xu and Yang Fu were waiting ahead, but he broke past them after an interval of slaughter. He then battled his way past Yin Feng and Zhao Ang.

After the slaughter a bare remnant of Ma Chao's forces, fifty or sixty riders, reached Licheng. The guards, assuming that Jiang Xu had returned, threw open the gates to welcome him. Ma Chao began a chain of attacks inside the walls, beginning from the south end and sweeping through the commoners' quarters until he had reached the home of Jiang Xu. Xu's mother was dragged before him, but she showed no sign of fear. Pointing at Ma Chao, she reviled him, and Chao dispatched her personally. The households of Yin Feng and Zhao Ang were also put to the sword. Ang's wife, Lady Wang, happened to be with the army and escaped the massacre.

The next day Xiahou Yuan arrived in force; Ma Chao abandoned the city, broke through the enemy line, and fled west. Less than twenty *li* away he encountered the army of Yang Fu deployed before him. His face contorted with hatred, Ma Chao lashed his horse to top speed as he trained his spear on Yang Fu. Seven of Yang Fu's brothers and clansmen sprang to Fu's defense; but Ma Dai and Pang De blocked off the reinforcement, and Ma Chao slew all seven of them. Yang Fu himself, wounded five times, fought till he fell. To the rear Xiahou Yuan was coming up; Ma Chao fled again, followed by Ma Dai, Pang De, and half a dozen riders.

Xiahou Yuan personally delivered the pronouncement comforting the people of Longxi. He had Jiang Xu and the other commanders defend the various key points, and he sent Yang Fu to the capital in a carriage. There he was received by Cao Cao, who wanted to make him an honorary lord. Declining the offer, Yang Fu said, "I have neither the merit of having suppressed the insurrection, nor the honor of having died with my lord. By law I should be executed. How can I accept office?" Cao Cao regarded him highly and insisted on awarding him the lordship.

· · · ·

Ma Chao, Pang De, and Ma Dai decided to go straight to Hanzhong and join Zhang Lu. Welcoming them gladly, Zhang Lu thought he now had the strength to gobble up Yizhou to his west and hold Cao Cao at bay to his east. He suggested giving Chao his daughter in marriage, a proposal Yang Bo opposed: "Ma Chao himself brought on the disaster that befell his family. Your Lordship should not give your daughter to him." Zhang Lu agreed and dropped the idea.

Ma Chao learned of the incident and wanted to kill Yang Bo. But Yang Bo found out and, together with his older brother Yang Song, began counterplotting against Ma Chao. Thus was the situation when Liu Zhang's appeal reached Zhang Lu. Lu refused initially, and so Liu Zhang sent Huang Quan, who went first to appeal to Yang Song. Huang Quan said, "Our two regions depend on one another for survival. If the western region falls, will the eastern endure? If you relieve us now, we will yield twenty counties to compensate you." Delighted, Yang Song brought Huang Quan to Zhang Lu and explained the new proposal. This time Zhang Lu agreed. Yan Pu of Baxi now took up the protest: "Liu Zhang and Your Lordship are mortal enemies. He has made this deceitful offer in desperation. Do not accede."

At this moment a man came forward. "I have little merit," he said, "but grant me a small force and I can bring Liu Bei back alive as a hostage to guarantee the twenty counties." Indeed:

> No sooner does a true lord reach the Riverlands
> Than crack troops from Hanzhong go forth against him.

Who was the man?
READ ON.

65

Ma Chao Attacks Jiameng Pass;
Liu Bei Assumes the Protectorship of the Riverlands

THE SPEAKER, MA CHAO, ROSE TO HIS FEET and cut short Yan Pu's argument against help-ing Riverlands Inspector Liu Zhang: "Allow me to thank Your Lordship for his kind-ness," Ma Chao said to Zhang Lu. "Give me a company of soldiers; I'll seize Jiameng Pass, take Liu Bei alive, and see to it that Liu Zhang hands over those twenty counties." Delighted, Zhang Lu sent Huang Quan back by a short route to inform Liu Zhang that help was coming; he also gave Ma Chao twenty thousand troops. Pang De remained be-hind in Hanzhong due to illness. Zhang Lu ordered Yang Bo to supervise the army. Ma Chao and his nephew Ma Dai selected a day for the campaign.

· · · · ·

Liu Xuande's forces were in Luo. Fa Zheng's messenger reported to him: "Zheng Du has advised Liu Zhang to burn all crops and stores of grain and to lead the people of Baxi over to the west bank of the Fu. He means to dig in and refuse battle." Alarmed, Xuande and Kongming said, "That would put us in great danger." But Fa Zheng smiled and re-plied, "Fear not, my lord. Liu Zhang will not use so vicious a tactic." Sure enough, to Xuande's relief Liu Zhang's rejection of Zheng Du's plan was soon reported. Kongming said, "We must capture Mianzhu at once; then Chengdu will be easily taken." He sent Huang Zhong and Wei Yan to Mianzhu with an advance force.

Fei Guan had Li Yan deploy three thousand troops against Xuande's approaching force. Huang Zhong rode out and fought forty or fifty bouts with Li Yan, but neither prevailed and Kongming sounded the gong. On rejoining the line, Huang Zhong said, "I was on the verge of capturing Li Yan. Why did you recall me, Director General?" "His martial skills are too great for you to win by force. Tomorrow feign defeat, lure him into the gorges; we'll surprise him there." Huang Zhong agreed to carry out his assignment.

The next day Li Yan and Huang Zhong met in combat. After less than ten bouts Zhong feigned defeat and fled. Yan gave chase and tracked him into the gorges. Suddenly, sensing danger, he tried to turn back, but the troops of Wei Yan were already before him. Kongming called down to Li Yan from a hilltop: "Surrender! Crossbowmen on both sides of the gorge are ready and eager to avenge the death of our Pang Tong." Li Yan dis-mounted at once, dropped his armor, and surrendered. Not a single soldier fell.

Kongming brought Li Yan to Xuande, who treated him courteously and generously. Li Yan said, "Although a relative of Inspector Liu Zhang, Fei Guan is a close friend of mine.

Let me see if he will join us." Xuande approved. Li Yan reentered Mianzhu; he praised
Xuande's humanity and virtue to Fei Guan, urging him to surrender to save himself. Fei
Guan, convinced, threw open the gates of the city, giving Xuande possession of Mianzhu.
Planning for the campaign against Chengdu had hardly begun when an urgent message
came: "Zhang Lu has sent Ma Chao, Yang Bo, and Ma Dai against Jiameng Pass. The pass
guardians, Meng Da and Huo Jun, are hard-pressed. The pass will fall unless we help
now." Xuande was alarmed. "Only generals Zhang Fei and Zhao Zilong can deal with
this," Kongming said. "Zilong is still away," Xuande said. "But Zhang Fei is back. He
should go at once." "Say nothing to him yourself, Your Lordship," Kongming responded.
"I know how to get him to do his best."

Zhang Fei had heard of Ma Chao's attack and went to see Xuande. "I come to say
farewell," he cried, "and be off to fight Ma Chao." Pretending not to hear, Kongming
turned to Xuande and said, "Ma Chao is attacking the pass, but we have no one to match
his strength—unless we call Lord Guan from Jingzhou." "Director General," said Zhang
Fei, "do I rank so low with you? If once I held Cao Cao's million-man army in check, one
miserable lout like Ma Chao won't bother me!" To this Kongming replied, "Yide, when
you held the river and cut the bridge, Cao Cao's ignorance of the art of deception saved
you. In this case, Ma Chao's bravery is known to all. In six battles around the River Wei,
Cao Cao had to cut his beard and discard his battle gown, choosing to disguise himself
rather than face Ma Chao; Cao nearly lost his life then. Ma Chao is no ordinary warrior.
I'm not sure Lord Guan himself could defeat him." "I'm set," Zhang Fei responded. "If
I fail, let martial law apply." "Since you're willing to make the pledge," Kongming went
on, "then take the lead. I would also like Lord Liu to go but to allow me to remain in
Mianzhu until Zhao Zilong returns." "I should go, too," said Wei Yan.

Kongming sent Wei Yan ahead with five hundred scouts; Zhang Fei followed, and
Xuande brought up the rear. Wei Yan reached Jiameng Pass first and closed with Yang
Bo. After ten bouts Bo fled in defeat. Wei Yan wanted to take the top honors from Zhang
Fei, so he gave chase. Ahead, Yan saw a company in position, headed by Ma Dai. Thinking it was Ma Chao, he charged forward wielding his blade. After a brief clash Ma Dai,
too, fled. Wei Yan gave chase. Ma Dai wheeled and shot an arrow through his pursuer's
left arm. Wei Yan retreated swiftly.

Ma Dai chased Wei Yan to the front of the pass, where he was met by a thunderous
cry from a commander racing out to confront him. Zhang Fei had reached the pass and
heard the din of combat. Spotting Wei Yan wounded, he dashed down to save him. He
shouted at Ma Dai, "Who are you? First your name. Then fight." "Ma Dai of Xiliang,
none other!" was the reply. "Then you're not Ma Chao? Begone! No match for me! Send
that wretch to me—Zhang Fei of Yan!" "You despise me?" said Ma Dai. He cocked his
spear and charged. The battle went less than ten bouts before Ma Dai turned and fled.
Zhang Fei began to pursue but was halted by a call from Xuande, who had just arrived.
Together, Fei and Xuande returned to the pass. "Your temper is too hot," Xuande said.
"That's why I came after you. Ma Dai is defeated. Rest tonight, and tomorrow we'll fight
Ma Chao."

At dawn the enemy began drumming heavily below the pass as Ma Chao arrived with
his troops. In the shadows of his command banners Xuande watched Ma Chao gallop
forth, spear held firm, helmet bearing a lion emblem, belt of worked animal forms. His
silvery armor gleamed over a white battle-gown. Such extraordinary raiment bespoke his
uncommon ability. Xuande sighed and said, "Men tell of Ma Chao the Splendid. The
man confirms the name." Zhang Fei wanted to descend, but Xuande checked him, saying,

"Do not engage him now when he is keen." Down below, Ma Chao demanded to fight no one but Zhang Fei; Fei ached to charge down and devour his foe. Time and again Xuande had to restrain him.

By afternoon Xuande noticed signs of fatigue among Ma Chao's forces, so he picked five hundred to ride down with Zhang Fei. Ma Chao motioned his men back the length of a bowshot. Zhang Fei's company stood its ground. More men were coming down from the pass. Spear raised, Zhang Fei finally raced out, thundering, "Remember Zhang Yide of Yan?" "I come from an old family of distinguished lords. How would I know a village lout like you?" Ma Chao replied, rousing Zhang Fei to fury. The two horsemen took the field and exchanged blows with their spears. After one hundred bouts neither had prevailed. "He's a tiger," Xuande sighed. Then, fearing for Zhang Fei, he sounded the gong, and the two warriors returned to their lines.

After resting his mount, Zhang Fei removed his helmet and wound a scarf around his head. He rode forth to challenge Ma Chao, and the two came to mortal grips once again. Uncertain of Zhang Fei's superiority, Xuande donned his armor and descended from the pass. Standing before his lines, Xuande watched the two warriors clash. After another hundred bouts their energies seemed doubled. Again Xuande sounded the gong and the fighting broke off; each warrior returned to his side.

Toward nightfall Xuande said to Zhang Fei, "Ma Chao is bold and brave. Grant him his due. Retire to the pass. Tomorrow is another day." But Zhang Fei's blood was up. How could he desist? "I'll die first," he cried. "It is dark," Xuande urged. "Fight no more." "Light the torches and we'll fight," Fei demanded. Ma Chao had returned to the field on a fresh horse. "Zhang Fei! Dare to fight in the dark!" he taunted. Zhang Fei's bloodlust quickened. He got a change of horses from Xuande and came tearing out of the line. "I won't go back until I have you alive," he swore. "If I don't win," answered Ma Chao, "I won't return to camp." Wild shouts rose from both sides, and hundreds of torches lit the field like day.

The two warriors resumed the ordeal of combat. At the twentieth clash Ma Chao wheeled and fled. "Where are you running?" thundered Zhang Fei. Ma Chao, realizing he could not prevail, decided to trick Zhang Fei into pursuing so that he could twist round and catch him with the brass hammer he held in his hand. Ma Chao's feint, however, had not fooled Zhang Fei. He ducked as the hammer flew at him, and it whizzed past his ear. Zhang Fei turned back, and Ma Chao gave chase again. Zhang Fei fitted an arrow to his bow, but Chao dodged the shot. At last the two generals returned to their lines.

Xuande stepped forth and shouted, "I treat people humanely and honorably; I never use deception. Ma Chao, recall your men and rest them. I will not exploit the advantage." At these words Ma Chao guarded the rear himself as his commanders slowly retreated. Xuande took his troops back up to the pass.

The next day Zhang Fei again prepared for combat. When the arrival of Director General Kongming was announced, however, Xuande went first to receive him. "I hear," Kongming began, "that Ma Chao is a ferocious fighter. In a fight to the finish, he or Zhang Fei will certainly fall. I therefore left Zilong and Huang Zhong at Mianzhu and rushed here. I have a little trick that should win Ma Chao over, Your Lordship." "Ma Chao is bold and brave. I admire him greatly. Can we get him?" Xuande replied. "Zhang Lu, Ma Chao's lord, means to set himself up as 'king of Hanning' in the eastern Riverlands," Kongming went on.[1] "Since Zhang Lu's adviser, Yang Song, craves bribes, first send someone to Hanzhong to buy his friendship; then write Zhang Lu and say that your struggle with Liu Zhang over the Riverlands is intended to avenge him, that you give no credence to others' divisive purposes, and that when it's all over you will recommend him as king of Hanning. He should order Ma Chao to withdraw, and we will be able to induce Ma Chao to surrender.''

Elated, Xuande wrote the letter and entrusted the mission to Sun Qian; Qian reached Hanzhong along narrow bypaths, bearing gold and pearls that would serve for the bribe. Yang Song was delighted with Xuande's proposal and introduced Sun Qian to Zhang Lu. On hearing Xuande's offer, Zhang Lu said, "How can a general of the Left[2] make me king of Hanning?" "The imperial uncle," Yang Song replied, "is entitled to petition the Emperor." Delighted, Zhang Lu sent orders for Ma Chao to cease fighting. Sun Qian remained in the home of Yang Song awaiting news from the battlefield.

Word came that day: "Ma Chao says, 'No victory, no retreat.'" Zhang Lu repeated the command, but Chao would not come back. After the third refusal Yang Song said, "The man was never dependable. If he won't suspend fighting, he means to rebel." Yang Song circulated rumors that Ma Chao meant to seize the western Riverlands and make himself lord of Shu in order to avenge his father, Teng, rather than remain Zhang Lu's vassal. Zhang Lu heard the rumors and turned to Yang Song for advice. "First," Yang Song told him, "have someone tell Ma Chao that if he is determined to win merit, we will give him one month more, but only on three conditions. If he fulfills them, we will reward him; if not, we will execute him. One, we want the Riverlands; two, we want Liu Zhang's head; and three, we want the removal of Xuande's Jingzhou troops." Yang Song went on: "Have Zhang Wei reinforce our strongpoints in case Ma Chao's troops rebel." Zhang Lu approved these measures.

Ma Chao was astounded at Zhang Lu's conditions. "What a turnabout!" he cried, and told Ma Dai that they would have to suspend hostilities. Meanwhile, Yang Song spread more rumors to the effect that Ma Chao planned to revolt on his return. As a result, Zhang Wei divided his men into seven units and put all strongpoints under strict guard to keep Ma Chao out.

Ma Chao's situation was hopeless. Kongming said to Xuande, "In his present dilemma, Ma Chao could be talked into surrendering. Let me go to his camp and put my arts of persuasion to work." "Master," replied Xuande, "you are my indispensable right arm, my most trusted counselor; what if something happens to you?" Kongming insisted on going, but Xuande would not agree.

At this juncture a letter from Zhao Zilong arrived recommending a defector from the Riverlands. Xuande summoned the man to his presence—Li Hui (De'ang) of Yuyuan in Jianning. "We have heard lately," Xuande said to him, "that you strenuously opposed Liu Zhang's cooperation with us. Now you offer your allegiance. Why?" Li Hui replied, "It is said that a wise bird chooses the tree it will nest on, and a wise vassal the lord he will serve. My protests to Liu Zhang went as far as a vassal's could; but when he rejected my views, I knew his cause would fail. General Liu, since all in Shu acknowledge your humane virtue, I know your cause will prosper and have come to offer my service." "There is much you can do for me," Xuande replied. "Ma Chao is on the horns of a dilemma," Li Hui continued. "I met him once in Longxi. Let me go and try to talk him into joining us." "We were just looking for someone to go," Kongming said. "Tell us what you plan to say." Li Hui whispered his arguments into Kongming's ear, to the latter's great satisfaction; the volunteer was sent.

On reaching Ma Chao's fortifications, Li Hui was announced. "I know the man," Ma Chao said. "A skilled advocate. He must have come to argue their case." He hid twenty axemen behind the curtains with instructions to hack the visitor to pieces on command.

Moments later Li Hui strode in. Ma Chao was in the tent, sitting erect, not stirring. "What are you here for?" he asked harshly. "I come as an advocate," Li Hui replied. "There's a fine sword in this box," Ma Chao said, "newly sharpened. Try your speech. If it's not convincing, we'll try the sword!" Li Hui smiled and said, "General, the end is near for you. My only fear is that your newly sharpened sword may prove itself on your own neck, not mine." "What?" said Ma Chao. "Do you remember Lady Xishi of Yue," Li Hui said, "whose beauty the most skillful slanderer could not cover up? Or Wuyan of Qi, whose ill favor the greatest eulogy could not disguise? The sun starts to set at noon; the moon starts to wane when full. These are universal principles. For killing your father, Cao Cao is your mortal enemy. In Longxi you have bitter foes. There is no way you can save Liu Zhang and force back Xuande's Jingzhou troops; nor can you break Yang Song's hold on Zhang Lu. Who in the world wants you, man without a master? One more defeat like the one at Wei bridge or Jicheng, and you will reap the world's scorn."

Ma Chao nodded and said appreciatively, "What you say makes sense. Have I a way out?" "If you are willing to listen," Li Hui said. "But what are the axemen for?" Shamed by the question, Ma Chao dismissed them. "Imperial Uncle Liu," Li Hui went on, "is courteous to the worthy and humble before men of ability. I have confidence in his success, and for that reason have transferred my allegiance from Liu Zhang to Liu Xuande. Your honorable father once made common cause with the imperial uncle in order to bring the traitor Cao to justice.[3] Won't you turn from the benighted Zhang Lu and make your future with the enlightened Xuande, not only to avenge your father but also to establish your own merit?" Ma Chao was delighted. He summoned Yang Bo and cut him down; then he took the head and went with Li Hui to Jiameng Pass to submit to Xuande. Xuande welcomed Ma Chao in person and treated him as an honored guest. Chao touched his head to the ground in appreciation. "Today meeting an enlightened lord is like seeing the bright heavens break through clouds and mist," he declared.

Sun Qian had already returned from his mission to Zhang Lu. Xuande had Huo Jun and Meng Da guard the pass, and sent his army to capture Chengdu. Zhao Zilong and Huang Zhong welcomed Xuande into Mianzhu. There was a report that Liu Jun and Ma Han had come to contest Mianzhu. Zhao Zilong said, "I'll take care of them." He mounted and rode off with his men. On the city wall Xuande feted Ma Chao with wine. Before the banquet had begun, Zhao Zilong presented the heads of Liu Jun and Ma Han. The astonished Ma Chao felt redoubled respect. "Do not tire your forces, my lord," he said. "I will call on Liu Zhang to surrender. If he refuses, my brother Dai and I will deliver Chengdu to you ourselves." Xuande was delighted. The day had proved a perfect success.

•   •   •   •   •

Remnants of Liu Zhang's defeated army reached Chengdu with the news of Ma Chao's defection. The alarmed inspector sealed the gates and would not appear. But when told that Ma Chao and Ma Dai were coming to help, he mounted the north wall and faced the two brothers. "We want to speak to Liu Zhang," they cried. Liu Zhang responded from the wall, and Ma Chao, remaining mounted, pointed with his whip and said, "I started out with Zhang Lu's troops to rescue you. Imagine my surprise when Zhang Lu heeded Yang Song's slanders and tried to murder me. Now I have submitted to Imperial Uncle Liu; I suggest you tender your territory to us and surrender rather than subject your people to further misery. Should you persist in your misguided resistance, we are prepared to attack your city now."

Liu Zhang turned the color of ash and fell over. His officials rushed to revive him. "How blind I was!" Liu Zhang said. "Now it's too late for despair. Open the gates and spare the people." Dong He, however, said, "We still have over thirty thousand troops in the city and the means to support them for one year. What's the point of simply surrendering?" "In our more than twenty years in Shu," Liu Zhang replied, "what benefits have my father and I conferred on the people?[4] In three years' warfare they have left their life's blood in the fields—and it is my fault. What peace can I know? Better to surrender and make them secure." All shed tears at these words.

Suddenly a man appeared and said, "Your Lordship's words accord with Heaven's wish." Everyone turned to Qiao Zhou (Yunnan), a man from Xichongguo in Baxi and a skilled reader of the stars. Questioned by Liu Zhang, he said "Observing the constellations, I have seen stars clustering over Shu, the main star bright as the moon. It is the imperial sign. Moreover, a year ago, there was a children's ditty: 'If you want fresh rice, you must wait till First Ruler comes.'[5] A clear omen: Heaven must have its way." Huang Quan and Liu Ba were angered, but Liu Zhang prevented them from executing the fortune-teller. Suddenly another report came in: the district governor of Shu, Xu Jing, had left his city and surrendered. Liu Zhang returned to his quarters in great distress.

The next day Liu Zhang was told that Jian Yong, ranking envoy from Imperial Uncle Liu, was at the city gate. Liu Zhang ordered the gate opened to receive him, but Jian Yong remained seated smugly in his carriage, eyeing the inspector. Suddenly someone with sword drawn shouted, "Upstart! Think you're above us all? How dare you snub the worthies of Shu?" Jian Yong descended quickly and offered his respects to the speaker, Qin Mi (Zilai) of Mianzhu in Guanghan. With a smile Jian Yong said, "Forgive me. I did not recognize my worthy brother."

Qin Mi took Jian Yong to Inspector Liu Zhang. Jian Yong explained that Xuande was a generous and understanding man who bore him no ill will. On this assurance Liu Zhang made up his mind to submit and showed Jian Yong every consideration. The following day Liu Zhang personally tendered his seal and cord and other official documents to Jian Yong, who then escorted him out of the city by carriage. Xuande came out of his campsite to receive Liu Zhang, taking his hands and weeping freely as he said, "Do not think we have forsaken the principles of humanity and honor. The situation was beyond our control." Together they entered the camp and, after transferring the instruments of office, rode side by side into the capital of the Riverlands.

Xuande entered Chengdu to a joyful reception. The people welcomed him at the city gate with incense and flowers and lanterns. He arrived at the government buildings, ascended the main hall, and seated himself. All the officials of the capital district prostrated themselves below, save Huang Quan and Liu Ba who refused to appear. The commanders wanted to put them to death, but Xuande hastily issued an order forbidding anyone to harm them on pain of clan-wide execution. Xuande went in person to their quarters and invited them to enter his service. Huang Quan and Liu Ba, moved by Xuande's gentle courtesy, finally accepted.[6]

Kongming said to Xuande, "We have the Riverlands. But there is no room for two lords: Liu Zhang should be sent to Jingzhou." "We have hardly taken possession of the capital district of Shu," Xuande answered. "We cannot command Liu Zhang to leave." "Indecision has cost him his estate," Kongming continued. "My lord, if you rule with womanish benevolence, this land will not long be yours." Xuande was persuaded. He held a grand banquet, requested Liu Zhang to gather up his goods, bestowed on him the insignia of General Who Exhibits Might, and had him take his family and household servants to Gong'an in Nanjun that very day.[7]

When Xuande assumed the protectorship of Yizhou, he richly rewarded all civil and military officials who had submitted and distinguished them with important titles. Yan Yan was made general of the Van; Fa Zheng, governor of Shu district; Dong He, Imperial Corps commander; Xu Jing, first lieutenant to the general of the Left; Pang Yi, officer in charge of the camps; Liu Ba, general of the Left; Huang Quan, general of the Right. Wu Yi, Fei Guan, Peng Yang, Zhuo Ying, Li Yan, Wu Lan, Lei Tong, Li Hui, Zhang Yi, Qin Mi, Qiao Zhou, Lü Yi, Huo Jun, Deng Zhi, Yang Hong, Zhou Qun, Fei Yi, Fei Shi, Meng Da, and all the surrendering officers and officials, over sixty in number, were advanced to positions of influence.

Zhuge Liang was confirmed as director general; Lord Guan, General Who Scours the Predators and lord of Hanshou precinct;[8] Zhang Fei, General Who Conquers the Barbarians and lord of Xin precinct; Zhao Zilong, General Who Keeps Order Afar; Huang Zhong, General Who Conquers the West; Wei Yan, General Who Displays Prowess; Ma Chao, General Who Pacifies the West. Sun Qian, Jian Yong, Mi Zhu, Mi Fang, Liu Feng, Wu Ban, Guan Ping, Zhou Cang, Liao Hua, Ma Liang, Ma Su, Jiang Wan, Yi Ji, and other officials and officers from Jingzhou were also promoted and rewarded.

A special envoy was sent to Lord Guan bearing five hundred catties of gold, one thousand of silver, fifty million copper coins, and one thousand rolls of Riverlands silk. Other officials and commanders were rewarded according to their deserts. Oxen and horses were slaughtered to provide a great feast for the soldiers, and the granaries were opened to relieve the suffering of the common people. Soldiers and civilians alike rejoiced.

Having conquered the Riverlands, Xuande proposed to grant his officials Chengdu's most desirable lands and buildings. Zhao Zilong, however, protested: "The people of this province have been through the flames of war so long that they have deserted their fields and dwellings. These properties should be restored to those who live here, for resettlement and economic revival—not taken away for rewarding our own. In that way, our rule will gain acceptance." Xuande gladly followed this advice.[9]

Next, Xuande instructed Director General Zhuge to revise the legal code, which provided for severe corporal punishment. Fa Zheng said, "When the Supreme Ancestor entered the Qin capital at Xianyang, he reduced the legal code to three provisions,[10] and the common people rejoiced in his benevolence. I would like the Director General to satisfy our people's expectations by easing the punitive provisions and curtailing the scope of the laws." "You don't see the whole problem," Kongming replied. "The laws of Qin were punitive and harsh, and the people detested them. That is why the Supreme Ancestor's kindness and leniency won their allegiance. But in this case, Liu Zhang was foolish and weak. His benevolence inspired no dedication, his severity no respect, so relations between lord and vassal have gradually broken down. Vassals he favored with office became cruel as their authority increased; vassals his generosity kept dependable became indifferent as his generosity was exhausted. Herein lies the true cause of Liu Zhang's failure. Our new administration must win respect through legal authority; when the laws are carried out, then the people will appreciate our kindnesses. Moreover, we must use rank to limit ambition so that when rank is granted, the honor will be appreciated. Balanced bestowing of kindness and honor will restore proper relations between lord and vassal, and the principles of good governance will again be manifest." Fa Zheng was persuaded and withdrew his suggestion. Henceforth there was good order in the army and among the population.

The Riverlands' forty-one subdistricts were placed under military control and pacified. Fa Zheng, serving as governor of Shu district, repaid the smallest favor and avenged the slightest grievance. Someone complained to Kongming that Fa Zheng should be rebuked for his overzealous administration. But Kongming replied, "I remember when Lord Liu was a virtual prisoner in Jingzhou, dreading Cao Cao to the north and fearful of Sun Quan to the east. Thanks to Fa Zheng, who lent our lord wings, he soared beyond anyone's reach. How can we restrict Fa Zheng or deny him his way?" Thus, the matter was dropped; but when the complaint came to Fa Zheng's attention, he began to show restraint in his conduct.

One day Xuande and Kongming were chatting, when a message came that Lord Guan had sent his son Ping to thank Xuande for the gold and silk he had been awarded. Xuande summoned the lad. After performing the ritual prostration, Guan Ping delivered Lord Guan's letter. "My father knows that Ma Chao's martial skill surpasses that of other warriors," Ping said. "He wants to come to the Riverlands for a trial of skill and has asked me to petition you, uncle, on this matter." Xuande was shocked. "If Lord Guan comes now to test his strength against Ma Chao," he said, "we will lose one of them." But Kongming said, "I see no harm. Let me send an answer." Xuande, fearing Lord Guan's hasty temper, had Kongming reply; Guan Ping sped the letter to Jingzhou. Lord Guan asked his son, "Did you discuss my trial of strength with Ma Chao?" "Here is the director general's response," Guan Ping replied. Lord Guan unsealed the letter, which read:

> I understand you wish a trial with Ma Chao. In my judgment, although Ma Chao is a fiercer warrior than most, he belongs in the category of Ying Bu and Peng Yue. He might prove the equal of your worthy brother, Yide, but could hardly compare with the unique and incomparable ability of our Long-Bearded Lord. Your present governorship of Jingzhou is no slight responsibility. If you came here and Jingzhou were lost, it would be the gravest offense. Please favor us with your discernment.[11]

After reading the letter, Lord Guan stroked his beard and said with a smile, "How well Kongming knows me." He had the letter shown to his companions, and lost all interest in traveling to the west.

• • • • •

In the Southland Sun Quan learned that Xuande had taken possession of the Riverlands and moved the former inspector, Liu Zhang, to Gong'an. Sun Quan summoned Zhang Zhao and Gu Yong. "At the beginning," he told them, "Liu Bei pledged to return Jingzhou province after taking the Riverlands. He already holds the forty-one subdistricts of Ba and Shu and is about to extend his rule to the Hanzhong districts on the River Han. Either he returns the province now, or the time has come for war." Zhang Zhao objected. "Our land is at peace," he said. "We must not start a war. I have a plan to make Liu Bei restore Jingzhou to us with all humility and respect." Indeed:

> As a new day dawns in the Riverlands,
> The Southland seeks to satisfy its longstanding claim.

What was Zhang Zhao thinking?
READ ON.

66

A Lone Swordsman, Guan Presents Himself at Lu Su's Feast;
Empress Wu Lays Down Her Life for Her House

ZHANG ZHAO OFFERED A PLAN for recovering Jingzhou. "Liu Bei relies above all on Zhuge Liang," he said to Sun Quan. "His older brother, Jin, is in our service. What if we arrest Jin's family and send him to the Riverlands with this message: 'My family's safety depends on the return of the province'? Out of fraternal sympathy Liang should agree."[1] Sun Quan replied, "Zhuge Jin is an honorable man. How can I arrest his family?" "Tell him outright it's part of the plan," Zhang Zhao returned, "and spare him any worry." Sun Quan approved. He sequestered Zhuge Jin's family in his headquarters and sent Jin west with a letter for Xuande. Not long after, Jin reached Chengdu.

Xuande asked Kongming, "Why did they send your brother here?" "To recover Jingzhou; why else?" was his reply. "How to respond?" Xuande asked. "Just do as I say," Kongming answered. Having set his course, Kongming received his brother outside the city wall and took him directly to the government guesthouse rather than his own home. After the ritual of expressions of respect, Jin let out a sharp cry. "Brother," said Kongming, "is there a problem? You have only to speak. What makes you express such grief?" "My family is done for," Jin said. "Not because of Jingzhou?" Kongming asked. "If your family has been seized on my account, how can I have a moment's peace? Set your anxieties aside. I have a very simple plan for returning it, once and for all." Elated, Zhuge Jin went with Kongming to see Xuande and deliver his letter.

On reading it Xuande said angrily, "First Sun Quan gave me his sister in marriage, then during my absence from Jingzhou he spirited her away. Imagine how I felt. I could have invaded the Southland to avenge the insult. And now you tell me he wants Jingzhou back!"[2] At this point Kongming flung himself to the ground, weeping, and implored Xuande: "Lord Sun has arrested my elder brother's family. If the province is not returned to Sun Quan, they will all be cruelly executed. If I lose my elder brother, how will I survive? I beg Your Lordship, if only for my sake, return Jingzhou to Lord Sun; preserve the fraternal ties that bind my brother and myself." After a show of resistance to Kongming's tearful pleas, Xuande softened and said, "In that case, in view of the director general's personal appeal, I will return one half—the three districts of Changsha, Lingling, and Guiyang."

"Since we have received your gracious consent," Kongming continued, "would you write to Lord Guan ordering him to make the three districts over to Lord Sun?" Xuande replied, "When Zhuge Jin reaches Jingzhou, it is imperative that he himself put this request to my brother in the most diplomatic terms. You know how volatile my brother can be; I fear him myself. Zhuge Jin, you must exercise the greatest delicacy." Provided with the letter, Zhuge Jin took leave of Xuande, bid his brother good-bye, and went to Jingzhou.

Lord Guan invited Zhuge Jin into the main hall, and host and guest exchanged salutations. Jin produced Xuande's letter. "The imperial uncle," he said, "has consented to restore three districts to Lord Sun. I trust, General, that you will arrange the transfer at once, so that I may return and face my master in good conscience." But Lord Guan's face darkened as he said, "My brother and I swore in the peach garden to make common cause in upholding the house of Han. Jingzhou is Han's sovereign territory. How could I give anyone an inch of it for no good reason? As they say, 'The general abroad may disregard the king.' Despite this letter, I simply will not 'restore' anything." "Lord Sun has imprisoned my family," Zhuge Jin pleaded, "and will kill them if he doesn't get Jingzhou back. Have pity, General." "That little ruse won't work on me!" responded Lord Guan.[3] "Have you no consideration, General?" said Jin. Lord Guan reached for his sword. "Enough!" he cried. "This sword has even less!" Guan Ping added his own appeal: "Father, for the sake of the director general, restrain your anger." "If it were not for the director general, you wouldn't get back to the Southland alive," was Lord Guan's final word to Zhuge Jin.

Thoroughly humiliated, Zhuge Jin exited speedily and sailed west to see Kongming. Kongming was away on a tour of inspection, so it was to Xuande that Zhuge Jin complained that Lord Guan meant to kill him. "My brother is swift to anger," Xuande said, "it is nearly impossible to reason with him. Return to the south for now, and give me some time to complete the conquest of the eastern Riverlands' Hanzhong districts. I will bring Lord Guan over to defend them, and then Jingzhou can be yours once again."

Zhuge Jin had no choice. He returned to Lord Sun and explained all that had taken place. "Your trip," the outraged Sun Quan cried, "dashing back and dashing forth—perhaps it's all a part of Zhuge Liang's plan." "Not at all!" replied Zhuge Jin. "My brother, too, pleaded tearfully with Xuande who finally consented to give back three districts. But Lord Guan stubbornly refused to comply." "In that case," Sun Quan responded, "send our officials on to govern those three districts and see what happens next." "An excellent decision, Your Lordship," Zhuge Jin said. Sun Quan let Jin take his family home.

The southern administrators Sun Quan sent were soon expelled from the three Jingzhou districts that Xuande had promised. "Lord Guan refused to accept us," they complained on returning to the Southland. "He drove us back the night we arrived and ordered anyone resisting to be killed." Enraged, Sun Quan summoned Lu Su. "Did you not serve as Liu Bei's guarantor when he borrowed Jingzhou? Now he has conquered the western Riverlands, but he does not return Jingzhou. Are you content to sit back and watch?" "I have a plan," Lu Su responded, "which I was on my way to offer to you." "Well?" Sun Quan said. "Station troops at Lukou and invite Lord Guan there to a meeting. If he comes, try diplomacy. If he resists, have hidden henchmen kill him. If he does not accept the invitation, sent troops for a showdown and recover Jingzhou." "I approve," Sun Quan replied. "Carry out the plan." But Kan Ze spoke in opposition: "Guan Yunchang is one of the fiercest generals of the age. No ordinary general can match him. Failure will be all the worse for us." "And when do we get Jingzhou back?" Sun Quan asked irritably, and commanded Lu Su to go ahead with the plan.

At Lukou, Lu Su arranged with commanders Lü Meng and Gan Ning to hold a banquet at the Pavilion on the River outside the camp at Lukou. Su prepared the letter of invitation and selected a skillful speaker from his staff to go across the river. On landing, the envoy was questioned by Guan Ping and then brought before Lord Guan to whom he conveyed Lu Su's good wishes and the letter of invitation. Lord Guan read it and said, "Since Lu Su invites me to dinner, I will come tomorrow. You may return."

After the envoy's departure Guan Ping said, "Father, Lu Su means us no good. Why did you accept?" "Do you think I don't know?" Lord Guan replied. "Zhuge Jin has informed Sun Quan that I won't give back the three districts. Sun Quan has therefore sent Lu Su to fortify Lukou and call me to a meeting to press his demand. If I don't go, they'll call me coward. Tomorrow I shall take a light craft down there, a dozen attendants, and my own trusty blade. Let Lu Su try to touch me!" But Guan Ping protested: "Father, for a man as valuable as you to walk into that den of wolves and tigers will compromise your duty to Uncle Xuande." Lord Guan replied, "When I faced a thousand spear points, ten thousand blades and arrows, and missiles flying from all sides, I charged in all directions as if traveling through uncontested ground. Do you think I fear a pack of rats from the south?"

But his adviser Ma Liang also voiced objections: "Although Lu Su has always behaved in an upright, self-respecting manner, he is unlikely to be altogether aboveboard in so vital a matter. Do not go, General." Lord Guan met this objection too. "Long ago in the time of the Warring States," he began, "Lin Xiangru of Zhao was too weak to tie up a chicken, but at the Mianchi meeting he held the king and ministers of mighty Qin in contempt. Need I, a master of 'one-against-many' battle tactics, feel fear? I cannot go back on my word." "If so, General, you must take precautions," Ma Liang said. "Then let my son, Ping, follow me with ten swift craft holding five hundred skilled marine fighters and wait on the river. Watch for my raised flag, then sail across," said Lord Guan; Guan Ping departed to carry out his order.

The messenger reported Lord Guan's ready acceptance and promise to come the next day. Lu Su asked commander Lü Meng, "What does it mean?" "In case he is bringing armed forces," Meng replied, "Gan Ning and I will each hide a company by the riverbank and at the sound of the bombard fall upon them. Also, have fifty men behind the banquet hall. If he comes without a company, kill him during the feast." Thus they laid their plan.

The next day at midmorning, Lu Su's lookouts on the shore spotted a boat manned by a few sailors and a helmsman. On it, a red flag boldly inscribed "Guan" flapped in the wind. As the boat drew nearer, they saw Lord Guan seated on deck. He wore a blue-green scarf and a green battle gown. Beside him Zhou Cang was holding a long sabre; and eight or nine husky westerners had broadswords at their waists. Perplexed, Lu Su welcomed the guest into the pavilion. After the exchange of courtesies Lu Su guided Lord Guan to his seat and offered him drink. But he seemed unable to look up into Lord Guan's eyes. Lord Guan, meanwhile, chatted away, perfectly relaxed.

Warmed by the wine, Lu Su said, "I have a small complaint to make, my lord. Vouchsafe your attention. Once your esteemed elder brother, the imperial uncle, required me to guarantee personally to Lord Sun Quan that his occupation of Jingzhou would be temporary; he gave his word that the province would be returned after the Riverlands was taken. Now the Riverlands has been taken, but Jingzhou has not been returned. Is this not a betrayal of his word?" "State business," Lord Guan replied, "hardly makes a fit subject of conversation for a banquet." "Lord Sun Quan," said Lu Su, "has but a modest territory in the Southland. He consented to lend Jingzhou only out of his concern to provide for you and your brother in your time of need. Now you have the Riverlands.

Jingzhou should be returned. But you refuse to turn over even the three districts designated by the imperial uncle. Doesn't this seem unreasonable?"[4]

"After Red Cliffs, in the battle at the Black Forest," Lord Guan replied, "General of the Left Liu Bei braved arrow and flying stone to join you against the common enemy. Why should he have toiled for naught, have not even a foot of soil in return? Sir, are you demanding the territory again?" "Such is not the case," said Lu Su. "My lord, when you and the imperial uncle were defeated at Steepslope, you were nearly done for; flight was your only option. Lord Sun did not begrudge the imperial uncle a place to plant his feet and aim for future accomplishment. But the imperial uncle has failed to reciprocate this kindness; he has failed to preserve friendly relations. He has the Riverlands and keeps Jingzhou—a greedy and dishonorable act, a scandal for all to witness.[5] If only Your Lordship would take cognizance."

Lord Guan responded, "This is entirely my elder brother's business, in which I should not interfere." "It is my understanding," Lu Su went on, "that Your Lordship and the imperial uncle are honor-bound by the peach garden oath to live and die as one. Indeed, Your Lordship and the Imperial Uncle are as one. How can the responsibility be shifted?" Before Lord Guan could respond, Zhou Cang shouted harshly from the foot of the dais, "The territory of the empire is for the virtuous to occupy and cannot be reserved for the Southland alone." Lord Guan's expression turned ugly. He rose and snatched the long sabre Zhou Cang was holding. Standing in the center of the yard, eyeing Zhou Cang, he shouted, "This is government business. What have you to say? Get out of here!" Zhou Cang apprehended Lord Guan's real intent and went to the riverbank. He waved the red flag, and Guan Ping raced to the southern shore.

Lord Guan held the sword in his right hand; his left was wrapped around Lu Su. Feigning intoxication, he said, "I have been your guest at dinner. May we drop the subject of Jingzhou while I am drunk, for the sake of our old friendship? I am planning a banquet in Jingzhou for you, when we can continue the discussion." Lu Su felt his affrighted soul part from his body as Lord Guan dragged him to the river's edge. Lü Meng and Gan Ning, set to strike, held off, seeing Lord Guan armed and Lu Su's life in danger. Lord Guan reached his boat and released his hostage. Then, standing in the prow, he bid his host farewell. Numbly, Lu Su watched Lord Guan sail away on a favoring wind. A poet has left this verse in praise of Lord Guan:[6]

> Less than men to him were southern liege men;
> Alone, he faced them down right at their feast.
> By this display of his heroic vein,
> Xiangru's feat at Mianchi was surpassed.[7]

After Lord Guan had set out to return to Jingzhou, Lu Su said to Lü Meng, "Our plan has failed. What can we do?" "Report to Lord Sun," he answered. "Ask him to order up troops for a deciding battle." The outcome of the banquet of Lukou was promptly made known to Sun Quan, who wanted to make an all-out attack on Jingzhou. Another report came in, however: Cao Cao was coming south with an army of three hundred thousand. Sun Quan, alarmed, reversed himself. He told Lu Su not to provoke the Jingzhou forces, and he shifted his army to Hefei and Ruxu in an effort to hold back the northern enemy.

•   •   •   •   •

When Cao Cao was preparing for his next southern expedition, the military adviser Fu Gan (Yancai) submitted a protest, which read:

It is my view that a fearsome reputation is a precondition for military action, while the art of civil government depends upon a reputation for virtue. When might and virtue are in balance, true kingship can be achieved. In times past Your Enlightened Lordship used military might to dispel the great disorders in the land, succeeding nine times out of ten. Today those who have yet to accept royal authority hold the Southland and the Riverlands. These two lands are difficult to overawe, for the one enjoys the protection of the Great River, the other of steep mountains. In my humble opinion, therefore, it would be preferable to cultivate civil government and personal virtue and to lay the weapons of war to rest. Raise up scholars and put down the sword until the time to act is ripe. If today you deploy a few hundred thousand men on the bank of the Great River, all the traitors have to do to check our divine authority is hide behind their deep defenses. That will deny us the chance to display our powers and to utilize our expedient tactics. Your Heavenly might will be adversely affected. If only Your Enlightened Lordship would consider this most carefully.

On reading this petition, Cao Cao canceled his southern expedition; instead, he established schools to which he invited men of learning. As a result, the privy counselors Wang Can, Du Xi, Wei Kai, and He He proposed honoring Cao Cao with a new title, king of Wei. This proposal was opposed by Chief of the Imperial Secretariat Xun You,[8] who said, "His Excellency has already been honored as lord patriarch of Wei, and his glory enhanced by the Nine Dignities. This is the highest honor one can hope to attain. Further promotion is unjustifiable." Cao Cao, angered by Xun You's objections, said, "He is simply following in Xun Wenruo's footsteps." When Xun You heard this, he was so exasperated that he fell ill and died some ten days later. Xun You was fifty-eight at the time of his death. Cao Cao buried him with honors; he did not pursue the kingship of Wei.[9]

One day Cao Cao entered the palace armed with a sword. Emperor Xian and Empress Fu were sitting together. Seeing Cao Cao enter, the Empress stood up hastily. The Emperor began to tremble. Cao Cao said, "Sun Quan and Liu Bei now rule their corners of the empire. They show the court no respect. What is to be done?" "That is entirely within Your Lordship's competence," the Emperor replied. "These words," Cao Cao retorted, "could lead outsiders to think I wrong my liege." "If you are willing to support me," said the Emperor, "it is most fortunate. Otherwise, I will be grateful to be left alone." Cao Cao glared at the Emperor, then left his presence with hate in his heart.

The royal attendants said to the Emperor, "We have heard that the lord patriarch of Wei wants to establish himself as king of Wei. Before long he will usurp your throne." Emperor and Empress wept. "My father, Fu Wan," the Empress said, "always wanted to kill Cao Cao. Let me write to him now in secret so that he can attempt it." "Once," the Emperor said, "Dong Cheng tried to do that. He was discovered and executed. If they caught us, we would be doomed." "Day and night we sit on pins," the Empress continued. "I prefer death to a life like this. Among our eunuchs Mu Shun is loyal and true. He could deliver the letter." Thus, Mu Shun was summoned into the Empress's presence for a private conference.

Weeping, the royal couple appealed to Mu Shun: "The traitor Cao wants to be king of Wei and may soon try for the throne. We want the Empress's father, Fu Wan, to move against Cao. But everyone works for Cao. Whom can we trust to take him a secret message from the Empress? We know your sense of loyalty and honor will not permit you to refuse us." Tearfully, Mu Shun replied, "I would gladly give my life to repay Your

Majesties' generosity. With your leave I shall go directly.'' The Empress wrote the letter
and handed it to Mu Shun. He concealed it in his hair, slipped out of the forbidden chambers, and delivered it to Fu Wan.

Fu Wan, recognizing his daughter's hand, said to the bearer, "Cao Cao's creatures are
legion. We cannot act precipitately. Sun Quan and Liu Bei will have to mobilize and draw
Cao Cao into the field. At this stage we must look for loyal and honorable men at court
to join with us. Only united action inside and out offers any chance of success.'' Mu Shun
replied, "Then, Your Worship, write back to the Emperor and Empress and request that
secret edicts go out to the Southland and to the Riverlands summoning them to arms to
punish the traitor and rescue the sovereign." Fu Wan wrote the letter, which Mu Shun
carried hidden in his topknot.

Unfortunately, Cao Cao had already been informed of Mu Shun's movements and was
awaiting him at the palace gate. "Where have you been?" Cao asked Mu Shun. "The
Empress was ill," he replied, "and had me fetch a physician." "Where is he?" Cao
pressed. "On his way," Mu Shun answered. Cao had the man searched but, finding nothing, let him pass. Suddenly a gust of wind knocked off Mu Shun's hat; Cao called him
back and examined the hat thoroughly before returning it. Using both hands Mu Shun
replaced it backward, reawakening Cao Cao's suspicions. He had his men look in Mu
Shun's hair and there discovered the letter calling for an alliance with Sun Quan and Liu
Bei. Angered, Cao Cao had Mu Shun detained and questioned in a secret chamber. Mu
Shun would not confess. That night Cao Cao surrounded Fu Wan's home with three
thousand men and seized the entire family. When he found the Empress's original letter,
he arrested every member of the Fu clan. The following morning he authorized Chi Lü,
general of the Royal Guard, to seize the Empress's seal and cord.

That day the Emperor was in an outer hall when he saw Chi Lü and three hundred
guards enter the palace. "What is your business?" the Emperor asked. "The lord patriarch has empowered me to seize the Empress's seal," the general answered. The Emperor
went weak inside, knowing the plot was discovered. When Chi Lü reached the royal couple's private quarters, the Empress had just risen. Chi Lü commanded the keepers to bring
forth the seal. The Empress realized her part in the plot was known and hid herself behind
the false wall of the Pepper Chamber at the rear of the main hall.[10]

After a short time the imperial secretary, Hua Xin, led five hundred armed men to the
rear of the palace and demanded the Empress. The palace attendants pretended not to
know where she was. Hua Xin ordered the vermillion doors opened but did not find her.
He then had his men break through the suspicious-looking wall; and with his own hand
he pulled the Empress out by her chignon. "Spare me," she pleaded. "Plead with the lord
patriarch yourself," he shouted. The Empress, disheveled and barefoot, was hustled out
by two guards.

Hua Xin, known as a talented man, was a close friend of Bing Yuan and of Guan Ning.
At the time the trio was called "The Dragon"; Hua Xin was the head, Bing Yuan the
stomach, and Guan Ning the tail. One day Guan Ning and Hua Xin turned up a piece of
gold while planting some garden vegetables. Guan Ning continued working, but Hua Xin
picked it up, examined it, and threw it down again. Another day, Guan Ning and Hua Xin
were reading together, when they heard a commotion outside as a man of importance
passed by their gate in his carriage. Guan Ning remained seated and did not stir, but Hua
Xin put down his book to look. From then on, Guan Ning held a low opinion of Hua Xin
and eventually ended the friendship. In later years Guan Ning secluded himself in a storied building in remote Liaodong. He always wore a white cap; and he lived and slept

upstairs, never letting his feet touch the ground, thereby demonstrating that he had never served the kingdom of Wei. Hua Xin, however, entered Cao Cao's service after leaving Sun Quan. Such was his story up to the day he arrested the Empress. A poet of later times lamented Hua Xin's conduct:

> Hua Xin furthered Cao Cao's foulest scheme:
> Breaking down the wall, he seized the queen.
> For one day spent, Cao's cruelty to abet:
> A name forever cursed, "Dragon Pate."

Another poet praised Guan Ning:

> Liaodong still keeps historic Guan Ning House;
> The name alone survives, no dweller there.
> He scorned the wealth and fame that Hua Xin craved,
> Who never had the "White Cap's" manly air.

Hua Xin marched the Empress to the outer hall. The Emperor saw her, embraced her, and wept. "The lord patriarch's order must be executed with dispatch," the imperial secretary snapped. Weeping, the Empress said to the Emperor, "Our life together is done." "My time, too, is uncertain," he replied. The guards removed the Empress. The Emperor beat his breast in despair. Seeing the general of the Royal Guard beside him, the Emperor said, "Lord Chi, how could such a thing come to pass?" He then collapsed in tears. Chi Lü ordered his men to assist the Emperor back into the palace.

Hua Xin took Empress Fu before Cao Cao. "I treated you all with sincerity," he ranted, "yet you planned to murder me. I must kill you first!" He ordered his men to beat her to death.[11] He then removed the Empress's two sons from the palace and had them poisoned. That evening he had Fu Wan, Mu Shun, and more than two hundred of their clansmen executed in public. Those in office and out were terror-stricken. This occurred during the eleventh month of the nineteenth year of Jian An (A.D. 215). A poet has left these verses lamenting Cao Cao's deed:

> Once in an age a man so fell and cruel!—
> Though loyal and true, Fu Wan could not oppose.
> We sorrow for the sundered king and queen:
> A better life a common couple knows.

After the loss of his Empress, Emperor Xian did not eat for many days. Cao Cao went to see him and said, "Your Majesty, be free of care. Your servant has no disloyal thoughts. My daughter is already a part of your harem, a woman both worthy and filial. She should occupy the Empress's place." How could the Emperor say no? On the first day of the first month of Jian An 20 (A.D. 215), on the celebration of the new year, Cao Cao's daughter, the concubine Cao, became the Empress of Han. And no courtier dared object.

Cao Cao's power and influence continued to grow. He summoned all the major ministers and officials to discuss absorbing the Southland and conquering the Riverlands. Jia Xu said, "We should recall generals Xiahou Dun and Cao Ren to take part in these discussions." Cao Cao immediately sent for them. Cao Ren arrived first and went straight to Cao Cao. But Cao had just lain down after drinking. Xu Chu, holding a sword, was guarding the entrance to the room and would not let Cao Ren pass. "How dare you block a member of the clan," Cao Ren cried angrily. "Though you are a kinsman," replied Xu

Chu, "your office is to control the outer regions; mine, though I am unrelated, to guard the inner sanctum. I cannot admit you when His Lordship lies drunk in his chamber." Cao Ren backed down. Cao Cao, hearing of the incident afterwards, exclaimed, "Xu Chu—a loyal servant indeed!"

A few days later Xiahou Dun arrived and the discussion on the campaigns began. Xiahou Dun said, "Neither Wu nor Shu can be attacked hastily. Attack Zhang Lu of Hanzhong first, and our victorious troops will subdue Shu easily." "Exactly my thinking," replied Cao Cao. And so troops were ordered up for a western campaign. Indeed:

> First he carried out an evil plot against the weakling Emperor,
> Then he sent a puissant host to sweep the regions west.

Would Cao Cao's imperial designs succeed?
READ ON.

67

Cao Cao Conquers Hanzhong;
Zhang Liao Prevails at Xiaoyao Ford

FOR THE WESTERN CAMPAIGN Cao Cao divided his army into three. Xiahou Yuan and Zhang He had the van; Cao Cao led his commanders in the center; Cao Ren and Xiahou Dun had the rear, guarding and distributing the supplies.

Cao Cao's movements were soon reported in Hanzhong, where Zhang Lu and his brother Wei discussed ways of repulsing their enemy. Zhang Wei said, "Yangping Pass is Hanzhong's strongest point; I'll fortify a dozen positions in the hills and woods on either side of it to oppose Cao's army. Once there, brother, dispatch grain from Hanning to meet my needs." Zhang Lu agreed and sent generals Yang Ang and Yang Ren to accompany his brother. The force reached Yangping Pass and built the camps.

Xiahou Yuan and Zhang He reached the pass and learned of the defensive preparations. They encamped fifteen *li* away and allowed their exhausted soldiers to rest. Suddenly the rear of their camp was ablaze; the two Hanzhong generals had moved in and struck. Xiahou Yuan and Zhang He took to their horses as troops stormed in from all sides. Badly defeated, Cao's army beat a retreat. Cao Cao received the two generals irately: "Two veteran commanders like you didn't know that 'troops tired by a long march must expect a raid on their camp'? How could you be so lax?" He would have executed the two to exemplify martial law but was dissuaded by the appeals of their peers.

The next day Cao Cao himself took the van. He viewed the formidable hills and dense woods and realized that their unknown pathways hid many dangers, so he returned to camp. To commanders Xu Chu and Xu Huang, Cao Cao said, "I would never have brought the army here had I known how treacherous the terrain is." "We are here now, my lord," replied Xu Chu, "do not shrink from the task ahead." The following day Cao rode forth with the two commanders to inspect Zhang Wei's fortifications. Rounding a hill, the three horsemen caught sight of Wei's positions in the distance. Pointing with his whip, Cao said, "Such well-built defense works will be difficult to break down." As he spoke, they heard a cry from behind, and arrows rained down on them as Yang Ang and Yang Ren closed in. Cao panicked. Xu Chu shouted to Xu Huang, "I will stand off the enemy. You protect His Lordship." Raising his sword, Chu charged ahead, strenuously opposing the Hanzhong generals. Overwhelmed by Xu Chu's charge, Yang Ang and Yang Ren retreated, followed by their men. Xu Huang hustled Cao Cao around a slope. There a friendly force under Xiahou Yuan and Zhang He, alerted by the commotion, had come to their rescue. The reinforcement troops beat Yang Ang and Yang Ren back and got Cao Cao safely to camp. Cao Cao rewarded the four commanders handsomely.

After this incident the two armies held each other at bay for more than fifty days. Finally Cao Cao ordered a retreat. Jia Xu said, "The enemy's strength remains to be tested. For what reason are you withdrawing, Your Lordship?" "They seem to me," Cao replied, "to be in full readiness every day. Victory is doubtful for us. I thought a retreat would make them careless; then we could have our light cavalry swoop down on their rear. That way we will certainly win." "Your Excellency," Jia Xu replied, "your ingenuity is unfathomable." Thereupon Xiahou Yuan and Zhang He were ordered to take three thousand light horsemen each around behind Yangping Pass while Cao Cao had the main camp completely pulled up.

Yang Ang, hearing of the retreat, proposed an attack. But Yang Ren said, "Cao Cao has an infinite number of tricks. We can't pursue him before we know the actual situation." Yang Ang, however, said, "I'll go alone, if you won't," thus overriding Ren's strenuous objections. Ang threw all five of his armed camps into the assault, leaving only a small force behind. It was a day of dreadful fog and mist, widespread and dense; even face-to-face the soldiers could not see each other. After marching a good distance, Ang had to call a halt and bivouac.

Meanwhile, Xiahou Yuan, having made a shortcut behind the hills, watched the heavy fog settle. Hearing the sounds of men and horses, he feared ambush and pressed his advance; unwittingly, he came to Yang Ang's base camps. The guards, assuming the hoofbeats meant the return of Ang, opened the gates. Cao's troops poured in and, finding the camps empty, burnt everything down. The men left guarding the five camps fled for their lives.

The fog lifted. Yang Ren brought his troops to the rescue and fought briefly with Xiahou Yuan; but Zhang He attacked Ren from behind. Yang Ren managed to fight his way to safety in Nanzheng.[1] When Yang Ang tried to return, he found his bases occupied by Xiahou Yuan and Zhang He; and Cao Cao's main force was coming on swiftly. Hemmed in all around, Yang Ang tried to break through the enemy lines, but Zhang He confronted him and killed him after a brief struggle. Ang's defeated troops returned to Yangping Pass, expecting to find Zhang Wei. Wei, however, had already learned of the flight of the two Yangs and the loss of the camps, so he had abandoned the pass himself and dashed for safety. Thus Cao Cao took possession of the pass and the campsites.

Zhang Lu was furious when Zhang Wei and Yang Ren informed him of the losses. He wanted to execute Yang Ren, but Ren said, "I pleaded with Yang Ang not to go after Cao's men. He refused to listen. Hence the defeat. Let me have another detachment to challenge the enemy. I'll kill Cao Cao for you or gladly face any consequences that the military code prescribes." Zhang Lu accepted his written pledge; and Yang Ren camped at a distance from Nanzheng with twenty thousand men.

Before advancing on Nanzheng, Cao Cao had Xiahou Yuan explore the roads. Yuan and his five thousand men met up with Yang Ren, and the two armies squared off. Ren sent out Chang Qi, a lieutenant commander. Xiahou Yuan engaged him and killed him in a brief encounter. Yang Ren himself then came forth, spear held high, and fought Yuan more than thirty bouts; neither prevailed. Yuan feigned defeat and fled, Ren in pursuit. Wheeling about, Yuan used the trailing sword maneuver and slashed Ren to pieces. Yang Ren's soldiers, badly beaten, went back to their base.

As soon as Cao Cao found out that Xiahou Yuan had killed Yang Ren, he advanced in force and camped before Nanzheng. Zhang Lu desperately called together his counselors.

Yan Pu said, "I know one man who can hold off Cao's commanders." Zhang Lu asked who he was. "Pang De from Nan'an," Yan Pu replied. "He surrendered to Your Lordship along with Ma Chao. Afterward, when Ma Chao defected to the Riverlands, Pang De fell ill and never went. He is still a beneficiary of Your Lordship's generous care. Why not have him go?"

Pleased by this proposal, Zhang Lu called for Pang De and provided handsomely for him. He then ordered up ten thousand men and commanded Pang De to take the field. Some ten *li* from the city, Pang De confronted Cao Cao's force and rode forth to challenge the foe. Cao Cao, having experienced Pang De's prowess in the disastrous battle at the Wei Bridge, advised his commanders: "Pang De is a bold Xiliang warrior who originally served Ma Chao. Though in Zhang Lu's service, he is not content there. I want this man for myself. You are to drag out the fighting—wear him down—then capture him."

Zhang He was first into the field. He fought several bouts, then retired. Xiahou Yuan, followed by Xu Huang, did the same. Next, Xu Chu came forth and fought fifty bouts before retiring. Pang De battled each of Cao's four generals fearlessly, and they praised his martial skill to Cao Cao. Inwardly pleased, Cao Cao said, "How can we get Pang De to surrender?" Jia Xu answered, "Zhang Lu has an adviser named Yang Song whose appetite for bribes is insatiable. Send him gold and silk secretly; have him slander Pang De in front of Zhang Lu. Then we can succeed." "How can we get someone into Nanzheng?" Cao asked. "In tomorrow's fighting," replied Jia Xu, "pretend you are defeated and abandon the camps to Pang De. At night we can raid our own camp and drive Pang De back into the city. We'll find a soldier who speaks well, have him mingle in disguise among the enemy, and thus get into the city."

Cao Cao accepted this proposal and chose an officer shrewd enough to carry it out. He paid him generously, supplied him with a gilded breastplate to be worn against the skin and the outer garments of a Hanzhong soldier, and sent him on toward the enemy. The next day Cao Cao had Xiahou Yuan and Zhang He conceal two detachments a good distance down the road and had Xu Huang go forth to challenge Pang De. After a few encounters Xu Huang retreated, and Pang De waved his army on for the kill. Cao Cao's troops withdrew entirely, and Pang De took possession of their camp.

Pang De was delighted to find Cao's ample stores of grain and reported the fact to Zhang Lu. He then held a banquet in the camp to celebrate the victory. That night shortly after the second watch, three companies of troops suddenly appeared in a blaze of torchlight: in the middle, Xu Huang and Xu Chu; on the left, Zhang He; on the right, Xiahou Yuan. The three squadrons moved in together and sacked the camp. Having no time to defend his position, Pang De took to his horse and fled toward the city, the three squadrons in hot pursuit. Frantically, Pang De shouted to open the gate, and his soldiers swarmed in.

Cao Cao's spy had already smuggled himself into the city and gone directly to Yang Song's residence. To Yang Song he said, "The lord patriarch of Wei, His Excellency, Prime Minister Cao Cao, has long known of your splendid virtue and has sent me with this gilded breastplate as a token of good faith. He has also sent this confidential communication." Yang Song was pleased and, after reading the letter, replied, "Tell the lord patriarch to set his mind at ease. I have a sound plan which will repay his generosity." Song sent Cao's envoy back and went directly to tell Zhang Lu that Cao Cao had bribed Pang De to lose. Zhang Lu angrily called in Pang De and condemned him. He would have executed him but for Yan Pu's strong appeal. "Tomorrow you fight," Zhang Lu told him, "and win—or I'll put you to death." Containing his resentment, Pang De withdrew.

The next day Cao Cao attacked, and Pang De went forth to oppose him. At Cao's command Xu Chu engaged De, then feigned defeat. Pang De gave chase. From horseback on the side of a hill Cao Cao called down to Pang De, "Why not surrender?" Pang De thought: "I can take Cao Cao; he's worth more than a thousand commanders." He raced up the hillside. Suddenly he uttered a loud cry as Heaven and earth seemed to collapse: man and horse had tumbled into a pit. From four sides hooks and nooses went into action; Pang De was delivered to Cao Cao alive. Cao Cao dismounted and dismissed his guards. After personally undoing Pang De's bonds, he asked him if he would surrender. Remembering Zhang Lu's hardness of heart, Pang De did so willingly. Cao Cao helped him onto a horse, and together they rode back to camp, intending that they be seen from the city wall. Someone reported to Zhang Lu that Pang De and Cao Cao had ridden off together, so Zhang Lu now credited Yang Song's slanders.[2]

The next day Cao Cao erected scaling ladders on three sides of the wall and attacked with stone-throwing machines. Zhang Lu realized his position was untenable and said so to his brother Wei. "Burn out our granaries and treasury and flee into the southern hills," Wei advised. "We can defend ourselves again in Bazhong." "Better to surrender," said Yang Song. Zhang Lu wavered. "Just burn everything," Zhang Wei reiterated. "All along," Zhang Lu said, "I have wanted to offer service to the Han, but I have never fulfilled this ambition. Now though I must flee, the granary and treasury belong to the dynasty and should not be destroyed." He therefore sealed up all the buildings. That night during the second watch Zhang Lu took his whole clan out of the city through the south gate. Cao Cao ordered no pursuit. Entering Nanzheng, Cao found the buildings intact and pitied Zhang Lu's plight. He sent a men to Bazhong to call on Lu to surrender. Lu was willing; his brother Wei was not.

Yang Song secretly assured Cao Cao that an attack on the city would have his cooperation. On receiving Song's letter, Cao Cao led his army to Bazhong. Zhang Lu sent Zhang Wei to meet the enemy. Xu Chu cut him down in the first clash. The troops reported the defeat to Zhang Lu, who wanted to continue holding the city. Yang Song said, "To stay inside is to await death passively. Let me defend the city while Your Lordship decides the issue with the enemy." Zhang Lu agreed, overriding Yan Pu's objections.

No sooner was Zhang Lu in the field than his rear guard deserted. Retreating swiftly before Cao's troops, Lu reached Bazhong; but Yang Song had barred the gates, leaving Zhang Lu no recourse. Closing in, Cao Cao shouted, "Surrender now!" Zhang Lu dismounted and submitted. Cao Cao was pleased and, grateful to Lu for securing the granary and treasury, treated him well and enfeoffed him as General Who Controls the South. Yan Pu and the others received honorary fiefs. And so Hanzhong finally came into Cao Cao's possession. Cao Cao ordered every district to appoint a governor and a commander and rewarded his troops well. Yang Song, however, was publicly executed for betraying his lord in search of profit. A later poet left these verses describing Yang Song:

> Thwarter of able men, betrayer of his lord,
> Hoarder of gold and silver—all for naught!
> No glory for his house, his death a shame—
> A laughingstock for all and for all time.

After the conquest of the eastern Riverlands, Cao Cao's first secretary, Sima Yi, advanced a proposal: "Liu Bei has overthrown Liu Zhang by deception and force; the people of Shu have yet to give him their true allegiance. Attack at once and they will fall apart.

Wise men know the value of timely action. This is a unique opportunity." Cao Cao sighed and said, "As they say, 'Man never knows when to stop; that's the trouble. Once you have Longxi, next you want Shu.'"[3] Liu Ye responded, "Sima Yi is correct. The slightest delay will enable Prime Minister Zhuge Liang, who is enlightened in governing, and Lord Guan, Zhang Fei, and the other generals to control the population and make the Riverlands impregnable." "Our troops are suffering from the long trek," Cao Cao argued back. "We must think of them." In the end he took no action.

·   ·   ·   ·   ·

When the people of Riverlands heard that Cao Cao had taken the eastern Riverlands, they assumed he would march on and take the western Riverlands. Fear and anxiety were rampant. Xuande asked his director general for advice. "I have a plan," Kongming replied. "Well?" said Xuande. "Cao Cao keeps an army near Hefei," Kongming continued, "because he fears Sun Quan. So, if we return the three districts of Jiangxia, Changsha, and Guiyang to the Southland and have a skilled spokesman argue the case, we may be able to get the south to attack Hefei. That would destabilize the northern position and force them to shift troops to the south."[4] "Whom could we send?" Xuande asked. "I volunteer," Yi Ji said.

A relieved Xuande wrote the letter and prepared suitable gifts. Yi Ji went first to Jingzhou to inform Lord Guan and then on to the Southland.[5] In Moling, he was received by Sun Quan. After the exchange of courtesies Sun Quan asked, "What brings you to the Southland?" "Some time ago," Yi Ji began, "we were fortunate to have a visit from Zhuge Jin, who came to recover Changsha and two other districts for the Southland. Unfortunately, due to the director general's absence, the transfer was not made. I have here the documents confirming your possession. Originally, we wanted to hand over all the districts of Jingzhou, including Nanjun and Lingling, but with Cao Cao seizing the eastern Riverlands, General Guan had to have a place to go. Now Hefei is vulnerable. We hope Your Lordship will attack it and force Cao Cao to move his army south. Once Lord Liu takes the eastern Riverlands, the rest of Jingzhou will be turned over to you." "Could you wait in the guesthouse," Sun Quan replied, "while I discuss this with my advisers?"

Zhang Zhao spoke first. "It's only a scheme," he said. "Liu Bei fears Cao Cao will take the western Riverlands. All the same, Cao Cao's campaign in the west means that we can take Hefei; and that is what we should do." Sun Quan approved. He sent Yi Ji back and began mobilizing for war with Cao Cao. He dispatched Lu Su to take possession of Changsha, Jiangxia, and Guiyang, stationed troops at Lukou, and recalled commanders Lü Meng and Gan Ning. He also sent for Ling Tong, stationed in Yuhang.

In a short while Lü Meng and Gan Ning arrived. Meng proposed a plan. "At present," he said, "Cao Cao has Zhu Guang, governor of Lujiang, stationed at the city of Huan. They are growing rice on a large scale there and furnishing grain to Hefei. We should capture Huan first, then attack Hefei." "Exactly my thinking," said Sun Quan. He put Lü Meng and Gan Ning in the van, had Jiang Qin and Pan Zhang take the rear, and assumed command of the main army himself, assisted by Zhou Tai, Chen Wu, Dong Xi, and Xu Sheng. Cheng Pu, Huang Gai, and Han Dang had been posted elsewhere and did not join the campaign.

The southern army crossed the river and captured Hezhou, then marched straight to Huan. Governor Zhu Guang sent to Hefei for help, all the while strengthening his defenses and refusing to come out. When Sun Quan reached the city walls, arrows rained down on him, and one struck his plumed helmet. Sun Quan returned to camp and asked his commanders how to capture Huan. Dong Xi replied, "Have the soldiers raise mounds of earth." Xu Sheng said, "Set up scaling ladders and towers so that we can see inside and then attack." "Either would take too long," said Lü Meng. "Once they get help from Hefei, anything could happen. Our men have just arrived and their morale is high. This is the moment for an energetic attack. We advance at dawn and by midday should have broken through the wall." Sun Quan approved.

The next day after mess at the fifth watch the whole army set out. From the walls of Huan arrows and missiles poured down on them. Gan Ning, wielding an iron chain, climbed up the walls, braving the volleys. Zhu Guang ordered his bowmen to mass their shots at him, but Ning fended off the bolts and knocked Zhu Guang down with his chain. Lü Meng beat the drums himself, and his men stormed the wall. Zhu Guang was slain in the wild slashing of sword blades; his force surrendered, and Sun Quan took possession of Huan by early evening. Zhang Liao, on his way to rescue Zhu Guang when his scouts told him of the loss of Huan, returned to Hefei.

Sun Quan entered the captured city, and Commander Ling Tong arrived with his men. After receiving them, Quan feasted the army and rewarded Lü Meng, Gan Ning, and the other commanders. All celebrated at a grand banquet. In the seating Lü Meng deferred to Gan Ning and proclaimed his merits and achievements.

Then something untoward occurred. Ling Tong, seeing Lü Meng praise the man who had killed his father, stared angrily at Gan Ning. Suddenly he took an attendant's sword and, standing in the center of the company, cried out, "We lack for entertainment. Allow me to perform a sword dance." Gan Ning knew exactly what Ling Tong wanted to do. He pushed over the table loaded with fruit and rose to his feet. Clasping a halberd under each arm, he strode forward. "Let me show the company how I handle these," Gan Ning said. Lü Meng saw that both were looking for trouble and, taking a shield in one hand and a sword in the other, he stepped between them.

"Neither of you is so skillful as I," Lü Meng boasted and, dancing with shield and sword, he succeeded in separating the antagonists. Sun Quan, who had already been told of the incident, rushed to the scene, and all parties put down their weapons. "I have told both of you more than once to set aside your enmity," Sun Quan said. "How could this have happened?" Weeping, Ling Tong threw himself to the ground. Sun Quan reiterated his admonition. The next day he led the entire army in the assault on Hefei.

Zhang Liao returned to Hefei, his heart heavy over the loss of Huan. Unexpectedly he was greeted by Xue Ti with a wooden box bearing Cao Cao's seal and inscribed "Open only when the rebels come." Having been told of Sun Quan's arriving with one hundred thousand soldiers, Zhang Liao opened the box. Inside was a note reading, "If Sun Quan attacks, Zhang Liao and Li Dian are to meet him, Yue Jin to guard the city." Zhang Liao showed the directive to the two generals. Yue Jin said, "What do you think, General?" "His Lordship is campaigning afar," Zhang Liao replied, "and the Southlanders think they have a sure victory. We should send our forces into the field to do battle with them and blunt their drive. That will reassure our own army. Then we can go back to the defensive."

Li Dian, who was often at odds with Zhang Liao, made no response. Yue Jin, seeing Li Dian remain silent, said, "The enemy is too numerous for us to engage. Better to mount a strict defense." "Gentlemen," answered Zhang Liao, "are you not regarding your private interests and forgetting our common cause? I will go out and fight—or die." He ordered his horse readied. Li Dian rose and said grandly, "In that case, General, how

can I let my personal chagrin distract me from public duty? I will do as you command."
Delighted, Zhang Liao said, "If you are willing to help, bring a company north of
Xiaoyao Ford tomorrow and place them in ambush. When the southern troops approach,
cut the Xiaoshi Bridge, and Yue Jin and I will strike." As commanded, Li Dian went to
order up the troops.

Sun Quan directed Lü Meng and Gan Ning to lead the van while he and Ling Tong
took the center. The other commanders set out one after another to join the battle at
Hefei. Lü Meng and Gan Ning confronted Yue Jin; Gan Ning and Yue Jin charged at each
other and fought several rounds. Then Yue Jin feigned defeat and fled. Gan Ning called
to Lü Meng to join the chase. Sun Quan, in the second battalion, heard of the victory of
the van and was pressing on to the north side of Xiaoyao Ford when a string of bombards
echoed around him. On the left Zhang Liao's company was coming; on the right, Li
Dian's. Sun Quan panicked and called for Lü Meng and Gan Ning to turn back and help,
but Zhang Liao was upon him.

Ling Tong had only three hundred riders and could not stand up against the onslaught
of Cao's forces. "Quick, cross Xiaoshi Bridge, Your Lordship," Ling Tong shouted. That
moment Zhang Liao's two thousand horsemen stood before them. Ling Tong dove into
the fray as Sun Quan rode to the bridge. But it had been torn down at the southern end,
leaving a ten foot gap. Sun Quan was at a loss. Gu Li, a garrison commander, shouted to
him, "Back up, Your Lordship, then race forward to vault the gap." Sun Quan retreated
more than thirty spans, then loosening the reins and swinging the whip, he urged the
horse over the missing planks. A poet of later times has left this verse:

> Once White Forehead took Liu Bei o'er the Tan;[6]
> And then Lord Sun vaulted onto land.
> He pulled back, laid on, sprinted hard;
> At Xiaoyao Ford a jade dragon soared.

Safely across, Sun Quan was met by boats piloted by Xu Sheng and Dong Xi. Ling
Tong and Gu Li, the garrison commander, checked Zhang Liao. Gan Ning and Lü Meng
came back to the rescue but suffered heavy losses, caught between the armies of Yue Jin
and Li Dian. All of Ling Tong's three hundred soldiers were killed. Tong himself, badly
wounded, fought his way to the bridge but, finding it impassable, skirted the river to
make his escape. Sun Quan, watching from his boat, had Dong Xi row over and take Ling
Tong on board. Then they all crossed again to the southern shore.

Lü Meng and Gan Ning also made it to the southern shore after desperate fighting.
This bloody engagement became so notorious and terrified the southerners so, children
crying in the night would hush at the mere mention of Zhang Liao's name. The southern
commanders got Sun Quan safely back to camp. Quan rewarded Ling Tong and Gu Li
handsomely. Then he led the army back to Ruxu to put his ships in fighting condition and
lay plans for a counterattack by land and sea. He also sent a call for reinforcements to the
Southland.

Zhang Liao heard that Sun Quan was at Ruxu preparing for a fresh campaign. Concerned that Hefei was too thinly defended, he sent Xue Ti to Hanzhong to solicit a rescue
force from Cao Cao. Cao Cao put the key question to his counselors: "Can we take possession of the western Riverlands at this time?" Liu Ye replied, "The area is somewhat
stable now and rather well defended. Instead of attacking, we should relieve our forces at
Hefei and then descend on the Southland."

So Cao Cao left Xiahou Yuan guarding the Dingjun Mountain strongpoint in Hanzhong, and Zhang He guarding Mengtou Cliff; he pulled up all the remaining camps and hastened back to the Ruxu barricade. Indeed:

> No sooner had his strong cavalry conquered Longxi
> Than he turned his war banners southward once again.

How would Cao Cao's southern campaign turn out?[7]
READ ON.

68

Gan Ning's Band Sacks the Northern Camp;
Zuo Ci Throws a Cup, Teasing Cao Cao

SUN QUAN REGROUPED HIS FORCES at the Ruxu naval base. Informed suddenly that Cao Cao was shifting four hundred thousand men from Hanzhong to Hefei, Sun Quan and his advisers decided to deploy fifty large concealed war-junks at Ruxu under Dong Xi and Xu Sheng. Sun Quan ordered Chen Wu to keep the shore of the river patrolled.

Zhang Zhao said, "Cao Cao has come a long way. Our first act must be to blunt his thrust." Quan put the matter to his commanders. "Cao Cao," he said, "is coming a long way. Who dares to strike first and blunt his thrust?" Ling Tong stepped forward and volunteered. "How many troops will you need?" Quan asked. "Three thousand will do," was the reply. But Gan Ning said, "Give me a hundred riders and I can do the job. Why use three thousand?" Angered, Ling Tong began wrangling with Gan Ning. "Cao Cao's power is enormous. Do not underestimate the enemy," Sun Quan said and sent Ling Tong with three thousand to scout the mouth of the Ruxu and to engage Cao's forces should they appear. As assigned, Ling Tong took his force near the Ruxu barrier. Soon dust filled the air and Cao's troops arrived. In the van Zhang Liao crossed spears with Ling Tong. They fought fifty bouts, but neither prevailed. Sun Quan, fearing for Ling Tong, ordered Lü Meng to bring him back to camp.

Gan Ning, seeing Ling Tong return, appealed to Sun Quan, "Tonight I want one hundred men to raid Cao's camp. If I lose a single one, count it no achievement." Impressed by Ning's courage, Sun Quan assigned him one hundred crack horsemen from his own command and in addition gave him fifty jars of wine and fifty catties of lamb to feast his men. Back at camp Gan Ning had the hundred seated in rows before him. Pouring himself two silver cups of wine, he addressed the warriors: "Tonight we have orders to raid their position. Drink deeply and advance boldly." At these words the warriors stared at one another. Seeing the men's reluctance, Gan Ning drew his sword and cried angrily, "I, a general, give no thought for my own life. How can you hesitate?" Before Gan Ning's wrathful look the men touched their heads to the ground and said, "We are with you to the death."

Gan Ning and the men consumed the wine and meat and set the action for the second watch. Each was identified by a white goosefeather in his helmet. They donned their armor and mounted; then they raced to the side of Cao Cao's stockade. They broke down the defensive staves, plunged inside with tremendous shouts, and headed for the site of the central army to kill Cao Cao. But Cao's command headquarters was sealed tight as an

519

iron barrel by an impenetrable circle of chariots and wagons. Gan Ning and his hundred horsemen thrust to the left and charged to the right, throwing Cao's troops, uncertain of the attackers' number, into great confusion. Gan Ning's hundred crossed the camp at full tilt, slaying anyone they encountered. All the camp was in an uproar as torches were raised, numerous as the stars overhead. The ground trembled from the shouting. Gan Ning cut his way out of the southern entrance of the camp. No one could withstand him. Sun Quan ordered Zhou Tai to bring up a detachment as Gan Ning and his hundred pulled back to Ruxu. Cao's men, fearing ambush, did not pursue. A poet of later time expressed his admiration for Gan Ning's charge:

> Army drums a-beating shook the ground;
> Southland soldiers struck; ghosts and spirits howled.
> Those hundred goose-plumes deep behind Cao's line
> Testified to Gan Ning's martial power.

Gan Ning returned to camp. Not a man nor a mount had been lost. Reaching the entrance to his camp, he ordered the hundred to beat their drums, blow their flutes, and give their battle cry. The southerners cheered wildly. Sun Quan welcomed the force in person. Gan Ning dismounted and prostrated himself. Quan helped him up and, taking Ning's hand, said, "Your raid should strike fear into the old traitor. I let you go only to witness your display of valor; it was not because I could spare you." He presented Ning with a thousand rolls of silk and one hundred fine swords, which Ning received respectfully and shared with his men. Sun Quan said to his commanders, "My Gan Ning is the equal of Cao Cao's Zhang Liao!"

The next day Zhang Liao came out to challenge the southerners. Ling Tong, having witnessed Gan's exploits, cried, "Let me face him." Quan granted his permission and Tong led five thousand out of Ruxu. Quan invited Gan Ning to observe the field. As the lines formed, Zhang Liao rode out, Li Dian to his left, Yue Jin to his right. Ling Tong dashed forth, flourishing his sword, and confronted them. Liao sent Yue Jin forth. They fought fifty bouts in a drawn battle. Cao Cao was told of the great conflict and rode to the beflagged entrance of his camp to watch. Seeing the antagonists absorbed in combat, Cao ordered Cao Xiu to shoot from hiding. Xiu ducked behind Zhang Liao and shot Ling Tong's horse, which reared and threw its rider. Yue Jin raced forward, spear poised for the kill, when an arrow struck him full in the face and he toppled from his mount. Soldiers on both sides came out to rescue their generals. Gongs sounded, and combat ceased. Ling Tong returned to camp and touched the ground in apology to Sun Quan. "It was Gan Ning whose arrow saved you," Quan said, and Ling Tong pressed his forehead to the ground to show his respect to Gan Ning, saying, "I never expected such kindness from you, sir." From that time forward the two men became sworn friends and buried their grudge.

Cao Cao sent Yue Jin to have his wound treated in his tent. The next day he detailed five armies to strike Ruxu: Cao led the central force; to his left, Zhang Liao and Li Dian; to his right, Xu Huang and Pang De. Each army had ten thousand men. They moved toward the riverbank to attack. On the southern side Dong Xi and Xu Sheng watched the enemy approach from their multistoried boats. Their soldiers wore worried expressions. Xu Sheng said, "The lord feeds you; you serve the lord. What are the frightened looks for?" Then he took several hundred of his fiercest warriors across the river on small boats. They struck deep into Li Dian's camp, taking a heavy toll. Dong Xi ordered those still on their ships to beat their drums and shout, thereby to heighten the fears of Dian's men. Suddenly a strong wind began blowing on the river. White waves leaped heavenward. Breakers churned and tumbled. Sensing that the boats might capsize, the soldiers struggled toward the lifeboats, but Dong Xi drew his sword and shouted, "We are under our lord's command, defending against the rebels. How dare you abandon ship!" He struck down a dozen of his own men. Moments later the ship went over, and Dong Xi perished in the river. Xu Sheng meanwhile continued slaughtering Li Dian's men.

By this time Southland commander Chen Wu had heard the cries of mayhem and brought his troops up. He was confronted by Cao's commander Pang De. A wild melee ensued. Sun Quan, at the Ruxu barrier, heard Cao's troops nearing shore and, together with Zhou Tai, came to help. Quan saw Xu Sheng wreaking havoc in Li Dian's camp and signaled his men to support Sheng, but Zhang Liao and Xu Huang trapped Quan between them. From an elevation Cao Cao saw Sun Quan surrounded and immediately ordered Xu Chu to fall upon the southern force. The shock of Xu Chu's attack caused the southern army to split; and neither part could help the other.

From the thick of the fighting, Zhou Tai reached the river but could not find Sun Quan. Wheeling round, he plunged back into the lines. "Where is our lord?" he asked his men. They pointed to the converging soldiers. "His Lordship is surrounded," they said. "It's serious." Zhou Tai broke through and found Sun Quan. "Follow me out of here, my lord," Tai said. By dint of hard fighting, Zhou Tai reached the shore but again lost Sun Quan.

He turned back into the fray and again found his lord. "We can't get out," Quan said. "Shafts and bolts are flying everywhere." "This time," Zhou Tai said, "you go first, and I'll follow." Quan raced forward as Zhou Tai fended off attacks left and right. He took several wounds and an arrow had pierced his armor; but he brought Sun Quan out. At the shore Lü Meng's detachment of sailors got Sun Quan safely on board. "I only made it thanks to Zhou Tai; he plunged three times into the thick of the fighting. But Xu Sheng is still trapped. How will he escape?" "I will go back," Zhou Tai said. He turned around, charged into the midst of the encirclement, and brought Xu Sheng to safety. The two commanders, severely wounded, climbed down to the boat as Lü Meng's archers raked the shoreline to cover them.

At this time Chen Wu, with no support, was battling Pang De. Pang De had chased him into the mouth of a gorge where trees grew dense. Time and again Chen Wu tried to turn and fight, but bushes snagged his sleeves and Pang De cut him down before he could defend himself.

Cao Cao, seeing that Sun Quan had fled, urged his soldiers to the shore; from there they shot their arrows to the opposite side. Lü Meng, his arrows spent, began to panic. But a boat came from the opposite bank, a general at its prow. It was Sun Ce's son-in-law, Lu Xun. He had brought one hundred thousand men, who, in a short spell, drove Cao's troops back with volleys of arrows. Seizing the advantage, Xun's troops climbed ashore and made off with thousands of war-horses. Cao Cao's army suffered countless casualties and went back to camp badly beaten. Chen Wu's corpse was found later in the carnage.

Sun Quan grieved bitterly over the loss of Chen Wu and Dong Xi. He had the river searched, and Dong Xi's body was found; it was buried together with Chen Wu's. Sun Quan then held a feast to thank Zhou Tai for his heroic rescues. Lifting the cup, Sun Quan rested his arm on Zhou Tai's shoulders and, face wet with tears, said, "Twice you brought me to safety, each time risking your own life, suffering so many wounds that they have patterned your flesh. What else can I do but show you a kinsman's kindness; what else but place in your hands a high command? You are my most deserving vassal, with whom I shall share every glory and success."

He ordered Zhou Tai to remove his coat and display his wounds: his entire body was carved with crosswise slashes. Sun Quan pointed to each and asked the occasion of infliction. Zhou Tai answered in full detail. For every wound he was ordered to quaff a flagon of wine; Zhou Tai became thoroughly drunk that day. Sun granted him the blue-green silk umbrella of chief command, ordering him to leave the feast and reenter with it raised to enhance his dignity.[1]

At Ruxu, Sun Quan held off Cao Cao for more than a month but could not gain the upper hand. Zhang Zhao and Gu Yong put forth a proposal: "Cao Cao's strength is too great for us to overcome. In a protracted war we stand to lose many men. It is better to seek a truce and give the people peace." Sun Quan approved. He sent Bu Zhi to Cao's camp for that purpose and promised to send tribute annually. Cao Cao, too, realized that no quick decision was possible and agreed to the truce. "Sun Quan is to remove his forces first," he stipulated. "Then I will withdraw to the capital." Bu Zhi returned this answer to Sun Quan, who shipped his entire army back to Moling, leaving only Jiang Qin and Zhou Tai guarding Ruxu.[2]

· · · · ·

Cao Cao withdrew to the capital, leaving Cao Ren and Zhang Liao stationed at Hefei. The entire court, civil as well as military branches, proposed establishing Cao Cao as king of Wei. The only strong opposition came from the chief of the Secretariat, Cui Yan, to whom the assembly said, "Have you forgotten the fate of Xun Wenruo?"[3] Cui Yan, in a fury, replied "Oh, what times, what times! The thing will come, but you will have to do it without me!" Those opposing Cui Yan reported his words to Cao Cao, who had him jailed and interrogated. But the prisoner—a man of tiger-round eyes and curling whiskers—simply denounced Cao Cao for treachery and treason against the throne. The security chief informed Cao Cao, who had Cui Yan beaten to death in jail. These verses of a later poet express his admiration for the secretary:

> Cui Yan of Qinghe,
> By nature hard and strong,
> Had curly beard and tiger eyes
> And insides hard as iron.
> Treachery must back away
> Before his high integrity.
> For loyalty to the lord of Han
> His name will live eternally.

In the fifth month of Jian An 21 (A.D. 216) the college of courtiers collectively petitioned Emperor Xian, lauding the merits and virtue of Cao Cao, lord patriarch of Wei: "To the ends of Heaven and earth he surpasses even Yi Yin and the Duke of Zhou; he should be advanced in rank to king." Emperor Xian commanded Zhong Yao to draft the edict confirming Cao Cao's elevation to king of Wei. Cao Cao unctuously made the three ritual refusals; but after three repetitions of the imperial will, Cao respectfully accepted the order making him king of Wei and at once assumed the appropriate trappings: imperial headdress with twelve strings of jade beads, a gilt chariot with a team of six horses, an imperial carriage with regalia.[4] Wherever he went, heralds cleared the way as if for the

Emperor. In the city of Ye he built the palace of the king of Wei and initiated discussions on establishing his heir.[5]

Cao Cao's principal wife, Lady Ding, had had no issue. His concubine, Lady Liu, was the mother of Cao Ang, who had died in Wancheng during the campaign against Zhang Xiu. Lady Bian had four sons: the eldest was Pi; the second, Zhang; the third, Zhi; the fourth, Xiong. Consequently, Cao Cao displaced Lady Ding and made Lady Bian queen of Wei.[6] Cao Zhi (Zijian), her third son, a brilliant scholar who could produce polished compositions in a single writing, was the heir apparent of choice.

The eldest son, Pi, who had been discouraged, asked Imperial Mentor[7] Jia Xu for a plan to improve his prospects. Jia Xu gave him certain advice. From that day forward, whenever Cao Cao went on a campaign and his sons saw him off, Cao Zhi would celebrate his achievements and his virtue in long rhapsodies. Cao Pi alone would bid his father good-bye, prostrate and weeping.[8] Cao Cao's attendants were deeply moved by this, and soon Cao Cao began to compare his favorite, Zhi, to his son Pi and to suspect Zhi of cunning and insincerity. Cao Pi reinforced his father's inclination by bribing Cao's close attendants to sing Pi's praises. As a result, Cao became torn over whom to name as heir. He took the matter to Jia Xu. "I want to establish my successor," he said. "Who should it be?" Jia Xu did not answer. Cao Cao asked why. "I am thinking," replied Jia Xu. "I cannot answer right away." "What are you thinking?" Cao asked. "I am thinking of Yuan Shao and Liu Biao and of their sons," said Xu.[9] Cao Cao laughed and subsequently named Cao Pi, his eldest son, heir apparent.[10]

The palace of the king of Wei was completed in winter, during the tenth month. Men were sent all over the realm to gather exotic flowers and fruit to plant in the royal gardens. One of Cao's messengers came to the Southland and was received by Sun Quan. After communicating the wishes of the king of Wei, he proceeded to Wenzhou where he acquired sweet oranges. At this time Sun Quan wanted to show his respect for the king of Wei, so he ordered someone in that city to select forty loads of large oranges and dispatch them to Ye. On the way, however, the porters had to stop and rest at the foot of a hill. There they were approached by an older man, blind in one eye and crippled in one leg. He wore a bonnet of white vine-stems and an informal grey Taoist robe. The man greeted the carriers, saying, "You have much to carry. Do you want this poor priest to lend a shoulder?" The workmen were delighted. And so the priest carried the entire load five *li* ahead. But to the workmen's surprise the loads he had carried suddenly became lighter. When he was about to leave, the priest said to the officer in charge of the shipment, "This poor priest, Zuo Ci, styled Yuanfang, with the Taoist name of Master Black Horn, is an old acquaintance of the king of Wei—from his native village. If you reach Ye, convey my best wishes to him." And with a flick of his sleeves, the priest was gone.

When the shipment reached Ye, the officer in charge presented it to Cao Cao. Cao Cao split a fruit and found an empty peel.[11] Astonished, Cao questioned the officer, who recounted his meeting with Zuo Ci. Cao Cao was incredulous. Suddenly a gateman announced, "An elderly man calling himself Zuo Ci seeks audience with the great king." Cao summoned the priest, and the officer identified him as the one they had met en route. Cao rebuked him sharply. "What black art did you use," he asked, "to draw the pulp from my precious fruit?" With a smile Zuo Ci replied, "How ridiculous!" and opened a fruit, showing him the succulent flesh inside. But the ones Cao opened were all dried out.

Beside himself, Cao bade the priest sit and explain it. Zuo Ci asked for wine and meat, which Cao saw to. Five measures later, Ci was still sober; after eating a whole sheep, he was still hungry. "What is your method?" Cao asked. "This poor priest," he replied, "has studied the Tao for thirty years on Emei Mountain[12] in Jialing of the Riverlands. One day I heard someone calling my name from within a stone wall on the mountain. I went to look but saw nothing. Suddenly a peal of thunder split the wall and I found three scrolls of divine text entitled *Avoidance Days, Text of Heaven*. The first was *Avoidances, Heaven*; the second, *Avoidances, Earth*; the third, *Avoidances, Men*. The first teaches how to spring into the clouds and straddle the winds in order to soar through middle space; the second, how to pass through hills and stone; the third, how to move freely within the realm hiding one's shape, changing one's form, taking an enemy's head with a flying a sword or a well-thrown knife. Your Highness has reached the highest ministerial office. Why don't you retire and come with this poor priest to Emei Mountain and practice the disciplines of the Tao? I will hand the three scrolls over to you."[13]

To this invitation Cao Cao responded, "I have long thought of retiring, having ridden the crest of success. The only thing stopping me is that we have yet to find the right man to assist the court." Zuo Ci smiled and said, "Liu Xuande of the Riverlands is a scion of the royal house. Why not yield this position to him? Otherwise, this poor priest will send a sword for your head!" Rage seized Cao Cao. "He is an agent of Liu Bei!" he cried, and ordered his guards to arrest the man. Zuo Ci only continued laughing. Cao Cao ordered a dozen of the jailers to take hold of Zuo Ci and beat him. They used all their might, but Zuo Ci remained as if deeply asleep, snoring away, showing no sign of discomfort. Next, Cao ordered a cangue fixed tightly on Zuo Ci's neck and wrists and had him imprisoned under close guard. Later the guards found the cangue and lock on the ground and Zuo Ci sleeping, unscathed. They kept him in prison for seven days with neither food nor drink. When next they looked, he was sitting erect on the floor, his face ruddy. The jailers informed Cao Cao, who had the prisoner brought forth for questioning again. "I can go for decades without eating—or I can consume a thousand sheep in one day!" he declared. Cao Cao was powerless to deal with him.

That day all the officials gathered at the royal palace for a banquet. As the wine was circulating, Zuo Ci appeared standing before the diners, wooden clogs on his feet. The assembly was shocked. Zuo Ci said, "Your Highness's table is fully furnished with fish and meat, and for the courtiers gathered at this great feast there is an abundance of rare delights. If anything is lacking here, I would like to volunteer to fetch it." "I want dragon liver to make a stew," Cao replied. "Can you get it for me?" "Nothing difficult about that!" was Zuo Ci's answer. With brush and ink he drew a dragon on the chalky wall. He waved his sleeve over it, and the stomach opened. Zuo Ci plucked out the liver, streaming with fresh blood. Cao Cao said contemptuously, "You had that in your sleeve!"

Zuo Ci said, "This is the coldest time of year, when all vegetation is dead. Is there any fine flower Your Highness might like to have?" "A peony, nothing else," was Cao's reply. "Easy enough," said Zuo Ci. He ordered a large flower basin brought before the company and sprayed water on it. In moments a peony stalk sprang up, bearing two blossoms. The assembly was astonished. Zuo Ci was invited to join the feast.

Soon after, the cook served minced fish. Zuo Ci said, "For mincing only a fine perch from the River Song will do." Cao Cao said, "How can we get one from so far away?" "It's not difficult," was the reply. The priest had a fishing pole brought to him and dropped a line into the pond below the hall. In a short while he had pulled up several dozen large perch and placed them in the palace hall. "Those fish were in my pond all along," said Cao. "Is Your Majesty trying to fool me?" retorted Zuo Ci. "Every perch in the world has two cheek pouches, except those from the Song, which have four. This can prove it." The officials verified the priest's claim.[14]

"You'll need purple sprout ginger to poach these fish," Zuo Ci went on. "Can you get that for us too?" Cao asked. "Easy enough," Ci answered. He had a gold basin brought out and covered it with his robe. In a few moments the basin was filled with ginger. Ci presented the basin, and Cao took it in his hands. To his surprise, there was a book inside bearing the title *New Writings of Mengde*. Finding every word in its pages to be correct, Cao was puzzled. Zuo Ci took a jade cup from the table, filled it with choice wine, and offered it to Cao Cao. "Drink this, Your Highness," he said, "and you will live a thousand years." "You drink first," said Cao. Zuo Ci removed a jade hairpin from his cap and with a single stroke divided the contents. He drank one half and proffered the second to Cao Cao, who scoffed at him. So Zuo Ci flung the cup into the air, where it turned into a white turtledove that flew around the hall. As the guests watched entranced, Zuo Ci vanished from sight.

"He left by the palace gate," said Cao's attendants. "This kind of black magician has to be eliminated or he will prove a scourge," Cao Cao said; he ordered Xu Chu to pursue him with three hundred armored soldiers and take him prisoner. Xu Chu raced to the city gate and there saw Zuo Ci in his wooden sandals sauntering along ahead of him. Xu Chu pursued him but could not seem to overtake him.

Chu dashed into a group of hills, where he saw a little shepherd driving a flock of sheep into the center of which Zuo Ci walked. Xu Chu shot an arrow at him, but he disappeared. Xu Chu slew the entire flock before returning to the palace, leaving the little boy in tears. Suddenly the lad saw a sheep's head on the ground speaking in human tongue. It called to him, "Place the severed heads against the necks of the dead sheep." The terrified lad covered his face and fled. But a voice behind him said, "Don't panic. I'm returning your sheep alive." Turning round, the lad saw that Zuo Ci had already put the sheep back together and was driving them toward him. Before the lad could question Zuo Ci, he was on his way with a flick of his sleeves, faster than the wind; in a flash he was gone from sight.

The shepherd boy reported the event to his master, who, fearing to keep it secret, reported it to Cao Cao. Cao had a sketch of the man made and sent it to various points with orders to arrest him. Inside of three days hundreds of men were arrested—in town and outside the walls—who resembled Zuo Ci exactly: one drooping lid, one lame leg, white vine-stem cap, grey casual gown, wooden sandals. A tremendous hubbub erupted in the city streets. Cao Cao ordered his commanders to sprinkle the prisoners with pig's and sheep's blood and then march them to the training field south of the city. Led by Cao Cao himself, five hundred soldiers surrounded and executed them. From each severed trunk a trail of blue vapor arose. The vapors coalesced in the sky and became Zuo Ci. Hailing a passing crane, he sat on its back, clapped his hands, and laughed, saying, "Earth rat follows golden tiger; the villain is shortly doomed."[15] Cao Cao ordered his commanders to shoot. But a great wind blew up, carrying stones and scattering sand. The bodies of those executed sprang up and, heads in hands, raced to the reviewing arena as if to strike Cao Cao. Officials and officers covered their faces and collapsed in disbelief, too frightened to help each other. Indeed:

> If the villain had power enough to overthrow the dynasty,
> The unearthly powers of the Taoist priest were even more amazing.

Was Cao Cao himself about to die?

READ ON.

69

Conning the Changes, Guan Lu Sees Things to Come;
Chastening Han Traitors, Five Vassals Die Loyal

STUNNED, CAO CAO WATCHED THE MASS OF CORPSES coming to life in the darkening day; then he fell to the ground. Moments later the wind ceased, the corpses vanished. Cao Cao was helped to his palace, suffering from shock. A poet of later times wrote in awe of Zuo Ci's black magic:

> He sprang to cloud and swept around our realm,
> Freely, harmless, avoiding days malign.
> Casually he worked his conjuries;
> But Cao Cao never understood his signs.

No medicine could cure Cao Cao. By chance, the assistant grand astrologer, Xu Zhi, was in the capital to see Cao. Cao ordered him to divine the matter from the *Book of Changes*. "Has Your Majesty ever heard of Guan Lu, the marvelous diviner?" asked Xu Zhi. "The name is familiar," Cao replied. "But I am unfamiliar with his craft. Can you tell me more?" "Guan Lu (styled Gongming) is from Pingyuan," Xu Zhi told him. "He is crude and ugly, fond of wine and unpredictable. His father was the elder of Jiqiu in the district of Langye. As a lad, Guan Lu was so fascinated by the constellations that his parents could not get him to bed at night. He would often say, 'Even chickens and swans know the time of day; how about men living in the world?' Once, playing with the neighbor's children, he drew the heavens on the ground, showing sun, moon, and star clusters. When Guan Lu got a little older, through a deep understanding of the *Changes*, he was able to observe the angles of the wind[1] and make miraculous numerical calculations; in addition, he was skilled at reading a man's fortune in his appearance.[2]

"The governor of Langye, Shan Zichun, invited Guan Lu to audience on the strength of his reputation. Attending the session were over one hundred scholars skilled in argument. Guan Lu said to Zichun, 'As I am young and diffident, I beg three jars of fine wine to drink before speaking.' Though surprised, the governor satisfied his request. Done drinking, Guan Lu asked Zichun, 'Are those seated here in Your Lordship's hall the ones to match wits with me?' 'I consider myself a worthy opponent,' was the governor's reply; and he began to discuss the logic of the *Changes*. Guan Lu waxed eloquent, speaking to the essence of the governor's questions. Zichun tried every way he could to confound the young man, but Guan Lu answered fluently from dawn to dusk; no wine or food was served. Zichun and the company were conquered by the child prodigy, as he came to be known.

"Some time after this event, Guo En and his two brothers, residents of Langye, asked Guan Lu to cast a divination concerning the lameness afflicting each of them. Guan Lu replied, 'There is a female ghost haunting your family graves, according to my reading of the hexagrams; it is the wife of either your father's older brother or of his younger brother. Some time ago, in a period of famine, she was pushed into a well and her head crushed with a rock for the sake of a few pecks of grain. Her desolate spirit now appeals to Heaven for justice, and the three of you suffer a retribution which cannot be warded off.' The brothers wept and acknowledged the crime.[3]

"Wang Ji, governor of Anping, on learning of Guan Lu's divining powers, invited him to his home. It so happened that the wife of the prefect of Xindu was suffering from fainting spells,[4] and her son from pain around the heart. The prefect therefore invited Guan Lu to divine for him. Guan Lu said, 'There are two male corpses in the western corner of this hall: one holding a spear; the other, a bow and arrow. Their heads are inside the wall, their feet outside. The former augurs stabbing in the head—hence your wife's spells; the latter, piercing of the chest and abdomen—hence your son's pain.' They began digging and eight spans down unearthed two coffins. One contained a spear, the other a bow and arrow. The wood had rotted away. Guan Lu had the bones reburied ten *li* outside of the city, and the symptoms disappeared.

"When the prefect of Guantao, Zhuge Yuan, was promoted to governor of Xinxing, Guan Lu went to see him off. One of the governor's men mentioned that Guan Lu could locate anything hidden. The incredulous governor secretly took a swallow's egg, a bees' nest, and a spider, placed them separately in three boxes, and ordered Guan Lu to perform his divination. After forming his hexagram, Guan Lu wrote four lines on each box. On the first:

> After brooding, it transforms;
> Till then, it needs its warm redoubt
> To let the male and female form
> And the fledging wings stretch out—
> A swallow's egg here!

On the second box he wrote:

> In homes hanging upside down,
> They throng at gates and doors;
> Hiding essence, brewing bane,
> Come the fall, the change occurs—
> A bees' nest here!

On the third Guan Lu wrote:

> On long and trembly legs he moves,
> Spitting gauzy silken thread;
> Seeing food upon the web,
> His advantage comes when we're abed—
> A spider here!

The entire company was astonished at Guan Lu's skill.

"Once an old village woman had lost an ox and wanted a diviner to locate it. Guan Lu's opinion was:

> North where a streamlet runs,
> A tasty meal for seven men!
> Swiftly go and look for him—
> Skin and flesh may still remain.

Indeed, the old woman found her ox. Seven men behind a thatched hut were dining on it, and some of its skin and meat was still left. The woman reported this to the district governor, Liu Bin, who arrested and convicted the seven. When the governor asked the woman how she had found the culprits, the woman told him of Guan Lu's divination. The incredulous governor invited Guan Lu to his quarters and bade him divine the contents of two boxes in which he had hidden a seal and a pheasant's feather. After divining, Guan Lu wrote on the first:

> Square within, outside round,
> A pattern in five colors,
> Holding the jewel of trust:
> Removed, the emblem of office!—
> A seal sack!

On the second Guan Lu wrote:

> Birds are perched upon those cliffs,
> Bodies brocade, vermillion coat,
> And wings a dusky yellow:
> Morning's never-failing note—
> A feather of the pheasant!

Liu Bin was astonished at Guan Lu's performance and treated him as an honored guest.

"One day while strolling outside the town limits, Guan Lu came across a young man tilling a field. Lu stood by the roadside watching. After a long time he asked, 'What is your honored name and age?' 'Zhao Yan,' the youth replied. 'I am nineteen. May I ask who you are, sir?' 'I am Guan Lu,' was the reply. 'I see the sign of death between your eyebrows. You are fated to die in three days. Alas, though handsome, you cannot live long.' When Zhao Yan returned home, he anxiously reported the prediction to his father, who ran out and overtook Guan Lu. Throwing himself to the ground, the father said tearfully, 'Please come home with me and save our son.' 'How can the decree of Heaven be forestalled?' The father reiterated his appeal: 'This old man has but one son. I crave your assistance.' The boy added his own pleas.

"Guan Lu saw how anxious father and son were for his help, so he said to Zhao Yan, 'Prepare a jar of pure wine and a piece of dried venison as a gift to two men whom you will find tomorrow playing chess on a flat stone under a great tree in the hills to the south. One of the men—unsightly and dressed in white—will be seated facing south; the other—fair of face and dressed in red—facing north. While they are rapt in their game, kneel down and present the wine and meat. After they finish, plead tearfully for longer life. They will augment your years. But make sure not to mention me.' The father had Guan Lu remain with him.

"The next day Zhao Yan took wine, meat, and serving utensils into the southern hills. After walking five or six *li*, he found the chess players at the foot of a giant pine. They took no notice of him. Zhao Yan knelt and offered the wine and food to them. Intent on their game, the two men consumed the wine and venison without being aware of it. Then a weeping Zhao Yan prostrated himself and pleaded for his life. The two men were astonished. The man in red said, 'This sounds like one of Guan Lu's ideas. After accepting the favor, we have to show him sympathy.' The man in white looked into a register he was carrying and said to Zhao Yan, 'You are to die this year, your nineteenth. I am going to add a 9 before the character 10, giving you ninety-nine years. And when you see Guan Lu again, tell him to keep the secrets of Heaven to himself or suffer the consequences.'

"As the man in red finished writing, an aromatic breeze passed; both men turned into white cranes and shot into the skies. Zhao Yan went home and questioned Guan Lu. 'The one in red was the Southern Dipper,' Lu replied. 'The other, the Northern.' 'I always thought the Northern Dipper had nine stars,' Zhao Yan said. 'Why was there only one man?' 'Dispersed, there are nine; concentrated, they make one. The Northern Dipper marks death: the Southern, life. Since they have already extended your span, what else are you worried about?' Father and son prostrated themselves in gratitude. From that day forth, Guan Lu was reluctant to divine lest he betray the secrets of Heaven. At present, he lives in Pingyuan. If Your Highness wishes to know what fortune holds in store, I suggest you summon him.'"[5]

Delighted with Xu Zhi's recommendation, Cao Cao sent for the diviner. Guan Lu arrived and, after paying his respects, was asked to divine the meaning of the wonders Zuo Ci had performed. "Simple black magic to delude you," he told Cao."What are you worried about?" Cao Cao took comfort from the seer's words and his illness gradually passed.

Cao Cao ordered Guan Lu to divine the state of the empire. The answer was: "Three and eight run crisscross; a yellow pig meets a tiger. South of the outpost, you will lose a limb." Cao ordered him to foretell the length of his line of succession. The answer was: "In the palace of the lion, the ancestral tablet takes its place. Kingship is renewed, his posterity will know the ultimate honor." Cao Cao asked for further explanation. Guan Lu said, "Vague and vast are Heaven's determinations. No man can foretell them. But in retrospect they are confirmed."

Cao Cao wanted to appoint Guan Lu grand astrologer, but the diviner replied, "My lot is meagre; my features bespeak adversity. Unfit for the office, I must decline." Cao Cao asked the reason, and Guan Lu replied, "My forehead is misshapen; my eyes lack luster; my nose has no bridge; my feet, no Achilles tendons; the marks of long life are absent from my back and stomach. I'm good for dealing with the ghosts on Mount Tai, but not with living men." "Then," responded Cao, "will you read my destiny from my looks?" "You are already the highest vassal in the land. What need is there?" said Guan Lu smiling, and he refused to answer despite Cao's repeated requests. Cao Cao then ordered Guan Lu to read the character of each of his officers and officials. To this, Guan Lu replied, "Officers to rule the age, one and all." Cao Cao asked his fortunes, but Guan Lu would not divulge them fully. These verses written in later times express admiration for the diviner:

> Guan Lu (Gongming), of Pingyuan, was a seer
> Who kenned the stars of north and southern poles.
> By the trigrams' arcana he reached the occult realm;
> By hexagrams' mystery he probed the house of Heaven.
> His predictions and readings sensed those doomed;

His innermost depths could activate the spirits.
Alas, the secrets of his ingenuity
Were never written down for posterity.

Once again Cao Cao ordered Guan Lu to divine, this time the prospects for the Riverlands and the Southland. Lu cast the hexagrams and said, "The south has lost a chief
general. The west sends hostile troops." Cao Cao was incredulous. But at that moment a
messenger from Hefei reported the death of Lu Su, the Southland general guarding
Lukou. Cao Cao was astonished. Next, he sent someone to Hanzhong, who reported that
Liu Xuande had sent Zhang Fei and Ma Chao to take the pass at Xiabian. Cao Cao was
enraged and asked Guan Lu to predict what his fortunes would be if he took his army
back into Hanzhong. Guan Lu answered, "Your Highness, do not be reckless. Next spring
the capital will have a disastrous fire." Cao Cao, impressed by Guan Lu's successful predictions, declined to act and kept to his regional capital at Ye. Instead, he sent Cao Hong
with fifty thousand troops to help Xiahou Yuan and Zhang He defend the eastern Riverlands; he detailed Xiahou Dun to patrol the capital with thirty thousand and guard
against the unexpected; and lastly, he had one of his senior advisers, Wang Bi, take command of the Royal Guard.

Cao's first secretary, Sima Yi, said, "Wang Bi is too fond of his drink, too lax to hold
that office." "Wang Bi has followed me through thick and thin," replied Cao. "He is loyal
and diligent, a man of iron convictions, and more than adequate to the task." Thus, Wang
Bi took command of the Royal Guard, which was stationed outside the Eastern Blossom
Gate of the capital at Xuchang.

There was a man named Geng Ji (Jixing) from Luoyang, who had served on the prime
minister's staff and was later transferred to the post of privy treasurer. He became close
friends with Wei Huang, security director to the prime minister. Geng Ji was outraged by
the fact that Cao Cao had been granted the title of king and that he went about in an
emperor's carriage. In the first month of the twenty-third year of Jian An (A.D. 218),
Geng Ji spoke confidentially to Wei Huang: "The treachery of the traitor Cao worsens.
He is bent on usurpation, and we servants of the house of Han should not be helping him
to do so." Wei Huang replied, "There is someone we can turn to: Jin Yi, a descendent of
the former prime minister, Jin Midi. Jin Yi has never wavered in his intention to see Cao
Cao brought to justice. Also, he is on close terms with Wang Bi. If Jin Yi joins us, we may
save the Han." "If he is already a friend of Wang Bi's," Geng Ji said, "why would he
want to join with us?" "Let's talk to him and see," was Wei Huang's reply.

Geng Ji and Wei Huang went to the home of Jin Yi, who welcomed them into his
private quarters. When they were comfortably seated, Huang said, "Because you and
Wang Bi are close friends, I have a special request." "What is it?" Jin Yi replied. "We
believe that before long the king of Wei will accept the abdication of the Emperor and
ascend the imperial seat. You and Wang Bi are both sure to attain high position; we hope
you will remember us and somehow manage to arrange for our preferment. We would be
deeply grateful." Jin Yi flicked his sleeves dismissively and stood up. At that moment his
attendants came in to present tea, but Jin Yi spilled the tea on the ground. Trying to look
startled, Wei Huang said, "Why should an old friend turn so unfriendly?" "We have
been good friends," Jin Yi replied, "inasmuch as you are descended from high ministers
of the Han court. But now, instead of being true to your origins, you seek to aid and abet
the rebels. I want no part of your friendship!" "Heaven ordains that we do what we
must," Geng Ji said. Jin Yi was outraged.

Realizing that loyalty and honor were uppermost in Jin Yi's mind, Geng Ji and Wei Huang told him that they had merely been testing him and actually wanted his cooperation in bringing Cao Cao to justice. Jin Yi responded, "How could a servant of the Han for generations follow a traitor? If you want to uphold the royal house, let me hear your esteemed views." "Although we want to show our devotion to the dynasty, we lack a plan for dealing with Cao," they responded. "I will work with you from within," Jin Yi said. "We will kill Wang Bi, take over the Royal Guard, and thus aid the Emperor. Then we can ally with Imperial Uncle Liu to destroy the traitor." Geng Ji and Wei Huang clapped their hands in approbation.

"There are two men," Jin Yi continued, "in whom I have full confidence and who hold Cao Cao their mortal enemy for killing their fathers. They live outside the city and will lend support to our efforts from there." Geng Ji asked who they were. "They are Ji Mao (styled Wenran) and Ji Mu (styled Siran), sons of the late Imperial Physician Ji Ping. Years ago Cao killed their father because he was involved with Dong Cheng in the secret edict affair.[6] At the time the two sons ran away to a remote area to escape Cao's vengeance. Now they have secretly returned to the capital. If you want their help, there is nothing they won't do." Geng Ji and Wei Huang were delighted.

Jin Yi quietly summoned the two sons of Ji Ping and explained the situation to them. Both men, so deeply affected that their eyes overflowed with indignation and their sense of justice soared skywards, swore to kill the traitor. Jin Yi then spelled out his plan: "On the night of the fifteenth day of the first month, when the Lantern Festival lights up the city in celebration of the year's first full moon, Treasurer Geng Ji and Security Director Wei Huang, you will bring your armed servants to the camp of Wang Bi's Royal Guard. The moment you see fire in the camp, form two companies and come in fighting. After Wang Bi is killed, follow me directly into the palace. I will request that the Emperor ascend the Tower of Five Phoenixes and in his own right command the officials to bring the traitor to justice. Next, I want the Ji brothers to force their way into the capital and set fires as the signal; they will sound the call for the good people to execute the traitors to the dynasty and block any rescue troops. After the Emperor's edict is delivered with an offer of amnesty to all who cooperate, we will advance on Ye, capture Cao Cao, and summon Imperial Uncle Liu. Today we have come to a decision. During the second watch of the festival night, we will act. Let us be sure not to fail as Dong Cheng did." The five men spoke their oath to Heaven and sealed their pact with blood. Then they went home to prepare men and weapons against the appointed time.

The household servants of Geng Ji and Wei Huang, numbering three or four hundred each, began readying their weapons. The Ji brothers added another three hundred. All arrangements were completed on the pretext of preparing for a hunting expedition.

Jin Yi called on Wang Bi and said, "Things seem calmer now in this vast empire, and the prestige and might of the king of Wei are already widely felt. Tonight, the festival of the first full moon, we shall have to light lanterns to celebrate the atmosphere of peace." Wang Bi agreed and issued instructions to the residents of the capital to greet the holiday with lamps and colored hangings.

When night fell on the fifteenth, the sky was clear and the stars and moon vied in brilliant glory. The whole city was given over to the display of lanterns. The soldiers on patrol let everything pass and did not enforce the discipline of the night watches.

Wang Bi and the commanders of his Royal Guard were feasting in camp, when a great hubbub broke out some time after the second watch, punctuated by cries of fire to the rear. Wang Bi dashed out and saw wheels of flame rolling every which way. The murderous shouts filling the air told him a coup was under way. He took to his horse and went out the southern gate, only to meet up with Geng Ji. Nearly felled by an arrow in the arm, Wang Bi turned and fled toward the west gate. Closely pursued, he abandoned his mount, ran to the home of Jin Yi and knocked frantically on the door.

Jin Yi's men were away—some had set the fires, others were fighting the Royal Guard—only the women were at home. Hearing the banging at the gate, the women assumed it was Jin Yi returning. His wife called from the other side of the closed gate, "Have you done away with that no-good Wang Bi?" The astonished Wang Bi thus learned that Jin Yi was a conspirator too. Bi fled to Cao Xiu and told him that Jin Yi and Geng Ji were plotting rebellion. Cao Xiu donned his armor and rode into the city with a thousand men to stop the enemy.

In the capital fires raged everywhere. The Tower of Five Phoenixes went up in flames, forcing the Emperor to take refuge in an inner palace while Cao Cao's trusted henchmen fought hard to hold the main gate. All over the city men were shouting, "Kill the traitor Cao! Support the house of Han!"

Earlier, Cao Cao had ordered Xiahou Dun to patrol the capital. He had thirty thousand men stationed five *li* away. Seeing the fires in the distance, Dun moved his men up and encircled Xuchang. Then he sent a detachment inside to relieve Cao Xiu. The battle raged until dawn. Geng Ji and Wei Huang fought on unaided until someone reported the deaths of Jin Yi and the brothers Ji. Geng and Wei then cut a path out of the city, but Xiahou Dun's troops captured them easily. Over a hundred of their attendants were slaughtered.

Xiahou Dun entered the city and put out the fires. The clans of the five conspirators were arrested and Cao Cao was informed of the events. Cao Cao sent back an order for an immediate public execution of Geng Ji and Wei Huang as well as the clans of the five conspirators. Cao Cao also ordered every official, high and low, brought to Ye for judgment.

Xiahou Dun marched Geng Ji and Wei Huang to the marketplace. Geng Ji screamed, "Cao, you barbarian! Alive, I couldn't kill you. But in death I'll be a fierce ghost and drive you to a traitor's death." The executioner thrust his sword into Ji's mouth, drawing gouts of blood. Ji died cursing. Grinding his teeth, Wei Huang struck his head against the ground, crying, "Heinous! Heinous!" until he died. A poet of later times commemorated their deaths in these lines:

> Geng Ji, loyalty pure; Wei Huang, integrity—
> With bare hands struggling to sustain the Han,
> Not knowing the mandate was soon to cease,
> Down to the Nether Springs they bring their grief.

Xiahou Dun exterminated the five clans and delivered all the court and palace officials to Ye. There, on the training field, Cao Cao set up two flags—red on the left, white on the right—and issued an order: "Geng Ji, Wei Huang, and other rebels burned the capital. Those of you who came to put out the fires, stand by the red flag; those who stayed indoors and did not try to help, stand by the white flag." The officials supposed that those who tried to put out the fires would be exonerated and thronged around the red flag. Only a third of the officials stood by the white flag. But Cao Cao ordered the arrest of everyone standing by the red flag. When the officials protested their innocence, Cao said, "At the time you were not thinking of helping fight the fires but of aiding the rebels." Cao Cao had over three hundred officials executed on the bank of the River Zhang. Those standing under the white flag were rewarded and sent back to the capital.[7]

The general of the Royal Guard, Wang Bi, had died of his wound and, by Cao's order, was buried honorably. Cao Xiu was given command of the Royal Guard, and Zhong Yao became first minister to the king of Wei. Hua Xin was made imperial censor. Six categories and eighteen grades of titled lordship were established and seventeen grades of lord within the passes. Each received a gold seal and purple cord. In addition, sixteen grades of honorary lord were established. Each received a silver seal, tortoiseshell buttons, and black cord. Lastly, five court retainers in fifteen grades were established. Each received a brass seal, round buttons, and black cord.[8] With grades established and officials enfeoffed, the court had a complete turnover of personnel. After that Cao Cao bethought himself of Guan Lu, who had predicted the fire. Cao offered him a handsome reward, but he declined it.

• • • • •

Cao Hong reached Hanzhong with his troops and ordered Zhang He and Xiahou Yuan to secure all strongpoints while he went forth to confront the enemy. Zhang Fei and Lei Tong were defending Baxi; Ma Chao, who had reached Xiabian, ordered Wu Lan to take the van. Wu Lan was scouting for the enemy when he met up with Cao Hong's army. Wu Lan wanted to retreat, but his garrison commander, Ren Kui, said, "The rebels have just arrived. If we don't break their spirit now, how can we go back and face Ma Chao?" So they charged ahead and challenged Cao Hong, who sprang forth at the call. They fought three exchanges; then Hong struck down Ren Kui and, gathering momentum, pressed the slaughter.

Wu Lan, badly defeated, went back to Ma Chao and was denounced. "How dare you engage in battle without my authorization?" Chao cried. "Ren Kui would not heed me," Wu Lan explained. "Hold all the key points and do not fight," Chao ordered and reported to Chengdu for further instruction.

Suspecting a trick when Ma Chao did not come out for days, Cao Hong withdrew to Nanzheng.[9] Zhang He came to see Cao Hong and asked, "Why did you withdraw after killing their commander?" "I thought Ma Chao might have another plan," answered Cao Hong. "Also, when I was in Ye, the seer Guan Lu said a top general would die in this region. His words made me cautious." Zhang He laughed and said, "General, you have soldiered half your life. How could you let your faith in augury cloud your judgment? Overlook my lack of ability; allow me to capture Baxi with the force I command. If I succeed, the district of Shu will easily be ours." But Cao Hong warned him: "The general guarding Baxi is Zhang Fei—an extraordinary warrior, not to be lightly engaged." Zhang He scoffed, "Everyone is afraid of Zhang Fei. To me he's like a babe. I'll take him this time." "And if you fail?" Cao Hong asked. "I will gladly submit to the martial code," Zhang He replied. Cao Hong had him write his pledge, and Zhang He went to attack. Indeed:

> Pride has ever been the ruin of an army;
> And few who underrate an enemy prevail.

What would be the outcome of the campaign?

READ ON.

70

Fierce Zhang Fei Takes Wakou Pass;
Veteran Huang Zhong Seizes Mount Tiandang

ZHANG HE DIVIDED HIS THIRTY THOUSAND MEN among three forts built against three strategic hills and named for them: Dangqu Fort, Mengtou Fort, and Dangshi Fort. From each, Zhang He took half the troops for the attack on Baxi.

Apprised of the situation, Zhang Fei summoned Lei Tong for his opinion. "This Langzhong region," Lei Tong said, "has rugged terrain and formidable hills well suited for ambushes. Go forth and fight them openly, General, while I mount a surprise attack. Zhang He will be taken!" Zhang Fei sent five thousand crack troops with Lei Tong. Fei himself took ten thousand and confronted Zhang He some thirty *li* from Langzhong. The two armies consolidated their lines, and Zhang Fei rode out to challenge Zhang He to single combat. Lance raised, Zhang He took the field, and they fought twenty bouts. Suddenly a commotion arose among Zhang He's rear troops: they had seen banners of Shu behind the hills. Zhang He lost his taste for battle, swung around, and fled. As Zhang Fei charged him from behind, Lei Tong appeared in his front, catching Zhang He between himself and Fei and worsting Zhang He's army.

Into the night Zhang Fei and Lei Tong pursued Zhang He to Dangqu Hill. Zhang He reconstituted his forces in their respective forts and maintained a strict defense, positioning catapults and missiles. Zhang Fei established a position ten *li* to the front of Dangqu Fort. The next day he came to provoke combat, but Zhang He remained on the hill drinking wine while his military band struck up a martial tune. Zhang Fei had to return to camp. The following day Lei Tong went to the base of the hill, and again Zhang He refused combat. Lei Tong charged up the hill; but timber and rocks pelted him, and he retreated. Troops from the Dangshi and Mengtou forts descended and defeated Lei Tong. The next day Zhang Fei again challenged the enemy; again they refused to respond. Fei had his men hurl up all manner of insults; and Zhang He hurled as many down. At a loss for an offensive strategy, Zhang Fei maintained his position for fifty days, making camp right before the hill. Every day he got drunk and sat before the hill reviling Cao Cao's commander.

Xuande had sent an envoy with gifts to cheer Zhang Fei's men; the envoy reported Zhang Fei's heavy drinking back to him. Alarmed, Xuande consulted Kongming, who said with a smile, "So that's how it is! Well, there's no good wine at the front, so let's send General Zhang fifty kegs of our best Chengdu brew on three stout carriages." Xuande replied, "In the past my brother has ruined things by drinking. Why on earth would you want to send him wine, Director General?'' ''Your Lordship,'' answered Kongming, ''don't you know your brother after all these years? Although he is willful and hot-tempered, his releasing Yan Yan when we took the Riverlands showed him to be far more than a foolhardy warrior. He has held Zhang He at bay for fifty days; after getting drunk every day, he sits beneath their hill camp reviling them with insolent audacity—this is no love of cups but a plan for defeating Zhang He.'' ''Nonetheless,'' Xuande replied, ''he should not get overconfident. Have Wei Yan go and assist him.''

Accordingly, at Kongming's command, Wei Yan transported the wine to the front in carriages flying yellow flags with the words ''Choice Wine for the Troops at the Front.'' Wei Yan came before Zhang Fei and conveyed Lord Liu's good wishes. Fei bowed low and accepted the gift. He then instructed Wei Yan and Lei Tong to establish themselves on his wings, each with a detachment, and to be ready to advance on the hoisting of a red flag. Finally, he distributed the wine, and the army drank heartily amid great flourishes of the drums and displays of banners.

Heeding the reports of his spies, Zhang He went to the hilltop and watched Zhang Fei drinking in front of his tent, enjoying a wrestling match between two soldiers. ''Zhang Fei provokes me beyond endurance,'' he cried and ordered a coordinated raid on Zhang Fei's camp with the units at Mengtou and Dangshi. That night when the moon was dim, Zhang He led his men down the hillside to the enemy camp. Farther ahead there were lanterns and candles alight while Zhang Fei drank in his tent. Taking the lead, Zhang He gave a great shout and, encouraged by thundering drums on the hill, cut his way into Zhang Fei's camp. But Zhang Fei sat perfectly erect and still as Zhang He plunged on toward him and thrust him through with his spear. It was a figure of straw!

Zhang He wheeled around frantically as a series of bombards shattered the air behind the tent. A commander moved to the fore, blocking his escape. He had the fierce round eyes and thundering voice of the real Zhang Fei! Fei raised his lance and sprang forward, taking He point-blank. The two warriors fought some fifty bouts in the glare of the lanterns. Zhang He was looking for rescue from the other two forts, unaware that their troops had already been beaten back and their positions seized by Wei Yan and Lei Tong. With no rescue in sight, Zhang He was at a loss. Then he saw fires on his own hill: his fort had already been seized by Fei's rear guard. With all his positions destroyed, Zhang He could only flee to Wakou Pass. The triumphant Zhang Fei reported to Chengdu. Xuande was exultant over the victory and delighted to discover that Zhang Fei's drinking was only a part of a plan to lure Zhang He into attacking.[1]

Zhang He retreated to Wakou Pass, having lost two-thirds of his army of thirty thousand, and called on Cao Hong for help. Hong was furious. ''You ignored my advice not to advance,'' he said, ''and lost a crucial strongpoint. On top of that you come for help!'' Cao Hong refused to send relief and had a messenger urge Zhang He into the field once again. Unsure of his next step, Zhang He dispatched two units of troops to concealed positions by a hill in front of the pass. His instructions were: ''I shall feign defeat. Zhang Fei should pursue. You cut off his return route.''

That day, encountering the forces of Lei Tong, Zhang He turned and fled after a brief clash; Lei Tong pursued. The two ambush forces emerged and blocked the road behind Lei Tong. Zhang He swung swiftly round and stabbed Lei Tong, killing him. The defeated troops reported back to Zhang Fei, who rushed to the scene to challenge Zhang He. Again He feigned defeat, but Fei did not pursue. Zhang He returned to the battlefield, only to flee again after a few clashes. Fei saw through the trick and withdrew to his camp. ''Zhang He sprang an ambush on Lei Tong and killed him,'' Fei said to Wei Yan. ''Now he wants to trap me. Why not try and turn the tables?'' ''How?'' Wei Yan asked. ''To-morrow,'' Fei answered, ''I'll go ahead with one company, and you bring up the rear with our best troops. When their ambushers come out, attack. Block off the paths with ten carts of brambles and set them on fire. That will give me a chance to capture Zhang He and avenge Lei Tong.'' Wei Yan accepted the assignment.

The next day Zhang Fei advanced and Zhang He met him. After some ten clashes Zhang He fled, and Zhang Fei pursued with cavalry and infantry. Zhang He fought and ran, on and off, drawing Zhang Fei past the hill where his men lay in wait. Zhang He then turned his force around, making the rear the front, and staked out positions for another battle with Fei, counting on his two wings to surround Zhang Fei. But Zhang He did not know that his troops were trapped in the gorge by the fiery carts and the smoky, blinding fires that spread out from them. Zhang Fei pressed his charge, crushing Zhang He, who, fighting now for his life, cut his way through to Wakou Pass. He collected his defeated troops there and did not emerge from his stronghold again.

Zhang Fei and Wei Yan, unable to subdue He's position, gave up and retired twenty *li*. Scouting the surrounding paths with Wei Yan, Fei spied a few men and women with bundles on their backs, clambering along the hill by clutching vines. On horseback, Fei pointed them out to Wei Yan with his whip and said, ''Those people are the means to take Wakou Pass.'' He instructed his men: ''Don't scare them. Gently call them before me.'' The soldiers did so. Fei reassured the travelers and asked why they had come there. The civilians replied, ''We are people of Hanzhong, trying to return to our village. We heard that heavy fighting in the area had closed the highway, so we crossed Blue Stream and followed the Zitong Range and the Guijin River into Hanzhong to get back home.'' Zhang Fei asked, ''How far is it down this road to Wakou Pass?'' They responded, ''There's a small road by the Zitong Range that takes you behind the pass.'' Delighted, Zhang Fei brought the travelers into his camp and gave them food and drink. He told Wei Yan, ''Go down and attack the pass, while I take some light cavalry and hit from the back.'' He ordered the civilians to lead the way, and he set out with five hundred riders.

Zhang He despaired of rescue. When Wei Yan's assault at the front of the pass was reported, Zhang He donned his battle gear, mounted, and was about to descend when the attack on the rear was reported: ''There are fires in four or five places behind the pass, and soldiers are approaching who cannot be identified.'' Zhang He turned to meet them. Where their flags parted, he saw Zhang Fei. Astonished, Zhang He fled by a side path; but his horse was spent, and Zhang Fei was closing in. Zhang He quit the horse and escaped uphill on foot. With barely ten men accompanying him, Zhang He made his way back to Nanzheng and there presented himself to Cao Hong.

Enraged at seeing Zhang He return with only ten soldiers, Cao Hong cried, ''I told you not to go. On the strength of your pledge, I let you go. Now you've destroyed an army. But you're still alive! What else do you want to do?'' Cao Hong ordered Zhang He executed. Acting Army Major Guo Huai protested, ''An army is easy to get, a general hard to find, as they say. Despite his offense, Zhang He stands high in the king's favor. He cannot be killed. Give him another five thousand men to take Jiameng Pass, contain Liu Bei's troops, and secure Hanzhong. If he fails, he can be doubly punished.'' Cao Hong approved and sent Zhang He to the pass with five thousand soldiers.

•   •   •   •   •

The defending commanders, Meng Da and Huo Jun, disagreed on how to meet Zhang He's impending attack. Huo Jun wanted a strict defense, but Meng Da was for combat.

He descended from the pass alone, therefore, and engaged, only to return badly defeated. Huo Jun sent an urgent petition to Chengdu, and Xuande summoned his director general for advice. Kongming gathered the commanders in the hall and said, "Jiameng Pass is in dire difficulty. We need to recall Zhang Fei from Langzhong to drive back Zhang He." Fa Zheng said, "Zhang Fei is posted at Wakou. From there he controls Langzhong, a strategic region. We cannot recall him. We will have to choose among the generals here." Kongming smiled. "Zhang He," he said, "is one of Wei's most renowned generals. No one but Zhang Fei will do." But a man stepped forward and said in an arresting tone, "Director! Do you make light of us all? Though I have no talent, I beg the chance to deliver Zhang He's head to your door."

All eyes turned to the veteran general Huang Zhong. Kongming said, "You are brave enough, but you may be too old to take on Zhang He." At these words, Huang Zhong, white beard bristling, replied, "Yes, I am old. But these two arms can still pull a three-hundred-pound bow. And my body has a thousand pounds of strength! Do you think I can't deal with a commonplace like Zhang He?" "General, you are nearly seventy," Kongming responded. Huang Zhong raced down from the hall, seized a great sword from its scabbard, and wheeled it round and round. Then he took stiff bows hanging on the wall and drew them till two of them snapped. Kongming said, "General, if you go, who will be your lieutenant?" "Let the veteran Yan Yan come with me," Huang Zhong replied, "and if anything goes wrong, you can have this white head!" Xuande was delighted and sent the two old warriors off to do battle with Zhang He. Zhao Zilong objected: "Zhang He has come himself to attack the pass. The director general should not play children's games. Losing this position will imperil the Riverlands. Why let two old generals go against so strong a foe?" "You think they are too advanced in years to do the job?" asked Kongming. "I predict it is they who will bring Hanzhong into our hands." Smirking broadly, Zhao Zilong and the others left the meeting.

When Meng Da and Huo Jun saw Huang Zhong and Yan Yan coming to the pass, they laughed inwardly at Kongming's ill-chosen commanders. "Why send those two old ones to such a crucial point?" they thought. Huang Zhong said to Yan Yan, "You can see from the way they're acting, they are scoffing at our age. Let us achieve a striking victory now and conquer their doubts!" "I am yours to command," Yan Yan replied, and the two men decided on their plan.

Huang Zhong led his men down from the pass and deployed them in opposition to Zhang He's. Zhang He issued forth and laughed at Huang Zhong, saying, "A man of your years and not ashamed to take the field?" Stung to fury, Huang Zhong replied, "A stripling like you mocks my years? The sword in my hand is not too old!" Slapping his horse, Huang Zhong raced forward, and the two warriors closed. After some twenty clashes shouts arose behind Zhang He: Yan Yan had quietly worked his way to the rear of Zhang He's army. Squeezed between two armies, Zhang He was defeated and driven some eighty li away; Huang Zhong and Yan Yan regrouped, and both sides held to their camps.

Cao Hong wanted Zhang He to answer for this latest defeat. But Guo Huai warned, "You will only force him to join the west. Send a commander to assist him and keep an eye on him so he won't think of defecting." Cao Hong approved and sent Xiahou Dun's nephew, Xiahou Shang, and Han Hao, younger brother of the surrendered general Han Xuan. Shang and Hao took five thousand troops to aid Zhang He. When the two rescuers reached the camp, Zhang He told them: "The veteran Huang Zhong is a great hero, and he has the assistance of Yan Yan. We cannot take them lightly." Han Hao said, "I saw

Huang Zhong's ferocity in Changsha. After he and Yan Yan delivered our territory to Xuande, they murdered my older brother. Now that we meet again, I will have my revenge!" Hao and Shang advanced from their fort.

It so happened that Huang Zhong, after several days' patrolling, had learned the roads and pathways. Yan Yan said to him, "Over that way is Mount Tiandang, Cao Cao's grain and fodder depot. If we can take the position and cut off their supply, Hanzhong will be ours." "My thought exactly," replied Huang Zhong. "Here's how we'll do it." In accordance with their plan, Yan Yan led away a detachment.

Huang Zhong marched forth to meet Xiahou Shang and Han Hao. Hao, standing before his lines, denounced Huang Zhong: "Faithless old traitor!" he cried and rode for his man, spear poised. Xiahou Shang followed to catch Huang Zhong in a pincer. Zhong fought the two commanders mightily, joining with each in ten clashes. Then he fled. Shang and Hao pursued him more than twenty *li* and seized his fortifications. Zhong established a bivouac. The next day Shang and Hao gave chase again. Again Huang Zhong met them and fell back after a few clashes. The two chased him another twenty *li*, seized his campsite and called on Zhang He to defend the one captured the day before.

When they were together, Zhang He warned, "Huang Zhong has been in retreat two days in a row. There's a trick in this somewhere." Xiahou Shang berated Zhang He. "It takes a coward to lose so many battles. Say no more now and watch us make our names!" Flushed with embarrassment, Zhang He withdrew.

The next day the battle resumed. Huang Zhong again retreated twenty *li*. The two commanders followed his track. The day after that, Huang Zhong retreated all the way to the pass and steadfastly refused to show himself. The two commanders pitched camp there. Meng Da secretly notified Xuande of Huang Zhong's situation. Xuande was disturbed and turned to Kongming. "This is merely the old general's trick to make the enemy overconfident," the adviser said. But Zhao Zilong and the others refused to believe it, and Xuande sent Liu Feng to the pass to support Huang Zhong. When Feng arrived, Huang Zhong said, "What do you mean, young general, by coming to 'help' me?" Feng replied, "My father sent me because of your recent defeats." Huang Zhong smiled. "I am only trying to make them overconfident. In tonight's engagement I shall recover all my camps and take the supplies and horses they've put there. The camps are 'on loan' for them to restock! Tonight leave Huo Jun guarding the pass. General Meng Da can help me move the supplies and horses. And you, young general, can watch me break the foe."

During the second watch Huang Zhong opened the barriers and raced down with five thousand men toward Xiahou Shang and Han Hao, who had grown lax watching the closed pass day after day. When Huang Zhong burst upon them, the two generals fled for their lives before their men could don armor or saddle a horse. In the stampede that ensued, the defenders killed many of their own. By dawn Huang Zhong had recaptured his three camps, and he transported the weapons, saddles, and horses acquired to Jiameng Pass.

Huang Zhong pressed his pursuit of the defeated army, refusing Liu Feng's plea that he rest. "'To get the cubs, go to the tiger's lair,' they say," Huang Zhong replied and took the lead. His soldiers pushed forward. Now the retreating units of the two northern commanders barged into Zhang He's own troops, forcing them out of their positions and sweeping them into the rearward flight, which took them to the shore of the River Han. All the camps and barricades were left to Huang Zhong.

Zhang He sought out Xiahou Shang and Han Hao and said to them, "We are near Mount Tiandang, our grain and fodder depot. Moreover, it connects to Mount Micang, another storage point. These are the lifelines of our troops in Hanzhong. If we lose them, we lose Hanzhong. We must think of a way to protect them." Xiahou Shang answered, "My uncle, Xiahou Yuan, has part of his force guarding Micang, which is adjacent to Dingjun Mountain.[2] No need to worry. And my older brother Xiahou De is defending Tiandang. We should go there and help defend it." Zhang He and the two commanders subsequently went to Tiandang and told Xiahou De what had happened. "I have one hundred thousand men here," Xiahou De said. "Use them to retake your positions." But Zhang He said, "It would be better to maintain the defense and take no imprudent action." At that moment the air was filled with gongs and drums announcing the arrival of Huang Zhong's army.

Xiahou De laughed loudly and said, "That old thief is no master of tactics. He relies on courage alone." But Zhang He answered him, "He plans well; he is more than a brave general." "It's hardly good planning for him to take troops fatigued from a long trek straight into battle," said Xiahou De. "Still," cautioned Zhang He, "it's better for us to defend than engage." Han Hao broke in, "Give me three thousand crack troops and victory will be almost certain." Xiahou De detailed the men, and Han Hao descended the mountain.

Huang Zhong deployed his troops to receive the attack. Liu Feng objected. "The sun has set," he said, "and the troops are weary from the long march. Shouldn't we rest a while?" "Not at all!" said Huang Zhong. "Heaven is handling us a rare victory; not to take it would offend Heaven itself!" So saying, he had the drums roll and the army move. Han Hao advanced for the battle. Whirling his sword, Huang Zhong raced for Han Hao, cutting him down in a single encounter. The soldiers from the west charged up the mountain. Zhang He and Xiahou Shang met them. Shouts went up, flames jumped skyward, and everything turned red. Xiahou De came to put out the fires, but he was accosted by the veteran general Yan Yan, who dispatched him with one swift stroke.

Earlier, Huang Zhong had had Yan Yan conceal men to await Zhang He's arrival. They put piles of branches and hay to the torch so that fierce flames stretched upward, illuminating hill and dale. After killing Xiahou De, Yan Yan came on from behind the mountain. Zhang He and Xiahou Shang, in utter disarray, had to abandon Mount Tiandang; they dashed headlong for Dingjun Mountain, which Xiahou Yuan then controlled. Huang Zhong and Yan Yan fortified Mount Tiandang and reported the victory to Chengdu.

Xuande gathered his commanders to celebrate the news. Fa Zheng said, "Previously, Cao Cao gained Hanzhong by Zhang Lu's surrender. But he failed to use his advantage to complete the conquest of the Riverlands—the Ba and Shu regions—only leaving two generals to hold Hanzhong while he took the main army back to the capital. What a blunder that was! Now we have our chance—with Zhang He defeated and Mount Tiandang in our hands—for Your Lordship personally to lead a major offensive and conquer Hanzhong. After that we can drill our men, husband our grain, and keep alert for any opportunity to bring the traitor to justice; we can also retreat and protect our position. Let us not pass up a moment vouchsafed by Heaven." Xuande and Kongming approved this suggestion strongly and ordered Zhao Zilong and Zhang Fei to take the vanguard. Xuande and Kongming led an army of one hundred thousand and picked the day to conquer Hanzhong. Orders circulated throughout the territory to remain on alert.

It was the twenty-third year of Jian An (A.D. 218); on an auspicious day in the seventh month Xuande's army came out of Jiameng Pass and established its camps. Huang Zhong and Yan Yan were summoned and richly rewarded. "Others said you were too old," Xuande said, "but the director general knew what you could do. Now you have rendered an extraordinary service. All the enemy has is Dingjun, which screens Nanzheng and holds their grain and fodder. If we take Dingjun Mountain, we will face no threat all the way to Yangping. General, are you game for another campaign?"

Huang Zhong was eager to take up his lord's challenge, but Kongming checked him. "Veteran general, though you are brave and brilliant, Xiahou Yuan is nothing like Zhang He. He is versed in the ways of war and wise in military movements. Cao Cao used him as a buffer against Xiliang. First, Yuan stationed his men in Chang'an and drove back Ma Chao; now his army is firmly planted in Hanzhong. Cao trusts his generalship above all others'. Your victory over Zhang He does not portend another over Xiahou Yuan. I think we should consider sending a man to Jingzhou to substitute for General Guan and bring Guan back before we go into battle." Indignantly, Huang Zhong retorted, "At eighty years of age, Lian Po, the famous veteran of Zhao, ate a bushel of grain and ten pounds of meat each day. The feudal lords feared him so much that none dared breach the borders of his state. And what of me? Not yet seventy. You say I am old, Director General. This time I am not taking a lieutenant commander, just my own corps of three thousand; and I'll deliver Xiahou Yuan's head to your command post." Kongming remained unyielding, but Huang Zhong insisted on going. Finally, Kongming said, "Since you are determined, General, let me send a military superviser with you. Agreed?" Indeed:

> Even a great general has to be stirred;
> A youth may not compare to the man of years.

Whom did Kongming send to help Huang Zhong?
READ ON.